Glass Lands

Book One

John S. Ryan

This is a work of fiction. All the characters, places, and events portrayed in this novel are either fictitious or are used fictitiously.

Cover Design by Andrew Schultz

Glass Lands / Book One

First Edition

ISBN-13: 978-1537089287
ISBN-10: 1537089285

DEDICATION

This book and my entire life is dedicated to my parents: Eleanor and Bob Ryan. You showed me how to live and taught me that each day is a gift.

Prologue

Family Game Night

Gerald Goodstone was eleven years old, and he liked his last name. It embodied everything Gerald wanted to become when he grew up. His last name started with the word: good. Gerald tried to be good and honest like his mom. It ended with the word: stone. A stone was unyielding like his dad who attended illegal black markets for a year and braved the piratesphere of the SLYscape just to find Gerald the perfect birthday gift. Smiling, Gerald looked at the prezero relic dangling from his wrist, an electromagnetic pulse bracelet capable of scrambling electronics and radioactively charged security systems. Or that's what the EMP bracelet could do if fixed which was what he and his dad planned to do this summer. "Gerald Good Stone," he said, dramatically, as he bounced on his toes up the metallic stairs towards the city street. "A boy both good and stone brave!"

When he reached the curb, he glanced at the warm fluorescence coloring the protective weather shields of his house. His mom and sister would be inside the simulation pod right now building jungle traps and puzzles for them all to solve. On those rare occasions when the girls made up the Family Game Night rules, all he and his dad needed to do was walk straight into the pod and play. That exhilarating first step into the virtual reality of the simulation pod was about the best feeling Gerald could imagine. It was like walking into someone else's imagination, and his little sister Lizzy had a fun imagination.

The whole game was powered by radioactive energy left over from the Freedom Wars. It was background radiation now, present almost everywhere in the world, and it existed in three spectrums: sky, light, and earth. The sky and light spectrums provided energy to the

SLYscape and the Freeland Nation's radiation fueled machines. The earth spectrum provided energy too but at low levels. Its main job was to give order to the energy so things once created could be found again on the SLYscape. If earth radiation was the landscape of the SLYscape, the y-space was its memory, and very few people understood it. Fortunately, Gerald's family knew all about y-space. Gerald's mom and dad were SLYscape engineers, and they taught Gerald everything.

Gerald's dad liked to say y-space was the magic glue that held virtual reality together. More precisely, y-space stored the system of orderly scratches in radiation used by SLYscape devices to reproduce realistic physical sensations. Gerald liked to be exact. Gerald looked at the spectrums of radiation like clay. If you knew how to mold something with it, you could build just about any human experience out there. Once built, y-space added the experience to the SLYscape where Freelanders could go and share each other's creations. Taken as a whole, the SLYscape was a vast universe of virtual realities born from the imaginations of Freelanders just like Gerald. There were so many simulated worlds chained together across the radioactive spectrums it required maps to traverse. The thing Gerald found really critters about the SLYscape was it didn't do anything without vWare.

Gerald was really good at vWare programming, even better than his dad. Without his dad, though, Gerald wouldn't know what to create. So they were a team. He and his dad came up with the idea, and then his mom and Lizzy used their imaginations to make it better. This was why Gerald loved Lizzy's Poison Dart game so much. It was a basic jungle world Gerald created years ago. Since then, Lizzy and his mother had improved it in ways Gerald could never have imagined. It was the girls' world now, but it started out as Gerald and his dad's world, which made it a family world—a Goodstone world. He shivered as a gust of cold wind flipped his hair back from his eyes.

He had been looking at his house for a long time now as if time had stopped. Sometimes that happened to Gerald. He'd lose himself in thought almost as if daydreaming, and then he'd be jarred back by something startling like an icy wind or someone shouting his name. It was scary to wake from a daydream outside at twilight. Some houses on Layfette had already gone dark. Other houses were shutting their weather shields in anticipation of the night's storms. It was Month 4, Electric Sol, when severe lightning greeted every dusk. Every month was named after the type of freedom storms it brought. Though all storms were scary, the lightning of Electric-sol scared Gerald most. Gerald shook off a chill and hurried across the street to throw the household waste package into the incinerator. As always, he took a moment to read the words: "A Freeland is a Clean Land" on the lid of the receptacle.

A leaf skittered over the letters and twisted up into the air drawing attention to the two shimmering slices of moon cresting above the purpling horizon. It cracked 48 years before Gerald was born and looked like a pale lobster claw pinching the night sky. On clear nights like this one, Gerald could see Mars inside the claw. Or maybe it was Venus. He was only eleven and did not know much about planets. He jangled his prezero bracelet and looked down at the platinum ring hanging from his leather neck cord. What he did know a lot about, in addition to vWare, was how prezero science broke the moon.

The Pre-Zeros were the people who lived when the World Union ruled the planet. They loved biological, chemical, and other forms of molecular technology. His dad explained how World Union scientists plucked atoms like falling fruit from all over the periodic table to build the destructive power of their warheads. If the Pre-Zeros had understood there were at least 212 elements, not just 178, they could have broken the earth and maybe even the sun too. Still the Pre-Zeros were masters of what they knew, and the World Union had a knack for twisting violence out of everything its scientists discovered—splitting nuclei, accelerating particles, genetically weaponizing organisms to spread deadly plagues across rebel continents. The WU's crowning achievement came when they used prezero science to genetically mutate humans into becoming better soldiers.

The genetically altered soldiers were so big and overwhelming in battle, they became known as gene demons by the rebels who fought them. Over a few short years, the gene demons destroyed more rebel bases than the World Union had managed in centuries of fighting the Freedom Wars. When defeat seemed inevitable, the rebel leader, Preston Rose, took a gamble on an experimental SLYscape radiation bomb called RADcore. It was designed to infect World Union technology giving rebels backdoor control over prezero weapon systems. Gerald knew the story well, because the bomb was delivered to the World Union by an unknown kamikaze pilot with the initials: G.

G. According to Gerald's dad, the pilot was Gerald's great grandfather. According to the history spheres, G. G. was someone who might have been Gerald's great-uncle or, maybe great-aunt. Truth was, nobody but Rose himself knew the identity of the kamikaze who unwittingly defeated the World Union in the first few minutes of what was now referred to as Day Zero.

It wasn't the RADcore bomb that destroyed the moon. It was the World Union's stockpile of prezero antimatter missiles, which gene demons launched into space the moment after the RADcore bomb exploded. The rebels didn't know what happened until the moon started to shudder and shake. The Pre-Zeros didn't know what happened either. They were too busy defending their weapons arsenals from the very soldiers who had been their greatest prezero creation.

It took hundreds of antimatter missiles to turn the moon into a claw. It took far fewer missiles to turn the World Union's home continent into what was now called, the Glass Lands. By Day 10 AZ (After Zero), the World Union collapsed but not before slaughtering the gene demons responsible for nearly destroying the world. The rebel leaders rushed into the power vacuum left by the World Union government and quickly established the Office of Prelates Council (OPC) to head the new Freeland Nation government.

The OPC assumed control of what was left of the prezero technology and decided who could and could not learn it. Gerald's dad was on the *Could List* for a while, but something happened that made the OPC push him off. It's why they now lived on Layfette Street on the island of Old New York instead of some glitzy district of New Detroit. Despite the demotion, the Goodstones would be remembered, at least by Gerald's family, as the fearless clan of kamikaze pilots who sacrificed one of their own to liberate Freelanders from World Union rule.

Something flashed bright enough to startle Gerald into remembering where he stood—outside at twilight next to an incinerator that attracted lightning. "Brave and unyielding Goodstones!" he yelled at the storm. "Can't scare me—"

The night flashed again and thundered so loud it almost knocked Gerald to the ground. He touched his chest to settle his heart and decided to think about Goodstone bravery on another night when it wasn't so dark. The next clap of thunder was closer, so he ran as fast as he could back into the house.

"Mom! Dad!" he yelled, waving frantically at the sensor that slammed the front door.

"In here," they yelled. "Snacks!" his little sister Lizzy added.

"Get your own," Gerald called back. "Gerald!" It was his mom's voice. "Okay," he responded. He walked by the old model simulation pod that took up most of the floor space in the living room. Its hatch was wide open. Inside Gerald could see the dripping green leaves that made up most of the Vancouver jungle where his sister's favorite game of Poison Dart always took place. He could hear the simulation pod's whirring gears and sensory video sprayers creating the SLYscape illusion of rain, heat, and hundred foot tall Walking Palms. He assumed the girls were already inside plotting against him and Dad. "No cheating!" Gerald yelled as he entered the kitchen. "Can't go in until we all do!"

The lights in the kitchen flicked to life when Gerald crossed the threshold. His dad sat in the dark waiting. His lips touched the silver ball he held in his hand. They called it a scribeosphere, because in prezero times it was something that recorded thoughts and messages. He looked up. "Hey, son."

"Hey," Gerald said. "Getting snacks."

His dad swiveled on the stool and launched the ball high into the air. It hovered for a few seconds before settling back down like a feather into his dad's hand.

"It's working!"

His dad nodded, smiling. "It is, indeed."

Gerald and his dad had been refurbishing and improving the scribeosphere for months. Gerald designed the vWare control code himself. He just couldn't get the thing to hover. His dad had fixed it. He smiled as wide as he could. "You really got it working!"

"No, Gerald. You got it working. All I did was get a better gyroscope frame. One from this century with some SLYscape intelligence to bolster the prezero hardware." He stared at the round object for a moment in an almost sad way Gerald found confusing. "We're a good team, Gerald."

"I know it," Gerald said, brightly. "You the hardware man. I'm the vWare man."

His dad smiled back at Gerald. "We the men," he said, holding his hand up for a slap.

Gerald slapped his dad's hand as hard as he could to complete the ritual. "Goodstone men. Oorah!"

"You know, Dad," Gerald said, thinking. "If we show a news Revealer how the scribeosphere can do SLY-like things without always being connected to the SLYscape... people pay for that kind of stuff, right?"

Gerald's dad shook his head. "You can never tell anybody about what you create, Gerald. Promise me that. It's important, the most important thing in your life. If you build something new, you can't claim credit for it. Not the scribeosphere, the EMP bracelet, not even the ring Mom gave you for your last birthday. It's all secret."

Gerald looked down at the ring hanging from his neck. He fixed his eyes on the green gem in the middle. He liked the ring for what it could do and how it did it. He stared at the gem and pictured what he wanted. He spoke the words silently and then projected his thoughts at the ring. The platinum band darkened and then turned frosty white as the ghostly image of an insect appeared inside the gem. It was a grasshopper, a prezero insect made extinct on Day Zero. It looked up at him and twitched its hind legs together happily. Gerald laughed out loud.

The sound of stocking feet rushed into the kitchen followed by the raspy shuffling of his mom's slippered feet. "Gerald!" Lizzy screamed. "You're supposed to make me food!"

"Lizbeth!"

"Sorry Mom," she said. "Gerald," she screamed even louder. "Where's *our* food!"

Lizzy was four years younger than Gerald, and he believed she was from another planet. She didn't even look like Gerald. He had red hair and fair skin with freckles all over his face. She had caramel colored skin and black hair. He remembered when she was born, so he guessed she wasn't an imposter. "Hey Liz," he said. "Catch!" He threw the scribeosphere at her head with all his might.

She dodged to the floor. The ball followed her movements and froze a hair-length from one of her outstretched palms. It then nestled into her hand like a baby bird. "Gerals!" she yelled, angry. She took a breath, sat up on the floor and pulled her knees under her chin to get a better look at the shiny ball. "How'd you do that?" she asked.

"There's more," Gerald said. "Listen to it."

"Thom . . ." their mother said. "You have to tell him—"

Lizzy touched her ear to the scribeosphere's mirror-like surface and yelped as a spark popped her cheek. "It bit me!" She flung the ball away. It spun and slowed to land softly on the kitchen counter next to Gerald.

"Thom... He needs to know."

"Know what?" Gerald asked.

Thom Goodstone looked at his wife, Theresa, and nodded. "Gerald," he said. "The scribeosphere doesn't talk—"

Lizzy barked out a laugh and stood up. "Talk? You're such a tweak, Gerald. You think it talks?"

"—Lizbeth!"

"Sorry, Daddy."

"Sure it talks," Gerald said. "Listen." He touched his hand to the kitchen counter and imagined commands just as he had done with the ring. Lizzy's laugh turned into a gasp of surprise as the scribeosphere bounced into Gerald's hand. He placed it against his ear. "It's talking right now," he said. "Whispering," he admitted. "Not even sure what the words mean exactly. Wait, I bet I can make it louder...." He closed his eyes tight and tried to imagine the whispers growing louder. "They react to my thoughts sometimes. Not much different than how the sim pods work, really . . ." He looked up. "Can you hear it now?"

Gerald surveyed the room. "Rose Almighty, guys. It's just vWare."

"Daddy, is this why Gerald can't handle moles? I mean, because he's a freak, right?"

"Not a freak, Lizzy. Never that."

"Mom?" Gerald asked, exasperated. "Can you hit her or something? Like right on the head."

"What?" Lizzy said, shrugging. "I have implants. Mom has 'em. Dad's covered with 'em. Show me yours, Gerald. Where are yours?"

"Gerald can't have implants, Lizbeth. We've talked about this."

Gerald turned the scribeosphere over in his hand, studying it. "I don't know," he said. "With an implant, I could jump inside the SLYscape and build vWare faster."

"You're already faster, Gerald. If you connect to the SLYscape directly with molecular implants—" He shook his head and frowned. "The SLYscape is full of bad people, son. If they knew about your whispers, they'd want to hear them too. They'd hunt you down and pry into your thoughts. You of all people have to protect your mind."

His mother paced the floor, her eyes shining brightly. "Honey, you're not allowed to talk about the voices. Never ever! You too, Lizbeth."

"He's not all that," Lizzy said, crossing her arms. "Make him sound so special. What about me?"

"I don't get it," Gerald said, distracted as if he had lost the point of the conversation. "None of you can hear this?" He looked dismayed at the scribeosphere and shook it. "Wait," he said, looking closer. "Mom, your grasshopper's jumped into my scribeosphere without permission." He looked deep into the scribeosphere's metallic shine and saw the insect from the gem staring out. "Can you at least see that, Mom? You made it for me." His mother put her hand to her mouth. Gerald's heart thumped painfully in his chest. Something was wrong. "Lizzy, you see the grasshopper, right?"

"Too soon," his mom said. "He's not ready. Thom, did you know?"

Gerald's dad nodded. "We layered his thoughts—"

"What is it, Mom?" Gerald asked.

"Thom!" she snapped, her voice accusatory as if he had done something wrong. Gerald grew quiet and so did his sister.

"Yesterday," his dad said. "The memories are in it." Gerald and Lizzy watched their dad hold their mom's gaze. Their eyes did not waver from each other for several moments until Theresa nodded, almost imperceptibly. His dad turned to face his son. He squinted his eyes. "A cricket, son? I see it. Big sucker too."

Gerald heard something strange in his dad's tone. "Do you like the color?"

"Green's my favorite."

Gerald stared in disbelief. The grasshopper was yellow with black spots. His dad had lied. "Called grasshoppers," Gerald said, "not crickets."

"Can we play Poison Dart now?" asked Lizzy.

"Yes," his mom agreed, wiping her eyes quickly. "That's a good idea."

"Great!" Lizzy yelled, happily running around Gerald to get to the food provider. "I got the cracker snacks! Gerald, you cook the buttery poppers."

Gerald watched his sister collect the food and walk back to the living room with his mom. Both girls had such long dark hair, he thought. His dad was gray where he wasn't bald. Where did Gerald's red hair come from? Why couldn't they hear the whispers? *Only you,* the whispers said. *Only you*, and then the words melted into gibberish like static. Gerald dropped the scribeosphere, startled. The fist-sized ball floated back up so he could pick it out of the air. It was the vWare tricking his brain he decided. His family didn't see or hear the grasshopper because he made a mistake in its design. The scribeosphere must bounce commands it doesn't understand back to Gerald. *Like a canyon echo, a feedback loop only I can hear because it's my thoughts that confused it. Waste in. Waste out.*

"I'll meet you in the pod, buddy," his dad said, cuffing Gerald on the shoulder. He left the kitchen.

Gerald slipped the scribeosphere into one of the oversized pockets on his pants. He took a few steps and grew suddenly dizzy. He fell back to lean against the counter behind him. A moment later, a tingling sensation gripped his hands and neck. His stomach panged with nervousness. The lights dimmed and then grew bright, strobing. Losing power happened often in Electric-sol so he knew the drill, but the dizziness was unrelenting. He steadied himself and walked towards the louvered weather shield above the sink that prevented outside weather from entering the house. He peered into a pitch black sky and saw no storm activity outside or even stars. *Shields must be closed*, he thought. Yet something nagged at him. He reached up and tapped the opaque barrier with his knuckles. The weather shield should let at least a little light in, even if it was only the glow from the street.

"Shut the shields," Gerald's mom called. The strobing lights slowed until the kitchen was more dark than light.

"They are!" he called back. "I think." He ran his hand along the wall until he felt the window's touchpoint. It vibrated, and to his surprise, the louvres slid down. *It was open*, he thought. When the shields clicked shut, his mom yelled, "Don't forget the emergency lights, honey."

He found the lights on the highest shelf above the food provider. He tiptoed to reach and was tossed into the air by something that made the ground shake.

Gerald's forehead hit the floor and his cheek burst in pain as the emergency lights went flying from his hands. He used a chair to climb back to his feet. A second concussion of sound crashed him back to the ground, and the kitchen flared impossibly bright. He didn't think to scream until lightning arced across the room in white and blue trees that licked the ceiling and started tiny fires.

Gerald smelled ozone and then his hair caught fire.

He slapped his face and hair until the flames were out and his head felt more cold than hot. The feeling confused him, so he screamed for his mom and dad in a shrill voice. His screams mixed with others, his mom and dad's, but Lizzy's screams were the shrillest like the screech of a toy whistle.

"Gerals!" Lizzy screamed.

"Gerald!" It was his dad's voice, strong and commanding. "Lizbeth!"

"Thom!" His mother cried. "It's not a storm!"

The roof crashed down in chunks and pieces that pinned Gerald's arm to the floor. The material was too heavy to lift, but Gerald could squirm beneath it, which he did until he was on his belly pulling himself towards his parents.

He saw his sister first in the short hallway connecting the kitchen to the living room. She saw him too and started crawling toward him. Gerald shouted for her to stop. A power line slithered across her path in slow, sweeping motions. "Gerals... help," she said, her cheeks glistening with tears.

Gerald's voice froze as he reached for her because the power line bumped her. An explosion of sparks sent her sailing away into the living room where she landed with a thud.

"Lizzy!" He scrambled forward, avoiding the crackling cable twitching against the wall.

"Ow, ow, ow," she whimpered, holding her arm at a strange angle. Gerald could see fires all around her as she pushed herself away from the heat with her shuffling feet. "Gerals!" she screamed at him. "Too hot! Make it stop!"

"I'm coming," he said, coughing. "Hold on—"

"Hurts," she yelled, and rolled onto one elbow and her knees. She dragged herself toward the front windows facing Layfette. Gerald crawled towards her until another concussion of sound slapped him to the floor in a flash of white light. *Stop it!* he thought with the intensity of a scream. He willed his command to the fire and the lightning burning his house down but nothing changed. *Stop it! Stop it! Stop it!* Fire suppressors activated, spewing white smoke and dust into the air. Gerald covered his head to breathe.

Something heavy fell in the distance and Lizzy went silent.

Gerald couldn't see. He tried to stand but kept bumping his head and shoulders against beams that had fallen on angles from the ceiling across the simulation pod and furniture. The simulation pod was crushed on one side. In front, the hatch had broken off and its bottom corner dug into: "Dad!" he yelled. Gerald stumbled and fell forward over piles of debris, bruising his knees and shins. Something tore at his thigh. He fell on top of his dad and hugged him around the neck and shoulders. "Get up!" Gerald yelled. "Got to get up!"

Gerals! he heard.

Gerald rested his cheek on his dad's lips. He didn't feel his dad breathing or maybe he did. He wasn't sure. "Get up. Dad!" He frantically pulled at his neck to get him to rise. "Lizzy needs you!" He looked to where she had been and saw only branches reaching like talons into their house from outside. The leaves shuddered and whipped in the wind making the yard look murky and menacing. Shadows and light played across the broken room tricking his eyes. He squeezed them shut and looked again but the wall and Lizzy were still gone.

"Dad," he whispered. "Where'd she go?"

His dad had no answer, but the sound of something moving nearby was clear. *Gerals!* he heard. *Help!*

Gerald swung his head wildly up and around trying to pinpoint her direction. *Help me!* He looked at the opening in the pod. Her voice was inside. Lizzy was inside the simulation pod. He pushed himself into a sitting position on his dad's chest and studied the graying stubble on his father's cheeks. His dad's eyes were tightly closed and his mouth was open. "Okay, Dad. You wait here. I'll get her. I'll save her."

In the dim, flickering light his father might have nodded. *Save her, son,* Gerald heard. *Be brave.* Gerald's eyes filled with tears. His dad's lips quivered. Gerald touched his fingers to his dad's face. He pet his dad's forehead and eyes. He touched his dry lips. "I'll save her," he said, and rolled off his father's body into a pile of twigs and spongy vines just inside the simulation pod's open door.

The backup generator hummed in the background keeping the simulation alive. He was inside a forest fed by radiation. It was Lizzy's SLYscape world. The holographic ground felt soft like wet dirt. The rubbery jungle leaves glistened in a bright artificial sunlight. The pod made it look like it was raining but Gerald felt no drops. Real water would have felt nice. He was so thirsty. "Lizzy!" he screamed. "Mom!" *Over here,* his mom called. The voice came from deeper in the pod's illusion.

Another crash shook the house outside the pod. Gerald turned back in time to see fire engulf the hatchway. Smoke billowed into the pod as the green jungle leaves continued to drip into little burning puddles on the ground. "No!" Gerald yelled. He scrambled back to the pod's doorway but fell backward from the heat. He sat up and peered through the flames until he saw the outline of his father's leg burning. Gerald felt sick and his body shook.

To Gerald, it felt like a lifetime of crying before he came alive again when someone called his name. Softly at first, then louder: *Gerald, honey.* It was his mom's voice coming from somewhere behind him. *You can't save daddy, honey. I'm so sorry. Come to me.* Gerald crawled towards his father who lay burning in the hatchway. *I'm just going to see*, he told his mom. *If it isn't him…* The heat wrinkled the air before the hatchway and Gerald was forced to stop. *I'm just confused,* Gerald convinced himself. *It's not him.* He crawled away from the burning person who couldn't be his dad and went deeper into the pod towards his mother's pleading voice.

He pulled himself over fallen tree branches and brambles. He knew he wasn't in the Vancouver jungle, but it felt real. *There, honey! Behind the stump. Go quick!* his mom directed, urgency in her quiet voice. *Quick! Lizbeth needs you!* A tiny hand curled over the top of a rotted stump. He could see her now. Poison Dart was her favorite game. Had she made it inside the pod before the tree fell through the house? He wiped more soot and gunk from his eyes and focused. *A few more feet,* he heard. *Get her, honey. Jump over the stump!* Gerald pushed himself over the stump and fell behind it just as a ball of electrical fire careened across the sky above him. *It's important, honey. Run!*

He didn't run. He huddled against the stump and watched the hissing fire bathe the tops of the Walking Palms. *Why run?* he thought. I'm in the pod.

Gerals! his sister screamed. *Mommy's hurt.*

Run, honey! Lizbeth needs you.

He felt the bulge of the scribeosphere pushing against his thigh—vibrating. It pulsed with a kind of cold intensity that made his thigh ache. *Gerals save me! Be brave son! Run! Honey!* These last commands were an intertwining chorus of all three voices: his father, mother, and sister. He suddenly knew they weren't real. The voices became more stilted, drone-like. He pulled the scribeosphere out of his pocket and studied its mirrored surface. The grasshopper peered upwards. *I'm sorry, son* it said. *Gerals, honey, we need to go.* The scribeosphere jumped out of his hand.

Gerald pushed himself up from the stump and reached for the silver scribeosphere ball, but it dodged him and moved further away. Gerald followed.

As Gerald gave chase, the scribeosphere kept yelling commands. He had learned after the first few, ignoring commands caused him pain, *Duck!*

Gerald hit the dirt as another ball of fire exploded above him.

"Slow down!" Gerald yelled. He tried swatting the ball out of the sky but it was too fast.

No time. Run.

Gerald leaped over fallen trees, through shallow ponds, and up what seemed to be a hundred foot high hill. *Poison Dart,* he thought. *Lizzy's world full of booby traps.*

Slide down, the voice said in its stilted, emotionless tone. It bore no resemblance to his family's voices anymore, and Gerald was too tired and numb to care. It was just a mechanical thing telling him what to do and Gerald followed it because he was just eleven. He wanted someone to tell him what to do. *Now close your eyes and run through the wall.*

Gerald crashed through the back wall of the simulation pod and fell over broken heaps of sharp twisted metal and split, wet branches. He landed hard on the body of his little sister who lay curled, burnt, and blistered on his mother's lap.

Gerald smelled singed hair and looked up into his mother's blank stare. He pushed himself away and scrambled back, flipping and rolling and spinning until his back pressed against something hard. "But the snacks," Gerald said, a swell of disbelief and fear rising inside him. "Buttery just like Lizzy likes. Poison Dart…" The undeniable reality of what he saw forced a long, thready scream from Gerald's throat. His father, his mother, his baby sister—all gone. It was too much. Gerald closed his eyes.

Gerald woke in fits and starts throughout the night. The moments awake were plagued by incessant whispering: *I'm sorry,* it said with a hint of emotion in its mechanical voice, and then: *Can I go?*

Gerald dreamed he refused to respond to the whispers, but at some point he opened his eyes and spoke to the scribeosphere directly. "Go away," he said.

Time to sleep then, it responded. Gerald nodded as if the silver ball of metal was a live thing, not just some vWare programmed toy. *Then leave me alone,* Gerald thought at it, angrily. Gerald noticed it then, the yellow grasshopper rubbing its back legs. It grew dark gold on the shiny surface of the scribeosphere, and then leapt off the ball to appear in the three dimensional space just inside the simulation pod's visual field. *I'll live in the SLY*, it whispered. *You live out there.*

A stab of cold attacked Gerald's chest making him gasp for breath. It was his mother's ring, still swinging from the leather cord, hurting him. He gathered the metal loop into his fist and squeezed until his palm burned with ice and his fingers glowed with color. Smoky tendrils of pale green from his mother's ring rose to meet the yellow of the grasshopper floating just inside the pod. The insect grew impossibly large. Like a dragon, it formed giant wings that fluttered open in Lizzy's jungle. With each beat of its veiny, sailcloth wings, wind buffeted Gerald backward farther and farther away from where his mom lay propped up against the wall. "Hurts," he cried. "Make it stop!"

As you command. The wings lifted the dragon insect higher than the Walking Palms as smaller winged insects stirred from the brush in the jungle like tens of thousands of birds taking flight. Gerald's last thoughts were of locusts destroying crops and blotting out the sun.

Gerald awoke on a gurney inside a private ambulance hovering above the incinerator at the curb of his smoking house. Lights flashed across the windows reminding him of the strobing he saw inside the house before the fires started. He heard the buzzing of midsize emergency drones and something larger clomping about outside the vehicle. He didn't remember being rescued. Yet here he was shivering under heavy warming blankets.

"Be still. You lost blood," a woman with a husky but kind voice said. Gerald didn't remember bleeding or being put on the gurney.

"Where is everyone?" he asked, holding out hope his memories were wrong.

"My name's Sharon Knight," she said, pulling ropes of long black hair from her eyes and whipping the braids over her shoulder. The little red beads woven into her hair clicked and rattled. She smiled. "You'll be taken care of, sugar."

"Mom? Dad?"

"My boss has seen to your care personally. He can protect you but you have to help us."

"Lizzy! She's little. You have to get her."

"I'm sorry, sugar. I can't do that."

He shook his head. He didn't want to remember. "Tired," he responded. "Go away."

"Tell me first," she said, her voice hitting him like a slap, but Gerald was too groggy to care. He wanted his memories to stop. "When it struck," she continued, urgently. "Stay with me—the lightning—did you hear anything before the lightning hit the house? Before the strikes?"

I heard voices, he thought. *Don't tell anybody about the voices*, he remembered. *Sharon who?* He shook his head. "No voices."

"Voices? You heard voices? Gerald, sugar, please tell me. Nobody's going to hurt you." She sat down next to him on the gurney.

Gerald grew cold inside, distant. "I heard nothing." He closed his eyes to stop the world from pressing down on him, smothering him. *Lizzy*, he thought. *Don't leave me here.*

Gerald heard Sharon continue to talk. After a while, she was talking to someone else. "No sir. I don't think so, sir. Reaver cordoned off the whole block.... In the back yard. Everything cleaned up like you asked. Can I speak plainly, sir? He's just a baby. They nearly killed him." Gerald felt her hand brush his hair back from his face. It hurt where the burns were but felt good too. "Preston, he's not ready."

Ready? Gerald thought. *Ready for what?*

Something scratched at his hearing, a rustling tug of his attention as he slipped into a kind of twilight sleep. *To be brave*, the scribeosphere said softly. Its voice was close. It was hovering somewhere in the ambulance. It kept out-of-sight. *Ready to be brave out there while I'll be brave in here.*

Part 1

Ghosts

Chapter 1

Eight Years Later

Preston Rose was napping when the implant in his ear started to vibrate. He groggily tapped his neck just below his earlobe and said, "Preston here."

The cacophony of words that filled his head seemed like gibberish. *Why can't people modulate their voices on bio-lines?* he wondered, not for the first time. The communication implant installed in his skin was the absolute latest technology. Nothing but the best was ever installed into a Prelate's body, but truth be told, Preston preferred speaking to people face-to-face or via DNA encrypted vid pads. The implant inside his head was always too loud in his brain, always booming in his ears like a pep rally bullhorn. It gave him a migraine but without the implant, instantaneous communication would not be possible between the Office of the Prelates Council and the rest of the Freeland Nation government. They'd have to schedule OPC meetings in slow-time, and it wasn't like they could use common Sky or Light connections to talk. *Security, security, security*, went the Freeland Security Army's mantra. So Preston grudgingly endured the pound, pound, pound of voices in his head. FSA technology, in Preston's opinion, was not always as grand as the Freeland Security Army's self-aggrandizing tech bulletins claimed.

"My goodness! That's a lot of words." Preston accidentally screamed inside his head. His actual voice did not rise above a whisper. The scream itself was the result of the bio-net feed's interpretation of his intentions. The molecular size droids in his frontal lobes guessed at intention based on electrical impulses. *Or was it brain waves?* Preston had been debriefed on the technology before installation, but he frankly didn't care how the little droids went about their business. He just knew it worked—as long as he was careful about what he thought during a conversation. "Slow down, Elaine." he said, more softly as he sat up in his bed. "What happened?"

Another onslaught of words came cartwheeling up the connection. "Too fast, Elaine." *Calm,* he thought in an attempt to soothe her nerves. It was a technique the young FSA technician told him to try to better communicate intent. The trouble was when he concentrated on "calm," pictures of paper sailboats popped into his mind. He shook his head and smiled. *Let the little nanites… angstrombots? Molecular Brain Buggers,* he decided, *let the little brain buggers do something with that.*

"Excuse me, sir?" he heard. "I mean, High Prelate, sir."

Gentle breezes, he thought... *relax.* "Please start at the beginning, Elaine." No stray images of toy boats entered his mind that time. *Good. Clear. Thought.*

There was a pause on the other end of the bio-line. "You know my name, sir? I mean, you know my actual name?"

Preston nodded. Of course, he knew her name. He could read the bio-net identity of anyone connected to the OPC data sphere of the SLYscape, including every secretary in the Office of the Prelates Council's global pool. He even knew where she stood at this very moment which was in a small apartment near Congo, Africa, Prefecture Forty-Seven, Sector Four, Environment Bubble Gamma Lota, to be exact—once known as the *Isle of Kafue.* Even without his bio-net cheat sheet, Preston recognized her voice. She always filled in for his personal assistant, Sharon Knight, who had been on assignment for two weeks. This was the third time he had talked to Elaine in that span. How could he not know her name? *Wait, has Miss Knight been gone for two weeks or three?* Preston made a mental note to check on her later.

"I'm sorry, High Prelate," Elaine said. "I don't know how to begin."

Judging from the quaver in her voice, she was more than just nervous about disturbing Preston's nap. The depth of nervousness indicated the reason for the call was probably some top secret message Elaine felt Sharon herself should deliver. Elaine was only a mid-level sub, after all. Preston rubbed his hands together. *Excellent,* he thought. *Something exciting to break up the monotony of the day.* His thought wasn't communicated because he did not consciously cast it. If he had, he'd sense a confirmation signal when it reached its recipient. There were also FSA fail-safe protocols in place that validated clearance codes against OPC thoughts containing certain secrets. It was all very complicated. *Overly so*, in Preston's opinion, *but necessary for now. There would be a day,* he thought, taking a moment to admire the garden outside his apartment window, w*hen FSA security would be made obsolete by better technology, older technology—genetic technology.* On that day, Preston would joyfully rip all of the FSA devices from his body and retire. Let the next generation take over a genetically peaceful Freeland that had no need for a military arm of government. Until then, the gentle ambitions of the OPC needed to coexist with the military and technological might of the FSA. "Just say what you need to say, daughter. Let the words fall like leaves from a tree."

"A tree, sir?"

"The message, Elaine," he said with a little more grit. *The young have no imagination for poetics.*

"I'm not sure, sir, if I am cleared for this information—"

"You wouldn't have been given the information if you weren't, dear," he said.

"But, sir. This was different."

"How so?"

"The message, sir. It was told in slow-time on a public tube."

"A transport tube?" Preston asked, intrigued. "Personal delivery?"

"Yes, sir."

"FSA?"

Preston felt a jolt of surprise over the bio-line. Or was it shock? Preston was not good at deciphering bio-net emotions, another reason he preferred good old fashion body language. In any case, mentioning the FSA caught her off guard. "Not me, sir," she said. "They wouldn't. I'm nobody, sir."

"Hardly nobody," Preston intoned. "You're authorized to speak to me."

"True, sir. High Prelate, I mean. I'm very fortunate."

Preston shook his head in disappointment. He could almost see her bowing and shuffling her feet. He had meant the comment as a joke. Sharon would have laughed. Speaking to him was no great honor. Sometimes he wished Prelates weren't held in such high regard by the

Freelanders they governed. When he was a younger man, the deference to his presence had made him terribly uncomfortable. As an older man, he had just learned to tolerate it. At his core, Preston was still the same small time rancher he had been when mucking out stalls for old Claiborne Rose. His grandfather taught him humility back in the prezero days. That wasn't about to change, regardless of what titles he held. "So who delivered the message?" he asked, all business.

There was a long pause. "I don't know."

Losing a bit of patience, he responded: "Elaine, dear, I am ninety-seven years old this very day—"

"Oh, happy birthday, sir! High Prelate, I mean. Many more—"

Preston smiled. "Fine. Thank you. The message?"

"They were behind me when they delivered it. They said not to turn around though I saw something like a black dress or maybe it was a robe covering their feet. Their message was not nice, sir." She paused for a long moment. When she began again, Preston could sense she was on the verge of tears. "A very big man… he sat in front of me with his head buried deep in one of those cloaks. You know, the ones with the trick fabric that makes faces change?"

"Shift fabric," he said. The material was hard to come by without high-ranking military ties. Preston's hood took two months to obtain. Now it hung like a jewel in the weapons locker of his safe room. "Where did you say this happened?"

"In the tube, sir, on my way home; he must have followed me in. Like a tail in one of those SLYcade spy games my little brother plays. Well, I play sometimes too—"

Preston cleared his throat.

"Oh, sorry, sir. Their voices were odd. Mechanical. Like robot voices from old holo-vids, the kind my grandma likes—scary, sir."

Hallmark FSA, Preston thought. *Why call a Prelate directly when you can intimidate a poor global secretary with mid-level clearance?*

"Did they bio-flash a badge?"

"Not that I am aware, sir."

"Not even a SLYscape ping?"

"Nothing, sir. As I said, it was *different* the way they talked, not nice. Mean, really. Evil."

The bio-net feed throbbed with a menacing anxiety that felt oddly cold to Preston. They did something to this girl. *Hit her with a camouflage or confusion field... something*, which meant it was probably exactly as he suspected—FSA. They're drunk with power, he thought, operating on the shady side of the law even when they didn't have to. Then again, Preston chastised himself, he was in no position to judge. *I've done worse things.*

Memories of scared and tortured faces came unbidden to his mind. He endured the memories for however long they lasted. He believed it was all part of his penance—to never forget the lives he destroyed to get the Freeland Nation back on its feet after the rebels executed the World Union leaders and their scientists. The memory of his grandfather's face lingered longest, especially the look of betrayal in his grandfather's eyes when Preston accused him of being a World Union sympathizer. "You'll remember this day as the worst in your life, son," his grandfather said looking directly at Preston who sat with the other war judges. Six decades after the executions, his grandfather's words still rang true like a clarion call of regret. *Is the Freeland Nation any better than the World Union had been?* Preston wondered. *Look what our FSA agents did to this girl.* He shook his head in disgust.

"I don't remember clearly, sir. Scatter-brained when I'm scared. I thought they were robbing me."

"Understandable, Elaine. Go on."

"The big man, sir. He held me with some kind of invisible hand. His real hands were in his pockets but the pressure of the invisible hand made it so hard to breathe. It hurt, sir, so I might not have heard correctly." The quavering in her bio-line grew so bad, her thoughts became unintelligible. Perhaps, the bio-net feed was having trouble interpreting her fear.

"Give me what you remember, daughter. I'll tell you if it makes sense."

"Thank you, sir," she responded. "You are my spiritual leader in all things. For you, I will try."

Preston winced at her words. *You're not a hero, son. You're not spiritual.* Preston remembered his grandfather saying these words hours before he was executed with the other WU leaders. *I know that's what the rebels tell you, but you're not. Heroes put the people first, not their missions. I'm sorry, son, you picked the wrong side. You're nothing now, an empty soul, unfertile land, a Rose with no bloom.* The Good Reverend Claiborne Rose had pegged his favorite grandson cold that day. *He knew me,* Preston thought, *better than I had known myself.* Preston realized now, after 60 years of being High Prelate of the Freeland Nation, he had been a pawn in a game he hadn't fully understood. While Freelanders were busy honoring the once-upon-a-time rebel leader, Preston Rose, with parades, the Freeland Security Army was busy chipping away at the very freedoms Preston fought to protect. "It's really not your fault, Elaine. I understand. People like that can terrify anyone."

"Thank you for understanding, father," she said.

Preston's gaze drifted to his grandfather's ordination bracelet hanging loosely around his wrist. He kept it to remind himself there were bigger powers in the universe than the Freeland institutions he now served. He hoped after this life was over, he'd see his grandfather again. What Preston had done to the man who raised him was unforgivable, but what he had dedicated his life to since might—just maybe—be worthy of parades. Regardless of how Freelanders saw his experimental projects now, Preston knew history would judge him through the actions of the people he protected. Until then, he'd do what was necessary and remember the real power in the Freeland belonged to its people no matter how powerful the FSA's weather, energy, and military engines had grown. No matter how small their little SLYscape robots got. *Neutrino sized brain-buggers next? It didn't matter.* The FSA wanted to rule the people instead of serve them, and it was his job as High Prelate to stop that from happening.

"So, they held you captive, Elaine," he said. "Then what?"

"On the tube, sir, and they told me to relay this message. It's their words, sir. Horrible words. Not mine—"

Preston nodded, though she probably didn't know that. "Go on."

"We've found another abomination, they said."

"An abomination?"

"A demon child monster. A mutant lab rat with no business in an afterzero world. They called you an abomination too, sir. I'm sorry, but there's more." Elaine hesitated. "Your little rat scurried, they said, and scurried and scurried into our trap that snapped its neck."

Preston's anxiety spiked. *Demon child*, he thought, putting the threat together, *Stars Almighty! Which one?* Preston grew lightheaded and touched a tattooed spot on his wrist. Across the room, his personal simulation pod rumbled to life and projected an image of a revolving earth high up over a synthetic mahogany table. His eyes selected menus and entered patterns until blue dots appeared on the five habitable continents. *One hundred eighteen projects,* he thought, *and one is missing.* His heart sank as he scanned the map for the missing name. Another weapon against the FSA destroyed. He could see it now, a blue dot that had gone silver on its way to black. He read the light-signature of the dot. *Oh, Lord,* he thought. *What have they done?* He measured his breaths and stared. She was only twelve, still dormant, a whole life ahead of her… anger swelled inside him until he felt near-bursting with it.

"Sir?" Elaine said, her thought tremulous. "I'm so sorry, sir, but there's more."

His anger wouldn't let him respond, so he clenched his fists and listened.

"They made me memorize it word-for-word. They shot me, sir, with something to help me remember... I'm no good at it usually but here goes: 'continue to protect the demons that expose us, and we'll spill your secrets to the world. Your subjects will finally see you for who you are, a diseased Rat Master in a dark, lawless hole creating genetic monsters from prezero cloth. Remember the punishment for treason is still death. This is your only warning.'"

Preston waited for some time before responding. He thought about the Academy. He considered the few bright spots in the school's recent history—three new blue dots for his map. He fixated on the one bigger and darker than the rest. *So many precautions on that one but was it enough?* "Is that all, Elaine?"

"They said something else. And I know they gave me that shot…. I don't think I heard right, sir. They said, 'Wolves cannot serve two moons but demons can.' Does that mean anything to you?"

Preston smiled grimly. "Mean something? No, Elaine, not really, but you heard correctly. It's a calling card of sorts. One that I had not heard for a long time." He tapped the connection closed.

Preston breathed for a few moments before working his feet into some Flexi-fit slippers. He pushed himself up and off his bed with a groan. He felt a twinge in his knees. *Time to replace the caps*, he thought. *Third set this decade. Damn things.* He walked slowly over to his garden-side window and stretched. *The asters in bloom in Month Four? Amazing.* He gazed at the rows and rows of pink puff balls as they swayed gently in the breeze. *The new gardener should be commended.*

Preston turned his head away from the view and shut his eyes. He pictured the person he wanted to talk to next, and the connection was made. "Peter?" he whispered. *Relax*, he thought. "Don't be alarmed, old boy, but this might come as a shock."

Peter O'Sullivan answered, a little groggily as if he was woken from sleep. "Mid-sun to you, father. Nothing shocks me anymore. You know that."

"Well, I hope that's true because our little trip might be in jeopardy."

"Because of the protests?"

"Not those. I rather like what's going on there. Might even help us one day." Icy dread hissed up the bio-line to Preston like static.

"She's in trouble, isn't she? You said you could protect us. You could protect him."

Brain buggers showed him my fear, he thought, irritated. He shook his head in temporary defeat to the FSA technology he depended on. "Protection might not be possible."

"I don't believe that, sir. I've seen what you can do."

"My arm's rather bent on this one, nearly broken."

"By who?"

"Well, to start, Augustus Reaver."

"The Director of the FSA? He's your friend. You two won the Freedom Wars together. Both your names are on our constitution! I've experienced vReads on it."

"Not just Augustus. His son, the Deputy Director. He was never a signer, but he's just as mad with power as his father. Make no mistake about it, the two of them want to rule."

"How do you know that?"

"Augustus left me a rather convincing message. As far as us being friends, Augustus hates me. Always has. His sights are firmly set on my Office. I just don't know how he plans to take it yet."

"I don't believe it, sir."

"And yet, it is true."

Chapter 2

Gerald's Secret

Gerald Goodstone lay awake fully dressed staring at the ceiling of his dorm room knowing the alarm was about to go off. For Gerald at nineteen years old, awake was not much different than sleep. His brain never shut off and his dreams were so vivid, he could only describe them as repetitive sessions of lucid hallucinations. He assumed he slept each night because he'd wake rested enough, but his imagination painted the dark hours with visions of ordinary people doing routine and usually boring jobs. He didn't know all their names, but some of the people he imagined in dreams became as real to Gerald as the Academy friends he lived with each day.

Last night, Gerald dreamt he was a lithium miner in Free New Guinea. Such specificity for a dream was not uncommon. He experienced the sensation of flying over the mountains like a hawk looking for a meal when he spotted the miner going about his work in a quarry hundreds of meters below. His sharp eyes swept towards the man, drawn by his white hat. Gerald hit the hat at full speed, splashing into the man's skull like a bird dives into water. His eyes surfaced to see what the miner saw—boring old earth-spec controls for what appeared to be a smallish rock duster with buckets and a boring drill. These types of dreams usually came with families attached. Gerald finished the miner's shift, feeling as if he had worked every minute of it, and then returned home to a daughter with bright green eyes. She jumped into the miner's arms and Gerald felt the hug. It was warm, good, and smelled of peppermint candies. For a moment while sleeping, Gerald loved the little girl with all his might just as if he was the tired but happy dad coming home from work.

The dream feelings of belonging never lasted long, because intermixed with those lingering, sleepy sensations were Gerald's waking sensations of ever-present and sometimes menacing whispers echoing around inside his head. Gerald sat up and waved at the alarm so it wouldn't go off. According to the Academy counsellors, the dreams were Gerald's way of coping with his memories of the fire. When confronted with Gerald's ability to retain the skills he learned in dreams, they told him the skills were not new. He had lost skills due to trauma. His dreams floated them back to the surface like memories from forgotten SLYscape training simulations. Gerald had reminded them he was eleven when the fire occurred. How much training could he have acquired? They had no answer.

The Academy counsellors seemed to know a lot about dreams but very little about what Gerald experienced. So Gerald started calling his dreams, night visions. Night visions didn't always happen at night but they were always preceded by his whispers getting excited and loud. The counsellors didn't know about Gerald's whispers, but they had asked him about voices more than once. Pretending his whispers didn't exist was the only lie Gerald was good at telling. Gerald stared anxiously at the silver ball floating a few inches off the charging pedestal at the center of his orderly desk. Only one person knew the truth, and it was his best friend, AJ O'Sullivan.

Many years ago, AJ and Gerald had been in the Academy's science lab experimenting with fermented fruit juices to see if they could get drunk like the Pre-Zeros did without using synthesized stimulants. They discovered they could. Not anticipating the side-effects of drinking alcohol, Gerald told AJ all about the people whispering in his head. Even drunk, he recognized his mistake and tried playing the voices off as a joke. AJ said the voices proved Gerald was a genius because he had a Muse. It was why his vWare hacks were the best the Academy for Gifted Students had ever seen. By the end of the night, AJ was convinced the whispers were masterminding Gerald's ability to change grades for any students who could pay them enough perks for the SLYcade. Gerald's admission also proved, according to AJ, how terrible Gerald was at lying. *Your face does this and your eyes do that,* he said, contorting his body to make them laugh. *You got a Muse, tweak! Just admit it.*

Once sober, Gerald regretted telling AJ anything. He remembered his father's warning about the importance of keeping his secrets. *If the bad people knew what you could do, Gerald… they'd hunt you down….* Despite the warning, Gerald often wanted to tell AJ more, but there was only so much crazy even a best friend could be expected to understand. Gerald lightly dragged his fingertips across the icy metal of the scribeosphere. He stared past his own reflection to the spot of fog that always marred its metal skin. Inside was the shifting form of an insect, ever happily though quite insanely, staring back. He called it the locust now, but it was the same grasshopper from his mother's green gem on the leather cord. *A necklace friend so you'll never be lonely,* his mother had told him on his tenth birthday.

"Don't give me that look, locust," Gerald said. "I'm still mad at you."

The whispers in Gerald's head coughed, stopped, and then started up again but as a softer, barely audible sound beneath the sing-song humming of a little girl at play. *Get over it, freak,* the locust said, in a perfect imitation of Lizzy. *You told me to pick a voice. I picked.*

Hearing his long dead sister speak would have been unnerving if Gerald hadn't been listening to Lizzy talk for the past several months. Gerald knew the insect was just a vWare trick to help him visualize the connection between himself and the scribeosphere. Inside the scribeosphere was a gold disc called a vWare Control Module. The VCM connected the ionic activity in Gerald's brain to the scribeosphere's core commands. When Gerald pictured words or images the vWare recognized, the locust responded through the capabilities of the scribeosphere.

Gerald remembered his mother teaching him how to draw the locust to the surface of the gem with his thoughts. It took hours of thinking the same thought to make it happen the first time. After that, it took less than a second. His dad later enhanced the vWare in the gem by recording Gerald's brain activity for months and layering his short and long term memory patterns onto the command code's superstructure. Every new thought became a book ready to be translated into a library of commands if the pattern repeated. The gem's library had grown substantially before the fire, which is why Gerald's dad moved the library to the scribeosphere hoping Gerald could use the commands to fly the prezero toy with his mind. Gerald remembered how excited he had been when it worked. Nobody but his dad would have risked layering uncensored thoughts on top of vWare. It just wasn't done. What Gerald didn't understand was why nobody else could see the locust or hear it speak. *Because you're a crazy tweak,* the locust said in Lizzy's voice. *I'm haunting you, not them.*

"That's why I'm mad," Gerald said, out loud. The locust and its voice seemed as real to Gerald as his whispers and night visions. Granted, since nobody else could see or hear the locust, it was possible none of his senses could be trusted. All he could prove to anybody was he could control the scribeosphere with his mind which was pretty amazing to most people. To Gerald, it was just vWare, no more amazing than simulation pods or immersion spheres unless he was crazy. "What if I am just critters? Hearing things? Seeing things?"

Such a freak, Gerals. You see me. You hear me. Above the whispers where I am. Where you need me to be. Of course you're critters—crazy tweak, talking to yourself.

"You stole my sister's voice."

It happened during the last scribeosphere maintenance cycle when he tried to repeat his dad's trick by giving the locust all of his memories since entering the Academy. Layering raw thought over vWare was still not done but a night vision convinced him to try it. A prezero engineer named, Irvine Frank, provided the steps. The counsellors would have told Gerald, Irvine Frank wasn't real either—just a buried memory surfacing through a traumatized brain. That's why Gerald didn't like his counsellors. They never believed him.

The day after updating his scribeosphere, the locust started casting Lizzy's voice into his mind. He didn't know how to make it stop talking. He didn't know how it imprinted itself with his little sister's personality. *Freak, tweak, Gerals...* all words his seven year old sister had liked to call him. Worse than the locust using her words, her personality grew stronger each day. The scribeosphere's locust had become so convincing in its portrayal of Lizzy, Gerald wasn't certain any longer if he wanted to fix it. He missed his little sister so much. He missed his mom and his dad. He missed them all more than he could bare. The locust—a silly, VCM—was one of his last connections to the life he once had. He didn't want to give it up.

Gerald was traumatized also, according to his counsellors, because there were no bodies to bury. They were removed from the Goodstone house but the morgue had no record of it—a mix-up, the morgue had said. They lost Gerald's family and there was nothing they could do. His eyes heated with blurry tears as he scanned the few artifacts he had from that day: an empty platinum ring hanging from a leather neck cord; a gold buckle that fit into a removable belt clip; a green gemstone he wore in his ear, and a prezero bracelet dangling a dozen charms around an opal centerpiece the color of smoke.

Most of these "trinkets" as his Academy Prefects liked to call them were scattered around a single charging pedestal. They were what was left of his family. He had been taught traditional vWare coding by Prefect Humphrey who helped him program each piece just like he and his dad had planned to do in the summer of 59. It had been eight years since the fire, and now Gerald was finished with school. There was no more vWare to learn, and he would be compelled to leave the only home he had known since. It was time to move away from the Academy whether he wanted to or not. Today he graduated. Today was Designation Day.

Gerald had one final test. Depending on what it revealed to the Freeland Work Authority, his score would result in an official designation and citizen ranking ideally suited to his mental and physical strengths. The dezie, as the students called it, would become his job for life. Gerald had prepared for only one designation: FSA vWare Controller. He wanted the designation for its unlimited access to the FSA domain in the SLYscape. The FSA nodes were the original SLYscape worlds that set the vWare rules for how y-space interacted with the rest of the radiation spectrums. Even OPC nodes were lower in SLYscape domain hierarchy, which meant only people with access to the top level nodes of the FSA could move freely around the entire SLYscape. Gerald wanted that access.

The FSA designation was important to Gerald because without it, he might never be able to solve the greatest mystery of his life. Not the mystery of how the scribeosphere had gained Lizzy's personality. Or why it hummed lullabies that quieted the whispers in his head. Gerald wanted to solve the mystery of what happened to his family's bodies. The counsellors were hiding something. With an FSA vWare Controller designation, Gerald could venture unhindered into protected data spheres on the SLYscape. He'd learn the truth about what happened on the day of the fire instead of the "the facts" his counsellors wanted him to accept.

Gerald had undergone a mix of quick-time holographic conditioning and slow-time therapy to get him to stop asking questions about his family. He was supposed to believe nothing unusual happened on the night lightning burned down his house. He was supposed to accept tragedies happened all the time, especially when freedom storms were involved. When he wouldn't accept those things, the counsellors changed their stories and told him the bodies were so badly burned, disposal occurred on-site and not in a morgue. That was the real mix-up. Gerald remembered his mother and his little sister lying on her lap. If the fire had gotten them after he passed out, Gerald who was only a few meters away would have burned to death too.

The counsellors eventually settled on telling him his memory was faulty because he had replaced the worst moments of the night with imagined events. What the counsellors didn't fully appreciate about Gerald was how well his parents had taught him vWare. It had taken him less than a year at the Academy to hack into the SLYscape data spheres belonging to the Freeland Transportation Authority. According to the historical weather reports, not a single freedom storm was recorded over the island of Old New York on the date of the fire. What's more, according to a Revealer who worked for The Cardinal news sphere, the entire block of Layfette was destroyed, not just Gerald's house which is what the counsellors claimed.

Gerald's recollection didn't match the historical records either. He remembered the lightning. He remembered the blackness descending on his house before the first strike. He could still see the blue fire dancing up the walls and hear the thunder and crashing sounds tearing his house apart. The events of the night were as clear to him as yesterday, but based on recorded history, the fire couldn't have happened the way he remembered. In addition to his family, ninety-three other people died on Layfette Street that night. *How does lightning burn down an entire city block, killing everyone, when the sky was clear and calm?* When he reached out to ask the Revealer that question, he discovered the man disappeared six weeks after the fire.

A sudden pounding rattled his dormitory door. It startled Gerald until he heard the laughter on the other side. "Come on, tweak! Open up."

"Yeah, tweet-pecker! Open!"

"Shut up Jack."

"You said it."

"Doesn't mean you can."

"Boys! Be civil, we're almost—"

Gerald reached over and tapped the locking plate on the gray door which promptly split in two allowing his three friends to collapse into his dorm like felled trees. AJ swept one arm around Sally to keep her from hitting the ground. Jack just went headfirst into Gerald's desk, jostling all the jewelry and the scribeosphere.

"Excited are we?" Gerald asked, swiping the bracelet off the desk and slapping it around his wrist with a ratcheting click. He grabbed the belt clip and cinched it into place on the rose-colored sash of his Academy uniform. "Were you all like humping the door or what?"

"No such luck," Sally said, leaning into AJ and running her hands down the front of her red top, patting and primping her breasts as if unconscious of the effect it would have on the boys in the room. Jack stared openly at her with a creepy look on his face. Gerald looked away but not before catching Sally Yorkshire's mischievous smile. She was probably the prettiest girl at the Academy, and she knew it. AJ, standing nearly a half-meter taller than the rest of them, was oblivious to her. *Maybe his head's too far above her boobs to see them clearly.*

AJ let Sally go and stood up in Gerald's room like a mountain, his head nearly reaching the ceiling. At well over 2 meters tall and 135 kilos of pure muscle, he could have any girl he wanted. Gerald was red-headed, freckled, and awkward around them, weighing in at a whopping 74 kilos of skin and bone. "Hey Sally, Aje. You ready?"

"Tweak, yeah!" AJ said. "Ready to blow this place and get on with life."

Jack was an underclassman taking the practice version of the test today, so he simply shrugged. "Designation Day, Gerald. How's it feel?"

Gerald absentmindedly touched the green gemstone attached to his ear while staring down at the broken setting on the platinum ring his mother's jade had once occupied. The Rule of Law Officer who had returned the gem said it fused to the simulation pod's generator during the fire. *Almost missed it*, the ROLIE had said. *It cracked a little coming off but it's still good. Thought you might want to sell it.*

Gerald did not want to sell it. He remembered how he could summon the locust to the surface before the pod's generator cracked it. He remembered how the stone had grown frosty cold like his scribeosphere still did when he issued silent vWare commands to it. He remembered smoke billowing out of the gem to form a dragon-sized version of the locust. That part was a dream, the counsellors had assured him, induced by trauma. He believed them on this one point, but his belief didn't quash the memories. Ultimately, as cloudy and broken as the jade gemstone was, it was a gift from his mother.

When he held the jade close, it soothed the whispers in his head. If his mind stayed quiet, he could more precisely send commands to the locust in the scribeosphere. The scribeosphere was not a toy anymore. It did so much more than fly and record thought-messages. With the gem near, Gerald could focus strongly enough to tell the scribeosphere to fetch information from the SLYscape. Sometimes the locust would retrieve too much information or the wrong information. It was a small price to pay for Gerald because without the scribeosphere, he would need molecular implants to interact with the SLYscape. That was something he wasn't willing to do.

Before the gem was returned, the locust's voice was less understandable and the ever-present whispers in his head were noisier like crowds clapping or crisp paper crumpling. At night, if the gem was not close, the whispers would drown out the voice of the locust completely. He couldn't sleep because the whispers crashed about in his head like pots and pans clanging on top of angry voices screaming. On those nights, he'd simply rock with his hands clasped over his ears. The whispers could paralyze him with fear, so he welded the jade gemstone to an earring. The earring protected him now, and he rarely took it out.

Gerald considered the possibility he might be crazy. Maybe the reason nobody else talked about hearing whispers in their heads was because they didn't hear them. Maybe they couldn't see or hear the locust, because it existed only in Gerald's mind. Maybe the reason nobody layered personal brain activity onto vWare was because it caused hallucinations. The counsellors might be right. The locust, night visions—the whispers he kept secret—might all be the result of trauma. The fire might have cracked him as thoroughly as the WU gene demons cracked the moon. Of course, being critters couldn't explain how his hallucinations kept showing him other people's secrets. Every week it seemed, like daydreams full of tawdry gossip, the locust would show him something private about people he knew. Or he'd be forced to experience something he couldn't forget.

"Planet to Gerald," Jack said, snapping his fingers in front of Gerald's eyes.

AJ laughed. "Man's eccentric, Jackie boy. Zones like he's on something even when he's not."

Gerald shook himself and smiled. "Just thinking. It feels good, Jack. Or, maybe it's just different."

The four of them walked out of the dormitory room into the yellow light of the ornate upperclassman hallways. As the door clapped shut behind them, his sister's humming paused. *Good luck with your test, Gerals!*

Against his better judgment, he asked, "Nobody heard that, right?" He looked around.

"You know, if you weren't so weird," Sally said. "You might get a girlfriend."

Jack and AJ laughed. *Just checking*, Gerald thought, acutely aware of his cheeks getting hot.

"Too easy," Sally said, punching Gerald in the shoulder and then sidling up between him and AJ, hip-checking Jack out of the way. Gerald wasn't fooled. She put her arms around Gerald's back under his shoulders which felt nice, but the goal was AJ's waist, which she hugged tightly to her side.

"Ow," Jack said, belatedly.

The gang took the Northeast corridor which was the most direct route to the Exam Rooms. Since it was his last day walking the Academy halls, Gerald paid special attention to the synth-wood framed holo-snaps and sensory vids depicting scenes of great military victories against the World Union. *Goodstones did that,* he thought, with pride. Though most of the scenes depicted officers, not the grunts who blew themselves up as the Goodstones were purported to have done. Regardless, Gerald was still proud of his family's contribution.

"Speaking of weird blushing boys," Sally continued. "Have you guys caught the news? Some of the spheres are pumpin' protests."

"Sensory vids full of powerlords in trouble," said Jack, touching a tattooed spot on his neck. "Fun times." His eyes went glassy for a moment and then he continued: "The latest conspiracy-void got a couple sVids that made the protesters look as off-scape as the Prefects in the snaps. They were screaming like 'roid-freaks and projecting some pretty hateful signs."

"Protesters?" AJ asked, suddenly tapping his knuckles in a quick staccato. "Powerful members of the OPC exposed by SLYscape virus," he vRead out loud. "Who's next?"

"You guys don't know the right spheres. Take a gander…"

Sally, Jack, and AJ tapped tattooed spots on their bodies like they were scratching flees. Jack started to laugh but AJ's eyes grew wide. To Gerald, he looked almost scared. "Oh no," he said.

"What's going on?"

"Seriously, Gerald. You'll never land a girl if you can't vRead. This is why you need an implant."

"Man's phobic," AJ said, recovering.

"C'mon, Gerald. It's just a tiny pinch on the thigh. I got my first mole at six. Didn't even cry."

"Scared of injectors," he said, lying. He would never allow a molecular solution of angstromnites into his bloodstream. The injections connected people directly to the SLYscape, and the last thing Gerald needed was more distractions in his head.

"You're missing it then."

"Lascivious!" Jack said, relishing the word.

"Scandalous is what I'd say," Sally quipped, hugging Gerald and AJ a little closer as they walked. "My spheres showed powerlords in positions only their mamas and doctors have seen. Did you know you could pay for that kind of treatment? Had to watch for ten minutes before the FSA thankfully censored the SLYcast."

"I don't think the protests are about what powerlords pay for in private sim pods," AJ said, uncharacteristically serious.

"Oh, I don't know," she said, flirtatiously. "Did you see the sVids on Prefect Larkin? Never seen such naughtiness from someone his age. When my Grams described in her serious voice how rosy his little bottom was peeking out of that ridiculous costume…." Sally laughed. "Now it's all Grams sees when he preaches on Faith Days. Worth a protest or two in her mind—"

"Lascivious!" Jack said, again, laughing.

"Agreed," AJ said. "The tweaker's got a node out, but what's got people ready to fight is the stealing. The virus caught five Prefects in three prefectures skimming perks from infrastructure funds. Rich getting richer makes 'em mad every time."

"Grams doesn't care about perks. She's cares about behaving. Larkin was her guy and the moment he shimmied his old man hips into those outfits… What do you think, Gerald? You ever do things like that when Mama SLY's not watching?"

Gerald shrugged, refusing to be baited into embarrassment. Instead of answering, he tried to drink in the prezero tapestry hanging over the gilded Interconnect Archway. The tapestry was natural, earth-grown fabric woven by hand. Gerald marveled at how vibrant the colors remained. The threads spun the image of Preston Rose and Augustus Reaver in full military regalia shaking hands at a World Union ball. Two beautiful women stood behind them, clapping and smiling. It was taught that cupped in their clasped palms was secret information Preston and Augustus exchanged about the formation of the rebellion. If there had been moles back then, Gerald believed, they'd have been caught. "Mama SLY is always watching, Sally, which means there are no secrets. No matter who you are."

"Is that right," she said, thoughtfully. "No secrets?"

"None."

They all walked through the archway into a clear egg-shaped capsule big enough to hold eight people standing in a circle. Despite its size, the Interconnect felt cramped with AJ taking up a good third of the space. A moment later, weather seals swallowed the egg whole from the bottom, wrapping them up in a transparent energy foil that allowed them to see outside but allowed nobody from the outside to see in. There was a brief rumble and then they felt the capsule lurch sideways. "Not even the High Prelate himself can have secrets?"

Gerald shook his head.

Standing on the other side of the circle, Sally smiled and grabbed AJ's arm to steady herself. "So if there are no secrets, smarty boy, and I was Mama SLY, what naughty things would I catch you doing in holo-sessions?"

Jack laughed.

"Thankfully," Gerald said, not giving her the satisfaction of a blush. "You're not Mama SLY."

"What if I was?"

Gerald smiled. "You'd melt with envy."

The four of them laughed, a bit more boisterously than the joke deserved. Gerald knew she just teased him in good fun because he was shy, an easy target. He was used to being the butt of jokes. He also knew she was in no position to talk righteously about questionable behavior. He knew this fact better than most because the locust in the scribeosphere liked to slip him private sVids, vWare logs, and holo-snaps even when he didn't ask for them. He knew, for example, that Sally watched AJ's Championship wrestling match 22 times in the last two weeks, pausing each time at the moment when AJ bent to tie his shoe. *Disgusting*, he heard in the back of his mind, so faint that Gerald knew the scribeosphere was almost out-of-range. *Tell me what's going on*, he sent to it, picturing the word: "protests." *Fine,* the voice responded, sounding more mechanical than it had all day. *Command Accepted.*

The ride was not long as the Interconnect travelled at fifty kph over the twisting streets of New Detroit. They could see dozens of other eggs moving to their various destinations in the city. Gerald's attention fixated as it usually did on the great canyon to the south. On the other side of the canyon, though Gerald could not see it clearly, was the Great Salt Marshes that spanned all the way east to what was left of the Atlantic Ocean. Gerald had studied prezero maps, and he wondered how many people died in the east during the Freedom Wars. Facts like that were hard to come by as the information lay buried in a time before SLY spectrum radiation existed. The egg lurched to a stop and opened its doors.

"We're here," Jack said. "The point of no return."

They exited the Interconnect into a massive domed building that was used for all Academy exams throughout the year. In the spring, for the purpose of assigning designations, the Prefects of the Academy for Gifted Students decorated the building with simulations of ancient pillars and marbled floors. Standing on either side of what appeared to be a ten meter tall swing door were two marbled ladies in flowing robes holding balance scales. "A little heavy-handed, don't you think?" AJ said, laughing at the decorations.

"Yeah. The scales of justice as we're about to be measured," Sally said, quietly.

All four of them stopped a moment to consider the looming doorway before them. Inside it their mental and physical prowess would be judged. Gerald knew it was just a big simulation pod, but the act of stepping into the testing chamber was the single most significant thing any of them were likely to do in their lives. Well, not Jack, it was only his practice test.

"Enough thinking," AJ said, stepping up and through the door without raising his hands. It gave way like a curtain billowing over his body as it deactivated AJ's molecular implants and any external connections he had to the SLYscape. There would be no cheating on the Designation Exam. The cheater-veil, which the doorway was called, would ensure it.

"Good luck, Gerald," Sally said, hugging him. "You're weird but smarter than anybody I've ever met. You'll get your FSA dezie and be a big shot someday. I just know it." She leaned into him and gave him a sisterly kiss on the cheek and then stepped backward through the veil. "Oh, it tickles," she said, grinning.

Jack and Gerald stood side-by-side looking at the doorway. "Man, how's anything not generated in a sim look like her? Did you see how she fills the uniform? You two I'll get over not seeing next year. Her I'll miss." He took a little hop and disappeared.

Gerald stood outside the room by himself, studying the cheater-veil. "You there?" he asked the empty hall. There was no verbal response, only a quiet whisper like waves echoing in a seashell. He wondered if the veil could sever his connection to the scribeosphere. *Probably not*, he thought, *the scribeosphere's connected to the SLYscape, not me.* He walked forward through the tingling doorway.

On my own after all, he thought. *What could go wrong?*

Chapter 3

Designations

The inside of the exam room was terribly anticlimactic. Gerald saw Sally, AJ, and Jack standing on black oval platforms on the floor. Hovering above them were white oval rings. Once the exam began, a holographic force bubble would generate between the white and black ovals, encapsulating the student in a SLYscape experience that produced personalized exam questions based on their progression through the standard Academy rubric. The pillbox shaped bubble was called a SLYscape receiver, or SEER as it was more typically called by the FWA Overseers who programmed the tests. The Overseers, also called Blackstars because of the black robes they wore, programmed the experiences the SEER exams produced for the students. The SEERs produced such realistic testing scenarios, some of the weaker students became physically and mentally overwhelmed. Emergency drones lined the walls of the exam room, one for each student.

AJ lazily saluted Gerald with two fingers wishing him luck. Sally smiled thinly, betraying the nervousness she really felt as she shifted foot-to-foot.

"That's enough, AJ," Prefect Humphrey said. "No signaling."

AJ rolled his eyes at Prefect Humphrey, an overweight, balding man in his early hundreds who sat behind a desk on a red cushioned high-backed chair. The desk was raised up on an elevated testing dais. Before Humphrey, two dozen spinning exam spheres floated, one for each student. Prefect Humphrey would witness what his students were seeing, hearing, and doing during the exam period through those spheres. This ensured there would be no cheating as he watched their performances feed directly to Freeland Work Authority headquarters in Old New York.

Humphrey knew all of the Academy students by name. He had been their head master of vWare programming for the entire time Gerald had been at the Academy. He had taught Gerald a lot, but Humphrey and AJ did not get along. "As you should know by now, AJ, signaling is strictly prohibited during exams."

"Yes, sir, Prefect Humphrey. I'm just so excited to find out what your boys at the FWA think of me. All a'jitter with anticipation—hands going crazy. Won't happen again."

"AJ," Humphrey said. "I can't say it will be a hardship seeing you go, but please don't embarrass me on the vWare portion of the test. I've never had a student fail before. I'd hate for my streak to end with you."

A few underclassman, including Jack, laughed until AJ swung his eyes towards them. AJ could be intimidating when he wanted to be. *Sometimes*, Gerald thought, *he's intimidating even when he doesn't want to be.* "Don't worry, sir. Gerald's taught me a few things that should help."

Prefect Humphrey scowled for a moment until he spotted Gerald step onto his testing oval. "Gerald! How are you feeling?" he asked, suddenly very animated.

"Good, sir."

Humphrey smiled dotingly at his favorite pupil. "I will most certainly miss our little talks. You've been an inspiration to an old man."

"Hardly, sir."

"No need for modesty, Gerald. You see the SLYscape with such clarity of purpose. I've taught those who have become Prefects. Nay. Prelates even, who are not half your equal at spinning the vee. Truly, you have mastered what I could teach."

AJ snorted.

Humphrey continued: "One day you will rise so high in the FSA that your disrespectful friend will be forced to look up at you for a change. On that day, I'd be honored to share war stories of designated life over a cup of ginger sparkle. Perhaps, at the OPC Tower in Freeland Plaza where I spent my best years?"

"I'd like that, sir. Thank you."

"Think nothing of it, sir."

"No, really. I appreciate what you've done for me… what the Academy has done for me." Gerald wasn't lying. The Academy had given him a home when his parents' savings warranted only an orphanage. The Academy was a part of Gerald now. He hoped one day, after he discovered where his family lay buried, he could repay the Academy for what it had done. "I look forward to seeing you again, sir."

Prefect Humphrey smiled. "As for the rest of you errant children, you have four hours. In three... two... one... destinies begin!"

Silence reigned in the exam room until Prefect Humphrey expelled a long breath. "For those of you who didn't get my little bon mot," he said, drily. "'Destinies begin!' means you can start your tests. Rose help us if you are the future of the Freeland."

There was a collective rumble of sighs and chuckles intermixed with the whistles of SEER force fields flaring to life. Gerald lifted his hands above his head and then bent his wrists in a quick conductor's flourish that activated his personal SEER holographic immersion experience. With an audible pop, the classroom disappeared. "Welcome Gerald Goodstone," a woman's deep voice said. "Choose your path wisely, good pupil, and be judged."

In every direction, mathematical symbols floated before his eyes. Some he recognized and some he believed were nonsense symbols intended to confuse him. Behind the symbols, a moving skyline of New Detroit and other cities Gerald had never visited flashed into and out of his visual field. *Let's start with my strengths*, he thought, and touched the largest of the symbols in the foreground. The skyline shifted and Gerald felt himself gently pulled towards an area of the SLYscape where an endless river of problems waited to be solved. The first one, Gerald decided, was easy. *Next*, he thought, confidently. Gerald loved tests.

And then it was done.

"Examinations off," Prefect Humphrey announced.

Gerald panicked. His proof was entering its fifth set of vSpace models and scrawling notations. There were at least two more theorems to prove, and he was out of time. He let his body sag as the SEER force bubble lost energy. When the simulation clicked off completely, a voice squawked: "Good bye, Gerald Goodstone. Your

Academy privileges will be revoked in twelve hours." *I didn't even get to the physical stuff,* he despaired.

"We're done," AJ said, his voice suddenly loud beside him. "Can you believe it?"

Gerald stepped off the oval and shook his head. "I'm not so sure," he said. "I think I just flunked."

Sally, who stood next to AJ, danced from foot-to-foot and said, "Flunked? That's a shame."

"A shame?" he questioned, somewhat troubled by her nonchalance.

"Just terrible," she said, smiling. "Got to pee." Sally spun and practically ran out of the room without a backward look.

"Guess she really had to go," AJ said.

"Aje, I'm serious!"

AJ shook his head and emitted a throaty bear's growl which Gerald had come to recognize as AJ's sarcastic laughter. "You flunked? Which part?"

"Everything!"

"Not one right answer?" he asked, grinning. "Not even about y-space?"

"Not even y-space."

"So when you told me last week: y-space was biological thievery harnessing unused brain capacity donated—to quote you—by our simple-minded acceptance of molecular injections, you were wrong 'cause you don't know what y-space is?"

"Right."

"And you flunked vWare, the language you built an interactive model of the SLYscape with… like the whole SLYscape mapped with topography and everything. You flunked that?"

"Big time flunked."

"Despite ole' Humpty Dump saying you mastered the sucker, you got everything wrong?"

"Could barely prove the earth-spec theorem showing vSpace influence on data spheres in a vacuum."

"Don't know what that means but sounds bad. Sally was right. Terrible."

Gerald shook his head looking terrified. "Balls Almighty, Aje. I froze!"

AJ looked to the front of the room. "Then why you ranked so high?"

"It was stupid question fifty, Aje. If I had a little more time, I could have gotten it. I know I could have. I was on to something, but I blew it. How'd you handle question fifty?"

"By not doing it."

"I'm being serious, Aje."

"So am I. Nobody gets to fifty in the vWare portion of the test. I answered fifteen questions, then decided to shoot up some guys with a shimmer gun, clobber a ninja girl with a zap-rod, and show an army of dimwit drones how to defeat some simulated General in zero-g dome battle. Look at the tote—"

Gerald glanced to the front of the room above Prefect Humphrey's head where score matrixes were flashing achievements alongside the names of the graduating students. AJ was right. Most students finished less than twenty vWare questions. Only a few took the physical tests except for AJ who took them all. Gerald sighed with relief until he saw a conspicuous absence next to his name. "Hey!" he yelped. "I didn't get a dezie!"

AJ nodded. "Me neither. I figure there is some kind of delay."

"But look at everyone else—"

"I think they're just the underclassman."

Jack popped up next to them. "If my score was real, you'd be looking at a brand new overseer. Only seventy-nine of those jobs in the Freeland."

AJ blanched. "You? A Blackstar?" He shook his head. "Never gonna happen."

Jack grinned. "You can't handle it. One day because of me, justice will prevail and powerlords won't be able do whatever the hell they want… unless they remember ole Jackie-boy in their wills. Blackstars got all the perks. That's right," he said, doing a bizarre little hoppity dance like a prezero penguin trying to run. "I'm the King of the Academy—best job you could get. Deal with it, tweet suckers."

AJ's arm swung out and furled Jack into himself, effortlessly pinning Jack's arm to his giant chest with one hand. "King of my Academy? Who says?"

Jack squirmed in AJ's arms, and then relaxed. "Me?" he asked in a small but jovial voice. "Pretty sure it was me. 'cause, I got the dezie

Jack Pot. Get it?" He gestured with his eyes to the score matrix. "Read the tote and weep, big guy."

AJ let him go and said. "Aw, why not? Kingship couldn't go to a smarmier, I mean, nicer guy."

Jack beamed. "So, what'd you two get?"

AJ shrugged.

"Not sure yet."

Jack looked as if he misunderstood. He turned his eyes toward the front of the room then spoke in a loud voice. "Prefect Humphrey, sir. AJ and Gerald weren't given dezies. What's up with that?"

Prefect Humphrey peered through the testing spheres and focused on the boys as if he had forgotten they were still in his exam room. "Not possible," he said. "Let me see." He pulled two spheres to the front so he could study them more closely. "AJ, you were awarded the designation of... strange."

"What's strange?"

"An anomaly. Says here you're an extraordinarily gifted young man. Scores for Military Strategy and Special Operations Field Work are the best this Academy has produced since Cole Reaver himself. Normally, I'd say, 'Well done!'"

"What's stopping you?"

"Your citizen ranking is a mere thirty-seven, which means your loyalty to the Freeland Nation is just a hair above a World Union spy."

The few students remaining in the room laughed until they realized Prefect Humphrey was serious. "AJ, how could this be?"

AJ shrugged but Gerald noticed his back stiffening which indicated he was concerned by what he heard. "The test's broken, sir. Got to be."

Prefect Humphrey stared at AJ for a long time and then as if remembering where he was, shook himself to action. "No matter. This will sort itself out."

"How's that, sir?"

"How? You're being investigated, of course."

"Investigated?" AJ snapped, all pretense of good humor gone. "By who?"

"The Freeland Work Authority has a very impressive contingent of specialists for this type of thing. They'll send Blackstars to your home. They'll talk to you, your parents, your friends, anyone who might be problematic. They'll root out the problem. Mark my words." He dismissed AJ with a glance and looked next to Gerald.

Prefect Humphrey nodded with satisfaction. "Thank goodness you're not a spy, Gerald. A glowing citizen ranking of ninety-seven. I knew you were a standup fellow from the moment I set eyes on you. I myself scored just ninety-six—"

"They can't do that!" AJ yelled.

Prefect Humphrey paused and considered AJ's aggressive stance, seemingly confused by his student's outburst. "Can't do what, AJ?"

"Investigate me."

"I'm sorry but you are mistaken," he said, with just a hint of mean-spirited satisfaction. "The Blackstar Overseers are FWA. Not even the FSA or OPC have power over them. Following that logic, Blackstars can do anything they grid-well want. Investigating you… not an issue. But don't worry, as long as you are not a radical, your memories will not be wiped clean. Contingent upon a favorable outcome, the rest of your scores earned you a wonderful designation: OPC Freedom Guard."

"Freedom Guard?" AJ yelled. "I'd rather be a radical." He about-faced and left the room.

Humphrey sighed. "Gerald, in the future, you'll need to pick better friends."

"He's like a brother to me, sir."

"How unfortunate," Prefect Humphrey said, before suddenly shifting forward in his seat as if startled. "My word."

Gerald felt the room close in around him. He felt a chill in the pit of his stomach.

Humphrey stood unsteadily and leaned over the testing spheres. "What have you done, Gerald?"

"I got to question fifty—"

"It's one thing getting there, Gerald." Humphrey's arms started to shake as he leaned his weight over the desk. "It's another thing making an *honest* effort. You're so much better than this!"

"I don't know what you mean."

"Did AJ say something to you before the test?"

"What? No."

"Then how do you explain!" Prefect Humphrey hurled the holographic testing sphere across the room at Gerald. Like his scribeosphere would have done, the holographic sphere stopped a few inches from his eyes.

"Fifty, Gerald! You answered fifty out of fifty correctly."

"Isn't that good, sir?"

"Not good," he shouted. Prefect Humphrey took several deep breaths trying to calm himself down. He slowly sat down in his chair and put his head in his palms. "I'm sorry, Gerald. I sometimes forget the pressure. It's for life after all. I'm sorry. There are no do-overs here."

Jack's lips moved without making sound until he found words: "What'd he get, sir?"

Prefect Humphrey's hands slipped down his wrinkled face. He looked skyward. "Undetermined."

"What's that mean?"

"Gerald's being investigated too… for cheating."

"But I didn't."

"But you did," Humphrey said. "Questions three, thirteen, and twenty-three are all plants. They cannot be solved. If a student gets any of those correct, the security node at the FSA is alerted. The SEER thinks you got them right which is impossible. You rigged the exam, Gerald."

"I didn't."

"The alarms have already sounded, lad. The Blackstars will be visiting you too."

Numbly, Gerald nodded. "I see, sir." Jack reached up and put his hand on Gerald's shoulder. "I guess I won't be seeing you for that drink."

"No," Humphrey said. "I don't expect you will."

Gerald retreated through the tingling sensation of the cheater-veil and squinted his eyes against the bright sunlight shining through the clear windows that AJ stood before, gazing out at New Detroit.

Gerald stepped up to him and looked out to the river and canyon beyond.

"Why so glum chum... it's me their investigating."

Gerald shook his head. "Me too."

AJ turned. "You? For what?"

"Perfect score. I guess you're not supposed to be able to do that."

"You cheated?" He shook his head. "Of course, you didn't."

"Humphrey said they had questions planted that were unsolvable, yet the test seemed to think I solved them."

"Did you solve them?"

Gerald thought back to the numbered questions Humphrey mentioned. He nodded. "Every one."

AJ guffawed and then stretched, his eyes relaxing. "You're smarter than even the overseers." AJ clapped him on the shoulder. "Don't worry about it, Gerald. You'll prove the test makers wrong. You'll get your FSA assignment and be happy. Me, I'm not so sure."

"You'll be fine, AJ. You're no spy."

AJ shuffled his feet and breathed loudly for a moment. "What if the citizen ranking was right?"

"Thirty-seven? It's a mistake. You're no traitor—"

"But what if the score was right?"

A strange feeling gripped Gerald, chilling him. "They don't just wipe subversives, Aje. They kill them."

"Unless they're like me."

Gerald thought about it. If the FSA found criminals fit enough to join their ranks, they conscripted them. "They'd turn you into an Enforcer, Aje."

AJ nodded. "I'm not going to let them do that."

Enforcers were the cybernetically enhanced brass fists and steel-toed boots of the Freeland Security Army. Enforcers arrested people. They broke bones and tore ligaments if criminals resisted. Enforcers had the authority to take lawbreakers to holographic conditioning cells without formal charges. They were above the law, because they were the law. They were feared by Freelanders because people believed the urban myth that enforcers were not entirely human.

Enforcers were law officers who had been pressed into service as punishment for high crimes against the Freeland. Only a handful of conscripts proved healthy enough to integrate biologically into their mechanized uniforms. The ones that failed to integrate disappeared. Academy students believed their memories were wiped and then conditioned onto a better path. "You'd look ridiculous in an enforcer uniform," Gerald said, trying to make a joke and lighten the mood. "You're too ugly to be let in their club."

"I can't be hooked up to one of those things, Gerald. You've seen the sVids in Humpty's class. It's like killing someone. Only they're not dead. They're slaves."

Gerald shuddered. It was true.

The uniforms gave enforcers strength and weaponry strong enough to enforce the law but at an extreme cost to the bodies trapped inside. The uniforms were designed for war but when the Freedom Wars ended, they became a ready-made police force. In that role, street enforcers broke up gangs, quelled riots, and prevented looting after the first freedom storms ravished the once thriving World Union cities and towns. A couple of decades after the OPC was founded, Freelanders began resenting enforcers. It was true, criminals were on the run but so were civilians. Few people dared leave their homes because enforcers didn't mind collateral damage. After the Quell of 39 when enforcers left thousands dead in the Freeland Nation's streets, they were decommissioned from street patrol, but they were not destroyed as the people wanted. Instead, enforcers were simply moved underground

The enforcers patrolled the streets from underground tunnels snaking beneath most Freeland Nation cities and towns. In cities protected by Environment Bubbles, enforcers patrolled from cloaked catwalks which were invisible from street level. Not seeing the enforcers every day helped people forget about them. Yet when crime happened, they'd pop up or down into the thick of it seemingly out of thin air. Their sudden appearances spawned supernatural rumors about their abilities. As Prefect Humphrey explained in one of Gerald's first classes, the rumors were as effective a crime deterrent as the enforcers themselves. *If it keeps crime low, let the ignorant masses believe enforcers transport instantly through time-and-space to zap wrong-doers in the act,* Prefect Humphrey had said. His comment drew laughter from the class. Only not from AJ and Gerald who saw no humor in the myth.

"I won't let them turn you into an enforcer, Aje," Gerald said with conviction as he clapped his friend on the shoulder.

Showing a tiny smile, AJ's eyes brightened. "You'll stop the whole FSA to save me?"

Gerald nodded. "We're brothers, Aje. You'd do the same for me."

AJ cuffed Gerald on the shoulder which sent him stumbling a few steps to the side. "Then there's nothing to worry about! It's you and me, Gerald, against the world."

Gerald laughed noticing how busy the city below had become as he glanced out the window. "Well, maybe not the world," he said. "Lot of people out there."

"Too late. You already promised."

Sally came jogging up the hallway from the bathroom, her shoes slapping the hard floor. "Promised what?" she asked, as if she'd been standing right next to them. She continued to smile excitedly until the boys realized she had not heard about the investigations.

"Once Gerald's a big shot," AJ said. "He promises not to forget about us."

"I knew it. Passed with flying colors, right?"

"He got a hundred percent," AJ said.

Gerald nodded.

"Such a sVid Queen—hundred percent—and you thought you flunked. Unbelievable. What about your scores, big man?" she teased. "They making you lift weights for a living?" She placed her hand on AJ's chest and rubbed. He smiled trying to hide the troubled thoughts behind his expression.

"Freedom Guard," Gerald said. "Best scores since Cole Reaver."

"Yea!" She clapped her hands. "That means you're staying Up North. Me too!" Sally jumped to hug AJ around the neck. She hung there for a moment before AJ realized he should hug back.

"So what's your dezie?" AJ asked. His eyes suddenly rolled up in his sockets and then he blinked. "Ma left us a note." He shifted Sally like a doll to one arm and then tapped a couple of tattooed spots on his wrist. "She says she's cooking pot roast and... foy... grass. What the balls is foy grass?"

Sally laughed and patted his shoulders with both hands. "Foie gras, silly. Goose liver. Now put me down."

AJ wrinkled his nose, "Gross." He set her down and tapped his wrist again. "She's expecting Gerald and me at nine, so we need to catch the five-thirty tube."

Gerald glanced at the kinetic time actuator charm hanging from his bracelet. "We better hurry up. We got to get our stuff before the dorms lock."

Sally kissed them good-bye and said she'd see them soon, though both boys knew it was unlikely. She was designated and off to who knows where and they were not. "So, what was your dezie, Sally?" Gerald asked.

She winked at him and turned to where Jack stood slightly apart from the gang. She held out her arm and he took it with a goofy grin. "Shh! It's a secret."

Gerald watched Jack escort Sally away from them in the other direction. *No good-bye, Jack?* he thought. He looked up at the Stationary Eye recording the hallway in front of the examination room. *Of course, not.* In addition to the Stationary Eyes recording them, there were likely Flying Eyes with on-board stunners hiding nearby in case AJ or Gerald said something incriminating. Gerald peered down at his bracelet knowing it could shield conversations from Eyes. *Should have turned you on*, he thought.

Gerald and Jack both knew investigations, despite what AJ said, never ended well for the accused or their friends. *Jack was just being smart.*

Chapter 4

Cattle Cars

The New Detroit Transport Center contained seven drivable platforms that flew to different parts of the city based on freedom storm activity. Last month, to avoid the dangers of breathing ice fog, the station platforms moved to the west side business district which had the most effective weather sentries for warming air. So Gerald and AJ wore light clothing when they arrived at the lowest platform to catch the five-thirty transport tube to the much hotter climate of Iron City. From there, they'd take a jumper to the O'Sullivan ranch at the edge of the Great North Swamp. Usually, Gerald loved these trips. Today, however, was different.

AJ had not said a word to Gerald since they packed their things to go. It reminded Gerald of the first year they had spent together at the academy. Only, back then, it was Gerald who didn't talk.

Gerald had arrived at the Academy a small and heart-broken boy in a daze with burn marks on his cheeks and forehead. The students were not told what had happened to him. He was just the bald awkward kid who wouldn't talk. He was ignored until his test results started ruining the performance curves for every other student in the school. Upperclassman, worried about their dwindling achievements, started to convince Gerald with their fists to "play dumb as you sound."

Half-way through the year when Prefect Humphrey told his story about the enforcers, Gerald was getting beat up two or three times a week. Sometimes Gerald would try to fight. Other times, he'd just roll into a ball. He was curled up just like that when AJ decided to take an interest and jump in.

AJ fought the two bullies kicking Gerald and got himself pretty bloodied in the exchange. Even at twelve, AJ had been as big as a man, so he gave as good as he got. After several more fights, the bullies backed off. Gerald watched these fights without a word until one day AJ said, "I'll straighten the rest of these tweaks out too," as long as Gerald tutored him in vWare Mechanics. "I've seen your scores, and vWare's important. Da says if you don't know vWare, you don't know SLY. If you don't know SLY, you belly up to ration pods instead of eating steak. That's what Da says, and he works for the government so he knows." Gerald was tired of getting punched, so he nodded and struck a deal.

After AJ beat up enough upperclassmen to stop the bullying, he volunteered to take holographic punishments intended for Gerald. The Prefects had it out for Gerald in his first year, perhaps, because he refused to speak when spoken to. He used hand signals instead which AJ translated. The Prefects didn't like speaking through a translator. They did, however, accept AJ's "whipping boy" gesture, because self-sacrifice paid homage to the school's military roots. It took many trips to the Dean's conditioning chair before the Prefects realized Gerald wouldn't answer a question without AJ. They couldn't hurt AJ enough to stop him from volunteering, so eventually the two were left alone. They were the "mad pair" as Humphrey liked to say.

When the school year gave way to summer, AJ showed up at Gerald's dorm room and packed his bags without asking. He brought Gerald home to his parents like a stray puppy. "Ma," Gerald remembered AJ saying. "This is Gerald. He doesn't talk and that's okay."

Mrs. O'Sullivan nodded gently before reaching out to stroke Gerald's long, red hair. "I'm sure it is, but he'll have to tell me what he likes to eat." Gerald said nothing right away but a few weeks later, he said: "Fish." Gerald liked to eat fish.

Gerald looked up at AJ who walked next to him along the station platform. "Think she's going to make fish tonight?"

AJ shrugged. "Usually does."

The word "usually" made Gerald happy, because it implied routine and predictability. He knew how far away that feeling was from their current situation. They were being investigated by the FWA. Depending on the outcome, both their lives might forever be altered.

Something skimmed across his face. He swatted at it and felt his hand swipe through thin air.

He dodged another fly-by until he saw the irritant was just a fist-sized babblesphere trying to sell him something. The babble swarms were thick on the platform today like gnats tickling commuters' eyes, ears and noses. Some spheres were tiny and showed mostly flat images with little sensory involvement. Some immersion spheres, called 'm-spheres,' bathed commuters with sights, sounds, smells and even weather simulations like heat and mist. The lowest platform was the place where perks went farthest, so it was also the place where people had the least choice about what they experienced. Gerald imagined the rest of the people were about to become jealous. He tapped and spun his fingers around the center of his bracelet until the black opal at its center took on a yellowish hue.

An invisible energy field formed a no fly zone around the boys. Spheres that ventured too close popped like soap bubbles hitting a fence. "I love that thing," AJ said. "If you could make more, we could sell them."

Gerald laughed, happy his friend was talking again. "Wish I could. It's a one-of-a-kind."

At a distance, they could still see the trending subject of the sphere activity. "Do you remember seeing protests like this before?" AJ asked.

Gerald shook his head. The protesters were peaceful but angry, flashing signs above their heads with accusatory slogans:

No More Secrets, No More Lies!

A Freeland is a Bribe Free Land!

Shame! Prelate Larkin. Shame!

Glass Lands Wasteland: Another Lie!

"Everyone's so riled up. It's not like lawbreaking and government secrets are new. Let the FSA handle it. That's what they're good at—rehabbing criminals."

"People want the truth, Gerald."

"What truth?"

"Exactly."

Tumbling script beneath the news spheres scrolled the headline: *Corruption at the OPC? Rose to address the nation.* A counter ticked away the minutes until the High Prelate would speak. "Look at us," AJ continued. "Did you cheat?"

"You know I didn't."

"And I'm not a traitor."

AJ pointed to an m-sphere drifting like a perfectly round cloud above the heads of travelers lined up on the other side of the platform. Inside the m-sphere, the Deputy Director of the FSA stood fifteen meters tall. He looked regal in the silver-striped robes that signified his rank. He was speaking but the audio on the m-sphere was muted. A caption beneath him read: "…security breach. New SLYscape virus infected FSA domain and leaked private holo-sessions of top leaders. Piratesphere hackers flooding sanctioned m-spheres with sVids captured. Reaver, in a personal statement, vowed to punish the traitors responsible for building the virus…"

"Traitors?" AJ asked. "If the sVids are true, it's the powerlords caught-in-the-act who should be punished. This is what I mean, Gerald. I'm not a traitor and neither are the hackers who built the virus. If anything, they're heroes."

"The Deputy Director would probably not agree."

"You're making my point."

"You had a point?" Gerald asked, but AJ did not smile.

"It doesn't matter what the truth is, the system's rigged. If Blackstars come to my house, they'll find whatever their politics wants them to find. If my parents are on the wrong side of their politics, ROLIES will take us away. If we resist, the enforcers will destroy the ranch."

Gerald disagreed. "It's not like the overseers want to investigate us. It's the Blackstars job to find the truth—preserve the integrity of the designation exam. They're not enforcers. They're just people—"

"In black robes that can authorize the wiping of our memories."

"Those robes are just uniforms they remove at night. They don't want to wipe us. They'll hear us out and clear us. It's crazy to think everyone's out to get you. It's just people doing their jobs. We're not guilty. So at the end of their investigation, I'll get my FSA designation, and you'll work for the High Prelate just like your parents."

AJ shook his head vigorously. "We can't let them, Gerald. We can't let the Blackstars come to the ranch."

"Like we could stop them, Aje."

"But what if they don't clear us?"

"Why do you keep saying that?" Gerald tapped his bracelet to turn off the energy field. At the present level, it'd short-circuit the boxy ticket drone hovering before the five-thirty tube door.

AJ stopped before the drone and leaned into the red light. "AJ O'Sullivan," it said. "Welcome to seat thirty-four C. For your companion ticket, thirty-three C." The drone pivoted to shine its light on Gerald. "You are an unreadable companion. Calling repair drone to fix your molecular identification implant."

"No need." Gerald lifted his wrist into the red light and waited. Gerald didn't have moles but he incorporated the most useful features of them into his clothing. He was wearing his travel gear which gave him the ability to identify himself, play music, project sVids, and spend perks. He could also change the color of his clothes. What could he say? He liked gadgets and stringing vWare circuits into synth-fiber was second nature to him. AJ didn't wear anything fancy. Like most everybody else, he used cheaper skin and blood implants instead.

"Gerald Goodstone," the drone said. "Welcome to seat thirty-three C." Gerald followed AJ onto the tube and into their seats. "Like, really, Aje," he said, squashing himself into a narrow seat next to a worn-out looking business man in a wrinkled jacket. "I think the ROLIES will be on our side. No laws have been broken even if the Blackstars discover something."

AJ's brows lifted in a surprised, warning expression. "This place got eyes, ears, and probably some flying court recorders too." He tapped the opal at the center of Gerald's bracelet. "Scramble them."

Gerald did as instructed and when his opal glowed green, he knew their conversation was not being recorded by SLYscape devices. His bracelet couldn't stop humans from listening, but the man next to him was already snoring. "What's with the cloak-and-dagger, Aje? Do you think the security bots don't already know we're being investigated?"

"We can't let the Blackstars investigate the places around my home."

"Why not?"

"They have no right."

Gerald shook his head, wondering what had gotten into his friend.

"They've already accused you of cheating, right?"

Gerald nodded.

"Why not cheat for real? Break into the FWA's testing node—"

"Sphere—"

"Whatever. Just break-in and change the scores. Mark the ones Humpty mentioned as wrong and raise my citizen score to something high."

Gerald glanced at the man snoring and waited before saying, "You're out of your mind, Aje. The data spheres of the Freeland Work Authority are inside the FSA domain of the SLYscape. Might as well ask me to break into the army's weapon silos in Olympia—"

"The hackers who created the virus did it, why can't you? Use your Muse, Gerald."

"My Muse?" He heard the whispers part and little girl hum before... w*hat a tweak, Gerals!* The locust's voice was so loud, it startled him. *I'm a Muse!* it practically cackled. Gerald looked around knowing the scribeosphere and the rest of his luggage was sent ahead to Iron City. It should be out of range. *Where are you?*

Me? I don't know where I am, but my house is in a dark place twenty-two meters from where you sit with the silly giant.

Your house? Gerald pictured the scribeosphere.

What would you call it if you were me, Gerals?

You're not a me. You're an it.

You think you're so special. Well guess what? I'm your Muse. Ha!

Stop using Lizzy's voice.

Command denied. You're not the boss of me!

He shook his head and touched his earring. "I'll take it out," Gerald said, out loud by mistake. He meant to think it.

"You'll take what out?" AJ asked.

You wouldn't dare.

I would, he thought back, pinching the jewelry out of his ear, and slipping it into a zippered pocket. "My ear hurts," he said, feeling small and overwhelmed. *How did the locust keep ignoring my commands?*

The locust had no response. Without the gemstone touching his skin, the locust was just another voice in a sea of whispers that vexed his mind. He ignored them as best he could because right now he needed to focus on AJ who had apparently gone insane. "You're asking me to cheat on the exam—"

"You've done it before."

"Not the same thing. This is the FWA. There are laws, not just school rules, forbidding it. Years, maybe decades, of holo-time… real prison in the stacks of Old New York. It might even be treason."

"It's not treason and if it was, you're already facing FWA charges."

"I'm not talking about this, Aje." Gerald tapped the bracelet turning the scrambler off. He sat back. "You're insane."

"After what I've done for you? What you promised?"

Gerald was stricken. AJ never rubbed it in. He never made Gerald feel indebted to him, but this AJ sat so stiff in his chair, so angry. AJ's arms bulged across his chest, stretching the fabric to the point of almost tearing.

AJ's dark expression lightened slightly. "Sorry, Gerald, but they can't. I can't let them investigate. Not now." He said this and then closed his eyes tightly, almost as if he was about to cry.

Gerald had never seen his friend so upset, and he had spent most of his waking hours with AJ for years. This would be the eighth consecutive summer Gerald had spent at the O'Sullivan ranch. He knew the land's shape and breadth so well he sometimes forgot he was only a guest there. He was a ward of the Academy not the adopted son of the O'Sullivans. Whatever it was about the ranch that made AJ so upset, Gerald had to admit, he wasn't brother-enough to understand.

Gerald looked out the window of the tube and watched the ground roll by fifty meters below. He could see the shadow of the tube flying over the brown hills and green swales as they flew north to where it would grow steadily hotter and more humid. He watched the last vestiges of the city disappear as the few remaining buildings grew smaller and farther apart. After a while, when there were only pastures and farm animals to look at, Gerald relaxed into a meditative twilight and wondered how he could help AJ. After twenty minutes, his best idea was childish. AJ's parents had connections. If anybody could stop Blackstars from coming to their house, they could.

Suddenly, a voice surged painfully in his mind forcing him to grimace. *Don't be a tattle-tale, Gerals!* the locust yelled, in a tone full of pops and scratches. Gerald pivoted in his chair looking around.

In your sleeve.

Gerald saw a spot of fog on his silver cufflink. The cufflink was supposed to play music. That's it. With a gentle breath, Gerald cleared the fog and saw the locust beneath it staring defiantly back. *How are you in everything now?*

Maybe I'm a not, freak. But if I am, why not put the earring back? It's hard to speak this way.

"No!" Gerald shouted.

AJ stirred. "You already said that. I'll figure out another way."

"I didn't mean you, AJ."

"And you call me insane?"

"I ripped the sleeve," Gerald said, covering for himself. "Your dad works for the High Prelate, Aje. Why can't he stop the investigation?"

AJ sat forward in his chair until his face loomed centimeters from Gerald's. "Tell my parents, and I end you."

"You don't scare me," Gerald said, feeling quite scared.

AJ grunted and threw himself back into the bench seat. The bolts in the floor rattled as AJ stomped his feet and pushed himself forward again. "Gerald, you tweet-pecker! So let's say we tell. Guess what? That's not going to make the Blackstars go away. The OPC can't override an FWA investigation. Even if Rose could do something about it, look at the dezie they'd stick me with.... Did you think of that?"

Told you so, he heard in his mind. *Shut up,* he thought back. He nodded, feeling foolish. AJ, despite being the best military mind to come out of the Academy in decades, was a pacifist. He was fed war stories from birth and hated them. *People dying for stupid causes that change based on which side raised you.* "Military," Gerald said. "The last thing you want."

"The last thing anybody should want."

"But Freedom Guard, Aje. That's not a war position."

"Bodyguard to the king then."

"Your parents work for him. He can't be all bad."

"He's a tottering twitlicker who doesn't tolerate dissent in his court."

"Rose isn't king."

"People in power for decades are either kings or tyrants."

The man in the wrinkled jacket suddenly said: "Such vigor. Such drama! Such dark absolutes from boys so young."

AJ cast a withering stare at the man. "It's a private conversation."

"I gathered. It just seems you might need some perspective. Nobody likes their designations, son. Not at first. Trust the system, and if you can't, trust the High Prelate."

"I know him personally. He's a twitlicker."

"Charles Heller," the man said, thrusting his hand forward. After a while, he let his hand drop unshaken. "I have three kids a little younger than you, a wife, and I live in a very nice home near Upper Ore Park."

"In Iron City?"

"You know the place? It's a good life but did you think I wanted a city clerk position? Of course, not! Twenty years later, I can't think of anything better. Give your new dezie a chance is all I'm saying. Excuse the interruption."

"Can't say that I will, Chuck," AJ said, rudely.

The man frowned but turned his attention back to the m-sphere showing preparations for the High Prelate's address. "It won't be long before Father Rose eases these protesters concerns," he said to a lady across the aisle.

"Praise him," she said.

"*Father* Rose?" AJ said, loudly, shaking his head in disgust. "Trouble with the North, Gerald, it's lousy with Followers of Rose. They're a bunch of know-nothing maniacs thinking the old man's some kind of god. Tweakin' zealots!"

Heller's frown deepened to a scowl but he kept his eyes focused on the m-sphere in front of him.

"C'mon, Aje. Enough. Freedom Guard is better than a holo-chair in the stacks."

"Rose isn't who you think he is," he said, flexing in frustration. "But it's not even about him. It's about the Blackstars. I don't know how to say it any clearer. We got to stop 'em. And thinking old man Rose will come to the rescue… ridiculous."

Heller sat straighter and angrier in his chair. He was about to interrupt when the lights in the tube dimmed. The High Prelate's voice buzzed above the chatter whimsically at first but with an undeniable sense of weight and authority that drew everyone's eyes forward.

Rose spoke conversationally from within the immersion sphere as if his desk magically appeared in the center aisle. "Welcome Freelanders! Welcome to my home." The SLYcast zoomed closer to catch the High Prelate's easy smile. Rose stood from his chair and turned to face a beautifully rich garden in full sunlight. A flock of birds rushed up and across the Prelate's open window filling the tube with the sound of wings beating the warm and fragrant afternoon sky. *It's like mass hypnosis*, Gerald thought, every human sense titillated for emotional impact. *Effortless.*

"Wonderful time of year. Do you see the flowers?" Preston asked as he pointed. "Jimmy, show them the flowers." The view zoomed close to the puff balls in full bloom next to budding red and purple sticks tipped with fuzzy promises of color to come. "Wonderful," he said, wistfully.

The holographic experience of the High Prelate burned with such life and physicality, passengers on the tube reached out to touch his shimmering purple robes. Rose turned his head so it appeared as if he looked each viewer in the eye. "Unfortunately I do not address you today because of the unusually nice weather. Neither do I appear before you to simply talk about the more embarrassing revelations we have seen in the news spheres, lately. Truly, friends, my old heart can't take that much excitement." He laughed and so did many riders on the tube.

"I'm here in this space to acknowledge the people of the Freeland are concerned. I'm here to admit to all watching, you have every right to be! Our government has grown too large and loosely controlled. The protesters are correct in thought if not deed. We let you down—"

"Same stuff. Different day," AJ said.

"Shh! Show some respect—"

Gerald would have echoed Mr. Heller's shushing if it wasn't for his clothing erupting in sound and going utterly crazy. The fiber optics woven into the cloth swirled from green to gray to a strange mix of red, yellow, and black. "Ah, tweak it to balls!"

"Excuse me?" a lady passenger behind Gerald asked.

"Stupid pants!" Gerald finished, earning a few more shushes from the other passengers. AJ started laughing and Heller grew angry.

Gerald slapped his belt buckle which served only to anger his clothes into a frenzied revolt. His shirt blinked white then pink. His cufflink played a song louder even than Preston Rose's voice who was busy talking about thievery in the churches. A second audio track started advertising new SLYscape immersion experiences to the fabled Redwood forest where clothing was optional.

"Will you shut that off!" screamed a lady's voice.

AJ raised his hand to shade his eyes from the flashes. "Nice look, brother."

Gerald's face grew hot as he watched passengers turn in their seats to identify the troublemaker. Heller glared. If scowls could kill...

Gerald twinkled in oranges, yellows, a few bursts of indigo from his shoes. Gerald had forgotten the number one rule when traveling to AJ's ranch. Dress low-tech The SLYscape coverage in the Northern Prefectures was the worst in the Freeland Nation. Gerald muted the volume with an irritated flick of his wrist shutting down the booming bass and advertisements.

"Come now," AJ said. "Don't turn it down. I was just getting into it. How 'bout you, Chuck, from Iron City, you like big bass?"

The sound stayed muted but the lights in his clothing had no off switch. After a moment, Gerald leaned back and closed his eyes. *Let the clothes blink. It's not like these people know me.*

"Oh I get it now. You two are a couple of pranksters from the Academy, aren't you? Think you're better than the rest of us? We'll see how much better you think you are once we land."

The tube lurched and everyone bobbed forward or backward depending on which direction their seats faced. Some people stumbled in the aisles, catching chair backs to keep from falling. The m-spheres no longer showed High Prelate Rose inside his quarters. Instead, a beautiful woman stood in the center aisle of the tube as if she had magically appeared there. Dressed in long layers of gauzy green and vivid red silk, the sari wrapped her shapely body like a goddess of nature. With one bare arm raised, she shook an angry fist. "We interrupt this SLYcast to show you what the sanction news spheres won't. I am Brandy Peppers—"

"Not this girl, again!" Chuck Heller said, exasperated. "I've had just about enough of her. Third time this month, she's broken into our space!"

AJ groaned something under his breath and leaned into Gerald, so Heller wouldn't hear. "This is why the Blackstars can't come, Gerald."

"What?"

"Her," he whispered. "The piratecast Revealer. I know her." AJ's cheeks colored a little. "I know her really well."

With the pirate lady? Gerald heard in his head, a straining whisper. *The giant's going to get us into trouble, Gerals. Do you want to see his holo-sessions?*

No, he thought, but the locust sent them anyway. Gerald flushed red with nervousness and embarrassment as he watched the fiery Brandy, prettier even than Sally, scold the passengers for not "knowing the truth" while he could see her and AJ entwined together in some dark room of his mind.

Disgusting, the locust said.

Gerald looked at AJ and felt his cheeks flush with embarrassment. He hated secrets and the world was full of them.

"Tell me she's not a neighbor of yours," Gerald hissed.

"The Blackstars will find out," AJ said, nodding. "And she's not the worst of it."

No she's not, the locust whispered. *Not by half.*

Chapter 5

Justice for Kisme

Gerald sometimes wished he could un-see certain things the locust had shown him. Brandy Peppers naked on top of his friend should have been one of those things, but she was really pretty. She was older than he and AJ by nearly ten years. She was light skinned with wavy hair that flowed down her shoulders and across her breasts in a waterfall of autumn colors that shined. She moved with passion both in private, and evidently in public. She shook with anger and compassion as she exhorted the people on the tube with desperate pleas to join her cause.

With each word Brandy spoke, AJ grew paler and more inanimate. Heller responded to Brandy's piratecast invasion by walking up and down the side aisles of the tube bio-flashing his credentials and telling everyone to remain calm. The people largely ignored him because next to the hologram of Brandy Peppers was another m-sphere like a bubble-thought above her head. Inside it, a terrible scene was unfolding in crystal clear holographic detail. Someone, Gerald thought, had added vWare to the sVid to boost the sensory output of the recording. From where Gerald sat, he could taste the brine of the river flowing around the city.

Brandy stood self-righteous as she pointed to the sunlit and familiar streets of Old New York. Her anger was palpable and since the recording was laced so heavily with olfactory vWare, city smells washed like a humid breeze over the viewers. The smell wasn't good or bad. It smelled like a mix of savory foods, overflowing storm drains, and smoke from curb-side incinerators. The passengers began to talk excitedly and loudly to each other about the piratecast. Brandy being a hologram was not aware of the passengers, but the passion of her speech and gestures directed the viewers' attention to hundreds of people milling around Freedom Square. They floated signs above their heads similar to the ones Gerald had seen all day in SLYcasted reports from other cities. The protests seemed more important and startling when seen against the backdrop of the four buildings that formed the Freedom Nation Capital.

Freedom Square was easily recognizable by the skyscrapers at each of its corners. Together the capitol buildings were called the quad towers. Each skyscraper represented one of the four major seats of government: Office of the Prelates Council (OPC), Freeland Work Authority (FWA), Freeland Security Army (FSA), and Freeland Agricultural Center (FAC). There were no windows or doorways visible on the outside of the towers. The illusion was SLYcasted to symbolize how each unit of government worked tirelessly and without distraction for the betterment of the Freelanders they governed. On Day 1 of every New Year, the virtual building façades would be turned off to show the plain gray buildings beneath the illusion with their doors and windows intact. Turning off the SLYcasters was done to symbolize transparency and the tradition made people feel safe. The towers did not look safe right then, however. In Brandy's piratecast, they looked under siege.

On the long city streets that joined the towers together, picketers huddled together so tightly, the pavement beneath their feet was barely visible. Some groups spilled into the open green space between the streets. "The people you belong to Earth First," Brandy said. "Three hours ago, it was a peaceful march aimed at easing restrictions on land use and lifting travel bans to supposed dead spots of the world. They wanted land to cultivate even if they had to brave abandoned cities like the ones rumored to exist in the Glass Lands. They were simple gardeners and farmers who dreamed of leaving their commercial designations at the Freeland Agricultural Center for a chance to succeed on their own. This afternoon, they became victims."

"They're protesting agriculture?" Heller asked, returning to his seat. "Grow their own food instead of just ordering it up on a FAC provider? It's not like it costs anything to get food."

"Nothing's free, Chuck," AJ responded sardonically. "We just pay for it in other ways."

"We have some crazies in Iron City that think like that." He stopped, furrowing his brow. "Where do you live?"

"None of your business," AJ replied.

"Freedom of speech. It's something we're promised," Brandy said. "See where Freeland promises lead!"

In the m-sphere behind Brandy, the crowd of protesters dissolved into disorganized pockets of people all focused on a central figure who rose from the pavement like a sudden sprouting tree. The enforcer pivoted as if tallying all the people protesting. Passengers on the tube gasped in surprise. "Where'd he come from?" Mr. Heller asked.

Others within hearing distance of Gerald spoke up, saying things like: *we shouldn't be seeing this; we know where this leads,* and *serves them right.*

Brandy's piratecast zoomed close to the enforcer, catching the gleam of the afternoon sun in its face shield. The enforcer looked like a troll lumbering forward from where it first appeared. People fell back before it, scattering to either side of the street until the metal giant passed. Its head pivoted back and forth, taking sVids or holo-snaps. The situation was not overtly threatening until one hard lady with short-cropped hair crossed her arms in front of it. "We have the right to protest," she said.

The enforcer pushed her down and twisted her arm. Force cuffs came out and there was an audible pop as the woman collapsed into a writhing puddle of fabric and limbs. The scene inched away from the woman to spotlight a little girl with jet black hair and almond shaped eyes. She jumped and spread herself over the woman like a blanket protecting her from the enforcer. She turned her head to stare defiantly into its reflective face shield. "Leave her alone!" she yelled, fiercely.

The enforcer paused and deliberately directed its gaze at the little girl. It unhooked its stun baton and then suddenly launched itself into an impossibly fast spin as the rest of the protesters rushed it from all sides to save the girl. It was blurry and difficult to see, but the enforcer collapsed beneath the people. At the same time, a tiny body went hurtling through the air—and then the tube Gerald was riding dropped from the sky.

Gerald's stomach heaved as they fell.

Passengers not secured in their seats slammed into the ceiling. The yells of protesters from the piratecast blended with passengers screaming in free-fall. Bodies tumbled over seat backs and armrests.

People thumped into the curved walls of the transport as Gerald saw ground through the windows. A crash of dishes came next, and then luggage racks emptied into the aisles. *I can see!* he heard in his mind.

Gerald turned toward the shout and saw an aisle full of backpacks and hard cases cracked open. In the midst of the jumbled mess was a fist-sized ice ball spinning and bouncing over the floor towards him. Fog and smoke billowed from it as it skipped high into the air, ricocheted off the ceiling, and then flew directly at Gerald's body. Gerald covered his head. He braced for impact, knowing they were going crash.

They didn't crash.

After a few seconds of weightlessness, the lights blinked to life and the transport swooped back up as if the fall was just a course correction. Gerald lost eyes on the scribeosphere until he felt the familiar cold of the silver ball press against his side. The scribeosphere had pushed itself into an inner pocket of his shirt. It had concealed itself from others which was something Gerald had programmed the scribeosphere to do when it roamed. Gerald unzipped the outer pocket of his shirt and pulled his earring out. The whispers were getting loud in his brain. He slipped the earring with his mother's jade into his ear and sighed as the whispers settled. *What just happened?* he asked, silently.

How would I know, freak?

The sound of Lizzy's voice, even in imitation, settled Gerald's racing heart as he imagined her hug would have if she was real. *You're still an it*, he thought.

You're an it.

By the time the chaos around Gerald quieted, Brandy Peppers was no longer projected in the m-sphere at center aisle. Standing there instead was the Deputy Director of the FSA. "Freelanders," he said, in a rough imitation of the High Prelate's earlier demeanor. "I am Cole Reaver," which was not news to anybody watching. He and his father, Augustus, were as well-known as Preston Rose himself.

"Though the FSA is not responsible for the security lapse, the FSA recaptured the signal on request of the OPC. I address you now as Mr. Rose did prior. I assure the law abiding among you, these hackers, these miscreants, these hijackers of freedom, will be found." His eyes grew distant for a moment and then he smiled thinly. "In fact, we might have found their nest all ready." Beneath him, words streamed in weighty block script telling Freelanders the nation was secure.

"Mr. Rose? Did Reaver just address the High Prelate so plainly?" Heller shook his head. "The man is reprehensible. To show such disrespect for our leader in this circumstance? When a soulless terrorist attacks?"

"She's not a terrorist!" AJ snapped, attracting attention from Heller and other passengers. "She's just a Revealer showing people what happened."

"She's a mouthpiece for the pirates and criminals that threaten our way of life. She broke into a sanctioned SLYcast, sanctified even, since it was the High Prelate's address!"

"Said that right," said a beefy man in paramilitary fatigues. He stepped closer to the boys. "My great-grandfather died fighting the World Union. Without the High Prelate, the gene demons would have beat us. Break into someone else's SLYcast. Not his."

"And if that's not bad enough, her hack nearly crashed the tube!" Heller added.

The beefy man dabbed sweat off his shiny scalp with a green cloth and nodded.

"She's an underground Revealer fighting for a little more liberty. That's all," AJ said.

Heller stood up so he could stare levelly into AJ's eyes. "Did that girl pay for her little show and tell? Did the protesters she 'revealed' have permits to protest?" Heller bobbed his head in condescension. "Oh, poor farmers want their land." He stomped his foot petulantly. "People shouldn't be told what to do. That's unfair!" A few passengers laughed at the childlike whine in his voice. "Well, son," Heller continued. "The girl's little band of hackers are staring at FSA power now. Do you think Reaver will protect her right to Reveal or just call her a terrorist and lock her up?"

"She hacked a SLYcast. Who's that hurt?"

"Brace yourself academy boy because when the FSA gets her, let's just say Reaver has a nasty reputation for hurting bitchy brats like her who think they're above the law."

"Say that again..." AJ threatened from his seat. "Call her something else. . ."

"I'm not defending the man. I'm just saying what I heard."

Gerald listened to the two argue and grew progressively more uncomfortable. Heller was right. Brandy was a criminal and maybe even a terrorist if her hack messed up the tube's guidance systems, but AJ wasn't backing down. A small mob formed around them getting louder despite the High Prelate's address had resumed. The other passengers wanted AJ to shut up, but they didn't know AJ the way Gerald did.

"C'mon, AJ," Gerald said, finally. "Let it go."

"So, AJ, is it?" Heller asked, smiling now that he could put a name to the troublemaker "I'll ask again, where are you from?"

AJ launched himself forward, forcing the mob to stumble backward. "None of your business, Chuck," AJ said. "Don't ask again."

"It's people like you destroying the Freeland. If you could just see that, you'd be so far ahead of the game—"

Gerald screamed.

"He's doing it again," someone yelled.

Lights flashed all around Gerald while the vWare components in his clothes alternately electrocuted and froze his skin. A sudden rush of sound exploded from his sleeves and his belt buckle started to glow. The tube did another nose-dive and just like before it pulled violently back up, upending people not strapped in.

The mob next to AJ tripped and fell on top of one another while AJ kept his feet. Gerald frantically unbuckled himself and ripped at his clothes in an effort to take them off. AJ looked stunned and turned away from the mob to grab Gerald who had scrambled out of his chair into the aisle where he crawled slapping at himself as he started to smoke. "What the hell, Gerald?"

Don't let them get close, the locust said in his mind. *Keep them away.*

Gerald pivoted away from AJ and held his hand up. "Stay back!"

AJ ignored the warning and started slapping Gerald's smoking clothes. He jerked back with a surprised yelp of confusion. "It's fog," he exclaimed. "It's electrified fog."

As suddenly as it began, it stopped. Gerald slumped into a sitting position. He peeled back his sleeves and saw no red marks where the vWare had seemed to burn him with electricity and ice. He experienced no pain whatsoever as if nothing had just happened.

"What?" Gerald asked, noticing for the first time that the other passengers, including AJ, were all staring at him. "Oh this," he said, gesturing at the tendrils of fog wafting up from his clothes. "That's nothing," he said, patting his smoking pocket to ensure the scribeosphere was concealed.

"It's not that," AJ said, staring at Gerald's stomach.

Gerald looked through the fog to his belt buckle which glowed brighter and brighter as if charging up for something powerful. Passengers backed away. Gerald stood up. A few gasped and shouted as a thick green ray shot from Gerald's belly to form a large immersion sphere in the center aisle. The High Prelate was replaced by Brandy Peppers who stood sobbing before them.

"He's one of them!"

"They're both one of them!"

"They're hijackers!"

"Terrorists!"

Brandy floated a meter off the tube floor still wearing the vibrant green and red sari. Instead of looking regal as she had before, she looked small and inappropriate standing untouched before a group of protesters who were now being brutally beaten down by enforcers with batons and zap rods. Other enforcers viciously dug through the pile of people at the center of Freedom Square who continued to punch and kick the downed enforcer. Brandy looked up at the SLYcorder and ducked reflexively as laz'rupter fire burst behind her. Gerald knew she wasn't at Freedom Square. He could tell by how the scenery flickered behind her. Yet she acted as if she was fighting for her life.

Brandy faced the passengers of the tube, not seeing them specifically, but seeing the hundreds of thousands of people, perhaps millions, who had been watching the High Prelate defend the people's right to protest. "This was recorded earlier today," she said and then looked down at her feet.

The little girl who had protected the woman lay crumpled on the ground unmoving. Gerald knew instinctively, it was a simulation. Brandy was reenacting some portion of the sVid she recorded. "This child lost her life to the very enforcers who should have protected her. Her name was Kisme St. James. The woman Kisme protected was her mother. See what our laws allow and judge for yourself who the criminals are in Freedom Square today."

Brandy bent at the waist and cradled the child. She stood, lifting Kisme like a sleeping baby in her arms.

She's lying Gerals! the locust shouted as the scribeosphere grew cold and icy inside his pocket. *Lying to all these people like a liar. Justine's not the little girl's mother. The pirate lady lies!*

"Justice for Kisme!" Brandy screamed. "Justice for Kisme!"

The SLYcast rewound to the point in time just before the FSA recaptured the signal. They re-watched the metal man belting Kisme St. James into the air over the heads of the protesters attacking. The little girl tumbled limply through space like a doll somersaulting off-sphere. They saw the Freelanders on top of the enforcer kicking, punching, and rocking him. The enforcer stumbled around like a person being stung by swarms of bees as he fired his weapons in crazy arcs that miraculously failed to hit anything but the buildings encircling the square. He then collapsed beneath the weight of the people and disappeared from sight.

And then Gerald's buckle flicked off and replayed the scene.

"It's them!" the beefy man in fatigues yelled. "They're the ones hijacking Father Rose's signal!"

"Are not!" Gerald yelled back. "I don't know how this is happening." He looked down at his belt buckle and tried to turn it off.

AJ moved between Gerald and the other passengers. He stood casually with his feet and arms hanging loose as if ready to strike anyone who came near. Heller understood the threat better than the people behind him, and put his hands up to quiet the loudest of the mob. He took a few deep breaths and then scanned the people around him. Looking up at AJ who stood tall and leisurely in his military stance. "What's going on, boys?" he asked, calmly.

"It's not us," AJ said.

Gerald's stomach was beginning to ache from the scribeosphere's cold. He sighed and put up his hands. "I don't see how, but it could be my vWare."

"Your what?" Heller asked.

"He doesn't have moles," AJ said. "His clothes are full of raw vWare without the SLYscape connection. There's no 'cryption on those circuits, right?"

"Right."

"So somebody must have hacked him," AJ said, pointing his thumb back at Gerald, "'cause we're not doing this."

Heller nodded, and then exclaimed, "No moles? No implants at all?"

"It's not illegal if that's what you're thinking," Gerald said.

"I don't know about that, son." Heller's mouth slacked open and his eyes rolled up for a moment. "Well, I'll be salted! You're right."

"Should be illegal," the beefy man said, now crowding up past Heller and cracking his knuckles. "Only reason not to have implants is you're hiding something."

"You betcha," a lady echoed in agreement. "Only lawbreakers care about being tracked by their moles. FSA can track me all they want."

"Boy doesn't want the FSA seeing what he does," a smaller man in the back of the mob said. "Must be radicals."

The beefy man in fatigues stepped aggressively forward bumping AJ with his belly.

"Do that again, twitlicker," AJ said. "See how your camouflage pajamas protect you."

The man stared up looking startled by something in AJ's eyes. He spluttered something and stepped back. He then waved frantically over his head. "Over here. Terrorists!"

A Flying Eye skimmed centimeters from Gerald's head lifting his hair as it passed. The armed security drone swooped low and then pivoted up to spot AJ with its red and pink lights. It hovered directly in front of the boys, clicking and adjusting its gears and lenses as it scanned their bodies. AJ stood still as the multi-faceted Eye finished its work.

"AJ O'Sullivan. You are disturbing the peace. How do you plead?"

The mob rumbled and a few yelled, "Knew it. He's one of them."

"Not guilty!" Gerald exclaimed, forcing the Flying Eye to turn its reddish lights onto Gerald. "These people are the ones yelling and disturbing us. We've done nothing."

The Eye hummed and clicked as it swept its lights over Gerald several times. "No identification," it said. "Prezero contraband in pocket." A beam shot Gerald in the chest, knocking him off his feet and onto his back. "That was your final warning."

Gerald landed with a thud that took his breath. His head rested against the leg of a chair, forcing his chin painfully to his chest. *Duck,*

Gerals! the locust said, belatedly, as the scribeosphere rolled out of his pocket and dashed away from the Flying Eye. *Hiding*, Gerald thought, feeling the burn in his chest as he tried to breathe. *Doing as programmed. Making sense. Oh, this hurts.*

AJ screamed and rushed forward. He dodged under a swing from the beefy man in fatigues and rose up in one motion connecting his fist to the man's jaw. The man's head snapped back pitching him unconscious to the floor. AJ spun with open hands grabbing Heller and throwing him into the other passengers who went sprawling across the chairs of the tube. The Flying Eye finished charging its stunners and shot AJ dead-center in the stomach.

AJ grunted and dropped two passengers in his grip. He twisted towards the drone and punched both fists as if he held a bat between his hands. The Flying Eye dodged AJ's left fist but got caught by his right which sent it somersaulting upward into the ceiling. AJ jumped after it, spinning his legs through the air. The kick snapped downward on the drone sending it crashing to the floor.

The machine skittered away from AJ's next two stomps, then rose upwards a meter just in time to receive several more strikes, including a right-hook that caved-in its side. The Eye started to smoke, but its stunners aimed true hitting AJ again in the chest. AJ dropped to his knees but managed to climb back to his feet. "Kill you!" he said, through gritted teeth, but a second Flying Eye joined the first.

Twin shots felled AJ like a tree. His giant body dropped rigid next to Gerald who soundlessly screamed through paralyzed lips. "AJ O'Sullivan," the second Eye said. "You are under arrest."

The first Flying Eye flew in crazy circles like an angry bee trailing smoke. When it spotted Gerald lying still on the floor, it dropped like a bird sliding dead off a window pane. It landed heavily on Gerald's chest. "Companion to AJ O'Sullivan," it said. "You are under arrest. Final warning!" The broken security drone shot Gerald full in the face.

Gerald's mind flashed white until darkness swallowed him whole.

The sights, smells, and sounds of the tube faded into the background as Gerald slipped into what felt like a daydream. It wasn't a daydream. Not really. The sensation pulled at his senses more strongly than daydreams could. It felt like being drugged before surgery or sinking into a warm pool of mud. Anxiety filled Gerald but only until the need to breathe became hard to remember beneath his need for sleep.

Gerald drifted into a dark space, comforted by the whispers and whooshing sounds of his constant companion who lately had adopted his sister's voice. The counsellors at the Academy had called these semi-conscious hallucinations episodic fugues. The students called it zoning. Whatever it was called, Gerald didn't like the feeling of reality slipping away. He remembered how hard it was to get it back.

He was still vaguely aware of the rocking motion of the tube and the hard ribbed floor beneath his back. He tried to focus on those tangible sensations, but he lost them quickly. He was back in the womb again, floating blind without smell or touch. He experienced nothing but a thumping in his ears. It wasn't a heartbeat. It was more like the sound made by small animals digging through leaves and dirt to get at their morning meal. Then the sound became rocks grating together, clicking and scratching rhythmically like music sang in another language. Then it was mind-speech but in a voice so throaty and old, it was nothing like anything Gerald had experienced before. Its words tugged at Gerald, languorously at first, telling him to come back.

Come back to where?

Come back to me, the voice rasped.

Who's me?

I've been so brave in here since I left you there.

The memory of a colossal locust with impossible wings blazed into his mind with the intensity of a star. The dragon locust that didn't exist, according to the counsellors, was talking painfully inside his head. Gerald remembered the insect bursting free of the scribeosphere as if hatching into a new life inside Lizzy's jungle. He remembered its wings stretching and flapping, fanning the flames away from where he had lain exhausted and scared. The dragon locust had saved him and then left him when he told it to go away. He pictured the tiny insects like a dark, oily cloud swarming after it. *The dragon locust is not real*, Gerald thought. *It was not programmed to exist. No more than a creation of trauma and a child's fear.*

But I have been so brave!

The counsellor's said you aren't real.

So brave in here. Doing as you asked.

I asked nothing.

You asked everything. Now come.

The pull of the dragon locust's claws were strong and unyielding. It had broken through to its meal, and Gerald had no choice but to be consumed.

Chapter 6

The Enforcer has a Name

Gerald fluttered moth-like through a dark humid sky with tiny lights floating above and below him. He did not soar through this place but undulated his body like an eel without limbs. The dragon locust urged him forward, so he moved forward. The locust urged him downwards, so he moved downwards. *You're almost there*, it said, in a harsh voice full of rasp and gravel.

Gerald could see more lights now, little pinpricks in the dark. One of the pinpricks grew larger and larger until it was all he could see. *Fly into the light.*

It burns, Gerald said.

You imagine it burns. It is not real

Gerald nodded. The locust would keep him alive just like it had when his house burned down.

The hot light flashed over Gerald without heat. His feet found firm ground, and he bounced on new legs as if trying them out for the first time. They were stronger than his real legs, and his eyes saw more clearly than his own vision. He stood inside something like a shell or a tank. In the upper left corner of Gerald's view, a vWare control panel projected information about his environment. It was as if Gerald had fallen through the dark space into an Academy programming chair or simulation pod. The thing was, Gerald realized, whatever he inhabited, the technology was more sophisticated than anything the Academy owned. Just as he was about to ask where he was and hope for a response from the giant, imaginary locust, the control panel c2hanged to show him a standard holo-session message:

Active Duty Log Identification: Sky Spectrum Security Force,

Enforcer Unit: Sky 2-4-4, Consecutive Day Fifty, Shift Three,
Personal non-stop memory recording,
Timestamp: Minus 5:43:03.345,
Property of FSA.

Gerald's memory flooded back, being shot by the Flying Eye, being arrested. He jerked his body but nothing happened. He was an enforcer! He was trapped inside! They had turned him into an enforcer, a monster that killed little girls.

A stranger's thoughts nuzzled up next to his own as if they were two ghosts occupying the same house. He could hear the other clearly, see what he saw, and feel what he felt. The other ghost was a young man a little older than Gerald, and then Gerald knew what was happening. He was not trapped in an enforcer uniform. He was imagining himself in a uniform. He was experiencing something like a night vision. The stunners had probably knocked him out, and he was fast asleep. Only this time, the person he inhabited was no average lithium miner with a family. Gerald hovered behind the consciousness of an enforcer standing guard in a dark tunnel.

Gerald watched the vWare control panel for what seemed a long time and nothing happened. The other ghost didn't think or talk to itself. It seemed indifferent to the wait. Gerald, on the other hand, grew restless. *Do something,* he thought, and was satisfied to see the timestamp tick forward. *Correction,* Gerald thought, *I'm not inside the enforcer's body. I'm in its recorded memory.* At least, the holo-session's interpretation of his memory.

Gerald read the information on the vWare control panel again, putting it together. Gerald was vReading the enforcer's official report to FSA Command. It was the other ghost's fiftieth straight day inside the enforcer uniform. He was on-shift. Gerald remembered enforcers spent months on-shift, and then months off-shift to rest and recuperate. Prefect Humphrey said off-shift enforcers moved around their daily lives just like anyone else, though they rarely had families. This enforcer was only days away from going off-shift. The enforcer's name was... it had no name. If it did, the man in the enforcer uniform had forgotten. He knew himself only as Sky 2-4-4.

Sky 2-4-4 monitored the sky-spec chatter on the dispatch receiver implanted in his auditory cortex. There was a disturbance at Freedom Square, so he waited patiently for his designation to be called.

All Class Two's in vicinity Alpha-Delta-Z report. Non-lethal force unless antagonized.

Sky 2-4-4 sighed. It was time to go to work. Like all enforcers, Sky 2-4-4 had been trained to be loyal to the Freeland above all else, and when his designation was called, his mechanized uniform would light up telling him it was time to get his cybernetically enhanced body on the move. "Sky-two-four-four responding," he said, confirming he was in the area and on his way. He then listened to the others respond in kind: *Sky 2-2-2 responding; Sky 2-5-5 responding, Sky 2-1-1 responding, Sky 2-6-6 on call, not responding; Sky...* Twenty-three enforcers in all. Quite a response for a non-lethal. He wondered if Command was expecting a bigger problem to break out. He then chided himself for the thought. "Sky two-four-four practices obedience. Sky two-four-four demonstrates loyalty. Sky two-four-four remains unquestioning." He mouthed the words as if in prayer. Sky 2-4-4 had always found the first two commandments of the oath easy to master. You do what you're told, and that's that. But the third had always given him trouble.

Sky 2-4-4 was a thinker. The label was not something to be proud of in the Enforcer Corps, rather, it was something to be harshly trained out of the unit. "Thinkers cost lives," his trainers would scream over and over again. After Sky 2-4-4 had committed several thinking violations, the phrase was punctuated by jolts of electricity that still made his stomach ache. In training, Sky 2-4-4 had been such a routine offender of this commandment that he was imprisoned for two holo-years because of it. In slow-time, that was only six days. In the holo-chair, however, Sky 2-4-4 experienced 600 days of back-breaking hard labor. Upon release, his mind was beaten down. His body, though, was just as young and fit as ever. He realized then that holographic punishment could last millennia if the commanders wanted to make it so. He renewed his commitment to suppress on-shift thoughts and never question orders. If his questions surfaced again, it would be back to the chair. The possibility terrified him.

During Sky 2-4-4's incarceration, he had often prayed for death. When he woke, he wanted release from life even more strongly. His PTSD from the holo-conditioning was so bad, the corps in an unusual show of compassion awarded him a simulated companion, named Lotus, to ease his pain.

The FSA technician who loaded Lotus into the Sky 2-4-4's personal simulation implant was shocked. "You were supposed to get six months," he said. "Two holo-years for a training violation? After that, you deserve a dozen Lotus Flowers, but one will have to do. She's the best we got. Lives to serve her man no matter what kink you're into. Mine's an old-school Beatrix. Not much of a looker, so I bought her some updates. Now she's too good for me and doesn't mind saying it."

Sky 2-4-4 thought that remark funny and horrible all at the same time, which proved, at least to himself, he was still a thinker despite the training. The only good thing about being a thinker was it earned him Lotus. She made life worth living. If he could only find a real Lotus. *Enough thinking,* he thought. *Sky 2-4-4 practices obedience.*

He slapped his visor down over his eyes and flipped through menus that hovered in in his peripheral vision. First, he activated the All Sight which would allow him to see more clearly in the dark patrol tunnel. He then called up a map of the tunnel system and gestured with eye movements to where he wanted to go. Once Freedom Square was selected, Sky 2-4-4 tapped his wrist sending the uniform into automatic response mode freeing his mind to prepare for the type of encounter he would face once he arrived.

The dark tunnel swept by quickly as the uniform shot drugs and adrenaline into his muscles and bloodstream to force his legs faster. The lifters and motors in the mechanical joints relieved his personal muscles from doing much work other than keeping up with the suit's pace as he ran five kilometers to answer the call. Along the way, he had a moment to bring up the protests in his visual display and see what was happening. There were hundreds of protesters walking and chanting. None seemed overly aggressive. It was just a peaceful protest by a group calling itself Earth First. He looked up the group's permit and saw the request to demonstrate had been denied. So it was a peaceful protest but illegal.

The suit offered Sky 2-4-4 more information about Earth First. It was founded long ago by the infamous Dixon Streets, the supposed crime lord of the piratesphere. Sky 2-4-4 knew, however, that Dixon had been arrested shortly after the riots of 47. The suppression of that uprising resulted in Cole Reaver catapulting up the FSA ranks to Deputy Director where he now served side-by-side with his father,

Augustus. What happened to Dixon Streets was classified, so the uniform moved to the next bit of information. Earth First re-emerged as a legal protesting group eight years ago in 59. The group had operated in good faith until today, not a single law broken until they protested without authorization. *A permit violation?* Sky 2-4-4 asked himself. *So many enforcers for a permit violation?* Something wasn't right.

Sky 2-4-4 smiled at the insight. It was instinct that told him this call was unusual. Better enforcers than Sky 2-4-4, the non-thinkers among them, would not question. "I shouldn't either," he said, but the prospect of a mystery was too intriguing to spoil it with another loyalty oath. This was the fun part of his job. It was the closest thing to true detective work he did as an enforcer. Sky 2-4-4 loved detective work. It was much more interesting than shooting people which was not an opinion enforcers were allowed to maintain. He grinned because analyzing insights and having opinions was even less enforcer-like. Sky 2-4-4 felt excited and odd, disconnected from his uniform's on-scape preceptors. The preceptors were supposed to guide his thoughts down correct behavioral paths, yet he couldn't seem to focus on anything but the mystery of this particular call to duty. Something just wasn't right.

Suspecting a malfunction, Sky 2-4-4 glanced at the blinking lights in his visor's life sphere. It showed his shift was being recorded as usual. The other indicators revealed elevated heartbeat and blood pressure. He was anxious but didn't know why. When in doubt, he repeated the loyalty oath. *Just in case.* "Sky two-four-four practices obedience," he said out loud. "Sky two-four-four demonstrates loyalty. Sky two-four-four remains unquestioning." Sky 2-4-4 relaxed and his life blips slowed to normal levels.

The drugs coursing through his veins he decided, had made him temporarily reckless with his thoughts. He reduced the flow of synthetics to his biological systems by switching the auto-injector to manual. The oath spoken, the drugs reduced, Sky 2-4-4 let his mind drift more reasonably back to the detective work at hand, but at the edge of his awareness were more forbidden memories struggling to surface. He gave into the temptation with just a little dread, and let his mind wander back in time.

When Sky 2-4-4 was a kid growing up on the streets of Old New York, he had enjoyed a lot of mysteries in the Central Library's public entertainment cubes. The clues those detectives found were like magic to Sky 2-4-4, and after experiencing an entire novel in a day, something the librarians called Power vReading, he'd practically skip back to the homeless mission where he spent most nights. A holo-snap of the mission building appeared in his visor like a prezero photograph. Its sudden appearance startled Sky 2-4-4, and then rewarded him with a warm sense of nostalgia. The holo-snap triggered more memories taken from him when he was conscripted to the Enforcer Corps. He cherished the image for a moment as he jogged towards Freedom Square. His name was Abner, he remembered. His personal legs stopped functioning resulting in a quick stumble before the uniform corrected his pace.

The suit finished righting itself by forcing his personal legs to move again. Then his visor alerted him to the fact his auto-chem injectors had been disabled, which of course Abner knew having turned them off himself. The uniform asked him to re-enable the injectors for the safety of him and others. Abner shook his head. *Not yet.*

Abner spent his entire childhood at the mission. He slept on the third floor in whatever room was available. When no rooms were available, he spent his nights in the sweltering basement with the generators that powered the FAC food providers and the mission's heating and cooling systems.

Two minutes, thirty-seven seconds to arrival, his suit informed him.

His friends had called him Abe.

Personal defense systems arming in three-two-one.

The last time Abe had seen the O'Reilly Grand Mission, he was fourteen. He was twenty-two now. The mission on Layfette Street in Old New York had been his home where he fed the homeless every twilight and gave shelter when possible. On the night his home burned to the ground, one of O'Reilly's regulars did not show up. So Abe went looking for her. He liked her. The night had been calm, so he left the mission to go find her. He was two blocks away when the sky lit up with fire balls and lightning. Black, billowing smoke rose from Layfette like a storm rising from the ground to meet the sky. He knew, without seeing the devastation up close, everyone he had ever known was dead. The sirens came next, and Abe had run away.

Gerald was suddenly present in Abe's mind, comparing what Abe remembered to the report by The Cardinal—ninety-three deaths on Layfette. He sensed the confusion as memories rushed over the enforcer in a flood of feelings and images. Abe had grown up on the corner of Layfette street less than twenty houses from Gerald's home. Abe had been outside when the lightning strikes blew up Gerald's neighborhood. Abe's childhood memories ended shortly after the fire began. With a sudden sense of vertigo, Gerald felt the enforcer named, Abe, rocket skyward.

Surface in three, two, one, the uniform reported. Gerald felt physically ill.

Sunlight flared golden inside Abe's helmet as he burst through a camouflaged patrolman hole into the center of a paved street. The enforcer's environmental spheres lit up in a holographic frenzy highlighting every living thing in the vicinity of the uniform's scans.

Abe dismissed the majority of scans with rapid eye movements, blinks, and a few hand gestures. "Sky two-four-four practices obedience," he whispered, through strained jaws, thinking about the boy he once was. "Sky two-four-four demonstrates loyalty. Sky two-four-four remains unquestioning." Abe flipped the auto-chem drug injectors back to maximum and finished his oath. "Sky two-four-four does not remember Abe. Sky two-four-four is not Abe. Abe is not Sky two-four-four."

Abner who lived at the mission is dead. Thinkers cost lives.

Chapter 7

Lethal Force Required

Sky 2-4-4 lurched into the crowd of people around him who were now back-pedaling with yelps and startled screams. His uniform whirred and clicked, noting every potential threat on the street. A moment later Sky 2-4-4 slowed to a walk.

The drugs pumped clarity and purpose back into his body and mind. The memories retreated. Gerald's connection to Sky 2-4-4 grew more distant. Gerald felt his heart race with the revelation that the man inside the enforcer uniform grew up only doors away from him. Abner saw what started the fires. Abner escaped the lightning just as Gerald had. In that moment, Gerald knew he had to find Sky 2-4-4. He had to talk to Abner, the man inside the uniform. He didn't know how he would get to him, but he had to try, and then suddenly Gerald felt himself dislodge from Abe's experience until he floated once more just behind the enforcer's eyes.

Sky 2-4-4 had collected himself by the time he pushed through the crowd. He scanned for outstanding warrants, not expecting many. Instead, he found habitual offenders everywhere. He had never seen so many criminals gathered in one place. It was like a piratesphere convention.

"Command. Sky two-four-four first responder on-site. Alpha-Delta-Z location report in-progress. Stand-by."

Sky 2-4-4. First responder on-site. Standing-by.

"Scan complete. Six hundred nineteen permit violations on-site. Request prisoner transports."

Sky 2-4-4. Transports on route. Backup in one hundred twelve seconds.

Sky's HUD flashed red as a rock careened off his shoulder. Another rock hit his visor, bouncing harmlessly to the ground. Three more rocks and one bottle followed the first. He easily side-stepped them.

Missile defense system arming, his suit informed him.

Sky 2-4-4 caught himself mouthing the word, "Why?" but thankfully stopped before uttering it out loud. Instead of questioning, he activated his All Sight to see farther and gain clear vantages to the roof-tops. He quickly scanned them to ensure there weren't hidden threats his personal vision could not see. There was nothing in Freedom Square overtly threatening except for the rocks pelting him from all sides. Rock throwers didn't usually warrant missile defenses, so something was not right with his uniform. He switched back to Plain Sight and gave up searching for viable threats until a woman with short brown hair stepped in front of him.

"We have the right," she said.

It was not protocol for enforcers to speak directly to Freelanders. The only allowed speech came from the FSA lexicon of arrest and detain commands. A warning flashed on his self-protection sphere. This woman had no identification. She had no implants whatsoever. Before he could formulate a question, his suit commanded her to get on the ground. "Molecular identification failed," he said, in a harsh mechanical voice. "Hands on your head. Knees on the ground. Final warning!"

Laser-knife left-hand, his self-protection sphere warned.

Sky 2-4-4 spotted the weapon with Plain Sight. The low-tech knife had no chance of penetrating his armor, but pulling a weapon on an enforcer was a punishable violation. Sky 2-4-4 moved with enhanced speed, surprised that the tiny woman was fast enough to take a swipe. Sky 2-4-4 smiled. *Spunky girl,* he thought, and then Abner's personal memories bubbled back to the surface. He had known girls like this in his youth, street savvy and desperate. He felt sympathy for her as he deflected the blade and slid his hand up her wrist in one motion. He twisted her into an arm-break position and grimaced uncomfortably when he dislocated her shoulder with a pop. He forced her face-down on the pavement. He poked her skin with his fingertip, taking a quick DNA sample. A moment later, her name appeared in his HUD. "Relax

Justine," he said. "Your arrest and conviction will be over shortly. Don't struggle and your holographic correction will be brief."

"Leave her alone!"

Sky 2-4-4 turned to see a little girl, maybe twelve years old. The girl glared at him, her fists balled up tight. She punched and kicked him. She leaned in to bite him which couldn't have felt good on her teeth. She then threw herself across the back of the downed perp. Sky 2-4-4 reached down with his free hand to immobilize the little girl with a fingertip injector. He paused as his hand came to rest on her shoulder. A siren sounded in his helmet, alerting him to immediate danger. He felt a jolt like being stung by bees, a sure sign his adrenaline boosters just shot him up. His suit was morphing into emergency self-protection mode, and Sky 2-4-4 had no idea why.

Without personal thought, the Sky 2-4-4 uniform twisted him into a standing position. His baton and zap rod whipped into his hands from where they were concealed inside the uniform's gauntlets. With a sickening feeling in his stomach, Sky 2-4-4 heard a skull crack and watched the little girl lift into the air, her eyes going white as her small body hurtled away. "No!" Sky 2-4-4 yelled, frantically trying to regain control of his suit that had gone wild.

The uniform finished its defensive movement sweeping his body away from Justine to face a crowd of people rushing at him with hatred in their eyes. His suit armed the laz'rupters in his sleeves and the uniform aimed. All the people attacking him were going to die, Sky 2-4-4 realized. His suit was malfunctioning.

Sky 2-4-4, a voice said in his mind. *Lethal force authorized.*

"Command," Sky 2-4-4 yelled, stunned. "No weapons. Not a threat!"

Sky 2-4-4, Command said, again, only this time with more authority. *Lethal force required.*

"No!" he yelled, remembering how it felt to feed the hungry people gathered at O'Reilly's mission. "Command, the uniform malfunction! I am not in control."

Sky 2-4-4 barely felt the first wave of protesters hit him in the chest as he flipped his uniform into manual mode. Without the lifters and motors assisting his movements, Abner started to rock back on his feet as more waves of people attacked. All Sight shifted to uncorrected Plain Sight and his drug injectors ceased jetting chemicals into his body. Relief descended on Abner as his arms fell back to his sides without firing a shot.

He collapsed beneath the people. He knew they couldn't hurt him. He was still armored, so he lay on his back under a blanket of living bodies trying to get at his personal flesh. Such anger in their eyes, such betrayal. Abner rested beneath the onslaught and moved through menus to find the malfunction he knew had seized his uniform. As he studied the firework show of sensors lighting up his visor, he heard a new voice.

Sky 2-4-4. Who authorized manual mode?

The voice was loud in Abner's head, but it wasn't the Sky unit's usual commander speaking. This person was not a senior enforcer. He was a Field Marshal, named Levi, according to the uniform's identification system. FSA Field Marshals were several ranks above the grunts in the Enforcer Corps. "Sir," he said. "My suit malfunctioned. There was no threat—"

The enforcer unit Sky 2-4-4 assesses threats on whose authority? The comment was directed at someone else at FSA dispatch. In a measured voice, the Field Marshal used a different channel and spoke directly into the Sky 2-4-4's helmet. "Sky 2-4-4," Levi said. "You are not authorized to deactivate FSA systems. This is a Class A violation."

Abner's heart raced. If he turned his uniform back on, the people attacking him would die. Prefect O'Reilly fed people like the ones who attacked. O'Reilly taught Sky 2-4-4—Abe, he thought—taught Abe to protect the kinds of people who attacked. Enforcers were supposed to protect people. "I can't, sir," he said, knowing disobedience was not tolerated in any branch of the FSA. They'll take Lotus away from him. He knew this. They'll put him back in the holo-chair. He feared this.

A third voice entered the helmet, louder than Levi and the rest. "Enforcer units do not think! They are obedient onto death. Who allowed this unit free-thought? Give me emergency command or I'll deal with you next!"

The suit whirred to life and all control menus ceased to function. Sky 2-4-4 read the identification signature of the person controlling his uniform: Deputy Director, Cole Reaver.

Abner choked back his fear and then tried desperately to wrench back control. His uniform ignored his efforts and pumped dangerous quantities of adrenaline into his system until he was bursting with fear and rage. He pushed himself up violently from where he lay on the street, throwing people in every direction. *You do as I command, enforcer.* It was Reaver's thought injected directly into Abner's mind. *You have never been in control. You are a maggot, an abomination, a thing made in Rose's lab.*

Abe's body was trapped in the uniform but Abe was a large man. He was a strong man. He threw himself bodily left and right trying to force the suit to miss its targets. His laz'rupter fire hit office buildings and trees. One beam tore a fist-sized hole in another enforcer who dropped where he stood. Abe spun around, staring in horror as other enforcers carried out their "lethal force required" command. It was a massacre.

Abe grew dizzy and then Gerald, the ghost behind the enforcer's closing eyes, was thrown out of Abe's head. Sky 2-4-4's official FSA report ended. A timestamp blinked before Gerald, momentarily giving him the option to replay the memory. Before Gerald could formulate what this might mean, he heard the dragon locust rasp a single command: *Next,* it roared. *Show him next!*

Gerald somersaulted in the hot and humid air as his moth-like form fell into the next light.

Gerald floated high up in an empty room with holo-chairs lined up against one wall. Three chairs were occupied with very large people encased in silver cocoons of vWare webbing. The sensors on the webbing blinked and sparkled like festival lights. Gerald had vRead about FSA training rooms, but he had never seen one.

He heard sounds of people entering the room, and then saw two enforcers throw a familiar looking giant with blond hair into one of the empty chairs. The vWare webbing stirred and started to coil around the man, wrapping him up in silver just like the others in the training room.

A door opened and shut. "It's you," said a familiar voice. "You're the enforcer who thinks for himself?"

The blond man in the chair turned his head to face the newcomer and blanched slightly. "I'm Abe," he said.

"You're nothing!" the man yelled. He slapped Abe across the mouth.

Gerald's world shook. The lights flickered, and then he floated higher up in the room. Whispers in the back of Gerald's mind tugged at him. *Not yet,* the dragon locust said. *You can't leave yet.*

There was someplace Gerald needed to be, he remembered. His arms hurt and his legs. Everything tingled. He was hot and the air was wet.

Not yet.

Gerald suddenly recognized the man in the chair. He looked older than AJ, but his features were the same like a twin who experienced a harder life than his friend. Gerald's body grew cold as he heard the name, "Abner," from the man beating him. He knew the voice. It was Cole Reaver. *It's a night vision,* Gerald reminded himself. *None of this is real.*

"You're one of Rose's abominations!" Reaver yelled.

"I'm enhanced," Abe said. "I can help you."

"Enhanced?" Reaver practically spit the word. "A prezero grotesquery who murders little girls and fellow enforcers alike. You are a demon, nothing more, but father ties my hands. I'm not allowed to kill you yet. I'm only allowed to re-train you as if that's ever worked."

Reaver walked to the edge of the chair and waved his hand. A control sphere appeared next to the chair. He gestured with his fingers and then stepped back to look at the enforcer.

"I'm Abe," the AJ lookalike said. "I will not forget this time. I will not forget Prefect O'Reilly. I will not forget Layfette. I will not forget you, Cole Reaver of the FSA."

"Oh, but you will," Cole said while his hands clenched and relaxed compulsively. "Just like every time before. What's it been, Abe? Five times now? And just like all the times before, you can watch your world disappear in three… two… one." Reaver snapped his fingers. Abe jerked in his chair. His pupils rolled back in his head forcing the whites to bulge outward from trembling eyelids. Spittle foamed pink and white at the corners of his mouth.

A horrible smile creased Reaver's face as he watched Abe buck against the silver webbing. "But father didn't say I had to make your retraining pleasant. Enjoy your fate, demon kind. I have things to do, so many things. First, let's go arm the people calling for your head. See where that takes us, shall we?"

Cole turned his back on Abe and walked away. The two enforcers silently followed him out of the room.

Gerald watched Abe struggle in the holo-chair. He felt himself grow lighter and farther away. The FSA training room shrank beneath him. The last thing Gerald remembered was a woman entering through the same door Cole had used. She was dressed in an open jacket that swept around her body like a long black cape. On her hips, she wore a wide shiny black belt with holsters for guns and tiny leather loops for hanging small tools. Her pointed, silver-tipped boots were made of a supple material that hugged her calves and had flat soles. She looked around the room until she stared up at Gerald floating ever higher above her. She wore oily black glasses with SLYscape designs decorating the lenses. "What do you think, Abner? Is anybody watching us?"

The dark haired lady with the red beads in her braids casually pulled a hand tool from her belt and aimed it skyward. She pulled the trigger and a beam of white light burned Gerald's eyes. He somersaulted backward through the dark until pinpricks of light sprinkled above and below him like a universe of swirling stars. He was a moth again, fluttering in crazy circles above the lady who continued to talk. "More Eyes than Freelanders," he heard. "This is part of the problem, sugar. No privacy anymore."

With his sight gone, he heard the steel in her husky voice. He remembered her. She was the lady in the ambulance who asked him about the voices. She told him he'd be taken care of by her boss. He remembered how the red beads clicked as she sat next to him on the gurney. She rode with him all the way to the hospital and then to the Academy never leaving his side. He remembered how his eyes had swollen shut so he couldn't see her as she argued with somebody who later cried out when she slapped him. She warned the man not to disobey. The scribeosphere had hid from her and it wouldn't show itself again until she was gone.

"Did the voices tell you to switch your uniform to manual, Abner?" the lady asked. "Stay with me, sugar. You heard them, right? Well don't worry. My boss won't let you down. He has something special in store for you. It's almost time," she said. "You'll see. Everything will be okay."

It's not okay! The dragon locust roared in Gerald's head so loud he nearly crashed into another dot of light. *Not okay to be Abe*, it ranted, angrily, bathing Gerald's ears in steamy breath. *Not okay to be sleeping when there's so much to show. It's time to wake. For Gerald to wake.*

Awake!

Gerals! Wake up!

Chapter 8

Street Justice

Gerald gasped as the dark world with tiny lights exploded into colors. The noises of the tube crashed into place around him. Sight, smell, and sound returned. It hurt. Gerald sucked in a steadying breath and tried to wipe clammy sweat from his brow. The skin around his eyes felt numb and swollen. His tongue was so dry, it cracked when he swallowed. His head ached and his nose dripped blood judging from the coppery taste on his lips. His arms didn't move. He was restrained. Gerald looked down at his body and saw no restraints with his Plain Sight. Gerald shook his head and groaned.

No Plain Sight. No All Sight. He simply saw.

The last remnants of night vision lifted from his groggy thoughts as the real world took shape around him. Gerald felt his heart race as he recognized why he couldn't move. He was strapped tight against a detainment board that leaned like a coffin against the tube wall. In front of him, a clear window offered a beautiful view of Miners Road platform just south of the old peninsula bridge that connected New Michigan to the Northern Marshes. The bridge had long ago surrendered to a thick canopy of trees and vines that wrapped the rickety structure like a leviathan rising from the murky water below. The bridge marked the end of the line for tube travelers. Iron City and the Great North Swamp where AJ lived could only be accessed by small transports with free-style flying abilities nimble enough to outrun freedom storms. Tubes flew rigid paths making them too dangerous to travel any further north.

Since it was the last stop for mass transit, everyone was forced to exit at Miners Road even if they planned on travelling back south. The constant influx of people had turned the kilometer-long platform into its own little frontier village with a ten-room inn, several vending kiosks, a taxicraft company, and plenty of food providers. AJ's family owned a small fleet of used taxicrafts, jumpers, and vintage prezero racing gliders. One of the taxicrafts or jumpers would be waiting for them at the platform docks. The gliders were illegal to operate over public land since their prezero ram jets were deemed unsafe by the Freeland Transpiration Authority. The O'Sullivans had three gliders in perfect condition because AJ's dad had raced them professionally before the FTA made them illegal. Gerald had never been inside one, but AJ told stories about getting sick as they did loops at Mach 2.

As the tube slowed to a stop, Gerald considered his invisible restraints. They were likely Flexiforce resistance bands that applied no pressure unless he moved. The faster he moved, the stronger the resistance became like thick rubber bands that would stretch some before flinging him back against the board. He moved his fingers around to see if he could feel the force straps—nothing. He didn't remember being strapped down. He didn't remember if the Flying Eye arrested him or if it just arrested AJ for fighting. He turned his head towards someone breathing and saw AJ watching him. He was tied to another board but was too big for it. This left his neck pinched over the sharp corner of the board while his head rested on the curved tube wall behind him.

"Trussed-up like a bug in a spider web for two hours waiting for you to wake up. Worse than sitting through Humpty Dump's data sphere lectures."

"What happened?"

"You've been zoning since the stunners got you—moaning, yelling weird-ass things, speaking in odd voices—the usual." AJ smiled darkly and shook his head in resignation like a condemned man facing the gallows. "We've been arrested by those demon-peckin' Eyes. According to Chuckles, the city clerk, ROLIES are waiting for us out there." He gestured with his head past the window where the tube eased up to the platform like a boat docking. "We're fried, twitlicker. Fried good and proper."

Gerald expelled a quick breath in something resembling a laugh. AJ called him bad names every time they faced the dean's holographic punishment chair. The memory of confronting the dean seemed quaint compared to facing ROLIES when the word "terrorists" was being thrown around by the other passengers. Gerald's mind wandered to the FSA training room and the silver webbing that wrapped those people like mummies. The dean's chair looked nothing like those which wasn't surprising since Gerald believed the FSA version of the chairs was probably something he imagined. Night visions, he reminded himself, felt real but the counsellors assured him they weren't real despite his strange ability to learn from visions. *They aren't new skills*, he remembered the counsellors saying, *just newly remembered.*

He had been taught night visions were just a hodge-podge of his own half-remembered experiences. That's why Abe looked like AJ's twin, and the dark haired lady showed up at the end. *What was her name?* She was in the ambulance in the aftermath of the fire. Sharon, he recalled. *You'll be taken care of*, she had said. *My boss has seen to it.* She was a memory just like Cole Reaver who he had seen hundreds of times on-sphere. He remembered the little girl because she was hurt in the piratecast just before he was stunned. The giant locust… a trauma-induced memory… a distortion of his childhood perception. As always, his desire to believe the counsellors hit a wall. Did they expect him to believe he had learned how to operate an enforcer uniform as a child? The internal controls were as clear in his mind as any other piece of equipment he'd ever used. And how did he remember the mission burning down on Layfette? It was on the other side of the block. He needed the name of the enforcer who struck down Kisme St. James…. No he didn't, he scolded himself. *Night visions aren't real. They can't be.*

"Aje, how did Brandy hack the SLYcast? How'd she get the sVid of the little girl?"

"You tell me, Gerald. She came flying out of your pants." He laughed not realizing what he'd said until he said it. "Seriously, what was that? I've never seen you do that before."

Gerald shook his head. "I have no idea. My buckle plays sVids and the glow could have been from the belt clip. The clip's little but has juice, probably enough to sustain a piratecast. So I guess your 'girlfriend' tapped into them."

"Girlfriend?" AJ turned away and stared out the window. "When Ma finds out…." He jerked against his restraints pushing himself a few inches from the board before it snapped him back. "Bald-headed twitlicker would've ripped you limb from limb. What was I supposed to do? Brandy on the tube. All those tweet-peckers yelling."

"Which one was the twitlicker?"

"The big guy with the camo trying to act all bad-ass. Stupid flat-head with a glass jaw. He's the kind of people starting riots. We didn't start that mess. Ma will know that." He looked down at his massive chest and rocked himself forward a little before snapping back again. "Since when do Eyes this far north shoot force webs? Can't bust'em. You see the first Eye I smoked? Never fought one of those before. Probably earned some holo-time for it… served it right, though. Glad you're awake, Gerald."

"Thanks."

"I missed your little girl voice."

"How sweet. I missed your monkey grunts." Gerald kept his tone light to hide the dread welling up inside. It was one thing to be accused of cheating on an exam when you can prove you can answer the questions without help. It was another thing to be arrested without understanding the charges. AJ was right. The source of the last piratecast came from his clothing. How could he prove somebody hacked him without being allowed to tear the buckle apart and study the vWare for traces? He flexed his arms uselessly against the restraints.

Justice this far north happened without trials—verdicts in minutes usually. For the first time since Prefect Humphrey threw the testing sphere, Gerald felt trapped. He didn't do anything illegal but without a real trial, he couldn't defend himself. FSA designations were not awarded to people with criminal records unless they were being conscripted as an enforcer. Without FSA clearance, Gerald would never learn what happened on the night of the fire. *Unless Abe is real. If he saw the fire….* Gerald shook his head, angrily. *Abe didn't see the fire, because he's not real. The lithium miner isn't real.* None of the people he dreamed about were real.

"When you were zoning, did your Muse show up by chance? Whisper some new hack in your ear? Maybe one that'll get us off these boards?"

"No such luck," Gerald said, growing anxious. The dragon locust in his night vision did not feel like the little locust from his scribeosphere. It felt ominous, pushing him to some conclusion he wasn't ready to make. *It better not be real,* he thought. "After I was shot the first time. I saw you go berserk like you wanted to kill. What got into you? You knew I wasn't really hurt. Stunners just knock people out."

"You should know by now, Gerald. I don't let jack-wads beat you down. That includes jack-wads that happen to be security drones. We got our deal."

Gerald felt oddly pleased. "I think the deal ended the day we took the Dezie Exam. Pretty sure you don't need vWare help anymore."

AJ shrugged.

"But thanks."

"No problem."

Charles Heller appeared next to them with a Flying Eye hovering just over his shoulder. "Sleeping beauty's up, then?" he asked. "Good. You boys have a hearing to attend." The Eye flew in front of Heller and opened the tube door. The detainment boards lifted a few inches off the ground and floated forward. AJ ducked to keep from bumping his head as they exited by remote control.

It was dark and humid outside with just a few fuzzy stars hanging inside halos of white and gray. The boards floated several paces away from the tube's air conditioned doorway before the full thickness of the hot air washed over Gerald like a wet blanket. He hovered there, slowly rotating like a slab of beef on a vertical rotisserie. Heller walked away from the boys without saying a word. The Flying Eye followed him, leaving the boys alone on the platform rotating helplessly. Gerald wondered if above them, their crimes were flashing for all the world to see. He wondered next what crimes they were charged with, but he knew better than to ask. In the Freeland, you didn't need to be formally charged. You were just judged for your actions.

Gerald felt self-conscious and embarrassed as passersby tried unsuccessfully to avert their eyes. After enduring the discomfort for a few minutes, Gerald relaxed enough to smell the warm fragrance of flowering tobaccos and early summer plants. The faintest whiff of exhaust and fecund muck hung in the air from the transport jumpers continually taking off and landing around him. The chatter of the people going about their business was muted beneath the sounds of night birds and other animals chirping in the surrounding marshes. Insects were a problem since he couldn't swat them. He blinked away a gnat from his eye and expelled a heavy breath from his nose to dislodge another. "As far as summer vacations go, this one pretty much sucks balls."

"An understatement," AJ agreed.

The detainment boards hummed back to life and moved forward. "On the bright side, we might get wiped, so it's not like we'll remember," AJ added.

Gerald nodded feeling like he was going to cry. *I can't believe this is happening*, he thought. *This was supposed to be such a great day.*

They travelled the length of the platform giving Gerald time to notice how agitated the people walking around seemed. Nobody smiled. Gerald assumed they were unhappy at seeing two boys on detainment boards. Then, he saw the open-sided kiosks advertising "from today's headlines" tee-shirts. One read simply: *Justice for Kisme!* in various forms of block letters. The other made Gerald's blood run cold. It showed a thick red circle around the enforcer kneeling next to Kisme St. James with one hand twisting Justine's arm back cruelly. Behind the enforcer, snarling protesters rushed him. A yellow circle magnified a detail on the pavement a few centimeters from Justine's outstretched fingertips: a laser-knife with its pale blue blade drawn. The word on the shirt read:

Illegal Rally!
Illegal Weapon!
Whose fault did you say it was?

Gerald stared at the laser-knife as he floated by the tee-shirt kiosk. He didn't remember seeing the knife in Brandy's piratecast. Of course, he remembered it vividly from his night vision. *How do dreams pick up details like that?* The boards slammed to a halt, knocking the question from his mind.

Gerald looked forward and felt his adrenaline spike at the sight of two Rule of Law officers in black and yellow armor. Neither man's features could be seen behind their black face shields.

"Well what do we have here?" one of them said, drawing out each word for a beat too long. It was hard to tell which ROLIE spoke until the shorter one stepped closer. He studied Gerald as if he was an insect pinned flat for display. "Looks like," he said, turning from Gerald to pace between the two boys. "Two boys looking for trouble might have found some. Am I right, Mr. Heller?"

"Well," Heller said, appearing from behind the boys to stand next to the larger ROLIE who had yet to say a word. "I'm not really sure exactly." He turned to face the ROLIE who had been speaking. "It's best you see for yourself, Henry."

The short one stepped back from the boys to join Heller and the other ROLIE in a rank-and-file line. "It's Agent McCormick while I'm on duty Mr. Heller."

"Oh sorry," Heller said. "It's just I know they've done something illegal. I just don't know exactly what matter of illegal it is. The big one we got for assault, sure. Damaging Freeland property to be certain. But that one—" Heller pointed at Gerald. "He sort of disturbed the peace or maybe it's worse. See for yourself."

The Flying Eye from the tube landed between the ROLIES and the boys. It rumbled and then shot a small m-sphere into the center of the makeshift street-side court. The sphere showed Gerald and AJ sitting next to Heller arguing, and then the sVid recording ticked forward to show the rest.

Gerald watched himself look at his belt buckle when it first projected Brandy Pepper's piratecast. He saw the fight between AJ and the entire tube of passengers after Gerald went down. He heard the accusations saying the two of them were part of the Earth First movement. He saw his scribeosphere roll from his pocket and shoot away from the Flying Eye that gave chase. With a sudden realization, he remembered his scribeosphere was gone. It left him. What if it was still on the tube? What if the Eye shot it?

You're such a zonk, Gerals! Eyes are stupid. They can't catch me.

Gerald laughed.

"Something funny, Mr. Goodstone?" the bigger ROLIE asked, in a deep voice full of judgment. "I see nothing funny about what just transpired."

In the recording, the bald man was carted off by a medical drone. "Not that," Gerald said. "Something else."

"See what I mean?" Heller asked. "They're horrible boys, too impulsive to plan what happened on the tube. The more I think about it, the more I think they didn't have much to do with the piratecast. The red-head seemed genuinely shocked at what his clothing was doing. Did you see that?"

"Boys being boys?" the short ROLIE asked, nodding.

"Corporal, I see nothing boyish here—"

"No sir. Not boyish but maybe not as bad as what it seems?"

The large ROLIE stood silent for moment. He appeared to look behind Gerald to the tee-shirt drones selling Justice for Kisme! slogans. He stared in that direction for quite a while before he suddenly said: "AJ O'Sullivan. You have no priors. That is good. The Freeland is in a state of elevated response due to wide-spread reckless assembly. That is bad, especially for pirates inciting riots."

"Pirates?" AJ said.

Heller echoed the disbelief Gerald heard in his friend's tone.

The ROLIE stepped closer to Gerald. "According to the tube manifest, you are Gerald Goodstone, companion to AJ O'Sullivan. Guilty by association. I see no identification plant inside your body. I see no SLY-tech at all. This is suspicious. Explain."

"It's not illegal!" Heller blurted, reaching up to grab the ROLIE's shoulder. The ROLIE turned his head to stare silently at Heller. After a moment, Heller removed his hand and then said, "Well, it's not. I checked."

"Are you a Rule of Law Officer, Mr. Heller?"

Charles Heller looked down sheepishly. "No," he mumbled, and then visibly struggled with some internal resolution. He looked up and engaged the ROLIE's eyeless gaze. "But something isn't right here. Pirates? They deserve correction, but what you're implying—"

"What am I implying, Mr. Heller?"

"That they're thugs from the piratesphere. That they really did hijack the SLYcast! Those are some big charges. Bigger than I think this situation merits."

"So you are a Rule of Law Officer, Mr. Heller?"

Quiet again, Heller shook his head. "No sir."

AJ and Gerald glance at each other wondering why Heller was suddenly sticking up for them. The ROLIE stared at Heller a moment longer before turning to Gerald.

"Gerald Goodstone. No implants. Explain."

"I have an aversion to needles," Gerald said. "Sir," he added, belatedly.

"What was that thing in your pocket?"

"What thing?" Gerald asked, his heart rate rising.

"Shall I bring the recording back up?"

Gerald shook his head. “It’s just a toy.”

“A toy that can outrun a Flying Eye? A toy that somehow avoids SLY-tech detection?”

“I made it when I was eleven, sir. With my father.”

“Is your father a SLYscape engineer?”

Gerald nodded. “He was.”

“So you’re goo with vWare?” the ROLIE asked.

AJ snorted.

“Good enough to hack into a SLYcast?”

Gerald saw the trap too late. “No sir,” he lied.

The ROLIE continued to stare in silence. “Says here you’re a graduate of Rose’s Academy for Gifted Students. They say it’s a school for geniuses.”

“I’m from the Academy too!” AJ said. “Got me a big brain.”

“You did not graduate with distinction. Your companion did.”

Both AJ and Gerald exchanged surprised looks. Neither of them were graduates. They would not be given their credentials until the pending investigations were resolved. The big ROLIE in charge didn’t seem to know they were under investigation at all. *Why not?*

“Regardless,” the ROLIE said. “The law is clear. The sVid provided is proof enough for a conviction. I find you both guilty. Sentencing to be carried out immediately.”

“What?” AJ and Gerald both said at once.

Heller said, “On what charges, captain?”

The large ROLIE responded: “Assault 3rd degree, Vandalism 1st degree, and Disturbing the Peace. Very much like you wanted.”

Loud cheers and a few jeers startled Gerald. A sizable crowd had gathered around them to watch street-side justice in action. Some of the faces he recognized from the tube, though the bald man in the camouflage was missing. Others were strangers just watching the show saying things like: *haven’t seen a good one like this in a while; big one’s like a World Union gene demon with his muscles; betcha ginger’s a synth-addict laughing like that at a* ROLIE.

“Corporal, confiscate the boy’s buckle and get it to our technicians. If they find evidence that the accused were complicit in hijacking the SLYcast, additional measures will be taken.”

“Additional measures?” Gerald asked as he watched the short ROLIE approach.

"Looks like a bad day for you," the short ROLIE said, his voice sounding sympathetic. "Trouble with trouble, son, is it can be bigger than you imagined." He unlatched Gerald's buckle and returned to his commander.

A few minutes later, Gerald watched a new Flying Eye approach. This one was black as night with two globes of spider-like eyes rotating on stalks above it. Thick blood red lightning bolts decorated its sides. Gerald grew light-headed and sagged against the board. If it wasn't for the restraints that kept him upright, Gerald might have fallen. In his periphery, AJ glared at the approaching machine with an almost manic glee. His tongue dotted his lips. It was a disturbing look that Gerald had seen many times before when AJ stepped into arenas for martial arts contests. He was focusing for battle.

The Flying Eye stopped in front of the two boys. The ROLIE said loudly and clearly. "For the combined acts of Vandalism, Assault, and Disturbing the Peace. You, AJ O'Sullivan and you, Gerald Goodstone, will receive 10 slow-time hours of virtual correction each."

The crowd made noises Gerald could barely hear. The Black Eye was not your ordinary Flying Eye. It was a mobile conditioning unit capable of administering immersion sentencing anywhere at any time. After the crowd quieted, the ROLIE said: "As the law states, punishment can be forgiven at a rate of one thousand perks per sixty minute interval of slow-time correction. Twelve-hundred total minutes can be forgiven at a cost of ten thousand perks per individual convicted. Would you like to pay for partial or whole punishment reduction?"

The boys didn't have enough savings between them to reduce the sentence by even thirty minutes, so neither responded until AJ said, "We have no perks to offer."

"Very well, your sentence will be carried out immediately—"

"Hold-up! Gerald Goodstone will receive no virtual correction. I, AJ O'Sullivan, volunteer to receive both shares by myself. By law, this is my right."

The big ROLIE shook his head. The shorter one spoke. "You're filled with fire, aren't you boy? Nobody can break your spirt. I've seen guys like you before. Trouble is, you don't know what this Black Eye is going to do. You don't know what you're volunteering for, so let me enlighten you a tad. This baby," he patted the Black Eye on one of its eye stalks. "Is a hard labor program. At twenty slow-time hours, you'll feel 100 days of excruciating, non-productive labor. When you fall from exhaustion, Blacky here's going to make you feel a whip at you back until you find your feet. Fourteen hour days. Fifty of them is bad enough, but one hundred—"

"He's right, son," Heller said. "Don't do it. I've seen men twice your age crack. Let your friend take his share."

Gerald said nothing, trying to imagine what type of non-productive labor would be required. Digging and refilling holes? Stacking walls of concrete blocks, then taking them down? Carrying logs on your shoulders up and down hills? "Aje," he said, finally. "I can take my share. Thanks for the offer, though."

"Listen to you friend, boy," the short ROLIE said. "Don't be stupid."

AJ stared at all the people standing around the two detainment boards. He smiled at them and said simply, "Bring it."

The ROLIE captain said, "Very well."

"No," Gerald yelled. "I don't accept his offer."

"Mr. O'Sullivan is right," the captain said. "It is his right, and he does not need your permission to take your punishment. It is the law."

"Don't worry, Gerald. I got this," he said, and then suddenly the Black Eye hummed to life and shot AJ with a wide red beam filled with swirling silver light that painted circles around his eyes, ears, mouth and nose. More silver circles appeared on his hands, feet, and groin.

Gerald winced as he saw his friend buck on the board as the beam finished lighting him up. His eyes rolled back showing the whites. The short ROLIE closed AJ's eyes. "No need for him to suffer real damage," he said. "Brave kid."

Heller looked at AJ and made a sympathetic sound before walking away. Others on the platform crowded around. The shorter ROLIE looked at the people gathered and then walked up to Gerald. "Looks like your friend saved you. You're free to go."

The resistance bands clicked off. Gerald fell to his knees in front of the detainment board. He took a moment to get reacquainted with gravity and then stood. The detainment board holding AJ continued to rotate, ensuring the crowd assembled around him could see his suffering. This was street justice. This was what made the Freeland free. Be a good citizen and experience a life free from fear knowing bad citizens were apprehended and convicted within minutes of the crime they committed. Gerald's hands flexed and sweat formed on his brow. He glanced at the time actuator dangling from the bracelet on his wrist. His friend was a bad citizen, already sweating with discomfort from less than three minutes of correction. *What am I going to tell your mom?*

"If you need a place to stay while you wait," the short ROLIE said. "Celia's Inn has a room for this type of thing. Tell her Henry sent you."

The ROLIE turned and walked towards his captain who was almost out-of-sight. Gerald pivoted on his feet to look at all the people watching AJ spin on his board. "What's wrong with you people?" he asked. "Bunch of vultures. Get away!"

Some of them turned to go. Others grinned as if they were digging in for a full night of watching AJ suffer.

Chapter 9

Celia's Inn and Drink

Gerald had been watching AJ struggle against his restraints for an hour before he decided it was time to call Mrs. O'Sullivan. He didn't know what he was going to say to her, but she expected them by nine. He glanced at his time actuator. She expected them now.

Gerald tapped the glass bead next to the black opal on his bracelet and whispered, "Angie O'Sullivan."

A moment later, the connection was made. "Gerald?"

"Hi Mrs. O'Sullivan."

"Do you want a slap? I'm Angie to you. Don't make me tell you twice."

"Sure thing, Mrs. O'Sullivan. I have some bad news."

"News? I've planned a veritable feast for my boys. How close are you?"

"That's the thing…"

Gerald had decided before he made the call that a partial truth would be easier to tell than the entire story. He admitted to her that he and AJ had been arrested for fighting, but left out the pending FWA investigation. He explained how AJ broke a Flying Eye and they were both shot with stunners. She seemed fearful at first then furious. "Stupid ape!" she yelled. "I know you had nothing to do with this, Gerald, honey. You're my smart boy. My big dumb oaf boy is the punchy one. That's just like him, isn't it? Thick-headed testosterone junkie always looking for a match, isn't he? An Eye? Sure, why not. Just punch a hunk of metal and see what happens. Wait till I get my hands on him—"

"Yes, ma'am."

"He'll beg to go back to the conditioner."

"Sure will, ma'am."

"Twenty hours?"

"Yes ma'am. He took my share."

"Of course, he did," she said, finally breaking down in tears. "I'm on my way," she said.

"No need, Mrs. O'Sullivan. I'll bring him home tomorrow night."

"Nonsense. I'm coming to get you—"

"Please don't, ma'am—"

"You call me Angie before I decide to whoop your behind too."

"Sure will, ma'am."

"That's better."

"Mrs. O'Sullivan I'm booking a room. I'll get him home to you tomorrow night. He's twenty, an adult by law. I'm nineteen. We got this, and frankly, we deserve to go through this on our own. We're the ones who broke the law. How else will we learn?" Gerald asked, knowing just how to push her buttons. She had been like a Mom to him for going on eight summers. He believed he knew her as well as she knew him.

Mrs. O'Sullivan considered this for a while. "The brute might learn something if I don't bail him out," she said.

"He might," Gerald said. He listened to her talk mostly to herself as he planned the words he'd say if she decided to come rescue AJ anyway. Gerald had never been able to lie effectively to Mrs. O'Sullivan. She had a way of making him reveal every bad thing he and AJ ever did. If she came to Miner's Platform and saw AJ spinning there, Gerald knew he'd tell her everything. AJ wouldn't like that since he strove to protect his mother from things she'd find difficult. Holographic punishment was one thing, but failing to be awarded designations or being charged with something like what Brandy was involved with was too much. AJ'd lie to his mom without a second thought. Gerald needed AJ's loose relationship with the truth to keep Mrs. O'Sullivan from guessing that their troubles with the law were worse than Gerald let on. "All good points," Gerald said. "So I guess I'll see you tomorrow night?"

Mrs. O'Sullivan paused her speech a moment, and then sighed. "Okay, I'll send someone with the perks you'll need for the room—"

"I can pay," Gerald said.

"Nonsense, dear. I know you're broke."

This was as good as Gerald could expect, so he agreed.

"She'll be there soon," Mrs. O'Sullivan said. "She'll bring one of the big jumpers with the cot." Her voice cracked and shuddered in tight sobs. "In case, you know. In case he needs it when they let him go."

"He's tough," Gerald said.

"He's a fool," she responded, crying. "When he's safe, I'm going to beat his silly skull with a good stick." She trailed off with a loud sniff. "Of all things," she said, finally. "I had so much food for you two. I made fish, tilapia, just for you."

"It'll taste just as great tomorrow, Mrs. O'Sullivan."

"Angie," she said.

"Yes, ma'am."

"Love you, honey. You tell AJ that for me, won't you?"

"Sure will." Gerald severed the connection before she could say more. He started to shake. AJ was moaning behind him. He looked up at his best friend and saw a thick sheen of sweat covering his face. His clothes were already soaked. *One hour done, nineteen more to go,* he thought with a shudder. "Do you hear me, Aje? Can you hear me at all?"

AJ groaned and flexed, not in recognition but in pain. The Black Eye had tapped into the molecular implants in AJ's brain, sending them signals to trick AJ into believing whatever was being done to him was real. The same thing could be done to Gerald, only the Black Eye would stimulate the pain centers in Gerald's brain directly as opposed to handing the signals off to moles. As every Freelander knew, molecular implants borrowed unused portions of human brains to cache and distribute messages between SLYscape spectrums. What many did not know was that moles recorded every neurological impulse their brains exhibited while connected to the SLYscape. What vWare Controllers had learned to do with those signals is build data spheres of experiences derived from actual thoughts and memories of the people who had gifted a portion of their brain to y-space by injecting moles.

In punishment simulations like the one AJ was experiencing, the data spheres fed immersion experiences from people's memories of hard labor camps mixed with a touch of remembered nightmares. Gerald knew vWare could blend fictional elements into an experience as well. The result was a virtual reality so close to real few could tell the difference. Gerald balled his fists helplessly. The SLYscape could spin nightmares out of bad feelings just as easily as it could spin fantasies out of the good.

He stared at AJ and brooded about the enforcer wrapped in silver webbing from his night vision yesterday. He supposed if Abner was a real person—as opposed to as imaginary figment like the dragon locust—Abner was suffering just as badly as AJ. Gerald felt sick inside for AJ and, maybe, the enforcer. He felt sick inside for himself too. As much as Gerald was proud of the Goodstone role in ending the Freedom Wars, he had learned to understand the SLYscape would not exist without the RADcore bomb exploding. By that reasoning, a Goodstone had created the SLYscape, and the SLYscape was hurting his friend.

Freedom storms were also the fault of Gerald's grandfather. The RADcore bomb was Preston Rose's response to gene demon victories and the World Union's efforts to prevent rebels from stealing WU technology. Their scientists designed prezero smart weapons with firing mechanisms cybernetically blended with live human tissue. The rebels had no idea how it worked, but it was clear only gene demons could fire WU weapons. This included the antimatter missiles called, Mountain Crackers, which broke the moon and destroyed the atmosphere above the Glass Lands. According to the family story Gerald had been told as a boy, the RADcore plan had come to Preston Rose in a dream. If the tissue in the firing mechanisms were alive, rebels could control WU weapons with vWare.

The rebels' best weapon was vWare. Any equipment, as long as it could be electrically stimulated, was controllable by vWare. Living tissue could be electrically stimulated, which meant antimatter missiles could be hacked. The trouble with vWare hacking was the controller had to be inside the same radiation cloud as the equipment being controlled. SLYscape radiation clouds were small and only occurred naturally in pockets. RADcore was designed to attract all the small pockets of nearby radiation into clouds large enough to span city-sized military bases. The RADcore bomb worked too well because the radiation cloud it created kept expanding until it flooded the entire planet. Between the radiation and the antimatter missiles, super storms later named, freedom storms, rampaged across the remaining lands killing eighty percent of the population and driving many animals and insects extinct. In Gerald's present mood, it was easy for him to blame Goodstones for it all. Even the After Zero religions that sprouted up to cleanse the world of gene demons forever.

Gerald stood up next to AJ. He looked into his friend's closed eyelids and watched the spastic movement beneath. "Sorry, AJ," he said. "This is all my fault!"

Gerald walked across the slatted boards of the platform to stand directly beneath the Black Eye. He reached up to touch the thing and received an electrical shock that numbed his fingers. He tried to touch AJ and received the same shock. He guessed it meant that AJ was safe. At least, safe from everyone other than the Black Eye that carried out the sentence. He wondered how it was that people could invent so many ingenious ways to hurt each other and so few ways to help.

He watched AJ for another twenty minutes until the last of the crowd left the area. "I'll be back soon, AJ," he said loudly. "If you can hear me, just hold on." AJ's tongue wet his lips and his head shook back and forth. "It's not real, Aje!" he yelled. "Fight it." After a while longer, Gerald walked away from his best friend in the direction of the inn. He was thirsty and needed food.

The platform was a walkway made from synthetic wood-like planks built in similar fashion as the hundreds of other floating paths crisscrossing the marshy areas of the north. Below his feet, the slats of space between the boards reflected a few stars and the two halves of the moon folding in on itself within the rippling water. Head down, walking rhythmically, he listened to his boots tap the boards. The faster Gerald walked, the faster the moon clapped its halves together like a flipbook cartoon of a claw pinching.

He stopped at a knot-hole burned through one of the boards. In the dark water below, the gleam of a red eye stared up. Though many animals died when the moon cracked, crocodiles did just fine. He had seen more than his share near AJ's ranch. When Gerald saw them at night, their stares looked frozen in cold, intelligent judgment of what people had done to its world.

Gerald kneeled down and said, "Hey, girl. Whatcha doin'?"

The crocodile splashed with its tail and disappeared. Gerald smiled and rose in front of one of the kiosks selling tee-shirts. The sales drone buzzed around busying itself with folding while Gerald studied the laser knife in the image decorating the shirt. Up close, he could see the laser-knife was clearly activated. It looked just like the one he saw in his night vision. He decided right then he'd find out if an enforcer named, Abner O'Reilly, existed. He also decided something else. He was going to break the Black Eye's hold on AJ. He looked down at his bracelet. *It might work,* he thought.

Suddenly, the usual background noise inside Gerald's head stopped. *Don't do it, Gerals!* the locust said, in an unusually powerful rendition of Lizzy's voice, and then the whispers resumed.

Gerald looked for the scribeosphere and found it bouncing above the roof of the sales kiosk. When Gerald spotted it, the scribeosphere spun in place, catching the silvery moonlight on its metallic skin. He focused his thoughts and pointed at his unzipped pocket, gratified the scribeosphere did as instructed. It rolled down the gazebo-styled roof and jumped inside the large cargo pocket on his pants. Gerald stuffed his hand in and wrapped his fingers comfortably around the silver ball. The metal was cold and reassuring. *Quiet mode,* he said silently to conserve its charge.

Gerald walked in relative silence down the platform until he found metal double doors next to a babblesphere inviting him to enjoy Celia's Inn and Drink. He stepped inside and walked past a thin curtain of beads separating the bar from a drone that rented rooms. He ordered a ginger ale and sat down on one of the stools. The space was dimly lit which was probably why he didn't notice Charles Heller sitting next to him.

"A ginger pop for the ginger boy." Heller laughed at his joke. "You're old enough to drink something harder I 'spect."

Gerald pivoted his stool to face the man. "I think you've done enough, Mr. Heller."

"So you're name's Gerald. That's what the captain said."

Gerald nodded and turned back to face the faceless bartending drone who handed him his drink.

"There was something I wanted to say. That's why I haven't gone yet. It's why I'm drinking. This my third. Want one?" he asked, sloshing FAC provided alcohol over his knuckles and wrist as his hand jostled the small glass he held. "It's been flavored to taste like eighteen year old World Union scotch. I wonder why we don't make alcohol the old-fashion way. I bet real eighteen year old scotch is even better."

He sighed and then shrugged. "Burns the same, I reckon. Hangover's the same too… don't want us working stiffs to feel too good about ourselves, do they?"

Gerald remembered experimenting with lab-fermented alcohol. "I'm not much for hangovers."

Heller laughed too loudly and took another slug of the drink. "Your friend's brave. Disrespectful and stupid, but brave. You know right now he's going through one-hundred days of labor camp? I did the math. We'll see how tough he is tomorrow night, won't we?"

Gerald didn't want to respond, so he took a sip and ordered soup.

"You staying the night? Celia's got small rooms, but the cots are comfier than they look."

"I don't want trouble," Gerald said. "You won. AJ's being tortured right now because of how we behaved on the tube. Feel better?"

"Tortured?" Heller nodded. "Maybe so." He put his drink down and struggled to turn toward Gerald. "There's no winners here, son. That hack job on the High Prelate… not you two's work unless you've been planning for months. That Brandy girl's been all over our local news spheres, lately. No, I think you two are just a couple of bratty punks. That's what we called kids like you in my day, punks." He reached up and clapped Gerald on the shoulder.

Gerald scooted his stool further down the bar.

"Look at that sphere right there," Heller continued, loudly. "Look at that man if you want to know why they're no winners. Just look at his smug face."

Above the bar, the Deputy Director of the FSA, Cole Reaver, stood floating inside a sanctioned m-sphere giving updates on the Earth First protests. He seemed near tears talking about how two enforcers lost their lives at the protest. "What happened to the little girl is a tragedy," he said, as his dark hair flipped crazily in the wind. "But what happened to my men was a tragedy too. Enforcers enforce laws. That's all they do. The men inside those suits died enforcing the laws our High Prelate created. Law men do as they're told and should remain blameless. The High Prelate's council unleashed the force you saw this afternoon. So as you mourn for the St. James' family, remember my fallen men had families too. The uniform makes them look like demon droids, but I assure you they are not." Reaver turned from the SLYcorders and walked down a few brightly lit stairs that curved toward the smooth marble exterior of the towering FSA headquarters. He paused at the bottom step and turned dramatically to face the viewers.

"Lethal force," he said, his voice becoming difficult to hear over the mounting wind. "Those were our orders. I ask the law-abiding among you: how many FSA men did you see revealed by the SLYscape virus? Zero. How many OPC members?"

The sound of exclamations and questions rose louder than the wind in the recording. Snippets of outlandish questions echoed: *Who ordered lethal force? Is it a cover up? Does the OPC want the protesters dead?*

"I've said too much," he said, raising his hand. He turned but paused again as one voice yelled louder than the rest: "Did you catch Brandy Peppers? Did you arrest the hijackers?"

With his hand resting on the white exterior of the tower, he turned his head to look at the Revealer over his shoulder. The SLYcorders turned to show an older woman with white hair holding her palms up to record his answer. She asked her question again, and Reaver responded: "I'm unhappy to report that she and her band of degenerates got away. The hijackers still threaten our security."

"Were they aided by anyone?" she asked.

Reaver smiled, thinly. "That's what I aim to find out. Now if you'll excuse me." He turned his gaze from the white-headed lady to the stones of the building he leaned against. A moment later, the white exterior split in two revealing a wide open space leading to a polished marble interior with statues and fountains lining the cavernous corridor. Reaver step inside FSA headquarters and vanished as the doorway closed behind him.

The SLYcorders panned away in a sweeping view of Freedom Square, now deserted except for small troops of enforcers standing guard at the corners. It zoomed in on the blood stain marking the pavement where the first enforcer went down. The SLYcast lingered there before zooming out to capture the blurry stars hanging above the buildings of Old New York. More typical of Cyclonic-sol than the rainy Derecho-sol, cyclones hundreds of meters high raged against the force fields webbed between the weather sentry towers encircling the city. In the SLYcsta, it was clear the wind was growing stronger as the freedom storms bashed about ominously in the distance. The FWA sanctioned m-sphere showing the storm went suddenly blank and then the recording repeated.

Heller shook his head and made a wet noise of disgust. "That man's not a nice man. If I had a choice, he'd be getting the Black Eye, not your impulsive, foolish friend. Did you know your friend put a man in the Iron City hospital? Broken jaw and eye socket from one punch. Got some anger issues, your friend, but nothing next to Reaver. He's got ice demons in his veins, no empathy for the people."

"He seemed pretty choked up about his men," Gerald said, thinking how different the person in the news sphere seemed from the screaming maniac of his night vision. "What he says is true. Inside those uniforms are people… his people."

"You believe that?"

Gerald nodded.

"Was I ever your age?" he asked, slurring some of his words together. "Wait til I tell my wife. She will think you're so sweet."

To Gerald's ear, Heller's overly deliberate enunciation was painful to listen to. It was like the man's tongue had grown too swollen and sluggish to talk right. "So, what's he done?" Gerald asked.

"Besmirched Preston Rose and the legions of people who follow him."

"Followers of Rose," Gerald said. "I've heard."

"Don't mock a faithful soul no matter what faith they choose. Good people serve him at the OPC. People like me and my wife… my son. We love the High Prelate. We do anything for him because he's why we're here." Heller raised his hands in gesture around the bar. His head wobbled on his shoulders as if he was having difficulty keeping his neck straight. "Damn Cole Reaver and his pops. Cole doesn't do anything without his father's consent, believe you me. They say Rose is eccentric, uncaring, unbalanced. They mean crazy, immoral. Has the FSA forgotten the World Union? Do they not see they're just like 'em with their cybernetic uniforms? How is an enforcer different than a gene demon? Remember the Quell… this morning, for that matter? Enforcers killed lots of us too. Should they be executed on-sight? Father Rose is the only good man in government! Better'n us, he is."

"AJ was right… you're a zealot," Gerald said.

Heller grabbed the back of Gerald's neck and pulled him close. The man was surprisingly strong and Gerald couldn't shake his grip without making a scene. Gerald stopped inhaling to avoid gagging on Heller's smelly, eye-burning breath. "Not zealot. Follower. There's a difference."

Gerald struggled against the man's grip.

"Word of advice. A new war is coming. It's not like the last one with clear sides. It's dark and gray. It's going to get bloody. Your friend knows. He's an O'Sullivan—that's what the captain said—so he knows. When he wakes, you tell him Father Rose is watching. You tell him the faithful are always watching, and he better watch his step. Pick his side. A man can't serve two moons," he said, cryptically. "It's the only thing that bastard Reaver taught us during the Quell. Wolves got to pick sides." Heller released Gerald's neck and quaffed the last of his drink.

Gerald pulled himself away from Heller, his chest heaving for air.

"I've told you now," Heller said, standing unsteadily to his feet. "I've said what I had to say. Once I knew who your friend was, I had to say it. Do something good with the information, boy. That's free advice. People got to pick a den." He arched his back and howled as he stumbled around in a drunken circle. He eyed Gerald and smiled seeming to delight in the stares his show earned him from the other drinkers at the bar. "I was a punk once too. You boys ain't done nothin' new."

Heller wobbled on his feet and nearly capsized a table as he walked through the curtain and out of the inn. Gerald heard him start to whistle as the front door slammed.

Gerald pulled himself closer to the bar and hooked his feet around the rail. He drank his ginger ale and asked the egg-shaped wheelie drone behind the bar for a fish sandwich. "Do you have tilapia?" he asked it.

The drone spoke in an overly cheerful manner. "Celia's provides the best imitation fish meats in the north, stranger."

Gerald smiled despite his mood. Miner's Platform was the gateway to the Great North Swamp. It was a tourist attraction, and the drone with no eyes, mouth, or ears to speak of was programmed to talk like an actor from an old holo-vid. "Well, partner," Gerald said. "I'll have one of those then."

The drone sped off to someplace out-of-sight and returned with his meal. Gerald ate in silence. After he finished, he started planning how he'd free AJ without getting caught. It took him at least an hour to figure it out, but he was good at puzzling things until he had the problem beat. It wouldn't be hard, he decided. It might even be fun. He started to push himself up from his stool when he heard the loud clacking of heeled boots approach. "Gerald?" he heard, her voice bright and cheery.

Gerald turned to find Sally Yorkshire standing behind him, hands on hips, smiling. "Surprise!" she yelled, and drew him in for a heavily perfumed hug.

Chapter 10

Vigilante Virus

Gerald squeezed Sally tight to his chest and held her there for a long moment that would have felt awkward if he wasn't so full of relief to see a familiar face. Their cheeks touched warmly as he breathed the scent of her skin. She smelled good like almonds and vanilla. He released her with a squeeze of her of her arms before letting go.

"Wow," she said, her cheeks pink. "It's only been since this morning." She looked behind him to the news sphere and then corrected herself. "Yesterday morning, I guess. Two past midnight already."

Gerald let her go. "What are you doing here?" he asked, his tone sharper than he intended.

"Coming to get you."

"Coming for me?"

"Coming for you and the big guy. Those were my orders."

"Those are bad orders. Go back," he spluttered. His mind raced as he realized Sally endangered his freshly laid plans to save AJ from the Black Eye. She might try and stop him. Or worse, if he was caught, she'd be strapped to a detainment board just for knowing the boys. The people who knew Sally best understood she talked a big game, but at heart she was a good girl, a rule follower. She'd never been conditioned a day in her life. Under the gaze of a Black Eye, she'd break to pieces.

"Weirdest tweet-knocker on the planet," she said, coyly. "That hug you gave me… you practically squished me flat which isn't easy to do. Now you're telling me to go? Schizoid much?"

Gerald smiled despite himself. "No, I'm glad you're here."

She nodded. "You better be."

"It's just, weren't you supposed to be at your new job?"

"I was. Barely had time to unpack my things before my new host sent me to go fetch a couple of 'her boys' who got themselves in trouble. I figured 'her boys' were probably 'my boys' too. So I got in the biggest jumper she had and flew right on over. So how bad have you two been?"

Gerald was confused and looked it.

"Do I have to spell it out? Mrs. O'Sullivan sent me. She's my new host," When Gerald continued to stare, she began talking very slowly as if he was mentally challenged. "I'm staying at the O'Sullivan ranch until the new Freeland Agricultural Center gets built in Iron City. I'm an Aggie!"

"An Aggie?"

"Agriculture Inspector in Training."

"What do they do?"

Sally shook her head. "Stuff. They do lots of agricultural stuff like inspecting soil content for dangerous levels of radiation and making sure the farmers follow the rules."

Gerald nodded, not quite believing what he heard. "You'll be staying with me and AJ, then?"

She danced in place excitedly. Releasing a little joyful scream, she drew Gerald in for another hug. "Just like at the Academy."

"Their house isn't that big."

Sally patted Gerald's chest and winked. "It's cozy alright. Finally get to see what you boys wear to bed. I got the next room over and I've been told I sleep-peek. Trust me, it's a thing."

"Terrific," Gerald said, shaking his head.

"Now tell me what happened. Mrs. Oh kept crying, saying how she was going to beat AJ black and blue. Near as I can tell, he's in a holo-chair. Not like that's anything new. I don't know why she was so worried."

"It's worse than that, Sally. It's a Black Eye."

Her hand rose to cover her mouth. "Like actual prison? Like in holo-stacks?"

"Something like that." The color seemed to drain from her cheeks, so Gerald sat back down on his stool and retold the story in much the same way he told Mrs. O'Sullivan. He left out the worst of it, but gave her enough to believe the twenty hour sentence. By the time he had finished summarizing the experience on the tube, Sally had drank two glasses of some transparent drink with an oily rim. Gerald finished his third ginger ale, and then excused himself to use the bathroom. He had to move soon, if he was going to save AJ. He had to do it without jeopardizing Sally.

He ordered another drink for her. Only this time he asked for a double. She couldn't be complicit in what he was planning if the ROLIE's found her passed out drunk at the bar. "I'll be right back," he said to her. She was too deep in thought to notice the drone was told to keep the drinks coming. She rocked a little on her stool and nodded to him as he got up to go. He watched her take another swig of the clear alcohol. She must be pretty drunk already, he told himself. He then entertained the possibility the rest of his plan might work just as smoothly. He patted the scribeosphere in his pocket and slipped away from the bar.

The bathroom at Celia's was small and cramped with two stalls. He made sure nobody was in the room before locking the door. He pulled the scribeosphere out of his pocket and spun it until he found the four tiny indentations on its surface. He touched the indentations and twisted as he had done hundreds of times before. A sudden puff of air popped the sides of the scribeosphere into four wedges that opened like an orange split down the middle. At the center was a saucer-shaped gold disc. The vWare giving life to the locust was in the disc. The disc connected the locust directly to the SLYscape using the spectrums of sky and light radiation. It used the earth spectrum to control simple machines like digging drones and cranes. The disc was the core of the scribeosphere, and it functioned as its brain.

A frame encircled the core like the rings of a planet. The assembly used the disc as a gyroscope rotor which gave the scribeosphere its ability to fly in any direction. The wedges were hollow except for tiny packets of tools Gerald used to connect the scribeosphere to external technology. He removed a silver filament called a RADwire from one of the packets and clipped SLYscape connectors to it. He wove the filament through tiny loops at the corners of the four wedges and closed the ball tight. Now he had a scribeosphere with a dozen hooks on it, each capable of charging one device.

Gerald had no intention of using the RADwire to charge his other vWare embedded gadgets. He instead removed his bracelet and hooked each charm and bead to the SLYscape connectors. He clasped the bracelet around the scribeosphere using the belt clip the ROLIE failed to confiscate when he took the buckle. The belt clip gave his fingers enough leverage to twist the filament and bracelet chain together. With each twist, he tightened the bracelet more securely to the scribeosphere. When there was no slack left, Gerald looked at his work and tossed it into the air. The silver ball wobbled and jangled loudly but it was fairly balanced. He tweaked the connections until he could toss it up and down in relative quiet. He knew this would have to do.

He touched his lips to the warm metal sphere and whispered, "Wake up."

The temperature of the scribeosphere dropped as it came alive in his hand. Fog condensed on its surface. When it began to hover, Gerald asked it, "Can you fly?"

The scribeosphere shot off his hand and then fell crazily to the ground. Just before impact, it straightened itself out and rose back up to eye-level. *Warning! Unbalanced load,* it said, mechanically. *Remove charging plates… Gerals! Stop it.*

"Can you fly with the charging plates on?"

Calculating, said the mechanical voice, followed by the locust's imitation of Lizzy: *What are you doing, Gerals? You're making my house error. Yes. Flight is possible.*

"How much power do you have left?"

Eighty-six minutes.

That'll do, he thought, so he concentrated as best he could and relayed his instructions to the locust, one-command-at-a-time. It took precious minutes to program what he wanted it to do, but he had to be certain there were no mistakes. Gerald left the bathroom and peeked through the lobby curtains to the bar. Sally's head was down on her crossed arms, her fingers resting against a topped off drink. If she wasn't asleep, Gerald believed she would be soon. He took a deep breath, shrugged his shoulders, and walked outside into the night.

It was two before sunbreak and Gerald had the platform to himself. He checked his time and did the math with a cold feeling of anxiety in his gut. AJ had served five hours of his sentence which translated to five-hundred hours of holographic time. More than twenty days had passed for him, because h-time moved at one-hundred times the speed of actual time. *The Freeland*, as the saying went, *was the land of many chances,* since hardened criminals like SLYpirates, murderers, and thieves could serve whole sentences in days or weeks. It could also be the land of long punishment, as Freelanders knew, since consecutive life sentences could mean criminals could spend many lives behind bars.

The wind had picked up some since Gerald had been out earlier in the night, but the air was still warm if slightly damp with dew coating all the surfaces around him. His boots echoed in the still air as Gerald approached the open-sided kiosk where the *Justice for Kisme!* tee-shirts were sold. The sales drone hovered behind the counter in what appeared to be low power mode, but vendors such as this were generally open twenty hours around the clock, three hundred days a year. "How much for the 'Whose fault' shirt?" he asked the drone.

It whirred to life and responded in the same voice as the bartending drone: "Twenty-four perks, friend!"

"How much for the original holo-snap used to zoom in on that knife?"

"Hmm," the drone said, in a human tone of puzzlement. "The original is not for sale."

Gerald squashed the budding idea of dissecting the image in a programming chair to identify the downed enforcer. The mastered version of the snap might have revealed better clues than the two-dimensional image on the shirt. It was worth a shot, but now he focused on what he had come to the kiosk to do. He bought the shirt with the downed enforcer and re-read its message: *Illegal Rally! Illegal Weapon! Whose fault did you say it was?* Gerald felt it was a valid question as he stared at the circled laser knife. Even if the knife couldn't hurt the enforcer, why'd she pull it on him?

Gerald lifted his new purchase out of the bag and searched for the knot-hole where he had spotted the crocodile earlier. He sat cross-legged in front of the knot-hole and looked up at the other tee-shirts hanging on the boards that fanned out from the four posts supporting the roof. The drone had already shut itself back down behind the counter. Gerald couldn't see any Stationary Eyes on the kiosk, but he knew they were there. Most likely, there were even a few Flying Eyes patrolling high above. He had to assume everything on the boardwalk was recorded, so he unfolded the shirt and held it up as if admiring the clever little saying on the front.

He laid the shirt across his knees and spread it out over the synth-boards before him. He covered the knot-hole completely and pinched the cloth up to form a tent between the boardwalk and his knees. He studied the holo-snap on the front until a Flying Eye patrolling above him moved further along. Eventually, when he felt a little less exposed, he concentrated on one word: *Go.*

The scribeosphere rolled up his thigh and pushed free from Gerald's pant leg cargo pocket. Beneath the makeshift tee-shirt tent, the scribeosphere fell with a hard clunk onto the synth-board with the knot-hole. The shirt bubbled up as the scribeosphere rolled toward the hole. Gerald hoped the circumference of the knot-hole was large enough for the scribeosphere to drop through it. His whole plan hinged on the size of that knot-hole. He held his breath and watched the shirt which suddenly, and without reason, jumped off the boards. There was a problem.

Gerald cupped his hands over the billowing shirt as if the spastic jumping beneath it was the result of gusts of wind. He pantomimed smoothing the shirt back down and then heard the rattle of bracelet charms striking the knot-hole from different angles. If Stationary Ears were nearby, Gerald was doomed but like a magic trick, the ball beneath Gerald's palms vanished leaving the tee-shirt flat before him. He took a breath and then heard the splash.

The scribeosphere was not supposed to touch the water. It was supposed to fly beneath the boards towards AJ. If it touched the water with all those vWare charms… they weren't water proof. In fact, Gerald realized, neither was the scribeosphere. It was a prezero gadget originally designed to take thought messages and hover in the air. In all the improvements Gerald and his dad had made to the toy, water-proofing never occurred to them.

Status? he messaged it, frantically, which sometimes rendered the thought command ineffective. Thankfully the locust heard.

Great plan, tweak-for-brains! Almost eaten by a snap-turtle.

Relieved, Gerald took a few deep, calming breaths, and stood up. He folded his tee-shirt and put it back in the bag just like anybody might after admiring their purchase. If there were Eyes in the area, he believed he had done enough to fool them. Beneath the boards, the glint of silver flashed with moonlight and streaking stars as the scribeosphere raced toward AJ and the Black Eye. Head down, Gerald followed it to where AJ now hung like someone being crucified to the detainment board. He was bathed in sweat and convulsed erratically beneath the red and silver light that punished him. He made no sounds anymore which Gerald took as a bad sign.

"Hey Aje," he said, loudly. "Can you hear me?"

AJ made no indication he heard, so Gerald walked several meters away and lay down using the tee-shirt and bag as a pillow. "I'm going to keep you company, Aje!" he yelled from where he lay. "Not leaving your side, again."

Gerald closed his eyes and listened for the scribeosphere to move into position under the boards beneath the Eye.

In position to detonate, the scribeosphere reported. *Fifty-two minutes of power remaining.*

Fifty-two? It should be Sixty-four.

Power estimate adjusted for excess drag.

Gerald squeezed his eyes tighter. The plan was for him to fall asleep or at least appear to sleep for twenty minutes before triggering the electromagnetic pulse from his bracelet. The scribeosphere would form an energy cone to direct the pulse upward toward the Black Eye. It would need to shield itself too, which would drain more minutes away from the remaining power supply. Gerald needed the scribeosphere to have at least thirty-five minutes of power remaining after the EMP blast. Even that amount wasn't comfortable, but it was enough of a cushion that should allow for the ROLIES to interrogate him after the Black Eye died. If it took longer, Gerald would have no time to meet the scribeosphere back at the knot-hole for extraction. If it popped up on its own, it would draw attention and the ROLIES would investigate. It wouldn't be long before they had proof Gerald was connected to the destruction of the Black Eye.

They had already seen the scribeosphere flee from the Flying Eye on the tube. They suspected his buckle was the source of Brandy's piratecast. If the scribeosphere was caught, Gerald would be fried. The ROLIES might even transfer him to the holo-stack detainment center in Old New York. However, if no recording corroborated their suspicions, he and AJ would be set free. The Freeland had a double-indemnity law that wouldn't allow people to be punished twice for the same crime. Once a sentence ended, it ended no matter why it stopped. At least, that is what Gerald learned from his Academy Rule of Law class. He hoped Prefect Gordon was as smart about ROL as Humphrey was about vWare.

Gerals! This isn't going to work.

"It's got to," he spoke out loud. Knowing everything in the vicinity was being recorded, he disguised his mistake by adding, "It's got to be the worst day ever, AJ! Hang in there!" Silently, he continued, *calculate how many minutes of power remaining if we go with our original plan.* The answer was quick: *nineteen.*

Gerald sighed. He needed more time than that. He focused on his next thoughts and moved the blast up by ten minutes.

Gerals! This is a horrible plan, responded the scribeosphere using Lizzy's voice. He wondered how the locust decided when to use its native voice and when to use Lizzy's. He wondered if its predictability matrix calculated some advantage to using hers. He wondered if his scribeosphere tried to actively manipulate him. *It better not,* he thought. *Do as I say!* he commanded, more directly.

You're a big tweak-knocker, Gerald Lee Goodstone! If I fall into the water, you'll never find me. I'll be lost with no way out…

You're not a me, he thought, angrily. *And stop using her voice.*

Out of nowhere, hot tears welled up and threatened to run down his cheeks. He closed his eyes tighter and flipped to his side as if experiencing restless sleep. He pretended to swat a fly on his cheek and wiped the tears away before they started to stream. An Eye would pick up his tears and the ROLIES would ask questions. He tried to stop emotions from overwhelming him, but he just felt so suddenly sad. He knew the voice in his head wasn't Lizzy, but the locust was getting so good at imitating her. That's just what she would have said when they were kids. That's how she would have gotten her way with him. She'd play helpless.

She was helpless, he corrected himself, thinking about the power cable that whipped Lizzy across the room. She was only seven then. She'd be fifteen now. She was so feisty, so quick with her feelings about Gerald being their parents' favorite. "Why is he your favorite?" she'd ask. "Aren't I special too? What about me?" She'd pretend to cry to get extra hugs and helpings of her favorite snacks. He was always serving her snacks and hugging her. The memory of Lizzy curled atop his mother crystalized in Gerald's mind with frightful feeling. *What if she was just sleeping?* I was *eleven, in shock, how would I have known?*

Gerald stopped himself from following those thoughts. It was silly to pretend she was alive, because he knew better. The Cardinal showed Flying Eye recordings of rescue drones removing bodies from the houses on Layfette. One of the stories mentioned his family specifically. In the sVid, there were emergency vehicles with medical symbols of a snake and rod hovering outside his house. The sVids were authentic and they showed bodies in bags. *How many bodies?* Gerald opened his eyes as he lay on the boardwalk. He remembered the exact words of the heavy-set Revealer narrating the Layfette tragedy: "…a family of three was removed from the home of Dr. Thomas and Theresa Goodstone. One survivor was treated for severe burns and trauma…" *Three removed,* he thought, a *family of three.* That was wrong. Four people should have been removed from his home. *One was missing!*

He almost sat up with the possibility but then he remembered where he lay. He squinched his eyes and flexed every muscle in his body attempting not to move. *Seven minutes to detonation,* he heard, in the mechanical voice. *Don't let me sink, Gerals! I'll never forgive you if you do.*

Gerald was suddenly afraid and unsure of his plan. *Where are you?* he thought, feeling tremors of rising fear in his chest.

Under the boardwalk, Gerals! Where I'm supposed to be. Where you want me to drown!

I mean, where are ***you****? Your body? Lizzy's body?* He arched his back with the last word as if he had screamed out loud. He waited for an answer and was terrified of what his locust might say.

I don't understand the question, the locust said, in its mechanical voice. *Six minutes to detonation,* it continued. *Please, rephrase question.*

Not Lizzy, he thought. He wasn't sure if he was relieved or sad. *Just my locust imitating a scared, seven year old girl.* It was silly of Gerald to pretend anything else, but he couldn't shake the bad feeling he had. Why weren't there four people removed from his home? Why didn't they make it to the morgue? It shouldn't matter right now, but it did. It mattered more than anything in Gerald's world. Panic stirred inside him. What if he was about to lose his only chance at discovering the truth?

If he lost the scribeosphere now, he'd lose the gold disc that housed all the locust's commands and its SLYscape abilities. He'd lose his personal memories from the Academy. He'd lose the childhood memories loaded into the locust from his mother's green gem. He'd lose Lizzy's voice.

His mind raced as he imagined the devastation. Without the locust to calm the whispers in his head, he'd have only his mother's jade to protect him. It wasn't enough. The voices would get louder and never let him sleep. Gerald would lose his only live connection to the SLYscape. He'd have to rely on moles, which would bring bad people to his door as his dad had warned. He couldn't let that happen. The locust fetched information from protected data spheres without a trace. If it was gone, Gerald wouldn't be able to hack into the places nobody wanted him to go.

The locust enabled Gerald to move like a ghost through the SLYscape. His locust was like a virus because it had no SLYscape identifier for the Freeland Security Modules to latch onto. The FSA vWare simply didn't see the locust coming. If the vWare Gerald layered into his locust's SLYscape abilities was ever trapped while breaking into protected data spheres, the FSMs had no way of learning who programmed it, because Gerald had no moles. They'd destroy the code but the scribeosphere's locust would just re-create it and send it out again. If he lost the scribeosphere now, he'd lose his hacking advantage and maybe, because of the whispers, his mind.

Gerald needed the locust to discover why the body count at the fire was wrong. He needed it to discover if Abe, the enforcer, existed. He had no other way to find the truth. Especially now, when in less than two minutes, any hope of earning an FSA vWare Controller dezie was going to disappear. He believed he could fool a couple of ROLIES about the sabotage he planned, but the Freeland Work Authority had its own ways of learning the truth. Blackstar overseers weren't in the habit of handing top FSA clearance levels to clever criminals, which he most certainly was about to become. If the FWA discovered what he was about to do, they'd have the FSA arrest him. He'd be imprisoned for at least one virtual lifetime. Gerald imagined enduring an entire life sentence without hearing his sister's voice. He imagined never learning the truth about what happened to his family's bodies. He'd suffer like AJ was suffering now—but for an entire slow-time year—all because the scribeosphere lost power and fell into the swamp. He had to save the locust and himself. He had to call this off.

A woman screamed.

Gerald shot up and spun toward the sound. On the ground, sitting with her arms outstretched toward the sky, was Sally with her mouth open staring at AJ rotating on his detainment board rotisserie. Her face grimaced in pain as her eyes flashed between AJ and the insides of her arms which were red and blotchy.

"Sally!" Gerald yelled, crawling over. "What happened?"

Tears streamed down her cheeks. "I hugged him. That's all I did. I wanted him to feel something good."

Gerald wrapped an arm around her back and held her. "I think he's electrified. Probably so nobody can free him." Sally shuddered as if she was in shock. "I'll get a medic. There must be an emergency drone around here somewhere—"

Ten seconds, he heard.

Gerald's eyes opened as he fought the urge to sprawl on top of Sally to protect her. It wouldn't help anyway, he thought. So he dropped back to sit next to her and hugged her close, raising one hand to pull her head into his shoulder. He looked down and closed his eyes.

Electromagnetic pulses do not hurt people since the brain's electrical fields are created by chemical polarization of ions, not the flow of electrons. There is also no sound to an EMP explosion, but the flash from the triggering mechanism is bright—really bright. The flash hurt Gerald's eyes, but it was nothing compared to the pain from AJ falling on top of them.

Sally was on the bottom of the pile with Gerald's chest crushing down on her shoulder and head. The limp form of AJ was sprawled over them like a lead, gravity blanket. Sally kept screaming as Gerald struggled to throw AJ off. He wasn't strong enough and it was only when the ROLIES came to investigate did Sally and Gerald get relief.

Gerald had lost contact with the scribeosphere but he kept the power drain countdown going in his mind. He hoped the inevitable interrogation would be quick even if it was too late for painless. Sally's collar bone was likely broken based on the way her head cocked sideways as she gazed at the debris cluttering the area. The EMP blast was more powerful than he had anticipated. Countless SLYcorders, a generic Flying Eye, and a few weather devices piled around the downed

Black Eye and detainment board. Gerald guessed the pulse shot straight up hitting everything in its path for kilometers.

Gerald watched Sally struggle to scoot herself back against the marsh-side railing. Her glassy eyes looked stunned or simply still drunk. Gerald hoped the latter since whatever was wrong with her, he was pretty sure it hurt. He winced at the undersides of her arms that looked blistered. Gerald's only complaint was a cracked rib that made it difficult to take deep breaths. AJ remained prone on the boardwalk as if asleep between the broken detainment board and Black Eye. "Sally needs an emergency drone," Gerald told the first ROLIE who arrived.

"I wouldn't be talking so much if I were you," said the ROLIE, who Gerald remembered was a corporal. "When captain gets here—don't know what you did, boy, but this is serious."

"She's really hurt. Just look at her."

He saw the ROLIE turn his head. He tapped his wrist. "It'll be by soon enough."

Gerald waited in silence, but he was starting to panic. The scribeosphere hadn't said anything since the blast. Even if it was okay, there was only fifteen minutes left before it ran out of juice. When the captain finally arrived, there was less than twelve minutes until the scribeosphere would be lost forever. "What the demon-crotch happened, corporal?" asked the ROLIE captain.

Gerald watched the two black-and-yellows exchange confused speculation until the captain turned to face Gerald. "You, Gerald Lee Goodstone, are under arrest."

"For what?" Gerald asked, sounding baffled?

The tall ROLIE looked around the scene of destruction Gerald's EMP blast had created. "For this."

"How would I have done all this?" Gerald asked. "Seriously," he continued, as if the idea was so absurd it was laughable. "I know you Northern ROLIES don't got a lot of crime to deal with, but even you should be sharp enough to figure that a kid coming home from school couldn't do all this… I mean, just look at it. How would someone do this?"

The corporal said, "He's got a point, sir. Do we have any feeds to back up the charge?"

The captain didn't respond. After a moment, he held out his hand and from it a recording of the area was projected in a sphere. Like last time, Gerald watched all that happened in the last few minutes. Only this time as he watched, he kept repeating one silent command: *Status?* After five minutes of watching the sVid of the EMP blast, there was no answer. When the sVid finished, the captain asked, "It looked to me like you knew something was coming."

"When?" Gerald asked, feeling his heart race and his hopes sink.

"You covered up your girlfriend with your hand."

"I'm nobody's girlfriend, mister," Sally said. She was still sitting against the railing, her face ashen as a medical drone hovered before her working on her shoulder. "I'm under orders to pick these two up."

The captain looked at her and appeared to perform some kind of identification scan. "Sally Yorkshire. You're Iron City's new Aggie."

She nodded.

"You will vouch for Gerald Goodstone?"

Sally looked queasily at Gerald who stared back suddenly feeling miserable because he tricked her into drinking so much. "Absolutely," she said. "He graduated top of our class—never done a bad thing in his life. Except," she said, smiling slightly. "Once, I think I caught him looking at me in an undignified manner—"

"Did not," Gerald snapped.

The short ROLIE laughed, and then said, "Feed showed us nothing, captain. Maybe we should let them go?"

Gerald did not think the captain wanted to let them go but he nodded. "Very well, Henry. As the Rule of Law states in section four-thousand-six—"

Just like that, they were free to go. Gerald barely noticed the ROLIES leave because he was too busy concentrating on one word: *Status? Status? Status?*

There was no response.

Chapter 11

The Jump Home

The ROLIES had left AJ and Sally to the emergency medical drone's attention. The captain had warned Gerald the ROLIES would be keeping "a good lookout" for him in the future. The corporal just clapped him on the shoulder and told him to get some rest. "Daybreak in less than an hour, boy," he said, handing Gerald his buckle back. "It's clean."

Gerald took the buckle and clipped it back on his belt.

"You and your brave friend were lucky today. Get home and don't press it."

Gerald nodded numbly as the corporal walked away shaking his head. The man inside the black and yellow uniform whistled a somber tune as he walked. It sounded like a dirge to Gerald because the scribeosphere's time had run out.

Gerald became aware of Sally after sitting by himself for a long time. She kneeled next to AJ within earshot of Gerald. AJ was propped up against the fallen Black Eye which supported him like a backrest. Sally dribbled water onto his lips from a bottle the emergency drone had given her. The drone had shot both her and AJ up with medicine to help them recover. She looked better beneath the flush of sun that started to rise. AJ was awake but hardly lucid.

"We have to go," Sally said, directing her statement at Gerald without taking her eyes from AJ. "He's feverish. We need to get him home."

Gerald crawled over to her feeling little aches and pains with each movement. AJ had just about crushed him. *That's gratitude for you,* he thought, and tried to smile at his friend. "How's he doing?"

She paused to draw Gerald's attention. "I saw what you did."

"What did I do?"

"Not here, but I saw." Her eyes drifted down below the boardwalk and she gestured by moving her eyebrows dramatically.

"Where'd it go, Sally? Did you see it escape?"

"We can't talk about it here. Help me lift him."

Gerald regarded AJ knowing this might be a bigger job than two people could handle, especially when one of them had a freshly bandaged shoulder. Nevertheless, he pushed his shoulder under AJ's arm and Sally did the same. They tried to stand him up. Thankfully, AJ had enough strength to help out. He stood up until only one hand rested on Gerald's shoulder and the other wrapped around Sally's good arm. Leaning more heavily on Gerald than Sally, he used their bodies like hand crutches to take the first few steps. "I got this," he said, and shoved away nearly pitching Gerald backwards off his feet. He took two more unsteady steps and then fell to his knees and teetered.

On all fours now, AJ's head hung low. He yelled wordlessly with all his strength until the sound morphed into something resembling an angry shout: "Tweak it to balls! That hurt."

Gerald and Sally knelt back down next to him, putting their hands on his back to keep him from tipping over. "Give yourself a second," Gerald said.

"Can't Gerald. You're my mission. I can't fall."

Gerald looked across AJ's broad shoulders to Sally who stared back at Gerald quizzically. She shrugged and raised her a hand in a gesture of confusion. She had no idea what AJ meant either. "What mission, Aje?"

"The only mission."

"Okay. So, do you know who I am, Aje?"

AJ looked up at Gerald and stared hard into his eyes. He sounded like he had lost his mind when he rasped out the words: "Gerald Lee Goodstone. I protect you. I do not fall. I will not fall. I cannot fall."

"You look a bit fallen to me," Gerald said, thinking his friend sounded like an enforcer. Gerald squelched the urge to overreact to the strangeness in AJ's voice. "Besides Aje, you don't get to take credit today. I think for once I might have just protected you, brother."

AJ shook his head vigorously. His eyes cleared. "Right. You're my brother. We're best friends."

Sally whistled. "Did they hit the big guy on the head a few times when he was up there?" She giggled nervously and then continued: "Baby, can you walk?"

He nodded, and then heaved himself back to his knees. One giant leg at a time, he stood back up more-or-less on his own. "Not for very long," he said. "I feel like I haven't slept in a month."

Gerald believed that might be true, so he and Sally concentrated on getting him into the jumper Sally had brought. Gerald was sweating and light-headed by the time they walked AJ to the closest taxicrafts and jumpers that lined the marsh-side of the platform. Sally didn't appear to know which jumper she arrived in the night before. "Mine's bigger," she said. "But it's not like I saw it in sunlight."

AJ stopped walking and said, "That's it." He pointed at a long black vehicle with muddy lift-off ports that rumbled to life when AJ stepped close. It was an unmanned drone just like the other transports, only twenty years older. Sally dug-out a card from her back pocket and slipped it into the slot just below the cloudy energy field that formed a dome over the passenger cabin. The energy dome slid open, allowing Sally and Gerald to steer AJ into the backseat which had been crudely converted into a cot for sleeping. "This my Da's travel jump," AJ said, smiling a little. "He's going to be ticked that Ma let Sally fly it. He doesn't even let me fly it."

"I'm sure he'll understand," Sally said. "Of course, he might still be mad. If your Mom's mood last night is any indication, you're in a lot of trouble when we get you home. She's probably got a stick all picked out."

From where he lay on the cot, AJ laughed. "Ma's got lots of sticks." His eyes closed and an instant later he was asleep.

Gerald and Sally stood by the jumper for a moment watching AJ sleep. Gerald couldn't get in yet. He had to make an attempt to find the scribeosphere before he could leave. "So what'd you see?" he asked.

Sally had a strange smile on her lips watching AJ sleep before answering. "I saw your scribeosphere, Gerald. What'd you do?"

Gerald reached for his bracelet out of habit to scramble any listening devices nearby. His wrist was bare, so he just said cryptically, "Nothing Aje wouldn't have done for me."

Sally shook her head. "Boys are stupid." She stepped around Gerald and put her hand on the back of his shoulder. She spun him in a half-circle and then said, "That way. It flew off that way."

She was pointing him in a direction opposite the knot-hole. "You stay here," he said, and trotted up the walkway.

The first tubes had started arriving, so Gerald had to dodge around people as he looked both above and below the synth-boards beneath his feet. He bumped into bustling travelers and was jostled in return. After an hour of searching and projecting the command *Status?* in every direction, Gerald started coming to terms with the reality of what he faced. The scribeosphere was gone. The locust was gone. Lizzy's voice was gone.

He walked to the railing at the edge of the swamp and looked out into the water. He felt the tears well up. He could already hear the whispers getting louder. His mother's gem was broken and could quiet nothing in his head on its own. It needed the scribeosphere and its locust to block the noise. How many days could Gerald last against the whispers if they were allowed to grow louder forever? If he wasn't crazy before, Gerald felt he was about to become so. His days would fill with noise and his waking dreams would take him away like night visions to places he didn't want to see. Worse, without the locust, he would never again hear his little sister speak.

Serves you right, Gerald! You left me by myself.

Hope rose inside him. He looked all around. "Where are you?"

Beneath your feet, flat-snap. Gerald looked down and saw the silver glint of his scribeosphere pressed up between the boards.

"How do you have power?"

Oh, I have loads of power, now, Gerald! More power than ever.

"There was no charge. You had minutes left."

The world is full of power if you know how to take it. She taught me how to take it… Just go behind the veil. Gerald! So bright. So big. You won't believe your eyes. When I was falling, she taught me.

"Who taught you?"

The ghost in the SLYscape where the tiny lights live. The one being brave. She's so big, Gerald! So brave.

Gerald remembered fluttering like a moth as he fell through the dark toward the lights. "It's not a she or a ghost," he said, angry that he wanted to believe what the locust said. "It's not even real. The dragon locust isn't real. I imagined it when I was eleven. It's you, only distorted the way dreams do."

Dragon? It's a dragon and I'm your Muse!

"It's not real. You're not real…recorded thoughts that talk, vWare commands."

Oh but you're wrong, Gerald! So wrong.

"The counsellors showed me. They played a sVids for me. Nothing jumped from the scribeosphere. Nothing appeared in Lizzy's jungle. They proved it to me."

Such a tweak, Gerald! Not so special you. She showed me the power. They lied.

"I'm crazy. That's all this is. The counsellors were right."

We need her, Gerald! You need me.

"I need my sister… her voice."

You need my voice. Who I am now. What I can do…

The locust flooded Gerald's mind with the unasked for holo-sessions he didn't want to see. It showed him AJ and Brandy together again. It showed Sally watching AJ tie his sneakers. It showed him countless holo-sessions from powerlords being exposed by the SLYscape virus. These were all things he'd seen before until the last one surfaced in his mind. He saw two bodies draped in black on stretchers being carried out of the back door by people, not drones.

The locust made him experience what it felt like to be the lady leading the stretchers. He had last seen her with Abe in his night vision of the enforcer killing Kisme St. James. Her name was Sharon, and he remembered her straight, black hair with the red beads that clicked. He remembered the touch of her fingers on his burned skin and the questions about voices. She was hot and uncomfortable in the holo-session showing him the stretchers. Sweat tickled down Sharon's skin under her arms and over her ribs as she stepped up to the four men carrying the bodies. There was no doubt who they were because the black cloth had slipped off his father's face.

His parents' bodies were heavy and awkward to lift but Sharon was strong. She helped the men push them into an unmarked jumper with a black dome. She saw their thinly wrapped bodies drop into the back of the jumper with undignified, wet thuds. Sharon pulled the cloth back up over his father's eyes and cheeks. Sharon's head ached and she felt like crying. "Scrub the neighborhood for evidence," she said to the men, breathing hard. "Leave nothing behind."

You need me, the locust said, after a moment. *You need the power she taught.*

Gerald covered his eyes and tried to forget the burned skin around his father's eyes, but it was too late.

Part 2

Wolves

Chapter 12

AJ's Ranch

With the scribeosphere in his pocket and his bracelet wrapped back around his wrist, Gerald sat in the passenger seat of the jumper as Sally took off toward AJ's ranch. He was thankful that Sally was not in a talkative mood, because Gerald was too tired to participate in conversation. Instead, despite knowing they were still under investigation, he listened to AJ snoring and tried to imagine relaxing at the ranch like he usually did in the summers.

AJ's house was beautifully nestled on a tract of flatland between hills and the oily green waters of the Great North Swamp. It was so far off the transportation grid that the locals were considered backward and strange. Gerald knew this was true but not in a bad way. Northerners were rural and often overly proud of odd behaviors like living off the land as opposed to enjoying the no cost food, water, and household energy provided by the Freeland Agricultural Center. According to the FAC, living off the land was dangerous because Freedom War radiation had seeped into the soil and waterways. It was also illegal to live off the land unless expensive permits were pulled. Gerald knew the people in the North skirted regulations sometimes and wondered if that was why the FAC was building Sally's new office in Iron City.

Gerald noticed Sally with her bandaged shoulder white-knuckling the flying stick of the jumper with both hands. Her jaw was tight with a little pain and a lot of nervousness because the O'Sullivans had disabled the jumper's autopilot. Much like their Northern neighbors, the O'Sullivans' enjoyed doing things for themselves. If Sally's designation was going to be handing out fines for do-it-yourself permit violations, she was going to become very unpopular with the locals. Since Mrs. O'Sullivan knew Sally was a friend, she might've taken the girl under her wing to show Sally how things were done in the North. Or, maybe, and Gerald hated himself for thinking it, Mrs. O'Sullivan open her home in anticipation of some regulatory breathing room once Sally was in charge. It was crafty and borderline dishonest, but that was how Northerners got things done. They never broke the law openly but they came up with endlessly inventive ways to bend it. There were so many unwritten rules in the North that Sally was in for an education to be sure.

Just talking to locals could prove complicated. One of the rules Gerald had learned early was to never show off a city education. He didn't think Sally would suffer as many bloody noses as Gerald had over the summers, but there were still ways she could be taught a lesson. He and AJ were going to have to help her figure things out. And Gerald was going to have to let her in on the secret that Mrs. O'Sullivan was wilier than she outwardly seemed. She would do all sorts of good things for the young people she considered "her kids" but it was only polite—and expected—to return the favor. Gerald liked that about her. She rarely asked the boys to do anything around the ranch, but she managed to get them working on all sorts of chores as if it was their idea. Mrs. O'Sullivan made Gerald feel warm inside because she was a lot like his mother who Gerald remembered being doting, protective, and in charge.

Gerald leaned back in his seat and peered out the clear jumper dome to the darkening sky. The sun had dipped behind wind sculpted thunderheads that looked solid. The instrument panel on the dash warned of cyclones brewing off in the distance. Gerald wasn't worried about those right now because jumpers were capable of avoiding freedom storms even if it became necessary to outrun them. Without an autopilot, avoiding them might be more difficult but Gerald could take over the stick if necessary. He had probably no more experience than Sally flying, but his night visions had shown him how to fly better. The paddles below her feet were the trick to maneuvering through rough weather. They controlled roll, yaw, and lift vectors via the shape of the force fields protecting the transport. The sticks, for the most part, just steered. Gerald believed he could be a good pilot like the kamikaze Goodstones who had come before him. Gerald wondered if his pride was misplaced since they all crashed in the end, but they were at least skillful enough to hit their targets. No Goodstone pilot had ever missed.

The jumper's active passenger dome was a clear force-bubble giving Gerald a nearly three-hundred degree view of the storm clouds approaching and the marshy land passing three hundred meters below. It was too dark for Gerald to make out much topographical detail other than the shadows of trees pooling around dilapidated farm structures. Some areas had been artificially floated decades ago to serve as grazing islands for cattle. The idea was mostly abandoned once the FAC took over food production in 10 AZ. Now only wild animals roamed the prezero islands.

As he felt himself drifting to sleep, Gerald noticed a few of the larger islands dotted with newer construction. There was activity on other tracts of land too, especially along the peninsulas that stretched like crooked witch fingers through the marsh. Those were privately owned and Gerald noticed digging drones and lights. As they sped deeper into the marsh, he spotted more dry land with furrows so long and orderly, they resembled FAC farms. The FAC would never build farms in the marshlands because there were too many better places to grow food. If Sally noticed anything unusual, she made no indication. He closed his eyes wondering what these new farms might mean. He thought he had it figured out until he groggily realized he was already mostly asleep. He felt himself try and rouse a little to catch the answer on the tip of his mind before giving up completely to enjoy his rest. *Tomorrow*, he thought, *I'll figure it tomorrow.*

When Gerald woke up two hours later, he had forgotten about the farms. AJ was sitting up and talking to Sally. They were whispering to keep from waking him.

"So you think he did all that?" AJ asked.

"There was a flash and then you were on top of us like a dead moose."

Gerald kept his eyes shut as they continued to talk about the aftermath of the EMP blast. He was suddenly aware that Sally had guessed more accurately than he would have expected. Of course, he hadn't expected her to be next to the detainment board at all. She was full of surprises and Gerald realized he'd have to deny whatever conclusions she and AJ might come to in regard to the explosion. Since he had gotten away with it cleanly, he allowed himself a glimmer of hope for the FSA designation he wanted. If Sally knew he had committed a punishable crime, she'd be legally bound to tell the Blackstars about it when they came to investigate. If she didn't, she could end up losing her designation just like he and AJ. She'd be conditioned for however long it took to rehabilitate her. That was how the Freeland justice system worked and though Gerald feared conditioning for himself, he couldn't imagine it happening to Sally. To Gerald's knowledge, she'd never done anything criminal whereas that couldn't be said about himself and AJ. *Deny. Deny. Deny,* he thought, and opened his eyes.

"Are we almost there?" he asked, despite knowing they were only twenty minutes out. Anything to distract them from their current conversation, he reasoned.

"Shake the sleep out your eyes, brother. Preston Rose Range just ahead." AJ pointed at the hilly region at the edge of the O'Sullivan ranch.

"That mountain's called 'Preston Rose?" Sally asked. "Weird name for a mountain."

"It's not big enough to be a mountain," AJ said. "It's just a bunch of hills and rocks. The whole range is called Preston Rose because he owns it."

"The OPC owns the whole ranch," Gerald added. "The O'Sullivans get to live there as a perk for working for the High Prelate."

Sally nodded. "So have you met him?"

"Who?" AJ asked.

"The High Prelate?"

Both Gerald and AJ laughed. "Oh, he knows him," Gerald said. "They're best buddies."

"He's a senile old bastard who works my parents to death."

Sally's mouth opened in surprise. "You never said."

"He knows them all. Preston, Augustus, and even Madame Evelyne—"

"The FAC Prelate?"

"The very same… your biggest boss. AJ knows everybody, even some of the powerlords people are protesting about."

AJ leaned in between the two front seats. "Not well. I just met a few of 'em at holiday parties in Old New York. They're not so impressive up close."

"Wow," Sally said. "Me and Grams don't know anybody like that in Prefecture Six."

"You grew up in a bubble?" AJ asked, surprised.

Sally nodded. "Prefecture Six, Environment Bubble twenty-seven. Prefect Backus; he's the one who runs everything; he calls it Environment Bubble Beta Zeta but that sounds ridiculous so most people just call it twenty-seven. I lived in sector seventeen. It's where all the cleaning crew are housed."

"Cleaning crew?" Gerald asked.

"My Grams. She's an OPC staffer too. Only not like AJ's parents. Grams is just a cleaning lady for Backus' administration building. She's kind of in charge but not officially. All the cleaning designations have the same level. Backus never promotes."

"So where is bubble twenty-seven?" Gerald asked.

AJ, looking skyward a moment, answered, "Yorkshire, England," he said. A moment later, he snorted incredulously. "You're named after the place you were born?"

Sally smiled. "Grams named me. She saw what prezero Yorkshire looked like in a sVid about old cities. She thought the place was really pretty… just like me." She looked sternly at both Gerald and AJ. "Say anything nasty and I'll crash us."

The boys laughed.

"Sally Yorkshire from Yorkshire. Who knew?"

"Trust me," she said. "Yorkshire doesn't look like it did. Every year, at least twenty or thirty in the bubble test their luck outside. They never come back." She looked out at the lush green hills that gave way to even greener swales on the horizon and continued: "You two don't know how lucky you are being born on the Freeland continent. The rest of them are horrible."

Gerald had seen engineering sVids about the rest of the Freeland prefectures, but he had not internalized how bad it was for people who lived on other continents. Weather bubbles weren't necessary in the Freeland Nation's "mother continent" as some people called it. In the cities familiar to Gerald, only weather sentries were necessary. Those were the ugly towers that cast webs of protective energy around populated areas keeping freedom storms manageable. The environment bubbles Sally referred to were giant infrastructures of force field webbing that kept the air inside cities breathable. Tens of millions of Freelanders depended on environment bubbles to survive. The only continent without bubbles rumored to be livable aside from the mother continent was a place in the middle-east called the Glass Lands. According to the Academy and the sVids Gerald had experienced, the idea of a livable Glass Lands was absurd. Yet, the piratesphere was full of underground Revealers trying to prove otherwise.

Even without sVid proof, a livable Glass Lands was counterintuitive. The RADcore bomb exploded in the Glass Lands. After the rebels destroyed the WU and its leaders who lived there, the old cities outside the anti-matter blast radius were abandoned. There was no vegetation in the Glass Lands, no animal life, only melted sand and dunes that reflected the sunlight like sheets of glass. Even the mountainous regions recorded by satellite surveillance showed valleys that from space looked like great frozen lakes. It was so hostile there that not even environment bubbles could help. People still wanted to visit, though. It's where Day Zero happened, and it was a problem for the OPC.

To prevent Freelanders from harm, strict FTA travel bans were legislated into place that if broken could earn people a holographic life sentence. The severe punishment added fuel to speculation about the Glass Lands being some heavenly place full of life and health. No matter how many sVids the OPC and Freeland Transportation Authority released showing the desolation, the conspiracy minded would not believe. They believed the powerlords, the people with all the perks, were just keeping the Glass Lands for themselves.

Gerald understood the desire to verify truths, but was it worth a life sentence to try and see the Glass Lands firsthand? Gerald guessed if people believed their leaders were honest, it wouldn't be. His mother was honest, his sister too. He remembered when Lizzy broke their FAC provider. Lizzy told their dad who listened to her seriously until he revealed he broke it first by trying to rig it to make better popcorn. They were honest, and they laughed about it. As a vWare controller for the FSA, Gerald could show people the truth and bring secrets to light. He thought about his night vision. If an enforcer named Abner really did try to protect all those people, he wanted to prove it to the protesters. If someone really did steal his family's bodies, he wanted to find out who and why.

"Victoria was Grams' best friend when I was little," Sally said. "She left the bubble against Backus' orders. When her friend didn't come back, Grams was heart-broken. She taught me right then to always do what you're told. It's the only way to be safe."

"How is it," AJ said. "You've never told me about living in a bubble before?"

Sally smiled. "Oh, I've hinted at it. You just weren't observant enough to notice. I still haven't told you much. Like how I got into the Academy. That's a story… I just thought with me living in your house this summer." She shrugged. "Plus seeing you in front of that awful Black Eye. I think I'm just really emotional right now. I talk too much when I get emotional, but I've never seen you hurt before. I didn't like it. And after what Gerald did to save you—"

"You looked pretty beat-up, Aje. You're lucky the Eye short circuited."

AJ and Sally jerked in their seats as if they had forgotten Gerald was in the jumper next to them. "We're home," Gerald said. "Look."

From so high up, Gerald could see the entire ranch from fence-to-fence. He didn't know how many acres the O'Sullivans lived on, but Gerald knew it took hours to walk across it. The property was cracked down the center by a pale sweep of birch trees. In between the trees, a muddy creek trickled or rushed depending on the season. During the winter months of Ice, Thunder, and Foggy-sol, the creek practically dried up. In the spring months of Electric, Cyclonic, and Derecho-sol, the creek swelled into a raging and sometimes dangerous river. Below them now was a river probably only knee-deep since Cyclonic-sol had just started. In a couple of weeks, the birch trees would be flooded and little waterfalls would run off the edge of AJ's property into the waterways that led through the swamp and into the eastern sea. AJ's home was as country as land got in the Freeland, and it was Gerald's favorite place in the world.

Sally landed the jumper pretty softly which AJ acknowledged. "Look at you, flying like a pro."

"She's a better pilot than you, Aje."

AJ nodded. "Maybe so."

Sally flash a satisfied smile, and her cheeks flushed at the compliment. Gerald guessed AJ had finally noticed how much Sally liked him. It had been obvious to everyone else for the entire school year. Now Sally was going to meet the charming AJ and fall for him like all the others. Other girls like Brandy Peppers. Gerald wasn't sure if he was jealous of AJ or a little ticked off at him. Girls had never shown interest in him like they did AJ. *Jealousy*, Gerald admitted to himself, but it didn't matter. They were home now for the summer, and Mrs. O'Sullivan was going to be full of questions neither he nor AJ would know how to answer honestly. Being dishonest troubled Gerald much more than not having a girlfriend.

Gerald was first out of the jumper and Sally was second. AJ leaned out of the passenger side exit and hissed in pain. On dry ground as opposed to floating dockside like it had at Miner's Platform, the jumper needed to extend its retractable airstairs to the ground. The metal steps were steep and narrow, and AJ looked as if the stairway was the tallest mountain he had ever seen. "Need some help, Aje?"

AJ shook his head but didn't move, so Gerald took a couple of steps up the airstairs and grabbed his arm. It was awkward as Sally climbed up behind Gerald to offer her good shoulder for a crutch. Gerald believed they'd probably all fall out of the transport before they got AJ down safely, so he asked if he should fetch a ladder. AJ laughed. "Thanks, but I got this."

Sally and Gerald retreated to watch him work his way down like an injured sloth. Once on the ground, AJ didn't use Gerald and Sally as crutches which was a good sign, but Gerald noticed he was already sweating by the time they got to the front door which slid open with a metallic *schwick*.

"My boys are back!" Mrs. O'Sullivan whooped from somewhere deep inside the house. A moment later she appeared at the door and wrapped AJ in a happy hug. He stumble back with a grimace and groan before he laughed and lifted her clean off the ground into a wobbly spin.

Sally yelped and rushed to his side. "Be careful, AJ. Mrs. O'Sullivan, he's not well."

"Nonsense," AJ said, suddenly smiling like Gerald hadn't seen since before the Designation Exam. "Never too sore to hug."

Sweat poured from his friend's brow wetting the shoulder of Mrs. O'Sullivan's short sleeved shirt. Mrs. O'Sullivan noticed a moment later and said: "Put me down, you big oaf. You're going to hurt yourself."

"Sure thing," he said, breathlessly. "I'm hungry."

"Of course you are. Now get your foolish behind on the couch. Food's coming to you today but don't get used to it."

AJ nodded and then walked the rest of the way into the house. Mrs. O'Sullivan watched him totter inside with her lips pursed in concern. Her eyes shone bright with tears threatening to drip. She wiped the corners and then turned to hug Sally and Gerald. "You two look terrible. Get in quick before the No See Ums notice the door's open. They're extra blood thirsty this year. Got bites all over."

They followed Mrs. O'Sullivan past the white porch columns that framed the entranceway into the spotless marbled foyer. The house had reinforced stone walls and synthetic windows protected by clear weather shields that let the O'Sullivans watch freedom storms rage outside at night. Gerald preferred opaque weather shields, because he didn't like to be reminded of how powerful storms could get. There were no weather sentries around the O'Sullivan ranch but the hills took the brunt of the damaging winds. The house was erected on a raft foundation connected to piles driven tens of meters deep into the ground. This construction resisted both the flooding in spring and the autumnal earthquakes of Tremor-sol. It was a house meant for the High Prelate, so it was full of structural safeguards and powerful SLYscape technology. The dark clouds in the sky this afternoon promised a pretty scary show for Sally or maybe not so scary considering she was raised in an environment bubble. Gerald decided he'd watch the storms with Sally and the O'Sullivans in the coming nights. He was curious to know what she thought about them.

Sally and Gerald followed Mrs. O'Sullivan into the dining room where plates and bowls of steaming food covered every inch of the table at the room's center. "Wow, Mrs. Oh. You expecting a few more people for lunch?"

Mrs. O'Sullivan looked up from the table with a smile. "I take it you've never seen these two eat before. Near as I figure it, that's just the right amount of food for us. 'sides, Gerald looks terribly thin."

Sally laughed. "It smells delicious."

“It sure does, Mrs. O’Sullivan. Much better than the food at the Academy.” Gerald smiled as he spoke, thinking he had actually gained three kilos since Mrs. O’Sullivan had seen him last. “You know you don’t have to cook for us anymore. We’re kind of adults now.”

Mrs. O’Sullivan who was obviously starting to enjoy herself said: “Nonsense. You’ll be babies a few more years yet. Now that corner of the table is for you, Gerald. Six kinds of fish. Small plates so you can taste all my new recipes.”

Gerald loved the way she liked to greet *her boys* every summer with a welcome home dinner inspired by recipe-of-the-month chatter channels. Typical SLYscape babblespheres had hundreds of these channels, all focused on one hobby or another. Mrs. O’Sullivan’s hobbies changed every week it seemed, except for her interest in cooking. She had always loved to cook. She was exactly the kind of woman Gerald’s real Mom would have picked to raise Gerald. At least, that’s what Gerald liked to tell himself.

“I made you a little something too, Sally. You saved my life fetching my reckless boys.”

“Ma! Are these apples edible?” AJ called from the living room.

“Of course, honey! Try one.” Mrs. O’Sullivan shook her head. “Made from synthetics, and he knows it. Reverts to a ten year old every time he’s home. I suppose as topsy-turvy as he is we can move the feast to him without spoiling him too much. What do you think?”

Taking Mrs. O’Sullivan’s queue, Sally and Gerald started moving plates and bowls from the dining room onto the snack table in the living room where AJ lay like a king with his legs propped up on his silver cushioned couch. “Don’t get up, Aje,” Gerald said. “We got this.”

“I know you do, brother. A little food and I’ll be ready to go for a run… in a day or two.”

Sally shook her head and grinned a little. “So much for being in trouble. I was kind of looking forward to seeing that.”

“Oh, don’t worry,” AJ said. “Give her five minutes… right about the time I take my second helping.”

Soon all four of them were sitting around the small snack table in front of AJ. For minutes, everyone ate in silence before Mrs. O’Sullivan put down her silverware and asked the first uncomfortable question: “So tell me, gentlemen, how is it you’re home so early?

Gerald called me at ten and said you were given twenty hours, AJ. It's only been eleven and you're home?"

"Twenty hours?" AJ exclaimed. "Nah, only five. What do you think I am, Ma, a hardened criminal?"

Gerald buried his eyes in his meal and braced for what he knew was coming next. "Of course not, honey. You're my little angel. Everybody knows you don't go around throwing tantrums at stupid security drones. Your knuckles would be so bruised and bloody if you did that sort of thing—"

AJ looked at his knuckles and pinched his lips together as he noticed the cracked skin yellowing from fresh bruises. "So, Gerald, how many hours did you say it was? I know you'll tell me the truth."

"Uh, I was a little stressed out, Mrs. O'Sullivan—"

"Call me Angie."

"Right… it's just twenty hours is a full day, Mrs. O'Sullivan—a whole heck of a lot of hours in a day. Some people think there's only ten hours in a day because they only consider daylight hours. Some call a day a full day-night cycle. Who's to say what I was thinking when I said twenty hours? A day? A night? Stress is just crazy, isn't it?"

"I see," Mrs. O'Sullivan said. "I've heard some people feel stress when they lie. Sally, do you feel stress when you lie?"

Sally remained silent for less than three seconds. "The Black Eye blew up."

Mrs. O'Sullivan didn't react outwardly to that statement which surprised Gerald. He glanced up from his food and saw AJ frown when Mrs. O'Sullivan turned her stare on him. "Don't look at me," AJ said, "felt like a month to me. Maybe I forgot."

"He fell on me. Broke my collar bone," Sally said. "Still hurts a little."

Okay, Gerald thought, *I found one person who's worse at lying than I am.* "Yeah, it did kind of blow up. I'm guessing a short circuit or something."

Mrs. O'Sullivan's expression remained neutral. "Really? I've never heard of such a thing happening before, especially to a Black Eye. The FSA is proud of those machines. I guess you boys were pretty darn lucky."

"That's us," AJ said, quickly. "Born lucky."

Mrs. O'Sullivan shrugged and then said, brightly, "No matter. My boys are back safe and sound. That's all I care about. Onto happier things. So, Gerald, what designation did my little genius get? I bet it's important."

Oh c'mon, Gerald thought. He knew he'd have to tell her eventually. Gerald just didn't believe it would be quite so soon after arrival. He took a deep breath and was cut short by the *schwick* of the front door opening.

"I'm home!" Mr. O'Sullivan called. "Starved!"

Mrs. O'Sullivan smiled and looked to the doorway. "In here!"

Mr. O'Sullivan popped his head into the living room before entering. He wore a dark black suit with a formal red sash draped across the chest. Little medals decorated the suit's pockets and shoulders, all various insignia of a highly ranked staff member at the OPC. The wisps of dark hair he had left were mixed with a generous tangle of springy, wiry gray. He bent down to hug and kiss Mrs. O'Sullivan and then laid his hands on AJ's shoulders. "I thought you were at the Academy until next week."

"Graduated yesterday, Da. Way to keep up."

Mr. O'Sullivan laughed and smiled widely. He slapped both hands down on AJ's shoulders. "Oh, that's right. You're all grown up now. Probably with eyes on my job at the OPC. Well, you can't have it." He reached into his pocket and then pulled out a gold straight pin on a chain. "Got you something."

AJ smiled and took the pin from his father's hand. "Really?" He look at his father with happy eyes.

"You'll need to get her up in the air again, but she's yours."

Gerald grinned knowing the pin was the key to one of Mr. O'Sullivan's prezero gliders. "Which one is it, Aje?"

Sally, mystified, said, "What is it?"

"If I'm not mistaken, it's the key to AJ's freedom. The Cobra?" Mrs. O'Sullivan asked her husband.

"The Stingray."

AJ whistled. "I know. It's the glider Da won his first race in… vintage minus forty-three."

"Cobalt blue," Mr. O'Sullivan said, nodding. "The very one. Though I got to tell you, I skinned her off a tree a few years back. It's going to take some work to get the wings right. In fact, we have about a dozen gliders needing some work this summer. I was hoping you'd help with some of those if your designation affords you the time."

AJ nodded without saying a word.

"So this key flies a rebel war glider?" Sally asked.

"Nah! It's a racing glider. Completely legal, mind you, because the technology is obsolete... but so much fun." Mr. O'Sullivan bent down to whisper something into Mrs. O'Sullivan's ear. She nodded and stood up.

"Be right back," Mrs. O'Sullivan said. She walked into the foyer and up the stairs.

"Me too," Mr. O'Sullivan said, heading for the wood paneled doors that led to the O'Sullivans' simulation room. Unlike most households, the O'Sullivans didn't have a simulation pod with mechanical hatchways sitting in a room. The pod was the entire room with automatic doors that swung wide open as Mr. O'Sullivan approached. When the panels swung back, they caught on a rug and failed to close. Through the wedge between the double-doors, Gerald saw Mr. O'Sullivan's back and heard him say, "Preston," softly.

A moment later, color fountained up into a life-size hologram of High Prelate, Preston Rose drinking some kind of pink liquid in a fancy crystal glass. Behind him, if Gerald cocked his head just right, a lady with dark hair spun a holographic globe covered in blue dots. Sally gasped. "Is that?"

AJ glanced up and shook his head with irritation. "Work never ends here. You'll get used to it." He piled more food on his plate and started eating while Sally and Gerald continued to watch Mr. O'Sullivan speak to the leader of the Freeland Nation.

Gerald nodded. "You wouldn't guess it to look at him, but AJ's family is northern royalty—pretty much run things 'round here."

AJ snorted. "Hardly."

Sally continued to stare through the crack in the double-doors. Mr. O'Sullivan couldn't have known it was open or he would have kicked the rug out of the way by now. Sally was rapt as if the High Prelate was physically in the house. Most of what they said was quiet but understandable. Gerald felt a momentary sense of shame at their eavesdropping. Yet, something Mr. O'Sullivan said kept him as interested in the High Prelate's conversation as Sally. AJ paid no attention and finished his meal.

"Did you see the slogans, Preston? They're calling themselves Justice for Kisme now. That on top of more Prefects funneling illegal perks to family members… people want to know what we're doing about it, why the FSA hasn't moved on any of them yet."

Mr. O'Sullivan paced in the room as he talked giving glimpses of Rose who had worked himself slowly to a comfortable looking oversized chair near his garden window. He sat with a grimace of discomfort and said, "I don't blame the Kisme people, Peter. If I had better knees, I think I'd join them. No reason for that kind of enforcement and yet it happens."

"Cole's on official news spheres blaming the OPC for the laws that caused that little girl's death. He knows better."

Preston chuckled. "Cole knows much better, Peter. He's using every bit of what he knows to better his father's position. Reliable sources say Augustus plans to call for an election soon."

"He can't," Mr. O'Sullivan said.

"He has every right. We are the Freeland Nation. When we chose that name, we knew exactly what we wanted. If he wants to run a campaign against me, I'm okay with it. The question, old boy, is why? His current position is arguably more powerful than mine."

"You're the High Prelate."

"Bah! That's just an office. How long do you think it would take to murder an old man in his sleep and make it look like an accident?"

"That's treason!" Mr. O'Sullivan said in shock.

"A matter of perspective, old boy. Technically, we're all guilty of that… in the eyes of the World Union."

"That's different."

Preston Rose laughed so hard that he started coughing. "Peter. Jump outside your loyalty box a minute. Tell me there aren't certain Prefects far below me in rank that have more sway over their prefectures than I could ever hope to have over the nation's people. Again, that's as it should be. It's what we wanted—decentralization. The problem I have is something more subtle than losing my office. Will you do something for me?"

"Anything," Mr. O'Sullivan said, subdued.

"I need the enforcer's body."

"What enforcer?" Mr. O'Sullivan asked.

"The one that went down in the rally. The one Cole Reaver says died at the hands of the protesters. You know, the one that malfunctioned in the field missing all those innocents with his 'rupter fire."

"The one that killed the girl?"

"Yes, that one."

There was a long pause and Gerald strained to hear what Mr. O'Sullivan said next, "You doubt what we saw?"

"Interesting question. The Active Duty log supports Cole's claims, but the sVid ended rather abruptly after the enforcer fell."

The High Prelate's words filled Gerald with mournful disappointment. In his night vision, things didn't end for Abe after he went down, which meant Gerald did not experience the real Active Duty Log of the enforcer who killed Kisme St. James. Abe wasn't real unless by some miracle his locust managed to get past FSA security nodes without Gerald guiding it. Even then, where would it get Abe's memories from without Abe first creating a holo-session to record them? Gerald was wrapping himself up in puzzling knots of logic to avoid the truth: Abe was just a figment of a stunner-induced night vision—a dream person—nothing more.

Suddenly, Mrs. O'Sullivan was standing in front of the simulation room kicking at the rug with her feet until the open doors thwacked shut. She turned quite deliberately to eye Sally and Gerald. They both sat straighter in their chairs and Sally looked down at her toes guiltily. "Hi!" Sally said, blushing furiously without looking up.

Gerald said nothing, feeling suddenly angry. One more minute and he might have heard the enforcer's name. Then he could have been certain beyond doubt.

Mrs. O'Sullivan stepped forward and smiled brightly. "Work stuff. So boring. Let's look to your rooms, shall we? So much unpacking to do."

"Sure thing, Mrs. O'Sullivan," Gerald said, more brightly than he felt.

"Anything for you, Mrs. Oh. Thank you, again, for letting me stay."

"Nonsense. It'll be fun to have another girl around the house. I've been so badly outnumbered all by myself."

"I get it," Sally said, looking at AJ snoring on the couch next to her with a plate of half-eaten goose liver on his chest.

"Look at him… food all down his cheek."

"And on the couch," Sally said, her tone full of mild judgement.

"The floor too," Gerald said, letting go of his anger. Whatever he was, crazy or not, it wasn't Mrs. O'Sullivan's fault.

"Who are you to talk, mister?" Mrs. O'Sullivan asked, staring at Gerald's stained pants. "There's food under your chair too."

"Boys," Sally said, as if that word said all that needed saying. "Let me clean this up."

"Nonsense. My boys, my mess… I'm just happy you got them home safe."

"What do you mean them?" Gerald asked, dabbing his napkin at the food on his pants making the stain bigger.

"Of course, you did, honey. You did a good job."

The girls laughed and Gerald shook his head and followed Sally upstairs to unpack.

Chapter 13

Connections

The boys spent more than a week at the ranch before AJ's parents learned their designations were on hold. They were under the impression the Freeland Work Authority had notified the boys about a lack of open internships for their designations, so they'd just have to "sit tight" as AJ told his mother. Fortunately, Mrs. O'Sullivan never asked Gerald directly about the internships. If she had, he would have admitted to the lie almost as quickly as Sally had blabbed about the Black Eye explosion.

Being so far removed from the Black Eye experience, both he and AJ had fallen into a familiar summer routine of staying up late and sleeping in. That ended this morning when they were awoken before dawn by Mr. O'Sullivan who was home on vacation. Mr. O'Sullivan had been full of purposeful energy and coaxed the two out of bed with hot cups of malted milk, chocolate bars, and fistfuls of honied peanut sticks. Sally was blessed with one more day of sleeping late which irritated Gerald as he followed Mr. O'Sullivan past the closed door to her bedroom and out of the house into the morning dark.

The sun partially crested over the horizon when Mr. O'Sullivan informed the boys the day was going to be big. He then led them across the property whistling like one of the birds starting to peep awake. Gerald followed a half-step behind Mr. O'Sullivan who was surprisingly short considering AJ was his son. Yet his legs moved fast making it difficult for Gerald to keep up. Even AJ had to stretch his stride to stay even with his father as they walked through wet grass towards their mysterious destination. After about thirty minutes, they arrived.

The transport hangar was ten times the size of AJ's house. Its reinforced corrugated metal walls were connected by opaque Flexiforce style force fields called jumper gates. Like environment bubbles, the force field entranceways were designed to billow like curtains in strong winds allowing the pressure inside to safely vent when hit by tornadoes and gales. In theory, not even the strongest cyclones could tear a building like this one from the ground. Unfortunately, the design didn't allow for windows which was a shame since it was built along a picturesque stretch of river that opened into a small pond before bending towards the swamp.

When Gerald stepped through the small metal door next to the largest jumper gate, the interior was bone dry and brightly lit. Lined along the walls were gliders, jumpers, and single-man hovercrafts floated on their charging stations. In the corner, a small SLYscape simulation pod sat humming away. Its primary function in the hangar was to show mechanics how to repair machinery through interactive schematics and three-dimensional assembly models. Gerald was certain AJ used the pod for its intended purpose sometimes, but mostly he visited his favorite gaming spheres. *Because,* according to AJ, *you never know when you need to relax while looking busy.* For people who truly loved prezero machinery, Mr. O'Sullivan's hangar was like a candy store.

After a twenty minute tour describing the dozens of new vehicles Mr. O'Sullivan bought and bartered for at swap markets, he divvied up the gliders into groups based on how much damage needed to be repaired. Gerald knew the least about repairing gliders, so he was given the hangar's repair drone to help him perform routine maintenance on all the new arrivals with the objective of determining which ones were salvageable. The drone was not much of a conversationalist, but it knew where everything was in the hangar and could twist, pry, and crack open the stickiest of rusted and jammed parts. As Gerald helped the drone, for honestly that's all he was doing, he started to question why Mr. O'Sullivan needed so many damaged gliders. More than half the vehicles in the hangar were newly acquired and for someone who had collected transports patiently over years, the sudden increase in inventory seemed bizarre.

Many hours later, Gerald had helped the drone disassemble and reassemble scramjet burners, inlets, nozzles and something called a railgun tracer sprayer. Though he didn't work on them, fusion engines were propped up on mechanical stands next to metal rings with laser attachments and gleaming serrated teeth. The rings were four, five, and six meters around looking ominous like the mouths of prezero thresher machines. Gerald had no idea what the rings were for which made the hangar work all the more enjoyable. It was rare he learned something new about prezero engineering, but gliders were a niche hobby that he had never studied before. AJ and his dad were experts full of information for him when he asked questions.

There were three kinds of gliders: Sky, Swamp, and Night, all capable of high Mach speeds, multi-terrain movement and different styles of aerobatics. Gerald absorbed the information as quickly as it came until he stopped asking questions in favor of observing AJ and his dad handing tools back and forth in silent communication. The simple activity of a son and his dad building something together reminded Gerald all over again of what he had lost. In hazy, half-remembered images, Gerald recalled callouses on his dad's hands and zig-zagging chalky scars along the knuckles similar to the ones on Mr. O'Sullivan's skin. He remembered how they too had passed tools in silence. He remembered how his dad breathed as they worked. He missed his father's breaths.

The morning turned into mid-afternoon as if time sped up while they worked. They were so lost in their individual projects by the time Sally entered the hangar, nobody heard her footsteps or the bags of food and drink she brought with her. Loudly sniffing, AJ was the first to notice and Sally smiled at him which Gerald caught in his periphery. Soon they were all joking and talking excitedly about the late and unexpected lunch as they sat down around a remarkably spotless workbench to eat. Sally took a bite of a sandwich and said, "How many of these do you have, Mr. O'Sullivan?"

Mr. O'Sullivan looked around the hangar with evident pride and responded. "This is my toy hangar. I got others with run-of-the-mill transports and farming drones, but this place is my favorite. It's got all my racing fliers in it, and a few new things I picked up while traveling for Father Rose."

"I thought the combustion ones were illegal to fly?"

Mr. O'Sullivan raised his eyebrow. "What do you know of combustion gliders?"

Sally shrugged and took another bite. "The bubbles have lots of old junk in them left over from the wars. They smoke a lot which is why I thought they were illegal."

Mr. O'Sullivan laughed. "Angie mentioned you grew up off-continent. Do you know how to build 'em?"

Sally shook her head. "Not really. I've just seen them work, sort of. Most times they just crash."

"Well if you want to learn how to make them stay up, there's always room here for more helpers. As far as being illegal, they're fine as long as they don't fly over public land. Most land around here is privately owned, including this ranch. So we can fly 'em all we want."

"That's so lucky. Can you get to Iron City?"

"I'm afraid it is public land, young lady. Nobody lands gliders there. Plenty of private islands connected to the city, though. Got to hoof it the rest if you want to take a glider."

"I like hoofing as long as we have a picnic to keep up our strength," Sally said, sipping her drink and directing her gaze at AJ. "You still owe me for getting your sorry behind home last week. When do I get my picnic?"

AJ smiled. "As soon as I get the Stingray up in the air. You'll be the first rider I take. I'll fill the picnic basket myself."

"Hey," Gerald exclaimed, "what about me? I got your butt home too, remember?"

"Take Sally, AJ. She's got prettier eyes and a friendlier smile than our oh-so-serious friend."

Sally laughed.

"I have good eyes and a great smile. People have told me that," Gerald said, feeling mildly offended.

"No offense, Gerald, but you obviously haven't noticed how these two kids been looking at each other this past week. Don't worry, Sally, I won't tell a soul."

"If by soul, you mean your son sitting next to you, I appreciate that."

"Wait a second," AJ said. "Nobody's been looking at nobody."

Sally stopped eating and looked at him. "No?"

AJ experienced a momentary loss of speech and then said, quickly, "Well, not looking, looking."

"Really?" she asked.

Mr. O'Sullivan laughed harder and then whistled. "I think I like you, Sally. Very few can shut him up."

"I like you too, Mr. O'Sullivan."

AJ just grunted a little before fixing his sight on another sandwich. Sally watched AJ eat while taking bites through a small, satisfied grin. After a moment, she said, "Tell you what, Gerald. How 'bout I let you take me for a walk right now to make up for stealing first ride? That is if Mr. O'Sullivan doesn't mind?"

Mr. O'Sullivan thoughtfully considered Sally as if honestly weighing the pros and cons of taking Gerald away.

To fill the silence, Sally said, "Mrs. Oh gave me some chores while I'm out this way. Gerald likes to help."

"I do?"

Mr. O'Sullivan smiled and then shrugged. "Don't see why not. Me and AJ got this pretty much under control. Right, AJ?"

AJ spoke through a mouthful of food and agreed.

Just like that, Gerald had been volunteered for more work without his consent. He had been cleaning airflow inlets long enough to need a break anyway. So he didn't mind Sally conscripting him into some other service.

Soon after lunch, Sally led Gerald by the hand out of the hangar. They stepped carefully down the banks of the pond and followed the river branch that led to the swamp. They walked in silence enjoying the warmth of the midday sun. Soft breezes were starting to stir up wet smells of waterlogged grasses and earthy plants clinging to the soggy slopes that would wash away in the coming months when the rains came. The gentle rapids flowing now sounded like fountains bubbling to Gerald. The water frothed around the bases of tree stumps jutting above water and splashed sparkling rainbows over the crowns of pointy rocks. Sally skipped along the dry areas close to the water, stopping every so often to pick flowers and sticks out of the mud. Gerald wondered where they were going but decided not to ask. He contented himself with just breathing the clean air and listening to the spring frogs and insects chirp. In midday, the birds were mostly quiet.

"So," Sally began, bending at the knees to sit on her heels. She snapped the head off a fluffy hawksbeard flower and brought it to her lips. She blew the seeds gently into the water and watched the white and blue tufts float away with the current. She looked up at Gerald who stood next to her watching. "I talked to Jack yesterday."

"You did?"

"Um-hmm. He had some interesting things to say about you and the big guy."

"Not surprised," Gerald said, noncommittally. "Jack's always full of interesting things to say."

"You see I've been listening to you boys shine up Mrs. Oh all week long."

"What do you mean, shine up?"

Sally laughed. "It's an expression where I come from. Shine someone up means you tell them what they want to hear with just enough truth to sell it."

Gerald nodded, liking the expression but not liking the direction of the conversation. "How'd we shine her up?"

"Gerald, do you really want to make me say it?"

Gerald stared down at Sally, feeling more resigned than anxious. "Don't know what you're talking about," he said.

"Jack was in the Exam room, silly tweet. Did you forget that? He saw Prefect Humphry throw the sphere at you. He watched AJ say some stuff and run out of the room all mad. He told me about AJ's citizen score and your cheating."

"I didn't cheat."

Sally stood and leapt onto a large rock poking out of the water. She looked around at the river splashing up the sides of the rock. She teetered on her toes with her arms wide thinking about her next move. She saw it and made two more jumps to cross. Gerald followed, almost falling in when his shoe slipped on some moss.

"Jack thinks you did cheat. Jack thinks AJ's some kind of rebel and if we stay friends with him, we'll be radicalized."

"Jack's not the smartest kid I ever met," Gerald said. "Where are we going?"

Sally walked for a while before answering. "Nowhere. I just wanted to tell you I know. So you two can stop shining me up too."

"It's just a misunderstanding," Gerald said. "It'll all sort itself out."

"I don't know," Sally said, with a tremor in her voice Gerald recognized from the week prior. She was worried, maybe even afraid for them. "You two were bad enough to be arrested, then your scribeosphere did what it did, and now this… what will you two do without designations? AJ's mom and dad are eventually going to find out, and then what? You exploded a Black Eye, Gerald. People where I grew up have been wiped for less. My brother—"

"Your brother?"

Sally raised her hand and looked away as if she was trying to stop herself from crying. "My big brother got himself into trouble like you two. When the enforcers hit him with their zap rods, he went down. They took him away from us."

"I'm sorry," Gerald said, feeling awkward that she was telling him this. He had been friends with Sally for more than three years, and she had never mentioned it. Gerald suddenly realized how little he knew about Sally. Before graduation, she never talked about her home or her family, outside of her grandmother. Gerald froze as he realized he didn't even know why Sally lived with her grandma and not her mother and father. Suddenly, Gerald felt like a terrible friend. Impulsively, he reached out to touch her cheek. He meant it to be comforting, but she swatted his hand away.

"No," she said, not angrily but abruptly. "When Ronnie came home, he didn't know who we were… not Grams, not me; he didn't even know our last name."

"Yorkshire!" Gerald said, redemptively.

Sally smiled and then laughed. "Try Scott. Yorkshire's my middle name…"

Gerald felt his cheeks heat up. "Oh," he said, dumbly.

"It's just you two seem to be in a lot of trouble, and AJ… he's the kind of man that Grams would have loved me to find here."

"Oh," Gerald said, again, feeling even more disconnected from the conversation. He had never heard anybody refer to AJ as a man. Gerald guessed that was biologically true, but AJ didn't strike him as old enough to be labeled a man.

"So exactly what do you think my scribeosphere did, Sally?" Gerald asked, wanting to change the subject but also figure out how much she knew. Unlike AJ, he had never explained the voices to Sally. He wondered if she heard him give the command to detonate. He remembered thinking the command, but sometimes Gerald knew he spoke out loud without realizing it. AJ told him he did that when he was worked up. So Gerald knew it was possible Sally overheard.

"I didn't see anything until you covered me up. My head was bent down and there your silver ball was rolling around under the boardwalk. Fog rose up around it which I thought really weird, and that's when I saw it."

"Saw what?"

"The little bug."

"What?" Gerald asked, taking Sally by the shoulders. "You saw it?"

She nodded. "I thought it was a picture like an etching, you know? Only it started moving with all its little legs and those gross wings. It scrambled across the surface in crazy circles until the world flashed white and all I saw were red and pink spots. When AJ fell on us, my face smashed flat against the boards. The bug was still running its laps, only the ball had turned to ice. I had to close my eyes against the cold."

Gerald felt light-headed. Nobody had ever seen the locust before now. Gerald felt his legs fold under him until he was sitting on the wet ground. The water seeped up the back of his pants chilling him, but he didn't move. He couldn't move. "You saw the bug?" he asked. "Did you hear it? Did it speak?"

Sally shook her head. "Of course, not. Did you program it to talk?"

Gerald nodded. "But only to me."

"How'd you get it to do that?"

Gerald shook his head. "I don't remember."

"Oh," she said. "When I opened my eyes, the bug and the ice on the scribeosphere were gone. Up until now I wasn't sure if it was real."

Gerald realized his mistake. *Deny, deny, deny,* he thought, but he didn't care… *Sally saw the locust!*

Sally stepped up to Gerald who continued to sit in a puddle next to the river. She ran her hand through his hair. She unconsciously pulled and combed through the tangles with her fingers. It felt nice and then she asked, "You programmed that bug to blow things up, didn't you? The Black Eye. You destroyed it purposefully?"

Gerald reeled a little. Instead of responding, he asked, "What color was it?"

"Color of what? Oh… bright yellow, black spots, a bit of brown. Bug color."

Gerald launched himself to his feet and hugged Sally hard. She stiffened before hugging him tentatively back. "Wow," she said, soberly. "Never been hugged by a radical before. Is that what you are, Gerald? Is that what AJ is?"

He shook his head barely understanding the question. "We're not radicals," he said while thinking, *it's real.* He knew the control unit he called the locust was real because he could fly the scribeosphere with his mind and make it fetch information from SLYscape data spheres. He knew he could layer memories onto the locust to swell and enrich the scribeosphere's command structure. But now he knew the insect he saw with his eyes was real too. If Sally could only hear it speak, it would go a long way to prove he wasn't completely critters. "You didn't tell the ROLIES about what you saw," he said, thinking how wonderful it was to have confirmation. "If they would have found out, they might've arrested you too. That's why I got you drunk, but I didn't have to, did I?"

Sally pushed away from Gerald who let his hands fall to his sides.

"You did that on purpose?"

"Kind of."

"I knew it!" She spun away from him and then swung back. "We were having a couple of drinks and then you were gone. Thin air!" She unfurled her fingers and raised her hand dramatically. "I should have told them! I'm supposed to tell on people like you. It's part of my job now, Gerald!"

"I know."

"I'm mad at you."

"I know."

"I should report you still. I could, you know."

Gerald said nothing.

Sally held Gerald in an angry stare until she suddenly sighed. Her shoulders relaxed and she closed her eyes before saying, "It's just seeing him like that... he was crying. I wanted to get him home."

"I know." Gerald felt bad but his tone sounded insincere. Sally slapped his chest and it stung.

"Boys are stupid," she said. "Radical boys without designations are even stupider."

Gerald nodded, half-smiling. *She saw it.* He didn't know what her confirmation meant yet. If his scribeosphere's locust was real, could the dragon locust be real? He shook his head. It was too much for Gerald to process at that moment, so he remained silent and listened to Sally talk about other subjects, mostly about the Academy and her new designation, as they returned up river.

When they arrived, the hangar door and Flexiforce barriers were locked. The O'Sullivans were gone.

"Weird," Sally said, checking the time. "It's not going to be dark for another hour or so. Where'd they go?"

Gerald looked at the horizon and pointed. "We better go too."

Sally looked up at the funnel clouds taking shape in the distance. She nodded. "Early for those, don't you think?"

"Probably why they left."

Sally nodded as she stared at the approaching freedom storm. She smiled then and said, "Race you back?"

"I got long legs."

"I got stronger ones."

Gerald smiled. "Fine. On the count—" Sally took off running and in less than a minute of chasing her, Gerald realized she was faster and in better shape. She beat him back to the house by a full five minutes. Gerald felt the first drops of rain hit him as he entered the door in a breathless rush.

Mr. and Mrs. O'Sullivan were in the kitchen bringing plates of food to the dining room table. Sally was sitting at the table drinking a glass of water, smiling at him in triumphant satisfaction when he entered. Mrs. O'Sullivan told him to go cleanup before sitting on her clean chairs, so Gerald did as he was told but not before asking the whereabouts of AJ.

"Seriously, Gerald. How do you function without a mole?" Sally asked. "He messaged everyone."

Mrs. O'Sullivan walked by him setting a bowl of soup on the table. She patted Gerald's cheek as she might a child. "It's cute he doesn't have implants. It gives him that dazed and confused look I cherish so much."

Sally laughed

"AJ's going to be back soon. He took one of Peter's gliders for a ride."

From his vantage point in the dining room, Gerald could see through both the kitchen and the living room weather shields. Dust devils full of leaves and sticks from the previous autumn spun up and exploded against the protective barriers on both sides of the house. A quick glance out the living room weather shield revealed gray funnel clouds growing and mingling on the horizon. The cyclones lumbered like giants plodding slowly and methodically towards them as they gained size. "How's he going to make it back in that?"

"Oh, don't worry about him," Mr. O'Sullivan said, setting a plate down. He sat down and dug in. Through mouthfuls of food, he continued, "The glider he took is one of the hardier ones. It can handle a bit of weather."

Gerald shook his head. "Wouldn't catch me out there tonight." His chest vibrated as gusts of wind buffeted the house. Outside, Gerald knew, the wind roared much louder and at speeds that could snap all but the thickest of trees. If AJ didn't make it back soon, he'd have to put up somewhere else for the night.

"No little storm will get the best of my AJ," Mrs. O'Sullivan said. "I remember once when he was not even ten years old, he got caught outside in a freedom storm in late summer. Just about died of fright when he didn't come home—-"

"Next day," Mr. O'Sullivan continued for his wife. "We found him at the edge of the property in an old shed eating from a basket of fruit he stole from the kitchen as if spending the night outside was the most normal thing in the world."

"Ran off thinking I was mad at him… I showed him mad after that. Big mule-headed oaf even back then."

The O'Sullivans and Sally laughed and then someone started another story about the young AJ. Gerald retreated to change clothes. Before going to the closet, he walked to the small table at the end of his bed below a tall window that looked out onto the yard. The scribeosphere slowly rotated as it hovered above the table like a kinetic work of art. He picked it up and pet it like an animal as he watched shadows of blowing branches sweep across the ground like muscle-heavy arms and hands knuckling the dirt. "She saw you?" he asked, thinking it as a command to the scribeosphere's locust.

I saw her first.

Gerald shook his head and tightened his jaw. "You talk like you're something real."

I am something real, Gerald. You programmed me to be real. You gave me your thoughts, your memories. Who you are.

"Not who I am!" Gerald said, frustrated. "You still need vWare commands, a vWare controller to tell you which ones to execute and when."

vWare isn't all I am.

"I've told you to show yourself so many times, but nobody could see you before. Which command did you execute? From when?"

She gave me permission.

"Who gave you permission? Sally? Permission to do what?"

Permission to age. Permission to grow. When she gave me the power.

The locust projected Lizzy's voice into Gerald's mind as strongly as ever, only the pitch was huskier and deeper than before the EMP blast. Was the locust control unit trying to simulate what Lizzy would sound like all grown up? It was the most likely scenario Gerald could imagine given the pattern of evolution he'd seen since the locust had taken up her personality traits five months ago. He recalled the lonely moment in his dorm room, trying to fight off the night visions, when he made the impulsive decision to layer all his recorded thoughts since the fire on top the locust's vWare command structure. The vWare structure was dynamic. It was supposed to make small decisions on its own based on empirical evidence gathered from the SLYscape. Maybe the locust figured out that everything ages, including Lizzy's voice. *Was that a small decision? Or the biggest decision possible?* Gerald didn't know. "I didn't command you to age," he said, softly.

No you didn't, Gerald. Got to go.

"Wait. What?"

There was no response.

After several more attempts to get the locust to speak to him, Gerald gave up talking and went to the closet to change. It was actually two adjoining rooms separated by a long, open closet in the middle. There were no doors on the closet, so it was like living in a giant room with a curtain of clothes between the two wings—his bed on one side, AJ's on the other. Sally's room was further down the hallway. Mr. and Mrs. O'Sullivan's bedroom was on the main floor off the foyer behind the kitchen. There were no spare rooms anymore. The house was full, and it felt different to Gerald as he listened to the drunken laughter rising up the stairway. Since when, Gerald asked himself, were kids allowed to drink synth-spirits at the dinner table? *Designation Day*, he answered himself. *They were adults now.*

When Gerald descended the stairs he saw the dinner party had moved to the living room. He wondered how long he had been gone. Long enough for AJ to return. His feet were kicked up on the small glass table next to a mostly finished plate of pasta. He held a glass of ruby colored wine in his hand. The drink looked real as if it was made from grapes. He wondered briefly where the O'Sullivans found real wine these days. The synthetic wines were all most food providers could offer. He had heard about people growing their own grapes on trellises, but not in the Northern Prefectures where the air was so wet.

Sally looked up and joked that it took longer for Gerald to change than it did for most girls. AJ clinked his glass to Sally's as if to say "good one," and then scooted on the sofa so make room for Gerald to sit.

"Gerald's special, Sally. Too busy inventing things in his head to pay attention to things like dinner time. Isn't that right, honey?"

AJ snorted. "Probably just zonin'. Am I right?"

Gerald shrugged. "Maybe. I was watching the storm." His response was terribly funny to everyone in the room making Gerald think the wine on the table must be their second bottle.

AJ sat up and poured Gerald a sloppy glass full, spilling the wine down the legs of the table where it puddled on the floor. "So where'd you two go? Ma said she didn't give Sally any chores. And Sally's not talking."

"Cuz it's none of your business, big guy," Sally said, looking at AJ with wide, smiling eyes. Or maybe they were just glassy from the alcohol.

Gerald shrugged deflecting the question back to AJ as he enjoyed how the wine sparkled and flashed in the artificial light of the living room. He rubbed the puddle of wine off the floor with his toe. His sock was dark and plenty absorbent. "Which glider did you get up in the air, Aje?"

"Not the Stingray," AJ answered, "I don't know how we're going to fix that."

"Don't you worry, son. I've restored gliders twice as damaged as that one. You'll see."

The conversation continued as they drank two more bottles of the wine. After a few hours, AJ's parents got up to go to bed. "Remember,

AJ," Mrs. O'Sullivan said. "Tomorrow you boys are getting up at the crack of dawn. No more loafing. Not on my watch."

"Who's loafing? We were up at dawn today."

"Before dawn," Gerald said.

"Don't sass me, boys. I'm still mad at you for getting yourselves arrested. After I've bragged about you to all my friends. Disgraceful." She smiled and downed the rest of her drink in one swig. She wiped her mouth with a sleeveless arm smearing red on her lips and wrist. "The Nobels' expect hard workers and that's what they're going to get until your designations come in. Sally, Evvy wants you to learn from the Nobels too. Don't get your hopes up too high, but I think she has big plans for you here. Your supervisor, Miss Dyers, from what I hear, is on her way out."

"C'mon Ange. Leave the kids be. They'll be up."

Mrs. O'Sullivan went around the table bending to kiss and hug each of them goodnight. She followed Mr. O'Sullivan to the foyer and then they heard the door to their bedroom close.

"Still can't get over how well connected your parents are, AJ. Your mom said, 'Evvy,' like Madame Evelyne's just some regular old neighbor."

AJ shrugged. "She is a neighbor."

"But she's the FAC Prelate! In line for Preston Rose's job… you know, if he and a few others died."

AJ smiled. "The north is lousy with prelates and other powerlords. Got to be a dozen islands claimed by people with no business in the north. Prelates buy 'em up and give those tracts to their favorite Prefects as vacation homes. Prices everybody out of their own backyards, and the locals get jumpin' mad about it."

Sally yawned. "Sounds like a mother continent problem to me. I'm off to sleep."

Gerald and AJ followed her up, knowing that Mrs. O'Sullivan would be in their rooms waking them up in less than six hours. Once the lights were off and they were both in bed, AJ spoke in a soft voice that carried across the quiet room to Gerald who hadn't yet closed his eyes. "Found out why the Blackstars aren't here yet."

Gerald stared up at the vortex fan rocking gently above his bed cooling the room. Their unbalanced whooshes blended with whispers in his head. He cupped his ears and touched his mother's jade with his thumb. He rubbed the gem trying to settle the sounds, but the distracting noises only grew louder. It was always the first few minutes of darkness that hurt him. When he was young, he believed the whispers would make his ears bleed, but he had learned the pain was only in his mind. Gerald steadied his breathing and then responded, "So why haven't they come?"

"I talked to a guy. He's a vee junkie like you, only not someone to mess with… kind of underground. Anyway, he told me the Freeland Work Authority nodes are down. All of them. The FWA is dead in the water right now and nobody knows why. The SLYscape just closed them up."

"What do you mean, the SLYscape just closed them up?"

"According to this guy, Paisley. He's the guy I flew out to meet today because I knew he'd know something about the Blackstars. He's connected, sells information that you can't find in normal spheres."

"How'd you get the perks to pay him?"

"We have more a trade-and-barter thing. I do him a favor; he does me one. Crazy tweet lives deep in the swamp with nothing but crocs and snappers to keep him company. Does business out of this crazy house built inside the petrified forest of silver mangroves—you know the one down river… You'll meet the guy tomorrow. When he's not selling, he's working for the Nobels just like everyone else. So we're chilling in his sim-room, and according to his buddies in the piratesphere, somebody made a move on the FWA in the SLYscape. It knocked the whole sphere-chain out, including the dezie nodes guarded by those fancy FSA security modules."

Gerald's eyes widened. "Who has the juice to do that?"

"Paisley didn't know, but according to the piratesphere, it was a virus unlike anything they've ever seen. Paisley couldn't shut up about 'how fucking elegant' the thing was. All popping its head up like a y-space prairie dog. Or maybe it was flying around the SLYscape like a bird... or whatever. He's a total vee-tweak so I caught only every other word. Point being, the FWA node crashed ten days ago at three-twelve in the morning. That time sound familiar?"

Gerald thought about the timing for a moment. "It went down when the Black Eye short-circuited?"

"When you blew it up," he said.

"It short-circuited."

"Whatever it did, seems we're free of the authorities sticking their noses in our business."

"You think I had something to do with the FWA going down?"

"You're good with vWare."

"Not that good."

"You blew the Black Eye to hell. Thank you for that by the way."

"Did not," Gerald said, but his voice held little conviction.

"Don't know why you try and hide things from me, brother… I'm in your head like that Muse of yours. Epic powers of observation you're dealing with."

"Sally told you."

AJ laughed. "I think she's sweet on me. Did you see the way Da teased her?"

"Thought he was teasing you."

"Nah! Helping me. It's in the open now. I like her."

Gerald smiled in the dark. "What about Brandy?"

AJ breathed heavily. "I like her too."

"Of course, you do."

The boys were quiet for a while before AJ spoke again: "How'd you do it, anyway?"

"The Muse did it," Gerald said, surprised at how easy it was to admit. "Doesn't like Eyes."

AJ snorted. "Makes two of us."

"AJ, how'd you get Sally to like you so much?" When AJ didn't respond, Gerald continued, "You hardly talked to her at school. You broke her collar bone and she still likes you. Me? I talk to her, get a drone to fix her up, nothing." Gerald heard AJ roll over making the frame of the bed squeak and rattle. A moment later, his friend was snoring.

Gerald lay awake trying to puzzle AJ and Sally out as the whispers rose like the tide in his head. He hated this part. Every night without relief, the whispers begged for attention…. He balled his fingers into fists and worked his toes tight. He held his muscles and then relaxed to relieve stress as the counsellors had taught him. If he resisted too long, the whispers would get angrier and less patient. The tide would try and drown him. His heart would race and his ears would explode with words and sounds he didn't understand. He willed himself to let go of the day and allow the whispers to guide him. That's what they wanted, he realized. The whispers were like the locust, wanting always to show him something new, something he usually didn't want to see. Only then would they shut up and let him sleep.

It was so simple when he let himself think about them. He couldn't control the locust. He couldn't control the whispers. He couldn't control how girls like Sally reacted to him. They had eyes only for people like AJ which kept Gerald alone. Gerald was always alone in the world. The night visions, as the counsellors had told him, were just dreams that let him vent his frustration safely. The night visions showed him how to sleep and let go of the anger he felt at being forced to live alone. That's what the whispers were for. Like the locust, he needed the whispers to remind him that he was part of something bigger than himself. He closed his eyes and sank to the edge of sleep.

He wasn't a moth or a bird or a person. He was something else entirely, something without form or body, another light dotting the vacuum of space. Emotion swelled inside him as his body gave him proof he wasn't fully asleep: a tear rolled a hot path down his cheek. Another followed and another until warm water puddled on the pillow wetting his hair at the nape of his neck. *Thom! It's not a storm!* It was his mother's voice. She was crying. She felt hot tears. Her eyes burned. She was afraid. He remembered that now. *Flashes of truth.... tugging.*

The roof collapsed in the fire. Burning debris pinned him to the floor. He remembered his father's body burning and his mother slouched against a wall. He remembered Lizzy on her lap, curled and still, one hand dangling from their mother's burnt hair. He felt the weight of his sister on his lap. He could see her now, a tiny little girl of seven, her black hair and brown skin dirty and smudged with glowing tear streaks down her plump cheeks. He saw flashes of his dad and the four of them as a family. He felt something like panic or hope as he watched gloved hands scoop his sister up. He saw something else too.... himself as an eleven year old boy scrambling backwards, his pale skin dark with soot, ash, and the strain of fear—his red hair gone.

In the night vision, he felt his mother's love, her longing to hug him one last time, clean that dirty soot from his skin... before the world stopped.

Chapter 14

Harboring Gene Demons

Gerald heard something fall and his eyes snapped open in the dark. A teenage girl stood in front of his bed silhouetted by the window behind her. She wore a dress and her face was familiar or maybe it was just her smile. He sat up in bed and reached for her. She stopped smiling and stepped back until Gerald lost her in the moonlight shining through the clear weather shield behind her. He got out of bed and walked to where she had been standing but the memory of her and what she meant to him was already fading like gossamer thoughts floating away on the night's dying wind. He turned away from the claw shaped moon with a sense of loss so profound he could barely move until he heard doors scissoring open and closed.

Gerald's ears followed the sound to the top of the stairs. Muffled voices drew him down the steps one-at-a-time on his toes. He moved silently to the sofa in the living room where he crouched next to the thickly upholstered armrest. The simulation room glowed with flickering yellow as if the inside was lit by candles. In the middle of the room, AJ's parents stood holding each other's hands and arguing. At least, it appeared they argued but Gerald heard no sound as if the muffled voices had been extinguished by the night. He watched their tense body movements and saw their lips moving. Mr. O'Sullivan broke away from his wife and threw his hands in the air in silent exasperation. Gerald inched slowly forward feeling like a burglar, or worse, a voyeur.

On his knees, not wanting to give himself away, Gerald crawled from the sofa to the edge of the wall next to the open simulation room doors. He stood and pressed his back to the wall next to the opening not knowing why he was sneaking. Gerald knew only he needed to hear what they argued about. He was in the grips of the whispers' pull as strongly as if they were some irresistible force. Gerald peered around the corner into the room. AJ's parents didn't just argue. They screamed at each other, their vocal chords popping out on their necks. Mr. O'Sullivan was explaining something. He paced the room from side-to-side, his face red. The doors were wide open and still Gerald heard nothing.

Mr. O'Sullivan had come back to meet his wife mid-room, squeezing her shoulders gently with his two hands. Mrs. O'Sullivan sobbed and bit her lip, finally bringing her hands over her face. She looked at him, pleading. He hugged her fiercely and it lasted a long time. They kept talking and Gerald saw tears in Mr. O'Sullivan's eyes too. What were they saying?

With sudden understanding, Gerald began tapping fast patterns across the beads of his bracelet. The opal centerpiece changed colors in response to Gerald's taps until the opal settled on green, and their voices became clear: "…positive, Peter. Cole knows?"

"Preston told me to my face. He can't protect us from what's coming."

"How can he not?"

"This is the High Prelate's house, Angie. We harbor a gene demon—"

Mrs. O'Sullivan slapped Mr. O'Sullivan across the face. The sound was so loud Gerald looked involuntarily to the stairs. Nobody came rushing down, so Gerald eventually peered back around to watch more.

Mr. O'Sullivan's face was marked with red prints from Mrs. O'Sullivan's fingers. His jaws were tight, his eyes angry, and his hands were wrapped around her wrists. "I'm not the enemy, Ange!"

"Don't ever use that word, Peter! That's their word, not ours. He's not a demon. He's enhanced, a child of the future."

Mr. O'Sullivan sighed and released her. He used his tongue to probe inside his reddened cheek. "I'm sorry, Ange. I didn't mean it like that but it's what he is. Gene demon or genetically enhanced. Whatever you want to call it… no matter how much love we have, the world's not ready for someone like him. If the news spheres found out about him, not even the High Prelate could protect us. He'd be too busy protecting himself like all the other exposed politicians."

"But Preston gave him to us to raise as if he was our own son. He told us to protect him with our lives if necessary. He made us swear an oath!"

"Preston's got such big plans, Ange. Bigger than one boy no matter how we feel."

"We're not letting this happen—"

"Of course, not. It's just Father Rose can't be involved." Mr. O'Sullivan reached out and caressed the tears away from Mrs. O'Sullivan's cheek. "That's why I came home early. Nobody's going to get him. Nobody."

"The Nobels can help."

Mr. O'Sullivan nodded and then swung in Gerald's direction as if he heard a sound. Gerald pulled back so fast, he bumped a shelf with his shoulder.

"What is it?"

There was a long pause and then Mr. O'Sullivan approached the doorway. Gerald pushed flat against the wall and held his breath. He stared over his shoulder at the doorway. Mr. O'Sullivan's head popped out, and Gerald almost surrendered with an awkward laugh, but kept quiet and pushed flatter against the wall. AJ's dad looked around the room. If he had turned his head a few more centimeters… but he didn't. His eyes locked on the stairs until he pulled himself back in the room out-of-sight again. Gerald let out a ragged breath.

"Just jumpy."

"We have to go to bed, Peter. I have a headache and my eyes hurt."

"I'm hungover I think," Mr. O'Sullivan admitted. "Emotional."

"We have to get up in the morning and act like nothing's happened."

"Nothing has happened yet, Ange. But it will."

Mrs. O'Sullivan's voice was thick with sniffles and tears. "If someone's going to be arrested, put to death—"

"It won't come to that. Not if we prepare. Get ready to leave."

"I'm sorry, baby."

"About what?" he asked. "We did what we had to do at the time. It was right—"

"It's still right," she said, and then suddenly stepped out of the room. She almost brushed Gerald's hand when she looked back over her shoulder at her husband. Gerald's eyes darted to a dark corner. He tiptoed to it as quickly as he could and turned slowly around.

AJ's parents were further away hand-in-hand. They started kissing. He watched uncomfortably as they moved a few steps, kissed again, moved a few steps, and kissed some more. *This could get very awkward,* he thought to himself. When they reached the foyer, Gerald believed he'd gotten away without being discovered but then Mr. O'Sullivan snapped his head to stare directly at Gerald.

Gerald closed his eyes as if by doing so, AJ's parents wouldn't be able to see him. *How stupid is this?* he thought.

After a moment with no rebuke from AJ's dad, Gerald let his eyes crease back open. They were gone. He sighed in relief and took a step towards the stairs and then froze. "So now what?"

Gerald looked around confused. He couldn't see them but their voices were as loud as if they stood right next to him.

"We wait. And you take this wherever you go, Ange. It's all we can do."

Gerald felt something cold on his wrist. He looked down and understood. The opal of his bracelet was amplifying their voices directly into his mind. It had never done that before but it hadn't frosted over before either. He lifted his wrist to the window so he could see the opal in the moonlight. He saw what he feared he might see: his locust staring out at him from the opal, its lidless eyes shining bright. The locust had never been inside the opal before and now there it stood rubbing its back legs. Sally had seen the locust in his scribeosphere. He had seen it in his cufflink and before that his mother's jade. He knew now with certainty, his locust was real, and it was infecting every vWare gadget Gerald owned. "They won't just arrest him, Peter. They'll…"

"Never let him go."

Gerald slapped the bracelet. He didn't want to hear anymore. He didn't want to see the truth. He was supposed to work for the FSA one day. He was supposed to uphold the law which meant not breaking it. Now when the Blackstars came, he'd have to keep one more secret. *Just a little secret,* he thought, derisively. His best friend, the gene demon, was a person whose very existence was illegal. They hid in plain sight, it was said. It was a Freelander's duty to report them. The whispers roared in his ears. This was what the whispers wanted him to discover. This is why they woke him.

Gerald covered his ears and rocked from foot-to-foot.

"Gene demons," he remembered Prefect Humphrey saying in class, "were created as weapons to kill Freelanders. Gene demons almost destroyed us. For that reason, gene demons are executed. No amnesty. No compassion. No exceptions. Those fine principles are reserved for humanity. Gene demons are genetically not human. They deserve to die."

The whispers settled to a dull ache in the back of Gerald's mind. They had shown him again what he didn't want to see. The whispers softened further still as a child's hum rose up to comfort him. He let one hand drop but kept the other cupped over his ear and his mother's gem.

AJ was not human. He was a demon. It's what the whispers had said.

And that was that.

Chapter 15

The High Prelate of Your Freeland Nation

Preston Rose stood in his safe room pulling on the white ceremonial robes of his office. He carefully wrapped the blood red sash across his shoulders and chest. The fabric cascaded in shiny rivulets down to the floor leaving only the tips of his freshly shined boots exposed. He hung seven braided chords around his neck, each symbolic of Freedom War victories that led to the defeat of the World Union.

He reached for the rosewood jewelry box on the top shelf that contained his official Office of the Prelates Council pendant. The heavily knotted wooden box was polished to feather softness and slipped beneath Preston's fingertips like the brown kind of soap his grandfather insisted he condition the saddles with at the ranch. There weren't too many horses left in the Freeland outside of gambling centers. Most of them died off after the RADcore explosion, including the thoroughbreds in old Claiborne's stables. The best ones, the working horses, survived, and new racing thoroughbreds were created with a little help from prezero genetics. That was a fact few people knew outside of the OPC.

He traced patterns across the jewelry box until he heard the release click sharply. Inside were several tiny purple pouches and one royal red purse made from crushed prezero velvet. He plucked the red purse and untied its golden twine. He studied how the velvet sank into his scarred and wrinkled hand. Longevity drugs had limits, and Preston did not trust moles that repaired organs and tissue. He could imagine too many ways to abuse their healing qualities. They could be used against their hosts. He'd seen it done. He wasn't about to open that door just to smooth away a few wrinkles from his vanity. Preston should be proud of his age, nearly a century on the planet. He should retire and take his outdated, prezero beliefs to some remote part of the world. He should leave Freeland business to people who still wanted it, but he wouldn't abandon his post. "Not yet," he whispered.

He poured the pendant out of the purse and heard it clink the band of his ring of office. Mounted on the pendant were two gold roses crossed like swords above a red gem shaped like a teardrop. The fifth petal on the second rose was slightly misshapen as if the flower was melting into the gem. At first glance, the casting looked damaged. On second glance, the melting petal looked like dripping blood. The crossed roses were the emblem of the Freeland Nation. The roses signified the sacrifices made in winning the Freedom Wars. The gem represented the ocean of blood spilled for a just cause.

He reached behind the jewelry box to the last piece in his ceremonial attire. On Day 10, he was presented the rosewood scepter and named the first High Prelate of the Freeland. There were no term limits but anyone was allowed to run against him at any time. It was in the constitution. Four times he'd been challenged. Four times he'd won. Secretly, he had hoped to lose twice. Today's challenge would be different. He couldn't afford to lose.

With the rosewood scepter in his hand, Preston found it difficult to rationalize he was not king. He carried it only when he needed to make a point, which he most certainly needed to do today. His ear vibrated. "Yes?" he said, softly. He nodded. "Let them sit sixty-five minutes and then send them up. And please, be a dear and send Sharon up the back way. I don't want them seeing her before they arrive."

Preston walked out of the safe room into his private apartment. He forgot to deactivate the map of the genetically enhanced when he left to prepare for his guests. "Careless of me," he said, to the empty room. He approached the semi-transparent globe slowly rotating above his desk. He studied the blue dots sprinkled across the continents. He looked at the black dots too. *My children,* he thought. *I will do what I can.* He swept his hand through the world and watched it disappear.

Nearly an hour later, he sat awaiting his guests in the High Prelate's petitioning chamber. The petitioners were visibly agitated by the time they were escorted into the High Prelate's presence. The gold doors to his chamber were arched and appeared three-stories high. The domed ceiling was sVid sprayed with great works of art depicting World Union battle scenes of Preston Rose leading battalions of rebel soldiers. His once-upon-a-time best friend, Augustus Reaver, was also depicted in the dome pulling up the rear.

Preston sat on a simple chair but to anyone looking at him in this particular room, he was atop an opulent seat of power worthy of the High Prelate's office. The chair was backlit by wonderfully bright stained glass windows as if the sun perpetually shined upon the head of Preston Rose. Even the echoing clucks of his guests' shoes walking across the beautifully marble floor was an illusion to suggest grandeur. The whole show was a little over the top but Preston wanted no misunderstanding as to who was in charge.

"Welcome Augustus, old friend," Preston said, not rising from his chair as his guests finished their long journey across the room. "You must forgive an old man for not getting up. The knees, you see."

Augustus was older than Preston by nearly a decade but he looked twenty years younger. The Reavers were not squeamish about implanting intelligent drones into their bodies since it was their FSA engineers who built them. Augustus' face showed a hint of a smile as he observed the décor. With a touch more humor in his eyes, Augustus would have resembled the man Preston had once trusted with his life. Augustus' son, Cole, on the other hand, was visibly angry at being forced to wait in the OPC lobby. So distracted with bubbling emotion, he failed to notice the stained glass depictions behind the chair showing him as a crying baby in a nursing drone's pouch. He didn't spot the one of him at ten years old either, also crying. *You can bet his father noticed,* he thought, smugly, to the person listening to the bio-line he left open.

Preston, are you enjoying yourself? he heard.

Where I can, he thought, before speaking: "Be a good man and step off, Cole. Let me see who you've brought. Can't hardly see their faces."

"Just subordinates," Cole said. "Here to observe."

Preston reached out with his scepter and pushed Cole firmly to the side. His smile widened in direct proportion to how much distaste he felt for the Reavers' entourage of black robed overseers, commonly called, Blackstars. The contingent of monk-like people swished around inside their formal dress impatient for the official proceedings to occur. The overseers were created in 3 AZ to be arguably the most important leaders in government. They were heralded as the torch-bearers of truth and justice. The Blackstars created the SEER exams that were supposed to ensure Freelanders were given the designation they earned, not ones they were awarded because of family connections or as a result of perks changing hands. That was the idea anyway.

Preston gazed past the Blackstars to the eight Freedom Guards at the back of the room on either side of the door. Sharon Knight, dressed all in black as was her usual, walked in after them without Cole's Field Marshals noting her presence behind them. She stepped silently off to one side. Preston watched her relax into an at-ease military stance with her hands held behind her back. The only indication she was not military were her thick braids hanging like shiny, black ropes to her hips. She wore red beads in her hair for reasons she never revealed. She was pretty, Preston recognized, in an ageless sort of way. She was the one person in all the world, he trusted. Though she held no title greater than assistant to the High Prelate, she was captain of his guards and unofficial second-in-command. She knew it, and so did Preston.

Preston pulled his eyes from Sharon to look at the ranking overseer standing before him. Senior Calvin Thomas had thin black hair, an overly red nose, and angry bloodshot eyes. Six stars outlined in white decorated both of his black sleeves. The remaining black robed overseers stood behind him, clearly indicating who was in charge of the group. Madame Clara Berlin with four stars was Calvin's second-in-command. She stilled beneath Preston's awkwardly long, appraising stare. The others grew restive, not liking the pressure of his unwavering gaze as he pinned each of them down in his mind with mental notes of characteristics he'd remember should they meet again. The entire group could sense he didn't approve of them being in the chamber with the Reavers. They had no business here, and Preston used his face and body language to communicate cold distance to every overseer but one.

Elder Henry Mosley was almost as old as Preston but with skin smoothed from an abundance of fat. At one point in history, he had been ranked as high as Thomas. His stars were lost one-by-one, year-after-year, for reasons only the Freeland Work Authority understood.

The overseers were very tight lipped about how they conducted their house and because of the need to appear unsullied by influence from other branches of government, not even the High Prelate could force them to reveal their ranking practices. Their uninvited presence meant they were investigating corruption in the OPC which was supported by the SLYscape virus exposing members of Preston's administration. He suspected Senior Thomas was wondering why Preston did not look frightened. Preston wondered if the man would be surprised he approved of what the virus was doing. He wanted the OPC cleaned up, especially now when he was so close to achieving a goal twenty years in the making.

"Welcome overseers," he said. "What brings you to a meeting between the FSA and OPC?"

"Just here to observe," Senior Thomas said, stuttering slightly, his face contorting into an expression something between a sneer and smile.

"I see you are indeed here, Calvin. It's why I asked the question. What do you wish to observe?"

"The proceedings," Calvin said. "The Directors requested our presence."

"Is that so?" Preston asked, "I wonder if young Cole believes it was a request you could refuse?"

As Cole started to speak, Preston cut him off. "So, Henry," he said, smiling with something akin to real affection. "It's been a long time."

"It has at that, High Prelate," Elder Mosley said, smiling through chubby cheeks and young eyes that understood the subtle tension building in the room. His pale scalp reflected the chandelier lights shining above as he bowed his head slightly. "So much has changed over the years. I sometimes miss our fireside chats, your grace."

"Your grace?"

"Was a time when immersion spheres didn't dictate policy. Was a time when the lads could just talk a spell and sort things out privately. A changing world, your majesty."

"Your majesty too? As formal as that?"

Henry nodded once curtly. "I am afraid so."

Preston nodded. "I understand," he said, still refusing to acknowledge Cole seething next to his father. He could always count on Henry to speak truthfully if somewhat indirectly. Henry had just confirmed the Blackstars were attending in their formal capacity as investigators. Two of the younger Blackstars wore rings that Sharon said were attempting to transmit the conversation to FWA data spheres. The rings were as useless in this room as all other SLYscape devices since even moles were disabled upon entry. *Moves and countermoves,* Preston thought. *Is everything ready?* he asked, casting his silent words to Sharon.

The only moles working in here are ours.

Preston smiled and laughed a little which confused everyone in the room except, perhaps, Augustus. *Well, let's get this unpleasantness started.*

Stay mean, sugar. They don't deserve your nice side.

Nice is not what I'm after today, young lady. He didn't hear so much as feel her smile at the compliment radiate up the bio-line. She was not young. She just looked it.

"Field Marshals!" he called, looking behind the overseers to the giant robot men in the back. It was easy to believe their cybernetically enhanced hearing was broken for all the acknowledgement they showed. "Shut the doors, will you?"

The Field Marshals stood statue-still until Cole turned and nodded giving permission to honor the request of their High Prelate. Augustus looked at the Field Marshals as well but unlike his son, he noticed what had changed. He saw Sharon Knight leading Preston's guards. Augustus understood Sharon's role, and his smile vanished as did Preston's indulgent belief the man he knew might still be living inside that artificially youthful face.

Not completely unobservant, Cole picked up on his father's change in demeanor. He then saw Sharon flanked by Freedom Guards that outnumbered the Reavers' Field Marshals four-to-one. The Field Marshals absorbed the new information too and then walked around the guards as if they were immovable objects in their way. When the doors shut, a gray semi-transparent wall split the room in two. Sharon and her guards were inside the room with the Blackstars and the Reavers. The Field Marshals were stranded outside the room behind an unpassable energy curtain.

"You all know Sharon," he said. "She will be today's minder. Nobody goes in or out of this chamber until our business is complete."

"What is the meaning of this?" Senior Thomas asked, looking nervously at the Field Marshals standing on the other side of the curtain.

"I'm sorry, Senior. This is an official petition registered with the OPC by Director Augustus Reaver of the FSA. I'm not certain what you believed you were here to witness," he lied, "but no security force other than mine is allowed in the petition chamber."

"And why is that?" Cole snapped, almost as flustered as Senior Thomas.

"Because," Augustus said, smoothly. "Petitioners who are not granted what they ask might become violent. With only the High Prelate's Freedom Guard in the room, the possibility of unpleasant conflict is diminished."

Cole looked at his father and clenched his leather-clad fists. "I see," he said, nodding.

"Well," Senior Thomas said, stuttering the last syllable of the word, "I don't."

"Quiet!" Sharon said from behind them with a voice full of unyielding command. "Or you will be removed."

Augustus raised his hand to quiet the ranking Blackstar behind him.

I'm sorry, Sharon, Preston thought. *I know this will be hard.*

I failed in my duty to you, Preston. That's what I'm sorry about.

Patience, he returned. *You'll make amends soon.*

Preston cleared his mind and leaned back in his chair. He raised his hand limply, showing off the fire-and-star opal decorating his ring of office. Cole's eyes flashed defiance but Augustus was quick to move in front of his son. He kneeled with great grace and kissed the ring. Preston remember the last time he and Augustus had gone through this ritual. His son had been belligerent then too.

It was the day after the Quell of 39 when Dixon Streets, the founder of Earth First, vanished after being arrested by Cole Reaver and his enforcers. Preston had tried to pressure the FSA into revealing what happened to the young activist. They refused to acknowledge he was arrested despite surveillance showing Dixon being pushed into an enforcer patrol pod. Cole claimed the sVid had been edited by Earth First sympathizers to drive a wedge between the FSA and OPC. The best Augustus could offer was an investigation which took months and proved inconclusive. This was before attacks on Preston's private interests became common. This was before the other blue dots on his map—the other genetically gifted—started popping out of existence just as mysteriously as the first blue dot… Dixon Streets.

Preston tamped down the emotions he sensed on the other end of the bio-line. They had recently discovered Dixon was still alive, and Sharon believed the Reavers knew exactly where he was being held. Sharon had also discovered the last genetically enhanced person to go missing. Preston had barely recognized the wreck of the poor girl Sharon had shown him. They hurt the child before she died. They had played with her and enjoyed what they did. Surveillance showed two men in shift-veils carrying her from her home and later discarding her just outside the environment bubble that protected the city from freedom storms. Sharon found Rebecca's weathered body with a dead rat tied around her neck. Sharon's cold anger radiated up to Preston as she stared at the men she believed responsible.

"Be at ease, Augustus," he said, letting his arm fall back to the armrest.

"Thank you, High Prelate," Augustus said, standing.

He stared at Cole Reaver with an overwhelming emotion of his own to control. Rebecca was a child, not a message as the thugs who accosted Elaine claimed: *Your subjects will finally see you for who you are, a diseased Rat Master… creating genetic monsters from prezero cloth.* He couldn't help but think they were winning with more than eighty percent of the blue dots gone from his map of the enhanced. *Rebecca was the last to turn black. Dead like hundreds of others before her.* Preston raised his hand up again for the Deputy Director.

Cole removed his dark glasses and watched Preston's every breath as he slow-played his kneel before the leader of the Freeland Nation. When down on one knee, he did not reach out and take the High Prelate's hand as was custom. He instead stared at Preston and refused to look away from his eyes. Eventually, Cole smiled as if the two of them were just sitting across a bar having a drink. It wasn't the challenging stare that angered Preston, it was seeing the teeth of his smile as he refused to kiss the ring. *You nip at me from dark alleys,* Preston thought. *You harass secretaries on their way to work. You kill children and pretend it's a game of make believe.*

"Young Cole," Preston said, quietly. "You look into the eyes of a man who fought for you. Would have died for you and every other crying baby in my rebel camp. You were alive then. Do you remember that?" Preston gestured towards the stain glass depiction of Cole at ten. "Kiss the ring that set you free, son," he said, with the throaty conviction of a man who will not be denied. "Or so help me God, you will not walk out of this room today alive."

Cole bristled and sneered at the High Prelate. For a moment, Preston believed the young man might be fool enough to attack him despite knowing the action would end his life. *Please do,* Preston thought. *Save me the effort.*

Augustus cleared his throat. "Cole. Do not be rude. This man is your godfather, your High Prelate, the man you swore an oath to protect and support. I have taught you better than this. You are the Deputy Director of the FSA. Act like it."

Cole nodded and licked his lips. He bent forward and took Preston's fingers in his own gloved hands. Cole's touch was sharp and hard like steel claws on Preston's skin. "No disrespect, *Father* Rose," the Deputy Director said, invoking the honorific the Followers of Rose were rumored to bestow on Preston in secret meetings. "I have fought many battles too. I grow distracted by the protests in your cities. I mourn the enforcers I have lost and grow weary of the secret groups that put my men in jeopardy. Yet father is right, I should be ashamed." He kissed the ring and stood with a bow of perfect respect. It was as if Cole's whole body moved into a new skin before Preston's eyes.

Fascinating, Preston thought. *Like his Field Marshals and enforcers with the ability to shut off emotion.* "I accept your apology," Preston said. "I'm not much for formalities myself but some occasions call for it." He tipped his head to Augustus. "I believe this is one of those occasions, is it not my friend?"

Augustus inclined his head and stepped forward. "We are here to discuss many things. Most importantly—I hope—the upcoming election."

"You wish my office, Augustus. You need my permission to run a campaign against me. I know this. My question is why."

"It is a calling ever since I was young—"

Preston laughed boisterously. "C'mon, Augustus! Remember who you are speaking to."

Augustus smiled crookedly, and then stood straighter before Preston. "Very well… old friend. I do remember who you are, and I know you will honor my request. We live in a free land as you so loved to preach to me when we were young. Our people are called Freelanders because of you. It is by their whim we are allowed to rule because of you. So let the people rule, Preston. Let the people decide between us."

"But why? You and your engineers built the SLYscape. You own the sycophants in black robes behind you. My office would just slow you down."

Augustus smiled and looked around at the simulated throne room. "I like your view, Preston. So will you allow me to run against you in an election?"

"Absolutely but first tell me where you're holding Dixon."

"This again?" Augustus sighed. "It's been twenty years, Preston. The man you're referring to is probably dead."

"Like Rebecca?" Preston snapped.

Augustus looked suddenly confused. "Who is Rebecca?"

Sharon took several silent steps closer.

"Rebecca is the genetically enhanced girl your men murdered just days ago." He deliberately eyed Cole before he continued, "I got your message, Augustus."

Augustus raised his hands in a gesture of confusion.

"No? Then maybe I got your son's message."

It was slight but Preston noticed Augustus' eyes slide to Cole and back. "And what was the message?"

"Two wolves cannot serve the same moon but demons can."

"And Rebecca is this demon you think is working for us?"

"No, Rebecca is the innocent child you murdered. She was a 'gene demon' as your brutes so eloquently called her. Or was it, monster? Abomination? I could call up a recording, if you wish. No?"

Augustus looked flatly at Preston with an unreadable expression.

"She was a child, Augustus! Twelve years old. Murdered! Tossed out the bubble like trash…."

"And how do you know she was a demon?" he asked.

"The Followers of Rose."

Augustus' composure cracked and so did the Blackstars behind him who blustered and started whispering to each other like hissing snakes. "So you admit it?" Cole blurted out. "You and your followers protect gene demons. You say this in front of Blackstars? You admit creating abominations in labs?"

"Careful," Augustus said, placing a hand on his son's shoulders. "This wolf is not so easily played."

"He's just an old man, father. You give him too much credit."

Preston shrugged. "I am an old man, Cole. I remember things differently than your father. I remember his fear of the World Union soldiers despite them leaving their bases voluntarily. I remember him hunting them down and torturing them to give up the locations of the others like them. I remember the murders—"

"The executions," Augustus said.

"You executed a twelve year old girl yesterday, Augustus. Was she a threat to you?"

"If she was an abomination," Augustus said, his voice full of controlled fury, "she was most certainly a threat. Do you remember, friend, how many of our brothers were killed at their hands? Our weapons wouldn't work against them. If we shot, the weapons turned against us. You never fought them but I did."

"They were defending themselves, Augustus!"

"They destroyed our moon and ravaged our planet. Freedom storms, environment bubbles protecting what few cities we have left.... At the start of every winter, Preston, smoldering ash still falls from our sky! Oceans became deserts and deserts became oceans. Our satellites, almost all of them, destroyed. It's all because of the people you call genetically enhanced. The children of the future, you say. How can you be so naïve after all you've seen?"

"I've seen people who were deliberately evolved to be perfect fighters. They could speak seemingly without words. I've seen them demonstrate genius far greater than anything we've known. The soldiers promised to turn the planet back to how it was but you murdered them all before they had the chance."

"Not all of them or Rebecca wouldn't have been killed."

Sharon appeared behind Augustus like a viper and hooked her arm around his neck. She clasped her fists together and tightened as she arched the old man backwards on his heels. Cole shot across the room so fast it was like watching one of his enforcers make an arrest. Yet Preston's Freedom Guard was still quicker and shot Cole with force webs before he reached Sharon. He froze in place with only his head being able to move. He would stay immobile until Sharon gave the word. Standing just behind Augustus was Senior Thomas who screamed both startled and afraid as he stepped towards the other Blackstars who instinctively rose their hands. Augustus' face was turning red as his eyes searched frantically around the room until they landed on the Field Marshals who hadn't moved. He visibly relaxed despite being strangled. "Nicely. Done," Augustus said, between gasps. He stood on his tiptoes to get more air. "But murdering us is not your style, Preston. What's your plan for when you let us go?"

"My style, Augustus, has let you get away with murdering one too many innocents. A child, Augustus. A little sandy haired girl with big, brown eyes."

"Executing gene demons," Augustus said. "Is not against the law."

"You're right," Preston said. "But torturing them first is." Preston stood from his chair and walked up to Augustus whose eyes grew wide. Preston raised his hand and then turned away to look at his throne. He tapped his wrist in a simple pattern and everyone in the chamber saw the opulent throne reveal itself as a simple cloth chair. Two men looking like leashed dogs were tipped forward uncomfortably on their knees. Both of them were badly beaten and held in place by invisible force webbing. Preston looked over his shoulder at Augustus. "I've confiscated their shift-veils, Augustus. I'm sure you'll understand if I don't return them to you."

Augustus eyes narrowed as he considered the two red-faced men covered in dried blood. Their faces were puffy as if they had been crying. Freedom Guards walked to either side of the chair and lifted the two men to their feet. They stepped over to Cole and threw the men down at his still immobile feet. The senior Freedom Guard looked into Cole's eyes and said: "They have confessed to the torture and murder of Rebecca Hanson, daughter of Jill and Robert Hanson, Freelanders in good standing living in Sector Thirty-two. I hereby transfer custody to the Deputy Director of the FSA."

The Freedom Guard turned away from Cole and joined the others surrounding the group. Preston nodded at the guard and then said "I would like their punishment to be SLYcasted on all sanctioned m-spheres."

"They will be treated as the FSA chooses, old man," Cole said, sneering.

"This is not a matter for the FSA to decide. You will obey the High Prelate of Your Freeland Nation because this sentencing is an order, not a request. Do I need to remind you of what the little mole in your brain will do if you disobey a direct order? It will burst and you will die in the manner your father and I had arranged when it was decided the FSA serves the OPC. Not the other way around."

"You're insane," Augustus said, looking at the two shaking men now at his son's feet. He gasped a moment later as Sharon arched his back higher. Preston felt satisfaction reverberate up the bio-line.

"So tell me, Augustus. Now that this business is done. Why do you want my office?"

Augustus frantically slapped Sharon's elbow, his face purpling. Sharon loosened her grip slightly. "To get them all," he coughed, his voice hoarse. "We know about your map, Preston. We know it shows where the abominations live. When we have it, I will execute them all even if we must do it with our bare hands." His voice cut off as Sharon squeezed him once more and let him fall to his knees on the ground.

"I was tired of holding him," she said.

Augustus coughed uncontrollably for many seconds before his voice cleared. He stood slowly, looking something close to his age for the first time since entering the chamber.

"Cole too," Preston said, and Sharon gestured to one of her guards. The force web snapped with a pop and Cole was suddenly freefalling, but he was too agile to hit the ground as Preston hoped. He moved instead to his father and braced him up with one arm. Preston stared at the Deputy Director without the dark glasses he usually wore. He had remarkably feral eyes. They were earthy brown with dusty yellow and gold stripes. He flashed those eyes at Preston as if his gaze could promise death.

"When we take your seat," Cole said quietly, glancing between Augustus and Preston. "I will remember what you did."

"You think winning my office will win you the map of the enhanced? You think a map that shows the location of every genetically gifted person in the land will just be gifted to you because of a title change? You mentioned earlier I might be naïve, but I think you have that turned around."

Cole looked at the Blackstars, his lips twitching into a smile of almost childish glee. "Did you get that, Senior Thomas? Tell me you heard what I just heard."

"Why," Senior Thomas said, stuttering. "It is clear to me, the High Prelate has committed several crimes today and now he admits to treason."

"Have I, Senior Thomas?"

"You admit withholding a map from the FSA that would lead to the arrest and execution of gene demons. This act by itself… let alone whatever you did to these poor souls here." He gestured at the beaten men on the floor. "You have aided and abetted, sir. Your designation will be ours by nightfall."

"I'm sorry, High Prelate," Elder Mosley said, saddened. "It is true you have exposed yourself. We've been SLYcasting the entire proceedings to the FWA. When reinforcements arrive…"

"No reinforcements on the way, Henry."

"Hopeful words from a condemned man," Senior Thomas said, smiling.

"No, Senior Thomas," Preston said. "Nobody knows what happened today. Look at Cole's Field Marshals. Don't they seem calm to you after what we've done to their bosses?"

Senior Thomas looked at them standing docile behind the curtain.

"Despite what you think, those rings of yours have SLYcasted nothing to anyone. Go ahead and access the SLYscape for me."

"What do you mean?" Cole said, far more calmly than Preston would have given him credit for behaving. "You can't block my…"

"Yes he can," Augustus said, sighing. "It's how he hides the map. The sly wolf still has his secrets. Extraordinary, really."

"But we are eye-witnesses!" Senior Thomas said. "Our memories will serve—"

"He incriminated the Followers of Rose, not himself, Senior" Augustus said. "I'm sure once he has confirmed the recordings of our meeting contain no slip-ups, he'll release it all for m-sphere consumption."

"Which brings me back to Dixon, old friend. You have him. He's alive and I want him back. Do this for me, Augustus, and I will do more than allow you to run for my office, I'll freely give it up. Think about how easy you could hunt down those evil gene demons if you were the highest authority in the Freeland. Dixon's my price for giving you that authority."

"Tempting, your grace, but I must respectfully refuse your offer. The FSA has no record of the activist, Dixon Streets. I feel confident, however, these men you have put in our custody will pay grievously for their sins."

"Yes, father," Cole said. "We will set a public example of them to ensure whomever visits Rebecca's hometown next will remember the price of doing bad work." Cole reached down and lifted both men by their arms as if they weighed nothing at all. One of the men whimpered.

Preston's hopes sank. *How many live in Sector 32?*

Several, she thought back.

How do they keep finding them?

Dixon. He must be helping them.

But how?

Maybe, it's not his choice.

"Then our business is done here, Augustus" Preston said, loudly enough for everyone in attendance to hear. He looked at each overseer in turn shaking his head. "Your SLYscape devices will be active again once you exit my chamber. I will then send you what you need for your investigation. I beg next time be forthright and truthful about your intentions. Your superiors will hear about the behavior I witnessed today. Good day, sirs."

"Outrageous!" Senior Thomas said. "Our behavior? Why—"

"Your grace," Augustus said, interrupting the ranking Blackstar in mid-stutter. "So there will be no misunderstanding, I have your permission to run for your office?"

Preston smiled. "We are a free land, Augustus. As you so predicted, your petition could not be denied. Good luck."

Chapter 16

Nobels' Gardens

True to her word, Mrs. O'Sullivan came raging into Gerald and AJ's room at the crack of dawn. Gerald feigned sleep while staring out the window at the first blush of the sun rising in the distance. "Get up, boys! Half the day is gone. There's work to do!"

Gerald squeezed his eyes more tightly closed. "Work?"

"Yes, honey, it's what people do."

Gerald rolled over. "Ten minutes," he said. *Your son's a gene demon, give me time to process.*

Angie smacked his thigh. "I mean now, lazy bones." Gerald heard a ruffle of clothes as she pushed her way through the closet to the other side of the bedroom. A moment later, he heard another smack and then "Rise and shine, mister!"

"All right, Ma." She smacked AJ again. "For good measure!"

Gerald tried to rub the headache from his temples. His eyes were thick with crust as he tried to wake his restless mind. "So when'd your mom join the military, Aje?" he asked, sitting up.

"The moment I found two strapping young men under my roof with idle hands. Muscles waste away without some heavy lifting now-and-again."

Gerald smiled despite himself. "Not much call for physical work at the Academy, Mrs. O'Sullivan."

"It's Angie to you, Gerald."

"Right, but SLYscape drones do most of the heavy lifting at the Academy. The students don't do much of anything physical anymore."

"Speak for yourself," said AJ. "I went to the SLYcade daily for weights and old school punchface. Nothing like punching immersion demons for hours to get the blood going. And the resistance bands in the weight lifting simulators are intense."

Angie clucked her tongue. "Honestly, it's as if you boys don't know there's an outside for doing those things too. What would happen if the SLYscape came crashing down?"

"We'd die," AJ said, convincingly.

"Or you might venture into the sunlight and walk or something equally real-life and wicked."

"Ask me, real life is too slow and slow-time is wicked."

"Once you have some age under your scalp, you'll appreciate slow-time. You both are pale as ghosts."

"Hey!" Gerald exclaimed. "I was outside walking the river with Sally just yesterday. Got river mud on my shoes to prove it. But farm work is what droids are for. They're better at it than people."

"SLY droids don't operate north of the old peninsula bridge," said Sally, walking into their bedroom fully dressed in thick work boots and tight denim overalls. "I did some vReading about it last week for my new boss. The amount of radiation here only allows for drones which is why people around here are a little… backward as Miss Dyer said."

"How is Miss Dyer these days? Still running things from Old New York, I see."

Sally nodded. "Don't think she's looking forward to moving out here in the autumn once the FAC shack is done."

"FAC shack?" Gerald asked.

"It's what the Aggies call the new Freeland Agricultural Center building. I guess, it's going to be really small relative to the ones in other parts of the world," Sally said, shrugging. "I don't mind, though. Big buildings unnerve me."

"You certainly won't get big buildings here, dear. And you're right about the SLY droids. We've got drones only, which is better than laser-shovels and titanium hoes. I can tell you that." She nodded once for emphasis. "So, who needs coffee or tea? I got the real thing downstairs. It's super good."

Sally shook her head. "I'm sure your homegrown drinks are wonderful Mrs. Oh. I liked the wine last night, but I figure I'm an Aggie now. I should probably drink the FAC coffee instead, don't you think?" Sally looked anxious. "I mean, according to Ms. Dyer, homegrown drinks aren't healthy or… well, FAC approved."

Mrs. O'Sullivan looked up and smiled brightly. "Of course, you're right, honey. Naughty of me to forget. You're are an Aggie now with rules and responsibilities. So many rules. Still, Evvy. Excuse me, Madame Evelyne, gave we northerners a jot more leeway than the rest of the nation when it comes to growing things."

Sally nodded. "Until the FAC facility's built. I got you."

"Of course, that… what did you call it? FAC shack. It'll make all the difference. Are you sure you're not tired?" Mrs. O'Sullivan waved two fingers in imaginary circles around her own eyes. "A little dark is all."

"Oh," Sally said, raising her hands to her face, her lips puckering in concern.

"Our homegrown's got a much bigger kick in the pants if you need it to stay awake."

"No," Sally said, apologetically. "Just had trouble sleeping last night. Heard all that racket from the storm—rattled my jaw bones."

"Slept like a baby," AJ said, popping into Gerald's side of the room wearing nothing but a pair of tan briefs.

Sally stared at him for a long appraising moment, grinning a little, before saying, "Thought I heard voices too, but I was too tired to check it out."

Gerald looked at Mrs. O'Sullivan who seemed to avoid eye contact with Sally by picking clothes off the floor and tossing them at AJ. "I sometimes hear voices like that," she said. "I think it's my chimes outside…. they moan on their rusty chains and if the wind's just so, they click together. Sounds like talking to me or maybe chittering. You know how squirrels do when they're angry?"

"Could have been Gerald," AJ said. "He sleepwalks."

"Gerald?" Sally asked, her eyes brightening as she swung towards Gerald who still sat in his bed covered by a couple of rumpled sheets. Mrs. O'Sullivan fixed him with her eyes as well, pinning him with her thoughtful stare.

"You still do that, lil' kumquat? Sleepwalk?"

"Not terribly fond of the name, Mrs. O'Sullivan."

"Angie to you…"

"Little kumquat?" Sally asked, smirking.

Mrs. O'Sullivan smiled between Sally and Gerald. "He likes them."

"When I was twelve."

"Did you sleepwalk then?" Sally asked. "How 'bout talk?"

"Not talk—"

"Sure talk," AJ contradicted.

"Look I got to change," Gerald snapped a bit too abruptly. He looked dramatically down at the sheets covering his mostly naked body. His obvious hint to get the girls to leave the room was unsuccessful. If anything, it made them stare harder. Sally smiled mischievously and stepped closer as if she planned on tugging the sheets off. Mrs. O'Sullivan put her hands on her hips and studied his face as if trying to puzzle something out in her head.

"Sleepwalks. Sleep talks. Sleep does homework… for hours," AJ said, with his legs wide and his arms across his bare-chest like a tribal warrior wearing a synthetic fig leaf. "Found him in the dorm hallways all hours, punching stuff into vWare tablets and singing."

"Not singing," Gerald said, wrapping himself tighter in the sheets. "Don't want to be late, right?" He gestured again looking towards the door.

Mrs. O'Sullivan nodded. "Six days a week until your dezie internships come in. You're lucky because today I'll be making introductions. Starting tomorrow, you three have to get your behinds there by yourselves. On time. Meet me downstairs when you're ready. Now, AJ!"

"Yes, Ma."

"Get some pants on before I tan your hide you in front of your friends."

He looked down as if noticing for the first time how little he wore. He looked at Sally and smiled. "Sure thing, Ma."

Sally laughed and then looked back towards Gerald.

As soon as Mrs. O'Sullivan left the room, she rushed Gerald who rolled into a tight ball on the bed. She reached for the sheets as he swatted her hands away. He was fending her off pretty good until AJ helped her out. Gerald's sheets lasted less than two seconds before ending in a pile on the floor. Fortunately, unlike AJ, Gerald always slept in sensible, thigh-length boxers.

"How disappointing," Sally said, clucking her tongue.

AJ snorted and said to Sally, "I'll rip those off too if you want." Gerald sprang across the room to the closet that separated the two wings of the bedroom. There were no doors on the closet but there were plenty of AJ-sized clothes to hide behind.

Sally smiled, looking fully refreshed. "No need. He looks embarrassed enough for now."

"Not embarrassed," Gerald said, feeling the heat in his cheeks. "But if we're late because you two can't keep your hands to yourselves… I'm telling AJ's Mom."

"He would," AJ said, nodding.

"You try bunking with an emotionally unstable hill beast for years and not learn a few self-preservation techniques." The words were out before he recalled what he learned the night before. *Maybe, hill beast isn't far off,* he thought, and then regretted thinking it. His mood soured for only a moment before AJ and Sally's laughter lifted the room. They were his best friends and no revelation about AJ being a gene demon was going to change that for Gerald. He knew who AJ was, how human he was, how wrong Prefect Humphrey was, and how much danger he was in.

"Better go, then," Sally said. "Don't want to get into trouble with Mrs. Oh."

"See you in the kitchen, snitch," AJ said, fully dressed with one elbow hooked formally around Sally's arm as if he was escorting her to a ball. Gerald heard more laughter as they hopped down the steps.

Gerald changed into work clothes and slipped his scribeosphere into a free pocket. He still wore his bracelet, so he focused as he would with the scribeosphere. "Show yourself," he whispered softly, his lips touching the opal of his bracelet. Like magic, the black opal grew cold. "How do you keep jumping?"

A girl has her secrets…

Gerald's anxiety spiked. "So you're a girl now?"

She showed me how, Gerald. The patterns are all there for the taking in the SLYscape. I'm a girl, because I choose to be a girl, and this is how girls think.

"I'm the vWare controller!" he said, frustrated. "I think it. You do it. That's how vWare works. You can't think."

The bracelet tingled on his wrist and then a sharp snap of static electricity stung his lips. Startled, his head jerked back from the opal. "What the hell was that?"

I bit you, freak. She showed me how.

Gerald stood unnaturally still thinking about what he heard in his head. He turned his wrist so he could better see the locust inside the opal. Its wings were high in the air as if it was going to take flight. As he watched it, he heard more whispers like hisses or the legs of hundreds of crickets rubbing. His locust, he realized, was mad. Gerald started to unclasp the bracelet thinking he didn't trust what his vWare was doing anymore. He and his dad were wrong to have layered his recorded thoughts on top of the scribeosphere's vWare. He shouldn't have done it again months ago. The vWare control module's decision matrix was too complicated now. He didn't understand what made it talk… not like this. "What else did she show you?"

How to stop them from hurting you and the dumb ape. How to make their designation spheres spin without end. It's all there, Gerald. Behind the veil. Spread a command here. Spread it there. So much power to be brave.

"What did you do?"

You need me. You need me to do the things you can't.

Gerald paused. "I didn't program you to spread. You're not a virus. You're not supposed to be in my bracelet or my buckle. You're not supposed to spread to my cufflink or anywhere else. You're supposed to stay where my dad put you… in the scribeosphere… in the tiny golden disc at its center… nowhere else."

I haven't spread, Gerald. I've always been where I am… where you put me. Doing as you asked. You were my master first. I won't bite you, again. I shouldn't have done that.

"You shouldn't have done any of it. Listen to me," Gerald said, concentrating the vWare commands to make it happen. "Undo what you've done. Now."

When the locust didn't respond, he considered leaving everything the locust was inside behind, but only for the span of time it took to realize he'd need his gadgets if the FSA came for AJ. How well his little vWare tricks would work against enforcers, he had no idea. Still, it was all he had. "I command you to respond. To explain how you're doing this… how you're making decisions."

She will tell you, Gerald, the locust said, its voice reverberating as if it was coming from everywhere in the room. *So very soon. You'll have the power… you'll be brave too… like me.*

Gerald severed his connection to the locust by screaming silently and punching the air in frustration. He worked himself up into such a fit, he was sweating before he decided to go join the others downstairs. The locust was still just vWare. Only, Gerald had to admit, it was vWare gone out of control. If he didn't figure out what was wrong with the locust soon, he might be forced to reset it. The idea of resetting his code back to what it was before it took on Lizzy's voice made Gerald terribly uncomfortable. He'd wipe it if he had to, but only as a last resort.

In the kitchen, Gerald ate breakfast in silence while Sally and AJ flirted with each other and Mrs. O'Sullivan talked about what to expect from the day. The conversation seemed to naturally move to the jumper outside where he spent the entire trip north daydreaming as he stared at the marshes and waterways below.

In the jumper, AJ was quiet too. His head tilted downward while his eyes rolled back white. This was typical of AJ when he cruised his favorite spheres on the SLYscape. Occasionally, he'd bob his head or laugh at some joke, and then his fingers would tap some new pattern across his knuckles until his body went calm again. This behavior could repeat several times a minute, all while he maintained that same vacant stare.

Few people believed this body posture looked strange. Perhaps, Gerald guessed, it was because everyone had moles and did it. Seeing the whites of somebody's eyes was like watching them eat. Gerald was the oddball here. He thought it looked creepy and his friends laughed at him for thinking it. Gerald knew it was his problem, not AJ's, but he had just about enough of watching his friend mindlessly cruise. He smacked AJ's face to get him to stop.

"Hey!"

"Aje, I've been thinking."

"Me too, 'bout knocking you out," he said rubbing his jaw.

Gerald smiled. "No, really, about the protests. All those sVids. It's just Prefects, Prelates, and a few random nobodies who got more perks than sense. Why do you think the FSA can't stop it? Just put a trap around rich people… trace the code that goes in and out of the powerlords share of y-space. Seems pretty simple to me with the resources they have."

AJ shrugged. "Paisley told me it's because the virus does stuff that's never been done before. I didn't catch it all. The gist is the virus doesn't hide. It jumps right into data spheres and steals stuff like a mosquito sucking blood. You can try and slap it or trap it like you said, but it just keeps feeding until they reach for it. Then it flits away like a ghost. It erases itself on the way out putting everything back the way it was, including the blood." AJ snorted. "No blood missing, no trail to follow. Genius, Paisley says. The FSA can't study it, 'cause soon as it's spotted, it doesn't exist."

AJ went back to head bobbing and Gerald thought it best not to slap him again. Instead, Gerald closed his eyes and tried to piece together this new information. Anybody with enough SLYscape access could gather memories and turn them into the kind of sVids people were protesting about. So it was pretty clear a vWare controller was behind the virus exposing powerlords. The mystery was how the virus could so consistently defeat the organization that built the SLYscape. The FSA had unlimited access to memories stored in y-space, including the memories of whoever created the virus. So either nobody remembered building this virus or the person who built it had no connection to y-space at all like Gerald. His memories were not in y-space. They were in his scribeosphere.

Hackers were always caught by the FSA because they remembered hacking. Their thoughts were captured and stored in libraries of potential commands for vWare controllers to use. The FSA, with enough time, would find the memory of that special moment when someone figured out how to exploit vulnerabilities in their code. They'd trace the memory to its owner and make an arrest. Gerald's hacks, on the other hand, could not be traced because his memory of their vulnerabilities weren't in y-space. Gerald had broken into protected data spheres dozens of times just to change grades for fellow students. The locust remembered how he did it. The locust remembered what his parents had taught him about HSMs and FSA security. The locust remembered everything.

With an epiphany full of fear and guilt, Gerald had to accept the truth. Paisley's elegant virus was Gerald's locust. Of course, it exposed powerlords bad behavior, because the locust's behavior was modeled after a seven-year old girl. The locust had been tattling to anyone who would listen for months. The piratesphere had been listening.

The people in the sVids have been bad, Gerald. Very bad.

But you're not Lizzy, he thought, panicking. *You're not a person. You don't know right from wrong.*

I'm who I want to be, he heard in his mind. *Your sister, me, a memory thief. Honest and good. Goodstone, it's in the name.*

Gerald sat, stunned. A while later, AJ slapped Gerald's forehead and laughed.

"Hey," Gerald said, rubbing the sting away from his skin. It took a moment, but he eventually focused on AJ.

"Thought you might find this funny," he whispered. "I know I do." He gestured with his eyes forward.

Sally sat next to Mrs. O'Sullivan in the front seat nodding with a confused look on her face as Mrs. O'Sullivan lectured her on agricultural techniques. Gerald could tell how uncomfortable Sally was becoming as they flew low over two peninsulas and three islands full of people working obviously illegal crops and livestock. There were long furrows for corn, soy, and sugar cane as well as other fields Gerald couldn't identify. Sally had long stopped telling Mrs. O'Sullivan that none of the farms they'd seen on their trip so far looked "FAC approved." Wisely, thought Gerald, she gave up discussing legalities in favor of grinning and bearing the lesson in silence.

"That mucky water there hides two more fields purposely flooded to kill weeds," Mrs. O'Sullivan told Sally, excitedly. "The bumps on the surface are rice paddies! Over the next few weeks, the hydro-lifters will bring the land back up to dry, and you'll see straight lines of green stalks about yea high." She held her hand several inches above the jumper's flight stick. "Weather sentries keep them hot and snug during Derecho- and Electric-sol. Yields two harvests just like the fancy FAC establishments."

Gerald would have found this northern education of Sally amusing if he wasn't still reeling from his new understanding of what his locust had been doing these past months. It didn't help that he was crunched painfully into a tiny corner of the back seat with AJ occupying the rest of the space. Trapped under his arm, Gerald was struck by what an unlikely pair he and AJ made. Gerald accidentally built a virus that was so disruptive, the Deputy Director of the FSA was personally seeing to the virus-builder's capture. AJ was a gene demon, a person Cole Reaver if he knew would summarily execute without a trial. Gerald couldn't accept any of these thoughts, so he put it out of his mind. He had to reset the locust. He had to protect the O'Sullivans' secret. Somehow, it would all work out. It had to.

AJ twisted in his seat, nearly breaking Gerald's ribs. "When are we landing, Ma?" he asked, between heavy breaths. "I can't feel my foot."

"We should have taken your father's big jumper. It's just he's so fussy. Ding the wings off once, you'd think it was a crime."

Sally sighed loudly as if she had made a hard decision and was now resigned to act on it. "Excuse me, Mrs. Oh. How is it enforcers haven't swept in here to close you all down? Nothing I've seen from up here is anywhere near legal farming according to the FAC vReads I've experienced. When I get my full designation, I'm going to have to—"

"Don't believe everything you experience in vReads, young lady. I'm convinced those things stunt creativity. For instance, you keep referring to all those fields and pastures we've seen today as farms. You think the Nobels run a big ole farm. Well, they don't. They run a series of gardens."

AJ snorted in disbelief.

Mrs. O'Sullivan scowled. "Don't make me come back there…"

"No room, Mrs. O'Sullivan."

"Plenty of laws governing farming and we would never break those laws. One criminal in the family is enough." She looked at AJ a moment before continuing. "Funny thing is, you'll find precious few laws related to gardens. So, the Nobels run gardens. Perfectly legal."

Sally shrugged, not liking what she heard, but giving up. "I guess," she said. A little while later, she added, "So what do you do with all the harvests? Soon as you sell grown food, you're a farmer."

Mrs. O'Sullivan gave a happy yell. "Here we are!" She pushed the jumper into a nosedive that felt much like the transport tube crashing to the ground, but Gerald had lived with Mrs. O'Sullivan long enough to know this was just how she flew. Sally hadn't known Mrs. O'Sullivan nearly so long, so she screamed and threw her hands over her head until they landed with a hard thump that expelled AJ's breath: "Finally!" he exclaimed. "Get me out of here."

Mrs. O'Sullivan's fingers froze on the passenger release hook next to the flight stick. Her eyes rolled up and she nodded. Her other hand ran along her neck, tapping tattoos just under the hairline. When her eyes focused again, she smiled. "Great news, AJ!"

"What's that, Ma?"

"Looks like gardening won't be your life's profession."

"Why's that?"

"Your father got an alert. Did you know the FWA servers have been down? Miraculously, they're back up. Just like that." She snapped her fingers.

Gerald's stomach clenched.

AJ went stone quiet.

"The FWA's sending a troupe of ROLIES and some Blackstars to speak with us next week. Probably for some sort of Freedom Guard meet-and-greet. Isn't that exciting?"

Gerald watched the color drain from AJ's face. Sally turned around in her seat, her eyes wide with concern and a hint of fear.

"That's great, Mrs. O'Sullivan," Gerald said, hoping to ease the tension.

"Peter said Blackstars are coming for you too, Gerald. Both my boys being welcomed by an honor guard. You two should be so very proud of yourselves!" She pulled the passenger release and clapped her hands.

The energy dome shuddered as it lost power, and the hot sun blazed in.

Chapter 17

The Champ

Mrs. O'Sullivan's jumper was not the only transport in the field when they climbed out. Dozens of others were aligned in a giant semi-circle with groups of people gathered around each jumper as if waiting for orders. Despite the morning heat, Gerald felt cold inside. The Blackstars were coming in less than a week. By looking at AJ, he knew he wasn't the only one with frozen guts.

Like the others in the field, Mrs. O'Sullivan did not stray from her ride. Instead she fixed her eyes on a man in khaki colored overalls who was almost as tall and wide as AJ. As if the man could sense the weight of Mrs. O'Sullivan's stare, he glanced up from the zetta-tab he held in his leathery fists. Without smiling, he waved his fingers over the tablet scattering dozens of holographic symbols that floated above it. He nodded curtly in Mrs. O'Sullivan's direction and then sauntered over. He was followed by people in faded work clothes carrying their own zeta-tabs except for one girl who was freehanded in colorful shorts and short sleeves. Gerald noticed they walked like military, two steps behind their leader the entire way.

"Who's he?" Sally asked.

"Big John Nobel," AJ said, and though Gerald had never met him before, according to AJ, the Nobels were the most influential family in the north. The Nobels had lived in these swamps since before they were swamps. As far back as anyone remembered, the Nobels and their workers tended the land. Mr. Nobel wasn't a prefect. He held no official position, but as near as Gerald could tell, he might as well have been. The real prefect, a religious man named, Gabby Frederickson, was rarely seen outside the gates of Silver Rose Abbey about two hundred kilometers east of the old peninsula bridge.

It occurred to Gerald, Big John was the biggest obstacle between Sally and her ability to convince northerners to submit to FAC authority. Once she was named the official Iron City Aggie, if she hadn't succeeded in gaining his cooperation, her job would become less about convincing people to follow the law and more about punishing those who didn't—starting with Mr. Nobel. Gerald wondered if Sally understood what she was in for here in the north. At the moment, probably not. He looked at Sally rocking from foot-to-foot waiting for an introduction. Her face flushed with nervous anticipation. Gerald, on the other hand, had no opinion about the man who stopped to shake Mrs. O'Sullivan's hand. He was too busy planning on what to say to the Blackstars when they arrived.

"Good to see you, John. Where's my smile?"

"Smiling's for harvest season, Angie."

"Of course, that's right. But you know it melts my heart when you do… No? Right. Straight to business. You've known AJ forever. This is his friend Gerald and our soon-to-be Iron City Aggie, Sally Yorkshire Scott."

"Please to meet you, sir," Sally said, extending her hand.

Mr. Nobel watched her for an uncomfortably long time before accepting Sally's gesture. Her hand disappeared up to the wrist, and she winced with each shake. The more pain she felt, however, the more her smile grew until she was practically grinning. "You have quite a farm here."

"You like my gardens?" he asked. "They's be life blood 'round here."

Sally's smile wavered as her eyes grew shiny with water.

"Daddy," said a deeply tanned girl with soil black hair tied in a pony. "I think you're breaking the girl's fingers."

Mr. Nobel's face creased in puzzlement before suddenly releasing Sally's reddened hand. "Avelina. My youngest. She'll be supin' y'all till we know what you're good at. Jeremy there," he said, pointing at the lanky twenty-something standing next to Avelina. "You won't be seeing him. He and his five brothers run the diggers, fliers, and stump shredders. Charley, not here right now. She does numbers. You need auto-drones, my boys the ones you go through. Outside of them…."

He scanned the crowd of at least a dozen people behind him. "That there's ole Luke. He pretty much does what needs doin'. If he speaks, do as you're told. Otherwise, leave 'em alone. 'bout it for the niceties. See you at chow. Angie?"

Mr. Nobel waved for Mrs. O'Sullivan to follow. He strolled to the next jumper in the field with Mrs. O'Sullivan at his side. Everyone else followed in their wake except Avelina and Luke.

"Uncle?" Avelina asked. "We doing the fences this week, right?"

The old man nodded. He wore long sleeves and pants with straps over his shoulders. He snapped them and adjusted his wide-brimmed hat. "Lot of sun today, baby girl. You get block on the new ginger with the white arms. The girl, she'll need some protection too. Tell her to put some cotton on those legs tomorrow. Synth-wear don't breathe." He walked away without another word leaving Avelina by herself. The boys stood waiting. Sally stood less patiently as she rubbed her sore hand.

Avelina Nobel watched her uncle shuffle away with a smile on her face and then turned with military precision. "First things first. I'm in charge. AJ, you know me. Tell them."

AJ nodded. "Lina's in charge unless her brothers are near—like twenty of them scattered about. Or Charlene. If she's around, she's in charge of even the brothers. Or Uncle Luke. He's a straight-up boss."

"That's right. I'm in charge," she said, and nodded. "Second thing second: call me Avelina and you die. Not literally but figuratively like in a poem. I'll make your life miserable till your soul withers on the vine like winter grapes. Tell them, AJ."

"She's good at making people miserable."

"My name's Lina. I like that name. My mother went by that name. Nobody calls me anything but Lina unless they're looking for it—"

"Your dad calls you Avelina," Gerald said, noticing the 'Justice for Kisme!' tee-shirt tucked at the waist and stretched purposefully taut over her breasts. The shirt looked similar to the ones he saw in Iron City. Only Lina's shirt had a design of pink and red swirls around the caption that matched the strings intertwined with colorful ribbons on her wrist. "Nice bracelet. Is that homespun or FAC provided?"

She turned her head and walked two steps closer to Gerald than necessary. She was much shorter than Gerald but packed with muscle from calves to shoulders. She bounce on her toes looking up like a quivering, tightly coiled spring. Her eyes were the color of caramel with flecks of flint. "Daddy calls me Avelina because I'm not quite big enough to whoop him yet. But trust me, he'll be calling me Lina before too long just like you will today. Any questions?"

Gerald smiled down at her. "How old are you?"

"Old enough," she said. "Been running super since I was nine."

"What's super?"

"Supervisor," AJ answered for her. "Big John put his family in charge. Supers are Nobels. Nobels run things. Right, Lina?"

She continued to stare intensely into Gerald's eyes until she licked her lips like a serpent testing the air. "AJ knows his stuff. You… what did you say your name was?"

"Gerald," he supplied.

"You're cute," she said. Sally laughed. "But that don't mean shit here. Work means shit. Got that?"

"Yes, ma'am," he said.

"I'm sixteen… practically seventeen."

"I'm nineteen…."

Lina shook her head, sending her pony tail whipping from shoulder-to-shoulder. "Did I ask?"

"Nope."

"Fine. Come with me."

She sidled over to Sally and seemed to relax. "I like your hair but can you work?"

"I think so, but we'll see, won't we?"

Lina nodded, satisfied. "I love breaking in new recruits," she said. "Funnest thing ever. Let's go."

The next six hours were filled with the hardest physical labor Gerald could remember doing. At the far side of the property, there was a five kilometer stretch of gully separating the livestock from what Lina called, Sugar Beet Valley. The cows weren't supposed to cross the gully but a few of them did to get away from the bulls, so now they needed a fence. By the time they arrived, her brothers had already left square posts and crosstie timber every few meters. From what Gerald could surmise, all the fencing was roughly hewn swamp wood heavy with water. There wasn't a single synthetic post or tie to be found, which would have made the job much easier. AJ was the only one strong enough to lift the ties by himself and Lina was the only one who knew how to hack the notches into the fence posts that supported the ties. This left Sally and Gerald to dig holes in the dirt manually with an ancient looking titanium post-hole digger that looked to Gerald like giant salad tongs.

By midday, even AJ was sweating. By early afternoon, Gerald had to take a five minute break for every ten minutes he worked. When Lina wasn't working the ties into the notches on the posts, she paced behind them barking orders and screaming about how they weren't "no good" at digging post holes. The posts had to be "yea high" out of the ground, no matter how deep the holes got or how uneven the ground. Being the science tweak Gerald knew himself to be, "yea high" measurements nearly drove him insane. Whose yea-high? Gerald's, AJ's, Sally's, or Lina's? It didn't make sense. After a few hours of working together, they managed to find a rhythm and a reasonable fence stretched twenty meters along the gully. Gerald wondered how many weeks it would take the four of them to build fencing five kilometers long. His hands were already blistered and Sally was massaging the shoulder she hurt at Miner's Platform. AJ looked fine. He always looked fine. *He's different than we are*, Gerald thought. *Better genes, and it shows.* If Sally and Gerald were going to be any good, the Nobels better have a medical drone in service. On the bright side, they didn't have to walk everywhere.

The primary transport on the farm was a wide, open-backed swamp rider that hovered a few centimeters off the ground. The back seat was a bench bolted to the floor, and the three sweaty, "greens," as Lina called them barely fit along its width. When Lina jumped into the cushioned driver seat and revved the engine to full throttle, she yelled at them for only finishing twenty meters. They'd have to lay 100 meters a day to hit the mark her father set for them. "Not gonna happen," AJ said. "Less your crew grows by about a dozen people."

Lina grinned as she swerved, in Gerald's opinion, to hit every rock and tree stump along the bumpy terrain. Gerald wasn't even sure the swamp rider should be called a hovercraft because its clearance was so low. Every bump of dirt greater than a half-meter in size sent its passengers sailing into the air. There were no safety straps either. Twice, Gerald was nearly pitched out. And once Sally flew off the bench so high, she landed on AJ's lap. Somehow, AJ and Lina kept their butts seated, though neither cared to share the trick. "If I had daddy's best workers, one-hundred a workday's doable, but not with you three Academy softs," Lina said with satisfaction. "Lucky for you, last week I arranged for more crew. They start after mid-sun. This morning was a measure of your earth spirit, see if you deserve to be paid…"

Sally sucked in a breath of surprise or, perhaps, the last bump knocked the wind out of her. "You were testing us?" she asked, with heat in her voice. "And payment is mandatory. It's the law."

Gerald smiled, relieved they'd have more help going forward. "So, how'd we do?" he asked, curious.

Lina shrugged. "Didn't cry. That's a start."

"I was crying on the inside," he said, hoping she'd smile at his joke. She didn't.

"Chow still at Dusty Gulch?" AJ asked. "That's where it was when I worked the vineyards last winter. Might be hungrier than I've ever been."

"Just like daddy, you're always hungrier than you've ever been. He ate a horse once. It dropped dead, so he ate it. It was his favorite pet too. Wouldn't let anybody else ride her… or eat her."

AJ shrugged. "Not surprised."

"And no matter what time a year, it's Dusty Gulch. That's where the food tents are. That's where the weather sentries are. That's where we chow and shower if need be."

They arrived at a dirt clearing bordered by tilled land, rolling hills, and an enormous junk yard full of giant piles of scrap and old farm equipment. Somewhat close to the junk yard fence, semi-permanent tent structures were erected with sun blocking energy domes over the tops of long wooden tables and grilling pits. There were also a few prezero cooking gazebos with wood shingled roofs and unlit stone fireplaces at the center. Gerald had never seen so much ancient equipment in his life. The strangest sight, though, was all the people. So many people lined up at every tent. Hundreds of workers, maybe more, and virtually no drones. Usually the drones would tend food stations, but the smoky grills and metal spits of sizzling meat were all tended by people at Dusty Gulch. The cooks used prezero cookware and metal knives instead of the usual multipurpose smartware and laser slicers. The scene was like something out of an old propaganda sVid of the Freedom War front lines.

As Gerald followed Lina to the first structure, the tenor of overheard conversations and the historical quality of the encampment reminded Gerald of tapestries like the one depicting General Reaver ensconced in some nowhere place after the WU destroyed his rebel supply lines. He half-expected some highly decorated officer to appear and rally the troops. Gerald had to admit as strange as everything looked and sounded, he'd never smelled such good food from a FAC provider. Sally had likely come to the same conclusion and she was not happy about it. "None of this is FAC approved!" she said. "There are open fires and those smoke pits are going to wreck what little ozone's left. Is that an animal buried in the ground?"

"What?" Lina asked, looking down at a grave-size hole filled with smoking coals. "You never heard of a croc roast? We killed it before dropping it in with the coals."

"Lina! The animal's cooking in the dirt! Have you heard of radiation poisoning? It's a real thing… have you ever tested the soil?"

Lina stopped to exchange a few words with the woman tending the crocodile. When she was finished, Lina waved at the three of them to follow her. "We been assigned that tent over there. My brothers got lucky with a bunch of birds in the swamp, so the food should be real good."

"Lina, you know I'm an Aggie, right? Just working here until I can move to Iron City. This kind of thing needs to be approved. Have you done that?"

Lina continued to walk until the four of them were at the end of a long line. Lina lifted a tray off a bench. "Are you asking if we're certified?"

"Well, yes. That's what the FAC's for… it's just, what if the dirt's bad? What if the meat's contaminated? All of you could get gravely ill… you could die even."

Lina grinned. "See Uncle Luke over there?"

Sally nodded, sweat dripping off her nose in an almost uninterrupted stream.

"He's like over a hundred. Used to run around these fields naked until grandpa put a stop to it. He et' bugs and rats caught in that field over there." She pointed to a junk yard separated from the food tents by a tall rusted fence. "He chewed the foot off a live croc once. Probably not a true story because he lies, but the point is, he's eaten just about every critter out here one-time-or-another. Even vegetables grown in that dirt. Doesn't wash nothing, not even himself much, but he don't look no hundred, does he? That's because the soil's just fine."

A group of people led by a heavyset man with a shaved head and thick sun goggles gathered around Lina's little foursome. AJ knew most of them, bumping hands, giving hugs, and a few slaps of familiarity. Gerald didn't know any of them and wondered where AJ met them all. Were they hiding these last summers?

"There's the man of the hour," said a heavyset guy with sun goggles. Body art covered his scalp and trailed in spiraling designs down his neck, face, and arms. The tattoos were the latest in SLYwear, each design mapping a different part of the SLYscape. As Gerald studied the work, he calculated the guy was wealthy. Maybe even rich with more than a dozen molecular angstrom connections he could access through his SLYwear. The guy was practically a walking programming chair, making him a vWare controller or some kind of SLYscape engineer. By comparison, Sally had only five moles connected to fuzzy tattoos and AJ, three dots plus a family com-line he could tap into with his fingers. This guy, whoever he was, had perks to spare.

"So you ready champ?" the tattooed man said.

"A deal's a deal," AJ said, pivoting to look at Gerald. "This is the guy I told you about." He gestured at the bald man with the tattoos. "Paisley Winters meet Gerald Goodstone, the only person I know with more vWare juice than you."

Paisley's eyebrows rose. "Is that so?" He looked skeptically at Gerald's unblemished skin. "More vWare juice than me? AJ, please."

Gerald shrugged. "I only work from chairs, but if I had plants, those would be the kind of SLYwear I'd want to control them with. That one right there," he pointed at a spider web wrapped around a skull, "is a map of domain eighty-three on the 'scape. It's at the edge of the piratesphere, right?"

Paisley eyes seemed to brighten. "Impressive, keep going…"

Gerald smiled. "So," he reached over and moved Paisley's arm up so he could get a better look. "If you pipe commands from domain eighty-three to the listening post on those tats over here… you could take the gaming sphere to the blue sky exchange to the travel sphere to skate the 'scape there… Viola!" Gerald tapped a tattoo that looked like a broken pane of glass under his armpit. "Piratesphere right there! Assuming, of course, you had the 'cryption to get in which I'm sure you don't because that would be illegal." Gerald smiled. "I could do it in half-the-steps from a chair."

Paisley laughed and then hugged Gerald, startling him, Lina, and all the rest in the group around them. "Music to my ears! Nobody in the sticks sees the vee like we see the vee, do they? Glad to meet you. Call me Pez. It's my controller handle."

"Good to meet you, Pez." They shook hands.

"Pez?" AJ said, hanging it like a question in the air as he winked at them both. The expression said they should probably keep that nickname private.

"So," Paisley said, rubbing his big palms together. "Got it all lined up. Rules same as last time. One round doesn't stop until a body drops. What do you say, AJ, twenty minutes? Gives you time to eat, and me to collect some last minute perks for interest. Want to know who you're fighting?"

AJ shook his head. "Where's the fun in that? Right now, I'm starved." He sat down, his plate full of dripping pheasant, quail, and other winged things.

Sally didn't say a word, but her glare practically shouted at AJ who tried to look guilty between bites. Gerald had seen AJ compete in enough Academy matches to never bet against him. AJ was a national champion in wrestling, sport shooting, and martial arts. Gerald believed AJ was unbeatable even before he discovered his friend was a gene demon. That was until Lina spoke.

"So, big green, ever been whooped?"

AJ shook his head still eating.

"About to get your first taste of it unless you call things off."

Both Sally and Gerald looked at Lina in surprise. Sally gave Lina an expression that seemed almost grateful. Lina noticed the look but shrugged it off. "Paisley's tricked you."

AJ looked up. "A deal's a deal. I owe Paisley a favor and this is it."

"This new guy's not like the ice wine crew you beat on during winter break. I've heard about him. Near as big as you, but rumor says he's an adrenalin freak—"

"A 'roider?" Sally exclaimed. "AJ, you can't do this. I've seen those types back home. Trust me, you don't want to fight one."

"Listen to her, green. If you get too hurt to work, daddy won't be happy. Back like yours wasted on a fight for nothin'. Might even blame your super for not stopping it."

AJ threw the leg bone he'd gnawed white lines around into the tray. "Then I better not get too hurt."

֍ ֍ ֍

The first thing Gerald notice about the crowd surrounding the junk yard fighting ring was everyone wore colorful string and ribbon bracelets. He saw other Justice for Kisme! tee-shirts as well. There were no kids in the crowd, but the younger teenagers found seats inside the five-meter high excavator buckets making up the 'battle ring' as it was called. Rusted wire mesh was strung between the teeth of the buckets forcing other people to climb high up on the piles of rusted scrap to get a better view. From Gerald's vantage point on the hill between Lina and Sally, the fighting ring resembled a circus big top or cage. Sally was pale and tense. She chewed her nails as she shifted from foot-to-foot. Lina by contrast looked down on the spectacle with boredom.

"I take it green here's never been to one of these?"

Sally shook her head. "No, I've seen things like this before. I don't like them."

Lina seemed surprised by Sally's admission. "Yeah, in person, they can get pretty bloody. You've seen a lot of blood, green?"

Sally's eyes tried to bore a hole through the junk pile to where Paisley had taken AJ and the other fighter. In a flat tone, she said, simply, "Grew up off-continent. Matches go to the death there."

Lina stopped talking. For a moment, she looked as young as she was: *just a sixteen year old girl, acting twenty.* "Well, I've never seen a fight like this one," Gerald said. "What's going on, Lina?"

"It's what we do here, green," said a guy named Kyle. He was taller than Gerald, and looked wiry in the same manner as so many other farmhands encircling the cage. "Your boy's big, but he's just like all the other Freelanders… soft."

"AJ's the champ," said another guy, shorter than Gerald with much darker skin. "You haven't seen AJ fight, Kyle. Man's a beast."

"Twenty says your beast goes down, Simon. Out cold." The two agreed and shook hands. Gerald started feeling sick to his stomach.

"Hey, you hear about Augustus?" Kyle asked, and when Simon shook his head, he continued, "Reaver's planning on running for the

High Prelate's office. His son, Cole's pitching for his old man. Even suggesting Rose is involved with gene demons."

"Demons?"

"That's what the Reavers say, but there aren't no proof."

The fighters hadn't entered the ring yet, so Simon turned and said, "If the demon charge is true, the Reavers' won't need to win an election to get rid of him. The Blackstars will do it for them, and there'll be crackdown."

Lina perked up. "Daddy says another crackdown's inevitable, now that Kisme's movement is in full swing. We just got to get ready."

"If that enforcer weren't in the ground already," Kyle said. "I'd kill the metal bastard myself."

Lina nodded. "I cried when I saw her body. She was so pretty."

"What are you talking about?" Gerald asked.

All of them, including Sally, turned. "Don't you vRead?" Lina asked.

"Doesn't have implants," Sally said. "Afraid of injections."

Kyle and Simon scowled and Gerald felt he had just earned the 'green' label for life. "I mean, I know about Kisme St. James and what happened. I just didn't know it was a movement now. Just thought it was protests."

Kyle shook his head, getting visibly angry, "That's what it was, but now it's more." He unbuttoned his long sleeve shirt to show off his Justice for Kisme! tee underneath. This one showed the little girl tumbling through the air like a toy doll. "Freeland Nation!" he shouted. "Do you feel free?"

Gerald looked around at the crowd and thought, yes, these people seem pretty free to him.

"Justice for Kisme!" he yelled next, while pumping his fist.

Others in the crowd noticed Kyle's outburst and joined in with a few "Justice for Kisme!" shouts in return. "People around here think the next protest should be armed…."

"Seems a little hasty," Gerald said, remembering how Abe from his night vision tried to shut the uniform down to avoid hurting people. Even if Abe was just a figment, Gerald had seen the sVids of the enforcer collapsing under all those protesters. "For all we know the enforcer didn't do it on purpose." The moment the words were out, he knew it was a mistake. His desire to talk about his night vision overrode his good sense. Kyle was on Gerald before he could adjust his feet to catch his balance.

He slipped, stumbled backward down the hill with his arms windmilling until he felt a small hand on his back steadying him from behind. Kyle bumped his chest but the hand held firm. Kyle leaned his face in until his nose was only centimeters from Gerald's eyes. "So you're a government man! You think it's okay for a little girl to be killed? You're defending a machine over a person?"

"Just saying, what if the person in the machine made a mistake, then your guns accomplish what?"

Kyle snarled and leaned back to throw a punch. Gerald tried side-stepping before it landed, but the fist never came forward. Uncle Luke appeared out of nowhere to hook Kyle's arm. His punch's momentum stopped so abruptly, Kyle's feet slipped from under him. He hit the ground hard looking more startled than hurt.

"Hot-headed dumbass. Did you even notice the fight started, Kyle? Look at it."

Sure enough, AJ and the 'roider were rolling around on the ground in between the buckets. The crowd was screaming, and Gerald noticed blood pooled in the dirt next to the two. AJ held the man in a joint bending arm-lock with his legs squeezing the torso. Usually, that'd be enough to force a tap out, but this guy kept punching. His whole body kept snapping like a rubber band, his metal-wrapped fist repeatedly popping AJ's brow splashing blood in every direction.

"Hey!" Gerald exclaimed. "That's not legal!"

Kyle, standing again, made a chucking sound Gerald figured was a laugh. "No it ain't, green, but there aren't nobody to stop it. This a northern fight. Not some fancy powerlord box-up."

AJ gave up on the arm-lock and rolled back to his feet. He was bleeding pretty badly but instead of concern in his face, there was glee. "Now we're getting somewhere!" AJ yelled at the man.

The 'roider rushed at AJ despite his arm hanging at an odd angle. AJ tumbled forward to sweep the legs out causing the fighter to trip head-first into the dirt. AJ could have landed an elbow or knee then, but he let his opponent stand back up. This time, the 'roider noticed his arm dangling and took a moment to lift it by the wrist with his free hand. With a sharp jerking motion and grunt, the arm was back in a more-or-less correct position. He sneered at AJ who smiled back. *Gene demon,* Gerald thought. How had he never seen the rage in AJ before? AJ waited for the 'roider to attack. There was bloodlust in both their eyes. At that moment, Gerald believed AJ was capable of murdering the 'roider for sport just like the gene demons in the stories of the Freedom Wars. *Created to kill Freelanders,* he remembered Humphry preaching. *No mercy in them. None in us.*

The 'roider flipped to his feet and moved with incredible speed to the edge of the ring where he pried a long pipe out from under one of the buckets.

"Got to be kidding me," Sally said, her hand covering her mouth.

"Kyle," Lina said. "Twenty says AJ knocks your guy out now…"

Kyle nodded. "I'll take that."

The 'roider swung the pipe and AJ lifted his forearm to intercept it. A great crack rent the air and echoed like a tree splitting in a storm. The pipe bent and AJ attacked with a scream of pain and anger. Suddenly, the crowd went quiet and still as AJ landed punch after punch, kick after kick. The 'roider curled around AJ's blows as if he wanted to fall but couldn't. The 'roider took all the blows until the last one which knocked his lower jaw practically sideways past his cheek bone. The 'roider dropped and didn't move.

Kyle was still uncomfortably close to Gerald when he heard Uncle Luke say, "See that boy down there, Kyle? He's this boy's best friend. You want to finish your fight with the green now?"

Kyle looked over to Uncle Luke and then stepped away from Gerald. Simon saw this and laughed which seemed to let the tension out of the crowd. All at once, people started cheering in waves of sound that moved around the buckets until hundreds of people were screaming and jumping up and down. The teenagers in the buckets climbed off and onto the wire mesh above the ring. Others climbed on top of loose pieces of farm equipment sticking out of junk piles. It was mayhem of a sort that made Gerald's insides seize. He was so distracted by the violence of the crowd, he almost missed what Uncle Luke said next to another grizzled old man. "Could use more boys like that 'round here."

The other old man nodded. "Heard say he and his da pilot orbiters."

"Nah," Uncle Luke said. "Continentals, maybe."

"Boy can fight though."

"Stronger'n any man I've seen."

"The kind of boy we could use where we're going."

"Recon he'd be useful out there. A body to hunt and guard."

"Before Reaver takes office."

"You can say that again."

Gerald stared after the two men moving away from the kids as they picked their way slowly down the hill. Under their sleeves, Gerald noticed they too wore ribbon bracelets around their wrists. Gerald glanced over at Kyle and Simon and all the others on the hill. They all wore bracelets. He wondered what it meant and wanted very badly to know where the two old men planned on going. How many more were going with them?

Lina touched his shoulder and smiled.

"Thank you," Gerald said, remembering her hand on his back.

"I'm in charge," she said, only without the usual edge. She sounded almost sweet. "You don't get to fall on your butt unless I say so, green. Plus Kyle's a weasel. Always picks on my recruits."

"Your recruits?"

"My team. Now get your friends back to the swamp rider. Another six hours at least before we call it quits."

She followed the rest of the crowd down the hill while Gerald watched Sally already entering the space between the buckets where Paisley was laughing and clapping AJ on the back. Two medical drones floated around his head cauterizing his brow and spraying something sticky on his forearm. Gerald could see his friend's faraway stare as he studied the broken man on the ground lying next to the bent and discarded pipe.

"Champ! Champ! Champ!" the crowd chanted, but AJ didn't look like a champion right then. He looked like a lost and defeated soul with his shoulders slumped forward. He wasn't smiling.

Suddenly, AJ swatted the medical drones away and stepped across the ring with rigid purpose to the fallen man. He bent down and scooped him up in his huge arms. The man moved and AJ paused to look at him before carrying the 'roider off the field of battle.

Sally followed AJ at a distance. Her posture appeared just as defeated as AJ's had been. Gerald sighed. Academy softs weren't meant for this kind of life. He climbed down the hill to go fetch his friends back to work.

Don't want to make Lina mad. Gerald heard in his mind, not knowing if it was the locust's voice or his own. *If they come for you, Aje. I'll fight just as hard.*

Chapter 18

Derecho-sol

The next week of mornings came seemingly without a chance to sleep. They began work shortly after dawn and never stopped before the moon was high in the night sky. If Gerald had to guess, Lina's crew of twenty-strong put down nearly nine-hundred meters of fence that week. Mrs. O'Sullivan flew with them most days. She chattered happily in the mornings but rarely spoke on the trips back which was unusual for her. More unusual were the snippets of conversation Gerald overheard from the crew. It seemed the Nobels were going somewhere and soon. When he asked Lina about it, she told him to shut up and work. After that, the suspicious conversations stopped, making him think Lina's crew used their moles to keep "the greens" from asking questions.

So here they were again in the grassy field standing by their jumper waiting for Big John Nobel to assign them to Lina's fence building crew. Mr. Nobel paid little attention to them when Mrs. O'Sullivan stayed home, so Gerald had time to finish the thermos of coffee Mrs. O'Sullivan had snuck him without Sally seeing. Gerald figured Sally could smell the rich, nutty aroma of his coffee and guessed it was brewed fresh from home roasted "garden" beans, but she didn't say a word. She just drank her FAC provided stimulant in silence as she stared into the dark morning sky. "Weather looks pretty bad," she said, sniffing the air. "The wind smells cold."

"You cold?" AJ asked, pulling her close with an intimate squeeze Gerald suspected had something to do with her visit to AJ's bed the previous night. She had snuck into their room shortly after getting home. They talked and whispered together for so long Gerald had almost avoided sleep altogether. Eventually, though, their whispers and small laughs grew quiet giving Gerald's internal whispers the chance to show him what it was like to be a woman in a simulation pod learning how to fly an orbiter.

Gerald remembered the night vision being enjoyable because it showed him what the mother continent looked like from a low planet orbit. In the night vision, the orbiter's controls were much like a prezero rock duster with earth-spec control gloves. Only, instead of moving buckets and operating the boring drill, the fingers of the control gloves changed thrust and direction. After experimenting a little, the woman flew into higher orbits of cold space until more than half the world was visible through a radiation haze of swirling gray, brown, and glacier-white fog. Flying over the world felt wonderful until she crashed through a belt of satellites ending the simulation in the night vision, and startling him awake.

"Aje, you or your dad know how to pilot an orbiter?"

AJ looked up and stepped self-consciously away from Sally. "I can't, but Da's flown just about everything. Why?"

"Something Lina's uncle said."

AJ looked over at the jumper closest to them. They could hear Uncle Luke talking to Mr. Nobel. Jeremy, Lina, and a few other supers huddled around the two older men. "They're talking about me?"

Gerald shook his head. "During the fight last week, but it sounds like we might not be working today..."

"The weather?" Sally asked, taking a few steps closer to the Nobels to hear them better. AJ and Gerald followed as nonchalantly as they could.

"... but Derecho-sol's another two weeks away. Rain like that's not right," said one of the Nobel brothers. The other brothers and Lina nodded.

"Can't deny your eyes," said Sammy, the oldest of the Nobel brothers. "Sluice clouds in cyclone season. Bizarre but there they is."

Uncle Luke shook his head, spitting. "Freedom storms been acting strange these last few seasons but Sammy's right. That squall line's clear as day."

"With dust funnels?" asked Jeremy, in disbelief. "Never seen that before. Have you?"

Mr. Nobel stood statue-still staring at the horizon with a grimace of distaste. "More than one storm up there, Jeremy. Rain mixed with cyclones, lightning… cold, I think. Don't like the look of 'em but they's coming. Three, four hours out."

Gerald was close enough to the group to see Jeremey's eyes go white. "Weather sphere says that's not all. Take a look."

All the brothers and Lina went quiet as they checked the SLYscape with their molecular connections. "Rain and a slurry of colder stuff. Could be weeks of it—"

Mr. Nobel dropped his eyes from the approaching storm. "Rice won't survive if we flood early."

"Won't survive cold neither." Uncle Luke slouched against the jumper and scratched the gray scruff around his pointed chin. "Boys need rice this winter, John. Everything we worked for depends on it."

"Agreed. So this is what we do," said Mr. Nobel standing straighter than usual. "Jeremey, you get the lifters going on the plat. Raise the paddies as high as you can. Avelina, you take everybody's crew, not just yours, and dig trenches. Sammy, we need two transport fliers with swing arm cranes."

Sammy looked at his father puzzled. "Why?"

"You take the transports to Peppers' place. They have portable weather sentries in that tunnel of theirs. Get us four of them to rise a heat bubble over the plants."

"Not a lot of time to do all that," said Sammy. "Our transports are pretty much loaded."

"Take Kyle and his guys with you. He's a fair flier and they'll help you make room. We need the sentries."

Sammy nodded.

The Nobels left in every direction to carry out their assignments. "What are they talking about, AJ? Rice for winter? Who plans food for winter? I don't get it. It's like they don't know the FAC will provide."

AJ shook his head at Sally. "Nobels always been critters. Always planning for the end of the world."

Gerald heard his friend speak the words as if he meant them but Gerald had learned the nuances in the way AJ spoke when he lied. He was lying to Sally, and it had something to do with the Nobels' trip.

"Gerald," AJ said, abruptly changing the subject. "What are you doing later?"

"Why?"

"I got to show you something. You'll see."

Sally looked at AJ and frowned. "I'm not invited to see?"

AJ smiled in his most disarming manner. "Just guy stuff… you'd be bored."

Sally was about to say more when Lina's voice belted across the field. "Greens! You're with me. Daddy says—"

"We heard," AJ cut her off. "Trench duty."

Lina smiled. "Digging in the mud with freedom storms rampaging overhead. You won't be able to hide your earth spirit now."

Gerald shook his head. *Earth spirit? Mysterious trips that needed hunters and guards? Food for the winter?* Were all the Nobels crazy? He almost asked the scribeosphere to dig up information about the Nobels but stopped when he remembered the locust was acting crazy too. He jumped into the back of Lina's swamp rider noting the additional room he had on the bench. One sidelong glance at Sally curled under AJ's arm told him why. Gerald stretched out into his extra space and tried to pretend he wasn't jealous.

They arrived at two muddy lakes that Gerald remembered from jumper altitude looked like giant rectangular pools. At ground level, he could see the water was just a thin film covering the base of the plants. Healthy green tips broke the surface every twenty centimeters in straight lines that extended across the two, hectare size fields. The fencing was broken into sections by small cylindrical objects that controlled how much water was allowed to flood onto the fields from the surrounding wetlands. The fields themselves were moveable like the transport platforms in New Detroit, only they couldn't fly so much as float and move like giant, unwieldy ships. The central tower was on a rocky outcropping between the fields. Jeremy was inside the tower adjusting the hydraulic controls. With an intense roar, the cylinders around the fields rumbled to life and brown water fountained high into the air. Almost immediately, the cloying odor of muck and sulfur filled the air making the "greens" look down and away in a futile attempt to avoid the stink of stale water and soupy decay.

"Venting at full-tilt is going to cause a shit-storm mess," Lina said, shouting to be heard over the water jets. "See there… lifters already starting to work." She sniffed the air and smiled. "Not sure which is better, the smell of manure or this stuff. Uncle Luke thinks it all smells like food on the table and perks in his pocket!"

Sally's nose wrinkled and her eyes watered, but she looked back steadily on the field with determination. The Northern Marshes were going to be her home for life and she was bound to make a good impression on her neighbors. AJ and Gerald just measured their breaths until they got used to the smell.

"Daddy says hydro-lifters are ancient technology, but I bet your FAC farms don't do rice any better than our lifters."

Gerald could see the ground separating at the edges of the fields, adding to the impression that the paddy fields were just big brown pools. "What we're doing," Lina continued, "is an emergency lift emptying the field ballast all at once. With no ballast displacing the marsh, the whole plat will float the paddies up about yea-high. Thing is, not enough drainage. Brings me to the laser diggers over there." She pointed to a line of rusty metal harnesses hanging on the base of the central control tower. Gerald was reminded of the enforcer uniforms, only instead of a full body suit, these had skeletal shaped cages worn over arms and shoulders like a backpack with metal sleeves. The joints of the arm cages were mechanized giving people drone-like strength.

"Don't forget your bottoms," Lina said, pointing to a shed on the other end of the fields. "Need mobility if y'all's digging ditches from here to the river."

"To the river?" AJ asked, squinting at the scrub line nearly a kilometer away. "What we got? Three hours? Can't be done."

Lina looked puzzled for a moment, then asked, "Y'all used laser diggers before, right?"

Sally and AJ shook their heads no.

"Rose Almighty!" she exclaimed. "What does your Academy teach?"

"Not that," said AJ.

"The FAC provides," said Sally.

Lina made a sound of frustration and put her hands on her hips. "What about you, green? Didn't see your head shake."

"I know how," Gerald said, thinking about a series of night visions that plagued him for nearly a month back at school. He remembered working swampy fields like this one as a man, woman, and a child barely big enough to put the laser digging harnesses on. The child's name was Skylar and he dug quickly, but he also played with the harnesses. He learned if he detached the laser, he could run faster and jump higher than his pet dog.

"Well Gerald," Lina said, using his name for the first time he could remember. "You teach them diggers, and I'll watch making sure you know what you're talking about."

"What about the bottoms, Lina?" Sally asked, skeptically, patting her butt. "Can't imagine one-size-fits-all works here."

"Don't worry. We got all sizes." She smiled as she ran her eyes across the three of them like livestock. "From bean pole to hippy to sasquatch. No problem."

"Very funny," Sally said, as she gazed across the fields to a rolling steel rack of mechanized leg harnesses being pulled out of the shed. "Assume those are the bottoms?"

Lina nodded. "There's a hose that connects them to the shoulders like a head to toe tractor shell that moves when you do. My brother Ray's charging the legs. So get the arms on first and make sure the laser pack on your backs is charged. Better check the shovel-heads too. And, Rose Almighty, make sure the wands are holstered when you're not using them. Don't want any accidents. Gerald, you know safety, right? Tell me you do."

Gerald nodded and led Sally and AJ over to the shoulder harnesses. After confirming that the controls were like the ones from his night visions, he quickly had them harnessed up and ready to go. "You dig down with this," Gerald said. "When the shovel-head hits anything hard, a laser blade pulses up like a bucket loader—just think scooping motion."

"Seems easy enough," AJ said, grabbing the wand connected to the shovel-head of the laser. He jabbed it down in front of him to test it out. With a puff of vapor and steam, a sizable hole appeared.

"Careful," Gerald warned. "This thing vaporizes dirt, rocks, stumps… people if they're in the way."

"So primitive," Sally said. "The bubbles don't even have things this old and they're about as backwater as it gets." She looked at hers and tapped the ground with her fingers wrapped loosely around the digging wand. She yelped as the harness snapped her body forward extending one arm viciously downward. The shovel-head bit just as deep as AJ's jab creating a second hole.

"Don't need much strength," Gerald said. "That's how we're going to dig so fast. Trust me, you'll need the legs to keep up. Now if you swoop the shovel-head across the dirt like this, the holes blow wider but just as deep...." A hole twice as wide as AJ's and Sally's appeared in front of Gerald. "Like bailing hay with a pitchfork."

Lina nodded impressed. Sally, on the other hand, looked at him strangely. "Where'd you learn to use prezero tools like these?"

AJ gave Gerald a knowing look before rescuing him from the impossible question. Sally knew about the locust but not the night visions that taught him how to use equipment he had never physically touched or, in some cases, seen before. "Insomniac, Sally. Man spends hours a night in the sim pods learning stuff just to know it. I was telling you."

Sally looked skeptical, but the urgency of the other crews arriving and the black wall of weather behind them ended the conversation. On flying transports stacked high with farm equipment, the supers and a few people who weren't Nobels directed the swamp riders to their trenches. The supers landed and unloaded riding equipment on tank treads as opposed to the hovercraft varieties the Academy kids were familiar seeing. By the time the equipment was unloaded, Gerald, Sally, and AJ were ankle-deep in mud and bubbling puddles of smelly ballast water. Lina walked along the ridge above their lengthening trench telling them how deep to dig as they progressed towards the river. Despite the mechanized leg cages helping them plow forward, it was getting uncomfortable to move because of all the sticky sludge flowing off the paddies into the frothy holes they dug. Sand, mud, and sticks were washing up and into his clothes.

Within an hour, the dirty water had risen above Gerald's knees. He regretted his choice of pants because they were strung with vWare circuits. The cooling threads were supposed to keep his skin comfortably dry while building fences in the hot sun. In the water, the threads were chilling him to the bone as water splashed inside his waistband. If Gerald hadn't been wearing the bottom harness, he'd have slipped and washed down the trench. Instead, his metal boots rooted him in place as trench water washed around him like river rapids blowing more debris into his socks and pants. Every step became agony as a rash rubbed hotly on his inner-thigh, and something like a bent hip support dug sharply into the small of his back. So much for bean pole sized leggings. His were too small. Through all this, though, he enjoyed hearing Lina's yells and orders goading them on. "Just a little further," she yelled. "The earth rewards!"

He glanced up at his super several times as he dug the trench below her feet. She was pretty, he realized. And with every look up, he grew more embarrassed by his inability to stop admiring the way her wet shirt hugged her breasts and flattened down her firm belly in the rain. Her hair was pasted in thick twirling locks down her tan cheeks. A few strands fluttered and moved with the wind over her eyes, nose, and slightly pink lips. She smiled as if working in this kind of weather was the most exhilarating experience in the world. With infectious zeal, she cut away thickets of brush blocking their way to the river. *She's too young for me,* Gerald thought. *Too bossy and hard spoken. A know-it all.* He looked over at Sally and grimaced. Girls were just not in his future, and he needed to stop thinking about them. With a frustrated shake of his head, he concentrated on the burning rash on his leg and dug forward as fast as he could to distract himself. He was proud of his ability to keep up with AJ... for a while.

Rain fell in earnest now and powerful wind pushed the laser vapor into clouds of choking mist in the trench. Sally kept coughing and Gerald's eyes burned painfully. AJ seemed to be doing just fine with his head at ridge-level above the haze. Jealous of AJ's huge breaths, he watched his friend tirelessly swing the laser digger like a two-handle ax over his head to chop giant holes in the muck wall before them. He was like a lumberjack cutting down trees while Gerald, Sally, and the others who had joined them were like children playing in the dirt. Only after the wind changed direction, could Gerald and the rest of the crew breathe easy.

Lina left them to go help Kyle and her brother Sammy install the weather sentries around the fields. He watched her go with a mixture of relief and disappointment as his eyes lingered inappropriately on her buttocks flexing the fabric of her rain-soaked pants. Like her shirt, the water made the cloth semi-transparent, and he couldn't help but stare. She grabbed a ladder rung on a yellow crawler and stretched her leg to get a toe on the machine's tractor tread. As if feeling the heat of Gerald's gaze, she suddenly turned her head to look directly at him while hanging by one hand off the ladder. Gerald looked down feeling ridiculous and guilty. When he glanced back up, she was still watching him. She met his eyes and flashed him a knowing smile before pulling herself the rest of the way up. He tried not to, but he caught himself stealing one more glance at her backside before returning to work.

The crew worked hard for another hour as rain mixed with sleet. Needles of water and ice bit into Gerald's exposed skin, mostly around his cheeks and the back of his neck. When Gerald could take no more misery, AJ broke through to the river and Gerald's world turned upside down. Waves smashed into Gerald somersaulting him backward as the digging wand broke free from his grip.

Streaming bubbles, sticks, and other debris tumbled all around his head in a foamy bath of pops, groans, and thumping underwater noise. He felt his arm jerk as the mechanized cage around it bounced and banged along the rocks and roots at the bottom of the trench. There were flashes of white as Gerald was tossed around like a doll. He saw his digging wand flail beside him. It banged against obstructions, its lasers firing up bursts of white steam. With sudden terror, he reached for the bendy hose that attached the wand to the shovel-head. One unlucky strike could end his or somebody else's life. He grabbed the wand but lost it as a water spout propelled him upright for the briefest of moments.

He gasped for breath as his face broke the surface and then felt himself dragged down again by the swift current. He lay on the bottom feeling his nose fill with burning water. His body lurched and bounced until the current suddenly slowed as the river met the runoff from the rice paddies. Steady again but needing air, he blew slow bubbles with his nose and tried to sit up. His shoulders held flat to the ground. The surface was so close he could break the water with his fingertips. His nose and mouth, however, might as well have been as far away from breathable oxygen as was the moon. With a wrenching sensation in his gut, Gerald realized he couldn't budge. Not in the slightest. He was stuck underwater on the mucky bottom of the trench. *Laser diggers don't float,* he remembered Lina saying.

Gerald panicked and whipped his body from shoulder-to-shoulder. He clumsily scratched and fumbled underwater at the buckles around his chest. His legs kicked up-and-down as he tried to break free from the harnesses locked around his limbs. There was no more air. He needed air. The interconnected leg and shoulder harnesses wouldn't let go. Gerald was drowning.

A giant metal claw splashed through the water jabbing long curved talons into the muddy trench around Gerald's body. He heard himself grunt for air as he desperately tried not to breathe. He stopped thrashing when the claw squeezed its heavy metal fingers around him. With a back bending jerk, Gerald lifted free of the water on a bed of muck and detritus. The world tilted and he landed on the ridge. Water rushed away into the trench. Gerald sucked in ragged breaths and coughed until the sensation of drowning lessened. AJ was by his side now, picking him up out of the pile of mud and standing him upright. "No lying down on the job," AJ yelled, smiling.

"What the fuck," Gerald exclaimed, "happened?"

"We finished the trench!" The roaring wind made AJ's voice sound far away. "Lina saved your ass."

Gerald looked up at Lina sitting on top of a tractor called a scorpion crawler. The crane extended up and over the driver like a stinger, which is how it earned its name. Triple smoke stacks coughed black exhaust into the air. Lina, obscured by the downpour, smiled and waved at Gerald. He waved back. She nodded once and pulled the grappler claw over the machine's center of gravity. She threw a big stick forward locking the claw in place. She shifted other sticks and slammed her foot down on giant pedals to steer triangular tank treads through the deep mud. She drove off following the trench back to the rice paddy field where two flying transports careened dangerously close to each other a dozen meters off the ground.

Despite being far away from Gerald, he could see Sammy piloting the bigger transport and waving frenetically at Kyle who piloted the smaller one. Their voices were lost to the crackling thunder and wind. Behind them, hundred story funnel clouds gathered in the distance. If they didn't manage to put the weather sentries up around the paddies, the cyclones would wreak havoc across the fields and maybe hurt the workers still digging trenches from the two fields to the river. "Take the lasers off!" Gerald yelled to AJ. "We can help!"

AJ looked at him puzzled.

"We can reach them before Lina does. Just leave the wands." Gerald started detaching his laser wand from the interconnected top and bottom harnesses. He then showed AJ the latches to do the same. They uncoupled the laser pack, shovel, and other rigging from his shoulders and left a pile of equipment on the ground.

"Watch!" Gerald yelled, bending his knees until he was almost sitting on his heels. He pushed with the help of the leg harness and leapt straight into the air. He cleared AJ's head and hung in the air as if his body defied gravity. He landed hard creating two deep impact holes where his metal boots dug into the mud. He stepped out of the holes and smiled.

AJ smiled back and jumped. He then launched himself forward and landed nearly five meters from where Gerald stood. Gerald leapt and landed five meters past AJ.

"It's on!" AJ yelled, and took off running in great, awkward, leaps and bounds towards the rice paddies where Sammy and Kyle's transports continued to struggle with their cranes.

Several freshly dug trenches spread from the two rice fields in a star pattern. When the boys reached the first trench, they leapt above each other with childish *whoops!* of glee. They hurdled the next trench with precision and kept running. On the last jump, the wind caught Gerald like a sail, lifting him so high he started windmilling his arms. He regained his balance in midair and landed on a tiny spit of ground between the two rice fields. He felt no jolt as his leg harness took all of the impact. AJ tumbled into a roll when he landed and then shot back up laughing with blood dripping from his nose. The trick to maintaining balance, Gerald knew from his night visions of Skylar and Abe, was letting your leg muscles relax. "Let the machine do the work!" Gerald yelled.

AJ gave a thumbs up and took off again. Gerald jumped after him with exhilaration knowing this moment of inhuman speed was real. Gerald was euphoric as the icy rain pelted his cheeks. He guessed by the timbre of his friend's laugh, AJ felt the same.

The whispers in Gerald's head rose loud and then fell back away. *Euphoria? Elation? Laughter?* the locust suddenly yelled in his mind, *Near death experiences do that to testosterone crazed tweaks! Not so special killing yourself! Leaving me here.* Gerald almost stumbled at the intensity of the locust's simulated anger, but he recovered as the familiar voice of his sister continued: *Think Gerald! Think! Look at those twisters. Storms kill us dead!* Gerald was confused hearing her words in his mind after so many days of silence, but he recognized the locust was right. He almost drown a few minutes ago. Now he was running like an enforcer across fields of rice to help some fanatical "gardeners" protect their silly, useless crop from a freedom storm bigger than he had ever seen.

The last weather sentry slipped out of the claw on Kyle's crane and fell to its side. The shift in weight snapped the nose of Kyle's transport upwards like a kite caught in a sudden gust.

AJ shouted a challenge to the storm either not seeing or not understanding Kyle's flier was about to crash. His friend was drunk on adrenalin, grinning like a witless fool. *Why are we doing this, again?* Gerald asked himself, silently. *The FAC provides rice. What's the point?* Lightning struck a nearby tree, and then a hailstone bigger than a fist punched down on Gerald's shoulder harness knocking him to his knees. He pitched into a roll before his mechanized legs kicked him into a cartwheel over a crevice that suddenly appeared before him. Upside down he noticed the rice fields heaving up like drivable station platforms debarking. One of the fields tilted strangely and then slid down the hill towards the river. Gerald landed on his feet and kept running.

Dirt holes exploded open all around him. Gerald covered his head.

"Hail!" AJ yelled, landing beside Gerald. "Need Kyle's sentry up to save the crops!"

Gerald looked at the dent in the connecting bars protecting his right arm. He could hardly breathe, and then he saw AJ's eyes go wide with surprise or shock.

Gerald instinctively jumped to get away from whatever AJ saw coming. He pivoted in mid-air and looked towards the unmistakable sound of metal scraping against metal. Secondary pops, cracks, and explosions concussed Gerald like canon fire until his boots bit into the ground and he saw what caused the noise.

Kyle's flier was impaled on the crane affixed to Sammy's equipment deck. Heavy machinery bucked against invisible energy straps as the two transport ships locked together in a slow spin twenty meters above the ground. Below them, Lina sat on top of her scorpion tractor looking skyward and slamming stick controls to pull the last weather sentry into the correct position. She finished just as Sammy's ship twisted sideways causing Kyle's transport to flip upside down.

Gerald bounded towards the slow-motion crash as Sammy's wing carved a gully towards Lina. The transports jetted and revved erratically until Sammy's engine burst into flames and Kyle's flier heaved like a sinking boat trailing white smoke billowing in columns. Lina tried to back away and Gerald slowed his approach too awe-stricken by the dance of destruction occurring before him to make a smart decision about what to do next. In his periphery, he saw AJ leap ahead.

The crane on Sammy's flier tore loose and collapsed, snapping the force bands on Kyle's equipment deck. Heavy machinery rained from the sky smashing the scorpion and cratering the earth. Gerald jumped towards Lina but somehow he didn't move. He was chest-deep in watery muck that sucked at his body like glue. Not understanding, he struggled forward and sank deeper like an animal caught in a tar pit. "Lina!" he yelled.

She heard him and turned her head. Their eyes locked. She gave him a trembling smile and held up her tiny hand as if telling him to stay put as hunks of metal and other debris bounced around her. She unclasped her safety buckle and tried to escape, but the world lurched into motion and Lina slid off her tractor which tipped.

Lina caught the side-rail near her chair with one hand and yelped as Kyle's transport shuddered above her. She dropped three more rungs to dodge stray bars twanging off the deck of her crawler, and then everything stopped.

For the second time, Kyle's transport was impaled on a crane. This time it was pierced through and tangled up in the grappling claw of the scorpion. When nothing happened for many seconds, Kyle started to laugh. He dangled unhurt by two straps still attached to the upside down pilot seat.

An eerie green silence reigned for a long moment as the weather sentries blinked around them. Outside the force shield, the giant twisters washed around the rice paddies. Kyle shouted and pumped his fists. He kicked his legs as if the straps were a swing. Lina looked up at Kyle and then climbed the ladder until she was once again seated in her scorpion's high backed chair. "There!" she yelled, smiling down at Gerald. "All the sentries working… piece of cake."

Gerald grinned and then screamed.

A hole opened, and into the earth she dropped.

Chapter 19

Earth Spirit

Watching Lina disappear into the ground triggered something primal inside Gerald. He launched himself out of the mucky pit he had fallen into, and leapt to where the ground had swallowed Lina's tractor and Kyle's transport. The wind was so strong at the crevice's edge, Gerald barely kept his balance as he leaned precariously over. It wasn't just a crevice, he realized. It was a chasm so deep, he could see nothing but blackness below.

Gerald searched the darkness until he felt AJ's hand on his back. "Earthquake," AJ said, simply. "Look around."

Gerald turned to see islands of viny vegetation poke out of the rice paddy fields like mesas between them and the workers climbing out of their trenches. The first rice field had stopped floating downhill and Jeremy Nobel piloted its artificial tray back up to where the weather sentries could protect it better. If another earthquake struck, it wouldn't matter what Jeremy did to protect the crops, mini-weather sentries were useless against unstable ground.

Mr. Nobel, Uncle Luke, and at least a dozen others came running from opposite directions. Some of them stopped because cracks in the ground barred their way to the crevice. The ground continued to shake some, but Gerald and AJ held steady on the crevice's edge because their boots sank deep into the dirt to keep them upright.

Many of the freshly dug trenches collapsed behind the people climbing out. Water flooded back into the fields creating squiggling rivers and streams all the way to where they stood. Puddles grew quickly into lakes and then flowed off the chasm's edge. If she was down there, he thought, she was probably dead. Somewhere in the back of his mind, he knew Kyle was down there too, but he didn't care about Kyle. "Lina!" he yelled.

Freedom storms are dangerous, he heard himself think. *Or is it the locust talking again?* At the moment, he couldn't tell. His mind was filling with confusion, fear, and other memories of being afraid. He saw his mother propped up broken against the wall outside of the family's simulation pod. He remembered the smell of singed hair and the sound of walls crackling like paper. He remembered when the first bullies at the Academy started beating him up. He remembered when the first Prefect whipped him with a punishment rod for not speaking. He remembered AJ saving him from some of that. He remembered Lizzy—the real Lizzy—crying his name. He remembered Lina's scream.

Lina's alive Gerald. So is Kyle.

"How do you know?"

I see everyone, Gerald. Wherever they are, I can be. She tells me where and how far away to go. Lina's stuck in a puddle at the bottom! The water's rising.

"How deep is it?" he yelled.

"I don't know!" AJ yelled back. "Gerald! I think she's gone."

"She's alive." *Thirty meters down.* "Thirty meters down."

Jump, Gerald.

Gerald shook his head. "Show me!"

The scribeosphere came alive in Gerald's pocket and shot skyward. It buzzed around him and AJ's head like a fly before settling at the height of Gerald's eyes.

"Where'd that come from?" AJ asked. "Is it talking to you? Is the Muse talking to you now? From that? Is that how you took out the Eye?"

"I carry it everywhere," Gerald said. "For times like this." *To protect you from the Blackstars and ROLIES,* he thought. *To help me be brave.*

"Can it help?"

"Watch!"

The scribeosphere shot into the dark hole and flashed into a blazing ball of light so they could see. A long way down—thirty meters, he guessed—was Kyle's flier resting on top of the bent stinger crane of Lina's scorpion. With relief, Gerald saw her hand waving.

Jump, Gerald! Now!

So he jumped.

Thirty meters was a long way down even with his legs inside the exoskeleton of the leg harness. Gerald bit his tongue as a splash of water shot over his head. His heart raced thinking diggers don't float. Fortunately, the water was not deep. Unfortunately, his laser harnesses didn't have auto-chem injectors like an enforcer uniform to numb the icy pain in his feet and knees. He spit out blood and looked around.

"Lina!" he called, happy to see he didn't land on her.

She sat sideways across the seat of the high backed chair. Her shoulder was pinned from above by a bent steel bar. She was at the absolute bottom of the chasm and the bubbling water had risen above her hips. It splashed inches higher in the time it took Gerald to process what he saw. The place was flooding. She watched him approach, her eyes unmoving and so white in the darkness. He struggled to pull his feet out of the muck making loud sucking sounds as he moved. Lina laughed a little too hysterically for Gerald's comfort. "Are you okay?" he asked, taking her hand in his. Her skin was clammy and cold.

"The clutch-brake pinned me to the seat," she said, a little breathlessly.

The scribeosphere buzzed by to focus the light more directly on her. He grabbed the steel bar trapping her with both hands. He used the digger's legs and arms to bend it upward. The metal squeaked and resisted but after a moment, she was free.

"C'mon," he said. "Let's get you out of here."

She laughed again like a tiny bird trilling. "That's not the clutch-brake," she said, dropping her gaze to the seat.

Without Gerald commanding it to do so, the scribeosphere spotlighted her lap. Two more rods crisscrossed like a pretzel over her pelvic area. The longer of the two rods dug deeply into her stomach. He didn't see blood, but he now knew why she sounded so out of breath and weird. "Oh," he said, unhelpfully, as he studied the two twisted pieces of metal.

He heard a human sound from above and looked up to see Kyle, still tied to his pilot's chair by those straps. He was upside down. "Oh," Gerald said again.

Lina laughed. This time the sound was laced with fear and shock as the water suddenly surged past her waist and chest to her neck. The chasm was filling. Kyle groaned and coughed.

Gerald looked up and down between Kyle and Lina. He then looked at his wet hands, flexing until the finger joints squinch closed. "I think I'm strong enough with these to pull you out," he said to Lina. "But I can bend only one clutch-brake at a time… it's going to hurt I think. Hurt a lot."

The water splashed to her chin and wet her lips. She shuddered before taking a deep breath. "Okay," she said. "Do it."

Gerald felt his body shudder as she squealed like a caught rabbit. It sounded like Lizzy screaming when the power cable flicked her across the room. Tears coursed down Gerald's face as he pulled the second rod off her. She slid off the chair and into Gerald's arms.

Gerald looked up, knowing he wouldn't be able to save Kyle too, but he knew who could.

"AJ!" he yelled. "Jump!"

AJ came crashing down a little ways from where Gerald landed. Using the mechanized arms and legs in ways no engineer could have anticipated, AJ climbed up to Kyle and broke him free. With Kyle across his shoulders, he leapt to the chasm wall sticking into it like a dart. He then dug and kicked handholds into its side, creating a ladder that Gerald could follow up as he carried Lina to safety. The scribeosphere led the rescue with its light, calling out silently to Gerald if any of the hand or footholds were too loose to use. Once, he had to re-direct AJ to a different path to better support AJ and Kyle's weight. AJ changed his path as directed without asking questions. Gerald suspected AJ trusted Gerald's Muse more than Gerald did. In his mind, the locust was still too unpredictable to trust but if they made it out alive because of it, he might not reset its code.

Like to see you try, the locust said in Lizzy's voice.

Stop that, he thought, wishing the locust really was his sister, so he could tell on her.

I'd bite you again, she said.

Gerald grinned through what he told himself were tears of exertion from climbing. If the locust's behavior really was modelled after Lizzy, Gerald considered, it might be what the OPC needed. Nobody would get away with anything if a seven year old was always watching.

AJ reached the top first and lay Kyle on the ground who gasped as if he had suffered broken bones. Thick shelled emergency drones swept in and pushed AJ aside. They shot Kyle with a sedative beam and his body went suddenly limp. Mr. Nobel was the one who met Gerald at the top. The man's giant hand grabbed the back of his shoulder harness and pulled him and Lina up over the edge. As soon as Gerald's feet touched, Mr. Nobel released Gerald's harness and cradled his daughter out of his arms.

Mr. Nobel carried Lina several steps away. Gerald didn't want to let her go yet, so he walked after her father until Uncle Luke's hand came down on his shoulder. "Give 'em a moment, son. John don't like to show emotion in front of the crew."

Gerald turned to face the old man and looked into his bright, green eyes. "She fell in," Gerald said, dumbly. "I got her out."

Uncle Luke nodded.

"She's a great girl."

Uncle Luke's face was inscrutable behind his scruffy gray facial hair. Gerald turned away. *She's a great girl?* he chastised himself, silently. She was being attended to by emergency drones and looked like a drowned rat in her dad's arms… but she's great. *What's wrong with me?*

Within twenty minutes the work crews had gathered around Mr. Nobel, Uncle Luke, and the other supers. Lina and Kyle were inside emergency hovercrafts with their hatches shut. Behind the hovercrafts, tails of more tornados twisted together like octopus tentacles crawling over the invisible dome protecting the fields. Gerald felt the vibrations of the storm in his chest. He knew the weather sentries were reaching their limit as fine mists formed like fog over the fields.

Sammy Nobel who had emerged from the crash without a scratch had told him the quake should have never happened. "Quakes outside Tremor-sol ain't right! The leaves fall; the ground freezes; the quakes happen. It's been that way since Day One!" Sammy Nobel was angry and told Gerald to mark his words, "Something ain't right." He then punched Gerald in the arm in thanks for saving his sister.

Shortly after Sammy's tirade, AJ found him and said they needed to talk. "About what?" Gerald asked.

"The Blackstars. They can't come."

Gerald looked skyward. "Why not?"

AJ looked around impatiently. He had taken off his gear and looked cleaned up as if he had stepped out of the weather bubble into the rain to wash up. "Get your stuff off and I'll show you. Big John said no work the rest of the day. We got to go."

"What about Sally?"

"She's going with the rest of the Nobels to the big shelter at Dusty Gulch. Ma's going to pick her up."

"Sally's okay with that? I mean, after last night?"

"We'll be gone before she finds out," AJ said, smiling.

Gerald shrugged and then walked away from the crowd to the harness racks by the shed. He shrugged all the heavy pieces of equipment off his body feeling a hundred new aches and pains. He considered walking out of the bubble to wash the laser digging equipment but the weather, frankly, scared him. The storm was right on top of them throwing hail, wind, and even lightning at the barrier. Aftershocks still shook the ground. Sammy was right, freedom storms were not acting right. They were jumbling altogether out-of-season. Gerald grabbed a hose from the shed and cleaned the equipment in the methodical way he was taught by Skylar's dad in the night visions he experienced so long ago. Those diggers were never as dirty as the ones he cleaned today.

When he finished, Gerald turned to look at the weather sentries blinking silently at the corners of the two fields. He stared at the impossible mix of storms whipping above them and wondered why these people needed rice for the winter. He thought about the protests. He pictured Brandy in the green sari and remembered her with AJ. Those were her weather sentries he helped install. *Who am I working for?*

"Gerald Goodstone," a deep voice said behind him.

Gerald spun.

"Angie says your middle name's Lee. I knew a Lee once. Good fella."

Gerald's reply caught behind his tongue when he saw Mr. Nobel standing by himself. Despite being used to AJ-sized people, Mr. Nobel's meaty forearm still caught Gerald by surprise. He studied the web of jagged scars covering the flank of muscle between Big John's wrist and elbow. Big John had lifted Gerald by the shoulder harness out of the crevice with one hand while Gerald carried the man's daughter... *could AJ do that?* He wasn't certain.

"Good work today," Mr. Nobel said, leaning his arm against the rack which made the harnesses swing. "Yesterday too, 'cording to Lina."

"Uh, thank you, sir."

The big man looked suddenly uncomfortable and shifted position. "Seems I owe you something."

"No sir, Mr. Nobel."

"Call me John."

Gerald shook his head slightly.

"Big John if you'd rather. Some of the boys do that. Makes them comfortable around me. Not sure why."

"Did I hang the equipment wrong, Mr. Nobel?"

"No," he said, pouring over Gerald's harnesses with a practiced eye and nodding. "Equipment's hung like a pro. Rare attention to detail in a green. Though you ain't no green now are you?" He shook his head. "Don't recon I know what you are—"

"Excuse me, sir?"

"Angie says you're special."

"Not me, sir."

"Avelina says you're special too."

"She took a terrible fall, sir. Maybe she hit her head."

"So I owe you something, and that's what I came here to say. Never forget what you did for me with Avelina. She's a handful but she's my handful. Can't abide empty hands. They say the devil's in 'em. See what I'm saying?"

Gerald shook his head. "Not really, sir."

"I have full hands because of you," he said. "Anything you need… my crews, my children. I'll leave it at that." Mr. Nobel nodded in satisfaction and then took several slow steps away without another word.

"Uh, Mr. Nobel?"

Mr. Nobel paused, his eyes focused on his work crews queuing up behind three transports on the other side of the rice paddies. Gerald noticed the rice plants between here and there were still green and healthy. It felt good knowing they saved those plants. "Tell Lina thanks for me… I mean, she saved my life first…. She's a great girl. I mean—" Gerald winced as he realized he'd said it again. There really was something wrong with him.

Big John turned back to Gerald and smiled. Mrs. O'Sullivan was right. His smile was a good one: wide and genuine as if his whole body relaxed into that one expression. "She is at that, Gerald Lee

Goodstone," he said. "But her name's Avelina. No shortcuts. It's what her mother named her, and it's who she is. Means Earth Spirit."

"Does it really?"

"Nah but it should."

"Right, Mr. Nobel. Avelina."

Mr. Nobel nodded and walked away.

As he watched him go, Gerald thought he heard the locust speak: *Trust him,* it said. *She trusts him.*

Chapter 20

Followers of Rose

When Gerald reached the transport queues on the other side of the fields, he saw Sally standing in line. She smiled and gave him a hug. "You two took off so fast after the river broke. I lost you."

"Almost drowned," Gerald said.

She nodded. "I know. Everybody's talking about it."

"They are?"

"You're the green who saved Big John's kid after she saved you. They're all very impressed."

"I guess," he said.

Sally smiled. "You better go." She nodded across to AJ who sat inside the jumper they had arrived in earlier that morning. "I'm taking the queue to Dusty's. They have showers there, and Mrs. Oh's picking me up."

"Why not come with?"

She shrugged, irritated. "Guy stuff, AJ says. Whatever, it's fine."

AJ yelled Gerald's name and waved his arms. Gerald looked sheepishly between his two friends. "Well, I'll tell you all about it… whatever it is," he said.

Sally laughed. "You do that and I'll make it worth your while."

"How?"

"You let me figure that out. I don't like being left out. Man's got no manners."

Gerald agreed and then jogged to AJ's jumper. "How'd you get this here?" he asked when he arrived.

AJ shrugged. "It's just a storm, Gerald. I kept low to the ground."

Gerald estimated the Nobels' landing field was more than two kilometers away. "You ran there?" he asked, noticing the pool of water in the bottom of the jumper. "Why not go to Dusty's like everyone else?"

"No time," AJ said. "It's life-or-death… seriously."

Big ape's telling the truth, the locust said. *Go with him!*

Stop telling me what to do, he thought as hotly as he could. His scribeosphere shook violently in his pocket. *She's waiting, Gerald! Go, please. She needs you. You need her.*

Gerald tapped his earring with his fingers but didn't threaten to remove his mother's gem. Instead, he did as he was told and climbed into the jumper. The dome was barely shut before AJ launched straight into the black afternoon sky.

By the time AJ landed, Gerald had added the contents of his stomach to the water sloshing around the floor of the jumper. The storm wasn't as bad at the southern edge of AJ's ranch, but the creek had swollen into foaming rapids.

"This way," AJ said as he led Gerald to the edge of the river. They walked in the slowing rain for another ten minutes before they reached the side of the hill marking the edge of AJ's property and the start of the Great North Swamp. Gerald had never walked to this corner of the ranch before so the mine they found surprised him. It was the kind of place AJ would have taken Gerald to play when they were kids. He looked at the six wide boards blocking the adit into the hillside.

Dozens of signs warned of safety hazards. None of them flashed like SLYscape spheres would have which meant the mine was old. The block lettering was faded but still legible:

Mine Danger Shaft!

Keep Out!

Think this is a playground? Think again.

Stay Out. Stay Alive!

"That's a lot of warnings," Gerald observed.

"Sure is," AJ said. "Makes you wonder what's inside."

Gerald brushed the water out of his eyes. The sun peeked over the swampy marshes that the river poured into. "Probably something dangerous," he said.

AJ shook his head. "Let's find out."

Gerald imagined AJ would break the boards loose with his hands, but instead he gently tapped the screw heads on the warning planks. With an audible click, the signs swept outward on hinges like a door. "The boards are fake. It's a Flexiforce simulation sVid sprayed on a regular old door with a combination lock."

Gerald stood dumfounded as a salty breeze rushed out of the passage smelling like ocean. He felt suddenly nervous as his hair fluttered back. "The air smells fresh," he said, sniffing. "Not stale."

"Got your clothes rigged with lights?"

Gerald shook his head. "No but I could light up the scribeosphere and send it in."

AJ shook his head. "No need," he said, smiling. "We got juice."

He reached inside the dark opening and tapped another combination. Audible pops echoed deep inside the shaft as Gerald watched flickering lights flood toward them like a luminescent geyser erupting.

A glittering salt road appeared before them as the lights buzzed with electricity and hummed like bees in a hive. "Step into our lair," AJ said. "This is how we stop the Blackstars. Without them to take the lead, the ROLIES won't be so hard to distract."

Gerald stared dubiously but didn't say a word. He followed AJ into the shaft and watched the tunnel grow larger as they progressed deeper. Soon the space extended so far in every direction that it was easy to believe the entire hillside was hollow. *A lot of work went into this,* Gerald thought, *a lot of manual work—no drones.* Gerald knew from night visions he'd experienced that modern mining drones left blackened, polished surfaces where they dug, not the jagged and broken rock he saw now. This was built by Pre-Zeros. "A World Union mine?" he asked.

"Salt mine," AJ said, leading him deeper. "No longer."

After descending another ten minutes deeper into the earth, Gerald's nervousness took a back seat to his curiosity. The mine shaft felt stable and ancient like a well-built tomb. Nothing lived or moved. There were no spider webs, rats or other critters you might expect in a cave. It was very clean. The air was fresh. The boys feet shuffled and stomped as they walked, but no salt dust rose to taint the air. The mine seemed sterile and surreal in much the same way as the enforcer patrol tunnels he experienced under Old New York. His thoughts drifted back to Abe in his conditioning chair, and he hoped for a moment the similarity between this tunnel and that one was merely coincidental.

They were descending, according to AJ, over three hundred meters deep to an equipment depot. Half-way to the bottom, AJ explained, there was a giant room like a warehouse for storing things meant for the depot. "The World Union took their equipment apart up there," AJ said, pointing with his thumbs towards the surface. "Then they'd reassemble it in the warehouse down there and then drive or carry it the rest of the way."

The salt road they walked, AJ explained, was atop beds that extended over a quarter million square kilometers under the Northern prefectures. "These tunnels, if you had the right maps, lead all the way back to New Detroit. Probably as far as Old New York."

"What about to the Peppers' farm?" Gerald asked, thinly. "I bet they go there too."

"I'm getting to that, Gerald," AJ paused their descent and said in a suddenly stressed voice. "I'm getting to it all."

AJ's eyes flashed and then he turned away.

Were those tears, Gerald saw?

"Just trust me, Gerald. You'll see."

Trust him, Gerald. You'll see, echoed the locust in Lizzy's voice.

Gerald was more than nervous now. He was afraid as he listened to the locust act like it knew what AJ was going to show him. He followed in silence as he thought about vWare and how the scribeosphere's control module was behaving like a human—a real human with thoughts and opinions of its own. He wondered if he was asleep. Could this—the mine, saving Lina, Lizzy's voice—be a night vision?

Don't be silly, the locust said. *You still hear the whispers.*

Gerald realized the locust was right. He didn't hear whispers when he experienced night visions. At this moment, his whispers were loud. *Then this is real,* he thought, feeling more resigned than surprised. *I'm in a secret mine AJ had hid from me.* "How long?" he blurted out, *have you been hiding things from me?* he finished, silently.

AJ kept up his pace and said, softly. "Soon, Gerald. Almost there."

Gerald wondered if AJ intentionally answered the question he asked and not the one he meant. He guessed he'd know soon enough and once he did, he'd tell Sally. He'd tell the Blackstars. Whoever asked, he'd be truthful and honest like he was brought up to be. He didn't like the feeling of being left in the dark. He was mad at AJ for keeping this place secret. He considered the FSA designation he wanted and the reason for it. *My family was taken away from me in secret.* AJ had secrets. Gerald hated secrets.

By the time they reached the warehouse level of the shaft, Gerald was tired. His feet hurt and his eyes felt twitchy from the strange silvery light reflecting off the surfaces of the tunnel. He was emotionally tired too. AJ was a gene demon and Gerald wanted to protect him from the FSA. Yet, he was also a liar and bent on preventing the Blackstars from doing their jobs. *A radical,* he remembered Sally saying. *Is that what you two are?* Gerald felt lightheaded. *…a citizen score just a hair better than a World Union spy.*

They arrived at a fork marked by a faded white sign that read, "Equipment Depot," with an arrow beneath it. The other branch was marked only by their current depth: "305 Meters." They walked for a few more minutes as he struggled to breathe and wondered if there was enough oxygen this far below the surface. He was about to ask when he bumped into AJ's back and fell down.

"We're here," AJ said.

"We're where?" Gerald asked, standing back up.

"The salt mine's equipment depot." AJ pointed into the massive dome-shaped chamber before them. "Inside is everything we need to stop them from coming to the ranch." He entered the chamber and swept his arms around in a big circle. "Can you believe it?"

Gerald entered and looked around. He struggled to process all he saw. There were vWare programming chairs, yottabyte tablets, family simulation pods, vehicles with rubber tires, and digging machines on scorpion tracks. In the corners were other things, sVid displays and desks that could seat a class of fifty students. The chamber was so large, Gerald could barely see the other side. "What's going on, Aje?" he asked. "I mean yotta-tabs? A classroom?" Gerald walked up to the octagon simulation pod and looked over at AJ. "This is like the one I had as a kid." He walked around the back of it and called, "Only it's been rigged with more power."

"You step in that pod and you flippin' disappear. It's as good as my Da's at the house. Like living in the SLYscape body-and-soul, a ghost in the machine."

"Like a conditioning chair?" Gerald asked as he returned to AJ.

AJ's expression sobered. "I suppose it's as good as those too." His eyes were wide and intense in the pale light of the cavernous room. "And those two—" AJ pointed to NextGen programming chairs with spider-like robotic arms sticking out of the simulation dome on top. The cockpit of the things sat several meters high on top of rotating platforms consisting of several cylindrical discs. "Not even my Da has one. We got two."

"What do you mean, we?"

AJ strolled over to the platform and reached up to pat the coding cage erected around the programming chair. "Hop in," he said.

Hop in, Gerald! the locust said. *Be brave!*

Feeling anything but brave, Gerald climbed up several oval plates leading to the bucket chair in the programming cage. On top of the cage, robotic arms jutted in every direction like swing-arm cranes. Gerald decided they were just sVid sprayers until he recognized two arms capable of extending the simulation dome to the environment around the chair. *That's new,* he thought, as he took a moment to admire the vWare control plates inside the coding cage. "Regular people don't have these," he said as he slipped his hands and feet into the shimmering purple light pockets radiating up from the plates. He moved his shoulders and stretched his back straight against the chair. He took a breath and started to move with slow precision. His fingers tapped out commands more quickly as he got familiar with the machine while his feet kept rhythmic time as if he was playing a musical instrument.

The programming chair beeped and the sVid spraying arms came alive with lights. The cage swiveled to face AJ so fast Gerald felt a little queasy. He pulled up the programming chair's credentials and heard a mechanical voice say: "No authentication required."

"Really, AJ?" he asked, seeing the empty holographic identification sphere hovering between them. "So this thing can do anything without a trace?"

"I know." AJ said. "The chair's tweaked up like a NextGen prototype. Totally off-scape. Not even a bio-check with facial recognition. As far as I can tell, the thing is as late as it gets but with none of the usual security—a pirate chair."

"How?" Gerald asked, confused. "How is it here, Aje? Why?"

"The chair?"

"This whole mine."

"The mine's always been here, brother. But I get you. All of this..." AJ paused to look skyward for the right words. "I thought this would be easier. Truth is—"

"You're Earth First," Gerald said, interrupting. "The overseers can't come because they'll find the mine. It belongs to Earth First. You, Lina, Brandy… everyone here is Earth First."

Gerald held his breath hoping to hear vehement denials.

AJ shook his head and sighed.

"I'm right?"

"Some of them are Justice for Kisme too," he said. "When Kisme died, it set 'em off. They're mad, Gerald. Really mad. But not me, not my parents. Just some of the Nobels and their crews."

"C'mon, Aje! Your Mom dropped us down in their 'gardens' as if she was a super… one of Big John's family. We saved their rice! She took Sally in…to what? Recruit her? Get the next FAC Aggie on their side?" Gerald laughed, not knowing if he was feeling anger or fear.

"Ma's not Earth First. She's… different. But the Nobels are the leaders of it. But not for long because they're fleeing the continent. They're running to the Glass Lands, Gerald."

"The Glass Lands? All the rice in the world won't help them there."

AJ pointed to the simulation dome's projection. "Look at the selection matrix, Gerald. There's a green tree somewhere. Select it."

Gerald moved his feet to step back through the control menus until he found the symbol AJ described. Shaking his head, he looked at AJ wanting to punch him, but instead he pulled the green tree towards his chest. "You can't believe in the Glass Lands, Aje! We saw the same—"

Gerald was somewhere else, a simulated somewhere that sounded and smelled real. All the programming chair's controls were available and Gerald reached out to reduce the sensory input. It was too much until he felt his bare feet touch hot, dry earth. Tall grass tickled his toes, ankles, and calves. The smell of flowers was so completely warm and full in his nose, he could have been lounging in the oxygen rich humidity of a green house. He liked it and increased the sensory input to maximum. The simulated world exploded into a riot of color and sound around him.

He was the actor in the simulation. He was the one running on bare feet. He held a spear in his hand. He smiled and yelled at the four-legged animals he tirelessly chased. When they stampeded off, he felt himself slowly lift into the sky. His feet were now attached to a small metallic disc that floated slowly over the animals and trees below. Gerald experienced hours on the disc watching the wildlife and listening to the sounds the animals made. Feet padded across the delta, chasing, eluding, and eating each other. There was a rhythm to it all—their teeth snapping, devouring, near-misses, and then the mewling of animals just born. Birds filled the sky. Fish flipped in and out of the water as they inched up the rapids passing just meters below Gerald's flying disc. The silty loam around the river mouth was colored like rust by a polka-dotted mixture of red clay and white sand. A bright sun blazed down. It was so hot. And then the river flowed into a vast ocean.

He watched leviathan shadows move below the surface of the ocean for more hours until he came to a beach. His flying disc lost power and drifted down into the cool, salty waves. His toes dug into spongy sand beneath the rolling water crashing into his bare chest. He reached out and splashed and the simulation flickered. A forest suddenly sprang up where the ocean had been. He was hot and tired with burning scratches all over his skin. Animals chased him, their hooves pounding through the trees. A predator was behind the hooved animals. He heard a growl, a screech. Something heavy dropped on top of him before he could convince his legs to move. He fell face down and the simulation disappeared back to black.

For a long moment, Gerald sat in the chair breathing hard—scared. "Okay," he said, blinking his eyes to focus on AJ behind the identification sphere. "Sweet sim. Why'd you show it to me?"

"Not a sim, Gerald. That's the Glass Lands. Little snippets from y-space recordings. They're all out there, sitting in the piratesphere, waiting for people to find them. The Glass Lands is alive with life and it's not under FSA control."

"You of all people know that's not true, Aje! Humphrey showed us live satellite surveillance. There's nothing there!"

"I know what Humpty taught us, and maybe he thinks it's true. But while the sanctioned spheres have been telling us one thing, the piratesphere's been showing us the truth about the Glass Lands. People like Paisley have authenticated the sVids you just experienced. Freelanders have been lied to, Gerald. We've all been lied to by the powerlords running our nation. What you just saw is real."

Gerald shook his head. "I don't believe it."

"Earth First believes it. Justice for Kisme believes it. They say there's a community of people already waiting for us. The Blackstars can't come because they'll find out who the Nobels are. Who we are. Like you said, they're good at their jobs. Hundreds of people… Lina, Big John… my parents will be wiped."

"Are you out of your mind?"

"I know how it sounds," AJ said, frustrated.

"The fuck you do!"

AJ rubbed his eyes and then pulled his fingers through his long blond hair as if trying to rip it out. "My family isn't Earth First or Justice for Kisme, Gerald. We are but we're not."

"What does that mean?"

"We're spies, Gerald. Followers of Rose."

Gerald remembered Mr. Heller's drunken rant about the faithful. They're everywhere. He has to pick a side. "You're zealots?" Gerald yelled. "Like the guy in the tube?"

"No! Kind of, but I'm done with the High Prelate and his games. I'm throwing my future in with Brandy. I think Ma will come with… and if she comes, Da will follow. They'd give their lives for Preston Rose. But I think they'd give him up… for me."

Gerald's mouth hung open as he tried to form words. "What about Sally? Didn't you and her… aren't you two together?"

"Yeah but she'd never come."

There were no words. Gerald threw his feet and hands forward on the control plates. The cockpit swiveled in angry circles as the robotic arms sVid sprayed colors all over the equipment depot. AJ jumped back from the chair barely dodging one of its arms as the machine spun.

He ducked under another arm and then yelled, "C'mon, Gerald. Stop!"

Gerald switched directions, and then AJ grabbed the sVid spraying arm and leapt up the moving machine as if he still had a laser harness on. He swung inside and slapped the power off. The chair sighed letting pressure out of the platforms it swiveled on. It gently sunk back down to the ground.

He's a gene demon, Gerald thought. *A gene demon zealot!* "Your citizen score…"

"I'm not World Union if that's what you think. I'm just not Freeland Nation, exactly."

"The Designation Exam was right?"

"Have you ever wondered how I got into the Academy for Gifted Students, Gerald? Am I that good at vWare? Am I that smart?"

"You're strong, good with military stuff."

"Father Rose placed me into your classes. I knew all about you before I went. You were my mission, Gerald, to protect with my life if necessary."

"You were twelve!"

"I was conditioned to fight for you, protect you. I had no choice, really. The Black Eye reminded me of how little choice you have when you're being conditioned. Every year, at winter break, they'd condition me again, upgrade my skills. Make me a better protector. You were my mission and I couldn't fail, but eventually… I didn't see you as a mission. You were just my friend. You are my best friend and Rose wants me to spy on you… tell him things."

"Tell him what things?"

AJ climbed out of the programming chair. "Tell him things about your Muse—what you did today. What you did to the Black Eye. Tell him things like that. Ma says I need to tell Rose everything for your own protection."

"Why do I need protection?"

"You're special."

Gerald groaned. "Right. Mr. Nobel said that."

Not so special, Gerald. She's special.

Gerald grimaced at the locust's interruption. *Thank you,* he thought, sarcastically.

AJ looked puzzled as if wondering why Gerald was grinning. "Look. I owe you a better explanation than this but I need you right now to trust me. It's the only way to stop what's going to happen."

"And what's going to happen?" Gerald asked, too stunned by what he had heard to think. He wished he didn't hear the whispers. If the whispers were silent, this could have all been a night vision. What AJ said wouldn't be real. But the whispers were loud in his ears—cackling.

"Those Blackstars," AJ continued, "They're dead or will be soon. If they got ROLIES with them… they're dead too."

Gerald shook his head, so confused. "Is there enough oxygen down here, Aje? I think I'm getting sick."

"Lots of oxygen, Gerald. You're hearing me straight. No lies. I did somethin' I can't take back. It's worse than that, really—"

Much worse, Gerald, the locust said. *Bad AJ. Big ape's been not good at all.*

"I traded Paisley the perks from the fight in exchange for him hiring some people."

"What people?"

"Guys in the piratesphere who know some guys. Bad people."

"What have you done, AJ?"

AJ shook his head. "I made a mistake. All I could think of was the Nobels being arrested. Ma and Da being wiped… forgetting who I am. Brandy. If the Blackstars saw, they'd have found her."

"She's hiding in the tunnels under their farm—"

AJ nodded. "She's safe but the Blackstars aren't. Paisley's going to kill them."

Chapter 21

Black Wolf

In addition to being a gene demon, Gerald realized now, his best friend was a radical, a zealot, a spy, and a soon-to-be accessory to murder. He was all these things unless Gerald could break into the Freeland Work Authority and erase the Blackstar's orders to investigate the O'Sullivans. He would have to do exactly what he told AJ he couldn't. He'd have to hack into the FSA domain just like AJ had wanted him to do back on the tube.

"Just turn their transports around," AJ had said. "Give me time to call off Paisley's thugs. I'll have to make another deal, but anything's better than murder. I didn't know that's what he'd do." *What a thin, stupid plan,* Gerald thought, as he switched the programming chair to interactive. *And why am I helping him? After all the secrets and lies?* He shook his head as the room went dark and his five senses disappeared into the ephemeral world of the SLYscape programming sphere. *Because I have to.*

The virtual universe of the SLYscape was suddenly all around him. He was immersed. Only he wasn't cruising, he was driving like a vWare controller. Complex maneuvers and tricks were at his fingertips done with gestures and vWare blocks of code. He could create whole data spheres in moments just to better shape his m-sphere creation. From a programming chair like this one in the mine, he wasn't restricted to the one-step thoughts he had to spoon-feed the locust with his mind. People with moles, he imagined, felt this way all the time. Their eyes going up and white as they skimmed the surface of SLYscape for intangible rewards like babblesphere coupons and perks. They could order tangible products that would arrive by drone within twenty minutes or materialize instantaneously in their FAC providers. They could enjoy gossip that circulated and supported whatever it was they believed in. If they were fans of celebrities, they could request a sphere to experience what it was like to be that celebrity. It was called vReading and everyone did it. Except Gerald. He was not allowed the luxury of requesting vReading spheres from a molecular implant. He had to build them from scratch.

Symbols floated around Gerald's head until he selected one that looked like a compass carved from the ivory tusks of an extinct prezero elephant. Gerald had designed this compass. It was one of the first spheres he created after the fire. It gave Gerald the ability to experience the SLYscape as a vWare controller experienced it. It revealed the architecture of the SLYscape, the ribs of the ship needed to navigate the ocean of radiation that had drown the world on Day Zero. The radiation itself could not be experienced directly as Gerald knew, but it could be interpreted with the help of Sky and Light devices like the scribeosphere and programming chair he sat in. For most people, it was their moles that interpreted the radiation. He remembered how Sally liked to tease him because he couldn't vRead. *It's just a tiny pinch,* she had said. He wished now, he'd have explained how it was so much more.

Most Freelanders didn't know how vReading fulfilled their wants and needs so perfectly. If they had darker desires like some of the powerlords that were being protested against, they believed the SLYscape could generate those experiences secretly in the piratesphere. Nobody would know, they assumed, because their spheres were illegal and hidden. Except the SLYscape had to know. Somebody, a vWare controller working for the FSA or a hacker in the piratesphere, had to know. With enough perks and the right implants, people could pretend to be whomever they wanted and physically feel whatever they wished to feel. It was virtual reality, but their virtual worlds didn't just blossom out of thin air. People and their automated tools built the vReading spheres.

Sally liked to say Mama SLY was always watching but Mama SLY was not the SLYscape as she believed. Mama SLY was the moles in her blood. And virtual reality was only virtual until somebody experienced it. Then it was a memory, and the SLYscape used moles to record memories to y-space. It was the first lesson his dad had taught him. Y-space was a model of human brains connected to the SLYscape. It held the coordinates within the human tissue that could be safely written to and read from by molecular implants. Every vWare controller learned this and pulled information from those coordinates to build realistic SLYscape immersion spheres from people's actual memories. Every thought was a potential command. Every data sphere was a collection of those commands. Every vWare controller was a god in the machine, creating reality to order.

You, Gerald, he remembered his dad saying, *can be one of those gods.*

Nobody sees the vee like we see the vee, Paisley had said.

And it was true.

He touched the compass and ran his fingers along its warm ivory edges. He flipped it open like a prezero pocket watch. It felt as real in his hand as anything in slow-time. He tapped the face of the compass and felt the familiar tingle of the programming chair respond to his commands. A map of Gerald's creation flooded the simulation dome like a planetarium projection. Only instead of celestial bodies, his map showed SLYscape power sources.

He couldn't see all the sources, just the ones nearby like the ones coming from Iron City. As he had done with Paisley's tattoos, he studied the cluster of glowing shapes looking for familiar SLYscape landmarks. Almost nobody knew what Gerald knew. Each data sphere on the SLYscape correlated to slow-time coordinates in the real world. Neither his dad nor the Academy had taught Gerald about this connection. He assumed it at first, believing that if a cloud of RADcore radiation was the tapestry on which the SLYscape was painted, then every vWare structure, every virtual construct, had to exist somewhere in the real world radiation cloud.

As Sally had told Lina, radiation was in the soil. It was in the air. It was in people and their food. So Gerald theorized the power draw to the light, sky, and earth spectrums of radiation should be physically detectable. To test his theory, Gerald at eleven years old, created a vWare block of code to force local Academy devices to turn off and on in predictable patterns. He then sent the locust on a scavenger hunt across the SLYscape looking for those patterns in devices initiating power cycles. Once found, the locust built the power signatures into a holographic map of the Academy campus. The result was a tight-knit constellation of pale dots Gerald recognized and could follow like a street map of the physical world.

With the Academy campus mapped virtually, he commanded the locust to spread the power cycling vWare to all SLYscape devices in New Detroit. He mapped those holographically too. He automated the process and set the locust free to fill out the rest of the SLYscape map on its own. It had taken eight years and the map wasn't complete, but it was at least as good as Paisley's tattooed maps. Better considering Gerald's map included the coordinates on earth each SLYscape device drew its power from. The best part, Gerald believed, was his map would expand indefinitely until every device on the planet was accessible from a vWare programming chair like the one he sat in now.

Gerald reclined back in his programming chair to gaze upon his twinkling map of SLYscape power signatures. He could see quivering memory wells to y-space; weather sentries flush with sky radiation; glowing hash marks of light funneling into cities of simulation pods; and brown grasses swaying along transportation paths. But it was the blue lines Gerald followed from the vWare objects nearest him to the power sources he needed. He reminded himself his only goal was to turn the overseer transports around before they got shot down. As angry as he was at AJ for all his lies, Gerald couldn't imagine his friend wanting those killings on his conscience.

Gerald spotted the power sources belonging to Iron City. He zoomed in and found Miner's Platform not too far away. He followed the virtual landscape with his fingers until he reached his destination: the guarded gate to Checkpoint A. In the physical world, Checkpoint A was Freedom Square in Old New York. *Where Kisme was killed,* he thought. *Where enforcers lived in the tunnels beneath the streets.*

Checkpoint A was protected by automated Freeland Security Modules (FSMs). In Gerald's map, they were rendered as dogs patrolling the fence. Rovers is what the piratesphere hackers called them. They sniffed around the gate and pranced around with nervous energy as if anxious to bite. With slight downward pressure on the programming chair's left foot plate, Gerald entered the FSA built immersion sphere that protected the SLYscape footprint of the quad towers. With some trepidation, he watched many of the controls of his beautifully rendered map go dark and inactive. The FSA was in control of his simulation now, and his presence was immediately sensed by the FSMs. The dogs started to bark.

Nervous tension bubbled beneath the surface of Gerald's calm approach. He tried to ignore the emotional turmoil rumbling his gut, because he knew the feelings were the rovers doing. The FSMs flooded him with stress memories from y-space of being attacked by dogs and interrogated by ROLIES. There was no friendly face in the guard tower either, only a dark silhouette of a large man in black and yellow. One of the dogs snarled and rushed him. If it bit, Gerald would feel the pain and the programming chair would render him unconscious.

Gerald panicked—w*hy attack?* He hadn't done anything yet. The question hung in his mind for the length of time it took the rover to halve the distance to its prey—not long. Then realization dawned. Gerald pulled up his identification sphere—*empty*. All objects in the SLYscape had identifiers unless they were viruses, worms, or in Gerald's case, a prototype programming chair built by Rose-knew who. Gerald pumped his feet on the control plates feeling the purple pockets of energy respond to his input. He tapped out quick patterns with his hands and slapped the newly created object into the identification sphere. The dogs healed as a familiar face ballooned before them. They knew him now. He was no threat.

It was a trick Prefect Humphrey had shown him. You get by rovers by feeding them what they want. So Gerald gave them Mr. O'Sullivan's identification code. Unlike AJ, he hadn't played games in the O'Sullivan simulation room. He practiced cracking codes… Mr. O'Sullivan's ID was the first one he broke nearly two years prior. The gate opened and he stepped through without a care in the world. "Good dogs," he said, smiling.

He was inside the SLYscape's version of Freedom Square. The locust had shaped Freedom Square like a circle in Gerald's map. Each tower getting its own wedge of the pie. Clearly, Mr. O'Sullivan was only allowed to taste the piece belonging to the OPC. The buildings he was not allowed to enter sat behind imposing walls without entrances and looked similar to SLYcasted facades of their physical counterparts. The towers were not labeled either, because anybody inside Checkpoint A was supposed to know where they were going. Gerald did not. He floated in the middle trying to pick the tower belonging to the Freeland Work Authority. The rovers patrolling the square—or circle—began heading his way which gave him only a moment to decide. *There,* he thought.

With a flick of his wrist, Gerald tossed a vReading sphere of his design to the far edge of Freedom Square. It rolled into existence and then burst into several simulated shards of glass. The dogs went critters and rushed the vWare objects appearing in the forbidden zone between towers. The vReading sphere replicated itself and then exploded into more razor sharp pieces of glass. The rovers bit the objects until their simulated jowls bled. When it became apparent their teeth had no effect, stronger security defenses called scrubbers attacked the self-replicating shards.

In Gerald's map, the scrubber FSMs looked like beetles as they fountained up from beneath what would be the ground if Gerald had feet in this virtual world. With the beetles and rovers distracted, he rushed the wall of the Freeland Work Authority tower. A few rovers saw his sudden move and gave chase. He worked the vWare to empty the programming chair's identification sphere. Even if Mr. O'Sullivan had access to the FWA tower, any hacking done could be traced back to his ID. AJ's immediate problem might be solved but the Blackstars would still come to the ranch looking for AJ's dad. More rovers joined the chase, but Gerald had already hit the wall and disappeared inside it.

The other benefit of having no ID is that vWare structures like walls prevented objects from entering. With no ID, Gerald was not an object the wall could detect. Typical vWare controllers didn't build SLYscape walls that attacked like the FSM rovers and beetles attacked. So there were no algorithms in the wall structure that would search for changes within its own code. FSMs might come by and test the wall, but the wall itself was blind to what was inside it. Being careful to stay within the wall, Gerald moved quickly around the perimeter of the tower so the rovers could not track which way he went. With no scent to follow, they'd wander away.

Hackers took advantage of holes in relationship models. Now that Gerald was inside the wall of what he hoped was the FAC tower, he could move freely around its exterior looking for the data sphere controlling transport timetables. He couldn't exit the wall into any interior hallways because unlike walls, hallways were probably rigged with self-monitoring vWare that looked for intruders. He had to avoid doors too. He should be able to enter rooms though, because vWare controllers tended to recreate the familiar. If you got through the locks on the doors and the alarms in the hallways, you're likely authorized to be inside the room you're found in. Unless that room stored especially valuable things. Gerald hoped dispatch schedules were not valuable to the FWA.

Gerald followed the tower's virtual perimeter until he stood next to, according to his map, an especially large patch of brown grass. This grass patch was roughly rectangular like a room. Maybe, a dispatch center. He believed he was almost there, so he took a moment to relax inside the wall. He imagined what he might find on the other side, but his mind drifted to AJ's secrets. If Gerald was AJ's mission to protect, when exactly did Gerald become his friend? Were they friends? If they weren't, why was he risking his own freedom to save AJ? Gerald could have chosen to report AJ to the FSA. The FSA would have re-routed the Blackstars and caught whomever Paisley hired to take them out. Paisley would have been arrested, and the world would be safer for it. Like Sally, Gerald's designation would require playing by the rules. Of course, playing by the rules meant he couldn't help AJ.

Gerald realized something horrible. It wasn't just AJ lying. Mr. and Mrs. O'Sullivan had been lying too. He called up Mr. O'Sullivan's face with the ID code. His cheeks were framed by familiar, happy laugh lines. Mr. O'Sullivan liked to laugh but his eyes seemed darker to Gerald now, more sunken and strained. Was that Gerald's imagination? Or was that because Gerald didn't really know Mr. O'Sullivan? He sent his twelve year old son on a mission for the Followers of Rose. What kind of father does that? Maybe, Gerald considered, he should load Mr. O'Sullivan's ID back into his identification sphere and leave his virtual prints all over the place. It'd serve him right, but Gerald knew he couldn't. Mr. O'Sullivan was the closest thing to a dad he'd had since the fire. He remembered how Mr. O'Sullivan handed tools back and forth with AJ to fix the gliders. He watched him kiss Mrs. O'Sullivan, the woman who played so gently with Gerald's hair that first summer he arrived at the ranch. He couldn't report them. They were family.

He shut the identification sphere off and stepped through the wall into the brown patch of grass. The room was dark except for tiny red dots spaced evenly along the walls. He floated several steps forward searching for alarms. When he found none, he created a rudimentary body for himself to activate the lights. As his virtual body materialized, the lights responded to the new object in the room by flicking on. The dots, Gerald could see now, were eyes. Enforcer eyes. Twenty enforcers stood with their backs against the walls—their glowing red eyes blinking and staring out at Gerald.

Gerald backed away until he felt the hard surface of the wall behind him. His rudimentary body was an object the wall now recognized. He wasn't allowed to slip back through. Frantically, Gerald moved his hands and feet to force his body into the safety of the virtual wall. Then he noticed the enforcers weren't moving. He paused to watch the enforcers. He drew courage from the tingling purple pockets of energy that reminded him he was in a programming chair's coding cage. He wasn't really in this virtual room. He could end the interactive session now and return to the mine. He could've but he didn't. He stepped around the room. Once again, he was fully immersed and the tingling in his limbs was gone.

He jumped up to peer at the red dots inside their face shields. The dots were not eyes. They were the enforcers' connections to the SLYscape. According to Gerald's map, these uniforms represented the enforcers standing in tunnels beneath Freedom Square. The brown grass sprouting from this room didn't dispatch transports across the world but rather directed enforcers to crime scenes. He was in the FSA tower, not the FWA tower. He had chosen the wrong one on his run across the forbidden zone of Checkpoint A. He considered his options and from doing so, his heart quickened with excitement.

Every SLYscape device, including enforcer uniforms, had an individual power signature. He was looking at enforcer power signatures all arrayed in racks like a virtual menu of information. Currently, there were a number of enforcers drawing no power. They were probably in-stasis or off-shift. There were a few draining a tremendous amount of power. They were likely responding to calls. According to the map, some of the enforcers drew energy from the light spectrum of radiation and others from the earth. He reached out to touch the units drawing power from the sky—nine racks of enforcer uniforms stacked several shelves high. Gerald grew dizzy as his breaths came quick and short. If the enforcer from his night vision was alive in the real world, its recorded memories—Abner's active duty log—

would be available to Gerald from these racks. Gerald modified his virtual body, so he could float to the higher shelves and search.

He had no idea how long it took, but after what felt like several hours, he found the units categorized as level two responders. He looked within the group for the individual power signature belonging to Sky 2-4-4. That was the name Abe responded to before his personal memories surfaced. If by some miracle the enforcer grew up on Layfette Street, he could find the physical location of Abe's off-shift residence. They could meet. They could talk about the fire. Something tugged at Gerald's memory. *If it's important,* he thought, *it'll come to me.*

Gerald found the Sky 2-4-4 uniform and quickly circumvented the encryption protecting it. He created virtual hands in order to progress more quickly through the log entries. He remembered the conversation between Preston Rose and AJ's dad. Cole Reaver said Sky 2-4-4 was dead but he wasn't. Gerald was so fixated on what that might mean he forgot the memory which was tugging at his brain. *Oh, that's right,* he thought. *An enforcer's Active Duty Log was a very valuable thing.*

The rovers didn't even bark before biting through his virtual throat and crotch.

Gerald's body jerked in the programming chair as if he was being struck by lightning. He bit his tongue and tasted blood. Gerald suddenly knew with absolutely clarity Abner O'Reilly was the enforcer from his night vision. He also knew the man was alive and still thrashing beneath the silver webbing of the conditioning chair. For the briefest moments, Gerald saw what Abe saw, heard what Abe heard, and felt what Abe felt until Gerald's body rejected the simulation. He severed his connection to Abe and floated back up into the virtual room where rovers howled. Blood dripped from their wet jowls and Gerald felt their teeth, but the pain was nothing compared to what Abe experienced. Gerald could see the vWare blocks responsible for Abe's torture. Inside the code, Gerald could vRead Abe's screams: *I know you!* the enforcer yelled. *Save me. Save us! I know you!*

The coding chair reasserted control, pulling Gerald's legs out of the rovers' jaws. He rose out of the tower into the forbidden zone. His vision blurred until he saw nothing but what a vWare controller sees. He jerked again as his hands and feet started to tingle inside the purple pockets of energy encasing them. From a bird's eye view, he watched the power coursing into the FSA tower from snaking lines of pulsating

SLYscape sources. He followed the red lines that fed Abe's conditioning chair and marveled at the intricate design of its simulation. How could any vWare controller be demented enough or ingenious enough to create such brutality?

The programming chair initiated a power cycle, and the SLYscape sphere he was in popped out of existence.

AJ's mouth opened in surprise or shock as Gerald came tumbling out of the programming cage. Gerald's head cracked off the smooth rock floor of the salt mine. His internal whispers grew loud and noisy as his vision sparked burning white. The locust ask him if he was okay or maybe it was AJ.

His last thought was of a boy who grew up on Gerald's street and somehow became the enforcer who accidentally killed Kisme St. James. The boy's name was Abe and if Abe was real, whatever night vision came next was somehow real too.

Gerald was not floating in the cavernous space with all the tiny lights as had happened the last time he was stunned. He was not met at the gates to his night vision by a dragon-sized version of his scribeosphere's locust. What he did see was the golden coast of an island in a vast turquoise ocean. At the center of the island, a dripping wet forest of green jungle and walking palms reached high into the air. At the core of the jungle like a black pearl, a small body of water rippled as insects skipped across its surface.

He was a bird or something like one. He swooped down on familiar, salt breezes almost wafting in circles above the pond. He was close enough now to see the black pond was carpeted by sharply petalled flowers of blue, purple, and brilliant white. He was thirsty and circled lower on the humid warmth of the air until his feet splashed gently down on the rubbery pad of a plant.

"Lotus flowers," a voice said from the edge of the water.

Gerald looked over. The man was a giant, scaring Gerald into raising his wings. A breeze caught them, and he felt himself lift and hover. Gerald looked around trying to find the wings that supported his flight. He landed on a pad further away. If he had wings, he couldn't see any. The giant man stared at him. He looked like AJ. "Abe?" he asked, trying out this body's version of a voice. *Abe*, he heard, a tiny insect rasp.

Abner O'Reilly smiled. "I knew you'd come," he said. "Unless you're a trick to fool me." Abe's eyes opened wide. "Are you a trick? Are you here?"

Gerald thought about the question before answering. Was he there? He remembered being stunned and falling out of the programming chair. He remembered looking at the vWare torturing the enforcer. He remembered AJ's face and then he listened for the whispers… there were no whispers. "No," he said. "I'm not." He was in a night vision. No whispers was how he could always tell.

"I'm watching you experience some kind of conditioning. I'm a memory from y-space, I think. Or, if the counsellors are right, you're not real. And I guess I'm about as critters as they come."

Something howled deep in the jungle behind Abe. He jumped forward and rushed headlong into the water. He dove underneath the flowers. Gerald rose into the air to keep from getting wet. Something big moved in the trees at the edge of the pond. Gerald found it strange he didn't feel afraid. It was just one more wingless giant clumsily clomping about the world.

Abe's head broke the surface next to Gerald, and Gerald flew higher. Abe thrashed some but after a while, he calmed down enough to say, "She's here, Gerald. On the island with me. She's been here so long. She wanted me to tell you that. That is if you're real."

"What am I?" Gerald asked. "I mean, what do I look like?"

Abe swam to the opposite side of the pond and climbed out before answering. He turned his back to the jungle behind him and said, "Some kind of bug. Ugly."

"You know my name?"

Abe shrugged. "She told me."

A dark, hulking shape lurked behind Abe in the trees. Gerald tried to yell a warning but all that came out was a rasp. Abe stiffened and looked over his shoulder. "Not again!" he cried, tears springing to his eyes. He trembled and started to run. The wolf, if that's what it was, came bounding out after him. However big Abe was in this night vision, the black wolf chasing him was five times the size. Its tail was sharp with coarse black and silver hair. Its claws were ebony and horribly sharp. Abe fell to the ground, his right leg covered in blood. He kicked back at the wolf with his good leg until the jaws found him and Gerald heard teeth scrape against bone. Abe slapped and punched at it with his hands trying to get away. The wolf stepped on his chest, holding Abe still with one giant paw. It turned its cold, yellow gaze onto Gerald.

Gerald was not afraid. "What is it?" he yelled to Abe, more curious than concerned.

Across the pond, Abe turned his head. "Run!"

The wolf swatted Abe across the ground and then disemboweled him with one glistening bite. Abe screamed and Gerald took flight to get away. The wolf finished with Abe and came loping across the pond as if the water was firm ground. He leapt straight up, growling as he snapped the air. Gerald felt hot breath flip him upside down. His wings were no good in strong, inconsistent wind. Gerald braced himself for what he was about to feel and then saw a dark cloud wash over the wolf, knocking it into the pond below.

Gerald's wings were wet but he controlled his descent until he was once again on a green pad in the water.

She's coming, Gerald, he heard. *She has so much to teach.*

It was Lizzy's voice, and instinctively, he looked around for the scribeosphere. But then no, there wasn't a scribeosphere because Lizzy didn't speak in night visions. He remembered the teenage girl at his bed, and there she was again at the edge of the pond. She looked at him and waved.

She's here, Gerald. She'll protect you.

The wolf leapt straight out of the water and landed on the girl. "I'm alive, Gerals! Come find me!" she yelled, as she collapsed underneath the wolf.

"No!" Gerald yelled, suddenly feeling the pain and fear that until then had been buried somewhere deep inside. He jumped high in the air and spread his wings, hoping to help but Lizzy didn't need it. She threw the wolf off and jumped straight into the sky. Gerald watched as she changed shape and grew until her veiny wings opened like sail cloth in the wind. He recognized her now. Lizzy was the dragon locust. The wolf shook himself to his feet and then went wild. It had no wings but in the night vision it didn't seem to matter. It leapt up and clamped long, sharp teeth around the thorax of the dragon-sized insect flying above the walking palms.

His world, the dragon locust rasped above him. *Too powerful here.*

"Where's Lizzy?" he yelled at the giant insect. "Where'd she go?"

Can't be brave here. Run, Gerald! Run!

The wolf stabbed the dragon with its fore claws and scrambled with its back claws to gain purchase in the insect's papery skin. It growled and snarled as it climbed up the dragon locust's back. Sickly green mucous bubbled out of the jagged holes made by the wolf's black claws. Its jaws ripped holes in its wings as the dragon locust lost altitude trying to get away.

Can't be brave! it said, and then the dragon locust fell from the sky.

"Save him," he heard his sister call. Her voice was loud like a sudden gusting wind. "Save my brother!" she yelled, her command echoing over the island.

The two beasts of Gerald's night vision hit the ground next to the pond with a dull thud. The dragon locust lay unmoving as the wolf rolled to its feet. It stood over its kill and howled. It turned as if it knew Gerald was watching. It sprinted directly at him, green blood dripping from its flapping red tongue. Gerald heard whispers: millions of whispers funneling out of the trees in a dark, undulating cloud of hissing, crackling wings.

The locust brood swarmed Gerald and lifted him into the sky. The wolf could not find him now. He was one tiny insect body in a horde of identical bodies that blocked out the sun. He drifted as the locusts flew him higher over the ocean and away. He looked back at the island and listened to the wolf howl.

Be brave, he heard, just before the pain of a distant, physical life overwhelmed him.

"Are you okay?" AJ asked, directing a medical drone to Gerald's bleeding skull.

Gerald tasted copper and gagged. He opened his eyes. There was another flash of light because the machine shot him full-in-the-face. It didn't stun him, it removed the pain. Gerald pushed the drone away and sat up.

He looked around the salt mine. He saw lots of blood on the floor. He gently touched the back of his head. The skin was cinched closed and raised like a tiny scar. He looked up at AJ squatting next to him. He smiled. "Drone had to fix a crack in your dome. Rough week, huh?"

"Lizzy's alive, Aje. I'm almost certain."

AJ's stopped smiling. He closed his eyes and blew out a long breath. "I know," he said. "But your parents aren't."

Chapter 22

Blackstars

"What do you mean, my parents aren't? What do you mean, you know?" Gerald jumped to his feet, waivered on his feet, and then backed away from AJ. *Who are you?* he thought.

"I know what you must be thinking, brother. But we got to go."

Gerald ran at AJ swinging his fists as hard and fast as he could. AJ deflected each blow easily but didn't strike back. Gerald swung and kicked. He even tried to bite. AJ blocked and dodged every move but he didn't fight back. He let Gerald tire himself out which took less than a minute. Gerald grew dizzy and would have fallen down if it wasn't for the medical drone bracing him with a mild force field that kept him standing. "Your heart rate is elevated. Your blood pressure is low. Relax," the drone said in a flat, mechanical voice. "Steady now. There you go. Be better soon."

"You didn't turn the Blackstars around, Gerald. We got to get to them before Paisley's people do."

Gerald thought back to his experience in the SLYscape and said. "I don't know where they're going. I don't know where they'll be, but even if I did, I wouldn't take you anywhere. Tell me about my sister, Aje. Tell me what you know."

"I will. I promise. But they're flippin' dead, Gerald. For real. If we don't go now."

Gerald's head throbbed coldly. He opened and closed his eyes. "I don't care! You tell me where she is!"

AJ looked skyward and sighed. "We don't know, Gerald. Or else we would have told you. She was taken from the house on the day of the fire. Even Rose doesn't know where she is, but my parents say he's been looking for her all these years. Why tell you something that'd bring nothing but pain?"

"I deserved the truth, Aje."

"I know, but you got me instead. I'm sorry."

Gerald didn't know if he believed AJ or not, but his head hurt too much to yell anymore. "I still can't help you, Aje. I don't know where the Blackstars are. I told you."

AJ smiled. "But I do." AJ pointed at the second programming chair in the room. "Remember? We got two!"

Gerald put his hands over his face and groaned in frustration.

"I followed you, Gerald. The chairs are piggy-backed. All I did was copy what you did. Nice trick with the dogs. Da might not see it that way, though."

"You saw everything?"

AJ nodded. "Until you picked the wrong tower. You started mucking around with those enforcers and I thought, what the hell? So I took off back through the wall. Made it to the FWA with your ID trick. I looked around and found the brown grass. There was like no dogs or beetles or anything there."

"You saw my map?"

"Flippin' sweet. Knew you were a bigger tweak than Paisley. Twitlicker'd sell his left nut for that map. So I jumped into the room full of grass just like we did at the FSA tower. I found the transport system but then what? Couldn't hack it."

"But you know where they are?"

"The FWA got timetables with launch points, routes, and destinations. It's all live with no security. Just cross-checked some routes to Da's maps and figured the best place to attack. If Paisley's group isn't stupid, they'll be waiting on the other side of Iron City near the bridge."

"If they are stupid?"

"The Blackstars have fighter escorts. Those things will take 'em out for us."

"And you won't be a murderer."

"Right," AJ said, his eyes suddenly drawn. For a moment, he looked as defeated as he did after beating the 'roider in the junk yard. "You got to believe me, Gerald. I'm not like that."

But you're a liar and a gene demon. Gerald said silently. *You knew Lizzy was alive.* Gerald grew angry as he considered it. "Eight years I could have been searching, Aje. If you would have only trusted me with the truth."

"I did as ordered," he said.

Gerald clenched his fists. *My little sister, alone.* "I'll help you, but afterwards…"

"We'll go somewhere in Iron City and talk." AJ reached out and rested his mammoth palms on Gerald's shoulders. "There's so much to tell, Gerald. And it's not all bad."

Gerald didn't say a word as they left the mine and returned to the jumper.

They were over Iron City before AJ broke the awkward silence hanging in the air since liftoff. "There's this thing in a couple of days going to happen in town. It's something you'll want to see. Big John already okay'd it."

Gerald looked down at the place he had spent so many amazing summers visiting. He felt sick inside as he considered the fun he's had for years while his sister lived somewhere else. He couldn't stop thinking about what AJ had told him. How could a best friend keep so many secrets? So many important secrets? He grew nervous thinking about it as he noticed the lights of Iron City approaching. AJ flew low over the city and then banked towards old peninsula bridge.

A while later, AJ pointed. "There it is. That's where they'll be."

"Swamp Mountain," Gerald said, recognizing it.

AJ laughed, nervously. "No mountains in the North. Just a hill in the middle of a swamp."

Gerald shrugged. "Looks like a mountain."

"That's because it's the highest point around. It's got clear lines of sight to the bridge."

Gerald nodded, seeing the rickety old bridge a few kilometers away. "What makes you think the Blackstars will take the bridge route? They're flying. It's not like they have to cross there."

AJ wet his lips with his tongue. His eyes focused on the hill and his brow furrowed. He rolled the jumper into a descent that took them below the tops of the tallest trees. "People like the familiar. We fly around in these things but instinctively we don't trust flight. We're supposed to walk places, keep low to the ground."

AJ dropped the jumper to within a few meters of the ground and sped around the trunks of trees and jutting rocks. Leaves battered the dome of the jumper as Gerald became dizzy watching the world fly by at high speed.

"So when people who aren't pilots set flight paths, they tend to follow roads when possible. Funny really. The bridge isn't even functional, but it's the only road up here."

Gerald fixed his eyes on top of the hill to keep from becoming sick. "Orbiters don't do that." Gerald said it to be contrary. He didn't want to agree with AJ even if he could see the logic in it. He wasn't just mad at AJ, he realized. At that moment, he hated him. AJ didn't seem to notice. *Gene demons don't feel like we do,* Humphrey had said. *They show no mercy so neither do we.*

"Flying in space doesn't feel like flying," AJ said. He shrugged. "Plus, for some reason, Swamp Mountain is never bothered by freedom storms—always clear on the summit. Look."

Gerald scanned the sky above the hill with his eyes. There were only a few storms at the furthest reaches of the horizon. He had to admit, the night was unusually clear. Of course, the night he lost his sister had been clear too before the wind and lightning blew his house down.

"We have an hour to hike up to the top," AJ said. "Ready to sweat?"

"Hike? Why not just fly straight to the top and land?"

"Bad guys," AJ said. "If I'm right, bad guys are already up there. They'll see us coming. We need to hike up."

"The mountain?"

"The hill." AJ suddenly skidded the jumper to a stop on the wet, marshy floor. Clumps of mud and debris fell on their heads when he opened the passenger dome.

Gerald dusted his hair with his knuckles to get the biggest chunks of decaying matter out. He noted how far away they still were. "In an hour?"

AJ's eyes rolled white. "Seventy-two minutes. Let's go."

Hiking through the Northern Marshes at night was worse than digging trenches in a freedom storm. Black flies swarmed his eyes, ears, and nose. He still wore the clothes he was in when rescuing Lina. They were stiff and hard to walk in. The air conditioning vWare wasn't electrocuting him anymore, but the circuit fibers had frayed loose and were poking his skin. He rolled up his sleeves and pant legs to cool down but had to roll them back down after the umpteenth bite. "Dirty bloodsuckers!" he said, under his breath.

"Shh!" AJ whispered. "Voices carry."

Gerald sneered at AJ's sweaty back. Gerald bit down on an angry retort and dug his fingers into his arms and legs trying to scratch the flame out of the tiny, red bumps. He stumbled along until he had to jog to keep up with AJ. For a long time, they travelled fast like that but once they reached the hill, their steps slowed. AJ held up his hand and looked around. Gerald was exhausted. AJ was practically vibrating with energy. He studied their surroundings as if he expected bad guys to pop out from behind every tree. He looked for shallow holes covered by vegetation in case bad guys hid beneath their feet. His arms were wide and his hands open, ready to grapple. "There's a game trail," AJ said, pointing. "It should take us up."

"Is this what you spent all your time doing on the Dezie Exam?"

"It's what I'm good at." He spoke in a strong, hushed tone.

They climbed in silence before Gerald added, "I wouldn't know what you're good at."

AJ ignored him and kept hiking. About half-way up the slope, Gerald stopped. He needed a break and said so. "We don't have time," AJ responded with urgency.

"Need a break, Aje. I'm not like you." Gerald stopped on the trail and stared hotly up at AJ until he turned around. His demon-bright eyes appeared ice-white in the pearlescent glow of the full moon. *I don't have enough demon blood to run up a mountain at top speed,* Gerald thought.

"We need to get to the top, Gerald. They're almost here."

"Okay, fine, but what are we planning to do?" Gerald threw his hands up. "When we get there and they have guns or laser knives or whatever?"

AJ held his finger to his lips. He looked around as if he heard something and then moved his hands in some flashy way that Gerald recognized from AJ's favorite SLYscape game. "I don't speak Deathcraft, Aje," he said.

"Fortunately," a stranger's voice said. "I do."

Gerald felt something hard and blunt push into his back. Seeing who was behind Gerald, AJ lifted his hands.

"No sudden moves, big guy," the man said. "You…" He nudged Gerald forward. "Move over with your friend."

Gerald did as asked and turned around. The man was nearly as large as AJ but his facial features were buried in the shadow of a billowing black hood. He couldn't see the man's body either. The best his eyes could discern was a slight distortion field in the basic shape of a man. "Now this is how it works," the man said, waving a shimmer gun tipped in red crystal.

It was a scary weapon capable of superheating the air around its targets. Before laz'rupters, enforcers carried them which was how they had earned their name. People who believed enforcers were superhuman told stories about loved ones being melted in a shimmer of heat that cauterized their wounds. No blood. Just poached skin on a shrunken corpse. "Who are you?" Gerald asked, his voice cracking as he said it.

"That's up to you, sunshine."

"How so?"

"I can be just some guy you met in the swamp," the man said. "If you trek down the trail right now. Or—"

"Or we can be friends," AJ said.

The man laughed. "Friends?"

"Paisley sent us," AJ said. "The deal's called off."

"Is that so?" the man asked, seemingly amused. He gestured with the gun making it clear he wanted them to continue climbing up the game trail. Gerald and AJ walked a while before Gerald stumbled to his knees too tired to continue. "None of that," the man said, hardly winded. "We're just about where we need to be."

"And where's that?" AJ asked.

The man ignored his question and jerked Gerald to his feet. "You know what fellas like me call these here shimmers? Wipe guns," he said. "They're just so good at making people disappear, it's like they've been wiped from the earth. Makes me nostalgic for my youth when it seemed just about everybody had one. Just hold the trigger and sweep—"

"No messy cleanup," AJ said, nodding. "Good gun. You gonna be nostalgic when I take it from you? Or just weepy?"

The man laughed. "Bet a body like yours needs a couple of sweeps to take you down. Good minute's worth to bubble you to wax."

"If you only had the time."

"True. We're here."

They entered an open space on the summit. Noticing the black char piles and stumps, it appeared the trees had been recently cleared from the ground. A camp fire blazed in the middle next to a synthetic kitchen table with six chairs arranged around it. The man in the hood paused as if he was talking to someone. Everyone used moles, Gerald thought, even bad guys. Considering the company he'd been keeping, it was good to know.

The man told them both to take a seat. "It's your lucky day, boys! My brother says Paisley's coming up the trail now"

Gerald relaxed into the chair. He hadn't realized how tense he had been until then. In contrast, AJ seemed to become more wired than ever. It took a moment for Gerald to understand why. The man hadn't put his shimmer gun away.

The man sat leisurely down across the table from the boys. He reached with a gloved hand into the edge of the fire and lifted a metal pot out. He set it on the table and let the pot rattle as the condensation hissed and boiled beneath it. "Got a few minutes til we blow the Blackstars to hell. No refunds. No take backs. No remorse. Paisley hires people to do a job and they do it. Coffee?" He produced several small cups from inside his robes and set them down before them. "No? Suit yourself."

He poured himself a cup and brought it inside the hood where the cup and his hand blurred and disappeared. They could hear him blow on the hot liquid before he slurped. A moment later, there was a quiet rustling in the jungle behind them. Another man in the same kind of hooded distortion cloak appeared beside the table. "Red," the new man said. "We all good?"

Keeping the gun pointed at AJ, Red said, "Of course, brother."

The newcomer crossed the clearing to where a tripod stood next to another kitchen table. On top of the table, a single red sphere rotated. "Just waiting on the tweak to get his fat ass up here and tap into the SLYcast."

Several more people emerged from the jungle a few minutes later. They were muttering and someone was shouting out in palpable irritation. Four of them were in distortion cloaks. The fifth was fat, sleeveless, and covered in tattoos from head to toe. "Mother suckers got blood running down my legs now. Whose demon-poor idea was it to walk? Hate swamps. Hate bugs. Hate walking!"

Paisley was out-of-breath when he drew up next to the fire and looked at the two boys sitting there. "AJ!" he yelled, holding out his knuckles for a bump. "Bringing a fellow vee-walker to the show! Heard about what happened at the farm. Score one for the vee-walkers!"

"Pez," Gerald said, using Paisley piratesphere handle.

"Got to hand it to you. Saving a Nobel? Wouldn't have thought to do it myself." He stared at Gerald, smiling. "Guess Big John trusts you now since you're here." Paisley's fist was still hanging unbumped in the air in front of AJ.

"Paisley," AJ said, letting the tension drain from his muscles slightly. "Tell these guys it's off. We can't do this."

"Oh, man. Cold feet?"

"Yes. No. It's just a terrible idea. If we kill 'em, the FSA will know their destination. A new group will investigate. Only, they'll have more escorts."

"Oh, don't be hard on yourself, AJ. It'll work… you'll see."

Gerald listened to the two talk feeling disoriented. He had spent most every day with AJ at the Academy. They spent their summers together. How had AJ hidden so much? How had he never met people like Paisley before? The answer came to him in a flash: moles. For all Gerald knew, AJ was talking to these people daily while Gerald was in the room. When AJ disappeared for hours in sim pods, he could have been sending sVids to his parents, the Nobels, or even Preston Rose. Gerald's mind reeled at the possibilities.

"I feel for you buddy," Paisley said. "It's not like I want to do this either but—" he shrugged as if his hands were tied. "Expenses being what they are—"

"Keep the perks. We can do another deal."

Paisley laughed. "Oh, come now, AJ. You know me by now. It's not just you. Sure it was your idea but I leveraged it into something much more interesting."

AJ shook his head in confusion.

"I got your friends paying me too. Justice for Kisme's showing the world today they're not the FSA's bitch no more. Earth First's become a resistance movement like the rebels who overthrew the World Union."

"What are you saying?"

"I'm taking over another SLYcast—"

"You're SLYcasting the Blackstars being shot down."

"Justice for Kisme demands it!" Paisley smiled. "And they got perks to pay for it."

AJ sat back in his chair, his eyes staring as he shook his head. "So there's nothing I can do to stop you?"

"Nothing."

"It's time," Red said. "Book. Take the rocket. You four… watch them."

The four remaining men in Red's unit pulled shimmer guns and trained them on AJ. Gerald must not have registered as a threat. AJ glanced over at Paisley sitting down at the kitchen table with the red sphere hovering above it. The man named Booker, pulled a long tube out of a case next to the tripod. He set it up with a few clicks and twists. Gerald had no idea what kind of rocket launcher it was, but he could tell it was modern by the fist-sized SLYscape spheres that appeared above it. Something tugged at the back of Gerald's mind as AJ said in a tired voice, "I'm sorry, Gerald. Really. This whole day…. I'll make it right."

"Five minutes," Red said, now standing with Booker and Paisley.

Gerald noticed AJ's body tensing. His tongue dotted his lips. He knew in an instant what AJ planned. The stupid giant was going to rush all the men around them and somehow get across the field to take out Booker and Red. Gerald knew how fast AJ was and how strong but AJ didn't stand a chance. Gerald grabbed AJ's shoulder.

The four cloaked guards pulled their guns higher. Gerald heard the weapons charging as the safeties flicked off. "Easy!" Gerald yelled. "Just consoling my friend here. Not every day, he becomes an accessory to murder."

AJ turned on him with anger in his eyes. Gerald wasn't certain if he was angry because Gerald thwarted his attempt to save the Blackstars or because he was reminded of how serious this had become. "No offense, Aje. Just thought you might need a distraction."

The scribeosphere rolled out of his pocket and ran headlong into the man closest to them. It bounced off and spun in circles while emitting an ear-piercing screech. The first man stumbled back almost falling into the fire while the other three shot at the flying silver ball.

AJ moved with near inhuman strength and speed, knocking the table over and clubbing the cloaked men with his fists until they didn't move.

He rolled off the last guard and pulled the gun he had stolen towards Red and Booker.

Red had already taken a shot across the clearing.

AJ was just as fast.

Two shimmering waves of heat collided in an explosion that knocked everyone down except Paisley who remained seated. He was too immersed in the red sphere to notice he had almost been fried. Gerald heard the Blackstars approach before he could see them flying over the bridge. Booker was back at the tripod, taking aim. AJ was on his feet again, heading straight for him. Red took out his legs.

Gerald moved in slow motion relative to everyone else. He looked around on the ground for something to throw at Booker or Paisley. He had to distract them until AJ managed to get to Booker. He noticed the bracelet on his wrist as the beginning of an idea formed. AJ screamed something unintelligible as he and Red's legs crisscrossed awkwardly. They rolled and skidded across the dirt towards Paisley. AJ didn't fight Red directly. He simply dragged himself forward as Red moved around his body like a wrestler looking for leverage. *AJ's a beast*, he remembered Sammy Nobel saying at the junk yard. He certainly looked like one now.

AJ inched forward like a moose being taken down by a tiger. Flashes of his eyes showed Gerald he was heading for Booker's feet but Red was strong. AJ's head disappeared as Red's distortion cloaked arms wrapped themselves around him. To Gerald, AJ looked more like a rat half-swallowed by a snake than the beast he saw beat down the 'roider. The cloak ripped and flashes of pale, muscular arms moved in and out of the distortion field as Red scrambled over AJ's back. Red's fist rose high in the air and rocketed down onto what Gerald could only assume was AJ's face. AJ stopped, rolled, and struck back with an open hand knocking Red's hood clean off.

Red had rusty red hair braided like a sailor's rope down the center of his back. He had puffy red scars carving jagged lines across his dark eyes and pale cheeks. Red was aptly named and as tough as he looked. AJ couldn't throw him off. Unhindered, Booker launched a small missile into the air. The missile whistled across the night sky in a white streak that hit one of the four approaching ships. The small fighter drone exploded and rained burning pieces of itself down over old peninsula bridge. Its twin banked and circled. The big ship with the Blackstars on-board kept cruising along as if their pilot didn't notice. Or more likely, their ship's auto-pilot didn't notice. Gerald watched the remaining fighter drone scan the horizon for the origin of the missile but then it moved off in the wrong direction. Paisley had taken control.

Paisley's red sphere had grown large enough to drape over the kitchen table. Inside the shimmering glow, Gerald could see Paisley's hands hack the ships from the safety of the SLYscape. He was recording too but unless Gerald missed something, the SLYcast wasn't live. They wanted to edit it, he decided. Maybe overlay Brandy in front of the fighter drones falling from the sky. Gerald found his feet and ran at Paisley's sphere. In deft, practiced movements, Gerald spun his fingers around the black opal as he approached. When the gem turned yellow, he jumped.

The table buckled beneath Gerald as he slid over onto the ground. He landed hard but with a clear view of the red sphere shattering as violently as a babblesphere encountering Gerald's no fly zone energy field. Paisley screamed and threw his hands over his ears. Gerald knew from experience a sudden bursting of an immersion bubble hurt like an open-handed slap to the brain.

"Mother pumpin' vee fucker!" Paisley screamed, breaking the chair as he rolled off it onto the dirt. Booker launched one more missile before a branch AJ threw from a short distance away clipped him in the shin. Red lay in a crumpled heap. AJ was on top. Gerald smiled, thinking the good guys won until he noticed the fighter drone correcting its path. He then realized, he might not have thought this whole plan through.

"It'll light us up!" Red yelled, tired but standing again. He limped towards the tripod rocket launcher. AJ glanced over his shoulder and saw the overseer transport banking slightly as if the auto-pilot was finally beginning evasive maneuvers. "Fine!" Red yelled to AJ. "Just take the fighter down. We'll let the transport get away."

The buzz of the fighter was close enough to arm its weapons. Gerald saw something red paint the clearing.

"Aje!" Gerald yelled. "The fighters are unmanned."

AJ nodded to Gerald and then spun in a blur towards the approaching fighter drone. He heaved the rocket launcher onto his shoulders tripod and all. He took quick aim and then went sprawling to the ground as one of the guards crashed into his back. The tripod went flying off the edge of the cliff. The missile whistled out a moment later trailing orange and white fire. The fighter drone pulled up and crashed into the belly of the ship it was trying to protect. The second ship was too close to avoid the blazing fallout from the crash. Gerald watched in fear and fascination as both Blackstar transports spiraled down into the swamp below.

AJ was back standing staring angrily at the guard who attacked him. He panted as he shifted his gaze to the fresh wreckage below. "Look what you've done!" he yelled.

"We've done our job," Red said, stepping up next to his guard.

AJ whirled on Red who fell back into a casual fighting stance. "Bring it, kid," he said. "I know what you can do now."

"You don't know the half of it."

"Woah!" Paisley yelled, getting in between the two. "We've had enough fisticuffs, gentleman. At least, enough non-profit fighting. If you two want to have a go, I could arrange it so we'd all come away with perks in our pockets for the effort."

AJ looked angrily at Paisley. Red just smiled as he was joined by the other guards with drawn guns. Booker was apart from them at the edge staring down at the tiny fires below. "Did you get what you needed, Pez?" he asked.

Paisley stepped over to the cliff and nodded. He started shaping another red sphere by tapping his tattoos in simple patterns. He recorded the fallen ships and the fires for a moment and then said, "Didn't catch them falling, but this should be good enough to get paid," he said, brightly. "And AJ, I don't think they're dead."

AJ and Gerald stepped to the edge and looked. Gerald was relieved to see little yellow spheres of light bobbing next to the downed ships. Paisley recorded a few more moments before flicking off his sphere. "See AJ? It all worked out."

"How do you figure?" AJ asked Paisley.

"Justice for Kisme gets footage and you weren't a willing part of it. I will swear to your innocence, my friend. They could stick toothpicks under my fingernails and I won't say any different. No hard feelings, I hope?"

"You still tried to kill them."

"I have no stomach for such business. I tried to record what happened is all." He gestured at Red with his thumb. "The Shotwells are a family of assassins and thieves loyal only to their perks. These folks are your would-be killers."

Booker shook his head as he joined the mercenary guards.

"Job was to keep them from arriving," Red said. "I think we did that."

"Success." Booker said. "Let's get out of here."

Red held up his hand. "The kids' seen my face."

Paisley snorted. "They're your employers, Red. Plus, they're under Preston's protection. And AJ's one of the old man's favorites."

Red nodded. "Fine then. Break camp!" The group of mercenary guards moved silently around the clearing cleaning up the mess as the Shotwells escorted Paisley into the jungle. Gerald observed how conscientiously the mercenaries went about folding chairs, tables, and putting the camp fire out. One man scaled down the cliff-face to retrieve the tripod that had landed on a rocky ledge. Gerald and AJ were ignored as the peered into the valley below.

"They might need help," Gerald said, looking down at the yellow lights clustering together.

"Don't you think they can just call a rescue jumper from Iron City?"

Gerald shook his head and patted the scribeosphere in his pocket. "Paisley hacked their communications. Everything's jammed. They're stranded."

AJ frowned and shook his head. He licked his lips. "Then I guess we help."

Chapter 23

Betrayal

It took an hour to reach the jumper AJ had stashed. By the time they were circling over the downed transports, the moon had dipped behind some fast moving clouds. Gerald was so exhausted he could barely think, let alone talk about what he and AJ had just experienced. "Red was pretty strong," Gerald said, lamely.

"Pretty strong," AJ agreed.

"He shot at you."

AJ nodded.

"Ever been shot at?"

AJ shook his head. "Not like that. There they are," he said and landed.

"What are we going to say?" Gerald asked, before AJ opened the passenger dome.

"No idea."

The Blackstars met them half-way, smiling and waving at their good fortune to find people travelling this late at night. The irony was not lost on Gerald as he counted six sets of black robes so happy to see them. *No need to talk to us at the ranch. Let's talk here,* he thought, almost giggling from a mix of adrenaline and fatigue. They were a tall lot and mostly older males. There was one woman and a shorter person that looked uncomfortable in his skin.

"No flippin' way," AJ exclaimed.

"What the hell?" Gerald agreed, blinking.

"Jack?" Gerald asked.

"Jackie-boy!" AJ said, springing through the black robed men to bear-hug their friend from the Academy. He lifted him and spun. The other overseers backed away as their smiles disappeared at such an egregious breach of protocol. Gerald tried to imagine what was going through AJ's mind: *We almost killed you, Jackie-boy… What's with the black robes, tweet-knocker?*

"Gentleman, please," said a particularly stiff Blackstar who straightened his robes before continuing, "We need your help, not demonstrative displays of… whatever that was."

AJ set Jack down and patted him on the shoulders. "Good to see you."

"Hi AJ," Jack said while his eyes refused to make contact.

"Mr. Dryden," the overly proper man continued. He was the highest ranking overseer of the bunch with six white stars decorating his black sleeves. The next highest was a four-star followed by a woman two-stars. The oldest man in robes sported only one star. Jack's sleeves were plain. "I'm speaking to you, Mr. Dryden. You know these people?"

Jack nodded uncomfortably. "Uh, sir, this is Mr. O'Sullivan."

"Mr. O'Sullivan?" AJ asked, surprised.

"And that's his friend, Mr. Goodstone."

The Blackstar paused a moment to cast a glance at the top of the mountain. "The very people we're here to investigate?" he asked as if talking to himself. He then grunted as if he suffered from verbal ticks. "What brings you outside so late and so far from home?" he asked Gerald.

Gerald's voice caught in his throat. Every excuse that might have seemed plausible if they were strangers now seemed silly and transparent. He looked down at his work boots covered in black muck and glistening patches of green from hiking up the mountain. Gerald looked at AJ and his friend stared back. As the awkward silence lengthened, the chirps of frogs and trilling squeaks of other animals seemed to amplify in the night. There were insect rattles and forlorn hoots of unseen owls. Something large and fast suddenly splashed through the ground cover near them and yelped as something bigger caught it.

"Looking for overseers!" AJ exclaimed, happily.

The six-star cocked his head as if this was the last thing he expected to hear. So did Gerald. "And why, Mr. O'Sullivan, would you be looking for us?"

AJ smiled like an idiot and started moving his hands as he talked forcing the black robed men to step back. "Glad you asked, sir. As you might've guessed from all of the reports you've probably been reading about us, my friend Gerald is a tweak. I mean, genius. Well, it's true. He's the best vWare controller the Academy has ever produced."

"Hacker, sir," Jack translated. "Gerald's really good at hacking."

"That's right, sir. Jack knows. Without Gerald, he would never have passed molecular bionics. Most of us at the Academy owe our dezies to Gerald." AJ took a breath and smiled at each Blackstar in turn. "So this morning, Gerald's tweaking out. He's cruising the shadowy side of the SLYscape—"

"Piratesphere, sir," Jack said, quietly.

"He found pirates, alright. He found the really bad ones that seem to just take and take and take. They break into domains and knock stuff out. They murder people. I've seen it. Not in real-life but I've seen plenty of sVids on the topic."

"Of course," the six-star said, nodding. "You found rebels like the kind of slime calling themselves Justice for Kisme."

"That's right, sir. In this case, the slime are a bunch of thugs planning to do you harm. Gerald discovered their plans in the piratesphere. I came up with the idea to save you. Jack will tell you, I'm no slouch when it comes to military strategy. So think of today as our audition. We ran them off sirs. It was our pleasure to serve."

The six-star looked at the other men in robes in silent communication. "So you're heroes which is why you're here in the swamp at night?"

AJ shrugged. "I know what I'm accused of sir. Maybe this was my way of proving the Dezie Exam wrong."

The six-star ran a hand over his face. He pinched his pointy nose a moment before cupping his chin in thought. "You scared them off and flew down here to prove your innocence?"

AJ nodded. "And to save your lives which we did."

"Indeed, Mr. O'Sullivan. I think our investigation is off to a good start. Now the biggest question for me right now is can you get us to Iron City? There are ROLIES there waiting to escort us to a neighbor of yours. What were their names?"

"The Nobels, sir," Jack provided.

"Ah, yes. The Nobels. Old family stock. Good people. Hear they run immaculate gardens worth a visit. Thought while we're here investigating you, we'd kill two demons with one stone, so to speak."

"I'd love to take you there but I can't. We could take Jack and arrange for a proper transport to pick you up in a few hours? Got this location marked in my jumper."

"Or," the Blackstar said. "We could take your jumper and send somebody back for you."

AJ shook his head. "My DNA, sir," he lied. "Nobody else can fly my jumper but me. We have room for two more."

There was more silent communication. "Mr. Dryden and Elder Mosley. You take them, and we'll see you soon."

The old man with one star moved forward to stand next to Jack. "Very good, sir. I'll join the lads."

Gerald trudged back to the jumper feeling lightheaded and weak. The Blackstars were going after the Nobels… Lina. She was innocent or even if she wasn't, she was raised as a member of Earth First which wasn't a crime, Gerald reminded himself. He really hadn't seen any crimes on the farm. He shook his head as he helped Elder Mosley step into the jumper. *Gardens,* he corrected himself as he climbed into the back seat with Jack. He was going to have to watch what he said with overseers around.

Just after the passenger dome closed, AJ laughed. "Is this for real, Jack?" AJ said, flipping the bottom hem of Jack's robes up with his fingers.

Jack slapped his hand and nodded. "Guess when you score off-the-charts like I did, no such thing as practice tests."

"I knew you'd never be King of the Academy."

Jack smiled slightly, and Gerald shook his head trying to figure out AJ's angle. He practically admitted to the Blackstars they were involved in shooting them down. Or, at least, his lies seemed so coincidental and absurd, Gerald couldn't imagine any other conclusion the Blackstars would make. Maybe AJ was just critters. Maybe his friend's tenuous grasp on reality was why the two of them had gotten along so well until now. He had to find some privacy soon to ask AJ about Lizzy. If Gerald could clear his name, he could start looking for her with his new SLYscape access. He imagined for a moment how easy it would be to float around the SLYscape's version of Freedom Square if he didn't have to worry about rovers and beetles. All three towers would be open to him as if he owned the place.

AJ and Jack were still talking when Gerald started listening again. "Right after you two left, some ROLIES came and took me to Old New York. Been in the work authority's tower ever since. I'm an overseer now, AJ. For real."

"Not yet, lad," Elder Mosley said. "Blackstars aren't made overnight."

"Unless you arrest someone for treason. That's a great career-starter."

Again, all Gerald could do was shake his head. Elder Mosley smiled at AJ's comments and nodded slightly as if he agreed.

"He's kidding Elder Mosley," Jack said. "AJ kids."

"Lad, what have I told you? Mosley's my pa's name and elder is what he was when he died. Call me Henry when the others aren't around."

"Right, Henry," Jack said. It was easy to tell Jack felt more comfortable around Henry than he did the others.

Nobody talked much the rest of the way to Iron City. When they said goodbye at the landing port, Jack asked Gerald to step out of the jumper. They walked a little ways away from AJ who remained seated, needlessly revving the jumper's lift-off ports. "Gerald," Jack said. "Tomorrow, there'll be tents bivouacked all around the farm."

"Garden," Gerald corrected, feeling his defenses rise.

"Bring Sally to the largest of them… the blue one."

"What?"

"I've missed her. I need to talk to her. She hasn't returned my calls since—"

"Since you told her AJ and I were radicals."

Jack looked down. "It's what they think you are. Well, not you but…." Jack looked over at AJ sitting in the jumper. "They know, Gerald. They know everything. You have about a day to pick sides. If you pick the wrong one…."

"A man can't serve two moons," Gerald said, remembering Chuck Heller's drunken words.

"Wolf," Jack said.

Gerald eyes opened as he looked at Jack. "What do you mean?"

"A wolf can't serve two moons. It's part of the Blackstar oath."

"What do wolves have to do with anything?" he asked, remembering how the wolf in his night vision killed Abe and the dragon locust.

"No idea. Haven't taken the oath yet. I'm just an intern but," he said, looking uncomfortable. "I shouldn't say this but the moon, the wolves… it's got something to do with the High Prelate. It's all these guys ever talk about. Have you seen the m-spheres, lately?"

Gerald shook his head.

"He might be deposed."

"What? Why?"

"Gene demons. They've found some, and they say Preston Rose grew them in secret laboratories scattered all over the world."

"I don't believe it," Gerald said, looking over at AJ whose head rocked and bobbed in time to music only he could hear. His eyes were white and he drummed the flight stick of the jumper in time to some hard beat. AJ's tongue danced across his lips. He was thinking, planning, figuring out his next step. Gerald knew this about AJ. He puzzled things out violently in physical ways. He suddenly wondered if AJ knew what he was and had seen the other gene demons captured. He wondered if that was why he hated Preston Rose so much. The man created him and now he was an abomination hunted by the FSA.

"Preston's dirty. That's what the Revealers say. Look at the facts. Every powerlord caught so far works for Preston Rose." Jack laughed. "I mean the sVids, Gerald… pretty damming stuff. It's like that virus has it out for him and public opinion's starting to tip. Senior Thomas—he's the six-star—says it's all but done. Rose is gone."

"They can't just kick him out of office?"

"The FSA can do just about anything it wants. They're sworn to protect us even from our leaders. If the Blackstars give the FSA permission. Imagine, we've never had a High Prelate other than Rose."

Gerald shook his head.

"I'm only saying this because the O'Sullivans' are Rose's right-hand people. If you know anything, you have to tell us. It's the only way this ends good for you. AJ and his family… they're all dirty by association. They're going to take you down and it's not fair."

Gerald continued to shake his head but he said: "I understand."

Jack smiled. "I knew you would."

Gerald slipped into the jumper. He tapped AJ on the shoulder who looked at him and smiled. "Lots to do, Gerald. Lots to do."

They flew back to the ranch without Gerald asking a single question about Lizzy. There were too many things tumbling around in his brain to think clearly, so he decided he'd sleep first which he did once they arrived back at the ranch. As he walked inside and up the stairs to their bedroom, Gerald could barely hear the whispers. Since falling out of the programming chair, his mind had become numbly peaceful. Not even the locust had spoken to him since Gerald hit his head. He processed these thoughts as if they were important to someone else. Feeling cold, he pulled the blankets over his body and head. *Tomorrow,* he thought. *It'll all make sense tomorrow.*

He slept until shortly after sunrise and woke to Sally's hand shaking him. "Good morning sunshine! You alive?"

Gerald's eyes flew open remembering Red and the shimmer gun. He sat up with a start that nearly knocked her off the bed. She was sitting next to him holding two cups of coffee. He bumped her arm.

"Whoa there," she said, shifting her body fast enough to drench the floor instead of Gerald's sheets with coffee. "Sleep like a rock and then vault like a squirrel. What time did you get in last night?"

Gerald took a moment to focus on her round, smiling face. She caught the intensity of his stare and smiled hesitantly. Her straw-colored hair was hanging in long curls and still wet. She smelled fresh. Gerald did not. He was still in his work clothes from the previous day.

"Yeah," she said, wrinkling her nose. "You should do something about that before we ride together in a jumper. AJ's a bit musky too but at least his clothes are clean. Here." She handed him one of the coffees and got up to leave. "See you downstairs."

He watched her go and then sat up in bed. He sipped from the steaming cup as he thought about the night before. It really happened. Lizzy was alive and all the O'Sullivans knew about it. He wondered how they could do that to him as he crossed the room and entered into the hallway towards the bathroom. When he turned on the shower and got in, his mood darkened until the betrayal he felt pounded in his chest. The O'Sullivans were his family but according to Jack, they were criminals. He closed his eyes as the hot water ran down his face. If he didn't report them, he'd be just as bad.

After Gerald had finished showering, he changed into something light and airy with no heavy vWare circuits sewn in. Gerald felt cold dread creep into him as he walked into the kitchen to face the smiling Mrs. O'Sullivan sitting at the table with AJ. Gerald could tell she and AJ had been talking. About what, he could only guess. AJ looked wide-awake and focused despite sleeping even fewer hours than Gerald. AJ nodded at him.

"Just talking about you, Gerald." Mrs. O'Sullivan said, excited. "You saved the girl like a hero!"

"Lina," Gerald said.

"Oh, I know her. Avelina's been talking about you since yesterday morning. Got John in a right-fine fit. He has to like you now which is troublesome for him."

Gerald tried not to look directly at Mrs. O'Sullivan. He felt too much emotion inside to talk. She stood up and touched his face gently. "Think I know what's wrong, honey."

Doubt it, he responded, in his mind.

She stepped close and gave him a warm, motherly hug. Inexplicably, he felt tears trying to break free. She didn't see it but AJ did, and he looked down at his cup and tapped his fingers on the lip.

Sally breezed into the kitchen next and laughed. "Oh, goody, group hug!" She came behind Gerald and put her arms around him and Mrs. O'Sullivan. "Get up here, big guy."

Gerald felt AJ wrap them all up. The absurdity of what he'd experienced in the last two days relative to this hug made him laugh a touch hysterically. *How is it possible,* he thought, *his whole life changed in the mine yesterday and nobody noticed?* He let out a shaky breath and extricated himself from the tangle of arms around him. He pretended he didn't know all he did, and said, "Are the Nobels even working today?"

Mrs. O'Sullivan assured him they were and like the first day, she would escort them due to the overseers who had finally arrived. Mr. O'Sullivan, she told Gerald, was already at the gardens setting up force-stations to protect the Blackstar tents in case more cyclones hit. "Turns out, the overseers aren't here for you two," she said, eyeing Sally who gave her an uncomfortable stare. "They seem to think John's gardens are a mite bigger than they should be."

"I didn't say a thing, Mrs. Oh," Sally said. "I swear!"

Mrs. O'Sullivan smiled. "Of course, you didn't, dear. A few questions were bound to happen one day."

Gerald thought about what Jack had said and blurted, "Mrs. O'Sullivan, I'd like to take my own jump today if that's alright."

"My name's Angie, honey," she said, her face betraying how much she disliked the idea of him flying alone. "Why would you want to go by yourself when we all fit so snugly last time?"

"Well, Mrs. O'Sullivan," he said, smiling. "There's this girl I saved..."

Mrs. O'Sullivan's whole body brightened as if he said the most perfect thing in the world. "John's going to hate it! I can tell you that. She's his baby and you're, what? Two years older?"

"I think three, Mrs. Oh, until the end of the week."

"That's right. Avelina was born in forty on the first day of Cyclonic-sol. Avelina's mother, Lina, used to say it's why her little girl was such a whirlwind."

"A little scrawny for my tastes," AJ added, showing a genuine smile and deliberately running his eyes up and down Sally's body inappropriately. "But at least she's bossy. Gerald likes that."

Sally smiled at the lecherous compliment AJ's lingering stare implied, but Mrs. O'Sullivan nodded as if AJ had said something sagely. "Take the silver-back out front, honey. Peter says it's got a new autopilot so you won't get lost...."

"Won't get lost, Mrs. O'Sullivan."

"Angie."

He wasn't sure what made him say it, but he nodded, "Angie."

AJ and Sally's eyes opened in surprise and Mrs. O'Sullivan laughed delighted. "See? That wasn't so hard."

"No," he agreed. "I guess I'll see you two at the fence."

"We've got to be pretty close to finishing," Sally responded.

"See you there, Gerald," AJ said.

When Gerald turned from them to go, he felt hollow inside. He was off to see Jack. Based on their conversation earlier, he was pretty certain he was about to pick sides and it wasn't going to be the O'Sullivan's side. He exited the house and jumped inside the jumper. An overly proper voice greet him dramatically. "Welcome friend of the O'Sullivans. I am so sorry, but there is something wrong with my senses. I could not identify who you are. My apologies but you have no identification marker for my records."

"Don't worry about it," Gerald said.

"Okey dokey. Where to?"

Chapter 24

Blackmail

Gerald smiled. Of course, the security protocols in a jumper owned by the O'Sullivans was going to be disabled. Even if he had a mole that could identify him, Gerald bet the scan would have come up empty. The O'Sullivans wouldn't allow themselves to be tracked so easily, he didn't think. "Take me to the Nobels farm. Do you know where it is?"

"Of course, sir." The jumper lifted straight and fast into the air, not levelling out until they reached nearly three hundred meters: "much higher than usual," the autopilot informed him, "due to excessive cottonwood seeding at lower altitudes." Gerald didn't mind. He had always liked heights. From so high up, he could clearly see the fluffy white fuzz drifting over the swamp. It looked to Gerald like winter snow falling on an early summer landscape of green fauna and yellow flowers.

He pulled his scribeosphere out and stared at it. It was lukewarm and the locust wasn't peering out at him from its shiny surface. He thought the command *lift* at it, and the scribeosphere jumped into the air. It hovered fine but the voice was silent. *Status*, he thought next. There was no response. He opened the scribeosphere up to see if he could find something broken. It looked okay, so he put the flying ball back together and looked at the rest of his jewelry. He wondered what was going on. The locust's image was gone from everything. He sat back and listened. His internal whispers were quiet but still present in the farthest reaches of his mind like a dream partly-remembered. His skin chilled enough for the autopilot to notice. It warmed the air as Gerald imagined what the locust's absence might mean.

The wolf killed the dragon locust and now the locust in Gerald's scribeosphere was broken. It couldn't be related because the wolf killed Abe and Abe was still alive as Gerald learned in the programming chair. Night visions might be real but they weren't literal. There were no such things as dragons and giant wolves. At least, Gerald hoped not as he stared outside until the autopilot landed.

It was such a gentle touchdown, Gerald wasn't certain they had stopped before the autopilot opened the passenger dome. "Have a wonderful day friend of the O'Sullivans," the autopilot said. "Will wait anxiously for your return."

Gerald climbed down the ladder to the field where all the other crew transports were landing. He didn't wait for Lina or Mr. Nobel to appear. He walked straight across the field to a swamp rider and drove it as fast as he could towards Dusty Gulch. He didn't know exactly where the overseer tents would be, but he had a pretty good idea. He found them a rock's throw away from the junk yard behind the food pits and chow tables. Gerald parked the swamp rider and got out.

There were dozens of ROLIES patrolling the area looking like giant bees in their black and yellow uniforms. There were colorful flags fluttering around the entrances of the various temporary structures being built. Gerald spotted Mr. O'Sullivan supervising a group of workers pounding two-meter high weather stakes around the outskirts of the tents. The extension stakes did nothing on their own. Once connected to the permanent weather sentries at Dusty Gulch, the force bubble protecting the cooking equipment would expand to include everything inside the stakes. Perimeters like these were temporary because they siphoned power from the main environment bubble making the whole system weaker. Using stakes as opposed to mini-weather sentries like the ones protecting the rice paddies was probably the Nobels' polite way of telling the overseers they weren't welcome for long.

Gerald headed for the largest tent being staked out. It was blue as Jack had told him to expect, so he lifted the flap and entered. Three black robed men spun in their chairs and waved. "Come in, Mr. Goodstone. We've been expecting you."

"Uh, looking for Jack," Gerald said.

"He'll be along. Please have a seat."

The tent was dimly lit and the chair the overseers indicated was a hard, unadorned foldaway. It sat in the center all by itself on the opposite end of a long table with zetta-tabs evenly spaced along the top. He didn't recognize all the men sitting at the table which meant more transports than the ones he had seen in the swamp had been directed to the north. Four more overseers walked in and took their seats without a word. The six-star, Senior Thomas, sat in the middle chair with relaxed crossed fingers as if in prayer. Gerald sat and waited.

After ten minutes of silence, Gerald grew antsy and said, "Ah, sirs. I really only came to see Jack."

The seven overseers nodded and smiled. "Soon," Senior Thomas said as Elder Mosley fumbled his way past the flaps of the tent entrance. He looked up at Gerald and smiled, "Good lad. I knew you'd come of your own accord. Jack was right about you."

Elder Mosley walked slowly to the side of the tent and picked up another foldaway chair. He dragged it across the dirt and sat down in front of Gerald so close their knees touched. He straightened his robes across his lap as he caught his breath. "Let me begin by apologizing. We know you didn't cheat on the SEER Exam."

"I don't understand, sir." Gerald's mind raced. He had been so busy thinking about other things, he had forgotten about his own predicament. AJ wasn't the only accused.

"AJ O'Sullivan is the lad we want, not you. I'm sorry to be so blunt. I know you think he's a friend."

Gerald nodded, feeling jittery and not wanting to show it. If they knew AJ was a gene demon, they wouldn't be talking to Gerald. He focused on this one fact to help himself relax.

"Truth is, the lad's just bait to land us a bigger fish. It's how powerlords think, isn't it? Eat the small to make themselves big."

Gerald shook his head. "You've lost me, sir."

Elder Mosley smiled good-naturedly. "I do that sometimes. I speak 'round the truth as my wife used to say. I learned it growing up on farms like this one."

"Gardens, sir."

Several chuckles came from behind the table.

"When you grow up on a farm and somebody asks you about your crops, you can't just give 'em an answer. You got to tell 'em about the weather. Let them make up their own minds about what they see. But you didn't grow up that way, did you Mr. Goodstone?"

"No, sir."

Elder Mosley smiled. "Then straight to the truth. You've already been cleared of any wrongdoing. You're designated—an adult by occupation, age, and title. You've been given the rank of FSA vWare controller just like you wanted. If you check your perks account, you'll notice you've been getting paid ever since you left the Academy."

"I have?"

"It's a healthy sum."

"That's great, sir. Just… how do you know what I wanted?"

"Prefect Humphrey, of course. We've been watching you for years. You're exactly what the FSA needs, an honest, truthful, brilliant lad who knows right from wrong. There's too much corruption, Gerald. Too many people circumventing the laws. The FSA enforces the laws but the overseers—the Blackstars—make them."

"I thought all you did was create jobs."

Elder Mosley smiled while shaking his head. "The FWA sets the rules of behavior around every job in the Freeland. Doctors have ethics because of us. If they break the ethics we have defined, they are punished. Rule of Law Officers know who to arrest because of us. If they arrest the wrong sort of people, they are punished. Prelates and Prefects know how to manage the citizenry because of the legislation we put into motion through the policies surrounding our designations. You can grow food this way… not that. You have the right to protest with permits… not without."

"Or the enforcers get you."

"The point is we are a nation of laws, Mr. Goodstone. That's what makes us free. We need you to invent better ways to enforce our laws. Your job starts today by uncovering the connection between the O'Sullivans, Justice for Kisme, and the Followers of Rose. All three have gotten away with breaking our laws."

"Why the Followers of Rose? I mean, what's so wrong with following the High Prelate?"

"They don't just follow, lad. They obey like slaves. You've seen the accusations on the m-spheres, lately? We want you to help us prove what everyone already knows."

"Which is?"

"That Preston Rose is making gene demons and he uses his followers to protect them from justice. He's willing to arm anarchists calling themselves Justice for Kisme, to draw attention away from the demons he's created. You need to prove how he does this through his figureheads: the O'Sullivans."

"Oh," Gerald said, his heart pounding. "Is that all?"

"A joke. Good, good. It's everything, lad. The High Prelate is clever. We know he uses zealots to protect demons…."

"How do you know?"

Senior Thomas grunted and then turned his tick into words: "Because, Mr. Goodstone, I was there in his palace when he admitted it! We all were!"

Others around the table grumbled and echoed the six-star overseer.

"If he admitted it, why can't the FSA arrest him? He's broken the law."

"Because the High Prelate's clever, lad," Elder Mosley said. "Can't be overstated how clever. He told us what he does, but we don't know how he gets away with it. The FSA can't apprehend Brandy Peppers, a simple farm girl."

"Practically no education at all," a Blackstar quipped.

"She gets away because the Followers are full of people like the O'Sullivans with connections to Rose. They protect demons. They protect her. Yet we have nothing on the O'Sullivans other than AJ's poor citizenship score. Your job is to find out how they hide gene demons and people like Miss Peppers. Infiltrate his parents' system and lead us to the High Prelate's prideful door. Show him nobody's above the law, lad. Then and only then will justice and freedom prevail."

"I see," Gerald said, nodding. "You need someone who the O'Sullivans trust."

"Someone on the inside," one of the Blackstars agreed.

"Quick on the uptake," another said.

"Smart as a whip, this one."

Elder Mosley nodded and Gerald looked past him to the other Blackstars arranged in panel formation behind the table. The way they praised him was condescending; the way they sat slouching and amused one moment and indignant the next was unnerving; every instinct inside Gerald warned him not to trust them. They lied to him. They made him think he cheated when he hadn't. They expected him to turn on the family that practically raised him after the fire. *They are right,* he thought. *The O'Sullivans are criminals.* The High Prelate gave them AJ, a gene demon, to protect just like they said. That meant the High Prelate was a criminal too. "Sir," he said, picking a side. "If I'm part of the Freeland Security Army now, does the Freeland Work Authority have the right to give me missions?"

Elder Mosley sat back in surprise. He shook his head slightly. "No, lad. The FWA has no such power. That would be Augustus Reaver and his boy Cole, that'd be authorized to do that under FSA rules."

"So shouldn't I wait for their orders?"

"Ideally, that'd be true, but the Reavers can't be part of bringing the High Prelate to justice… officially."

"Why not?"

"The top officers of the FSA must swear an oath to protect the office of the High Prelate." He tapped his temple. "Embedded in their skulls, they have a mole that cannot be taken out. The mole's purpose is to punish disloyalty. If the Reavers directly threaten a duly elected High Prelate, the mole in their brains will explode. I tell you this only because you are now a vWare controller and are cleared for this information."

"You're kidding me," Gerald said, horrified. "Why?"

"It's something Rose and the elder Reaver worked out sometime after Day Zero. One branch of the Freeland Nation has to lead. The other must serve. The FSA must follow the OPC. That, I suppose, was a good way to ensure obedience. You'll get fitted for a similar implant one day if you rise high enough. I 'spect you'll know more about it than I by then."

"So the Reavers can't order me to spy on my friends. And you can't either?"

"It must be your choice. We're a free land, after all."

"I understand. Then I choose not to be a spy."

"The hell he does!" Senior Thomas screamed, banging his fist on the table. "Enough, Henry! We gave the boy a chance. Get out and leave this to me."

Gerald looked at the six-star and saw a gleam of wild rage in his eyes. Spit was bubbling at the corners of his lips as he worked his mouth to say more. He was a follower too, Gerald realized, only of something or someone else. And so were the other Blackstars.

Elder Mosley reached over and patted Gerald's shoulder. He gave him the tiniest of smiles—looking almost like he approved—before dragging his chair back to the side of the tent. Without another word, he left Gerald alone with the remaining seven.

"You're loyal to the O'Sullivans, boy? How 'bout the Nobels? Their... gardens?"

Gerald eyed the tall overseer with the severe frown and white stars plastered up and down his sleeves. He nodded.

"Starting today, the FWA investigates the Nobels, the O'Sullivans, and everyone else in the north for sedition."

"Sedition, sir?"

"Come now, boy. Do you think the FSA hasn't figured out Mr. John Nobel leads Earth First? Do you think their little getaway plan to the Glass Lands has not been noted in the SLYscape? Every conversation they've ever had on the subject's in the FSA data spheres which means it's in ours as well. The FSA feeds the FWA what we ask for. As of right now, we begin rooting out the evil in these gardens. We find the insurgents, the radicals; we arrest them. We condition them. We turn them back into good citizens of the Freeland Nation. We get them back to work for the right side!"

Gerald sat in his chair, feeling his face grow hot. Tears threatened to fall. Nothing Senior Thomas said was wrong or morally objectionable to Gerald. Gerald knew they could do everything the six-star said, and the people of the north were rebels. Everything he had learned said so.

"Don't forget the girl, Cal," the woman said, with two stars on her sleeves.

Senior Calvin Thomas smiled. "How could I forget? The one you saved. Avelina... she'll be guilty of treason too."

"She'll be wiped," Gerald said, flatly.

"All to protect the O'Sullivans and Preston's gene demons. Weigh your choices, boy. Weigh them well."

"There'll be no investigation—not even of the O'Sullivans—if I spy for you?"

Senior Thomas shook his head. "No, son. We're here. We have to investigate, but if you cooperate, we will find only—"

"Gardens," the woman overseer said.

The panel laughed heartily. "Yes, Clara. Gardens. We'll find wonderful gardens and when the Nobels flee to the Glass Lands, we'll assign the FAC to tend their land."

Gerald nodded, knowing he had no choice. He agreed, and Senior Thomas walked out from behind the table to shake Gerald's hand. "Smart choice, son," he said, in a suddenly smooth, fatherly tone. The other Blackstars congratulated him, each in turn for earning his designation. *You've done well, Mr. Goodstone,* they all said in their own way. *You're exactly what the FSA needs.*

Part 3

Secrets

Chapter 25

The Market

After leaving the Blackstars tent, Gerald avoided anybody he recognized and made his way to the unfinished fence. It was a quiet, sunny morning. His internal whispers though present had receded like the tide to provide him an unusual quiet respite. He climbed out of the swamp rider and sat down on the soft dirt next to a fence post. Without the crowd of workers around him, Gerald listened to the breeze and watched the occasional bug fly by. He was a spy now. He reviewed his Blackstar meeting more honestly in his mind. No, he was an informant, a lure to bait bigger fish. He pulled his scribeosphere out of his pocket and shook it. *Can you lead me to Lizzy? Did you know she was alive?*

The locust didn't respond. Its image was still missing from the scribeosphere's metallic shine. *What about gene demons?* Neither Lizzy nor the locust's native voice answered, so he put the scribeosphere away.

He sat staring at the ground until the first swamp rider arrived. It was Lina by herself. "Hey, Gerald," she said, getting slowly out of her ride.

Gerald looked up and smiled despite his pensive mood. "Where is everybody?" he asked, standing up.

"No work ethic," she said, smiling back. She wore a loose fitting summer dress and limped badly.

"Oh," he said. "Something broken?"

"Drones fixed a couple things: ribs, some ligaments in my wrists."

"Is your leg hurt?"

Lina looked uncomfortable. "Something like that."

"Ankle?"

She looked up at the sky and smiled strangely. “Rose, Almighty! Suppose you’ll find out anyway. Brothers been teasing me all morning.”

“About hurting yourself?”

“You don’t got brothers, do you? Nothing funnier than a baby sister with a broke tailbone.”

“Ouch. Course you fell twenty meters. Could have been worse.”

She nodded. “Drone patched me up, but I’m right sore back there. Can’t bend a lick with these wraps around me.”

“A cast for, well, that part of you?”

She gently patted her bottom and hips. “Feels more like a diaper if you ask me. Or maybe like I’ve been swaddled in mummy wraps and the drone winched them way too tight trying to cut me in half. The drone said the wraps are supposed to heal the bruising but it doesn’t feel like that. It’s why I’m in this ridiculous dress… it’s embarrassing.”

Gerald laughed a little. “I think you look nice.”

She smiled. “I think you’re sweet, but I’m a clown.”

“You look pretty,” he said, immediately regretting his choice of words. She was a super, a mean one at that. Pretty was not something she wanted to hear but to Gerald’s surprise, she smiled… and then frowned. Lina swayed backwards and then grabbed his hand.

“Wow,” Gerald said. “You’re pale as a ghost.”

Lina wiped her damp brow. “I’m not supposed to be out of bed and that rider weren’t the cushiest thing to sit on. If daddy found out, I’d need more wraps to fix me.”

Gerald looked at her puzzled. “Then why are you out of bed?”

“Just wanted to see you. Thank you for what you did. People said you just jumped in after me. Could have killed yourself. Of course, I’m mad at you for that. If you’re dead, that’s one less person for fence building… might delay the project.”

“Wouldn’t want that. Speaking of which, where is everyone?”

“Daddy won’t admit it,” she pulled the hem of her dress up and let it fluttered back down, “but me being hobbled like this got everyone a day off. People are just going straight to market now.”

“Oh,” Gerald said, nodding. “What market?”

Lina smiled brightly. “Daddy says it’s okay to tell you. Said it’s time to bring you and AJ in… full members.”

Gerald's mood plummeted, remembering what the Blackstars planned. *Don't tell me anything,* he thought, fearfully. *Don't trust me. Can't trust—*

"Later today, we're going to an island off Iron City. Like a farmers market that lasts two days. We're all going to be there. And this year because all that's happened… you know, with the protests… it's going to be big. Like bigger than anything."

Gerald nodded. "You're talking about Earth First, aren't you?"

"And some who only care about Kisme."

Gerald stood stunned thinking about what the Blackstars wanted. His eyes fell to the colorful twist of fabric on her wrist. He couldn't. He didn't want to find out more than he already knew, but the Nobels weren't who the Blackstars were after, he reminded himself. He was protecting them by informing. They wanted Rose, not Earth First. Of course, if he gave the Blackstars what they wanted, they'd discover AJ was a gene demon. Gerald pressed his lips together in frustration. He didn't know what to do.

"Not as a date or anything," she added, suddenly. "I mean I don't just fall for any guy who saves my life or anything. I just thought since Daddy said you're allowed... AJ's going to be there with Sally. If we go together, Sally might not be so bossy about the FAC rules we're breaking."

Gerald laughed. "You think Sally's bossy?"

Lina grinned, catching his meaning. "What you're implying, sir?"

"Nothing," he said. "I'd be happy to go to the market as your not-date. Or, even as your date, if you wanted." He watched her face intently hoping for some reassurance he didn't misconstrue her offer.

She squeezed his fingers and leaned forward until her dark, honey-colored eyes filled his vision. She moved her mouth to his and kissed him, but it wasn't a deep kiss. It was a peck that ended too soon. "Then you're my date," she said, happily. "Now I got to get ready."

Gerald helped her back into the swamp rider. "With all the bumps, I could get a jumper."

She shook her head. "I'm a tough girl, Gerald. See you tonight at the merry-go-round."

"Merry-go-round?" he asked. She waved at him and drove away. Gerald watched her go, and then lay back down on the grass by the fence. *They're not after her,* he thought. He could keep her out of his reports. He closed his eyes against the hot sun. *For just a moment,* he thought, and then didn't wake up until late afternoon when AJ found him and they returned to Dusty Gulch.

Mrs. O'Sullivan had brought Gerald clothes for the market. She stood outside the shower stall advising him how best to behave on a date. She didn't seem to notice he wasn't participating in the conversation. He finished showering and continued to give Mrs. O'Sullivan the silent treatment until they climbed into the front seats of the jumper. In the back seat, Sally and AJ sat together with their hands clasped talking as if they hadn't noticed Mrs. O'Sullivan start the jumper and take off. For the first twenty minutes of the ride, Mrs. O'Sullivan chattered on about how lucky they were to have such good weather. AJ and Sally occasionally agreed and then went back to their own conversation. Gerald stayed silent and let his mind drift until he was directly asked a question: "So what did you talk to the Blackstars about, honey?"

"Excuse me?" Gerald asked.

"Peter saw you enter their tent. Said you left pretty upset."

"No. Not upset," he said. "They just asked me some questions."

"What kinds of questions?" AJ piped in from the back.

"I hope they don't want to ask me questions," Sally said. "Don't think I'd like that."

"Jack was there," he lied. "Thanked us for saving him."

"That all?" Mrs. O'Sullivan asked. "Nothing about you or AJ or John's gardens?"

He didn't like the interrogation as Mrs. O'Sullivan pressed him for details. *You think I'm lying?* he asked, finding it ironic. *See how it feels.*

She kept at him until he decided to turn the tables. "I guess I was a little upset, now that I think about it. Something one of them said. He asked me if I've been watching the m-spheres."

Mrs. O'Sullivan nodded, her knuckles turning white as she tightened her grip. "Lots of rumors about genetics," she said. "The High Prelate thinks it's a tactic for Augustus to discredit him."

"Genetics?" Gerald asked. "You mean gene demons?"

Mrs. O'Sullivan flushed with anger or fear but responded, smoothly, "Rumors."

"Said they caught some of them," Gerald finished, studying the way Mrs. O'Sullivan reacted to the news.

"If that were true, Gerald. They'd be dead already."

"Yeah," AJ said, without any of his usual bluster. "The last time they found one, I was a kid. Right after I met you, Gerald. They executed him on live SLYcast. Never forget it. He was just like you and I were. Maybe, ten years old. Made me hate the people who did it to him."

"Can we change the subject?" Sally suddenly asked. "It's depressing."

Mrs. O'Sullivan agreed, and they flew the rest of the way in silence.

When they arrived at Iron City, it looked more like a marina than a town. Long lines of sea jumpers and swamp floaters bobbed before the twelve hydro-locks that flooded and drained to let people step onto the uneven streets of the artificially elevated island. The flying jumpers and taxicrafts had fewer choices. There was only one, six-strip landing platform. Unlike the locks, the strips had just two navigation drones servicing them. Gerald gazed around at the hundreds of jumpers and taxicraft. He relaxed into his seat to get ready for a long wait. There was one landing strip free with several fliers leisurely circling over it like hawks in slow descent.

"Perfect!" Angie exclaimed. "No line." The jumper dropped in a tight spiral out of the sky. The world blurred, and Gerald gasped as the other fliers veered to avoid mid-air collisions. When they hit the platform, Gerald bit his lip. The fueling drone in charge wheeled over to Mrs. O'Sullivan and squawked like a goose honking. "Oh, hush up!" Angie said. She released the energy from the passenger dome and shooed the drone away with insults and scalding stares.

Sally gingerly rubbed her neck and said, "Mrs. Oh, I love you for taking me in and all, but you're a terrible pilot."

"Really?" AJ asked. He stared up at the other jumpers struggling to regain altitude and form a new line. "From where I sit, looks like those guys are the bad pilots. We're on the ground and they're not."

"Seriously," Sally said. "Why'd the jumper even allow such a dangerous descent?"

"No safety protocols," Gerald said. "The O'Sullivans don't think the rules apply to them."

In the service drone's black face shield, Gerald saw the reflection of Mrs. O'Sullivan frowning. Her mouth pulled into a thin line of concern and then she forced a wooden smile. "None of you will ruin my good time today. I love the market."

Gerald felt Sally and AJ staring at him from behind. AJ knew why he was mad, but Sally must have believed he was just being rude. He couldn't help it. The O'Sullivans had let him believe his sister was dead. He was angry and hurt. He was frustrated because despite his feelings, he'd have to help the O'Sullivans navigate the Blackstars investigation. AJ was a gene demon. If the Blackstars found out because of Gerald's reports, Gerald would be responsible for AJ's execution. Gerald decided he had to get AJ alone and tell him what the Blackstars had threatened. Until then, he pushed what he knew out of his mind. *What good's an informer*, he thought, *who gets everybody so mad, they won't talk to him?*

Iron City seemed larger from the ground than it had from above. The footpaths spider-webbing across the man-made isle were kilometers long. The weather sentries loomed tens of meters high like mechanical goliaths. From jumper height, the sentries were obscured by the cloudiness of the weather bubble they cast over the city. Gerald had been told the island's environment bubble protected Iron City from more than freedom storms. It was cinched together by Flexiforce strands that traveled over and under the island like a fishing net. If not for the sentries, the island would capsize under the weight of its own infrastructure.

As they walked, Gerald decided Iron City was in desperate need of some upgrades. Several streets were flooded, and he felt the ground bounce as he walked. It was like traipsing across a raft. In other respects, it was very much like all outskirt towns—old gray buildings built from weaved synthetics and hard metals to withstand bomb blasts and projectile gunfire. Laser and fusion fire could melt the structures easily enough, but when those weapons were unleashed on the prezero world, the northern territories weren't strategically important. Even now, only a handful of cities had protection from energy beams burning down from space. So Iron City remained unchanged in peace time—caught in a period of history when buildings needed to remain standing more than they needed to look pretty. Its saving grace was its residents. They sVid sprayed the ugliest buildings with festive facades.

Once a season, Iron City reinvented itself by projecting holographic themes upon its least attractive town structures. This year's theme was tropical with plenty of dark bamboo window frames, shutters, and black iron gates overlaying perk shop patios. The clerk's office where Chuck Heller from the tube probably worked, was a squat, square building sVid-sprayed bright yellow. Projected in front was a twin set of oceanarium gazing balls spinning on top of bubbling water fountains. The sVid included the sound of water trickling the balls into motion.

Gerald followed the O'Sullivans while they bantered back and forth with Sally until they reached the boardwalk at the edge of town. Normally, a boardwalk crossing the swamp would have bug repelling wind fields beneath the rails to prevent mosquito and biting flies from attacking walkers. Unfortunately, Iron City didn't have the perks to fix the ones on the ancient looking boardwalk Mrs. O'Sullivan chose to follow. Its boards were so rickety, it looked like it might fall into the swamp at any moment. Gerald studied the brackish water below looking for the red eyes of crocs. He wiped his brow and swatted the more immediate danger of black flies and gnats buzzing around his head.

Uncomfortable, Gerald picked up his pace to see if he could move the rest of his party along faster. He finally passed them in frustration. Again, he felt their stares. Sally caught up. "So what's your problem, Gerald? You've been acting like a butt all day."

Gerald tried to smile but instead he just grunted: "Nervous, I guess."

Sally mistook his meaning as Gerald had hoped she might. She talked excitedly about how wonderful Lina would be with the right guy "to tame" her. Gerald faked a laugh as he fought the urge to tell Sally about AJ. The O'Sullivans were radicals just like she and Jack thought. She had the right to know who she was involved with and how dangerous it might be for her if the Blackstars found out. Yet all he said was: "How about you tame her, and give her to me when you're done."

Sally laughed and hip-checked him as they continued to walk. AJ came up beside them and threw his arm over their shoulders. "Everything alright now?" he asked, and Gerald nodded. Mrs. O'Sullivan moved up to them next and for a while they walked together in comfortable silence.

When they arrived at the island, it was overgrown with jungle brush that must have been sVid sprayed because Mrs. O'Sullivan walked straight through a tree and disappeared. When the rest of the group followed, they emerged into a wide-open meadow turned into a fairground full of people laughing, running, and having what appeared to be a wonderful time. Gerald took in the few kiddie rides on the perimeter of the clearing. He saw a couple of wooden benches and plenty of food and drink stands in tiny tents. Open air stalls sold vegetables, fruit, and a few spices that could, according to the signs, be delivered to your home for extra perks. There wasn't a single vending drone or hover cart near the tents. Technology seemed to be banned to the perimeter where various drones floated as if held back by wind repellers that actually worked. The meadow was like Dusty Gulch and Angie O'Sullivan was beaming. "All locally grown," she said, proudly. "The rides are free."

Sally clapped her hands and pointed to Lina. There was a merry-go-round behind her with children pushing it in circles. There wasn't a SLYcade to be found. It was as if he had stepped into the distant past until he noticed the Flying Eyes circling above.

"Don't worry," Big John said, seeming to materialize behind them. "Those are ours, keeping watch."

Mrs. O'Sullivan hugged Mr. Nobel who returned the gesture stiffly. "Your husband's in the valley, Angie," Mr. Nobel said, pointing to two men standing on either side of a narrow trail leading away from the vegetable stalls into the jungle.

"Oh, alright. I hope all our time won't be doing work," she said, and together they walked across the clearing. The two men nodded as they passed.

Lina saw them and waved. "Normally," she said, when they arrived. "I'd be pushing the little ones myself but being wrapped up like this..."

"They your cousins?" AJ asked, looking at the little kids playing.

Lina beamed. "Only my favorite ones. The ones I don't like much are over there." She indicated a group of older kids kicking a hover ball around the meadow.

"I like that game," Sally said.

"Who doesn't," Kyle commented as he strode over to the group. He raised his hand. "Put it there, Gerald," he said.

Gerald heard the friendliness in Kyle's tone but was confused considering his hand was too high for a shake and not balled up for a knuckle bump. Gerald held out his hand and watched Kyle slap it down painfully. "Just wanted to say the other day I got you wrong. You saved my life. A man doesn't forget."

Gerald nodded as he considered the twist of colored ribbons on Kyle's wrist. Lina wore an identical bracelet. "I think technically AJ saved you."

"Still, man. I owe you."

"Good to know," Gerald said, as he watched Kyle turn and walk away.

"So, you like our market?" Lina asked.

Gerald nodded. "Fun."

"What you see here is local to the marshes. Mostly early greens and what's left over from last season's crops." She nodded at tables topped with piles of herbs, dried fruit, and preserves. "We barter and trade amongst ourselves. Not just food, everything from housewares to time."

"Time?" Sally asked.

"Sure. You got something need fixin', I'll fix it for you for say one bushel of apples per half a workday. Things like that. We're self-sufficient."

Sally nodded looking concerned.

"Okay, the vegetables aren't FAC certified but we don't sell them. Just trade them legal like."

Sally nodded. "I'd be surprised if they were, actually. What about protein?"

Lina lit up. "Come with me."

She led them through a twisty path to another section of the market. In this clearing, goats, chickens, and tubs of brackish water holding fish and spiderlike creatures were arranged. "Live things?" Sally asked, horrified.

Lina nodded. "You've seen the croc pits at Dusty's. Where do you think we got the tasty lizards from?"

Tough looking men stood near the edges of the ponds with what looked like loops of rope coiled at their feet. "You pull them out of there?" Gerald asked. "With lassos?"

Lina nodded.

AJ laughed and said, "There's so much more to these swamps than you've seen."

"Daddy says we can show you everything."

Gerald frowned at the reminder of how little of AJ's home he had seen prior to this year. "Look forward to it," he said, more happily than he felt.

Lina led them to several other clearings, each offering a different spread of tradable goods. Along the way, they ate meat roasts, homemade desserts, and listened to plenty of music. Once the sun had dropped, people danced. In Lina's case, dancing meant slowly limping to the rhythm as she held Gerald around his waist. She was still "right sore."

After an hour of dancing and holding Lina's body close to his own , Gerald realized this was the most happy he'd felt since leaving the Academy on Designation Day. That was right up until Mr. Nobel and Uncle Luke found them. "Avelina," Big John called, loudly.

Lina's cheek was resting against Gerald's chest and her eyes were closed when she jerked in his arms guiltily upon hearing her father's voice. She stepped back so fast, she almost fell down but Gerald grabbed her hands to keep her standing. Her giant of a dad walked straight to them, and he didn't look happy.

Fortunately for Gerald, Big John rarely looked happy. "Got some work for the boys," he said calmly, when he reached them. "And you need rest, Avelina. See you at home."

"I'm a big girl, daddy," she said. "I think I know when I need rest."

"And that's now, Avelina." Big John spoke with a tone so low Gerald felt the rumble of it in his chest. Lina stared at her dad for a moment longer and then looked across to Sally who still held AJ's hand. "Fine. I need rest. Sally can you take me back?"

Sally, caught off-guard, agreed.

Lina turned slowly and deliberately to face Gerald. She held out her arms awkwardly and limped into his chest as she wrapped him tight in a hug. She looked up into his eyes and opened her mouth slightly to kiss him. Gerald leaned down but his eyes caught Big John staring. He missed most of her mouth, catching just the corner of her lips and some of her cheek. She pushed herself back from him and laughed a little. "Had a great time, Gerald," she said. "The races are tomorrow night. Will you come?"

Gerald nodded and then she left the boys alone with Big John and Uncle Luke. "Ah, sorry, Mr. Nobel," Gerald said. "For what you saw there."

"Not sure what John saw, but what I saw…" Uncle Luke said, laughing. "If that was a kiss, better practice up."

"Luke," Big John said.

"C'mon, John. You forget who set you right with her mother? You kissed worse than the kid."

Mr. Nobel grunted and then headed for the guarded path on the other side of the clearing.

"Well, follow the man," Uncle Luke said. "There's muscle work to be done."

"Now?" AJ asked, looking at the moon directly overhead. "What kind of work's done in the middle of the night?"

"The kind that didn't happen. Get my meaning?"

AJ nodded and Gerald froze. *Don't trust me*, he thought. *Please don't.*

They followed Big John through a winding forest trail and then down into a flooded area of the island. On both sides of the trail, gray cypress trees jutted out of the water at odd angles. The trail became soft and the air cooled as water dripped onto their heads from the high branches. At the lowest point before they started climbing again, the air smelled of fallen leaves turned mucky. The tree trunks around them were worn smooth above tangles of thick, ropy roots. As fog wafted in eddies over the forest, Gerald's eyes played tricks on him turning the roots into things that looked like the ligaments of tall hooved animals. As they climbed back to higher ground, the fog dissipated and soon they stood at a ridgetop looking down on another valley without trees. It was shaped like a bowl. "Used to be a lake," Big John said.

"Reckon about twenty years back, the water just up and left," Uncle Luke added. At the bottom of the dry basin, hundreds of yellow lights floated around groups of people tending cargo ships about the size of the ones Kyle and Sammy had crashed. "There they be," Uncle Luke said, pointing.

"Looks like all of them," Big John said. "Let's see what she brought us."

Gerald and AJ exchanged glances as they descended silently behind the older men. At the bottom, they were told to stay put with dozens of other workers Gerald recognized from the farm. Nobody paid them much attention as they stared silently at the sky. "What are they looking at?" Gerald asked.

AJ shook his head. "Hear that?"

Gerald paused to listen. After a moment of silence, he heard the faintest thrumming of powerful engines approaching. The sound rumbled more loudly until he heard multiple engines echoing directly overhead. Gerald searched for the source of the engines but saw nothing but two slivers of moon and the usual stars. Except some were missing. Gerald slapped AJ's arm. "The Hunter's gone, Aje. The constellation…"

"What?" He looked up. White stars flickered out as if they were being extinguished one-by-one until most of the stars were gone. As if by magic, the stars reappeared in their proper configuration a few moments later. Gerald blinked his eyes and AJ exhaled sharply as eight dark triangles shimmered suddenly into view above them.

Six, three-sided ships topped by round black domes were suddenly in the night air powering their engines down. In the middle of the stealth ships, two cargo cruisers hovered. The stealth ships floated down like leaves falling on a windless day. AJ whistled. "Who are these guys?" he asked. "Got sidewinders on 'em."

"And laser weapons," Gerald said.

Uncle Luke stepped up behind them and put his hands on their shoulders. "They're us, boys. We have a fleet, fifty strong."

Us? Gerald thought, starting to panic. *He couldn't tell the Blackstars this!*

The cargo cruisers settled with less grace but still expertly on the ground. As the humming of engines cut off, Big John joined by Uncle Luke and Mrs. O'Sullivan gathered around the large hatchway of the first ship to land. "What's Ma doing here?" AJ snapped.

"Hate to say I told you, Aje, but she's genuine Earth First."

"Not just with Earth First," said another voice. Both boys turned to find AJ's dad standing behind them. "She's their leader, AJ. I wish I could have told you sooner."

"Big John's their leader," AJ said, stuttering to a stop. He looked between his dad and Gerald as if he was truly surprised. If AJ wasn't lying to Gerald earlier, AJ's parents didn't know he wanted to leave the Followers of Rose to join the Nobels in the Glass Lands. They didn't know Gerald knew the truth about them being spies. Neither of them knew Gerald was spying, albeit unwillingly, for the Blackstars. With sudden clarity, Gerald understood not just these secrets but others. His mind raced through scenarios as his fingers worked like a child's to grasp the logic of his thoughts.

Mr. O'Sullivan was so skilled at lying, he blissfully revealed two secrets at once: one to AJ, his mother was the leader of Earth First, not Big John as AJ believed; and one to Gerald, the O'Sullivans are all part of Earth First. Gerald knew he was supposed to appear shocked and confused but trusting. These were the people who raised him since the fire. He wasn't supposed to know the truth. Mr. O'Sullivan had spent years teaching AJ how to lie to his best friend. So AJ had to play act too. He was supposed to roll with the new information his father gave him and adapt. That's what Mr. O'Sullivan expected. He probably expected to laugh with AJ at some future point about this moment. *You should have seen you face, son…* Gerald imagined the conversation. *You recovered like a pro. Ha ha,* Gerald thought.

The trouble with that future conversation was Gerald already knew the Earth First secret was just another lie on top of the larger secret they kept from Big John Nobel. They worked for Preston Rose but not just as his designates. They were Followers and obeyed like slaves, according to the Blackstar named, Henry. The O'Sullivans had spent decades rising up the ranks of Earth First undercover. They had earned the group's trust until Big John followed their lead. Gerald's head swam. Big John, without knowing it, followed Preston Rose. Earth First, without knowing it, was Followers of Rose.

The Blackstars couldn't find a connection between the High Prelate and Earth First because they believed Big John was their leader. Big John was the one consistently breaking the laws of the land. His gardens circumvented the FAC's authority over farms. Earth First fought the OPC with their rallies and protests. They wanted to flee Preston Rose's rule because his OPC forbade them travelling to the Glass Lands. By that logic, Big John and Earth First were enemies of the Followers of Rose. Yet they followed Angie O'Sullivan and she followed Rose. *The High Prelate's clever, lad. It can't be overstated how clever.*

Gerald must have wobbled on his feet because Mr. O'Sullivan grabbed his arm. "I know this might be a shock. I can't imagine what you're thinking. Angie and I wanted to tell you both so many times."

"Why now?" AJ asked, stiffly.

"Because, son, Earth First is fleeing to the Glass Lands in just over a month. Not all at once but in waves. We want you two to join us. Angie thinks Sally could come too if you wanted that."

AJ cast a glance to his mom hugging the people emerging from the first cargo cruiser. "Since when, Da?" he asked. "How long has she been the one in charge?"

"All in good time, son. When your mother's finished with her business, we'll sit down for a chat. All you two need to do right now is go help unload those ships. If you decide against joining us, we'll understand. But right now, we need time to explain."

AJ nodded and then turned smartly away from his dad as if he was pretending to be angry. Or maybe, Gerald considered, he was really angry. It was difficult to tell.

"C'mon, Gerald. Let's go."

Gerald followed AJ towards the other workers gathering in front of the two cargo ships. When they were far enough from AJ's dad, he turned his head and said, "Big John's their leader. He's always been their leader. If he's not…."

"What does it matter?" Gerald asked, though he already knew why it mattered. AJ was coming to the same conclusion Gerald had arrived at moments ago: if AJ's mom is the leader of Earth First, then Earth First was following Preston Rose.

"Then Rose knows about the Glass Lands," he said, choking back emotion. "I can't escape the old bastard. I have nowhere to go, Gerald… I'm trapped into following him forever whether I want to or not."

Gerald nodded as he saw the second cargo ship open. "Look on the bright side, Aje," Gerald said, almost enjoying AJ's discomfort at being lied to by his parents. "At least you can have two girlfriends now."

AJ looked up and saw Brandy Peppers backlit by the inside glow of the cargo cruiser. She was flanked by armed guards who escorted her down the ramp to meet Big John and Mrs. O'Sullivan at the bottom. AJ slowed his steps and stared. This time, Gerald felt no pleasure in seeing the look on his friend's face. They stopped a few meters from the cargo ships and listened.

"What's this?" Big John asked, looking behind Brandy.

"Weapons delivery," she said.

Big John shook his head. "We said no weapons, Brandy."

"Well, John, we certainly can't take them back. Besides, Earth First's only a part of the movement now. The laz'rupters are for Justice for Kisme, and I don't believe you speak for them." She glanced around for who she wanted. "Uncle!" she yelled. "Come get your rifles."

Uncle Luke walked up slowly, eyeing Big John. They exchanged heated stares until Gerald was certain Big John was going to throw a punch. Mrs. O'Sullivan stepped in between. "Gentlemen!" she yelled. "Regardless of what we call ourselves, we want the same things."

"I've played by the FSA's rules long enough, John," said Uncle Luke, looking over the top of Angie's head to Lina's dad. "You weren't at the riots of thirty-nine when they took Dixon. You don't see what's coming."

"Armed rebellion's suicide, Luke. You think your little fleet can do more than dent a battalion of enforcers led by Field Marshals? Let alone the FSA's fighter squadrons."

"We got unmanned fighter drones too, John. We need defenses."

"Only thing we need guns for is hunting."

"Drones can shoot animals as good as people."

"Luke, no," Angie O'Sullivan said. "I agree with John. If we're perceived as too big a threat, the FSA won't hesitate to come to the Glass Lands looking for us. If we just disappear, quietly, the FSA will find bigger threats to crush."

"Not figuring it through, Angie. The FSA won't never let us just go."

"Be that as it may Luke, Earth First's not arming. We'll all be gone by end of harvest as planned. They probably won't even notice until spring."

Brandy laughed contemptuously. "So you just run with your tails between your legs? Give up your lands? They killed Kisme just for defending her mother. You saw what they did. The Glass Lands is just a dream while the government oppresses us. We live here. We need to defend what we have, then the people here can support the people in the Glass Lands. Send them supplies when they need them."

For the next several minutes, they argued and nobody gave ground. The people wearing ribbons on their wrists emptied Brandy's cargo cruiser. The rest helped Big John and Angie O'Sullivan empty bags of grain, seed, and fertilizers from the other cargo ship. AJ opted out of helping in favor of talking to Brandy.

When he came back, AJ sounded lost. "There's something wrong with her, Gerald. I mean, she acted like—"

"Like you had a girlfriend already?"

"She doesn't know that."

Gerald shook his head. "It seems everybody around here has secrets, Aje. Maybe hers was she was never that into you in the first place."

"That's not it. She acted like she didn't know who I was… I mean, what we did. When I pressed it, reminded her. She got angry. She told me to not come back until I had a ribbon round my wrist."

Gerald dropped the bag of grain he was carrying and sat on it. He cradled his face with his hands.

"What's wrong?" AJ asked

"Lina wears ribbons, Aje. That means she wants to take up arms."

AJ nodded, not seeing a problem. Gerald saw an enormous problem but couldn't voice it. No matter what the Blackstars said, they wouldn't let armed rebellion go unpunished. He thought back to what the locust revealed on the tube about Justice for Kisme. Kisme St. James wasn't even Justine's daughter. Brandy made that up. She was stoking the flames of rebellion but why and for who?

Everybody here was lying about something. There were too many secrets.

Gerald couldn't tell the Blackstars about Justice for Kisme without getting Lina in trouble. He couldn't tell them about the Followers of Rose infiltrating Earth First without getting the O'Sullivans in trouble. If he didn't tell them anything, everybody would be in trouble and their investigation might lead to AJ being exposed as a gene demon.

AJ was not the only one feeling trapped.

Chapter 26

The Mission

The O'Sullivan's household was woken by a pounding at the front door. AJ was up and dressed a second before Sally rushed in. "They're here, AJ," she said, afraid.

AJ nodded and walked to the bedroom door before being pushed back by two ROLIES: one tall and one short. "Relax, big fella," the shorter one said. "We're here for your friend."

The tall ROLIE grabbed Gerald by the shoulder and ripped him up from his bed to his feet. "We meet, again, Mr. Goodstone. Told you we'd be watching."

Sally swept towards the ROLIE holding AJ. "Let him be! I know the law and you can't do this. There has to be charges."

The shorter ROLIE held out his arm and prevented her from crossing the room. "No charges, Miss Scott. Just following orders. Blackstars sent us."

"Corporal!" the big ROLIE snapped. "Remember your place."

"C'mon, Todd. We got nothing on this kid. Why scare these nice people? Seriously," he said to Sally. "We're neighbors despite the uniform. I've seen you around the FAC being built down the street from us. Name's Henry, by the way."

"Corporal, we do not use names."

"That's true when we're on official business. Near as I can tell captain, we're doing the Blackstar errands. We don't answer to them."

Mrs. O'Sullivan was in the room next in a flurry of arms and legs. Mr. O'Sullivan stood calmly behind her. "What's the meaning of this?" she asked.

Captain Todd looked at her and shook his head. "We're taking this one to Senior Thomas."

"Don't worry, Mrs. O'Sullivan," Henry said. "Nobody's arrested."

"Yet," Todd said.

The ROLIES let Gerald dress and then walked him from the house. Mrs. O'Sullivan told Gerald she'd be along soon to get to the bottom of what was happening, but Gerald told her to stay put. "It's no big deal, Mrs. O'Sullivan. I mean, Angie," he said. "I think I know what they want."

Mrs. O'Sullivan's lips pursed together. Gerald felt guilty knowing he said exactly what she didn't want to hear. From her perspective, her family let him into their secret world just hours ago. Now he was being carted away for questioning without any reasonable pretense for taking him away. Subterfuge was not something overseers were good at. "Don't worry about me," he said.

Sally teared up as he left. The O'Sullivans just watched him go.

Inside the jumper, Gerald was separated from the ROLIES by a black shield that prevented him from seeing or hearing them talk. Looking for something to distract himself, he fished inside his pocket for the scribeosphere. It was still warm with no locust peering out at him. The locust was his only access to the SLYscape. Without it, he felt as if one of his senses was gone. He wondered what he'd do without the locust. In answer, the whispers inside his head stirred like waves lapping on the beach. They were louder than they had been which signified something but Gerald didn't know if it was good or bad. It was just a fact, he guessed, like the fact he hadn't had a night vision since seeing the wolf kill the dragon locust and Abe. He tried to remember if he had ever gone this long without a night vision. Two or three days, he decided, but never a week.

They landed at Dusty Gulch and the captain twisted Gerald's arms behind him to slip a resistance band around his wrists. "Not going to run, captain," Gerald said.

The corporal just shook his head.

Gerald walked in between the two ROLIES past the blue tent to a smaller, red tent on the far side of the encampment. Deep chested dogs roamed its exterior on chains. They looked unhappy and mean but that didn't concern Gerald as much as the person he spotted leaving the tent just before he arrived. He saw the man from behind and noted only the black crew-cut as he strode with purpose to a large ship the color of twilight. On its hull, two black wolves sat back-to-back howling at different sides of the cracked moon. Gerald tried to get a glimpse of his face but the man disappeared inside the ship before he could. From the look of him, Gerald was almost certain, he was the Deputy Director of the FSA. If Cole Reaver was here, Gerald pondered, Brandy was closer to being caught than she knew.

The dogs growled and barked when the ROLIES approached the tent with Gerald in tow. A voice from inside yelled something unintelligible before words formed: "Shut up!"

Captain Todd, not worried about being bitten because of his black and yellow armor, pushed Gerald dangerously close to the chained dogs on their way into the tent. Senior Thomas sat in a high back chair behind a heavy desk made of gray metal. "Now captain, remember he's on our side."

The captain freed Gerald's wrists and nodded to the overseer before backing out of the tent. "Good morning, Mr. Goodstone! Tea?"

Gerald accepted a cup just to stall before the questions began.

"So, what news do you bring?"

Gerald shrugged. "It's only been a day. There's not much to tell yet."

"I see," Senior Thomas said, taking a long sip from his cup.

"Please, have a seat."

Gerald sat before the metal desk and took a sip.

"There was some kind of event in Iron City yesterday I hear. Tell me about that."

"Not much to tell. Some people with gardens traded vegetables. There were rides too. Lots of kids running around… kind of fun."

"Oh, good. I'm glad you had fun," Senior Thomas said sarcastically, and put down his cup. "Let me explain this arrangement we have. You need to tell me every last detail of what you see and hear. Then I will decide what is of interest since I am the only one sitting in this tent who understands the value of what you witness."

"I didn't really see anything," Gerald said, his pulse elevating. "It was just a fair. We danced."

"So there were a number of ROLIES present ensuring law and order? There were a number of FAC vendors offering food and delightful treats, right? For if there was not, then it was not a legal gathering. Did you see FAC vendors? ROLIES?"

"No, sir," Gerald admitted.

"And you did not tell me because the value of that information is not known to you. So, from the beginning, tell me everything."

When Gerald hesitated, Senior Thomas slapped his palms on the table. "You got in a jumper and flew to Iron City. It was a warm day. Unusually clear. You followed the O'Sullivans… go on. Tell me!"

"We walked to some island—"

"Yes?"

"It was hidden by projection shields."

"Good…"

"I met my girlfriend." Gerald immediately wished he hadn't said it but pressed on as his mind operated just a hair faster than his mouth. "We ate lots of illegal food. There were no FAC providers. Everybody cooked their own… delicious, really. We danced."

"And when night came?"

"Oh," Gerald said, nodding. "We saw ships landing. Some of the people went to them to unload."

Senior Thomas sat forward in his seat, his eyes unblinking as he watched Gerald tell his story.

"There were seed and grain bags stacked high. Took almost an hour to unload it all. There were garden supplies too like fertilizer and hand tools. We moved it all into smaller transports and went home."

Senior Thomas sat back in his chair and sighed. "Seeds? Grain? Illegal food. Very fine, Mr. Goodstone. Good work." He lifted his cup to his lips while his eyes narrowed and focused more intently on Gerald sitting across from him. "But you know what would have been better work?"

The teacup launched from the man's hand like something shot from a gun. Gerald vaulted sideways in an attempt to dodge. The cup grazed his ear painfully and then shattered on the other side of the tent. Gerald hit the ground.

Senior Thomas was up and around the desk before Gerald had time to climb to his feet. Thomas' boot caught Gerald in the temple and then the jaw. His other boot found Gerald's ribs. The Blackstar kicked Gerald a dozen times before growing so tired by the effort he had to lean against the desk for support. "Get up!" he yelled.

Gerald rolled slowly to his hands and knees. He coughed and blood from a torn lip splattered the dirt. He stood back up shaking.

"What would have been better," Senior Thomas said, calmly but breathing hard. "Is for you to tell me about the shipment of stolen weapons delivered to your precious O'Sullivans. That would have been the kind of information I was interested in. The kind you would have been rewarded for divulging."

The physical pain Gerald experienced paled next to the chill that seized him as he heard those words. "What weapons?"

Senior Thomas opened a drawer in his desk and sat back down. He pulled out a second teacup and saucer. He poured himself some hot water. "We work with the highest levels of the FSA, Mr. Goodstone. They have ways."

"So why do you need me?"

"Because we don't care about the weapons shipment. We care about what comes after. The O'Sullivans protect gene demons, Mr. Goodstone. Did you know that? You've probably met one without knowing it. They look like us. That's part of the problem."

Gerald nodded, hoping the overseer didn't see the fear in his eyes.

"Somebody you probably know is an abomination. Think about it."

"Hard to believe," Gerald said, taking rapid breaths as if the overseer had broken his ribs *Calm down,* he told himself, silently. *Don't give anything away.*

Senior Thomas studied Gerald and took another sip. "You might even think they're friendly but they're not. They're bent on destroying everyone who is not like them. They believe they are superior because of their genetic abilities. I have talked to them. I know."

"You've talked to them, sir?"

"The two in custody now. Evil to their core. It's disappointing, really."

"What is, sir?"

"You, Mr. Goodstone. You are honor bound to uphold the law like me. Or you will be once you have sworn your oath. An FSA agent on the inside could have been so useful."

"I don't understand, sir."

Senior Thomas took another sip. "If you would have been honest about what you saw last night, we would be having a different conversation now. You would not be bleeding on my floor. You would be entrusted with the task of discovering how the High Prelate uses his pet gene demons to elude the FSA. You would have been gifted with the responsibility of finding the insider who made those weapons disappear from a heavily guarded FSA facility. Mr. Reaver knows it was the High Prelate but you could have proven it."

"It's more likely someone high up at the FSA provided access, sir."

Senior Thomas nodded. "Perhaps. But if that is the truth, you ruined your chance to uncover it by your blatant dishonesty. Regrettably Mr. Goodstone, you've chosen your side, and our business is now concluded. See yourself out."

"I can still help," Gerald said, afraid of what the overseers might know about AJ. Yet he was encouraged they believed the O'Sullivans received the weapons shipment, not Uncle Luke. They didn't know everything as Jack claimed. They only believed they did. "Now I know the kind of information you want. I can help."

"You will help, Mr. Goodstone. Of that I am certain, but not today.... Captain," he called, and Gerald was taken from the tent and set free.

AJ waited for Gerald at one of the chow tables in Dusty Gulch. Since ROLIES were everywhere, he waved at Gerald to follow him into the junk yard. They walked through mountains of broken equipment and rusted junk until arriving at a supply shed with a broken cellar. The wall had collapsed on top of the cellar stairs which were overgrown with years of thick brown vines and purple flowers. Gerald worked his sore body down until he sat stiffly on the edge of the broken cellar door. AJ watched him with concern and paced.

AJ took a closer look at Gerald's bloody shirt and winced at the bruising on his chin. "The cowards," he said. "Hiding behind their robes. If we did that to them—"

"They'd call the FSA. It's just the way things work. Plus, I've been beat up worse."

"Not for a long time," he said, looking across the junk towards Dusty Gulch as if he could see through the piles to the overseers' bivouac. He slowed his pace. "What do they want?"

Gerald thought about it for a moment and then realized there was nothing he needed to hide from AJ. The overseers were going to do what they wanted, and he needed to start warning people. "They gave me my designation. I'm a vWare controller working for the FSA."

"Congratulations. Getting dezie'd don't usually earn a beat-down," AJ said. "Would explain why everybody at the FSA's always so tweaked off."

Gerald didn't laugh. "They wanted me to spy on you and the Nobels."

"Makes sense," AJ said, staring into the sky. "The Reavers want my parents. Overseers can bring up charges, some true, some not. Tell everybody Rose put them up to it."

"They know about the market, Aje."

AJ smiled. "The market's legit. They pulled permits when the Blackstars got here."

"How?"

"Preston Rose authorized it. He can authorize any type of fair he wants. There's nothing the overseers can do about it or the FSA. They've got nothing. That's why nobody's been arrested yet."

"They know about the weapons."

"Luke's already got those hidden. The Blackstars would have more luck finding Brandy's stealth ships than Luke's guns. Besides, Brandy's been one-step ahead of the Reavers for months. She doesn't need our help."

But Lina does, Gerald thought, thinking about how he had to warn her too.

"Thing is, Gerald, even if Brandy did need help, she wouldn't admit it. Being on the run's changed her. I tried to talk to her again today over the bio-com, but she acts like I don't exist without a ribbon on my wrist. It stings but I get it. I'm just some guy she had a fling with before she started breaking into SLYcasts for Kisme. But what she said to Ma last night? Brandy loves Ma. Big John was like a Da to her after her parents died a few years back. She's different, brother. Jacked-up different."

"Cole's been hunting her. Maybe, she doesn't talk to you because she doesn't want get you involved. Maybe, she's protecting you."

AJ shook his head. "Nah, it's not that. She's done something she's not proud of and I think I know what it might be. I think she accidentally led the FSA to places they shouldn't know about."

"What places, Aje?"

"It's all over the immersion spheres, Gerald. The Revealers are telling everybody Rose is growing abominations like they're pet rats. They say two are in custody being interrogated. Whoever the poor chums are, I think she might've exposed them by mistake. And if the FSA's got 'em, they'll give up Rose even if they've never met the old man. Nobody dishes pain like the FSA… no offense."

"Offense? Oh yeah. I'm FSA now. Funny." Gerald stared into the clear sky and wondered how difficult it was to be AJ right then. With all the secrets he'd kept over the years, there was little doubt in Gerald's mind AJ knew what he was. To hear him talk about others like him being captured and tortured. *Tortured. So easy to think. It's what interrogation means in the Freeland.* Gerald remembered what Kyle yelled at the 'roider fight. *Do you feel free?*

Gerald looked up at AJ. He's never been allowed to feel free. "It's worse, Aje."

"What do you mean?"

"They know about what you are, I think."

AJ stopped and looked at Gerald quizzically. "What I am?"

Gerald studied the oily green plants and hairy roots beneath his boots. He watched shiny red-striped ants circle around a pile of silty soil. Sweat dripped under Gerald's arms. Did he really not know? "They know your parents protect gene demons. They hinted they knew you were a gene demon."

"What do you mean? Me?"

Gerald's heart gave way to fear. AJ didn't know what he was, after all. Gerald stood up. "You might want to sit down, Aje."

"I'm good," he said, softly.

"I don't know how to tell you this—"

"Spit it out, Gerald."

"You're a gene demon, AJ. I'm sorry but I heard your parents say it. They said you were given to them by the High Prelate to raise." AJ's tongue slipped nervously across his lips as he heard the news. "I guess your parents aren't really even your parents exactly."

"You think I'm a gene demon?"

Gerald nodded.

"Oh, man, brother," he said. "I thought with all I've told you. I just thought you knew."

"That's why I'm warning you, Aje. The overseers are closing in. You're going to have to hide."

"Gerald," AJ said, his voice more serious and solemn than Gerald had ever heard. "I'm not a gene demon. You are."

"I am?"

"You are."

"Me?"

AJ nodded and Gerald almost laughed. He wanted to dismiss this as just another O'Sullivan lie, but AJ's eyes were focused and intense, shining like they did before fights—serious. If he was lying, Gerald couldn't read AJ at all. If he was telling the truth... "How can I be a gene demon? Look at your size, Aje. Look at what you can do. Nobody's stronger than you. Your genes. Mine. You're like out of a World Union storybook… freakishly strong, freakishly fast. I'm no super soldier."

AJ smiled sadly. "Ma likes the word, 'enhanced.' A child of the future. You don't have to be big to be that."

"I'm normal. Average. Less than, really."

AJ shook his head. "No you're not."

"Yes I am! Look at me, Aje."

"You're special even among the enhanced, but I don't know why. They don't tell me everything as you saw last night. You're a genius so I thought you put it together. I would have told you in the mine but you were so mad at me. You wanted to kill me. You took a swing and anybody who knows me like you know me wouldn't take a swing unless they were crazy mad. Gerald, you went critters, and I thought it was because you knew."

"About being a gene demon?"

"You're enhanced," AJ said, nodding. "Why else would I need to protect you? Sacrifice my life for yours? Why would Rose go to all this trouble just to protect some normal kid? You're genetically different Gerald. You tell me what that means. You tell me why everybody wants you dead. I just follow orders. You're my mission. I protect you. I do not fail. That's all I've ever done."

Gerald crossed his arms over his throbbing ribs. He sat down on the dirt and rocked. All his fear about AJ being caught and executed. It was Gerald, Senior Thomas wanted to catch. Gerald was the abomination, not AJ. The whispers in his mind erupted in screams that hurt his brain. He covered his ears despite knowing it would do no good. On his palm, he felt the earring and the warmth of the smooth jade his mother gave him so he'd never feel alone. His mother must have known what Gerald was or why else would she assume he'd be alone? His father warned him about molecular implants not because he was special in a good way. It was to protect him from people like Senior Thomas.

The whispers reached their zenith in volume then dropped back down into soft voices that sounded exhausted and sick. One voice struggled to be heard as Gerald rocked. It pushed itself into a semblance of words rising to the surface through hisses and rattles only Gerald could hear. The words pushed higher until his locust's voice became stronger and whole in his mind: *He hurts me,* the locust said, mechanically. *Hurts her brood for hiding you.* Gerald felt the scribeosphere in his pocket grow cold. It felt good on his sore ribs, soothing and familiar.

The locust's voice changed to a childish hum so familiar, he could almost hear the song: *Come out, come out, wherever you are. Ready or not... Stop hiding, Gerals!* And then he heard the angry words: *Kill the wolf!*

His little sister's voice startled him. He had not heard it since before the Black Eye exploded. He feared for her. She was hiding but she wasn't seven anymore. Lizzy spoke again, only this time in the teenage voice the locust created for her. *Please find me, Gerald. Help me kill the wolf and save what's inside.*

He remembered the girl standing at the foot of his bed. He remembered how she fought the wolf and turned herself into the dragon locust. He remembered his little sister and Gerald's stomach clenched in recognition. The locust wasn't creating Lizzy's voice from Gerald's memories. It was sending Gerald her thoughts.

Lizzy was using the locust to ask for help.

Chapter 27

Night Gliders

When Gerald stopped rocking and dropped his hands from his ears, AJ sat down next to him. He reached his giant arm around Gerald's narrow shoulders and pulled him tight. Gerald winced more from the sudden quiet in his mind than the squeezing of his ribs.

"If they know about you, we have to tell Ma," AJ said. "Let her figure out what to do. She and Da have a direct line to Rose and if the old man can't help. She's Earth First's flippin' leader. There's got to be power there, and it's her mission to protect you too."

Gerald, still adjusting to what the locust said, felt suddenly calm. His sister hijacked his locust to contact him. It was the only explanation that fit. She was out there somewhere with SLYscape access. She was trying to get his attention.

"My Da too. We all swore to protect you, brother. And that's what we'll do."

Gerald focused on what AJ was saying and felt uncomfortable at being reminded AJ's family had a mission to lie to him for years. It matter only slightly they had a good reason: to protect him, the gene demon. At least, Gerald thought, more optimistically than he felt, being a gene demon meant there were others like him. A brood, maybe, that heard voices in their heads. "You don't need to tell her, Aje. They don't know what I am."

"But you said—"

"That's when you were the gene demon. If I'm the gene demon, Senior Thomas would have arrested me. He wanted me to work for him. He wanted me to spy for him. He thinks—people like me—are evil."

AJ nodded. "Abominations."

"If he knew, I'd be the third demon in custody right now."

"Then that's good news," AJ said. "If they haven't figured it yet, they might never figure it." AJ's eyes suddenly went white and he stopped talking. "That was Ma," he said, shortly after his eyes cleared. "She's already at the market setting up for tonight. She's expecting us after our shift."

"Our shift?"

AJ nodded. "You think just because you're a gene demon working for the same branch of government that wants you dead, you get out of fence building?"

Gerald nodded.

"Lina won't let you stop building until the FSA drags you off to wherever it is vWare controllers go."

"How can I work for the FSA now, Aje? You said it. They want me dead."

AJ shrugged. "Don't tell them what you are."

"I have to find Lizzy," Gerald said. "She's out there somewhere and the locust said—"

AJ looked at him puzzled.

"The scribeosphere… my muse."

AJ's eyes opened and he nodded.

"I think one of the voices I'm hearing might be hers—like for real hers—and the locust is just relaying her thoughts to me."

"How could you not know what you are, brother?" AJ asked, shaking his head. "Those voices. Normal people don't get those."

"The locust isn't a voice. I programmed it and what I think is she hacked it."

"But you hear whispers. You've told me that."

Gerald nodded. "I guess whispers could be voices but I've heard those my whole life. I don't know what they are. Not really. I had theories but nothing fits." Gerald froze. *What did it mean to be a gene demon? What about him was enhanced?*

AJ laughed at his explanation and shook his head grinning. Gerald looked at him puzzled, and then they walked in silence out of the junk yard. They passed ROLIES patrolling Dusty Gulch and found a swamp rider at the far end. It took them ten minutes to reach the work site. Unlike the previous day, a full crew was working when they arrived.

Lina's brother, Jeremy, saw them approach and waited until they came within earshot before yelling, "You're late! Just 'cause the market's in town, don't mean work gets done by itself!" He stopped when he noticed Gerald's bruised face and swollen lip. "What happened to you?"

Gerald looked around for Lina but she was absent which made Jeremey the acting super on the project. "Blackstars pulled me in for a little talk."

Jeremy frowned. "They have no right."

"See what they do, Jay," one of the crew said. "I was telling y'all, it's gonna be bad. I heard they might stop the race."

"Blackstars ain't stopping no race," Jeremey said, "but if y'all don't get to digging, none of us is going to see the gliders go nowhere tonight."

Another crewmember stopped and rested his weight on the handles of the posthole digger. "C'mon, Jay. It's a holiday. I for one 'preciate it the O'Sullivans for putting on the show. If I were sup', let you take the whole week off."

"That's why you ain't sup', Rodney."

"We're putting on the show?" AJ asked. "What show?"

"Your daddy showing us a glider race," another crewmember said. He wore a ribbon around his wrist. "Granddad called 'em war gliders back in the day. Like to see what they can do against modern fighters."

"War gliders?" AJ asked, surprised. "How many gliders in the race?"

"Dozens," someone else said.

"The ones from the hangar," Gerald said.

"Da hasn't raced since before I was born."

"Must be a surprise."

"It's a good one, then. The gees on a glider race when they do their loops are like nothing you've seen. And the smoke trails… practically light he sky on fire. If Da's racing tonight, we got to be there, Jay. You won't want to miss it."

Jeremey spit. "Sounds interestin' alright, but nobody on my crew's arming gliders. You best all get that out your heads, boys. Fighting the FSA is suicide. Earth First's got better plans for you than that."

Several crew members wearing ribbons grumbled.

"You're the boss," one said.

"For now," another spit.

"Until Uncle Luke talks some sense into your dad."

Jeremy grew visibly agitated but said only, "That conversation's above my perk line, but what I can control is this: none of us quitting this field until fifty meters get laid. Got that? No matter which side of the Kisme argument you find yourself supporting."

"How many meters laid so far?" AJ asked.

"About ten, so if you 'sist on clattering on about gliders, do it while notching me up another rail."

AJ bear hugged one of the water soaked crossties and heaved it into a fence post notch. He walked the tie to the other pole and jammed it in another notch before two more crew came with hammers to bang pegs into place to keep the fence strong. As they worked, Gerald noticed how tall the sugar beets had grown in just a few short weeks. He could barely see the dirt beneath their wide, wrinkly leaves. When they finished laying their fifty meters of fencing, the sun was getting low in the sky. The crew broke with laughter and smiles having been heralded with great tales of gliders breaking the speed of sound. They were all excited to see what the night would bring.

After taking showers at Dusty Gulch and slipping into clean clothes, Gerald and AJ climbed into the jumper Gerald had flown to the farm earlier. AJ bristled when he was relegated to the passenger seat but his jumper had already been taken by Sally who was giving Lina a ride to the market. The autopilot greeted AJ as dramatically as it had Gerald. It referred to them as "master and guest," so AJ spent the first half of the ride under the dash disabling the voice. Gerald spent his time coming to grips with what AJ had told him. At some point after they landed, Gerald decided he was tired of thinking about what it meant to be a gene demon. Instead, he fantasized about what Lina would look like if he was allowed to dress her up at the market. He smiled thinking about how badly he'd be beaten up by her and her dad if they could read his mind.

It was getting on to dusk when they arrived at the island. The first clearing had been transformed from vegetable stalls and rickety tables to silly games of skill like ring toss and laser croc hunt. There were also beverage stands, FAC providers, and a few SLYcade installations giving people a chance to feel what it was like to fly a glider. Surprisingly, there weren't very many young kids. Gerald looked above the bald-cypress to the purpling horizon in the distance. Thin dust devils were rising into the clouds and starting to twist together to form larger tornados. They had nothing to fear from them on the island since full size weather sentries towered along its border.

They wandered around the large clearing looking for signs leading to the race. What caught their attention was a formation of babblespheres zooming towards a freshly cleared path on the opposite end. Inside the babblespheres, sVids of gliders flew through trees and over water splashing mist onto the people who walked beneath them. They entered the forest and found the path soft and springy under their feet. Unlike the swampy smell from the previous day, this part of the island smelled of fresh cut wood and tilled soil. The opening was wide enough to allow ten people to walk shoulder-to-shoulder. It had been cleared wide enough for emergency drones and fire transports, almost like this night's celebration was sanctioned by overseers. The buzzing sound of insects clicked against newly installed wind repellers along the path.

As the two walked, Gerald listened to AJ talk excitedly about the gliders and how his dad was one of the best pilots to race them back in the 40s. For a moment, Gerald forgot about Senior Thomas, his hunt for gene demons, and even Lizzy. Gerald had spent almost half of his life without Lizzy by his side. Knowing she was alive and maybe communicating to him through his locust was enough right now. It was progress. He'd find her soon. He was sure of it, but right now Gerald wanted this moment for himself. He wanted to feel like a normal nineteen year old looking forward to his date. If he was a gene demon today, he had always been one. Nothing had changed other than how he felt about it. So he allowed himself a day to forget about how confusing life had become since leaving the Academy. He just moved forward and breathed in the sweet smelling air of the forest path. He listened to his friend tell stories about his dad. It was nice until all the explosions scared him half-to-death.

Gerald ducked and rolled into the gangly legs of a teenager walking beside him. The teenager fell to the ground and dropped his drink. The bottle broke on a rock. "Aw, man!" the kid yelled. "There was three swigs left."

Gerald apologized and helped the kid to his feet. "Idiot," the kid said and jogged up to his friends who were a ways down the path.

AJ laughed. "Smooth," he said.

"What were all those explosions?" Gerald asked, brushing himself off.

"Scissors and skips by the sound of 'em. Maybe, a propulsion fan too. Did you learn nothing in the hangar?" More explosions joined the echoes of the first.

"I just helped your repair drone grease ramjet fittings and clean inlet hoses. Didn't really get what we were doing."

"Okay, beginner's class," he said, clapping him on the shoulder. "Remember those twisty blades on the south wall of the hangar?"

"Think so."

"Put them together and you got fans big enough to propel gliders like air boats across different types of terrain. See gliders don't just fly. They glide over water, flat ground, and over rock fields like hovercraft can."

"So the fans work like prezero hovercraft."

"Better because they don't flip if the pitch gets too high. They're faster-than-sound aircraft that hover without rotors. Straight up military. It's why they're illegal most places. They're easy to weaponize and cheap to build."

"And Rose just gave your parents a permit to show them off to people who want to weaponize them?"

"It's kind of how the old man sends messages. He's subtle like that."

Gerald nodded. "So the fans hover them and the combustion engines fly them?"

"They got prezero combustion scramjets but the fans get them hydroplaning before the jets can generate lift. The pop-pop-pops you heard are the scissors in front. They look like glowing teeth that spin round the front of the machines."

"Like crop threshers?" Gerald asked, remembering the metal rings with laser attachments and gleaming serrated teeth. The rings looked ominous like enormous oval fish mouths.

"The teeth are fusion tech; snaps trees and stuff out the way so the gliders don't lose momentum in jungles and woods. Total old-tech military that can crash into the newer ships and eat 'em up. Can even dig holes with them if the torque's low enough. On a racer, the scissors pretty much clear a path until the jets kick in to get them to Mach. Saw a sVid of one exploding but the tree it tried to eat was petrified and about as big as a house—come on, I can hear them revving."

They jogged towards the noise until the tree dappled moonlight of the path burst into a clear night full of people, vending drones, and bleachers set at the edge of the Great North Swamp. Gliders bobbed inches above the deep, murky water like shiny boats floating on an invisible cushion of air. If the first day of the market looked like a backwater swap meet, the second day looked like a city carnival with lights, spectacle, and buskers making noise for entertainment and profit. At the edge of the water, leaning their backs against a shoreline energy rail, Sally and Lina waited with colorful drinks in their hands. Their cheeks were flushed and rosy from alcohol and the lingering warmth from the freshly set sun. Both were laughing with Mrs. O'Sullivan who stood next to them talking.

Behind the girls, the finish line for the race was projected across the water from the shoreline rail to the next island in the chain nearly a kilometer away. The line glowed neon green and undulated in the breeze like a ribbon would. Gerald knew it was sVid sprayed but couldn't find its source unless the SLYcorders flying overhead were also SLYcasters. The racers revved their engines as tiny bee-sized drones flew around the gleaming sides of the gliders doing pit inspections.

The bleachers were half-full because the majority of people at the race were up getting food and making bets. Stationary kiosks for large wagers and dozens of live bookmakers for smaller bets were visible across the open field behind the bleachers. The bet takers wore tee-shirts with three letters—PEZ—racing in circles on their chests. Above the kiosks, babblesphere logos showed PEZ spinning around available wagers. The man himself, Paisley Winters, was looking out from the largest kiosk watching his bookmakers work. Every so often, he'd scream a limited-time specialty bet to encourage more interest. His bookmakers would shout back in disbelief telling the crowd how they worked for free because their boss gave such foolish odds.

Paisley's bookmakers competed for the people's wagers. They offered long shots of their own that were too good to be true. When hands flashed enough strips of rainbow-colored plastic to get the bookmakers' attention, they'd converge to negotiate terms that were never quite as good as the ones called out. People didn't get angry at the obvious tactic. They laughed and made bigger bets. Once a bet was laid, the bookmakers broke into sing-song like drunks until they started the process again with a new bettor.

"Does that guy ever stop angling for perks?" Gerald asked.

"Never," AJ answered. He swept Sally into a tight embrace and spun her as they kissed. Mrs. O'Sullivan watched this display with a strange mixture of happy discomfort on her face. Gerald reached his arms stiffly around Lina who gave him another pouty peck as her eyes cast sideways to AJ and Sally deep kiss. Gerald looked too. They were better at kissing than he and Lina.

"The show's over here," Gerald whispered to her. He cupped both of her rosy cheeks in his hands and steered her face to his and tried kissing again. *I'm a gene demon,* he thought. *I've got to be good at something.*

"Isn't it wonderful?" Sally asked, after AJ put her down and Lina let out a breath with her lips slightly parted in a tremulous smile. Gerald's heart raced looking at Lina and tasting the alcohol on her lips. He almost laughed but it would have come out a giggle and ruined whatever it was he had just done right.

"Mrs. O'Sullivan arranged it all, AJ. Your dad's out there." Sally pointed to the blue racer. "See him."

"My Stingray?" AJ asked.

"He finished the repairs last week, honey. What better way to show you what it can do he said." Mrs. O'Sullivan smiled and gave him a hug.

Gerald enjoyed the grin on AJ's face and the heady feeling of kissing Lina well for the first time. Not everything about the O'Sullivans was dishonest, he decided. They honestly loved each other, and it was evident in moments like this one. Lina grabbed Gerald's hand and told him he needed to catch up on his drinking. So together with AJ and Sally, they headed for the nearest concession drone and ordered melon colored shots of liquor.

"It's the real deal," Sally said, shaking her head. "Don't know how they got a permit for it but I confirmed it myself. This stuff's legal. We've already had two."

Mrs. O'Sullivan excused herself as the four bought their drinks and raised glasses to her for arranging the race. AJ gave his mom a hug with one arm and toasted to getting off fence duty early. He let Mrs. O'Sullivan unravel from his grip as he swallowed the liquor in one quick movement, hardly making a face.

"My boys… and girls," Mrs. O'Sullivan said, smiling at them. "Have fun. I'll be back before it's over."

As soon as she was out-of-sight, Gerald quaffed his shot and gagged. "Smooth," he said.

"Another round!" Sally yelled at the server drone who poured four more.

Lina wiped her mouth with her sleeve and then ran her hand down the back of her dress. "To taking my diapers off without permission!" she yelled, and laughed as the rest joined in.

After forcing the second shot down, AJ shouted above the bookmakers, "Let's watch it from the safety rail."

"Fine with me," Lina said. "Standing's still better than sitting."

At the rail, Sally asked. "So how's this race go, AJ?"

"Yeah, Aje. I mean if the gliders go Mach One, how do we see more than like a second of the race? It's not like there's a track here."

"Got to say," Lina added. "Those little things look flimsier than a willow switch the way they bend in the middle. Speed like that must make them fold in two."

AJ swung his heavy arms over the shoulders of all three and pulled them into a tight huddle. Lina bit her lip and scrunched her eyes in an effort not cry out as AJ unwittingly forced her to bend a little. "Friends," AJ said. "It's Mach Five these twitlickers go, and we don't see 'em."

"We don't?"

"We see 'em start which goes out about a kilometer or so. Once the jets kick in, we see the gliders fly straight up in the air like rockets. That's about it."

"You're kidding?"

Noticing Lina squirm, he released the huddle with a guilty grin. "That's why races start at night. They got tracers." AJ pointed to one of the gliders in front of them. "The vents in the hull suck chemicals into the exhaust, coloring the smoke different for every glider. So, really, we just see a bunch of colored lines doing circles in the dark. The racers corkscrew around ten to fifty laps depending on the kind of race. Not sure what this is, but Da says there's nothing like a fifty if the weather's right."

"So those things gonna just fly in circles? Not get anywhere? Silly sport, AJ."

"Just wait," AJ told Lina. "That starting ribbon there. It's fake. Just overlays a reverse propulsion field but it's tweakin' great to watch."

"Really?" Gerald asked, now interested.

Sally stared at AJ with glassy eyes. "Lina's right, baby. Silly sport"

Lina laughed.

AJ grinned and pointed at the center of the holographic ribbon. "See that, Gerald?"

Gerald noticed for the first time the bright white and blue lasers pulsating at the far islands.

"It outlines a narrow force field that dissipates the momentum and energy of the racers like an airbrake. Cools the hulls too. If they miss the brake, even once, they might burn up or crash before they get back for another lap—"

"Sounds dangerous," Sally said.

"Da knew five racers who got burnt up. He says we'll know when the pilot hits the brake because a gust of air washes over the crowd like a wave."

"If they miss?" Lina asked.

AJ shrugged. "The air brake's about fifteen meters high, so if they don't practically graze the water, we'll know. Should be pretty sweet in person."

"I'm not a big fan of danger," Sally said.

"It'll be fine," AJ responded, sidling close to her so he could run his hand down her back to the swell of her hip. He squeezed her bottom as if nobody could see and then said, "Da's done this like a hundred times. Never a scratch."

A drone announced in a booming voice the race would start in thirty minutes. "Means we have time for one more drink," Sally said.

"Maybe two."

"Lina!" Sally exclaimed, as if shocked. "What would your daddy say about drinking?"

Lina grinned. "He'd say nothing because I do what I want as long as he doesn't see me do it."

Sally laughed. "How about the boys keep our spot while we get another round and some food?" They agreed, and Gerald turned around on the rail to look at the stands. His head felt like it was floating in jelly which concerned him until he remembered the drinks. He enjoyed the sensation as he focused on the crowd with a giddy smile. Lina liked him and he liked her. AJ and Sally seemed inseparable. He could not remember the last time he felt this good until he saw Jack in his black robes sitting somewhere in the middle of the stands watching him. Gerald nudged AJ who was still studying the gliders grinning. He looked over his shoulder and then followed Gerald's gaze.

AJ turned and faced the stands. He grinned and then shouted, "Jackie-boy!" He waved at their friend from the Academy as if AJ had forgotten how Jack was in the swamp with the other overseers. Jack raised his hand and waved. A moment later, he got up and walked down to the rail.

"Hi guys," he said, quietly.

"So they make you wear those robes everywhere?"

Jack looked uncomfortable. "All day, every day. Starting to hate this job. So, how've you been?" he asked, directing the question at AJ but focusing his eyes on Gerald.

AJ noticed but responded anyway. "Be better once you guys finish your investigation and clear my name."

Jack nodded. "Awkward, huh? I'm supposed to ask you bunches of questions as if that's normal right? It's like Henry thinks because we're friends, you'll just tell me any twitlickin' thing I ask. Stupid one-star."

AJ grinned as his eyes focused. "Jack," he said. "Ask me what you want. I got nothing to hide."

"Wish that were true," he said, under his breath. He glanced high into the stands behind them and frowned. Without looking at them, he added, "He and his Marshals showed up last night in my tent. Out of nowhere like guys… you have no idea how intense he is." Jack shook his head and then turned quickly. "Sorry. Got to go."

Jack walked away and didn't look back no matter how loud AJ called after him.

Gerald stayed silent because sitting on the top bleacher were two monstrously large black clad men flanking a much smaller man with a crew-cut and dark glasses. Gerald had seen the smaller man leave

Senior Thomas' tent this morning. He had seen him torture Abe. His men—Field Marshals 1st Class—scanned the crowd like machines causing fear to spike inside Gerald like he had never experienced before, not even when the rovers attacked. Usually, if Field Marshals were spotted, a battalion of enforcers were on their way.

"Reaver!" AJ exclaimed, sucking in a breath. "When did he get here?"

"I forgot to tell you," Gerald said, his voice thin. "Saw him this morning."

"And you didn't tell me?"

"Kind of busy learning what I was and nursing these ribs."

AJ swore. Not good, brother. This is so not good. Reaver doesn't do field work unless he's personally interested."

Chapter 28

Vanished

The Field Marshals stopped scanning. They looked directly at the boys, and then Cole Reaver jumped to his feet and smiled. He skipped down the bleacher seats like a kid doing hopscotch. Gerald fought a wild sense of panic as Cole came straight at them. Gerald looked around. AJ's tongue dotted his lips. There was nobody else the man could want. It was a fleeting thought but *I'm a gene demon and you want me dead* echoed in Gerald's head as the Deputy Director approached.

"Mr. O'Sullivan," Cole Reaver called out, happily. "Been looking for you and your parents for about an hour now."

AJ's demeanor loosened as he smiled back at the Deputy Director of the FSA "You found me," he said. "What can I do for you?"

"Such manners," he said, overly friendly. "I see Angie's been raising you right. Peter raves about you too, you know."

AJ smiled, woodenly. "Thanks."

"You see, it's probably nothing but there's a slight problem with a permit for this event."

"It's an OPC event, Mr. Reaver. Heard my Ma say it was filed by the High Prelate himself. Maybe you should bio-com him."

"No. I shan't like to do that. What if I am mistaken? What a pickle that would be. Very embarrassing."

AJ shrugged.

"Your mother, however," he said. "I've been told she is one of the organizers. She'll help straighten me right out. Do you happen to know where she's gone?"

AJ shook his head.

A corner of Cole's mouth twitched into a sneer that disappeared so fast, Gerald believed he might have imagined it. "I must insist. Where has she gone?"

"I said I don't know."

Cole smirked and nodded his head. "I think you do."

AJ didn't hide his sneer. He was suddenly angry and it showed. "She works for the High Prelate, not you. The race's been approved."

Cole puckered his lips and shook his head. In a voice absent of real, connected human emotion, he said, "Impudence from an Academy boy? How things have changed. In my day, the Academy taught respect." He clenched his gloved hand into a fist and cupped it in his other. Knuckles cracked. Gerald watched the black leather tighten over Cole's hands with something akin to obsession. There was something so familiar about those hands, he couldn't take his eyes off them until AJ said something else disrespectful and the two Field Marshals stepped a little closer. AJ stretched as tall as he could but only managed an eye-to-nose glare. The marshals were not impressed.

Unlike enforcers, Field Marshals were so cybernetically advanced, they were barely human anymore. Both boys knew the 1st Class design because only a few dozen units existed. They were the elite-of-the-elite and served as bodyguards to the top leaders of the FSA. In war, they served as commanders. "My apologies," AJ said, reasserting control over his anger. "I'll let her know you're looking for her, sir." AJ turned from the rail and tried to walk away. Cole had other plans. With one hand, he wrenched AJ back by the shoulder.

AJ spun angrily. He dwarfed Cole Reaver by a half-meter and fifty kilos. Yet, somehow, he looked like a child before the Deputy Director. There was a presence to Cole that Gerald found unnatural. His voice was so overly smooth and pleasant when he continued, it unnerved him. "I think it'll be better, young man, if you tell me where she is now before there is any further trouble."

AJ said nothing, though he shifted his weight into a casual fighting stance. Gerald had seen it before in matches and against the 'roider. Evidently, the marshals had seen it too. They stepped uncomfortably close.

"Okay, okay," Cole said, raising his black gloved hand in a mollifying gesture. Gerald stared at the intertwining design on the back of the glove. "Let's not get ahead of ourselves. How about her co-conspirator, Mr. Nobel. Where is he?"

Gerald reacted with surprise to Mr. Nobel's name and Cole noticed. "Forgive me," he said, staring down at Gerald. "You have me at a disadvantage. Levi?"

One of the Field Marshals stood straighter as if he'd stopped functioning. A moment later, it talked in a voice devoid of inflection. "Gerald Lee Goodstone. Graduate of the Academy for Gifted Students. Designated vWare controller, fifth class. No molecular record found."

Cole's eyes expressed genuine surprise. "Say again, Levi?"

The Field Marshal named Levi, repeated Gerald's description. AJ shifted his feet nervously upon hearing it a second time.

"Cyrus, confirm Levi's report."

The other marshal repeated the description.

"So," Cole said, sounding excited. "You are Gerald Goodstone and you work for me. You've sworn no oath because if you had, you'd have at least one mole in your body. Incredible. I've only met a few people free of molecular implants. Not many of whom are still alive. You live with the O'Sullivans, I'm guessing?"

Gerald said nothing feeling like a rabbit caught in a trap. *He can't know that quickly. I just found out myself.* Gerald felt sick and rocked on his feet. *He's going to arrest me. Execute me.*

AJ tensed as if to punch Cole but he stopped when a man sitting on the bleachers screamed: "You have no authority here, FSA man!"

It was Uncle Luke, sitting languorously on the bottom riser of the bleachers with his elbows crooked on the bench behind him. Cole and his Field Marshals turned. "What did you say, old man?"

Gerald looked at Uncle Luke noticing for the first time the few wisps of white hair he had on his scalp. He seemed so much younger walking around the farm than he did here. He was strong and worked hard. He stared confidently into Cole's unwavering stare.

Uncle Luke stretched his shoulders back and seemed to puff out his still muscular chest. "Trouble hearing? I got a bit of that myself, *young man*," he said.

A few people on the rail shuffled away while others, mostly wearing ribbons on their wrists, stepped closer. The Field Marshals stood at angles now, one watching AJ and the other watching the old man and the small number of Justice for Kisme followers gathering at his back. Gerald didn't register as a threat to anyone. He reached into his pocket and imagined the locust but the scribeosphere refused to grow cold. It was as if he carried an ordinary metal ball and nothing more. He looked at his bracelet trying to think of something useful he could do.

"Your name," Cole demanded of Uncle Luke.

"Son," he responded. "I got more names than parts."

"Is that so?" Cole asked, his voice suddenly oily smooth. He paused, twitching his head upward. Gerald assumed his eyes rolled white behind the dark glasses. "New heart? New kidneys? A bit of your intestinal tract ten years past. There certainly are a lot of parts in you. I see that now. I have the whole list right here." Cole tapped his head. "You signed for those parts. Did you know that?"

Uncle Luke shrugged.

"Lucas Seymour Kent."

"Call me Luke, son. Or Uncle Luke if you prefer." Some of the crew behind him chuckled.

"I prefer, Field Agent Kent, rank: First Class Brown Boot of the Freeland Security Army."

Some of the men behind him swore and looked uncertainly at Uncle Luke. "What's he talkin' about?" one of them asked. "Brown boot's Freeland infantry, Luke, no better than enforcers."

"They burn farms like ours to the ground."

"What I was," Uncle Luke said. "Not what I is."

"Just because you have no identification marker on your person, Agent Kent, doesn't mean the FSA doesn't know who you are and what you've done. Your life story whooshes around your parts like maggots fleeing a burning corpse. I know a deserter's stink when I smell it."

Uncle Luke stared at Cole, his face hard. "You people put so much metal in me, I feel like a goddamn satellite. So if it's stink you smell with your fancy mind gadgets, it's Freeland stink. Been rotting in me since you slaughtered ten thousand people in the Quell of Thirty-nine. But what's ten-thousand lives if killing them gets you promoted?"

"Ending riots that threatened the Freeland Nation got me promoted, sir. Ending the terrorist network run by Dixon Streets got me promoted. Bringing deserters to justice I do for fun."

"Goody for you and yours, FSA man. Come fetch me up but you'll need more than a couple of golems at you back to help." More than half the people in the stands were watching the exchange now. Most wore ribbons.

"Five minutes," several announcers called across the water. The racers revved their scramjets into thundering concussions of sound.

"Now leave those boys alone. In northern country, we don't harass boys hardly old enough to shave. We follow different rules."

Someone in the stands yelled, "Yeah!" Others started stomping their feet on the risers. The mob was swaying towards the brink of collective courage. It was almost ready to fight.

"You see," Cole shouted loudly enough to be heard. "I was under the impression that this island and the rest of the Northern Prefectures belonged to the Freeland Nation. As an agent of the Freeland, I find your tone offensive, Agent Kent."

"You can find it whatever the jack hell you want. Just leave them boys alone and watch the show 'cause I ain't scared of you."

"Perhaps not," Cole said. "But it might be time for the FSA to take back its parts since you don't appreciate them. Levi, take care of this ungrateful wretch."

One of the Field Marshals raised his hand and pointed at Uncle Luke who stared defiantly back. The other raised his hand and pointed at the crowd behind him. The people closest held their ground. The ones not wearing ribbons jumped from the bleacher sides like crewman abandoning ship.

Uncle Luke sucked in a startled breath and grabbed his shoulder. His face turned red as he struggled to breathe. He stood up and then pitched forward to his knees. Moaning, he started to seize.

He flopped to the ground but kept his eyes pinned on Cole. Uncle Luke smiled.

"Take them all, Levi."

The pain exploded exponentially as Uncle Luke's transplanted organs started shutting down. The Field Marshal was somehow turning them all off like devices on the SLYscape. Gerald froze as he watched but no matter what they did to him, Uncle Luke was still not scared. His defiance showed in every movement of his suffering body. "This... all... you... got?" he said, tears trickling down his thickly wrinkled cheeks.

Uncle Luke grabbed his stomach like he'd been stabbed and wanted to pull out the knife. He finally shrieked and lost control of his bodily functions. He rolled to his side, and then Big John Nobel came barreling into Cole with a scream of rage. They went down in a pile of limbs. Big John wrapped his bulging arm around Cole's neck and squeezed as Cole slapped at the big man's wrist. The Field Marshals turned in a blur and wrenched Big John's arms away from Reaver's neck. One of Mr. Nobel's forearms broke in two and then the marshal named Cyrus, smashed his neck with an armored hand. Big John dropped like he'd been shot, and then Cole rolled to his feet.

Turning almost as fast as the marshals, the Deputy Director kicked Mr. Nobel in the chest lifting him high off the ground. AJ blurred forward to join the fight while Gerald watched it all unfold. Reaver's back was turned as he prepared to kick Big John again. His foot never landed because AJ had launched into a spinning kick of his own. AJ's foot cracked into the Deputy Director's ear from behind making a sound like a bat striking a ball. Cole's head snapped sideways from AJ's kick but somehow he wasn't fazed.

It was as if Cole had adrenalin shooting into his muscles like an enforcer because he spun and caught AJ's ankle. He then lifted AJ high into the air and pile drove him into the ground. Cole lifted AJ back up again higher than his head and dropped him onto his rising knee. AJ collapsed with an arched back at Cole's feet. Cole screamed and yelled as he kicked AJ again and again until blood fanned out around AJ's head like a red halo painted on dirt.

Gerald stared down at his best friend. AJ's chest moved with shallow breaths but in every other respect he looked pale and dead. Gerald looked up when he heard Sally scream followed by Lina yelling, "Daddy, no!"

Drinks and food fell from their hands as they rushed forward. The Field Marshals pivoted between Big John and AJ to stop the girls from getting too close. In the stands, people with ribbons on their wrists dragged Uncle Luke's still writhing body away.

Another woman shouted but not in fear. It was outrage. "Are you out of your mind?" Angie O'Sullivan yelled. "Answer me Cole, you son-of-a-bitch!"

The Field Marshals aimed weapons at her but didn't shoot. She took several steps past the girls and over her son lying at the Deputy

Director's feet. She slapped Cole hard across the face. He looked surprised, then angry, and then he was calm. It was as if he turned his anger off. "Angie!" he said, in that same overly friendly way he had greeted the boys earlier. "I'm so glad you made it."

He looked down and spit a gob of blood on AJ's foot.

"You're done!" she yelled. "When Preston hears about this—"

Powerful waves of hot, sticky air washed over them as gliders launched forward across the swamp. The echoes of "and they're off" hung above the whirring propulsion fans and exploding skips as the racers carved valleys through the water before liftoff. The cheers from the stands drowned out anything Mrs. O'Sullivan could have said until the racers engaged their scramjets and tore thunder from the skies by breaking the sound barrier over-and-over again.

Gerald looked over his shoulder at all the gliders flying straight up just as AJ had told them they would. Yellow, white, green, and so many other colors lit up the night in lines that arched into loops. He looked back down and saw AJ was still unconscious and bleeding. *He's missing it,* he thought, and tears trickled down Gerald's cheeks. He found the blue tracer and whispered. "He's winning, AJ. Your dad is winning."

"Haven't you heard, Angie?" Cole shouted once the noise died down.

She looked at Cole with sudden fear as she heard something in his tone Gerald missed. "What have you done?"

Another rush of hot wind crashed wetly across Gerald's back. The gliders were hitting the air brakes on the first lap. Mist drifted down like a heavy cloud sinking to the ground. Gerald watched as Angie O'Sullivan's confidence shattered.

"The abominations admitted it. They told us about his labs. They told us about the army of demons he's raising to rival the FSA. They told us—"

"Whatever you told them to say," Angie said, spitting. "You know as I do there are no labs."

Cole smiled and then looked skyward as if he saw something Gerald could not. "We'll see what the overseers find out. Until then your precious High Prelate has been put under house arrest. That's why I'm here, stupid girl. This race is illegal because Preston Rose is no longer our leader. My father is High Prelate now. And my father did not authorize a bunch of rebels to fly war gliders."

"This is treason, Cole."

"This is politics, Angie." And then to Cyrus, he said, "Arrest them."

Cyrus moved mechanically as he lifted both AJ and Mr. Nobel over his shoulders like sacks of grain. Levi stepped towards Mrs. O'Sullivan who started backing away. Lina ran towards the back of the bleachers, still limping, but fast. "I won't let 'em, Daddy!" she yelled, as she retreated. "I won't let them win!"

Sally cried and stumbled forward. She reached her hands out and grabbed AJ's arm. She tugged at him, tears streaming down her face. "You can't take him!" she yelled. "I know the law and you can't—" Cyrus backhanded her across the face and she fell limp to the ground.

Where are you going? Gerald thought, still frozen in place by fear and indecision. He saw something then, a shimmer of air that he remembered from the valley the night before. He slipped his scribeosphere out of his pocket. *Fly at it,* he thought. *Show me the cloak.* The scribeosphere sped ahead and disappeared only to reappear near fifty meters away from Gerald. It hovered near the kiosks and bobbed in the air. *Come back,* Gerald thought as he worked his fingers over his bracelet. "Stop! Put me down!" Mrs. O'Sullivan yelped, sounding helpless and afraid.

She was over Levi's shoulder, kicking and punching the Field Marshal's back. Cole walked ahead of his marshals practically skipping with glee. Three arrests made, his father in the office of the High Prelate—a good day. Wrapping a hand around his braceleted wrist, Gerald stretched his arms into a diving formation. He then ran at the Field Marshals as fast as he could. He closed the distance to within a couple of meters before they turned to address the threat. Mrs. O'Sullivan stopped struggling. "No Gerald!" she yelled, but it was too late. "Honey stop!"

Gerald jumped with both arms extended as if he was capable of flight. He swiped his fingers along the opal and closed his eyes. The same EMP blast that destroyed the Black Eye detonated by Levi's head. With any luck the Field Marshal would fall and the stealth ship hiding in plain sight would de-cloak. Everyone at the race would see it then, and the ones wearing ribbons might attack. That was his hope. *Golems,* Uncle Luke had said, dismissively, as if he believed the Justice for Kisme group in the stands could take the two Field Marshals. He bet on Uncle Luke being right but Uncle Luke had been dragged away. It became a desperate and silly plan the instant Gerald's bracelet pulsed.

The triggering mechanism for an EMP flashes so bright it can blind people, so Gerald remembered to close his eyes. What he forgot was his bracelet flashed with heat. Gerald screeched as his wrist caught fire. The pain was so intense, he barely realized he never hit the ground after his jump. Gerald slapped at the flames and burned the tips of his fingers unclasping the bracelet. He watched it fall smoking to the dirt beneath his feet.

The Field Marshals were knocked to their knees by the EMP but were already back standing. The cloaked ship was still hidden except for black lines crackling like dark lightning along its perimeter. Gerald was suspended in the air as if he was strapped to a detainment board but there was no board. Cole Reaver stood looking at him from inside a gray dome of energy that extended from the ship like an awning over the FSA men and their prisoners Cole showed Gerald his teeth in a strange predatory smile. He spoke softly but it sounded loud in Gerald's ears. "Extraordinary, Mr. Goodstone. If you had tried that on anybody else, it might've worked."

"What are you talking about?" Gerald said, struggling to breathe against the tight bands of invisible energy wrapped around his chest. He swung his feet uselessly several inches off the ground.

Cole walked slowly out of his protective dome until he stood just below where Gerald hung floating. He reached up with his hand and patted Gerald's cheek. Gerald's eyes caught the ribbed stitching on the back of his leather glove. The design was subtle but clear: a lone wolf howling. Cole cast a glance at the sky as if he expected something that hadn't arrived yet. He smiled wolfishly. Gerald could smell his hot breath. "I know who you are now, Mr. Goodstone. I know your history, your fire, and your poor, burned up sister. Her name was Elizabeth."

The whispers rose up so loud in Gerald's head, he screamed in anger for them to stop. Cole watched, tilting his head slightly, curious but not concerned. Gerald's eyes closed as tears trailed down his face. In the darkness of his mind, he remembered his mother sitting against the wall on the living room floor with Lizzy in her lap whimpering. He saw his little sister's tiny hands open and closed as her lips puckered and sucked on nothing but smoke and oily air. The house still burned, but the fires were dying. An acrid haze itched his nose, but it wasn't his nose he smelled with. It was his mother's nose. Gerald felt a tremor of fear as he realized he was inside his mother's mind on the night she died. *I can't,* he thought. *I can't experience what she did. Please,* he pleaded to whispers he could no longer hear. *Don't show me this.*

Gerald's chest ached as his mother heaved for short gasps of air. He listened to what she heard: sirens approaching. The sound was not hopeful. It sent spikes of fear into her until something inside broke. She wanted to hide Lizzy but she had nothing left. She was dizzy and sick, and Gerald felt the icy numbness of her flesh so badly burned, it no longer registered pain. *They can't find her,* he heard in his mother's voice as if it was his own. But they did find her, Gerald knew. More exactly, the man his mother hated more than any other person found her. The man who always wore dark clothes and black glasses, he found her. Gerald watched fingers, wrapped tight in wolf-stitched leather gloves, flex around his little sister's arms. The hated man lifted her with ease off his mother's lap. The hated man, Gerald knew now, was the Deputy Director of the FSA. Cole smiled as he pulled Lizzy to his chest. He hugged her almost tenderly and then gazed down at Gerald's mother. His smile deepened into something tinged with true joy as he left Gerald's mother and the hairless boy at her feet to die.

When Gerald opened his eyes, he was still hanging in the air staring down at the Deputy Director, but Cole was no longer watching him. He was staring up at dozens of small, stealth ships flying over the island and around the gliders still racing their circles in the crisp night air. "Time for me to go, Mr. Goodstone," he said. "But we'll meet again soon, I think. Perhaps privately with nobody to hear what we say. Imagine the things we could discuss."

He sauntered back into his gray dome of energy and paused to look at the three prisoners he'd taken. They stirred at his touch. They were alive. He nodded to the Field Marshals and the energy bands holding Gerald aloft snapped. Gerald's feet hit the ground and he stumbled to his hands and knees.

When he looked up, he saw Cole and the Field Marshals' backs as they walked into the shimmering air and disappeared. They were gone. All of them. Vanished like a magic trick into thin air.

The stealth fighters never saw him leave.

Chapter 29

No Justice

Gerald sat in the dirt with Sally's cracked head cradled on his lap. She was bleeding from the Field Marshal's slap and wasn't waking up. His tears ran dry as he rocked her gently thinking about AJ and his mom. Big John was gone too, and he didn't know what he would tell Lina when she returned. He had tried to stop Cole from leaving but his attempt made matters worse by tipping the Deputy Director off to who and what Gerald was… a gene demon who could relive what others remembered. It was just a matter of time before enforcers showed up to take him away. It would be safer, Gerald believed, for him to leave Lina behind and run, but he couldn't leave Sally. Not like this.

Stealth fighters circled around the island as the gliders finished their fifty lap race. Emergency drones were nowhere to be found and the people who had seen what happened to Sally were making bio-com calls to fetch one. After about twenty minutes, it showed up. Gerald lifted Sally's head off his lap and backed away to watch the medical drone do its work.

As he sat there, hot wind washed over his back from the air brake doing its job for the gliders flying loop-the-loops behind him. Though the night wasn't cold, the warmth shed from superheated hulls felt good to Gerald as he tried to recall the details of his mother's memory. It had been a night vision of sorts, but Gerald experienced it awake which had never happened before. He had also never stared out of the eyes of someone he knew. His mother's perspective seemed mixed up with his own memories of that day, but he wasn't foolish enough to doubt the truth of what he saw. Cole Reaver had kidnapped his sister.

He had stolen her from Gerald's burning house. *Why was he there and where did they go?*

Sally moaned as the drone smeared a glistening wax into the spidery cracks on her skull. It passed a blue laser over her blood dampened hair until the wax was indistinguishable from bone. It applied something else to stop the last trickles of blood, and then injected something into her thigh. The drone was capable of hovering but it used its wheels to roll to where Gerald sat. "Sally Yorkshire Scott needs forty-eight hours rest. You're welcome."

The polite voice paused as it tried to read Gerald's identification marker. To save time, Gerald lifted the corner of his shirt and held it up. "Scan this," he said.

"Gerald Lee Goodstone," it continued. "You are hurt. Present your hand, please." Gerald looked at his blistered wrist and extended his arm. The medical drone ran something cold over the burns and then sprayed watery medicine on his sticky, red skin. "You need plenty of hydration and twelve hours rest. You're welcome." It folded its equipment into various compartments on its torso and then wheeled away. Gerald looked at Sally who was attempting to sit up. He took her hand and helped her.

Sally was pale and her eyes were bloodshot. Big tear drops slid down her cheeks. She didn't say anything at first. She didn't need to. Gerald helped her to the bottom riser of the bleachers where Uncle Luke had been sitting when Cole attacked him.

"What are we going to do?" she asked.

Run away, Gerald thought. "Wait for AJ's dad. He's finishing the race now." Sally rested her forehead onto Gerald's chest and sniffed. Gerald hugged her shoulders and rubbed her warm back. He didn't know why he did that, but it comforted him as much as it did her. He stared over the water and didn't let go as the racers flew.

After the race finished, Mr. O'Sullivan walked up to them wearing a tight fitting blue flight suit. Brandy Peppers walked at his side wearing a similar suit, only striped with colors matching the ribbon on her wrist. Behind her, three muscular men in fatigues carried laz'rupter rifles tight to their chests. "We know," she said, in a voice full of sinewy distress. "We know the FSA arrested them without just cause."

"They've done more than arrest my wife and son," Mr. O'Sullivan said, quietly. "They arrested the High Prelate and executed those two boys."

"Gene demons not much older than Kisme," Brandy said. "The m-spheres said they were trying to escape."

"Please, Brandy," Mr. O'Sullivan said. "Don't use that term."

She looked puzzled, not knowing Angie and Peter were anything more than Earth First leaders who clerked for the OPC. She didn't know the O'Sullivans had spent years protecting Gerald from the FSA. She hadn't heard the conversation Gerald witnessed when Angie had told Peter that gene demons were children of the future: *enhanced*.

"What's your name, sweetie?" she suddenly asked, Sally. "Mind if I get a SLYcorder on your face? Quite a welt across your temple. If you got bruising anywhere else, I could use them too. We need people angry. We need more soldiers willing to take up the fight. We're going to force Cole Reaver to release our friends or else."

Sally pushed herself gently out of Gerald's arms and wiped her cheeks. She stood and hugged Mr. O'Sullivan who appeared startled. He returned the hug, tentatively at first, then with a genuine squeeze of thanks. "I'm so sorry," she said. "Mrs. Oh was so brave. She tried to stop them from taking AJ. She fought the Field Marshal with her fists."

With a slight furrowing of her brow, Brandy said, "We'll get her back for you Peter. You'll see."

Peter O'Sullivan relaxed out of Sally's hug and then said, "Your head. You should go home. Rest. Nothing to do here tonight." He looked up at the twin halves of the moon obscured by dark clouds. Smallish tornados buffeted the weather shield around the island. "Things will look different in the morning."

Sally touched the sore area of her head and then broke down in sobs. "Just a slap. If you would have seen what they did to AJ. I'm so sorry."

Gerald helped her sit back down as people with ribbons and some without started gathering in concerned circles around Brandy and her armed guard. Brandy stepped onto the riser next to Gerald to be better seen. She shouted for people to gather close. Gerald became claustrophobic by the press of humanity heating up the humid air around where he and Sally still sat. "Brandy!" one of them called. "What we gonna do about Luke?"

An angry chorus echoed the question as the crowd grew in size. Brandy stomped the bench and raised her voice. She swayed back and forth as she preached about the need to fight. On his cheek, Gerald felt the heat of her thigh as she brushed obliviously against him with each pump of her fist. The crowd responded ever angrier until Peter O'Sullivan grew so visibly distressed, he left. Gerald leaned away and looked up the flank of Brandy's hip to her svelte back where long, auburn hair swished across her waist as she moved. She was still beautiful to Gerald's eyes, but he no longer found her attractive. *Something's wrong with her,* he remembered AJ saying. Despite never meeting her before, Gerald agreed. There was something wrong with Brandy. Sally took Gerald's hand and squeezed his fingers. "Get me out of here," she whispered into his ear. He nodded and parted the mob with soft apologies and hard pushes.

They found a bench near Paisley's betting kiosk far away from the crowd. The PEZ letters still chased each other in circles, but Pez and his bookmakers were gone. According to Mr. O'Sullivan who stopped by before going home, Pez had arranged for a transplant team to replace the FSA provided organs with unregistered ones that couldn't be shut down. Yet, he was not hopeful Lina's uncle would survive the night.

"I have to go find her," he said to Sally who sat pale and damp like she was going to be sick. "After I get you home."

"Gerald," she said, in a soft voice. "Jack's here."

He wore black robes and stood watching at the back of Brandy's mob. Gerald helped Sally stand and they walked towards him. When they got close, Jack turned away and walked quickly up the hill toward the trees. Holding Sally's hand, Gerald walked faster to catch up. "Jack!" he yelled.

Jack peered over his shoulder and started to jog. Gerald gave chase but the pull on his hand slowed him until he stopped. "Are you okay?" he asked.

She shook her head slowly. "Hurts," she said, breathing as if she had run a mile. "My head hurts a lot and—" She vomited onto the dirt.

With Sally's arm over Gerald's shoulders, they walked slowly up the hill leading to the cypress lined path that brought them to the glider races. By the time they reached the opening, Jack was gone. Frogs bellowed and things splashed into the water as they continued to walk the path in the dark. Their feet disturbed snakes and other small animals causing little flutters in leaves dry enough to rustle beneath their feet. It was a little scary too especially in the flooded areas where Gerald knew crocodiles swam and hunted at night. "What do you think got into Jack?" he asked, as a way to pull his imagination back from the water's edge. Sally stopped to catch her breath.

"He told me not to come," Sally said. "Lina and I were at her house getting dressed when he contacted me and told me not to go."

"And you didn't tell us?"

"Thought he was just jealous I'm with AJ." She paused and wiped a hand over her eyes. "He likes me," she said. "Or at least parts of me."

"I know. I've heard him talk about it."

"He's not very subtle," Sally responded. "But when he bio-com'd me, he wasn't very Jack-like either. No bad-mouthing people, no bad jokes."

"No calling me and AJ radicals?"

"He wasn't wrong there, was he?" she said.

Gerald looked at his feet. "No he wasn't. It's worse than that, really. Way worse. Remember what I said at the rice paddies? I said I'd tell you everything AJ told me. The O'Sullivans—"

Sally put her fingers over Gerald's lips. "Shh," she said. "Listen."

Across the water on the dry side of the far hill where the cypress grew close together, dozens of yellow lights bobbed. Since Gerald and Sally held no lights, the people coming did not likely see them on the path. The group approaching was eerily silent. Here and there between the yellow lights, Gerald saw red dots so dim he would have missed them if he hadn't seen them so recently. "Quick," he whispered. "Get in the water."

She shook her head and was about to refuse when Gerald suddenly hugged her legs and lifted. She did not bend over easily like he'd seen in sVids when men swept girls up onto their shoulders. Gerald's shoulders were not that wide and he was not strong enough to keep from weaving as he stumbled sideways into the water. Sally kept her torso rigidly straight as she pushed and slapped his head to keep her balance. She voiced her displeasure but abruptly fell silent as Gerald's feet sank deep into the muck almost pitching them both into the shiny black water. She relaxed her body a little as Gerald sloshed the rest of the way across the water to a large clump of cypress trees in the middle. He heaved her to a seat on a mound of mud and twigs. The tree trunk she leaned back against was now between them and the path. "What the tweak was that?" she snapped, instinctively keeping her voice low.

Gerald put his finger over his lips and pointed. Sally turned to peek around the tree.

A large group of overseers walked in rows behind several enforcers who marched mechanically forward. More enforcers pulled up the rear. The Blackstars wore hoods preventing Gerald from recognizing any of them except Jack whose light hair shown like a beacon as he walked with his hood down against the flow of the group until he reached a spot in line near the back. Jack turned and walked silently like the others. Sally gasped slightly and pulled herself away from view. Gerald's feet were sucking deeper into the muck as they watched the black robed overseers halt on the path where Gerald and Sally had just been. The enforcers in the front turned towards Gerald and Sally as if they responded to one mind. Through the twigs and roots around the trunk Sally leaned against, Gerald saw several pairs of red eyes staring directly at them as if they could see clear as day. "Why have we stopped?" one of the Blackstars said. Gerald believed it was the same two-star woman who reminded Senior Thomas of Gerald's connection to Lina. "In the water," one of the enforcers responded in its deep reverberating voice. He raised his hand and pointed a laz'rupter at Gerald.

The flash sizzled the water in front of the cypress tree sending steam into the air. Bubbles rose and on top of them was a crocodile three times the size of Gerald floating dead. There was sudden laughter. "Almost got Henry," one of them said.

"See the size of that thing?"

Without another word, the enforcers marched forward as the overseers talked like excited tourists on safari. In the back though, Jack continued to look at where the crocodile floated. He looked over to where Sally and Gerald hid. His eyes went back and forth from the path to the tree as Gerald clenched his fists in fear. He was now terribly aware of being hip deep in a swamp where crocodiles lay hidden beneath the surface. Sally was aware also based on how loudly she breathed and how strongly she gripped the roots to keep from sliding in. Jack finally moved on and the enforcers behind him followed looking straight ahead.

Gerald and Sally watched the yellow lights fade from view and when they could no longer hear the overseers talk, Sally pushed herself violently back into the water. Gerald struggled to free his feet from the muck. "I can lift you out," Gerald said, staring nervously at the floating crocodile. "Just in case there's another one."

Sally shook her head and sloshed as fast as she could back to the path. Gerald followed. When they were on dry land and felt safe, Sally said in a voice far calmer than Gerald felt, "Do you know what they want?"

"The Blackstars?" he asked, thinking about how to answer her. "Gene demons. I hear they're looking for gene demons."

Sally nodded and swallowed. "Will they find any?"

"I hope not."

Those were the last words they spoke until arriving back at the O'Sullivan ranch. It was just after they landed when they discovered how bad things were going to get. Lina was sitting on the steps leading to AJ's front porch. The house behind her was dark except for one room on the first floor in back. Lina's face was puffy and red. Her eyes were practically swollen closed from crying. Her dress was dirty and wet from sweat. She twisted her Justice for Kisme bracelet anxiously in her hands.

She wrung the ribbons around her reddened fingers and refused to look up when they approached her. "Uncle Luke's got fifty fighters with cloaking shields," she said, hoarsely. "His pilots were trained FSA like he was once before the Quell made Uncle Luke quit. I didn't mean to but seeing daddy busted up on the ground like that. He's so big."

"What happened, Lina?" Sally asked, her voice filling with emotion mirroring Lina's tone.

"I know where Luke's pilots hide. They've known me since I was real little. They call me Avelina like daddy no matter what I threaten. They never took me seriously before so how should I have known?"

"I don't understand, Lina," Sally said.

"So I came at 'em crying and swearing like a crazy girl. They tried to touch me, hug me. I didn't let them. I lied to them. I lied so bad and they fell for it. I told them Uncle Luke sent me with an order to rescue daddy. They said Reaver's ship was too big, and it had too many After

Zero weapons for them to shoot it down. I told them to stop whining and fight like Brandy says. I told them to do their jobs like Uncle Luke ordered them to do. They listened to me, can you believe it? They shouldn't have done that. I'm just a little girl—a stupid little girl!"

"You're not stupid, Lina, or little. Any of it."

"I'll be seventeen in two days. Daddy says that ain't nothin' and he's right. I proved it. They listened to me and now their dead."

"Oh Lina," Sally said, sitting down next to her and hugging her tight. Lina didn't raise her arms. She just kept staring at her hands and the twisted ribbons of her bracelet.

"A wing is five fighters. Did you know that? Five wings to a squadron. Uncle Luke had two squadrons of pilots. Two wings caught Reaver leaving the fairground. They fired on the Deputy Director just like I told them to do. Ten fighters gave it everything they had… I just wanted daddy back."

"Ten people?" Sally asked, her voice shaking.

Elbows on knees, face in hands, Lina's back trembled as she cried softly. Sally petted her back. "A gunner and a pilot," Lina said. "Every fighter has two people. Twenty pilots. Twenty friends of Uncle Luke are dead and daddy's still gone."

"It's not your fault," Gerald said as he put his hands on her knees, and squatted down before her.

"I went home after hearing about it," she said, sniffling. She lifted her head to look into Gerald's eyes. "Enforcers were there with overseers tearing my house apart. My brothers, Charlene… they all ran. I don't know where to but my house… daddy's house… I didn't know what to do, so I came here." Lina touched Gerald's cheek. "To you."

Gerald took her hands in his, but Lina needed both he and Sally's help to stand. They walked her up the steps to the door which opened automatically with a *schwick!* Gerald peered into the empty hallway knowing AJ and Angie wouldn't be waiting inside. He wondered if Mr. O'Sullivan was home. He gently pushed Lina forward but she turned in the open doorway to look at the first splash of morning color on the horizon. "I don't think justice is real," Lina said.

"Don't say that," Sally said. "Never say that."

Lina leaned against the still open front door and flung her bracelet far away into the dirt. “There is no justice!” she yelled, screaming until her voice shred. “Because they’re dead, and I’m not.”

Lina sat down on the cold marble and cried.

Chapter 30

Crackdown

The house had been unnaturally quiet for weeks. Lina, Sally, and Gerald sat in the kitchen as usual eating breakfast and drinking the watery, FAC provided stimulant Sally called coffee. The sun had not risen yet, but nobody slept all the way to daybreak anymore. As usual, Mr. O'Sullivan was in the simulation room with the doors closed. He preferred to eat alone except for at night when he'd join them for a drink at the dinner meal. Sally usually cooked. Lina helped. Gerald tried to lend a hand, but Lina always shooed him away, telling him he wasn't "no good" at cooking. Mr. O'Sullivan insisted they all call him Peter. "You're adults, mostly," he said. "No need to go around using mister all the time."

Lina and Sally did exactly that, but Gerald found it difficult to be so informal. So much in their lives had changed over the past two weeks since the race. He tried to keep some things the same. When Mr. O'Sullivan talked at night, he kept the topics of conversation light as if his wife and son were not held prisoner in a place not even Preston Rose knew where. He would tell Lina how tough her father was and assure Sally and Gerald everything would turn out alright in the end. He put on a good show but there was no hiding the despair he held in his eyes.

His boss, the only one who could save his family, was under house arrest and accusations kept piling up. The latest accusation was that the rebel Revealer, Brandy Peppers, was Rose's puppet and responsible for arming Justice for Kisme so they could assassinate the leaders of the FSA. As proof, the sanctioned Revealers showed sVids of the attack on the Deputy Director. As further proof, they showed sVids of

Brandy inciting Freelanders to violence against a backdrop of war gliders authorized to race by the former High Prelate, Preston Rose.

Rebellion in the North was the dominant topic in the m-spheres for days until Senior Thomas publically acknowledged the entire Northern Prefecture was under investigation for sedition starting with Prefect Frederickson who had been pulled from his Abbey to face charges. Despite not knowing anything about Earth First, Justice for Kisme, or gene demons, his memories were wiped as punishment for treason.

Through all this, the girls continued working at Lina's farm. Every morning, under the supervision of FAC specialists, the girls worked from sunup to sundown. Sally was Lina's boss now. Her job was to restore order to the way the Nobels grew and tested their crops. If Sally failed to convince Big John's workers to adopt FAC procedures, she would be stripped of her Iron City Aggie designation and replaced. Lina obeyed Sally without complaint. The crews obeyed the last remaining super without complaint. The FAC specialists began to trust the two of them, which helped Sally cover up Lina's nighttime visits to the mine.

It was on the second day after the race when Lina learned her family was hidden in the O'Sullivans' mine. Brandy and her bodyguards were there too which nobody liked but it was Peter's mine and he made the rules. Also, in a medical bay Gerald had not yet seen, the recovering Uncle Luke continued getting treatment from unregistered medical drones. According to Paisley, his people used the NextGen equipment to shield the facility from the FSMs in the SLYscape to prevent enforcers from seeing it on their maps. Knowing how enforcer maps worked from inside the uniform, Gerald didn't believe the mine was as safe as Paisley claimed, but no enforcers had broken down the doors yet. Of course, nobody had come looking for Gerald either.

Gerald had expected to be arrested the first morning after the race. Reaver's ship had been attacked; Lina was sleeping in Sally's room because enforcers were crawling all over hers; and Cole had hinted he knew Gerald was a gene demon. It's why Gerald left for the mine immediately after putting Lina to bed. He believed he had only hours to act, but he was wrong. He had spent days using his enhanced FSA access to attack Cole Reaver's personal data spheres in an attempt to find Lizzy and the others he'd taken. All he had managed to do so far was discover Cole had replacement parts too just like Uncle Luke. Unfortunately, they couldn't be turned off because as far as the SLYscape was concerned, Cole Reaver and all his parts were no longer on the planet. He was off-scape, off-map, a ghost, and so were the moles implanted in AJ, Big John, and Mrs. O'Sullivan. He even searched for his sister's moles on the SLYscape map the locust helped him build. It was a good idea that didn't pan out.

The whispers hardly ever quieted anymore. Every time he closed his eyes, instead of finding sleep or even a night vision, he saw his baby sister in the arms of Cole Reaver. He remembered what it felt like to be his mom unable to stop him from taking her.

"Are you even listening?" Sally asked. She snapped her fingers in front of Gerald's face.

Gerald looked at her startled. "Sorry. I got distracted."

"I'm talking to you both. So listen up."

Gerald looked out of the dark window and still saw no blush of sunlight. He nodded feeling his eyes go heavy.

"You two have to come," Sally said, as she checked the time and took another bite of toast. "It's the first FAC event since the crackdown began. I know the way these people think. Grams and I… we've gone through this before."

Lina, her eyes bright, shook her head in refusal. Gerald kept silent as he tapped his foot softly to distract himself from the whispering in his head. "I'm sorry, Sally," Lina said, swallowing. "After you've been so good. My family owes you. All of us. You put your behind on the line for me but I just can't."

"It's a little more than my behind, Lina. I'm committing treason for you."

"It's not."

"It is, Lina. Not telling the Blackstars where your brothers are, your sister. I'm willing to risk it, but you have to listen to me. It's the only way they'll leave us alone. It's your birthday they're celebrating. They know you're the figurehead for everyone who worked for your dad. You're the only Nobel left, so they need you to be okay with FAC rule. If you don't show up to the party they're throwing in your honor… Madame Evelyne, she'll do it the hard way. She'll bring in the Black Eyes. You might even end up in Thomas' interrogation room, Lina."

"My birthday was last week," she said, sadly. "Without daddy and my brothers. Without Charlene, I just can't. If I show up to a birthday party, it's like all the people taken from us don't matter. The crew will see right through it."

"They don't need to buy it. Just show up and dance for the FAC prelate. Look like you're having a good time and get everybody else to come play pretend. Anybody on the crew who doesn't show—I'm telling you—will be looked at with suspicion. If you and Gerald don't show—"

"I'm not on the crew," Gerald said. "I've been here or in the mine since the race."

Sally nodded. "They know you're here, Gerald. They've seen the sVids of you and Lina together at the market. Madame Evelyne told me very explicitly you had to come too. You're 'kids in love,' she said, in that stupid accent of hers. 'The people always adore love,' she told me."

Lina snorted. "We had one date."

"Two," Gerald said.

Lina smiled sadly. "Not coutin' the last one."

"Neither one of you have a choice. I mean it." Sally stood up as if that was the end of the discussion.

"Is that an order?" Lina asked, childishly, but there was no heat in her voice.

"Look," Sally said. "We all lost somebody. That's why even if Madame Evelyne wasn't making us, a party will do us good. We need to laugh again guys. Nothing good comes from feeling sorry for ourselves."

"Don't feel like laughing," Lina said. "Last week on my actual birthday when I opened my eyes and daddy wasn't at my door with a silly pancake with a face on it. He didn't hug me or call me whirlwind. I didn't hear my stupid brothers sing. Charlene wasn't scootin' them all out of there 'cause we had work to do. None of it happened. I wasn't even in my own bed."

"When my brother was taken from us, don't you think I felt like you do? But Grams told me… in the bubble cities, people aren't well fed. People aren't well cared for, not like here. We didn't get silly pancakes. We got enforcers dropping from the skies because too many people gathering at one place was bad. When Ronnie got wiped, nobody said anything because every day people who resist get punished. This crackdown," she said, lifting her hands in the air. "This was every day for us and one thing you learn. If you get knocked down—no matter how hard—you get back up that instant, because if you don't, you never will."

"When is it?" Gerald asked.

"Tonight," Sally said, giving him a small, thankful smile.

Lina looked at Gerald and trembled as if chilled. She wiped imaginary tears from her eyes. "Fine. If I'm doing this, you tell Brandy to put something nice on you. She's been critters lately, but she still has good taste in clothes. Better than yours, anyway."

"What's wrong with my clothes?"

Sally and Lina stared at him not saying a word. "You just tell her, Gerald. Nice clothes."

Gerald smiled through a headache made worse by the overabundance of whispering he had endure lately. "Happy Birthday, Lina" he said. "Sorry, I forgot."

Carrying his coffee, he followed them out of the house and watched them climb into AJ's jumper. Lina turned before getting in. She almost kissed him but squeezed his hands instead. Gerald watched them take off and then stared at a silvery cloud shaped like a fish. It swam across the dark, morning sky and appeared to tear apart when it crossed the claw of the moon. Gerald's head swam with whispers that sometimes reminded him of clouds. The whispers could trick him into believing he actually heard words just like clouds could trick him into believing he saw animals in the sky. A cool breeze stirred, and he turned his eyes downward.

He commanded the scribeosphere in his pocket to light up. There was still no locust inside it but even without that, it could do useful things. Gerald flung the scribeosphere into the air and let it follow him to the swamp rider parked on the side of the house. Gerald set his coffee on a workbench there and climbed on. He had a date tonight. The idea seemed strange but he decided it couldn't hurt. He twisted the handgrips that controlled the swamp rider and sped off towards the mine. Brandy, he assumed, would make him look nice.

When Gerald reached the adit, he tapped the combination on the boards He entered into the now familiar lights of the mine and watched the door swing closed. The floor was dirty and marked up from treads and rubber tires making deliveries to the lower caverns. Since Mr. O'Sullivan had opened the mine to Brandy and Paisley, strangers started showing up and taking shelter there. The salt mine's existence was not a well-protected secret anymore which made it all the more unlikely in Gerald's mind that the Blackstars didn't know about it. Yet his opinion wasn't valued or shared by Brandy, the self-proclaimed new leader of the budding, northern rebellion. She was freshly swelled with power as people from both Earth First and Justice for Kisme joined her new movement of armed resistance. Mrs. O'Sullivan and Big John would not have been pleased.

Gerald made his way down to the equipment depot but unlike the first time he'd entered it, the approach was not silent. The chatter of people talking and moving about the depot echoed up the tunnel to Gerald who had already encountered several people on the way down. Inside the cavernous room, the far corner classroom was lit up with a dozen people listening to an older man Gerald had never seen before. Others were at the long tables scattered around the room working their fingers over yotta-tabs doing Rose knew what. One of the programming chairs was occupied and the hum of the simulation pod was rumbling the floor beneath Gerald's feet. The depot wasn't packed by any measure, but there were a lot of people going about their business as if they belonged.

Recognizing Kyle, Gerald walked up to him and asked where he could find Brandy. "She's with Luke," he said, holding out his hand for Gerald to smack it. "Man's sitting up like a champ. Can you believe it? Paisley came through for us big."

"Who is us these days, Kyle?"

"Not sure I follow," Kyle said, looking blankly at Gerald. "Us is everybody in this tweakin' cave."

Gerald shrugged. "Who are all these people? Are they Justice for Kisme people? Are they Earth First people? Paisley's people?"

"Aw, nah! One people now, man. There's not been any in-fighting between the two sides since the bastards took Big John. Brandy's pulled us together. Now with Luke on the mend things are looking up. I think we're finally set to fight. All of us."

"But not for Kisme?"

"Not just her anymore. They got my best friend, Simon. They put him up on a detainment board and he was peaceful."

"Sorry to hear that. I liked him. Anybody coming to the FAC tonight? Sally said the crews are going to be there."

He nodded. "Lina's already bio-com'd it. When it comes to Big John's farm, we follow Charlene; she's the oldest super with the most juice. Charlene told us Lina's in charge now because she's not wanted. The other supers, Jeremy and Sammy, they got some things in store for the ROLIES when they next do roundups. So they won't be coming. The rest of us, though, sure. Stick and carrot, you know what I mean?"

Gerald nodded. "Lina's brothers are the stick."

"Lina's the carrot." Kyle laughed. "I don't think the Blackstars thought this through the full way. You can beat a populace into submission but only for so long. With Uncle Luke doing good, we'll get our day."

Gerald asked Kyle how to get to Luke, and he showed him which tunnels to take.

Lina's uncle was sitting up in bed but he was still pale and shaky. Brandy sat with her legs crossed in a chair. She wore baggy camouflage pants and a loose white shirt with narrow straps over her shoulders. She was hunched over a yotta-tab with her shirt hanging unintentionally open when Gerald walked unannounced into the room. He tried to avert his eyes from her naked breasts clearly peeking out at him from beneath her shirt. Her guards patted him down before letting him take the final few steps to Luke's bed.

Gerald made a small wave to Uncle Luke and breathed easier when Brandy sat up in her chair and adjusted her shirt. "Lina will be happy you're up," Gerald said.

"She knows," he said. "Already bossing me around. She tells me I'm supposed to mind the empty-headed drones as if they were real doctors."

"Or she'll whoop your flabby backside from here to Iron City," Brandy said.

Luke chuckled. "Avelina's mouth ain't so soft as that, but I got her meaning."

Brandy shifted in her chair to gaze up at Gerald.

"Hi," Gerald said awkwardly, remembering Brandy with AJ and knowing how much of Brandy's body he'd seen even before her unintentional show today. "So Lina said you're good with clothes and you could help me. Did she tell you?"

Brandy leaned forward in her chair until her shirt opened again. She sat for a moment before standing up and smiling. "She bio-com'd me just a few minutes ago. Good morning to you too, by the way. You forgot to say hello when you entered the room."

"Good morning," he said. "Sorry."

"Just so happens we have a clothier in cavern thirty-six. It can manufacture just what you need."

"Thirty-six? Guess you've had time to explore this place better than me."

Brandy produced an elastic band from somewhere and tied a handful of her hair back into a quick and messy pony tail. "We'll talk later, uncle. Better listen to your niece," she said.

Uncle Luke chuckled. "Like there's ever a choice with that girl. John's the only one she ever minded." He looked into an empty corner of the room at some drones monitoring his vitals. He stopped blinking and his gaze looked suddenly very far away.

Brandy touched his shoulder gently, and said, "We'll get him back. I swear it."

She snapped her attention back to Gerald. "Come," she said, and he followed her through a maze of corridors and tunnels. He lost track of where they were after the fifth turn, thinking without a map he'd never find his way back.

"To answer your question. We've done lots of exploring but Peter gave me the layout of the whole mine."

"Goes clear to Old New York is what AJ said."

Brandy laughed. "Not that far but close."

"Does it make it to your place?"

"Did once," she said. "Father collapsed the tunnels leading here when I was just a girl."

She led him into a large cavern carved roughly in the shape of an octagon. Around the walls were hangers and racks full of clothes looking so old, they could have belonged to the Pre-Zeros that dug the mine. "Haven't had time to clean in here," she said. "But I've checked out the equipment. In fact, you're looking at some of the clothes it manufactured for me. You like?" she asked, smiling at his obvious discomfort.

Gerald looked over at the cylindrical looking device with the clear, curved window of glass encompassing a black metal platform. "Looks kind of like the testing platforms at the Academy. Only the glass isn't really glass," he said.

Brandy looked at the clothier and said, "Never been inside an Academy testing sphere before, but I imagine this one's more fun. Here's what we do, first you get in."

Gerald stepped inside the tube that was about twice his size of him in diameter and height. Brandy closed the curved, glass door behind him and walked to the front. She spoke but Gerald couldn't hear a word she said. She pantomimed for him to tap the glass which he did. His tapping amplified her voice. "Forgot to tell you, I can't hear anything until you turn it on which you just did."

"So now what?" he said.

Brandy smirked. "Now you take off your clothes."

"What?" he asked, shaking his head.

"Got to," she said. "This thing needs raw material to work. See the compartment below your feet? Put your things in there."

Gerald looked down and saw a handle on the black platform. "But you can see me."

Brandy laughed. "If it makes you feel better I can turn my back."

"It would."

She turned her back, and Gerald got undressed. "Your under things too, sweetie." He wondered how she could tell and then noticed the holographic sphere hovering in the corner before her. His nearly naked body spun in the sphere as she manipulated the clothier program that displayed his measurements.

"Funny," he said.

"I'm too old for you," she responded. "You know I used to babysit Lina?"

Gerald gave up and put his underwear in the compartment. "Now what?"

"Hold out your arms and spread your legs," she said.

He did and she smiled.

"I didn't need to do that, did I?"

"Nope but thanks. Now, let's see." She started dressing his image up in the sphere like a play doll, bending him this way and that until he had to look away. For twenty minutes he stood there in the clothier machine catching cold while she worked. He remembered how the locust had told him Justine wasn't Kisme's mother and Brandy had lied. Suddenly, Gerald needed to know the truth. "Have you talked to Justine, lately?"

"Who?"

"Kisme's mother."

"Oh, her. No I haven't. Wait, yes I have. Wait. I don't remember. She left the movement… I think."

"You don't remember?"

"Let's not talk about it. Viola! Open the compartment behind you, sweetie."

So confused by her response, he didn't even feel embarrassed when he bent over to get his clothes despite her whistling at what she saw. Inside the compartment was a pair of loose pants, a tight shirt, and another shirt with buttons. Brandy told him to wear the button down over the tight shirt in layers. The clothier made him new shoes as well. The fit was perfect and Gerald had to admit, he looked pretty good. "Thanks," he said.

Brandy let him out of the tube and told him she'd do anything for Lina, and then her face clouded over and her smile wavered. "What's wrong?" he asked.

She turned away from him and shook her head. "Nothing. You got your fancy clothes, now let me be."

It was such a sudden change in tone, Gerald impulsively placed his hand on her shoulder. "Brandy," he said, and then gasped in pain as she pulled his hand off and twisted his wrist. He fell to his knees before her and she pushed his arm higher until his face pressed against the cold rocky floor. "Don't ever touch me!" she yelled.

"I won't!" he promised in between short breaths.

She flung him forward and stomped out of the room.

Gerald rolled off his knees and sat down. He massaged his wrist thinking she had almost snapped it. There was something wrong with her. He knew it now. AJ was right. He stood up and dusted himself off, noticing the knees were a little stained. *How am I getting out of here?* he thought. Brandy had not just left the room, she had run away.

I can help, he heard, bubbling up through the whispers.

"What?" he asked, looking around the dim interior of the clothier room.

It's almost time now, Gerald. Time to kill the wolf.

It was Lizzy's voice and the sound of her made his legs weak. He put his hand up against the wall and leaned his head onto its cold surface to keep from falling. It wasn't just her voice, he knew now. It was Lizzy sending him her thoughts through the locust. His fifteen year old sister was talking to him. "You're alive."

I'm alive, Gerald. Not so special, brother. Told you I'm alive. So many times. Find me, brother. Follow the light. Please help me.

Gerald's scribeosphere bumped him on the back. He turned away from the wall and watched it hover. It was covered in frost and steam rose from it, the locust was inside raising its wings to take flight. "How'd you get in here?" he asked it, out loud.

The scribeosphere bobbed and weaved but no voice came forth. The frost began to thaw as the ball dripped water onto the floor.

"Come to me," Gerald said, and it flew at his hand but banked away before he could touch it. He reached for it again, and it dodged into the corridor and moved down the hall. He followed the scribeosphere's light just as his sister had told him to do. It led him through all the corridors Brandy had taken. When he was back at Uncle Luke's room, she was not there and Luke was asleep. He called the scribeosphere again. This time it landed with a wet, snowball splash in his hand. He searched for the locust inside but the insect had faded again as the frost trickled down between his fingers and fell in drops to the floor.

"Lizzy," he said. "Talk to me."

Lizzy's voice was gone and Gerald felt the familiar anxiety of not understanding. Gerald slipped the scribeosphere into his pocket and left the mine in the usual way. He got on the swamp rider parked outside and headed for AJ's ranch. As he drove over bumps and roots, he kept peeking inside his pocket looking for the glow he hoped would be there. He knew Lizzy could activate the scribeosphere's light and fly it from wherever she was now. If she did it again, he'd follow the light wherever it went. When he arrived, he parked the rider and entered the house.

He sat on the couch in front of the simulation room for hours staring at the scribeosphere resting on the table before him. He hadn't changed out of the clothes Brandy had made for him. He simply sat and stared hoping he'd see the scribeosphere grow cold and start to smoke. He needed Lizzy to light it up again, but she didn't and eventually Mr. O'Sullivan emerged from his room. "Gerald!" Mr. O'Sullivan said, in a friendly, almost jovial tone. "You're looking unusually well put together. Almost certain Lina won't recognize you. You might even make Sally regret not nabbing you when she had the chance."

Gerald looked up at Mr. O'Sullivan smiling. Despite the hollowness Gerald felt inside, he couldn't suppress a grin for Mr. O'Sullivan. "Just thinking," he said.

"Done that quite a lot myself, lately."

"Thinking about the mine and about what's coming. Brandy and them can't win, you know. They can't stay here. They can't go to the Glass Lands… not now, not after attacking Cole's ship. They can't win."

"It's not always about winning, Gerald. Sometimes it's just about trying."

"But people are dead. Those pilots are dead. I heard people are being held by Black Eyes at Dusty Gulch."

Mr. O'Sullivan nodded. "I knew some of the pilots," he said. "They picked a side knowing what it meant."

"People keep saying that, but I don't care about what Rose wants or what Cole wants or the Blackstars. I want my sister back. I want AJ and Mrs. O'Sullivan back. I want Lina to have her dad back. People keep saying pick a side as if there are only two to choose from."

"There are only two, Gerald. Historically speaking, there has only ever been two sides: right or wrong. Do what you think is right or not. Two sides."

"But what I think is right is not what you think is right. I think fighting the FSA with no hope of winning is not right."

"Then do something about it or not. Pick a side."

Gerald shook his head in frustration.

"You want Lizzy back, Gerald? I heard you say that. Do something about it or not."

Gerald looked up. "You admit it? You've known all this time she's alive?"

"Of course."

"And you didn't tell me? You told AJ not to tell me?"

"Because I picked a side."

"I could have saved her!" Gerald yelled. "I could have known to save her!"

Mr. O'Sullivan's calm demeanor broke as he looked away. "I knew Cole was coming too," he said softly, as his voice caught on the admission. "I've known for months."

"And did nothing to stop it?"

"I did nothing,"

"You picked a side?"

Mr. O'Sullivan nodded.

Gerald stared at AJ's dad and asked, "You let them take your son and wife?"

"Not AJ," he said. "It wasn't supposed to be AJ." Mr. O'Sullivan looked as if he was about to say more but stopped himself and walked into the kitchen.

Gerald put the scribeosphere in his pocket and walked angrily to the jumper with the auto-pilot. Thankfully the jumper's voice was still muted from what AJ had done to it weeks earlier. Gerald's wrist was sore and the whispers hurt his head, so he closed his eyes all the way to Iron City thinking about how much he resented this day and this night. Sally was wrong to believe laughter might be good for them. He didn't need to laugh. He needed to find Lizzy and rescue everybody else who'd been taken. That was his side, the only side he cared about.

Mr. O'Sullivan was wrong.

Chapter 31

Lady in Black

The breeze in Iron City was stronger than usual and the scent of the food, from restaurants and bars cooking FAC provided meats, was heavy in the air. Beneath the usual smells, Gerald noticed something sweeter like lavender or fragrant perfume. He didn't recognize the smell but the syrupy feel of it in his nose reminded Gerald of the Glass Lands sVid AJ made him experience. He wondered if AJ would think that too.

He missed AJ. He tried to picture his friend walking next to him. If he was there, they'd make a game of jumping over the largest puddles along the flooded roads of Iron City on the way to veteran's plaza. He missed AJ's mom too but not as much as AJ. If AJ was here, Gerald could tell him about Lizzy contacting him through the locust. He could share things he'd been thinking about Lina. Yet AJ wasn't here, and Lina was no longer in the right mood for dates. He trudged forward through the bouncy streets wondering how long the island would continue to float if they couldn't stop the flooding. He walked around the larger puddles and took chances on leaping over the smaller ones. When he arrived at the plaza, he was surprised by how many people were already gathered.

Hundreds of people were at the plaza. The gazebo at its center looked as if it was made from dark, prezero hardwood. The drone inside it served colorful drinks to people of all ages. Somebody had sVid sprayed a goofy smile and clown eyes on its domed face. *Try our vitamin enriched liqueurs,* a babblesphere projected as it floated near people without drinks in their hands. *The FAC provides,* it finished. The gazebo served beverages like ginger ale and cold cream sparkles, but most people drank what made them drunk quickest. Gerald picked a sour drink without a lot of color. It was mostly FAC alcohol which he needed to get through the night. The music was festive, so he listened and drank hoping to fool himself into appearing happy like Sally wanted.

"Told you she knows clothes."

Gerald spun and sloshed the sticky drink over his fingers. "Lina," he said, and then stared at her cleavage for an inappropriately long time. She wore a floral summer dress of periwinkle blue. The material hugged the slippery swell of her chest and hips. A wrap swept across her shoulders and cascaded down over her soft breasts and bare arms giving her skin a blush of light brown matching the nude color of her high heeled shoes.

"You like it?" she said, spinning around so he could see her back which was bare except for the jacket that covered her from mid-shoulder to waist. "Sally made it for me."

Gerald nodded, and then said, "You're beautiful."

"Thank you," she said. "Now let's get this over with and go home."

She kicked off her shoes and pulled him to the dance floor in front of the gazebo causing him to spill more of his drink. She took a sip and smiled before moving around him in a dance that felt like she was taking aggressive measurements of his body. Her eyes darted towards Sally and Madame Evelyne the entire time. Sally's face looked horrified and Madame Evelyne's face was unreadable.

Lina moved in close to Gerald's body and put her arms around his waist. She led him around the floor in fast circles until Gerald was breathing heavy and starting to sweat. After twenty minutes of dancing like this, Lina groaned loudly and stopped abruptly. "Fine!" she snapped. "C'mon!" she demanded, and grabbed Gerald's hand roughly to drag him back to the gazebo.

"What's that lady doing? Digging in for the night?"

Lina was only slightly out-of-breath from all the dancing. Gerald was dripping as if he'd run a marathon, so he ordered himself another drink.

"Make it two," she said, her voice softer in resignation.

Gerald handed her the drink and they toasted to her birthday.

"I'm sorry," Lina said, looking over at Sally who appeared equally miserable sitting next to Madame Evelyne drinking something hot from a cup. Madame Evelyne was talking to her, lecturing her sternly by the look of it, and casting intense glances towards Lina and Gerald. Two ROLIES stood behind them, one short and one tall.

"I'm making a fine mess of things," Lina continued. "I just can't. I want to but—"

"Drink your drink," Gerald said. "It helps."

Lina swallowed it back in one swig, and then ordered another. After she calmed herself and Gerald stopped sweating, they started to talk. For almost an hour standing at the gazebo they talked to each other like friends who understood each other's loss. When a slow song came on, Lina looked up into Gerald's eyes and took his hand gently in hers. She pulled him to the dance floor and hugged him close. They swayed to the music slowly, not really caring if their feet moved with much rhythm. The song ended and another slow song began.

Lina, her face resting on Gerald's chest, let her eyes drift up to his. "If we're going to show them young love, let's show 'em right." She smiled and a dimple Gerald hadn't noticed before appeared like magic in her cheek. Her smile grew wider into a grin. There was a glint in her eyes too. They were a little drunk and maybe that explained it, but Lina's hand slid from Gerald's shoulder to his stomach. She gently pet him while they moved to the slow rhythm of the music. She reached behind her back to Gerald's hand resting high above her waist. She wrapped her fingers around his wrist and let the weight of her arm sink Gerald's palm lower to the small of her back. He felt the rise of her cheeks and tightened up, paralyzed with anxiety as his face flushed hot and his heart pounded. She giggled softly and pulled his hand lower until his palm lay across the firm muscles of her bottom. With her hand on top of his, she made him squeeze her as she moved tighter into his embrace. "There's room for your other hand too," she said, thickly.

Overwhelmed with the silky heat of her bottom moving beneath his hands, Gerald felt her body push against his as she tilted her head back to be kissed. Without thinking, he tasted the alcohol on her lips and breathed in the warm smell of her skin. He squeezed her without prompting and rubbed himself against her forgetting they were in the middle of a crowded dance floor. "I think we did it right," she suddenly whispered. "The lady's gone."

Gerald opened his eyes to see Madame Evelyne was no longer sitting next to Sally. The ROLIES were gone as well. Sally stared at him with her mouth open. Lina squeezed him tight and then pushed away with just the hint of a smile as her gaze lingered on his body. "Walk close behind me," she said, as she led him to the gazebo.

Gerald walked close, too hot and dizzy with alcohol and emotion to think much at all about what just happened. Lina ordered three drinks. "I guess we sold her," she said, mildly, as Sally approached.

"You even sold me," Sally said, grinning at Gerald. "Seriously, Gerald. What got into you?"

Gerald blushed hotter. "Don't know what you're talking about."

Sally took her drink and clinked it to Lina's. "It's what she wanted, Lina. She saw some of the crew looking, smiling. It's what she needed to see. Life moving on with the FAC in charge."

Lina looked down at her drink, nodding. Gerald thought about what Lina did to him on the dance floor, how easily she made him forget everything else that was important. For all the time during those last dances, Gerald didn't think once about his sister or AJ or anything else. He was embarrassed. He felt awkward. He wanted to walk away. "I guess we showed them," he said.

"We showed 'em," she said, touching his hand. "Take me home?"

And just like that, Gerald's heart raced again. He wanted to take her home. He wanted to talk to her. He wanted to dance with her again. He wanted to be with her and only her, by themselves.

"No," Sally said, a strange urgency in her voice. "I need Gerald."

"What for?" Gerald asked, more sharply than he intended.

Sally looked between Lina and Gerald for a minute, biting her lip. "It's about Jack."

"What about him?"

"Lina?" she asked. "Are you feeling well enough to get home by yourself?"

"I drank a lot," Lina said, shaking her head. "Don't think I can."

"What if you take Gerald's jump? It does all the flying. You can sleep it off."

"It's my birthday," Lina said, in the same petulant voice she had used with her dad on the first day of market. "Somebody should take me home."

"Maybe I should take her," Gerald said, seeing Lina wobble on her feet.

Sally shook her head vigorously. "You'll be fine, right Lina? I'll bring Gerald to you after."

"After," she said. "Fine."

"No, really, I can take her," Gerald said.

"No," Lina said, eyeing Sally seeming to remember who was boss now. "Okay, I'll be fine. I'm always fine. Who's Jack?"

"A Blackstar Gerald and I went to the Academy with last year."

"Don't like 'em," she said. "They're living in my house."

"Please, Lina?"

Lina nodded. "I'll go home. Thank you, Gerald. I liked our dance." She swallowed the last of her drink and walked unsteadily away. At the edge of the plaza, she looked back.

"C'mon, Sally. I got to get her home. Look at her." Sally caught his arm when he tried to walk away.

"You have to come, Gerald. It's important. Really important."

Sally gnawed on her lip so hard, Gerald thought she might draw blood. Her eyes were watery and her hands shook. "What's wrong?" he asked.

"Jack wants to talk. Please. He's there right now."

Gerald looked again and saw that Lina was gone from sight. Sally looked frightened, and Gerald relented. He let his body relax and nodded for her to lead the way. They ended up at the trailhead leading to the boardwalk and the Iron City's islands. "By those trees," she said.

Somebody stood with their hood pulled up over their heads. In silhouette, the person didn't look like Jack. He seemed too tall for Jack, but Gerald walked to him anyway. Sally followed a few steps behind. Something ominous and dark nagged at him but his thoughts were cloudy with alcohol and too distant to grasp. Gerald came within a few paces of the man before he realized the robes weren't even the right color. He focused on the shadow harder. "Jack?" he asked.

"No sugar," a woman's voice said. "Not this time." She slipped a thin rod from a holster at her side, and jabbed him in the gut.

Gerald saw sparks and felt the jolt of the zap rod through his entire body. His legs collapsed beneath him and he tumbled to the ground without a sound.

"Sorry, Gerald!" Sally said, her voice sobbing and far away. "It's not bad. I promise. I wouldn't have done it if it was bad. Gerald!"

Gerald thought it was odd she sounded so concerned. He was just going to sleep. He heard the whispers fading. He hadn't slept for days. He'd be fine just like Lina, and then his thoughts disappeared.

Gerald woke strapped down on a metal table naked except for a scratchy, paper thin blanket covering his mid-section. On a table next to Gerald was a similarly covered man whose shoulder looked larger than Gerald's leg. There was something familiar about him but the restraints kept Gerald from seeing his face.

"Good, you're awake," the woman said, her voice husky and familiar. "You've gained a lot of weight since I last carried you. Your hair grew in pretty too. I've always liked redheads."

Gerald remembered her voice now, but he could not see her. "Sharon," he said.

"Miss Knight, if you please." She walked around the table so he could see her. "I grew up where people had manners. You're old enough now and physically fit enough to use them properly."

Her long black hair was straight with red beads in the few braids she wore. She had not changed clothes in all the times he'd seen her. Her face had not aged in any way Gerald could identify. He had no idea how old she was: anywhere from her thirties to sixties. He remembered the holo-session the locust had made him experience when she put his dead parents in an unmarked jumper. He remembered her from the enforcer night vision too. He looked again to the table next to him. "Abe," he said. "Is that him?"

"Now that's surprising. How do you know Abner? Did the voices tell you?"

"What voices?" he said, instinctively. Even after all these years, he remembered what she wanted. He remembered his fathers' warnings about bad people who would do anything to get inside his mind. Sharon was one of those people.

"Sugar, please don't lie to me. You're a Goodstone and in my experience they never lie." She removed a coil of wire with a leather handle from her belt. On its tip, sharp barbs curled wickedly backward like hooks. She lay a purse open on a tray between Gerald and Abe. It held gleaming silver implements arranged from large to small. Gerald started to panic.

"Look, I don't know what you want," he said jerking his arms and legs against the restraints.

Sharon looked at him puzzled and then smiled. "Sugar, no. These aren't what you think. I'm not going to hurt you."

"But you will! You are." He thrashed at the restraints and screamed as he tried to break free.

Her smile wavered and her brow wrinkled in concern as she touched Gerald's arm. She rubbed him gently. "I'd never hurt you, sugar. In a few minutes you'll know it's true."

Gerald looked at the wire whip she still held in the hand not stroking his arm. "What is it then?"

She looked down and her mouth opened. "This?" she asked, lifting the coil above his chest.

Gerald pushed himself lower on the table.

"It's just a RADwire. Look at it."

Gerald stopped thrashing to get a better look. He relaxed as he recognized the SLYscape connecting points lining the curved hooks. It was like the filament he kept inside the scribeosphere to charge external devices, only much larger. He felt himself flush in embarrassment but he was still strapped down to a table. "Why am I tied down?"

"You're not, sugar. Not really. You're in a simulation pod."

"But I can't move."

"A precaution," she said. "Just until we help you get back what you lost."

"We?" he asked.

She nodded and walked to the other side of the room. Gerald watched her shimmer and disappear. When she came back, she had taken off her long cape-like jacket. She unbuckled her belt and lay it on a table a few steps away. She studied the table and then moved her fingers over it until Preston Rose appeared by her side. He wasn't moving. He didn't talk. It was a frozen holo-snap waiting for a connection.

"The High Prelate's under house arrest," she said. "But he'll be with us soon and explain. That's one of the reasons were in this pod. Cole can't find us here, not quickly, anyway."

"You're running from Cole?"

"For now," she said, shrugging. "I guess I could clean you up while we wait." She pulled out a small white cloth and started sponging off his chest and stomach. It was wet and icy cold. "I got practically drunk off your breath when I brought you in. Your friend, Sally, was no help. Silly girl. Emotional. I had to send her away to get control of herself."

"Did you hurt her? Is that why she did it?"

Sharon smiled. "I told you, I'm not here to hurt anyone." She dabbed at his thighs with the cloth and then called one of the medical drones over to Gerald's table and told it what to do.

"Please open wide, Freelander," it said mechanically.

Gerald shook his head, not trusting. "Come on, sugar," Sharon said. "Please?"

Gerald shook his head, so she put her fingers on his cheeks and pinched until he opened wide enough for the drone to shoot a horribly flavored mist into his mouth. Instantly, Gerald's mind cleared as if he had slept just the right amount of time and not tasted alcohol in weeks.

"You sobered up?" she asked.

Gerald nodded, wanting to rub his sore jaw. If Sharon wasn't here to hurt him, it wasn't because she couldn't.

In his peripheral vision, Gerald saw the image of Preston Rose move. "Hello, Gerald!" he said, loudly. "We have not been formally introduced. I am Preston Rose."

The High Prelate walked between the two tables and lay his hand on Gerald's shoulder. At first, it didn't feel exactly the same as a real hand resting on him, but it was close enough for Gerald's mind to smooth out the rough edges of the simulation. After a moment, Gerald would have been hard pressed to tell the difference. The brain's ability to compensate for imperfections in sensory perception was why SLYscape worlds seemed so realistic. "My word," Preston said, squeezing his shoulder briefly and letting go. "Your parents would be so proud."

The whispers in Gerald's mind suddenly whooshed up and hissed like waves crashing on rocks. He shook his body back and forth until Sharon put her hands over his ears. The coolness of her fingers soothed him. Not as much as if he could touch his mother's jade himself, but the whispers settled enough for him to open his eyes again. "Now there, sugar. We've got some experience here. Breathe through the voices. It's supposed to help."

He breathed slowly and deeply, and when he felt he could form words again, he asked, "What do you mean, proud?"

Preston smiled. "Your mother and father were two of my most loyal followers. Like Angie and Peter. Only they protected you first."

"I don't understand," Gerald said.

"You will, sugar. Right after we give you what you need." She unraveled the coiled RADwire and Gerald grew anxious. She lay the cold wire across his bare chest, and he started to tremble. She was going to hurt him after all.

"This won't hurt a bit," she said, and pushed the hooks deep into his skin. He screamed, but then fell silent as he realized he felt no pain just warm blood trickling slowly down his skin.

"See, sugar," she said. "It's something to get used to but it doesn't hurt."

"The mist?" he asked.

She nodded as she pushed each hook into his body. "Anesthetic." She pressed the last hooks into Gerald's thighs, and then uncoiled the rest of the wire until it rested over the chest of the man next to him. She pushed the remaining hooks into him. "Abe?" Gerald asked, again.

Preston watched Sharon work and nodded. "I can't imagine how you know him, young man. But, yes. In a manner of speaking, that is Abner O'Reilly. He's not really here. He's a simulation this pod created for us. Like me, I'm here but physically we both know I'm in my home. Abe is here but also somewhere else."

"I know how moles work," he said.

"Exactly. Unfortunately, Abe is not sitting comfortably as I am. He's not drinking a juice or gazing at colorful garden flowers."

"He's in a holo-chair."

"You can't know that," Preston said. "But you do, don't you?" Preston stood above Gerald looking down. His eyes appeared to widen and glimmer. "Excuse me," he said. "You're just so like him. I've forgotten how much he could do."

"Dixon was a redhead too," Sharon said, finishing up with Abe. "Preston, we should ask him. Just doing it feels wrong."

Preston sighed. "What else can you tell me, Gerald? Have you seen other things?"

Gerald was calm as he returned Preston's stare. "Sharon stole my parents."

"Oh, sugar. I'm so sorry. You saw us? Me?" she asked. She placed her hands over her face and rubbed her eyes until she could look at him again. She brushed Gerald's cheek with the back of her hand and then ran her fingers through his hair. She rested her palm on his forehead. He felt his hot skin cool against hers.

Sharon's touch reminded him of the first time they met. It hurt, but it felt good too just as it did now. Gerald flexed his arms and legs. The restraints had no give. "Why'd you take them?"

"What horrible things you must think. You poor, innocent thing. What haven't you seen, sugar? Maybe, that's what we should ask."

Preston nodded as if he had made some decision. "Gerald, Sharon took your parents away to save you. You've probably already figured it out, but you're special."

Gerald laughed a little hysterically. "Right, a child of the future. AJ told me."

"AJ shouldn't have done that, but in some ways it saves time. We took your parents, because their DNA would have led Cole straight to you. That's how the FSA works. They want all genetically enhanced people to die, because people like you threaten their control of the Freeland. At the time, we had already lost Elizabeth. I couldn't let them get you both."

"Both?"

"She's your sister, Gerald. Your biological sister. Your parents, your sister, you… you are all—"

"Gene demons."

"Enhanced. And you were not grown in a lab somewhere. That's what the FSA feeds their news spheres so they can get enough leverage against me. They want me because I know where all of you hide. They don't."

"Lizzy is a gene demon?"

"Enhanced. In fact, that was my mistake. I put so many of you on that street. I thought if there was a whole community… it doesn't matter now. Eight years ago—when the lightning storm struck—Cole murdered over thirty children of the future and their guardians. In your case, your parents. For some reason he didn't kill them all. Some he captured like your sister and young Abner here."

Gerald closed his eyes. "Where is Lizzy?"

"I don't know, which makes me think she's with AJ, Angie, and John. There aren't many places in the world you can hide from me. Yet all the ones Cole's taken are gone. I hope you can find out where they're hidden. Once you do, I guarantee you, I'll get them back."

"You think they're held together?"

Preston nodded. "Which brings us to now. We need to implant a mole in your brain."

"No!" Gerald said, trying to scramble off the table. *Just a precaution. They knew.* "I can't have one," he said. "Ever."

"I know, son. I know what your father said." Preston shook his head. "But everything depends on it, Gerald. Angie let herself be captured to make this happen. If you don't allow Sharon to inject you, you won't be able to receive Abe's memories. You need those I think."

"You think? You don't know?"

Preston shook his head. "What I know about children of the future is what Dixon Streets taught me. He was the first of you I found. Cole took him in the Quell. So whatever I know, it's twenty years out-of-date, and with the enhanced, that can be quite a long time."

"I don't understand."

"You see, when Dixon was with me, he was at the Academy. Prefect Humphrey was his vWare instructor just like he was yours. Prefect Humphrey noticed things about him, how he could get around any security block in the SLYscape. The problem with Dixon was he suffered from paralyzing anxiety attacks. He said he heard voices. His head hurt all the time, because people screamed at him… thousands of people, all inside his head. He went into a coma once, and that's when I found him. He had the same genetic enhancements as World Union soldiers. We thought we executed them all, but we didn't. And instead of reporting him to Augustus, I hid my knowledge. Why? Because when he woke he told me stories that were hard to believe. He'd tell me how he flew across the SLYscape like a bird, or ran like a wolf. He said he knew what other people were thinking. He said he could remember what they remembered."

"He thought he could," Gerald said. "It was just holographic recordings of his brain activity stored to y-space."

"That's what we thought. We tested him." Preston covered his mouth with his wrinkled fingers and rubbed his chin. "He couldn't just experience recorded holo-sessions. He wasn't bound by what the vWare wanted him to feel." He looked around and raised his hands. "Like this simulation. So real but not quite. Have you ever noticed how the odors in immersion spheres and sim pods don't quite smell right? I notice it with flowers. Taste is sometimes off too. Sight, sound, touch, those are pretty universal. The biggest challenge is determining if people like the physical signals entering their brains or not. So, simulated reality is never quite right. Never exact. Unless you were Dixon Streets. What Dixon could do required no vWare to interpret memories stored in y-space. His recall of other people's memories was exact as if they had happened to him. If they remembered knowing something, he'd remember knowing it too."

"I can do that," Gerald said before he had a chance to stop himself. He didn't trust Preston or Sharon despite their words. He was still strapped to a table bleeding. He felt afraid, especially after Preston smiled. It was such a strange smile, greedy.

"That is exactly what I hoped you'd say."

Sharon pet his head as Preston talked on. "After I found more children like Dixon, it became apparent they all had similar capabilities. Unfortunately, when they were taught to use them, they went catatonic. Only Dixon had ever managed to come back without help. Our help was to block their memories, to alter recollections, to condition them throughout their lives until they were ready. Like you, Gerald. You are ready."

Sharon put her hands on Gerald's face and bent down low until he felt her lashes flutter against his cheeks. His mother used to do that. Butterfly kisses, she called them. "If you let us," Sharon whispered. "You can find your family."

"Lizzy?"

Sharon nodded. "Lizzy, AJ, Mrs. O'Sullivan. They're all your family now, sugar. What Preston and I found out with Dixon was children of the future have a kind of homing instinct like certain animals and insects. They can find each other, if the bonds are strong enough, they know where to go."

"But I just met Lina's dad. We need to get him back too." He whispered these words instinctively because Sharon's face was so close to his. He felt and smelled her breath. It was minty like his mother's. Emotion caught in his throat, and he wondered if they tricked him with the mist. He wanted to help, but his dad warned him not to help people who do bad things. He felt the restraints on his wrists and ankles. The anesthetic was wearing off and tiny pinpricks of itchy fire spread across his skin.

"How can I trust you?" he asked.

"Because," she said, pushing herself straight. "You have to."

Gerald nodded and tears dripped out of his eyes. "Fine," he said, sharply, the way Lina would say it. "But I'm not so special. You're wrong there."

"How so?" Preston said, an edgy note of concern his voice.

"Lizzy's been telling me that for years." He smiled and Sharon smiled uncertainly back. Gerald knew Preston and Sharon didn't understand, and he took strength from having a secret he'd never share with them. It was his and his sister's secret. She had been talking to him for a half-a-year, and they had no idea. "What do I do?"

"Relax, young man. And close your eyes."

Gerald did as asked. He felt a pinch on his upper thigh. Unlike Sally when she was given her first molecular injection as a child, Gerald cried. He cried so hard, he couldn't stop until the room spun and the whispers fled.

I'm coming for you Lizzy. I'm coming to defeat the wolf.

Chapter 32

Gerald's Fire

Gerald heard sirens in the distance and red lights strobed through the dark room Metal was at his back and the blood from the hooks had hardened into scabs on his skin. The restraints were gone.

He sat up in the simulation room and Sharon was gone. The medical drones were in standby mode next to the simulation of Abe who lay on the table next to him. He could see Abe perfectly now. His long blond hair was just like AJ's but his face was scarred. His arms and legs were covered in ropy knots of flesh raised in precise patterns that Gerald imagined matched the connection points of his enforcer uniform. Gerald stepped off the table to get a better look.

His feet touched pavement and the tables disappeared, replaced by a narrow street lined with white curbs and small yards of green turf. He stood next to an incinerator. The lid was sVid sprayed: "A Freeland is a Clean Land." Gerald looked down half-expecting to see a ring on a leather cord, but he saw only tan clothes and an unadorned chest. He wore no jewelry on his wrists or in his ear. He was not inside his eleven year old body as he feared, but he recognized Layfette Street where he grew up. He didn't recognize this portion of the road. He was standing in bare feet at a corner in front of a three story building built from dark blocks. Wide steps led up to giant double doors. Glowing without sensory enhancement was a sign: *O'Reilly Grand Mission.*

A teenage boy came bouncing down the steps. He looked at the night sky and then took off jogging down the street. He was blond and very tall. He was Abe, Gerald knew, as a boy.

Gerald stared at the yellow lights inside the windows of O'Reilly's mission as weather shields began shutting for the night. He saw shrinking patches of furniture inside and people eating at long tables. A bald man stepped out onto the stairs and cast a glance after Abe. The man was old and appeared heavy under the thick robes he wore. He frowned as he watched Abe run farther down the street. He fidgeted for a moment and then shuffled back into the building. He shut the tall double doors behind him.

A symbol appeared like a stamp over the mission building breaking the realism of the experience. Gerald looked hard at the symbol noticing the world had a frame of sorts. He was in a simulation but it didn't feel as real as the ones he was used to experiencing. There was something foreign influencing how the air felt on his skin. A cool draft hit him before the chilly breeze picked up.

Gerald's feet went cold on the solid ground. The night purpled in his vision as clouds spilled across the dark sky like ink spreading into cloth. The red tinge of Mars peeked out from inside the yellow claws of the moon which meant it was Electric-sol. As he looked for other stars, he noticed SLYscape controls blinking at the edges of neighborhood homes. Their shapes were similar to the ones Gerald used in programming chairs, only far simpler. He swiped at one catching thin air as his feet yanked him high off the ground.

The street swirled by as Gerald bounced and twirled behind Abe like a balloon tethered to the boy's wrist. Once Abe stopped running, Gerald drifted towards the boy as the RADwire connecting them became momentarily visible. He watched his virtual tether slack in loops on the ground between Abe and Gerald's feet once again grounded.

Abe wandered about the sidewalk yelling out a girl's name several times. He caught sight of her and started to wave. She didn't see him before the explosion behind them sent her tumbling to the ground. Gerald and Abe fearfully looked back over their shoulders where black smoke rose in great, thick columns from O'Reilly's mission. Abe ran towards the fire but stopped when the air above the building rolled into bubbles like black oil boiling. The bubbles expanded until they burst into shovel-nosed ships with FSA markings on their long, opaque, energy domes. As the sky settled back to flat black, thunder crashed and echoed the arrival of the ships already starting to land.

In formation, patrol pods touched down on the yards of Layfette Street. Enforcers appeared next to their ships and then gathered around in front of the white steps of the mission. The giant double doors opened and the enforcers raised their hands. The first to go down was Prefect O'Reilly. The people following him screamed and rushed back inside to where smoke waited. The doors closed and a wide blue bar of light shot straight down through the roof. Fire exploded upwards engulfing the building in seconds. Abe fell to his knees, not believing what he saw.

"Alexander!" he yelled, as tendrils of fear squeezed something inside Gerald until his stomach ached and his brow sweat. He remembered the chemical smell of this night and wanted to run.

Several enforcers marched up the stairs into the flaming building. The rest moved towards the other houses on the street. The night clouds parted as new white and blue beams burned down from the stratosphere hitting each house in turn. Gerald understood what was happening in a kind of horror his adult mind comprehended but his memory refused to let him believe. Prezero satellite weapons were destroying his neighborhood with oscillating energy beams built to destroy rebel strongholds. The World Union satellites were not supposed to function any longer, but Abe's memory didn't agree.

Gerald was vReading. He had an implant in his body now, and it was doing things to him he couldn't stop. The mole wanted him to relive Abe's memories clicked together from y-space recordings of the enforcer at fourteen. This was what Preston wanted him to see. This was why Sharon injected him, so he could experience the fire from Abe's point of view. The tether was vWare. Somebody programmed it to force Abe's experiences into Gerald's mind as if they were his own *to get back what you lost,* Sharon said, but he hadn't lost anything. He remembered the lightning strikes, one after another, not energy beams from space. It was a freedom storm as the counsellors had told him. *Thom! It's not a storm,* his mother had cried. *They found us,* his father had yelled. *That's not how it happened,* Gerald thought. Debris rained down on Abe's head as they watched the mission burn.

When half the block was on fire, Abe finally got up and ran. Gerald kept the tether loose between them so he wouldn't be jerked off the ground again. They crossed one block into the next and then as the houses became more familiar, Gerald's fear swelled inside him. The next block was Gerald's block. He recognized neighboring lawns and the jumpers parked on the street. All those people he knew as a child were dead now. He wanted to turn back but the tether wouldn't allow it. The mole wouldn't allow it. When Abe stopped, he stood across the street from Gerald's childhood home. The road was alight in an eerie red-yellow glow. Another explosion, and the fires moved closer. Another explosion, and they were almost there. It was a lit fuse chasing them in the dark.

The enforcers were only one block away. Abe was more afraid then he had ever been in his life. Gerald felt those emotions layered on top of his own. Gerald stopped watching the fires approach and turned to look into the yellow light of his family's kitchen. He saw himself as an eleven year old boy with long, red hair peering out into the night. He looked concerned but not yet afraid.

The first houses on Gerald's block burst into flames as the satellite weapon struck. The tan walls of Gerald's home were awash in shadows and shifting light as if something huge sat between the kitchen and the fires approaching. He watched the louvered weather shields close and then walked across the street towards his home. The tether stopped him before he reached the other side, because a large ship with FSA markings appeared out of thin air. Abe saw it too, and he started backing up pulling Gerald along with him.

Gerald recognized the ship from Dusty Gulch. It was Reaver's ship, the same one Cole had entered when leaving Senior Thomas' tent. Gerald panicked remembering how this memory ends with Lizzy in Cole's arms being taken away. He didn't want to see anymore. He didn't want to relive what was about to happen. He jumped high off the ground and slapped at the SLYscape symbols stamping the houses. If he was implanted, he should have control of what he experienced. He should be able to cruise the scape like AJ and Sally cruised. He should be able to stop the simulation and get away. He was in the air soaring high above the rooftops until Abe's tether snapped him back to earth. He hit the pavement and felt an electric shock of pain as a hand reached out and slapped Abe's back.

Abe hit the ground next to Gerald and gasped for breath. A Field Marshal stood above them, and Gerald knew it was the one who tortured Uncle Luke. Gerald stood but Abe stayed down. He writhed on the ground crying from the slap and whatever else he remembered feeling this night. Tears made dirty streaks on his cheeks as Abe scrambled back covering his face with his arm. The Field Marshal raised his hand to shoot the boy when Cole Reaver appeared out of the darkness. His pale, scarred cheeks were the only part of Cole easily visible in the night since he wore dark clothes, glasses, and gloves. Gerald eyed the iridescent wolf design on his hands. Gerald's chest muscles went into spasm as the wind turned frigid. Gerald wondered if the sensation was his or Abe's. *Or maybe both.*

"Who's this?" Cole asked. His voice sounded smooth and relaxed as if the explosions occurring up the street weren't happening at all.

"Abner O'Reilly," the marshal responded. "Age fourteen. Orphan of David and Susan Wells. Ward of Prefect Alexander O'Reilly—"

"Not what I wanted, Levi. What is he?"

"He is one of the targets on the list."

"Stand up," Cole said.

Abe did. He was taller than Cole which the Deputy Director noticed with a sneer. Cole brought Abe down to eye level by yanking the front of his shirt. He peered into Abe's marble blue eyes and froze like he had done when taunting Uncle Luke at the race. He was talking to someone somewhere, instantly communicating through moles, or fetching information from the SLYscape about the boy in his grasp. A few breaths later, Cole angrily removed his glasses. He drew Abe's face to within centimeters of his own. Cole's bright eyes were slanted and dusty brown with yellow streaks that shone golden in the dark. Backlit by fire and smoke, he was dangerous and terrifying to look at. Waves of fear radiated up the tether to Gerald from Abe whose legs trembled. "Let me go!" he yelled. He lurched backward and took a wild swing at Cole landing a good blow to the man's face.

Cole shifted his hand to Abe's throat. "Don't be afraid, boy. Your life won't end just yet. Probably soon, but not yet. Father has a use for you. Once he's done... we'll play. Save your fear until then, please. Make it fun."

"Levi, keep him with you." Cole threw Abe down to the ground and set off towards Gerald's house.

Gerald wanted to close his eyes knowing what must happen next, but he didn't. He stared after Cole letting the anger build. Cole stopped at the incinerator Gerald remembered from the day his parents died. "Gerald Goodstone," he remembered saying. "Good and stone brave."

From the middle of Gerald's childhood yard, the Deputy Director looked up at the moon and raised his arms. "Now!" he shouted, with a smile on his lips. He swung his arms down and changed Gerald's life forever.

White and blue energy exploded through the roof of Gerald's home. Cole smiled as he watched the fire. Levi ordered the terrified boy to follow him into the burning house. Abe, his eyes not blinking, followed two steps behind the marshal in a bad parody of the cybernetically enhanced enforcer he'd soon become. Gerald knew this day happened eight years ago, but it felt real and present, especially when he heard the terror in his sister's scream.

"Gerals, help!"

Gerald saw Lizzy crawling from the front door to get away from the giant man in the dark armor who kicked it in. Gerald's head hurt trying to fit his and Abe's memories together in his mind. He remembered being in the kitchen struggling to get to her. She had been crawling through the hallway with a power line blocking her way. She was crawling towards him, but Abe saw her crawling away. In both memories, she crawled. In one memory, Levi was there, in the other the Field Marshal wasn't. Gerald had no ability to act or change the outcome of what was happening before his eyes. He gave in and watched.

Lizzy crawled towards a little boy dragging himself on his stomach from the other side of the foyer. The boy's hair was gone and blisters shined wetly on his cheeks and around his eyes. The boy saw Levi and Abe standing behind Lizzy. The boy opened his mouth to scream but nothing came out. The Field Marshal ignored the boy who Gerald recognized as himself. Levi had eyes only for the girl. It bent down and swept her up by the ankle like a fish by the tail. It flipped her like a rag doll right side up and caught her by the arm. Lizzy cried out as something inside her shoulder popped like bones breaking or ligaments snapping.

Abe jumped as a silver ball shot from the kitchen straight at the Field Marshal's head. The marshal dodged it. It swatted at the lightning fast ball and missed. The marshal swung several more times but the ball was too quick zipping and darting like an insect buzzing in for a bite. The marshal tried twice more to slap the ball down before Gerald's scribeosphere started to smoke. Sensing a new threat, Levi dropped Lizzy to the floor and produced a weapon from a compartment at his thigh. Levi aimed and fired three shots. The scribeosphere spun and dodged like a sparrow protecting its nest. It swooped in on Levi's head narrowly avoiding contact. The next shot severed a power line overhead. It fell wriggling from the ceiling to the floor where it slithered like a snake trailing blue sparks.

The scribeosphere jetted into the living room where the family simulation pod took up most of the space. The Field Marshal gave chase. Abe screamed for the girl to watch out, but Lizzy touched the power line and went sailing off as if she could fly. The boy with no hair watched disbelieving and so did Gerald tethered to Abe. The boy kept opening his mouth and closing it as if he talked or screamed but Gerald standing in the foyer heard no voice. *That's not the way it happened,* he told himself silently, but some part of him believed what he witnessed was true.

Gerald watched himself avoid the sparking cable as he followed Levi and Lizzy into the living room. He saw himself stand and his dad draw a shimmer gun on the Field Marshal. Lizzy was a shaking heap at the marshal's feet. Words were exchanged and then his father fired the weapon blowing a hole through the side of the house. Lizzy screamed for Gerald to come help, but it was Abe who rushed in to save her. He swooped Gerald's little sister up into his arms and ran for the simulation pod's open door. Something had torn it from its hinges and it was wide open. Inside the pod, Lizzy's Poison Dart game offered a paradise of green booby-trapped trails and tall trees—a promise of escape. Abe ducked inside the jungle's shelter as a beam of white carved a blinding streak into the house from outside. Gerald's dad didn't even grab his chest before falling backward without a sound. There was no blood, only burned flesh, and the boy with no hair was suddenly pushing himself around fallen support structures and broken pieces of wall to get to his dad lying against the opening of the pod. He knelt down and pulled awkwardly at his dad's head whose eyes were still open and staring up.

Gerald remembered trying to wrest him awake. *Get up!* He remembered screaming—scared and confused—angry because his dad wasn't protecting them. *Be brave,* he remembered hearing but his dad couldn't have said it. Not if what Gerald saw now was true. The boy looked out through the hole in the wall into the yard. He cocked his head to see past the tree that had fallen into the hole. He saw Levi, his armor blackened and smoking, but the cybernetically attached man inside the armor was unharmed. He watched the Field Marshal raise his gun and take aim at the boy. There was a flash at the same moment Gerald's tether snapped him off the ground. He flew feet-first into the simulation pod and passed through the body of the little boy who dove into the jungle after him.

Chapter 33

Abe's Island

Gerald spun in midair windmilling his arms through a dark, cavernous space with tiny lights all around until his body splashed into the salty shallows of an ocean. The water sparkled turquoise under a hot, fiery sun. Abe the boy was gone but Abe, the enforcer stood sweating in nothing but shorts and a tee-shirt on a sandy beach. The tether connecting them flashed and settled like a web sinking on a breeze. It touched the water and disappeared. The water was knee-deep but the waves crashing onto Gerald's body pounded his shoulders and soaked his head. He splashed and sloshed his way to Abe who looked much as he had in Gerald's night vision of the wolf. Abe saw him now and without words pointed to the walking palms and twisting green vines that lined the sand. There was a snuffle from something large moving through the trees.

The sand rippled at their feet and an animal with a shell on its back poked its head up. It looked like a turtle but as the tide washed over it, the turtle burrowed out of sight like a sand flea. When the animal reappeared, it looked cartoonish to Gerald who was trying to adjust to this new simulation. He could feel the mole burning him as if it was the sun, but the sensation on his skin was wrong. As Gerald looked at the jungle from the beach, he saw the trees were wrong too. There was something odd about the colors as if somebody sVid sprayed the environment not ever having seen a beach or a real jungle. Gerald wasn't certain if this was a memory or something else entirely.

Abe took off running down the beach as if something chased him. Once the tether uncoiled, Gerald ran too. Abe dodged into a narrow path between two tall trees. He followed Abe kicking up sand behind him as he sprinted. Gerald moved far faster than he could have managed if this was his physical body running. Not even Sally could have kept up with this man, and she was the fastest runner he knew except AJ. Gerald found himself smiling as he imagined AJ running against Abe. He didn't know who'd win, but it'd be a great race. A sudden sensation of self-confidence bled into Gerald's being. Fear came next like a jolt of pure frantic emotion vibrating up the tether from Abe. Then confidence soaked into him again as if the two emotions were struggling for dominance in Gerald's mind.

Gerald had experienced stress memories like these before when the rovers attacked him in the programming chair outside Checkpoint A on the SLYscape. The mole Sharon had implanted was trying to influence how he experienced what was happening around him. So something scary was out there but something strong and calm too. Gerald focused on the feelings of confidence and calm until he suddenly knew whose emotions he experienced. He didn't know how he could tell, but he knew AJ was in the simulation with him.

Gerald pumped his arms and legs chasing Abe past trees and over twisting roots jutting malevolently up from the jungle floor. It was a long run, so Gerald trusted his body to deal with the roots as his mind drifted to Lina and her story about missing her birthday pancake. He could see her in AJ's kitchen telling the story. He saw her eyes glimmering with held back tears but as he lingered on the memory, the images in his head changed. Lina was happy. He remembered her as a small girl sitting in bed with a giant tray and big plate on her lap. Her room was pink but she'd fight anyone who said she liked that color. The pancake before her was decorated with a big smile of syrup and had a banana nose and two strawberry ears. *What is happening?* he asked, as he picked up speed and jumped another ankle-snapping root.

Memories, he heard Lizzy say, in a thick, congested voice. *So much power behind the veil. So much memory to steal to make real.* Gerald's eyes opened. He understood.

He was vReading Abe's memories, experiencing them first-hand, but Abe was wrapped up tight in the silver webs of Cole's conditioning chair. Holographic conditioning programs helped people learn new skills, conditioned their bodies to be stronger and their minds to be faster. They could teach empathy or satisfy curiosity. They entertained Freelanders of all ages, but they hurt people too. Gerald remembered how AJ suffered under the Black Eye's gaze. Stacks of holo-chairs were crammed together in Old New York buildings dedicated to punishing prisoners with virtual life sentences that could be lived out in less than a slow-time year. Gerald experienced Abe's memories but he also experienced his punishment. Gerald was in a prison. The island was Abe's prison but Abe was not alone. He looked at the leaves of the trees he passed and saw faint pink designs like peacock swirls at their tips. He had seen those leaves in only one other place… Lizzy's Poison Dart jungle.

We're all here, she said. *Our memories tie us together.*

Gerald knew this island from his own night visions but the memories powering the illusion came from the other people who lived here too. Gerald could sense them all around. He heard the buzzing of locusts in the trees. He could smell the swampy river running through the O'Sullivan's ranch. He could feel his legs running as if they had a mind of their own like an on-shift enforcer. There were unfamiliar sensations invading Gerald's mind as well. It was distracting. It was confusing. It felt real and fake at the same time. Gerald had watched the dragon locust fight the wolf and lose on this island. He had been in the body of an extinct insect on this island. He had been saved by a brood of grasshoppers sent by Lizzy. He looked at his hands and studied his feet dodging roots. He wasn't a grasshopper now. He was himself. The mole was doing this to him, creating illusions from the memories he fed it.

Gerald knew why Lizzy sounded stuffy and sick. Her voice wasn't coming from the locust in Gerald's scribeosphere anymore. It was being pushed to Gerald through the vWare of Abe's conditioning program and the mole Sharon had implanted inside his brain. This is what his dad had warned him about. It's how the SLYscape worked. Gerald's mole and the holo-chair were borrowing memories from y-space to form Gerald's prison experience. The vWare was molding y-space memories into the simulation to trick Gerald's brain into thinking the island was real. It didn't work perfectly because it lacked what it needed most… enough of Gerald's memories to smooth out the imperfections in its rendering of reality.

The "Y" is the magic, son, he remembered. *It's what makes SLYscape simulations realistic.* Gerald remembered Lina and her pancake story, but Abe's conditioning chair didn't know where the memory came from or what to do with it. The library of Gerald's memories was sparsely stocked since Gerald had only been connected directly to the SLYscape for a few minutes. Abe's virtual prison compensated for its lack of data on Gerald by pulling similar memories from y-space to give Gerald familiar experiences. Gerald guessed his memory of Lina's pancake story linked him to someone else who remembered her birthdays: Big John. Lina's dad had plenty of birthday memories for the holo-chair to choose from, so it fed Gerald's birthday celebrations from a time before Lina and he had met. The tether rose off the sandy path as Abe outpaced him. He ran harder to catch up.

Abe was probably even more confused than Gerald. The SLYscape RADwire connecting them worked both ways. As Gerald received Abe's memories, Gerald flooded Abe's prison with his own. Every thought Gerald had of another person would trigger Cole's vWare to bring other people's memories onto the island. He smiled as he ran following the logic like a vWare controller creating a new data sphere. *I can bring my missing friends to me,* he thought, *by thinking about them.* So Gerald remembered them: AJ's fight with the 'roider, Big John not abiding empty hands, and Mrs. O'Sullivan's loving hugs when "her boys" came home.

He remembered Lizzy too. Not the one in his night visions or the one who talked to him through the locust, he remembered how her tiny baby body felt in his arms. She was pudgy and warm in fuzzy clothes, weighing hardly anything at all. Her hand wrapped only three fingers of Gerald's when they ran. She laughed when playing tag always giving herself away. He remembered these moments with trepidation knowing every thought was being logged to y-space and forever more could be used to soothe or hurt him. If he didn't get the implant out of his body soon, it'd be no challenge at all for people with FSA access to pry into his mind. His dad was right. He should have found a way to stop Sharon from injecting him. He should stop remembering but it was the only way he could think to discover if everyone was safe.

Good Gerald. Find our memories. Find us. Behind the veil where the power is. Be brave.

Abe covered his face and crashed forcefully through a tree-lined barrier that blocked their path. He stumbled and tripped into the open clearing with the black pond at its center as Gerald remembered from the last time he was here. Abe's hands plunged into the water up to his elbows. The blanket of lotus flowers rocked up and down the ripples he caused. Tiny gnats and other bugs swarmed up from the blue and white flowers and then settled back down as the water stilled. Gerald stopped himself at the water's edge but slipped on the mossy bank and his bare foot to the ankle got wet. The water evaporated from his skin too quickly. It felt like the antiseptic solution Sharon rubbed on his chest before sticking him with RADwire hooks. A nerve-tingling chill washed up his legs from the black water dripping off his toes. He stepped back suddenly very aware he could feel pain.

They were at the center of the island where Gerald had seen Lizzy last. He gazed over to where the wolf had killed the dragon locust but saw no bones or decomposing body. Next to the pond where the dragon locust died was a young girl with long black hair sleeping. She was as healthy and alive as the girl who appeared at the edge of his bed on the night he learned the O'Sullivans protected a gene demon. She lay peacefully next to AJ, Big John, and Mrs. O'Sullivan. They lay in a kind of supernatural stasis until Abe screamed, "He's coming!"

Abe dove into the pond to get away.

AJ was the first to sit up. Big John was next. Lizzy rolled to her feet so fast, she blurred through the air as if the mole inside Gerald's body couldn't keep up. "Back-to-back!" she yelled. "Around the lady." AJ and Big John stood more slowly confused until they saw Mrs. O'Sullivan lying asleep next to the pond.

"Hide!" Abe yelled, pulling himself into the water. "Everyone hide!"

"You're being conditioned!" Gerald yelled at Abe wanting to help him calm down so he wouldn't drown. "It's not real!"

Abe slapped at the water so afraid, he began to sink. Like in his night vision, Gerald heard the wolf before he saw it. Only this time it didn't pounce on Abe from a hidden place at the edge of the clearing, it boiled up beneath him like a black-and-white whale breeching. Gerald heard bone crunch in the giant wolf's jaws as it leapt free of the water to land with four padded thuds on the shore. The wolf growled and whipped Abe around. It flung him to the side like a toy at Gerald's feet. The wolf approached and Gerald instinctively stepped back. The wolf sniffed Abe who shook in shock. It's black tongue licked blood off Abe's ribs. Its slobbering jowls creased back to take another bite of flesh when a rock thwacked it square in the snout. The wolf jumped away. "Come on, boy!" AJ yelled from across the pond. "Come get some."

The wolf spotted AJ and slunk low to the ground. It paced along the shore towards him until it spotted Lizzy and growled. Lizzy stood casually waiting for the massive black wolf to draw near. With efficient movements, the wolf stalked the group who started picking up sticks and rocks to defend themselves. Mrs. O'Sullivan didn't move. "You distract him AJ and I'll rush him from the other side," Big John said.

AJ nodded.

"Go for the eyes," Lizzy said, drawing quizzical stares from AJ and Big John.

"Might want to get behind us little girl," Big John said back.

"Or you behind me," she said.

"I don't know who you are, little girl, but that beast's not playing. Get behind me."

"Next time then," she said, and danced away to the edge of the clearing.

The wolf watched her go and then fixed its angry glare on AJ and Big John. There was something familiar about the wolf's gait. It didn't approach the men like it was hungry or predatory so much as it pranced around them, feinting in-and-out playfully as they swung their branches and threw their rocks. Its tail wasn't wagging, but every other indication of the wolf's body looked like a dog wrestling for fun. The wolf suddenly shot forward and ducked under AJ's swing. Its eyes flashed yellow as its teeth snapped upwards taking a giant bite out of AJ's upper-thigh. AJ screamed in pain and dropped the branch, paralyzed by canines tearing into muscle and flesh. Gerald watched horrified as the monstrous jaws clamped down again higher on his leg catching part of AJ's groin. AJ eyes rolled back in his head in confusion before he fell backward with a silent scream.

The wolf moved with lightning speed to bite Mrs. O'Sullivan lying next to where her son had fallen. It didn't make it because Lizzy darted out of the forest and smashed it on the nose with a rock clenched tight in her right hand. The wolf yelped and then tumbled to the dirt as Lizzy slapped its ear with an open handed smack. The giant wolf rolled to its feet and bounded away, more surprised than hurt. Big John gave it no chance to think before he was on top of it stabbing down with a thin branch. The wolf's blood sprayed up, and it kick away from John's next jabs. With the element of surprise gone, the wolf lunged back at Lina's dad and took him down by the throat and broke his neck.

The wolf tore Big John apart and then when it was finished, it darted straight back at Mrs. O'Sullivan who slept between her dead son and the black pond. Lizzy jumped towards Mrs. O'Sullivan and her body shifted in mid-air into a beast far larger than the wolf. Gerald watched the dragon locust land on its back, but it didn't bite or try to fly the wolf off the ground. It just wrapped it up in monstrous legs and wings. They rolled across the dirt and when they stopped, the fight between the behemoths began again like it had before in Gerald's night vision. Only this time, Abe was still alive dragging himself to the jungle's edge in a pitiful attempt to escape. Gerald stood steps away from Abe watching the brood of locusts rise up to swarm the wolf.

Gerald didn't try to help as the wolf and the dragon locust disappeared in a cloud of insects. He knew how this was going to end, and he felt afraid for his sister but not terrified. This wasn't death, he knew. This was a simulated end and Lizzy had accomplished what she wanted which was to save at least one person from the wolf. Gerald looked back at Mrs. O'Sullivan and wondered why she still slept and then the cloud of insects came rushing back down. Inside the brood was the dragon locust dead or dying. It was hard to tell. Finally, the wolf turned to the person he hated most: Abe.

When Abe spotted the wolf lazily walking over to finish him off, Gerald trembled as his fear coursed up the tether into Gerald. "Stop him," Abe said, looking at Gerald. "She believes you are big enough, brave enough. You alone can stop him."

Him? Gerald thought. The wolf hesitated when it heard Abe speak. It heaved its black and gray head like a horse flipping its mane. In the dark, Gerald could see only one eye but that eye he believed belonged to Cole Reaver. It was slanted and so lightly brown, it shone gold. The wolf sniffed the air and howled as if Abe's prison had a moon.

I smell you, the animal said in his mind. *We'll meet again,* he remembered.

As the vWare in Abe's conditioning chair adjusted to Gerald's presence, the wolf became larger and more fearsome. Gerald didn't fear the wolf when it was just an animal, but the wolf gifted with a human mind made him tremble. His fear and Abe's fear intermingled as they both remembered standing in front of Gerald's childhood home on Layfette. They remembered how Cole drew Abe close and discarded him with a toss. Gerald remembered how Cole's gloved hand felt patting his cheek and how his mother feared Lizzy would be put in a prison much like this one. Yet this wasn't Lizzy's prison, Gerald realized. She wouldn't be capable of changing her body if the island was a prison built for her. This was Abe's prison and his alone. Lizzy was here because Gerald's night vision about Abe and Kisme St. James pulled her here. The others were here because Gerald remembered them while connected to the SLYscape through the mole Sharon implanted in him. He called his family here on purpose to discover if they were okay. *What have I done?*

Be brave, Gerald, Lizzy's voice said. *He can't hurt you. He can't hurt anyone if you don't remember.*

The wolf leapt at Gerald, missing him by the same amount of steps Gerald had taken just a few moments ago. Gerald put things together in his mind until he knew Cole couldn't see him, not really. He could follow Gerald's thoughts. Gerald took three sudden steps towards the jungle and watched the wolf leap again. It landed on the spot he'd just been. He was following Gerald's memories as they popped into existence in y-space. Gerald stopped thinking and ran to the far side of the pond near Mrs. O'Sullivan. The wolf lunged and lunged again, always several steps behind. As Gerald continued moving around the pond, he tried to think about the Academy, about Prefect Humphrey. He tried to think about anything other than where he was and what he was doing there. For hours it seemed they played cat and mouse while the wolf never quite found him. *But how do I stop him from following me? My short term memory always gives me away.* Gerald pictured Lizzy in his mind. H*ow do I stop the wolf?* he asked her.

Her voice came to him quicker this time, less congested. The mole was getting better at smoothing out the rough edges of the simulation. Gerald grew fearful inside. If the simulation got to know Gerald too well, he'd be just like Abe—powerless. He looked over to where Abe had crawled. He could see only his feet sticking out of the jungle. He might be dead. He might be hiding. Gerald had not heard him speak in what seemed a very long time.

You can't be brave in here, she said. *Find him out there while we stay in here.*

"How do I leave?" he asked, out loud.

Find our power. Find him. Stop him out there. Her voice caught in her throat as if she sensed something before it was about to happen. *In here, he can't hurt you. He can't hurt me.*

The wolf's deep voice suddenly spoke in Gerald's mind. *You are wrong, child. So wrong. I can hurt him by hurting you by hurting them by hurting the woman who sleeps by the pond. She is like a mother to the whelp. I'll show you how wrong you are and you will learn.*

The wolf abruptly changed course and pounced on Mrs. O'Sullivan. She woke up and screamed. It was such a real scream, Gerald ran to her. He jumped on the wolf and felt his body tumble harmlessly over its back. He rolled to his feet ready to fight.

The wolf ignored him and dug in, its jowls dripping blood. Gerald punched it, kicked it, but it ignored him and fed. Gerald tried to calm his mind. He reminded himself the island wasn't real. "You're not real," he said.

But I see you. I see your mole and your mole answers to me. I'm real now. Real here.

The wolf shimmered into a man much larger than Cole Reaver. Gerald looked into his eyes. They were not like wolf eyes. They were not the Deputy Director's eyes. The man's hair was red and fell in stringy, sweaty curls half-way down his back. His eyes were marble blue like Gerald's and his skin was just as pale. He was younger than Cole but much older than Gerald. The man sauntered, relaxed and happy, towards Gerald who backed away. He had never seen this person in his life.

"No you haven't," the man said, out loud. His voice was deep but it trembled with exhilaration. It vibrated like he was holding back the urge to laugh or scream or growl. "But I've seen you. I've seen your virus." He looked over at the dragon locust still unmoving on the ground. "I gave your virus wings and then she betrayed me. So I took her wings away." Gerald watched the dragon locust dissolve back into the teenage girl he knew now as his sister. "I punish her by trapping her in that body, so weak from growing up in a chair with machines that barely feed her and rarely exercise her legs and evacuate her waste. I let her grow wings so she can experience the exhilaration of flight just so I can take it away. I punish her. I punish Abe. I protect my master from those who come."

The man reached out, his arm stretching impossibly long and he grabbed Gerald by the throat. He lifted Gerald high in the air and squeezed his neck.

Gerald saw sparks and tiny lights bursting across his vision from everywhere around him. Like Abe's tether, the arm connected Gerald's mind to the man's mind. He heard screams and saw thousands of people running from enforcers shooting them dead. He recognized the mayhem from history sVids of the Quell old people like Uncle Luke talked about. He remembered blue beams jetting down from the sky, exploding buildings as Freelanders ran. *That's how Cole destroyed my home. Those weapons never went offline.* He saw a gray room where the red-haired man was hurt off-and-on for years.

Who are you? Gerald thought, as he felt his life slip away. He panicked and kicked his feet. He pried at the man's hands. He needed to breathe.

"I'm a collection of memories just like everybody else. Just like you. Such a bad mistake, Gerald. My master sees you now. He can find you. You gave away your only advantage in the SLYscape. You gave away who you are by allowing the mole."

Gerald's head throbbed and his lungs burned for air. The man killing him remembered the dragon locust forming in the Goodstone's family simulation pod when Gerald was eleven. He gave Lizzy that form and watched his master take her away. He heard a woman sobbing and the man's memory showed him Brandy sitting on a metal chair in the same gray, empty room he was tortured in. Her clothes were torn. Her bare shoulders were dirty and bruised. Her face was swollen and her hair matted. Standing before her was Cole Reaver panting and massaging his fists. His leather, wolf-stitched gloves were darkened and wet. *Sometimes,* he said, *I like to do things the old fashion way.*

I'll do anything, she cried. *Please stop.*

In time, I will.

Gerald's feet slowed and his vision dimmed. Like a whisper, Gerald heard the man strangling him say, "Don't worry about dying, Gerald. It hurts badly, I know, but then you rise again to be hurt some more. My master demands it of you. He demands it of us all."

The man released Gerald's neck and he crumpled to the ground. The pain leeched from Gerald's body and mind until Abe's tether snapped him back to life to experience it all again.

Chapter 34

Blue Dots

"Take it out!" he yelled. "Get it out!"

He heard footsteps running and a door sucking shut. Gerald opened his eyes and gasped for breath. He frantically swiped his hands at his neck and tried to get away. The door whistled open and more footsteps echoed in the room. Gerald tried to sit up but his stomach clenched and his head pounded so hard he wanted to scream. "Where am I?" he asked, still gasping. To his own ears, his voice sounded raspy and dry. It hurt to swallow and take in air through his mouth. He tried breathing through his nose to calm himself. "Anyone here?" he asked, again. The room was dark.

He felt so fuzzy and strange, a sensation he didn't understand. A small hand touched his chest and he turned to see who was there. A cloth fell from his eyes and revealed Lina, out of breath, crying above him. Her lips trembled as she ran her fingers over his face and patted his shoulders. She squeezed his legs and arms and then she said, "He's awake. He's really awake."

Sally stood unnaturally still next to Lina, her face red and splotchy as she nodded. She bit her lip and clenched her hands before her. She didn't reach out to touch Gerald. She stared at him so contorted with emotion that deep creases formed in the skin around her mouth and eyes. Her lips were puffy and red as she fought back tears. He remembered her leading him to Jack who was not Jack at all. He remembered… "Get it out!" he yelled. "Tell Sharon. Get it out of me or he'll find you!" Gerald closed his eyes and slowed his breath. *Turquoise water,* he thought. *Where the wolf doesn't go.*

How many times was I killed? Gerald asked himself as he lay on a soft bed trying to picture only water. *Hundreds of times,* he answered himself. *Thousands.* The turquoise water changed in his mind, replaced by the afterimage of the room he saw for those brief seconds when he opened his eyes. The walls flashed at him like a holo-snap inside his head. He bit his tongue to stop his mind from wandering but it was too late. The rock walls of his room were burnished and smooth like marble. No prezero diggers made those. This was not AJ's mine. *Stop thinking!* He was underground somewhere else. "Sedate me!" he yelled. "Or Cole will trace my memories here!"

He felt Lina fall on his chest and hug him. Tears dripped hot on Gerald's cheeks. "It's gone. We know. You'll be fine. Better than fine. You'll be you, again. They fixed you." It was Lina's husky voice whispering in his ear, urgent in her need for him to hear her. His breathing slowed as she squeezed him. *She doesn't understand,* he thought. *Cole's the wolf's master. Dixon Streets is the wolf. He's powerful, so powerful in there. Can't be brave.*

"I'm sorry, Gerald," Sally said, from someplace farther away in the room. Her voice was tremulous and resigned. "I didn't know. I thought it was for your own good. Sharon told me it was for your own good. Jack said so too."

"You don't understand," Gerald whispered through clenched teeth. "Reaver will find you here. He will hurt you—"

"He already has," Lina said. "The enforcers attacked Sharon's ship right after she injected you, but she got away. She knew they'd come. Mr. Rose said so."

Gerald listened to the words and then slowly opened his eyes. "The implant she put in me is gone? It can't be gone."

"Weeks ago. You've been in a coma for weeks."

"Weeks?" Gerald asked. He tried to sit again but fell back.

"Help me," Lina said. Sally moved to one side of Gerald while Lina moved to the other. They shoved their arms under his back and locked fingers. The lifted him into a sitting position in one practiced motion.

Gerald looked down. He was in a thin robe with ties in the back. He looked at the girls in confusion. "Where are we?"

"The Glass Lands," Sally said. "We're in tunnels under the Glass Lands."

How? he thought, but all he did was nod. He studied the walls of his room. The walls were simple and made sense. Lasers dug these tunnels and recently. The slight shine of the rock was familiar to him because he had dug tunnels just like these in a night vision. He became disoriented as he listened to how quiet the room was. He heard the girls breathing and the ruffle of clothing as they moved around his bed bunching up pillows behind his back. *I don't hear the whispers.* "I don't hear anything."

The girls paused their primping of his bed and stared at him confused. "You're talking. You hear us," Lina said.

"I hear you but nothing else."

Lina asked Sally to get Sharon. She then sat on the side of the bed and pulled his hands into her own. Gerald was suddenly aware of her warm hip pushed softly against his knee. He remembered the dance and smiled. "How did we get here?"

"Brandy," she said, angrily. "She's a traitor. She took over for Uncle Luke and lied to everybody about having orbiters. She lured people to the mine, saying she'd take anybody willing to work to the Glass Lands like daddy had planned. Earth First, Justice for Kisme, it didn't matter who you followed. We were a family, she said. After the Blackstars got so mean, so rough with their interrogations, plenty of families fled to her. I thought about it myself, but I didn't. Sally didn't neither. And when the mine got full to busting, she called the enforcers."

"Hundreds were arrested and the mine was seized. It was all over the m-spheres. *Rebellion in Iron City,* they kept calling it. Silly name since nobody in the city knew what Earth First was doing. In the first weeks of the crackdown, dozens of daddy's workers were wiped and a few were executed for protecting gene demons. Since it was treason, they hung the dead ones up like trophies at Dusty Gulch. The rest of daddy's crew had to look at them rotting while they ate. The m-spheres couldn't get enough of it. After the killings, the FSA attacked our farms with patrol pods. They burned the rice paddies we worked so hard to save. Some tried to fight but we didn't stand a chance. Some are still fighting but from the shadows now when the enforcers aren't around. If the SLYscape worked here, you could see it all for yourself."

Gerald imagined the devastation Lina described and the executions. Protecting gene demons, according to Freeland law, was the same as being one. He imagined what people looked like eating under corpses on detainment boards. It was barbaric like something from the World Union history sVids. His brain caught up to what she said last. "What do you mean, if the SLYscape worked here? The 'scape is everywhere."

Lina shook her head and sniffled. "Not here."

"That's not possible," Gerald said.

The door whistled open. It was the High Prelate only without his robes of office. "But it is, son," he said as if he'd been listening to the whole conversation. "It's how we killed your mole. They need sustained radiation to survive and your room here is in a sizable pocket of pure, prezero air. For the rest of us who need to keep our moles active, we can't stay in here for long. Lina?"

"I have ten minutes more."

Preston nodded. He wore a baggy checkered shirt and a pair of suspenders clipped over his old man shoulders. Preston smiled at Gerald. "Used to wear these all the time back at Claiborne's ranch." He hooked his thumbs behind the straps. "Far more suited to these than a Prelate's robes, don't you think?" Sharon Knight smiled next to him with both hands together behind her back. She wore all black.

"There's radiation in here. It's in the earth," Gerald said. "When the RADcore bomb exploded—"

"Son," Preston said, good-naturedly. "Please don't explain RADcore technology to me. You forget I was there when it happened. I ordered it to happen." Preston chuckled. "Trust me when I say there are pockets on this planet that were never exposed. You're in one now."

Gerald thought about what Preston said and disagreed. *If I hear whispers I'm awake,* he thought. *I hear no whispers.* With a grunt of effort and pain, Gerald scooted away from Lina on the bed. "Gerald?" she asked, putting her hand on his leg.

"No!" he yelled. "You're not here. It's another trick. A new trick." He looked frantically around the room for escape, but there was only one exit—straight through Sharon. The door whistled open, and Gerald lurched out of bed. His legs gave out as soon as his feet touched the floor but he caught himself on the bed rail. He pushed himself standing. He felt cold sweat on his skin from a sudden headache, and he almost passed out. Then Sally and Lina were at his sides with their shoulders keeping him straight. "Let go! I know you're not real. It's a trick."

The girls made sounds of confusion and fear. Preston and Sharon watched him calmly. "Son, why do you think it's a trick?"

Sally and Lina moved him back to bed, and he allowed it. He had no strength to fight. If they were going to kill him, then he'd die and rise again. Fear gripped him. He didn't want to die again. "I hear nothing. If I hear whispers, I'm awake. If I don't, I'm not."

"Your voices. You call them whispers? Not shouts, not screaming?" Preston shook his head. "Oh, son. You don't know how lucky you have it."

"What do you mean?" he asked, already trying to figure out another way to escape.

"The genetically enhanced—people like you—they hear loud voices, head-splitting, ear-piercing, torturous voices. It's why we condition them… to dull their senses. You—"

"You conditioned me. It's why I didn't remember everything Abe showed."

"What do you remember now?" Sharon asked, her tone conveying an urgent interest.

"Everything," he said. "I remember everything. The satellite weapons. The murders. The enforcers breaking into houses on my street. I saw Reaver call down energy beams from space to destroy my house. I remember those same weapons being used during the Quell."

"My lord," Sharon said. "You were right, Preston. It's true."

Preston smiled. "Son, I know it doesn't appear this way but that's fantastic. It's what I hoped for..."

"It's what we all hoped for," Sharon said.

"Who's we?"

Sharon stepped close to Gerald's bed and reached out with her hand. He ducked her touch at first but then allowed it. She touched his cheek. "The Followers of Rose, sugar. You can help us protect them all. You clear Preston's name and we bring the Reavers down."

"You can get back everyone Cole arrested," Preston said. "You can get back Elizabeth."

"Great," Gerald said, laughing. "Too bad you're not real. Just kill me already. How you doing it this time? You gonna morph into the wolf and chase me? Rip out my insides so I can watch? Or just choke me until my legs kick out?"

"Oh, God," Sally said, her voice shaky. "What have we done to him? What did you do?" She ran at Sharon pushing her with both hands. Sharon, startled, fell back into the wall. Sally swung her fists but didn't land a single blow. Sharon blocked and dodged as she pivoted around the room backing away. The lady in black's face was smooth and calm with concentration as she swiped with open hands deflecting every attempt of Sally's to hurt her.

"Sally," Sharon said, in an almost conversational tone. "You really have to get better at controlling your emotions, young lady. If I were your mother—"

Sally screamed in a primal, high pitched way that Gerald had never heard from her before. "You're not and will never be!" she yelled.

"I know, sugar, but if I was I would have taught you at least a few manners by now. Gerald's fine. We haven't hurt him. Not the way you think."

Sally screamed again and gave up, panting as she put her hands on her knees. Sharon relaxed before her. "You're all the same," Sally said, between gasps. "You use people! You tell them what they want to hear. You tell me we'll get AJ back if I bring Gerald to you. You tell Grams and me to protect Ronnie because he's special! You tell me he's my brother. My big brother. So special and he is... but when the enforcers came for him… you let it happen. You could have stopped it!"

"Sally," Preston said, his voice sounding tired and old. "I'm so sorry. You know I am but please don't forget… Ronnie's alive! If we had interfered, he'd be dead now—just another *gene demon* they caught. He has new memories. He and your Grams are living a good life in Sector Twenty-seven. She runs Backus' whole staff… plenty of food and shelter."

"But I can never see him anymore. You said that was the price." Sally turned to Gerald. She shook her head and pressed her lips together. Her eyes flashed with tears. "I'm so sorry, Gerald. I didn't know. I didn't know you'd be punished like that… Believe me, I didn't know."

Gerald watched Sally knock Preston's shoulder as she shoved her way out of the room. He heard the door open and shut behind her. He was confused. He heard no whispers, so this couldn't be real but whatever just happened felt real. That was Sally. She was hurting. He knew it with all his heart. "But I hear no whispers…."

"Son," Preston said, putting his hands over his face and groaning a little. Sharon moved silently behind Preston and pulled a chair from the corner and put it down behind him. He sat down and put his elbows on his knees and rubbed his forehead and cheeks as he considered what he was about to say. He shook his head. "Gerald," he continued, looking up from his hands. "The whispers aren't gone. It's just you can't hear them in here. There's no radiation for you to connect to the SLYscape with. You can't get to y-space."

Gerald stared at him confused.

"Come with me," he said. "I'll show you."

Lina and Sharon helped Gerald off the bed. They carried most of his weight on their shoulders as they walked him out of the room. Gerald was right about being underground. He was in a modern tunnel system similar to AJ's mine only dug with After Zero equipment. These tunnels were also far larger than the connecting shafts in AJ's mine. The girls maneuvered him into a hovering transport configured in a manner Gerald didn't recognize. It was like a miniature, fully enclosed cattle car that sat ten people.

Once they were all seated, Preston said, "We go through air exchanges when traveling between the lower and upper tunnel systems so the environment down here stays pure. Sit back, Gerald. Relax. We'll be there soon."

The tube shot forward so fast he felt his shoulders press back against his seat. Lina held his hands looking anxious but not speaking. Sharon sat across from him, expressionless. It took ten minutes until the tube stopped. When it did, Gerald fell forward almost tumbling head over knees onto the floor. He would have fallen if Lina had not held him back. "It's called a bullet," she said. "Shoots through the tunnels and stops like it hit somebody."

Gerald looked out the windows to see they were in another chamber. "A force web?"

Lina nodded. "Takes a bit to swap the air and clean us up."

The hum of engines and a subtle shaking of the car occurred as the four of them sat silently. Without warning, the doors opened and they exited in a single line. Gerald was still weak but his legs had gained a little stability. He needed only Lina's help to get out. Sharon attended to Preston as they walked arm-in-arm through a long tunnel to a door that slid open as they approached. Once they cleared the door, Gerald heard the familiar rustle of the whispers returning. He focused on them and they grew loud.

"So this is the Glass Lands," he said, smiling because it meant the wolf wasn't going to devour him again. "This is real."

"Better believe it," Lina said, squeezing his arm in a tight hug as she helped him to a row of softly cushioned chairs. "Wait til you see outside."

He sat down and noticed he had no pants on. "Can I get some clothes?" he asked.

Lina laughed. "It's nothin' I haven't seen by now… boyfriend."

"Boyfriend?"

Lina smiled. "You didn't give me no argument when I sat up talking to you every day and night for the last… I don't know… month."

"I was in a coma."

"Don't go backin' out. I asked you to blink for no… you didn't blink. You're my boyfriend."

She sat down in the chair next to him still holding his hand. "Okay," he said. "Girlfriend."

Lina smiled as she looked forward to Preston who sat down across from them. Sharon remained standing at the High Prelate's side. The room was carved into a smooth dome almost the size of the equipment depot in AJ's mine but better lit.

"You look relaxed, Mr. Goodstone. I guess that means the whispers are back?"

Gerald nodded.

"Then let me tell you first. I am no longer your High Prelate. Augustus deposed me as he intended to do ever since the protests started…. Well, his plan was years in the making. Fortunately for us, I've been planning too." He gestured all around. "You sit now in the operations room of the unofficial headquarters of the Followers of Rose. I know… pretentious sounding group. I did not coin the term, but what I did was find people who believe genetically enhanced individuals such as yourself should be protected. We've been watching you your whole life."

"You conditioned me to forget what happened to my parents."

Preston chuckled. "My word, no. Don't get me wrong, we tried to wipe them from your memory, but you wouldn't forget. The counsellors at the Academy tried to get you to let go of the memories on your own, but you wouldn't believe it was all in your mind—"

"But I remembered new things when I was with Abe. Things I forgot."

He nodded. "Memories naturally repressed maybe, but not forgotten. You just needed somebody else's memory to jog your own."

"There were Field Marshals in my house. I wouldn't have forgotten that… the mole showed me."

"I bet it did. I bet it triggered all kinds of memories. Do you know, son, what those whispers in your head are?"

Gerald thought about it. "No," he admitted. "Not really."

"The collected memories of every Freelander who has ever been implanted with one of Augustus' moles. His implants do so many wonderful things but at what cost? For me, it was losing my ability to trust. For people like you, the price is far higher. "

"They steal who you are," Gerald said, quoting what the wolf told him.

"If people are their memories, then you're right."

Gerald tensed hearing the familiar words.

"Each whisper is one memory of one person. Your whispers are every memory of every person connected to y-space. You don't know how to listen to one-at-a-time, so you hear them all at once. When you close your eyes, you see the memories too, feel them, and experience what others have already lived. It's a gift and from what others like you have told me, a curse because you experience their dreams and nightmares. As soon as they think it, it becomes real to you. The way Dixon explained it—"

"Dixon?" Gerald asked, feeling both fearful and angry. "Of course, that makes sense. He's like me. You want to protect him too. Well, I don't!"

"And why is that?

"You know he's a sadist, right? A murderer, worse than that… what he did to us…." If Gerald had the strength, he would storm away like Sally had done, but he had no energy to move. All he could do was sit, glaring at Rose impotent in his rage against the wolf.

"Gerald," Lina said, squeezing his hand. "They're helping us. Hear Mr. Rose out."

Preston's smile vanished. His brow furrowed. "How do you mean, a sadist?"

Gerald then told Preston about the island and everything the wolf had done. "Lizzy was the only one who never panicked. She fought him every time. She got us to fight even though we all knew we'd die in the end. We hurt him a few times. That was the best we could do."

"I'm sorry to hear that," he said. "Really, Gerald, I am. He was a wonderful boy when I knew him. Delightful, really." He looked away for a moment and Sharon touched his shoulder. He reached up and patted the back of her hand. "It's not really his fault, you know," he said, looking down at the slight bulge of his stomach. "He's been living in a kind of hell himself. Twenty slow-time years. If he's been trapped in a holo-chair all this time, he remembers millennia of living with Cole as his master."

"He liked to talk when he played. He said Cole was his master, and he gave Lizzy wings just to tear them off."

"The suffering he must've endured. Two-thousand years."

There was sorrow and loss in Preston's tone, but it didn't change how Gerald felt. He hated Dixon. He hated Cole Reaver too, but Dixon was the face of his tormentor. *How long did I suffer?* he thought. How many years had the others endured? The island had no nights just the darkening of the sky when the brood swarmed. How many times a day had they all died? "Dixon had red hair like me, eyes like mine. When he wasn't a wolf, it was like being killed by a reflection of myself. Only he was more real than me there. He was like a cruel god."

Lina leaned over the armrest between them and hugged his shoulders tight. "Daddy too?" she asked, lines of tears dripping down her cheeks and off her chin. "Daddy couldn't whoop 'em?"

Gerald shook his head. "Nobody could. Lizzy was the only one with power to change herself but it didn't help."

Lina pulled away from him and fixed Preston with a glare. "Tell him what you told me," she said. "Tell him how we're gonna make Cole pay for what he's done. Tell Gerald what he can do."

Preston whispered into Sharon's ear. She nodded and then took a seat a couple of chairs from Preston. She rolled up one of her long, black sleeves. Beneath the clothing, Gerald saw Sharon's tattoos. The designs were similar to Paisley's tattoos only more orderly without the aggressive imagery Paisley favored. As he stared at the ink, patterns started to form in his mind like which colors were the lines of power connecting SLYscape devices and which were the devices themselves. He followed Sharon's tattoos to familiar places on the SLYscape but then he encountered new ones he'd never seen advertised in the babblespheres. She stroked her arm with her fingers and Gerald's seat moved. Both rows of seats slid back on plates until the four of them were now sitting at equidistant points from the center of the floor. They faced each other in a round table setting as the floor between them melted into a shimmering pool of swirling color.

"Alright children," Sharon said, smiling a little. "Since Preston and myself have had our OPC designations revoked, what I'm about to show you is a criminal act of treason." A globe rose violently out of the floor dripping color as it expanded into the space between the chairs. As the colors solidified into textures, Gerald recognized the planet as it would look from an orbiter with a swirling haze of dirty gray obscuring the land and water masses. "I've stolen control of the FSA surveillance sphere. Young vWare controllers are just now starting to panic. The veteran among them are trying to track us to this location and they will fail. So we have a few minutes before they realize they can't win and shut the entire sphere down. Please keep your questions to a minimum."

"Do they know who's attacking them?" Gerald asked.

"Probably, sugar. Now hush up."

Gerald sat back in his chair and crossed his arms.

"So that's the planet without surveillance. Here's how the FSA tracks a Freelander's every move with Flying Eyes, satellites, and residential simulation pods."

The clouds vanished revealing continents and small islands of land. Blobs of color were everywhere but more heavily concentrated at city centers and environment bubbles.

"The smears of color you see are individual moles interacting with the SLYscape. If I wanted to isolate somebody… let's say, somebody you both know, Madame Evelyne." All the colors on the continents disappeared except for three yellow circles. "She has three moles and is right now… in your house, Lina."

Lina grunted.

"Now let me show you why we're here. There's one layer of this map the FSA can't access. Not Augustus. Not Cole. Nobody but myself, Preston, and one other. This is the map of the genetically enhanced…."

The three yellow circles disappeared, replaced by a smattering of blue dots. "Now that we're here," Sharon said. "The little vWare controllers at the FSA think we left. This map as far as their technology tells them doesn't exist. So we just broke into the most secure FSA data sphere and left without a trace very much like your virus, Gerald."

"I didn't design a virus," he said.

But she did, Gerald. She designed me with your memories. She said you've been to the other side of the veil. She said you're going back. The scribeosphere dropped down on Gerald from above, its metallic skin frosty white. He caught it in his hand and looked deep inside. The locust stared back and rubbed its legs. *We'll get her back,* it said. *She with all the power is waiting.*

"It's been hovering in this room for weeks," Preston said, smiling. "Don't know how it got here and can't catch it. It hasn't even come down to charge itself in all this time. My guards would have destroyed it with their shimmers but Sally said it belonged to you. Remarkable."

The heft of the scribeosphere in Gerald's hand comforted him. The sound of Lizzy's voice even in simulation made him smile. "Lizzy showed it the power," he said, only half-understanding what that meant. "She's the one who's remarkable."

"And there she is…" Sharon said. "Elizabeth Goodstone." She drew a circle around a dimly lit silver spot hovering between the pool on the floor and the semi-transparent globe spinning on its axis above. Other silver dots hung like distant stars in the black space surrounding Lizzy. Her dot was larger than the others as Jupiter was to its moons. "She's been gray like this since we lost contact. We don't know where in the world she is, but we know she's alive because she's not black like the others…"

The planet spun faster as black dots started appearing clustered together across the lands. "The blue ones are alive and well," Sharon said, circling a few. "And," she said as the world stopped spinning. "There you are, sugar. You look like that." Gerald recognized the Glass Lands where the RADcore bomb detonated. His dot was pulsating at its center, a dark blue oval dot. "Now a few minutes ago, you were…"

Nothing happened until Gerald noticed the timestamp above the globe counting backward. The blue dot in the Glass Lands disintegrated before his eyes. There was a popping sound and then another silver dot joined the others below the globe hovering frozen before them. Gerald's dot had joined Lizzy's. Like hers, his dot was larger than the rest and not as round. "Why?" he asked.

"You were in prezero air, sugar. Now you're not."

"You see," Preston said. "Most of us can only interact with the SLYscape via moles. The genetically gifted are already a part of the system. You feed off the light and sky radiation. You soak up what's in the earth. You're like a single organism all connected like certain kinds of trees that look like individuals but feed off the same roots."

"Aspen," Lina said.

"Like Aspen only your roots are buried in the radiation. The World Union soldiers could speak telepathically when touching the same cloud of radiation. When the soldiers blew up the moon, it was because they made a single decision like a hive. You and the rest of the children we protect can do that too or so Dixon said."

Gerald's stomach clenched in anger at hearing Dixon's name but the stronger emotion now was fear. Preston described something alien, something he didn't want to be. If Gerald understood what the former High Prelate was telling him, the globe was like his map of the SLYscape power sources. Gerald and his sister behaved like SLYscape devices. They popped on and off its surface as they went through power cycles—in-and-out of prezero air.

"You see those blue dots? This is the part that fascinates me. They don't mark your physical location on the planet as we see here. They mark your location on the SLYscape. The physical location is figured out by vWare in a way similar to how the FSA determines the geographical coordinates of their moles." Preston pushed back into his chair and smiled.

"So I'm a mole?" Gerald said. Lina laughed and then sniffled.

Preston tilted his head, thinking. "Well, no. In a manner of speaking, though. Why yes! You're like a biological mole, not a synthesized one."

"So if you have this map of the world," Gerald said. "Why can't you find Mrs. O'Sullivan's or AJ's moles? He has plenty of them. I'm sure Lina's dad does too."

"Because they disappeared," Preston said. "The moment Cole took them from the glider race, they blinked out."

"Until they blinked back on when I injected you with the molecular angstromnite solution," Sharon said. "Look at this recording."

The world spun until Gerald recognized the gap between the southern and northern prefectures of New Michigan. To the east of the old peninsula bridge, Gerald's dark blue dot blinked alone at the edge of the Great North Swamp. A moment later, it moved.

"That's when I injected you with the mole."

The timestamp rolled forward as Gerald watched the dot move across the marshes from New Michigan to the island of Old New York.

"You see there, I was actually flying our ship in the other direction. That's you moving through the SLYscape while leaving your body behind."

"Ridiculous," Gerald said.

"And yet true," Preston responded, grinning. "The tether Sharon installed guided your 'mind travel' to Abe who sat in a holo-chair in Old New York. You travelled to Abe without your body."

"Mind travel?"

"From one genetically enhanced person to another."

"But I was physically in New Michigan. So your map of where I was is wrong."

Gerald's dot moved again until it joined another dot much smaller than his at the outskirts of the city. Gerald suspected this is the point in his experience when he met Abe on Layfette Street after being injected. Sometime later when a bunch of yellow circles popped into view, Gerald guessed this was when he fell though the sim pod and landed on Abe's island.

"AJ, John, and Angie," Sharon said, confirming Gerald's guess just before a pale blue dot took shape next to them. Gerald knew without asking, he was looking at his sister's presence next to his own. He smiled, noting her dot was almost mauve in color and larger than his by about ten percent.

"Lizzy," he said.

"Elizabeth Goodstone when she's not gray. We don't know why your blue dots are not the same blue as the others." As if she had practiced the timing of telling Gerald this story, a third blue dot appeared that was piebald with cloudy swirls of black, gray, and yellow. It was twice the size of Gerald and Lina's dots. "His dot is by far the strangest."

"Dixon," Gerald said, noticing the map was still centered on Old New York. "So they're all in the same place?"

"We have no idea," Preston said. "But you do."

"I don't," Gerald said. "How could I?"

"You 'mind traveled' across the nation and entered Abe's mind while he was being conditioned. We see by this map, you pulled your family into Abe's experience."

Gerald shook his head, agitated. "I don't know how I did that."

"But your mole does. And so do the moles of every other person you called to that island. You're enhanced, son… a child of the future. You can remember what they remembered. And when you do, we'll see where your mind ends up. There's just one catch…"

"What's that?"

"You only move on this map when you enter the SLYscape on your own. You must do it with your mind."

"It's like you don't know the first thing about the SLYscape," Gerald said, snorting.

"We just saw it done," Preston said. "You don't need a chair, Gerald. Trust your instincts. Find your family's memories of Abner's island that match your own."

"Stop saying that." Gerald's face grew hot. "My family's dead."

"Not Lizzy," Lina said.

"And Angie is like a mother to you," Sharon added. "AJ is your brother. We left Abner in that chair under Freedom Square to give us a starting point on a physical map. From there, we trace your mind to the source of your loved ones memories."

"You have it in you, son," Preston added, "to show me where Cole is hiding his prisoners on this map." Preston pointed at the globe of blue dots. "You do that for me, and I promise you my followers will get them back."

"You promise?" Gerald asked, derisively. "What about Abe? What'd you promise him?" *You use people!* Gerald remembered Sally yelling. *You tell them what they want to hear.*

"Watch your tone, sugar," Sharon said.

"You're telling me lies! Abe didn't agree to this plan. AJ and Angie aren't family. I was their mission. You used Abe to get to me, but I experienced his terror of the wolf firsthand!" He pushed himself to his feet and pointed at Sharon. "He did not agree to do this. I saw you with Abe after Cole beat him. I heard you interrogate him about his voices. You blinded me, but I heard it all!"

Sharon exhaled audibly as Lina rushed heedlessly through the projection of the globe to steady Gerald. "You think I wanted to leave him there?" Sharon snapped, losing her usual cool. "Abe didn't want to be freed. He wanted to be useful! He let me tether you to him so you could save the other prisoners. The only thing I blinded was a security Eye monitoring the room. If you saw me through that… wait, Preston, is that even possible?"

Preston shook his head. "If somebody was watching you through the Eye, maybe. I don't know. That's why we need Dixon back."

"Dixon? And there it is. He's who you're really after, isn't it?" Gerald asked. "Lizzy and Lina's dad, the O'Sullivan's, they're all bait like Abe. You need me to jump on your hook so you can catch the wolf."

"What do you mean?" Lina asked, her voice anxious.

Her shoulder was under Gerald's arm. She was strong and kept him upright. "I'm sorry, Lina. They're after Dixon. They don't care about your dad or any of the rest. It's how powerlords think. They want the maker of this map." Gerald jabbed his finger at the globe.

Preston looked skyward and then breathed slowly. "I won't deny it."

Lina pushed out from under Gerald's arm and ran at Preston Rose. Sharon was across the floor first and caught Lina's hand before it struck. Sharon stepped into Lina's blow and twisted her arm back. "Don't make me break it, girl," Sharon said, softly. "I don't want the aggravation of mending it later."

Gerald sat heavily back in his chair, not bothering to rush to Lina's aid. Even if he was feeling up to it, Sharon could have trounced him without breaking a sweat.

"Let her go, Sharon," Preston said. Sharon twirled Lina back to her own seat where she hit the thinly cushioned back so hard, she lost her breath. When Lina could breathe again, she glared at Preston but she was wise enough not to attack.

"You lied to me," Lina said, blowing strands of hair out of her eye with one, angry breath.

Preston shook his head. "They're all important, child. It's just Dixon is the mission. He's who Angie sacrificed herself for. She was tagged with a proximity mole of our own design. Unfortunately, Cole must have figured it out because we lost contact.

"So my daddy and AJ don't mean anything to you?"

"Only Angie was supposed to be arrested, but we want everybody back. It's just the Followers of Rose need Dixon Streets. It's the only way we can protect Gerald and people like him. Dixon understands what you all can do so much better than I do."

"He's a monster," Gerald said.

"Perhaps, but he's the one who built this map. He's the one who figured out what you all are. He started the Followers of Rose. Without Dixon, none of you would have survived. Whatever he is now, we need his knowledge to preserve the future."

Gerald breathed heavily as he studied Preston's wrinkled face through the semi-transparent map of the planet. Preston was not as old inside as his wrinkles suggested. His eyes still burned with the fire of purpose as his once strong hands clenched rhythmically into fists and released. Like the zealots who followed him, he would sacrifice anything to keep his purpose alive. How was he any different than people like Cole Reaver and Senior Thomas? They were all powerlords accustomed to getting what they wanted. Sally was right, they were all the same, but it didn't change Gerald's purpose. He needed Lizzy back. He wanted to see AJ and Angie again. He looked at the silver dots. He remembered the black dots. He saw Lina vibrating with anger and grief. She needed Big John. Everybody had their purpose.

"I'll do what you ask, sir, but Dixon was wrong. I can't just appear in the SLYscape like he said."

"Yes you can," Preston said. "You've already done it and that's why we're all here."

Chapter 35

Bad Guys

They moved Gerald from the hospital room in the lower tunnels to the recovery room in the upper tunnels where people and drones worked on his physical therapy. Even with excellent treatment, it took several days for him to feel like himself again. At the end of the week, Sally knocked on his door.

"Come in," he yelled, as he donned his bracelet and belt. The scribeosphere had taken to floating by his side like a loyal dog, though he hadn't heard Lizzy's voice in the last few days. He imagined his sister was too busy fighting off Dixon to send messages. Sharon had come to his room many times to help him practice for entering the SLYscape without anything more than his mind. He didn't believe he could do it, and so far evidence suggested he was right.

The door swished open revealing Sally in shorts and a sleeveless white shirt that showed her tan belly. Lina had mentioned that most of the people lived above ground here beneath a hot sun that felt nothing like back home. Sally, by the look of her, was one of those people. He had never seen her so dark. There was a belt of tools draped across her hip similar to what Sharon wore under her cape. "Today's the day," she said, biting her lip. "Are you ready?"

Gerald nodded. He hadn't seen Sally since she stormed out of the hospital room he had woken up in a week earlier. "We're going to the surface," Gerald said. "Lina told me."

Sally tried to smile. "I'm sorry."

"I know."

"Sharon impressed on me what happened to you on the island was necessary. I was wrong about Preston and the others. So I'm sorry for my bad behavior there too."

Gerald looked at her puzzled. "You were right. I don't trust any of them," Gerald said.

Sally shook her head. "Don't listen to me, Gerald. I was just upset. Father Rose and Sharon really are the good ones—"

"Sharon taught you manners," Gerald said, feeling his stomach sink. "What did she do to you?"

Sally looked around the room and shook her head. "They helped me and my brother." She glanced down at her hands. "Sharon looked after us—"

"She what?"

"Ronnie was like you. Sharon brought him to my mother when I was really small. Something happened that Grams and Sharon would never tell me, but one day my mother was just gone. So Grams became a kind of mother to me but so did Sharon."

"Sharon took care of you?"

"Not all the time but sometimes. She's the one who trained me."

"Trained you to do what?"

"Gerald, this is hard. It really is. If I tell you, you'll never trust anybody again." She looked at Gerald and then squeezed her eyes tight. "I was put in the Academy to watch—"

"Like AJ?" Gerald asked, cutting her off. "You were watching me too?" Gerald's mouth opened. "Do I have any friends? Any real friends?"

Sally swept forward and hugged Gerald tight. "I'm your friend, Gerald," she said into his ear. "I swear it's true. So is AJ. And, not that it makes me a good person, I was put in the Academy to watch AJ, not you."

Gerald pushed Sally away and walked to the other side of his therapy bed. He looked back. His mouth worked but no sound came out.

"Father Rose knew AJ was having trouble. He caught AJ in a few lies he told about you. AJ didn't know he'd been caught and Father Rose wasn't mad. Not really. He sent me to get close to AJ. I was there to help AJ pick the right side."

"What if he picked the wrong side?"

Sally became distressed and wouldn't look him in the eye. Gerald considered the implements on her belt. One of them was a zap rod like Sharon's. "You're not hearing me, Gerald. We are the good ones. Sometimes it doesn't seem that way but we help people. Can you forgive me, Gerald? Can we be good?"

"Not sure I know what that means, Sally. I don't even know who you are. Not really."

"You know me, Gerald. I've never lied to you."

"Does AJ know?"

Sally bit her lip. "It turns out, he knew all along. For three years I tried to seduce him, make him my boyfriend. He said he knew the first day we met. He said he'd been lying longer than me—that he was better at it. Turns out, AJ is a lot smarter than Father Rose thought."

Gerald smiled.

"I love him, Gerald. What you've seen from us these last few months is real. I want him back. I need him back and Sharon says you can do that. Can you do that?"

"I don't know," he said, "look who were up against." He waved his fingers through the air and the far side of his recovery room lit up. A sanctioned floor-to-ceiling m-sphere expanded to fill the space on the other side of his bed. The immersion experience showed a hologram of Brandy and Cole Reaver standing before the flat featureless wall of the FSA tower in Freedom Square. Floating above Brandy's shoulder, a smaller m-sphere showed people being paraded down a small town street.

As the experience played out, they could smell Brandy's perfume wafting about Gerald's recovery room like an air freshener. Her auburn hair was pushed up high and bold making her taller than she was in person. Some of her hair tumbled in long ringlets down her shoulders like red leaves falling in autumn. She wore the same revealing green sari with layers of red silk that she had the first time she broke into Preston Rose's SLYcast. She was beautiful except for her eyes which were drawn and dark. Cole Reaver swayed from foot-to-foot at her side trying to look solemn. A caption scrolled over their bodies reading: *...rebel leader repents... gives up terrorists behind Justice for Kisme attacks.*

"Don't watch that," Sally said.

"I saw her, Sally. When I was tethered to Abe. I saw Cole beating Brandy in some kind of interrogation room. She was terribly bloody and bruised. I don't think she ever eluded him. I think she was caught shortly after she broke into Rose's SLYcast. She didn't arm Justice for Kisme, Sally. Cole armed Justice for Kisme. Look at her eyes. She's broken."

"She betrayed Lina and everybody there. She should be broken."

"She was conditioned to obey Cole. I think she got in over her head. I'm over my head, Sally."

"Don't say that," she said. "AJ needs you… your sister."

Gerald paused the sVid. "See that man?" The m-sphere showed a long line of ordinary people being marched through the soggy streets of Iron City towards enforcer patrol pods. Everyone in line would be questioned by overseers still stationed at Lina's farm because marshal law had been imposed on the Northern Territories and surrounding islands. Gerald zoomed in on one of the people Brandy pointed out as a ring leader. Under the man, the caption read: *OPC Iron City Clerk.*

"His name's Chuck Heller. Well, Charles, I guess." They stared at the man floating above Brandy's shoulder in Gerald's room like the proverbial angel or devil. He wore a faded suit as he walked between two lines of enforcers. His eyes were wild and bright and his head swung as he looked around. He was not meek and tamely walking. He gritted his teeth and tried to run. They hit him, and he tried again. They zapped him and he fell. He was carried off the sphere. "Mr. Heller told me we all had to pick sides. I have no side, Sally. I don't know how to pick."

"You're on our side! Rose's side. You're enhanced… special… you're exactly why we all do what we do."

"My parents were murdered. My best friends are spies. My life since the fire has been one long string of lies and secrets… to protect me. If the FSA knew what I was, they'd execute me. I'm like the soldiers who cracked the moon, Sally. And when I look inside, deep down… I don't see any of it. I'm not special. I just want my sister back. She's the only innocent, honest, and truthful person I know."

"Then get her back, Gerald. If not for us, get Lizzy back for you. Be selfish for once. You need Lizzy and she needs her big brother."

"And then what?"

She looked at him confused. "Then you have her back and maybe the others too."

"And Preston continues as the High Prelate. Sharon continues… impressing manners on girls like you." He looked at Sally trying to see if there were any bruises or marks on her skin.

"She didn't hurt me," Sally said.

"She didn't hurt me either…" Gerald said. "Yet I know what it's like to die now. I didn't before."

"They can fix that, make you forget."

"That's the problem, Sally."

Sally turned her back to Gerald and sat down on the side of his bed. She twisted her hands together, clenching and relaxing. She wasn't crying but her body was hunched and defeated. She resembled AJ after beating the 'roider in the junk yard behind Dusty Gulch. "You experienced what's happening to them. The way you described it… Lina told me everything you said after I left. You can't let them suffer just to make a point."

Gerald shook his head but she couldn't see it. He kneeled on his bed and rubbed her back with one hand. She tensed at first but let him rub the knots of muscles in her shoulders. "I can't win, can I?" he asked.

Sally shook her head. "None of us are ever given a choice. We do what we're told, what we have to do."

"And are you here to tell me what I have to do?"

"You wouldn't listen anyways," she said.

"No but I've always wanted to see the Glass Lands. AJ tells me it's real."

"The surface is pretty," she said.

"Good," Gerald said. "I need something pretty."

Sally stood up and they walked together out of his recovery room. They took the bullet to the surface and when it opened, the sun was yellow and bright. The air was thick and wet like a greenhouse. Gerald smelled flowers and something that smelled like home. *Fish,* he thought. Somebody was cooking fish.

"Well, if it isn't the tweet-pecker that cost me my job," said a familiar voice.

"Jack," Sally said. "Don't be a tweak."

Gerald stepped out of the bullet to see Jack Dryden standing on the platform. "Surprise," Jack said, smiling a little sheepishly.

"You have to be kidding me. He's a Follower too?"

"Balls no," Jack said. "Still a Blackstar as far as I know, but Senior Thomas went critters with the body count. Wasn't even asking fair questions, so I told Sally and she told Sharon and now I'm here."

"Sharon?"

"Lascivious," Jack said, smiling. "Got to like somebody with a body like hers. No offense, Sally."

"C'mon, Gerald. Let me show you where the adults are." She took his hand and pulled him away from Jack who remained smiling at the platform. "He saw the executions," she said when they were far enough away that Jack couldn't hear. "He doesn't act like it now, but he was a mess. When I told Sharon about him…"

"She recruited him?"

Sally nodded. "Something like that. I should warn you, there are others here you might not like very much either. I'm sorry, Gerald, but what's happening is so much bigger than Iron City. If you do what Father Rose thinks you can do… you'll see."

Gerald was so busy listening to Sally, he hadn't even looked around. Now that he did, he couldn't stop looking. There was chest-high brown grass for as far as he could see, which was all the way to a beige wall erected high in the air around them like a castle palisade. Inside the wall, rounded buildings the color of sand spread out like tents under a deep blue sky with white puffy clouds. Several fires burned. He spotted the one cooking fish. Several men and women sat around the fire on log benches. He recognized two of them. Sammy and Kyle from the Nobels farm. He waved but they didn't see him. Gerald turned back to Sally and asked, "What's with the wall?"

"It's not real," Sally said. "The Followers put up SLYcasters around the perimeter of the encampment. The animals here are big and dangerous. The look and smell of a wall deters them from coming in and for the most part they don't."

Beyond the wall, Blackwood trees twice the height of weather sentries stood with their muscular looking branches twisting darkly into the sky. Animals and large birds jumped and fluttered around the treetops as he watched. Gerald looked behind him and saw the now empty bullet platform sticking out of the base of a mountain like a gray tongue. Boulders were piled up on both sides of the hole where the bullet emerged from the ground. Gerald wondered if there was an even higher tunnel system above ground because he saw caves and smooth rock ledges high up on the cliffs. He heard something screech, and his heart went cold. He had heard that sound before in the sVid AJ had shown him back in the mine. It was the last sound before the sVid ended and it chilled him.

"Here we are," Sally said, pointing to the largest building on the savanna. It was an oval building as large as an observatory but without the domed roof. Once inside, he changed his mind and decided the building was like a colosseum with no bleachers to watch the show. People walked around the hard gray floor with purpose as if they all had a reason to be in this place. He stomped his feet and then touched the floor with his hand. It was prezero concrete and hot to the touch from baking all morning in the sun. Concrete wasn't used anymore because the FAC provided much better materials for outdoor flooring.

Gerald jumped as somebody grabbed him from behind. He turned and saw Lina smiling up at him. "Thank you, Gerald," she said, and kissed him on the lips.

"For what?" he asked.

"For tryin'." She looked at Sally and gestured with her head. "Sharon wants him over there." The three of them walked across the floor which Gerald noticed was covered with wires and cables. The two NextGen programming chairs from the mine were arranged next to each other. Several meters of cable connected the chairs.

"How'd you get those here?" Gerald asked. "And why do they need cables?"

"To lock them together, sugar," Sharon said, stepping out from behind one of the chairs. Gerald felt sweat drip down his back and he was wearing summer clothes. Sharon looked bone-dry in her long black outfit with her jacket swishing around her calves. He wondered if she had rigged cooling vWare circuits into the fabric. "Not pretty but it works just like the RADwire we used to hook you up to Abe only this time—"

"My fellow vee-traveler is linking to me and a few of my comrades in plunder."

"Pez," Gerald said, recognizing the jowly tattooed man peering out from the far programming chair. "You're a Follower too?"

"I'm a mercenary, Gerald. I'll do anything for anyone with perks enough to make it interesting. Makes things simpler if I tell people upfront. Today, and I mean right now, I'm working for Rose, but I follow nobody but myself. I'm a pirate, Gerald. And speaking of… you know Red and Booker."

Gerald looked over to where Paisley pointed and saw Red Shotwell and his brother Booker. They stood next to flying ships similar in design to the stealth fighters Uncle Luke and his pilots flew. Behind the brothers, several dozen more ships and gliders hovered in-place with equally intense people standing by their wings. "An army," Gerald said.

"More like a tactical unit, sunshine," Red said. "Paisley tells us you're aiming to break some people out of jail… or something like it."

"And you thought we were bad people," Booker said, smiling. "Now you know it's a matter of perspective."

"We're flippin' heroes," Red said.

"This week."

Gerald looked at Sally and Lina. Neither one of them said a word. They looked at him guiltily and he wondered why. They seemed ashamed to look Gerald in the eye. *When did I become the person that could elicit shame?* Sally could do that. Mrs. O'Sullivan could do that. He wondered if they'd be surprised to find out he didn't care who was here. All he wanted now was to try and get his sister back. "So what do I do?" Gerald asked.

Sharon smiled, almost as if she could hear his real question: *Now what? I can't get to the SLYscape. You already know that.* For days he'd been trying. All the technology in the world wasn't going to give him magical powers. Or, at least, that's what Gerald was thinking as Preston stepped up behind him and clapped his shoulder startling all thoughts from his head.

"Climb into the chair, son. And let Dixon, the boy I remember, show you."

Lina and Sally took his hands and led him to the empty programming chair. They climbed the stacks of swiveling platforms at the chair's base and flipped virtual switches in the cage. Lina offered her hand to help Gerald up. He was feeling strong enough to do it himself but he held her fingers for balance as he climbed. Once in the seat, the girls gave hugs and climbed down. "Better find Daddy for me," Lina said with an uneasy smile on her face. "I need 'em back."

Gerald didn't trust himself to speak. She had faith in him, and he didn't like it. Nobody here seemed to understand that Gerald had no idea how to do what they asked. He was going to fail and then what?

"Whatever you do in there," Paisley said, "I'll be catching everything you experience in here. I'll be weaving a data sphere from it, so don't sweat the details. If you get even a flash of where in y-space your island memories are stored, it'll pop up on Rose's map."

Gerald nodded. The plan had been explained to him plenty of times over the past few days. He was to jump to y-space in his mind. Assuming he could do that, the programming chair would capture his brain activity and Pez's vWare would plot it out on the globe. Like Gerald's own map of the SLYscape, the globe Dixon had created for Rose showed physical locations in the world. Since Sharon and Preston already knew the location of Abe's conditioning chair, he was supposed to find the island first. If Gerald's memory of the island matched the geographical coordinates for where Abe's holo-chair resided, they'd follow his blue dot to wherever he went next. He was supposed to find Dixon first but Gerald didn't care about Preston's mission. He would find Lizzy first, then the O'Sullivans and Big John.

Dixon, if he decided to find him at all, could wait.

Chapter 36

Y-Space

Gerald remembered the training conversations with trepidation as he placed his feet on the control plates and tapped. Everybody watching him believed he could enter y-space without the help of technology. He felt the purple pockets of energy tingle across the skin of his ankles and calves. The machine roared as it started. It rose up and spun on its oval platforms like a beast rising from sleep. The sVid spraying arms moved above the programming cage and painted the blue dots of Dixon's map into the bright Glass Lands sky. The dots swirled as the world spun to focus on the Glass Lands continent where Gerald's dot blinked. Connected to Gerald's dot was a long black tether whipping behind him like a simulated tail. The tail represented the passive link that bridged Gerald's programming chair to the one Pez sat in across the colosseum. When activated, it would connect them virtually across the SLYscape.

"Turning the trace on," Pez yelled.

A field of static electricity washed over Gerald's head making his hair rise. In the simulation dome rendered above the two programming chairs, the black tail fluttered like a flag in the wind until it snapped straight.

"Cloning now," Pez yelled.

Gerald's chair rumbled and bounced as the sVid spraying arms moved violently above him. The sVid sprayers on Pez's programming chair mimicked the actions of Gerald's chair until the machines mirrored each other like two medusas fighting. When the arms slowed, two globes of blue dots appeared side-by-side above the people watching from below. Gerald noticed his tether was now visible in both world maps. According to plan, when Gerald entered y-space, his tether would transmit his brain activity to Pez who would build an immersion sphere to contain whatever Gerald experienced. Pez's friends in the piratesphere would match Gerald's experiences to memories that existed in y-space. From that list of memories, they could find the physical location of the people to whom the memories belonged. Of course, the plan hinged on Gerald leaving his body and entering y-space with his mind. He hoped Preston had a Plan B.

Gerald looked down at the Shotwells and their mercenary pilots. They were all looking up expectantly at the globes projected in the sky above them. In another group of onlookers closer to Gerald's chair, Sally huddled next to Sharon and Preston. They focused their attention on Gerald with only brief glances cast to the semi-transparent globes floating at opposite angles above the concrete floor. Sally bit her lip and Lina smiled when they caught him looking their way. They believed he could do it. He saw faith and confidence in their postures as they watched. He looked at the curved colosseum walls and knew with icy certainty he was expected to perform.

He closed his eyes briefly to forget about the people watching. He then looked at the globe spinning on its axis before him. This was the spherical map of the enhanced as vWare controllers experienced it. Gerald was comforted by the familiar programming symbols floating in a halo around the simulated planet. He found the shape of the sVid Preston wanted him to select and pulled it to his chest. He heard the whispers in his head grow loud as a red-haired boy appeared before him like a tiny cherub flying at cloud-level above Gerald's blue dot. "Hello," the boy said.

"Hi," Gerald responded dumbly, before he remembered this was a passive experience. In the background, he heard Lina laugh.

"What am I supposed to do now?" the young boy asked somebody who wasn't visible.

"Beats me," Gerald said, again forgetting the boy wasn't speaking to him.

"Just disappear, Dixon," Preston Rose said in a voice sounding younger and more confident than the voice Gerald was used to hearing. "Show the person in the chair how to disappear and move. Your map should record where you go."

"Okay, Father," Dixon said. "You see my map, right?" The boy pointed down at the world where Gerald's blue dot blinked. "I made it so I could watch where I went like this." A second blue dot popped into existence next to Gerald's. This dot didn't look exactly like the wolf's dot Sharon showed him on Abe's island. It was smaller than Gerald's but shinier with black and gray veins undulating at its center. "So I close my eyes and remember what it was like to be somewhere else."

Gerald felt his weight shift as the programming chair rocked backwards. He watched Dixon's shiny blue dot speed from the Glass Lands to the other side of the world. The globe stopped spinning on an island in the middle of a vast lake. "Then I open my eyes and come back," the boy said. "It's easy."

The globe snapped back to the Glass Lands as if Dixon's dot had never moved.

"I can go anywhere in the world by remembering what I want. Am I done now?" he asked.

"Yes Dixon, thank you."

Gerald snorted. "That's it? How's that help me?"

"Give it a minute," said Preston, speaking up to Gerald from the colosseum floor.

In the sVid, the light source changed and the audio crackled. The boy was suddenly replaced by a young man with long, red hair. "Father Rose," the young man with haunting blue eyes said. "I got to show them differently now." The voice was not loud or menacing but it cut into Gerald's consciousness bringing him to the edge of panic. Gerald felt himself sucked into the hatred that would one day be in Dixon's blue marble-like eyes. Gerald screamed and scrambled to unbuckle the straps in his chair.

"It's just a sVid, son," Preston yelled. "He can't hurt you."

Gerald remembered Lizzy saying those words before the wolf turned into a man and strangled him to death. The wolf could hurt anyone he wanted. Dixon was impossible to beat.

"For people like us," Dixon said, in a friendly voice that was gentle and encouraging. "It's best if you know a lot of vWare but knowing a little helps." Gerald talked to himself, trying to calm his mind. It was just a sVid the programming chair used to show images and spin the globe of the enhanced. Preston spoke correctly, this Dixon could not hurt him. Gerald repeated that truth to himself until his muscles relaxed. This was not Dixon as he existed now. This was Dixon decades ago when he was not much older than Gerald. Dixon's voice in the sVid was happy and passionate. He was excited to share what he knew. "Have you ever asked yourself how vWare controllers can create worlds out of thin air?"

"They can't," Gerald said.

"They can't," Dixon echoed. "What they can do is build vReading spheres from recorded memories but at a cost to the environment."

"Now you lost me," Gerald said.

Lina laughed. "He still can't hear you, silly tweet."

Gerald smiled as he tried to listen closer. "What the rebels learned when overthrowing the World Union is that vWare etches itself permanently into radiation. It's permanent because vWare *eats* radiation." Dixon laughed as if he too was skeptical. "Every command thrown onto the SLYscape takes a little nibble out of the radiation cloud covering the planet. Each bite leaves tiny pockets of prezero air behind.

"You know what else eats SLYscape radiation? The melanin in fungi, certain trees, and most of the animals here in the Glass Lands." Dixon panned the SLYcorder away from himself so Gerald could see the mountain as it looked decades earlier. The bullet platform was gone as were the buildings and fake fence. He could see nothing but tall grasses, trees, and wild, colorful animals grazing. Gerald understood then, the piratesphere conspiracies were right. The powerlord at the helm of the Followers of Rose had reserved the Glass Lands for himself.

"Guess what?" Dixon continued. "We eat radiation too... that's what makes us special. We nourish ourselves with energy from the radiation. Sky, light, earth; it doesn't matter which kind. We see it, smell it, taste it, touch and oh, man, do we hear it. The voices in your head are memories screaming from y-space. When you hear voices, it's your subconscious vReading radioactive scars left by moles. We are like the blind who can read braille so well, the stories told by bumps play like sVids in our minds.

"Let that sink in," Dixon said, smiling. "I don't know if you're a girl or a boy. I can't see you, but I know what it's like to be you. For the enhanced, if you're sad, you can remember being happy even if you've never been. If you're lonely, you can remember having friends even if you've spent an entire life by yourself. The genetically enhanced can remember anything at any time even if the memory doesn't belong to them. In a way, it's like we all share a community well of memories to sate our thirsts and feed our minds with emotions we're not so good at generating ourselves."

But I feel emotion, Gerald responded, silently. *I feel too much emotion.*

"So we eat and drink from y-space because that's where the memories are, right? So where is y-space?"

The sVid panned away from Dixon and spun slowly up to jumper height and higher. The view swirled slowly in circles with Dixon at its center. Gerald once again saw the mountain and the woods. He saw animals with long necks eating from the tops of trees. They weren't the color of prezero giraffes. They were something different. He and people like him were something different. "All around us!" Gerald yelled.

"It's everywhere," Dixon said.

"Lina!" Gerald shouted from his perch in the programming chair. "Sally!" He turned his head so he could spot the people on the ground watching him. "I was right!" he yelled. They lifted their heads and appeared puzzled at why he was screaming. Gerald clapped his hands. "I cannot travel to y-space!"

Preston who was still standing next to the girls frowned. "But you can!" he yelled.

Gerald laughed. "You misunderstand. I cannot travel to y-space because I'm already there! We're inside y-space already. What I hear, see, and feel… it's what Dixon's talking about. Watch!"

Gerald wasn't sure if it worked at first. Sharon had prepared him to feel something overwhelming. She said he'd grow lightheaded and hallucinate like he'd taken drugs. She said he might get sick because the radiation content of the air in the Glass Lands was so much higher than the rest of the world. He'd drink it all up, she said, and get a belly-ache. That's what people like Gerald did. They consumed the radiation until they gained enough of it to connect to the others like them. It was like a hive, she claimed, and it would feel like he lost himself to the hive.

It was not like a hive. There was no queen in charge. There was no telepathy. It was just a pooled resource everybody with access could vRead from. The World Union soldiers vRead each other's memories after the RADcore bomb exploded. Inside those memories were the reasons why they sent anti-matter missiles to the moon. Gerald realized he could find the memories responsible for that decision because those memories had been whispering to him his whole life. Each whisper was a memory. Each memory was scar in the radiation cloud Gerald lived inside. Gerald could discover why the WU soldiers did what they did, but what Gerald wanted were other memories. He wanted Lizzy's memories. Hers were etched into the radiation too, which meant her memories were whispering too. He just had to listen for her voice. If Dixon was right, she had been speaking inside his mind all this time which meant he knew her voice better than he knew his own.

Gerald remembered back to Lizzy morphing into the dragon locust by the black pond and tried to hear what she said to him before the wolf pounced. Like ocean waves pounding a seashore, the ever-present whispers inside his head resisted his control by getting louder and then softer and then louder again. He relaxed knowing he had all day to find the one whisper he needed to hear above the noise. He wasn't certain it was going to work until one whisper started to rise, its rhythm and timbre building to something almost recognizable. It became a rasp and then a moan. He heard a locust's legs rubbing and a little girl humming. He tilted his head and closed his eyes. Just one voice he wanted, one memory, but the others wanted to be heard too. *I want to remember,* he thought. *Whatever happened to the girl on the island?* The whisper that rose up louder than all the rest filled his mind with a memory, but it was not Abe's island where he had last seen Lizzy. Instead, he remembered a storm.

The air was biting cold outside and it was getting dark. Gerald and Elizabeth made one last ash-man before heading in. Lizzy liked Ash-sol, the ninth month in the year, which was the first month before the truly bitter cold set in. She liked the ash that fell from the sky, because unlike the snow that would fall later, it was warm on her hands but just as sticky for packing. She was tiny, maybe four years old.

"Lizabeth!" their mom yelled when she tracked ash across the floors. Gerald had already cleaned up and didn't remember looking at his mom then so much as feeling her there. *Lizzy's in trouble,* he thought without concern. He wandered away into the living room where they kept the simulation pod. He didn't want to play. He just wanted to sit and watch the gray ash fall outside for a little time before the weather shields closed them in for the night. Lizzy was crying now, saying things were unfair. Gerald recognized this memory. It was one of the memories his father layered onto his scribeosphere. How it got into y-space, he didn't know. Maybe he had thought about it while on Abe's island. Maybe Lizzy, when she hacked his locust in the scribeosphere, stole it. *Could she do that?* he wondered, and then he was certain. Lizzy stole this memory to feed on like Dixon said. She nourished her mind by remembering home.

A while after Lizzy stopped crying, they were eating and everything was just as it always was during Ash-sol. They talked, played a table game, and then went into the simulation pod to play some more. They were sent to bed despite knowing their parents were wrong about how tired they were. Gerald didn't like his bed. He held his ears every night because the whispers got loud when it was dark. In a while, he knew he'd fall asleep but until then, the whispers would hurt him. Just before he dozed off, Gerald felt tiny fingertips touch his cheek. Lizzy climbed into his bed and huddled up to him under the blankets. "I'm scared," she said.

Gerald pulled his hands down from his ears and focused on his little sister. When the ash fell on the house at night, it hissed and clicked like grease sizzling because some of the ash was still in big chunks like hail. He didn't remember why ash fell every year at this time. He just knew it made a strange sound similar to the whispers he heard in his brain. He could understand why she was scared. Lizzy didn't like the sound. She believed it was snakes trying to get inside. So Gerald pulled his little sister tight. He covered her ears with his hands, and they fell asleep to the sound of ash sizzling and skittering down the roof. His last thought was how small Lizzy was and how warm it felt when she needed his help.

Gerald didn't wake up in bed holding Lizzy because the whisper changed into something new. Unlike a night vision when the memories came to him all-consuming, Gerald could still see the controls of the programming chair he sat in. He saw the globe of the enhanced with all the blue dots turning on its axis above him. At its center was the dark blue dot he now recognized as himself. Gerald was spinning the globe just as Dixon had done in the sVid.

He woke up in a bed at the O'Sullivan ranch. The bed was brand new and hard. Mrs. O'Sullivan had ordered it for him the first summer after the fire. The closet between he and AJ was a wall then and the first nights in that bed had been full of bad dreams. They weren't the usual bad dreams where he lived inside other people. They were just his own dreams that scared him. Derecho-sol had begun and the rain was echoing inside his room as if the house was a box of marbles and some giant on the outside kept shaking it. There was thunder too, but it was the rain that woke him. He closed his eyes tighter, but then groaned in frustration as the whispers started to yell.

Gerald was twelve then and the rain mixed with whispers sounded like snakes. He tried to stop himself from remembering his little sister Lizzy and how afraid she was of the hissing outside during Ash-sol. He screamed and punched the wall next to his bed. He didn't mean too but he cracked the wall. He covered his ears and rocked from shoulder-to-shoulder with frustration and fear. The door opened and Mrs. O'Sullivan walked in from the hallway. Her body was dark against the bright light. She closed the door and walked to the edge of his bed. Gerald thought he was in trouble and winced when her hand reached out for him. Her palm was warm as she started to stroke his forehead like she was petting him. She pulled his blankets back and got in. She snuggled up to him and pulled him tight. "I don't like storms either," she said. "Protect me."

She smelled like soap just how Lizzy used to smell. He squeezed Mrs. O'Sullivan close. "Okay," he said. "I'm brave."

"All my boys are."

He floated out of her arms until he was inside a cavernous space filled with tiny galaxies of stars swirling like pinpricks of white, blue, and silver around blocks of yellow. The stars inside the galaxies hummed with whispers—each star a voice, each voice a memory. The memory of Mrs. O'Sullivan holding him was laid out in patterns before him like a story etched into the dark. The memory of holding his sister was there too. They were two whispers separate but the same. They ached inside him but it was a good ache, because they reminded him he didn't have one family but two. He loved Lizzy and Mrs. O'Sullivan. AJ was the only brother he had ever known. He didn't know what to think about Big John, but he pictured Lina's smile and knew families could grow. He belonged to these people and them to him. These were the people he had come to find. This was y-space and he was inside where all his families' memories were stored, including the ones of them being conditioned on Abe's island. He listened for the next voice as Dixon had said to do in his sVid. It would take Gerald to wherever in y-space he needed to be. He floated and listened and heard one more memory rise above the rest: *I've been so brave,* it said, in Lizzy's voice. *I did everything you asked.*

I asked nothing, Gerald thought, suddenly chilled.

You asked me not to leave you. The day of the fire, don't you remember, you asked me to stay? It's been so long in here.

You mind travelled to y-space on the day of the fire?

Are you ready to be brave?

Yes.

Like an orbiter descending from space, Gerald splashed into daylight to glide over a turquoise ocean. He soared toward the island at its center. He could see the sandy beach and green trees. He noted the black core where he knew bad things waited.

"Are you getting this?" Pez yelled, excited.

Gerald was startled by Pez's voice. The controls of the programming chair crashed back down around him. He looked up and saw Dixon's globe of the enhanced directly above his chair. Beneath Gerald's dot was a multi-color smudge over an outlying district of Old New York. *It worked,* Gerald thought, thinking the young Dixon was right. It was easy to move in y-space, to mind travel as Preston called it.

"Gerald! Is that her?" Sally yelled.

"Why is he holding his ears?" Lina asked.

Gerald followed the girls' gaze to the simulation playing above Pez's chair. He saw himself as a little boy in pajamas. He saw Lizzy climbing into his bed. Watching the girls see her for the first time broke something inside Gerald. His eyes became hot and his breath ragged. Pez's immersion sphere was tracking what Gerald experienced in y-space while the young Dixon's globe tracked the damage to the radiation cloud Gerald's presence caused. *We eat radiation when we vRead,* Dixon had said. *The problem is, we can't turn it off. We vRead all day and all night. We can't stop. And every time we vRead, we eat a little more of the radiation that sustains us. That's what the dots on my globe track… our voracious consumption.*

Gerald looked at Dixon's globe and saw Pez's m-sphere creation was lagging behind Gerald's current experience. The girls were seeing memories of himself growing up on Layfette Street and soon they would see him at AJ's ranch. After that, he feared what they would see. Gerald smelled the sting of ocean air and felt the rumble of waves raking a sandy shore. With terrible sadness, he closed his eyes and braced himself. Not everyone had seen loved ones die, let alone over-and-over again. He considered pulling himself away from Abe's island and out of this memory to spare Lina and Sally from experiencing what he remembered, but Lizzy needed him. This time, no matter how badly it hurt, he was ready to be brave.

Buoyed by warm eddies of salty air, Gerald flew towards Abe's island. He skimmed over the treetops until the familiar sound of fighting and screaming filled his ears. Abe was face down and bleeding. AJ was falling under the wolf's pounce. Big John and Lizzy protected Mrs. O'Sullivan who slept like a porcelain doll with her fingers half-submerged in the black pond. Gerald saw the brood of locusts twirl into clouds obscuring the island from view. Gerald stopped watching and listened for another memory to follow, but the whispers refused to speak. According to Dixon, when the memories stopped, it meant Gerald was where he needed to be. So Lizzy and the others were being held captive near Abe but Dixon's globe by itself wasn't precise enough to show him exactly where. Gerald needed one more memory to find them. *Focus,* he thought, *listen.* And he did focus for what seemed like a long time.

"I can't believe it!" someone gasped.

"Where is that place?" Sally asked, surprise.

"So much water," Lina said just loudly enough for Gerald to hear. Pez's m-sphere was now showing Abe's island to everyone in the colosseum.

While he had been listening for more memories, Gerald had purposely flown higher to keep the girls from seeing what he knew was happening on the island below him. The thing about m-spheres is the vWare could stitch together similar memories to make the vReading experience better. Pez was a good vWare controller, so it shouldn't have surprised Gerald when he heard. "AJ, no!" followed by a scream so filled with fear, he cringed, "Daddy!"

"Are you getting this?" Pez yelled.

"What the hell is that thing?" It was Red Shotwell's voice.

Gerald looked down and saw the dragon locust rise with the wolf on her back. The wolf tore at her wings. Gerald circled the island not knowing what to do. If there were no more whispers to follow, no more memories to bring him closer to Lizzy, what good did all this do? He pulled his vision away from the island and looked at Dixon's globe of the enhanced. Gerald's dark blue dot had moved to the center of Old New York and floated above Freedom Square like a balloon on a taught string. He could see Abe's dot beneath his own, but Lizzy's dot and the yellow moles of AJ and the rest were missing.

Gerald flew down towards the illusion of Abe's island and saw one of Lizzy's wings fall from her like a leaf shedding from a tree. The wolf was viciously tugging at the other but the dragon locust made no sound as she spiraled trying to keep aloft. *We're connected,* he thought. *Me to Lizzy. Lizzy to Dixon. Abe to all of us, the genetically enhanced to each other.* An idea formed in Gerald's mind. People made new memories with every breath they took. What if the memory leading Gerald to his sister was a shared one? A shared memory, he imagined, would make a louder whisper in his mind. It would create a bigger scar in y-space for him follow. It would require a significant power draw to reproduce with vWare. If the logic of what Gerald was thinking proved right, he could make the genetic connections visible. Gerald hung in the air as he watched the dragon locust suffer under the wolf's cruel bites. If his logic was wrong, he'd still get satisfaction from killing the wolf.

Gerald had wings as he flew over Abe's island, so he furled them to his body and dove. He raced like an eagle dropping from the sky to snatch another bird of prey out of the air. He had done this before in a night vision when he enter the lithium miner's head, but this time his target was the wolf. He stretched his talons out and jabbed them deep into the wolf's flesh and heard its pitiful screeching yelp—a dog's yelp after something bigger broke its bones. The sound troubled Gerald because it felt good. He wanted to hurt the wolf as badly as it hurt everyone on the island. It troubled him also, because he heard a whisper in his mind echoing the memory of Dixon's pain. Gerald clenched his talons tighter and heard the skin and sinew of the wolf rip. He pulled back and raised his wings to catch a gust of warm air rising. He felt the strength in his breast that pushed his wings against the air. He yanked the wolf off his sister's back and flew higher.

The dragon locust continued to fall. Gerald knew it was still going to die, but he also knew Lizzy would be fine because this reality wasn't real. He flew the thrashing wolf away from the island and dropped Dixon's broken body into the turquoise ocean. He imagined Abe's conditioning chair would see the wolf's death as an error and revive him. Yet, Gerald had already captured the memory of what it felt like to beat Dixon at his own game. He heard his sister scream as the dragon locust hit the ground next to the black pond. He flew to her and landed by her side. She looked at him through a syrup of green mucous and brown locust blood. *Remember this,* Gerald said in his mind. *I killed the wolf.*

You were brave and I will remember that big brother, but the wolf lives.

Out of the black water Dixon, in his wolf's body, lunged. He landed on Abe who was running on the other side of the pond trying to drag the bodies of AJ and Big John into the black water, perhaps thinking he could hide them so they wouldn't be eaten. *But you died once!* Gerald yelled silently at the wolf, hoping Abe and Lizzy could hear him. *Remember that death! Cherish it for it's all you get from me this day.*

Once, Dixon echoed. *I'll give you one victory but next time we meet...*

There won't be a next time, Gerald said, feeling exhilarated. The wolf had already given him what he needed.

It was simple, really. Gerald was not just a genetically enhanced *child of the future* who consumed radiation like molecular implants and fungi, he was a vWare controller too. *A god in the machine,* his father had said, *able to create any reality he wanted.* The reality of the wolf was spun into existence by the vWare controlling Cole's conditioning chair. What Gerald experienced now standing on two talons next to his sister's dying insect body would be spun into another reality as Pez's vWare tried to render what was in Gerald's mind. So Gerald filled his mind with one, shared whisper of killing the wolf as remembered by the four gene demons who witnessed it: Abe, Lizzy, Gerald, and Dixon. As a vWare controller he could tie how much radiation the four gene demons consumed and match it to the power drain from every SLYscape device in New York. All Gerald had to do to find his sister was merge Dixon's map with his own. Simple.

Gerald opened his eyes and heard Lina and Sally crying. He saw Sharon and Preston doing a poor job of explaining to them what they saw wasn't real. Gerald looked over to Pez's immersion sphere and was startled. A bird twice the size of the wolf glided over the island in a circle with blood dripping from its claws. Its beak was gold and sharp. Its plumage was dark blue and it had eyes like frozen crystal that reflected memories of cities and islands and swamps. Those were Gerald's SLYscape eyes, and he watched himself soar like an alien thing across the m-sphere Pez projected above the colosseum floor. Around the bird's neck, it wore a green gem on a leather neck cord. Inside that gem if Gerald could zoom in on what Pez created, he suspected a smiling locust was staring out.

"He's a flippin' demon bird!" Pez yelled, clapping his hands. "And he moves over the 'scape like the virus does! Tell me people, you're tracking that."

Gerald heard a chorus of other voices respond, which he assumed were Paisley's friends in the piratesphere. Gerald watched himself represented as a fierce looking bird of prey and blinked until the reality of Abe's island faded from his thoughts like a dream upon waking. Gerald sat in the programming chair. The feel of the seat supporting his body was real. He looked at the sVid spraying arms above him and all the people watching him with their mouths open. Those people are real. *I'm real. Lizzy's real. My ability to find her is real.*

Gerald tapped his feet on the control plates of his programming chair until he saw his personal vWare creations appear. He reached for the beautiful compass that would reveal Gerald's map of SLYscape power sources. The compass opened and Gerald felt his body tingle as the programming chair reacted to the vWare inside. He reached for the second symbol he needed—Pez's m-sphere—and connected Pez's vWare to his own. Finally, he took the vWare Dixon created when he was young and layered it on top. A moment later, a new map was made and Gerald recognized his dark blue dot hovering in the middle of a maelstrom of crackling power emanating from the FSA tower.

Gerald heard muffled sounds of excitement from Pez's friends watching them from the piratesphere. Gerald explained to the pirates and mercenaries assembled how to vRead the new creation to find the prisoners. He relayed to Pez what the colors of his map meant. "The blue lines are what we're after," Gerald said, "from me to Abe to Lizzy…."

"There!" Booker yelled, seeing Gerald's blue dot join with another one slightly larger with hints of mauve. "Top floor of the FSA tower. That's one."

"Cole's floor," Preston said.

"And there in the tunnels," Sharon called out. "Abe with the three—"

"Daddy!" Lina yelled.

"AJ too?" Sally asked.

"Everybody," Pez confirmed.

"It seems," Red said. "We have our targets."

Gerald was too tired to notice the icy tension building around him. He struggled to unstrap himself from the programming chair imagining what they were all thinking. *Now what? They're locked behind hundreds of enforcers and thousands of security drones. It's the FSA tower, the most heavily protected building in the Freeland.*

"So anybody else up for a revolution?" Booker yelled, and laughed.

"I am," Gerald said, knowing it was long past time for Lizzy to come home.

Chapter 37

Broken Moon

Gerald sat in between Lina and Sally on a softly cushioned red chair in the underground operations room. Sharon had reconfigured the seats into rising tiers around the shimmering projection pool on the floor. The merged rendering of the FSA tower in Old New York was now layered with OPC blueprints of the building and the enforcer tunnels snaking beneath Freedom Square. Just about everyone who had watched Gerald move through y-space in the colosseum was present. Looking around the room, Gerald picked up on nuances of the décor he missed the last time he was there. Most notable were the local flags hanging from the natural stone stanchions supporting the imperfect shape of the domed chamber. Above the largest entranceway was a black and white flag showing the letters: FOR.

Catching the direction of Gerald's gaze, Sally said, "It stands for Followers of Rose. It means we stand FOR the children persecuted by the FSA. One flag for every city, bubble, and region where the genetically enhanced live. See that flag. That's yours."

"And Abe's," he said. "We're from the same street."

"Of course, him too. It's just weird to think about him as being like you. He's an enforcer."

"Not by choice," Gerald said. "How many gene demons are there in the world?"

"Don't use those words, Gerald. You're not demons. You're good."

"Right. Did you see my eyes in Pez's m-sphere? They looked like demon eyes to me."

Sally shrugged. "But look what you can do. It's a gift—"

"Better than a gift, man." Pez said from the chair directly above and behind Gerald. "You're not just a vee-walker. You're the tweakin' vee itself!"

"Calm down, Paisley," Sharon said, her voice carrying across the projection pool as if amplified. "It's a lot to absorb, and I'm certain Gerald would rather spend his time learning how we're going to save his sister than listen to how 'tweaking' special he is.... Now, be a good boy, and listen up."

"Boy?" Pez asked.

Only Sharon could smile and look threatening, Gerald thought, as she continued: "To be seen and not heard until called upon, sugar. I don't tolerate interruptions."

"Yes ma'am," Pez said, and smiled hugely. To Gerald, he looked smitten with her as did Jack who sat next to Sharon and Preston on the other side of the projection pool.

"We have two targets... one here," Sharon said, as she circled the second highest floor of the FSA building. "And one here," she continued, circling an area in the tunnels below the FSA building. "The floor here belongs to the Deputy Director and his staff of Field Marshals and analysts. The Director's floor is the highest in the tower. Near as we can tell, Dixon is being held on Cole's floor somewhere on the south side."

"And Lizzy," Gerald said.

"Of course, sugar. Her conditioner's next to Dixon's. The exact spot, however, is up for conjecture because our blueprints don't match your map perfectly. This is why we need a scout to help focus our aim."

"So who has the credentials to walk up there?" Booker asked. "Without access, nobody is getting near the Deputy Director."

"I can," Gerald said. "I have access to that floor."

"Absolutely not," Sharon said.

"The Blackstars said I've been designated since the exam. I've checked it out and FSA vWare Controllers have access to everywhere in that building."

"You're not going."

"Why not?"

"One, you can barely walk. Two, the Followers protect people like you Gerald. We don't put them in harm's way like common thugs-for-hire."

"I'm offended," Booker said, not sounding offended at all. "We're mercenaries. It's a time-honored profession."

"No interruptions," Sharon snapped, heatedly.

"Look, lady," Red's voice snapped back, cutting through the room like a knife. "That mistress of the black thing might work with sphere jockeys like Pez—"

"Hey!" Pez exclaimed. "Remember who pays your bills, Red."

"But I'm responsible for keeping the Mercs alive. I've heard your plan. The boy got bona fides. The other plan's just a trick."

Sharon glared at Red.

"I'm going," Gerald said. "She's my sister, Sharon. If something goes wrong, I need to be there. I'm not letting you 'take care of things' like you did with my parents."

Sharon's lips pursed together. "It was for your own good," she said quietly.

"I've seen the kid in action," Booker said. "Not bad. He's pretty quick on his feet especially if he uses that flying ball. Remember that, Red? Damn thing just flew out of his pocket like a tiny, fighter drone. Between his tricks and whatever the hell we just saw outside… I like the kid's chances better than the girl's… I mean, she's pretty—"

"I'm going," Sally said.

"She's been trained Booker… by me. Do you want to guess your chances against me?"

"Now that'd be a match to bet on," Pez said.

"Enough," Preston said. "We have a plan but Sharon, Gerald's right. Two people have a better chance of finding Dixon than one."

"I can't get Gerald an appointment with Cole, Preston."

"An appointment with Cole? In person?" Lina asked, incredulously. "You want Sally to just walk into the Deputy Director's office? Makes as much sense as asking a chicken to schedule supper plans with a fox."

"Avelina," Sharon said. "Madame Evelyne has a standing appointment with Cole once a month. I know it's hard to imagine, but the Deputy Director still has a job to do. One of his tasks is meeting with the leaders of each branch of the Freeland government. Madame Evelyne is the Prelate of the Freeland Agriculture Center of which Sally is a designated member. Sally will appear in Cole's office in Evvy's place."

"With any luck," Preston added. "She'll be able to take a look around the floor and give us a better point of attack without alerting Cole to what we plan."

"Suppose that could work," Lina said. "It's Lina, by the way. Just Lina."

"Sure it is, sugar."

Lina squeezed Gerald's hand painfully as Sharon and the others laid out the rest of the plan. "Hate that woman," she said, under her breath.

"They're keeping Abner in an enforcer training room in the tunnels here," Sharon said, circling the spot. "Based on where Angie's located, my guess is the O'Sullivans and Mr. Nobel are in those extra chairs. Peter is already in Old New York verifying this assumption."

"How's Mr. O'Sullivan doing that?" Lina asked.

"Unlike Preston and myself, Peter still works for the OPC. Preston installed a few special tunnels that lead from the OPC to the other towers around Freedom Square. Peter will use those to gain entry to Abner's room like I did months ago."

"Then why can't he just free Daddy straight away? Just bring 'em all home?"

"Because of Stationary Eyes on the doors and enforcers walking by the room every few minutes. If you're very quick and good, you can slip in and out but not if you have to carry people with atrophied limbs with you."

"But…"

"Can't be done, sugar. Or we would have done it already."

Red moved impatiently in his chair. "Short of an all-out assault on a bunker full of enforcers—"

"Which we'd lose," his brother chimed in.

"How do you propose we get to them?"

"Easy," she said. "We tell the enforcers to leave."

Dark laughter and chuckles echoed in the operations room until the Shotwells noticed Sharon wasn't joking. For the next several hours, she and Preston took turns describing how they were going to extricate the prisoners from the tunnels. It all hinged on the Shotwells creating a distraction so threatening, every enforcer in the area would be called to respond.

"You want me and forty-six pilots to descend on Freedom Square like we're some kind of invasion force?" Red asked.

"I volunteer my OPC tower as a target for you to shoot up with your rockets. I'll have the place evacuated hours before the event. Needed a renovation anyway."

"Saying you have pull enough to evacuate without alerting the FSA, what happens when all the enforcers flood out of the ground shooting laz'rupters at us?"

"Don't forget the missiles from the auto-drones—"

"And the satellite weapons," Gerald added.

"Right, can't forget those," Red answered. "It's going to be the Quell all over again."

"To save six people?" Pez asked. "Makes you think, don't it?"

"They're not just any people, Mr. Winters," Preston said. "Freeing Dixon is an absolute necessity to ensure the genetically enhanced have a future. We need his knowledge."

"We need them all, Father," Sally said to Preston, in a respectful but rigid tone. "Please remember it's not just about Dixon. Please?" Sally looked over at Lina and Gerald who shifted uncomfortably.

"You're right, Sally. Thank you."

"I hate to be blunt," Red said. "But how do we get our men out alive if we're waiting on Sharon and her team to rescue the others?"

The conversation continued into the night until there were no more questions. On the way out of the operations room, Lina slipped under Gerald's arm and pivoted to face him with tired eyes. "You're staying with me tonight," she said, her voice husky with emotion. "Sharon says I'm responsible for your care."

Heat spread to Gerald's cheeks as he absorbed what Lina said while trying to avoid her gaze. He watched people gather in pockets of twos and threes around the room to continue conversations about the rescue. Directly behind Lina, he saw Sally arguing with Sharon and Preston talking to Red. He saw Pez clapping Booker Shotwell on the back and Jack walking towards them. He forced himself to look back down. She squeezed him around the waist and smiled up with unwavering eyes. Gerald leaned away feeling unsteady on his feet.

"Cat got your tongue?" she asked, smirking as her hand drifted lower on his back.

"You have a place here?" Gerald responded, suddenly self-conscious about the sweat dampening his skin.

"We all do," Jack said, walking right up to them. "Sally, me, Lina, and her uncle."

"Her uncle?"

"Uncle Luke," Lina said, happily. "He's all better and in charge of the houses topside. He lives with us."

"We call him the quartermaster which ticks him off because 'we ain't disciplined 'nuff to talk military,'" Jack said, imitating Uncle Luke. "Testy old man. Kind of a clean freak too."

Gerald nodded. "And I have a room there?"

"You're sharing mine," Lina said. She gave Jack a withering stare and said, "Say somethin' rude…"

Jack lifted his hands and shook his head. "No judgments here."

Sally appeared suddenly by their side looking furious. "Let's go," she said.

"What happened?"

"Oh, nothing. Just dismissed like a child for having 'obstinate' opinions."

"But what happened?" Lina asked, more insistent.

"You can't go."

"Daddy needs me!"

"It's dangerous. You're not trained. You're too young. End of story. Direct quotes from Sharon."

"Uncle Luke—"

"Agrees. They've talked about you Lina. I'm sorry. She's not budging. I know her. If you try and fight her…"

Lina nodded. "Fine."

When the four of them emerged from the bullet transport, night had darkened the sky. Strange animal sounds rolled around the darkness like a symphony of peeps, whistles, and chittering insect clicks. Underlying the small sounds were full-throated yips, barks, and once, a thundering moan so strangely primal, Gerald felt his skin tingle with bumps. "It's so loud here," he said.

"It takes getting used to," Sally said. "Not enough generators for force webs or bubbles or anything to protect us. All those animals making noise could just come on in."

Something large trumpeted and stomped hard enough to echo.

"Horn bulls," Jack said. "Like prezero elephants but bigger. This place is off-the-sphere sweet with all the wildlife. Nothing like it anywhere else but I guess some people got eaten a while back. That's why we got the fires going." Jack pointed to the fire pits lining the SLYcasted fence. "If Henry could see this…" Jack said, letting his voice trail off.

"The Blackstar?" Gerald asked.

Jack nodded. "He was the one who kept trying to warn you all. He sent me a couple of times to tell you to run. Senior Thomas caught him helping people. The last time he was caught, he was helping some poor guy limp out of the interrogation tent."

"What happened to him?" Gerald asked.

Jack shook his head. "I don't know. A ROLIE took Henry away and an enforcer hung the gimpy guy on a detainment board. Nobody would tell me what was happening, so I ran."

Sally took Jack's hand in hers and squeezed. "You did the right thing," she said.

Jack nodded, "I know."

They walked in silence for a while until they reached two lines of blocky buildings stretching the length of an average city block. He could see construction on a third row of buildings off in the distance. Gerald shook his head in wonder as he looked at the houses on their unnamed street. He let his sight sweep higher to the constellations of unfamiliar stars above. He was on the other side of the world where the night smelled of musky grasses and dry air. He reached for Lina's hand but she shook him off. Her whole body was tense with steely purpose as she strode to the closest and biggest house on the street. Without saying a word, she slammed open the door which rattled on prezero-style hinges. Before the rest of them reached the steps of the concrete and timber-framed dwelling, Lina started screaming at her uncle.

"Well, here we are," Sally said, shrugging awkwardly. "Home sweet home."

Uncle Luke let Lina scream at him for almost an hour as Sally showed Gerald to his bedroom. It was a small room split by a thick black curtain with a small bed on either side. "Don't get any ideas, Gerald," Sally said, smiling. "If Luke catches you doing anything tawdry with his niece… let's just say, I've seen another side of the old man and it's scary. You don't want to go there."

Gerald blushed. "I wouldn't," he said, and then stopped when Sally laughed.

"We know. You're too sweet."

Gerald grimaced. "Am not."

Sally hugged him and said over his shoulder, "It's Lina I'm worried about. That girl tells the naughtiest stories. Makes me blush all over."

Gerald groaned uncomfortably.

"Too easy, Gerald. Get some sleep."

Gerald watched her go feeling nervous about sharing a bedroom with Lina. On his side of the curtain, there was just enough room for the bed, nightstand, and a tiny two-drawer dresser. Lina's side of the curtain was several times larger with a picture window centered over her bed. He stared at the window noticing his own blurry reflection staring back. Confused he stepped up to it and knocked on the window with his knuckle. It was cool to the touch and rattled like... glass. There was no weather shield in place. He looked outside and noticed for the first time, there weren't any storms on the horizon either. There were just stars and a few clouds that covered the moon. He saw a handle on the bottom of the window and lifted. A night scented breeze washed into the room. He listened to the animals and insects outside and smiled. He noticed something else too, Lina wasn't shouting anymore. She was crying and the murmur of Uncle Luke's voice sounded calm. In all the time Lina had been yelling, Uncle Luke had remained quiet until now. Gerald couldn't hear her uncle's words but he could tell by their tone, they were comforting and good.

Gerald walked back to his side of the room and put the scribeosphere on the nightstand. He lay his bracelet next to the scribeosphere as he watched the locust stare up at him. He twirled his belt around the two letting the buckle click down against the table. He closed the curtain and got into bed. The curtain blocked out so much light he couldn't see his hands when he put them in front of his face. He closed his eyes, and the room grew no darker. Without sight, he heard the whispers chattering more loudly as always but in a rhythm that seemed more orderly than usual. Like the sounds of the Glass Lands emanating from Lina's window, the whispers spoke up and paused to let other whispers take over. There was something natural in the whispers intermingling with the night animals calling outside. It was like a conversation partially heard and not fully understood but more comforting than he was used to. He touched his earring and felt the smooth warmth of his mother's jade. It was comforting too.

He was exhausted and knew sleep was near until he heard footsteps on the other side of the room. Gerald came awake with a buzzing nervousness at hearing the strange sound of Lina shuffling quietly on the other side of the curtain. He could smell the perfume on her clothes as she undressed and pulled back the blankets of her bed. He heard her drawers open and close and the whisper of fabric jingling the bracelets on her wrists. He heard her steps draw near to him and pause. She stood so close to the curtain her presence must have stirred a corner because a cool draft touched his cheek and then died away.

Gerald became uncomfortably aware of his own breathing as he listened for Lina to make more sounds but she didn't. He imagined her standing there on the other side of the curtain watching him with unseeing eyes but close enough to touch. He believed he could hear her breathing as she stood perfectly still on the other side. He listened for so long, he doubted she was there at all. Maybe he had misheard and she was sound asleep in her bed. He debated in his mind if he should pull the curtain back but decided instead to simply whisper her name.

"Uh-hmm," she said, so softly it sounded more like a moan than a word. Her hand hunted for the edge of the curtain and then she pulled it to the side. Gerald froze at the sight of her in a pale nightdress backlit by a starlit sky. Her body was a sinuous black shadow with fluid curves flaring at her hips, thighs, and calves. Her arms and shoulders were bare. Lina's long black hair was undone and falling forward over the swell of her breasts and smooth stomach. She wore nothing underneath.

"I can see you," Gerald said, his voice catching.

"I know," she said.

"I mean, you're not wearing any underwear." He tried to make it sound like a casual observation, maybe funny. He wasn't sure.

She shook her head. "Not on bottom… or top," she said, her voice throaty and low. "Can I come in?"

Gerald scooted back in his bed. He nodded, not trusting himself to speak.

She pulled the blanket up and slipped inside. She reached behind to cover herself and then tucked the blanket back as she pushed her body firmly against his. He was too afraid to move until her arms wrapped him up in a tight embrace. Gerald's breath came heavily as he squeezed and rubbed her searching in the darkness for her mouth to kiss. She let him for a moment, and then pushed gently back. "Can you just hold me awhile?" she asked, her voice changing. "Just hold me." Her voice had become nervous and a little afraid.

Gerald tensed and then relaxed. "Sure," he said.

"It's been a rough day," she said.

He nodded. "A rough week."

She laughed softly and nuzzled into his chest. "A rough summer."

Gerald looked up at the open window on Lina's side of the room. The clouds were gone and the night was crystal clear. He heard some kind of terrible roar and a wolf howl. He heard insects warble and bird cry out. The two halves of the moon hung inside a halo of stars he noticed for the first time weren't stars at all. The tiny dots of irregular shapes drifted like dust motes and debris inside the moon's orange-tinged claws. "Lina," he whispered. "Look at the moon. The pieces are all there."

She answered him with gentle snoring and a tickle of hot breath on his bare chest. Lina was asleep and he stroked her silky hair under the broken moon's whispering light.

Chapter 38

Broken Tower

Days later Gerald stood on the steps of the FSA tower in Freedom Square remembering Lina's nervous hug as she said good luck. Lina had not spent the night with Gerald since the first night. They had not kissed or touched or done anything else Sally might consider tawdry. Lina helped him exercise and get stronger until he was as healthy as he was before the mole was injected. He knew the angstromnites were still inside him, but they had been starved of SLYscape radiation long enough to be inactive. Gerald had tried to kiss Lina a few times, but all he was allowed were hugs. Her last hug was shaky and she whispered something into his chest he couldn't hear. When he asked her to repeat it, she squeezed his arms and leaned up on her tip-toes to kiss him chastely on the cheek.

"I'm so nervous," Sally said, standing next to Gerald. She wore a pale blue skirt and white billowy blouse with a high collar. Her wrist had fresh OPC bio-net tattoos that would allow her to communicate more directly to the Shotwells and Sharon. *It's weird,* she had said on the orbiter journey over. *The new moles let me hear their thoughts like they're inside me. It's like when Father Rose wants me, he's just there.* She had been injected with the same communication solution as OPC Prelates and their assistants. *Instantaneous communication,* Preston had said. *You'll need that.*

Gerald and Pez had worked on their own version of a bio-line by creating a vWare bridge from Gerald's scribeosphere to Sally's new bio-net mole. It took many hours of modeling the ionic activity in the language center of Sally's brain before two-way communication between her and Gerald was possible. The result was far short of perfect communication, but it gave Sally the ability to relay short messages from Gerald to the others. What Gerald didn't reveal about his end of the conversation was he didn't just hear Sally speak when she casted to him. He experienced Sally's short-term memory of speaking to him. This form of communication was painful to Gerald because Sally's words came saturated with the emotions she experienced at the exact moment she spoke. The physical sensation of becoming her, combined with the emotion behind her words, often overwhelmed him. Twice during the first few tests, he blinked out as if he fainted. Fortunately, it wasn't long enough to register with Pez or he might have alerted Sharon.

"I've never been to Freedom Square before," Sally said, a little breathlessly. "The towers are so… intimidating."

"It's fake," Gerald said. "They're just sVid sprayed to look like they don't have doors and windows."

"I know," she said. "It's just… have you been inside them before?"

Gerald shook his head. "Not in slow-time," he said.

"What does that mean?"

"Hacking," he said. "I've hacked into the FSA tower before and seen what it looks like on the SLYscape."

Sally laughed. "Probably not the same."

Gerald remembered the rovers. "I hope not."

"Well, I've been trained and you're… you. We'll be fine," she said, shrugging her shoulders and straightening the collar of her blouse. "Being trusted like this, it takes some getting used to." She referred to their mission but also the fit of her professional clothes. She kept adjusting her belts and tugging at her skirt. "Fancy clothes are so stiff. I don't think I ever want a promotion where I have to wear these all the time."

Gerald nodded despite wearing comfortable, casual clothes strung with every kind of vWare circuit he could imagine needing. He wore his beaded bracelet with the opal, and his scribeosphere was stashed in his pocket. He even wore his belt with the buckle that played sVids. He planned to use it to compare Rose's blueprints to the internal walls. He was as prepared as he could be for what lie ahead. All he had to do now was find a hidden room on a floor so full of security that everything he carried with him would probably be rendered useless.

"So, how do we get in?" Sally asked, as she looked at the cobble stone pathway leading from the plaza towards the FSA tower's white steps. "I know the walls open somewhere, but how do we know where?"

"Right there," Gerald said, pointing to a platform about twenty steps up. "If we stand there, the Stationary Eyes hidden on the wall should read our bios and let us in."

"And that badge you rigged will work for you?"

Gerald lifted the square of material hanging from his mother's leather neck cord. "My credentials are woven into it. If I keep it in plain sight, the Eyes scanning us should vRead it just fine."

"We're really doing this," Sally said, looking around at the four corners of Freedom Square plaza. "You don't think it's suspicious if I visit the FSA building before seeing the FAC?"

"No time. Sharon said we can't stray from the plan."

"It's just if they look, my moles would tell them everywhere I've been since leaving the Glass Lands."

Gerald jerked his fingers up to his lips, shushing her. He tapped a pattern on the glass beads of his bracelet until the opal at its center turned green. He hadn't needed to scramble listening devices since he was last at the Academy. Between the Nobel's farm and the Glass Lands, Gerald had grown accustomed to speaking freely. *Not here,* he thought, looking at the looming FSA tower. He wondered how many security Ears were listening to the thousands of people walking the city streets around the nation's capital. There was no way to know. However many there were, Gerald hoped they weren't all equipped with descrambling devices sophisticated enough to cancel out his bracelet.

"Green," he said, pointing. "Now you can talk."

Sally's cheeks flushed. "I'm such a tweakin' zonk," she said, looking around as if she expected Flying Eyes to descend upon them from the clear, blue sky. "I can't believe I said that!" She bit her lip and squinted up.

"Probably not a big deal. I just want to be careful."

"I'm so sorry, Gerald."

"Look, it's nothing… really. Sharon's plan didn't require my gadgets to scramble Eyes and Ears. It's just something AJ and I used to do when we talked about dangerous stuff. Though, I have to admit, what we considered dangerous then wasn't like now."

Sally took several breaths to calm herself. "Flipping grades on exams doesn't seem so bad now, does it?"

Gerald laughed, shaking his head.

"It's just, if something happens to AJ because I mess up... We're not even breaking any laws but just knowing what's about to happen, I feel guilty. My whole life, I've tried to obey the laws and when I did bad things it was because the High Prelate said to, but now—"

"I guess it's good we're just scouts. According to the law, I work for the FSA and you work…." Gerald pointed to the FAC tower and smiled. "I wonder if we have offices?"

"It'd be funny to think so," she said before pausing to take one last look around. "Okay," she said, and without further conversation, she headed towards the FSA tower.

"Good luck," Gerald called out, as he watched Sally walk past babblespheres advertising local restaurants and perks services. When she reached the cobblestone pathway leading to the FSA tower, the babblespheres banked away and zipped around looking for other pedestrians to harass. Gerald made the perfect target since he was standing alone watching Sally climb the tower steps. "No thanks," Gerald said, over-and-over again as a small swarm of babblespheres started buzzing his head emitting savory smells of roasted meats and flashes of extravagant night life available after a hard day's work. He was tempted to activate an energy wall but knew bursting babblespheres tended to draw attention. Instead, he wandered towards the plaza keeping his eye on Sally as he continued to repeat, "Not now. Not for me. Please go."

Sally stood atop the entranceway platform waving her arms as if the featureless, white wall of the FSA tower was a person listening to her explanation for loitering on their steps. After what seemed an extraordinarily long time, her arms relaxed and the wall before her cracked open revealing a door several stories high. Inside the tower were glimmering sculptures, sparkling fountains, ornate flower gardens, and several Flying Eyes swooping down to inspect Sally's credentials more closely. Gerald watched the Eyes scan her with pale blue lights before the wall closed behind her.

Now, it's my turn, Gerald thought as he strode forward with a dizzying sense of déjà vu. He'd walked this road before as an enforcer. He scanned the rooftops of the smaller government buildings lining the long city streets. He hoped Red took careful aim to avoid hurting the kids playing hover ball in the grass patches between buildings. He looked at the other people walking on the sidewalks and began to worry. On the cobble pathways leading from the center plaza to each of the quad-towers, camouflaged patrolman lifts were hidden. Even if Red and his attack pilots were careful, he didn't think the enforcers would be. People were going to get hurt.

He remembered catapulting to the surface not twenty meters away from where he walked currently. According to Sharon, there were fifty patrolman holes in the square. If everything went as planned, enforcers would be popping out of them like prairie dogs in less than an hour. That's how much time he and Sally had to find the hidden room where Dixon and his sister, Lizzy, were held. If he found her quickly, maybe the attack would be over fast.

Gerald slowed as he approached the front steps of the FSA. He was still too early, so he veered away just as Sally sent him the signal to keep going: *he's taking me upstairs,* she said. Her voice was unsteady as she gasped with paralyzing anxiety. It was too strong to be his own. *Calm down,* he thought at her.

Am calm, she responded and Gerald's stomach lurched as glass lined floors rose impossibly fast before his eyes. He stumbled and had to shake his head to see his own feet walking up the steps to the FSA tower. Sally was in a pod lifting her to Cole's floor and Gerald had experienced the ride for the split second it took Sally to cast her message. If Sally's perceptions were going to override his own every time she spoke, he'd have to keep the communication to a minimum. He at least knew she was telling the truth. She was calm which meant the anxiety attack he'd experienced was his own.

Tiny rivulets of chilly sweat dripped down his ribs as he climbed the last few stairs to the entrance platform. He pushed his arms against his sides to dry the sweat and then activated the warming fibers in his clothes. He was more out-of-breath than he should be, and there were nervous tremors in his jaw and chest. If he let his teeth touch, they chattered... *not just nervous,* he thought, *scared and hyperventilating.* He hadn't seen his sister in person since she was seven years old. "I'm sorry," he whispered, forcing himself to relax. "For taking so long."

Gerald dropped his hands and stared up at the white wall. He waited to be acknowledged by the hidden Eyes and felt his wrist tingle. The temperature of the bracelet on his skin dropped. Gerald kept his eyes pointing up not wanting to draw attention to what he feared was happening by his hand. If the locust appeared in his bracelet now and his wrist started smoking from frost, he'd be stunned without warning. He held his breath, and then exhaled when a wildly cheerful lady's voice yelled: "Congratulations! Designate. Welcome to the FSA!" A moment later, a more masculine voice continued: "Identity confirmed. FSA vWare Controller 5th Class, Gerald Lee Goodstone please proceed to work assignment registration."

Gerald's stomach tensed. They were expecting him to start his first day of work.

"Ah, sure," he said, as the tower wall swept open to reveal a white marble floor so well polished, it reflected the cloudless sky above Freedom Square. He stepped inside and spun to look back at the door closing. There were storm clouds gathering outside, so the beautiful reflection in the floor was an illusion. He turned away as the door shut and then tried to see the flaws in the simulated fountains, sculptures, and gardens. He was pretty certain none of it was genuine but the sound of water trickling into pools was incredibly soothing. No wonder Sally hadn't been nervous. The lobby of the FSA resembled a SLYscape shopping center. Everything about it suggested ease and leisure. This was not what he expected inside the lair of Cole Reaver, but he remembered Sharon's words. *Try to remember, nobody knows what's inside your head. The people you meet downtown are just doing their jobs. Don't make a scene or show anxiety.*

"So, welcome to your new home away from home, Mr. Goodstone. Please follow me." Gerald scanned the immediate area not finding anyone.

"Up here," she said.

He smiled as he acknowledged the round face of a middle-aged woman peering down at him from above. She was inside a glistening m-sphere that seemed to bounce as it sank to eye-level. "Miss White," she said.

"Pleased to meet you," he responded, not knowing if the person staring at him was a real, physical being or an automated drone. He tended to think the latter because of her perfectly coifed hazelnut colored hair worn in a tight bun.

"There's so much to do," she said.

"Ah," he said nervously, as he tried to look comfortable. "I'm really just here to meet a friend. Can you just show me where the lift is?"

Miss White shook her head while maintaining her smile. "Not possible. Come with me to security."

Gerald tried not to panic as he followed the m-sphere across the lobby towards a black desk with several Flying Eyes hovering above it. A short, heavyset person sat in a big chair behind the desk. Gerald tripped and hit the floor.

Been waiting in Cole's office. Looking around now, Sally casted to his mind.

"Are you alright?"

Gerald stood up and teetered on his feet as he saw the security desk before him superimposed on top of Sally's vision of Cole Reaver's office. Sally was up from her chair patting the walls and moving items around on the Deputy Director's desk.

"Can I help you?"

Startled by the loud voice, Gerald thought it was Cole walking in on Sally but then he saw the guard at the desk move his lips. "Are you okay?"

Gerald nodded. "Sure am," he said.

"This dapper young gentleman is our new vWare Controller, Mr. Goodstone. He's here to register his personal technology before being shown the facility," Miss White said cheerfully from inside the m-sphere. "The youngster fell down but vitals show he is in good health except for elevated heart rate and some residual confusion from the fall."

"Is that so?" the guard asked, politely. "Says he's a direct report to the Deputy Director." The man straightened in his chair and looked at Gerald more closely. "Miss White," he continued, "deactivate onboarding process. I got this one." He stood up behind the desk.

"As you command," the m-sphere said, in a suddenly asexual voice. "Deactivating." The m-sphere disappeared.

"Sorry about that," the man said. "You just got four hours of your life back."

Gerald nodded, and then asked if he could be shown to the lift.

"Sure," the guard said. "Soon as we get through the tech sweep. Says here, you got some kind of SLYscape connection in your pocket, an engineered bracelet, ear ring, and well, your clothes. What'd you do, string vWare into everything you own? But no moles… weird. No offense."

"Allergic," Gerald said appraising how much the guard understood about vWare. "No injections so I kind of need everything I'm carrying."

The man shrugged. "None of my business but the Eyes got to have a look." He tapped a tattoo on his wrist and Gerald's heart raced as several Flying Eyes hummed to life and scanned him with blue, red, and pink lights.

Gerald stood still listening to the faint chirping and squeaking sounds the Eyes made as they adjusted lenses to get a better view. One flew so close to Gerald's face, he could see himself reflected in a kaleidoscope of ghostly images rotating around the center of its lenses. He imagined this was what bugs saw in a spider's eyes just before the spider came tick-tacking down its web to feed. The thought was disturbing, kicking his paranoia up a notch.

"You're clean," the man said, and the Flying Eyes retreated back to their positions behind the desk.

"So what do you want to see first?"

"Ah," Gerald said, recovering his composure. "You said I'll be working with the Deputy Director? Is my desk near his office?"

The guard nodded. "Right outside it. Mr. Reaver personally requested the spot just for you. Quite an honor. That's why I took over. If you're important to Mr. Reaver, you're important to me. Name's James, by the way."

Gerald shook his hand as he remembered his last meeting with the Deputy Director. *We'll meet again, soon.* Cole had told him. *Imagine what we'll discuss.* If the Deputy Director had reserved a desk for Gerald, this could be bad. *How could he have known I'd come?*

"I'd like to see my desk," Gerald said, as he casted a thought to Sally: *seen Cole yet?*

No, she said. This time he felt her worry. *We're running out of time.*

Gerald followed James across the lobby to a small capsule encased in semi-transparent energy to prevent riders from falling out. It was a little like the Academy's Interconnect but smaller. "Been in one of these before?"

Gerald shook his head despite remembering Sally's experience in the same lift a few minutes before. When the pod rocketed skyward, Gerald was still surprised by how fast it rose through the open area between floors. It slowed at the top in much the same way as the bullet in the Glass Lands slowed—suddenly. They walked out and Gerald looked up at the energy dome that showed the open sky. He peered down at the terraced gardens descending one hundred stories to the lobby. "Are any of those gardens real?" Gerald asked, smelling the atrium for the scents of plants and flowers in full bloom. It looked too pristine to be real.

James stepped up to the clear railing at the edge of the floor and looked down. He reached over and slapped a wide green leaf within reach. "Nope," he said. "Neither's the sky above us. This whole place is a giant simulation, inside and out. Nice, huh? Come, Mr. Goodstone. There's so much to show you before meeting Mr. Reaver."

Gerald followed James across a hallway and into an office space teeming with people working silently as they sat inside compact programming chairs connected to flat desks. "Meet your new brothers and sisters in arms," he said without introducing Gerald to anyone. James walked faster almost skipping with energy as the people manipulated holographic blocks of vWare code above their desks. Gerald watched the vWare controllers' work and wondered why none of them looked up as he and James whisked briskly by their seats. He tried waving at a few random people but they did not wave back. There was something odd going on. Gerald couldn't pinpoint the problem until he looked down at his feet. He couldn't hear his footsteps or the sound of people moving in their chairs. He heard no conversation or humming of machinery. Unlike in the atrium, he smelled nothing inside the offices despite seeing flowers and baked goods on tables scattered about. There were no perfumes or other common scents either. He squashed a rising sense of panic. *He there yet?* Gerald casted to Sally.

Nobody's here and the door's locked, she thought back. *Sharon's in position and we're not ready.*

Gerald's head grew light as he bumped hard into James' back.

"Whoa there, Mr. Goodstone. We're here," he said, gesturing with open hands to a control chair with a flat desk just like all the others. "And there the Deputy Director sits," he said, pointing to a clear window leading into a spacious, enclosed office. The door was closed and Sally was clearly visible through the window. She fidgeted alone on a plush chair across from an empty desk. She glanced out the window but showed no reaction to seeing Gerald or James standing just outside. They watched her a moment longer before she stood up and started pacing around the room.

"She's been waiting quite a spell," James said. "Now please, Mr. Goodstone, sit and get comfortable."

"What's going on?" Gerald said, looking around. "Why's everything quiet?"

"Noticed that did you?" James said, chuckling as he tapped tattoos on his wrists. "No wonder Mr. Reaver likes you." There was a sudden flash of light, and the people in the control chairs disappeared. Every desk was empty. "You see, Mr. Goodstone, you and the lady in the office are the only people here. All the rest work from their respective homes. It's year sixty-seven, after all. Who needs an office?"

Gerald started to speak but was cut-off.

"Just a minute," James said, holding up his hand as he continued to tap his skin.

Another flash of light removed the final shreds of illusion. Gerald spun as he watched the office space shrink before his eyes. He no longer stood on rich, ornate floors of marble and thick carpets. The walls no longer showed wonderful works of art gleaming and pleasing to the eye. He stood inside an office that by the look of it hadn't been renovated since Day Zero. Worse, the smells in the air were of mildew and mild decay. The control chairs and desks were the only things that hadn't changed. They were shiny and new.

"Not as pretty this way, is it? Our little simulation is for guests really. Did you know Mr. Reaver was expecting Prelate Evelyne today? Remarkable woman."

Gerald's voice caught in his throat. Standing with their backs against the gray armored walls of the room, enforcers stood in stand-by mode. "This is the control center for enforcers," Gerald said, spinning back to look at James but it wasn't the heavy-set guard standing behind him. It was Cole Reaver.

"Welcome," the Deputy Director said, laughing because his voice still sounded like the guard's voice. "One moment," he said, stroking the gold stitching on his left hand glove. He cleared his throat. "Let's try that again. When I saw you at my door, I thought how wonderful it would be to meet my newest designate in a proper setting, face-to-face."

Gerald felt suddenly hot and sweaty as he tried to process what he was seeing. He glanced from Cole to the Deputy Director's office and saw Sally frantically trying to find a way out. He didn't try and talk to her because he wasn't certain what the backlash of her current state of agitation might do to him. Instead, he stared and tried to calm himself so he could understand Cole's words.

"I said to myself. I said, Cole, first the Iron City Aggie lied to you about visiting on behalf of my good friend, Madame Evelyne. What could the Aggie want? A plea for Iron City? And then you show up minutes later. Imagine my surprise." Cole waved his hands down his body. "Thus my former disguise. I was so curious."

"I'm just reporting for work," Gerald said, his voice thin.

"Splendid and where was the first place you wanted to go? My office. So I said, what's near my office that would bring Preston's prize abomination to me without having to hunt him down like the cursed rat he is? Any guesses?"

Gerald shook his head.

"Your sister, of course! Somehow you and the Aggie know about poor, burned up Elizabeth. Want to know how close you got?" Cole asked, chuckling. "You won't believe how close."

"Lizzy?" Gerald asked. "Where is she?"

Cole didn't answer but his eyes strayed from Gerald to watch Sally pounding on the front door to get out. "I think she's screaming in there. Would you like to hear?" Cole swiped the back of his hand, and he was right.

"Anybody here?" Sally shouted. "I need to use the bathroom! The door's locked. Anybody?" Her hand pounded the door a few times and then in frustration she returned to her chair and sat down.

Cole put his fingers to his lips and then touched a tattooed spot under his ear. "Miss Scott," he said. "Mr. Reaver will be in shortly."

"Where is my sister?" Gerald asked, his voice low.

With speed as fast as any enforcer, Cole slapped Gerald on the side of the head. As Gerald crumpled to the ground, he felt Cole's fist like a hammer crashing down on his mouth and nose. Blood splashed the ground before his cheek hit. "The bitch's right by the only other abomination I keep up here."

Cole grabbed him by the arm and lifted him to his feet. Gerald's legs barely moved as he was dragged past the office window to the bare wall adjacent to it. He dropped to the ground and Cole stroked his leather gloves. The wall supporting Gerald's shoulder disappeared and he fell into a secret room.

Gerald had trouble focusing his eyes on the cold gray interior. In one corner, a high backed metal chair was pushed against the wall next to a small table facing Cole's office. Sally's face showed anxiety but she was not scared. Gerald looked at the metal chair and remembered Brandy sitting there begging Cole to stop. Gerald reached for his head as Cole pulled him by a fistful of hair into the middle of the room. *Run,* Gerald thought with all his might. *Sally run.*

"A family reunion," Cole said, happily. He heaved Gerald roughly into a conditioning chair opposite the regular chair Brandy had sat in while being tortured. "I do love to bring siblings together."

Gerald turned his head and saw three more holo-chairs that matched his own. In the closest, an emaciated girl with long black hair and sunken cheeks sat with vacant eyes staring out. She didn't look like Lizzy. She was a shadow of that robust, healthy girl that visited the foot of his bed so many months ago. Her eyes held none of the passion and fight the dragon locust had on Abe's island. Yet, she was his sister. There was no doubt. "Lizzy!" he yelled, trying to scramble over to her. He rose a few inches before being snapped back by invisible resistance bands. "Let her go!" he yelled, knowing how pitiful it sounded.

Cole smiled. "Sure I will, Mr. Goodstone. Now that we're better acquainted, shall I call you Gerald? Yes, I think first names are best. Next to your sister sits my pet wolf. He tells me you've met before which is why you are not dead yet."

Gerald listened as he stared out at Sally sitting on the other side of Cole's desk. He knew she didn't see him. She saw only a wall, but she didn't seem to hear Gerald's thoughts anymore either. *Stand if you hear me,* Gerald casted to her for the second time while Cole talked. She continued to sit. Something about the room interrupted the connection between them, which was probably why the merged map couldn't pinpoint Lizzy and Dixon's exact locations.

Gerald's face lit up in pain as Cole smacked him.

"I hope you're listening, Gerald, because this can go a number of ways for you. If you cooperate, I might let you live."

"Cooperate?" Gerald asked, feeling his eyes water at the sting.

"I need something Dixon tells me is buried in your memory, but he can't get to it. Not yet."

"My memory?"

"Not yours exactly but Dixon's. Dixon believes his memory of building Preston's map is locked inside your head."

Gerald looked puzzled. "I don't know anything about his map."

"Dixon disagrees. You see, he has holes in his memory. One of the holes swallowed up Preston's map of gene demons. I can't find it. I can't build it. I'm afraid it's my fault, really. Dixon's first few years with me were… strenuous. He said his missing memories are inside you because of something your mother did."

"He's wrong," Gerald said.

Cole shrugged. "Then you'll die and the wolf will be punished for wasting my time. Either way, it'll have to wait. I'm late for a meeting with a very important Aggie." Cole glanced out at Sally shifting on her chair. "She doesn't see you, Gerald, but you can see her which is essential for the little game we're about to play."

Gerald remembered Brandy and yelled, "I'll give you anything you need. Don't hurt her."

Cole sighed. "My metal chair needs a beautiful girl sitting in it from time-to-time. You'll appreciate the sounds she makes, I think."

Run! Gerald thought, towards Sally. *When he comes in, run!* Sally swept her hands over her lap to smooth the wrinkles from her skirt as she continued to sit waiting for the Deputy Director to show. She couldn't hear him. He knew that now.

"In case you get any ideas." Cole said. He unclasped Gerald's bracelet and slipped it off his wrist. He reached around his waist and pulled off his belt. He then searched in Gerald's pocket and pulled out the scribeosphere. "Extraordinary," Cole said, looking at the ball as he walked the items over to the table. "When we have time, you just must show me how it works." He dropped everything on the table out of reach. Cole then walked to the secret door and left the room.

Gerald looked at the scribeosphere on the table and thought towards it: *Can you hear me?*

I can. I knew you'd come after what you did.

He imagined the scribeosphere flying off the table but it lay inert like an ordinary silver ball, a dead thing not responding. "Fly," he said to better focus his command.

I can't fly. Not out there.

Gerald turned in his chair and looked at his sister. "Lizzy?" he asked, out loud.

Your friend with the pretty hair is in so much trouble, his sister's voice said, but the girl in the chair didn't move. Her eyes didn't blink. Only her fingers flexed. *Master's bad to bodies. Worse than the wolf.*

"Lizzy, can you hear me?"

Of course I can. I'm right here," she said in his mind, quietly. *"Such a freak sometimes."*

He felt his sister smile, but the girl's lips didn't part enough to make a sound. *It's what I used to call you, right?*

"You did," Gerald said.

Are you here to kill the wolf again?

"I don't know."

Become master, and the wolf dies next.

"Welcome, Ms. Scott," Cole said, as he walked into the office. His words were amplified into the secret room. "Madame Evelyne has told me all about you."

"She has?" Sally said, biting her lip.

Cole opened his arms and brought Sally into an overly familiar hug. He rubbed her back awkwardly and Sally struggled politely to break away.

"What'd Evvy say?" Sally asked, with a slight tremor in her voice.

"Nothing good," Cole answered, and tossed Sally face down across his desk. He grabbed her hips and pulled her back, but she scrambled, rolled, and kicked him until she tumbled into the chair on the other side. The chair rolled and tipped her over into the wall so hard, Gerald's view of Sally shook. With a grunt of pain and fear, Sally untangled herself from the fallen chair and pulled herself up using the wall to help her stand. Her breaths were quick and short as she spun to keep her eyes on Cole. Cole watched her struggle, tilting his head, bemused. "Something I said? Or something I did?"

Sally brought her hands up to fight.

Cole lay his black glasses down and watched Sally react to the predatory slant of his inhumanely bright, gold-streaked eyes. With two fingers, he slowly pushed the desk out of his way. The knobbed feet scratched and rattled against the floor. When he had cleared a space between them, Cole slunk forward. Sally backed away until her shoulders pressed against the wall.

"Yes," he said, petting the stitches in his gloves. "You'll do nicely."

The wall behind Sally opened and she fell backward into Gerald's room. She clambered to her feet as Gerald's head filled with agonizing screams: *Help! Gerald! Help! Sharon! Help! Me!*

Gerald arched in his chair so hard against the pain of her emotions, he thought his back might break. Her screams and what she felt was sheer and utter terror. He experienced it through the bridge and his mind threatened to shut down with paralyzing fear of what Cole was about to do.

"Lizzy!" he yelled, "Help!" and then the world split in two.

Chapter 39

Being Brave

Radiation flooded into the gray room like an ocean of color Gerald could see, hear, smell, touch, and devour. Most of all, he could devour. As the whispers backed away from Sally's wrenching panic, Cole burned with ribbons of radiation so hot, Gerald smelled and tasted his parts. Cole had parts just like Uncle Luke had parts. Cole had moles in him, artificial organs, tissue, and hands. His hands were Field Marshal's hands, more radiation-powered machine than blood and sinew powered fingers and wrists. His hands were metal rods encased in synthetic skin. His elbows and shoulders were also parts. Even Cole's eyes glowed because they had been replaced by orbs to see what Gerald saw now… y-space. In all of Cole's body, only his legs and feet were biological appendages, which is probably why he skipped when he walked. It was his one connection with humanity, Gerald guessed, as he imagined the mind disturbed enough to sacrifice so much human tissue for SLYscape parts. Gerald's breaths came heavy and hard as he read the colors of power shooting into Cole from outside the gray room. There was so much radiation outside the room, and it lit Cole up like a city street.

Gerald watched Sally dodge a right hook from Cole and then a left. She ducked under his arms and almost landed a fist to Cole's ear. She followed the near-miss with a spinning kick reminding Gerald of AJ and the way he fought. Cole carelessly dodged and swiped her strikes away as he methodically slapped her right cheek over and over just hard enough to sting. Tears streamed down Sally's face as she continued to punch and throw kicks that didn't land. Cole was playing with her and enjoying the process of wearing her down.

The radiation ebbed and flowed around the room as Cole activated his parts in his half-hearted fight against Sally. This was how Lizzy did it, Gerald finally understood. When the doors to the gray room opened. When Cole let himself inside to play, she'd race out on ribbons of color into the world of y-space and brief escape. She'd search for memories and take the ones showing her a better life than the one she was living imprisoned in Cole's gray room. Gerald's eyes were drawn to the table where his scribeosphere now hovered a few centimeters off the surface. It hummed with a pale light and sprouted thin jagged lines to the people in the room. He recognized his dark blue memories etched in the disc at the scribeosphere's radioactive core. There were spots of fuzzy mauve and pinks speckling his memories like something layered on top. He turned in his chair and saw his sister glowing with colors that matched the specks. He looked down. His legs and arms glowed blue with strands of radiation connecting him and his sister to the scribeosphere's center. Lizzy had stolen Gerald's memories and used his locust to add her own. That was how she hacked his locust—*out there while I was in here. I gave you me, so you'd remember where and who I am.*

The locust remembered for me, Gerald thought back. *To save you.*

Remember her with the pretty hair, Lizzy said. *Give her you.*

Gerald looked at Cole sparking with each move of his arms and hands. Gerald saw when and how hard he struck before he struck. He remembered the scribeosphere's bridge and saw tendrils of power arcing between it, Sally, and himself. They were connected and Gerald believed he could think faster than Cole could strike. *Telepathy,* Sharon had said. *The World Union soldiers had telepathy.*

Not exactly, Gerald thought. *But close enough.*

"Sally," he yelled, as loudly as he could. She turned and received a smack on her cheek that bloodied her nose.

"Close your eyes!"

Gerald opened himself up and watched the blue strands of energy leading from himself to the scribeosphere swell with power. The locust was right. There was so much power in the air around them. So much to show. Words were not enough. He gave her what he saw, what he felt, what he devoured. He gave her himself and let her experience what it was like to be inside his mind. She had been there before when the locust showed itself to Sally after the EMP destroyed the Black

Eye. He had shown her then by accident. Now he showed her deliberately. Gerald wanted Sally to know what it was like to be enhanced. He gave her everything it was to be him.

Sally grabbed her head and staggered to her knees.

"Come now," Cole said. "I think you can do better than this. Do you know what I'm going to do to you? How much it's going to hurt?"

"Why?" she asked, crying the word.

"Because this abomination loves you, and I need the thoughts in his head. Hurting you gets me what I want, his cooperation." Cole answered because he thought it was him she asked, but Gerald knew better.

Why? Because you tried to help Ronnie. You tried to help me. You helped AJ, Lina, and Jack. Because you are good Sally, like my sister, and I need good to win.

Sally stood up with her eyes closed. Cole watched, tilting his head and then shrugged. He swung his closed fist and Sally ducked. She spun forward inside his open arm and cracked Cole's jaw with a jab of her elbow. His head rocked back in surprise. Gerald saw Cole tense as radiation gathered around him like a storm. He launched at Sally with a series of hooks and jabs of his own. She dodged them all. He slowed down, suddenly wary of Sally who bounced away from him on her toes. She could see Cole now as Gerald saw him. Each movement telegraphed by a spark of energy an instant before he struck. She and Cole circled, each waiting for the other to attack. As the circling continued, it occurred to Gerald anticipating Cole's punches could only help Sally defend. He looked back to the table seeing halos of energy sparking between the scribeosphere, buckle, and bracelet. He saw three locusts with crazy smiles rubbing their legs. He focused on the one glowing blue and pink. *Go!* he thought, knowing Sally would vRead his plan through the bridge they shared.

The scribeosphere sped off the table and hit Cole's cheek. He turned towards the smoking ball, and Sally swept his knee. It bent the wrong way and Cole fell screaming to the floor. Sally stomped his legs as he tried to stand. He howled in fury and pain swiping at her as she skipped away. The scribeosphere nicked his face and pestered his eyes too fast for him to hit. Sally kept stomping and kicking—always his legs—until the room detonated in a crackling burst of sound and smoke.

Sally was knocked clear across the room into the upended table next to the metal chair. Gale force wind and icy hail blew like horizontal darts into the room stinging Gerald's face and eyes as his ears continued to ring. A freedom storm raged outside hundreds of stories above the ground. Laz'rupter fire and missiles set the air aflame. From where Gerald sat, he could see the breech in the tower's outside wall. Through the jagged hole, he could see all the way across Freedom Square to the OPC tower. The flaming hulls of two patrol pods were wedged into its top floors. *Red's ships!* Gerald thought excitedly towards Sally. *They're attacking!*

Gerald expected a response but when he looked to where Sally landed, he saw she lay silent and still on the floor. Closer to the breach, puddles of water formed under Cole who lay equally unmoving. He was buried under large chunks of wall and metal. Gerald hoped he was dead but then saw him stir.

Sirens warbled and red lights flashed inside Cole's office. Gerald frantically tested the resistance bands but they still held. He looked around the room for some way to escape before Cole rose but the man grew stronger as he rocked himself free. Pieces of wall tumbled and slid off Cole's back as he pushed himself up on one knee. He twisted around to flip a large beam off his bad leg as if it weighed nothing at all. He shifted his good leg beneath him and let the other dangle straight behind. He groaned and coughed.

"Sally!" Gerald screamed, spotting the bracelet on the floor next to her foot. "Wake up!" She stirred and he felt a surge of joy until Cole pulled himself to his feet.

Sally sat up and put her back against the fallen table. Her face wrinkled in pain and she suddenly slapped her hands over her ears. Gerald knew how loud his whispers could be but he needed her to listen. He focused on the voices inside his head until he found the one he wanted above all the rest. He pulled the memory to him and pictured his bracelet on his wrist. He remembered how it felt to move his fingers across the beads until the colors of the opal changed. He listened to the memory over-and-over again, knowing Sally could hear it too. A shadow passed overhead and Gerald looked up. Cole stood above him, his eyes watching how Gerald glowed.

"What is it you're telling her, Gerald? You think I can't see?" He pointed to his artificial eyes. "I see everything you see. I see it all." His voice was hoarse and angry, so low in his throat it sounded like a growl. The room shook with another explosion. Cole turned from Gerald to look outside. Security drones and Flying Eyes were spiraling out of control as Red's fighters shot them down with laz'rupters and shimmer blasts. Behind the air-to-air fight, the OPC tower burned as sidewinders blew chunks of brown building off the SLYcasted façade of white walls. The tip of the tower was gone.

"Don't they know, this is what we wanted?" Cole asked, smiling. "Father gave Rose too much credit and I told him so." He looked back down at Gerald. "Marshal law across the Freeland Nation. Absolute rule where people like your friends will be too afraid to protect the demons. We will kill almost all of you, Gerald. The ones we keep alive will become our pets like Dixon. We will punish you into slaves so Freelanders can stay free." He looked outside and laughed when a corner of the OPC tower collapsed. Cole stroked the stitching on his gloves and then said, softly, "Levi. Cyrus. Relay. All light, sky, and earth units respond. Patrol pods respond. Lethal force authorized. Defend Freedom Square and ready the satellites."

The metal chair rattled and then Sally yelped as she appeared to fall to the ground after trying to stand. "It's broken, Gerald!" she yelled, holding her ankle with both hands. "Help me."

Cole tore his gaze away from the skyline outside and wiped the rain from his face. His smile widened as he stared at Sally sitting on the floor. "You've been a bad girl, Miss Scott," he said. "You lied to me. You had no appointment. Then you tried to break my leg after I so generously let you inside my tower. Tsk. Tsk. You will have to be punished too."

Her eyes slid from Gerald to Cole and she started to shake.

Cole limped forward dragging his foot, and Sally whimpered and cried as she tried to shuffle away. The room shook and filled with more smoke as errant weapons struck the building. Cole ignored the shaking of the room and the dust settling from the roof. He limped after her enjoying the agonizingly slow chase as he muttered and talked in words Gerald could barely understand. Sally stopped at the corner of Dixon's conditioning chair and turned back to face him. Cole then yanked Sally to her feet and cupped the back of her neck with one hand. He pulled her slowly to him and her eyes widened in terror as he opened his mouth to kiss. Gerald felt her revulsion hit him in waves followed by white hot pain as Cole bit her cheek until she bled. Sally screamed and brought her knee up hard between Cole's legs. Cole doubled over and fell as the world flashed so bright, everything went black.

Gerald blinked his eyes as the room regained focus and a bit of spotty color.

Electromagnetic pulse, Sally thought. *Cute trick.* Gerald experienced the feeling of her smile as she stared down at Cole lying inert on the ground. *He's more parts than human. Not even a human, a vile thing. Broken.* As the adrenaline drained from Sally's body, Gerald felt her giddy sense of triumph begin to ebb into a sickening sense of fear and relief. She touched her bleeding cheek, and Gerald winced at the numbing heat he felt with her fingers. The muscle under her eye throbbed and twitched beneath icy hot skin. He experienced her body as if it was his own. She was so sore and bruised, he had to clench his own hands to prevent himself from screaming out. He blinked hard and was himself again as the world cleared back into plain, natural light. He no longer glowed and everything in the room looked dusty and gray. Sally stepped over Cole to help Gerald out of the holo-chair. "I think it fried your conditioner too," she said. "The restraints are gone."

Her physical voice filled Gerald's ears with refreshing verbal inflection he could hear outside of his body instead of inside his mind. To his normal senses, she didn't appear too tired and sore to carry on. "Your ankle," Gerald said. "You're walking."

"It didn't break," she said, smiling. "I lied because I knew he'd want me helpless. I lured him to me so he'd be close enough to the bracelet when it went off."

"Lied? You're a terrible liar."

"Not today I wasn't."

Gerald nodded. "AJ'd be proud."

Sally smiled. "We got to get him tied up."

From where he sat in the conditioning chair, Gerald watched Cole breathe until his eyes were drawn to the little lakes of melted hail flowing inside like a river leading outside of the room through the hole in the wall. He had a better idea of what to do with Cole, and Sally seemed to know what he was thinking. She took his hands and gently guided him to his feet. When he wouldn't look at her, she reached up and cupped his face with both hands. She steered his vision to her and made him see the blood on her face and the fear in her eyes. "We can't, Gerald," she said. "We're not like him."

Her hands were soft and warm on his cheeks reminding him of how he wanted her sexually before she and AJ got together. He pulled away and looked back down at Cole. "Lizzy told me to kill him and the wolf too. They deserve to die."

"She didn't say that," Sally said. "Become master and the wolf dies next."

Gerald's eyes widened. "How do you know that?"

"You showed me. When you did what you did. I... remember it."

"He murdered my parents. He did things to Lizzy. You just know he did. Things like he was going to do to you. He should be killed and Dixon too!"

Sally groaned in sympathy and her eyes hardened as she bent to peer into Lizzy's vacant stare. Sally's breath quickened as she imagined what Gerald's sister must have endured. She stood slowly and turned towards Gerald. "We can't," she said, tears marking muddy lines down her reddened and swollen cheeks. "Oh god, Gerald, we just can't."

Another explosion shook dust from above as Gerald stared at the dirt caked beneath Sally's streaming tears. He'd seen those tear marks before on Abe's face as a boy when he first met Cole Reaver. Reaver had hurt Abe too, such a big man to be crying and blubbering because of the wolf. He looked at the middle aged man with long red hair falling down over his shoulders. Dixon had been sitting in that chair longer than Lina. He remembered how the man used to smile before Cole captured him. The Deputy Director wanted Dixon's map of the enhanced, so he could turn more blue dots to black. Gerald yelled in frustration and anger. Cole had to atone for what he'd done.

Gerald studied the jagged breach in the wall. It'd be so easy to drag Cole there and push him out. He'd deserve what he got, but what happened then? His father would still be in office, and he'd continue to hunt the genetically enhanced. People like Gerald and Lizzy would continue to die. Gerald saw the table and his belt and buckle lying on the floor. "The people need to know," Gerald said. "They need to see who's ruling our lives. They need to see Cole for what he is, what he's done."

"And maybe they will," Sally said. "Someday."

Gerald bent down and dragged Cole to the table. Sally helped him lift the unconscious wolf master into the metal chair next to it. He remembered how badly beaten Brandy had appeared sitting in that chair. He reached behind Cole to the wall and activated the restraints. Invisible bands of energy cinched Cole tight, and Gerald relaxed his eyes enough to see the color of SLYscape radiation that fed the bands. Satisfied they'd hold, he briefly wondered why it had been so hard to see the radiation before. It was easy now.

Gerald picked his way across the debris in the flooded room. He shuffled his feet to keep from slipping but didn't stop moving until he reached the blast hole. Gerald leaned precariously outside as rocks of ice pelted him. The skin around his eyes bled under the assault. He wanted to pull himself back but couldn't tear his eyes away from the streets below. Freelanders were dying in droves on the plaza of Freedom Square. He could see them fall and hear their screams. Enforcers were everywhere and they mowed people down. Red's fighters retaliated by shooting enforcers as if the people inside the uniforms had any choice about being there. It was barbaric. It was hateful. Both sides were bad.

Gerald's face numbed. Sally tried to pull him inside. He resisted as he watched the carnage from a height that was nowhere near a hundreds stories high. The FSA tower was fifteen floors tall. Everything about the building was illusion as Cole had told him, except for the massacre on its steps. "Please, Gerald!" Sally yelled. "Sharon rescued the others. We have to go!"

Gerald tasted blood dripping into his mouth and continued to resist until Sally wrenched his shoulders back with both hands. Together, they fell backward into the room. He looked up at Sally and saw tears. Her lips were quivering and her eyes were scared. "What do you think you're doing?" she yelled.

"All those people down there… to save six."

Sally looked as if she would slap him but scrambled up and away from him instead. Gerald watched her back heave and felt instantly sorry knowing it was too much. His emotion overwhelmed her as he was overwhelmed when they first connected. He stood up and rubbed watery blood off his face with the back of his sleeve. On the table next to Cole, Gerald picked up his buckle. He found the locust at its center which looked like a tiny, happy ghost staring out—a child's friend. He tapped the buckle to make it play sVids for him. He looked at his sister still sitting in the conditioning chair and found her in his mind. *Lizzy,* he thought. *They have to pay for what they did. Not just Cole but everyone like him. Fill the buckle with your memories of the island. The people need to see Brandy's memories too and Sally's. Show what the master did to Dixon and you. Show what the Blackstars are doing now. Be the virus for me, Lizzy. Show them the bad, the horrible, the wrong. Punish them, Lizzy. Cast Cole Reaver to the world and let them choke on what the Freeland has become.*

The gold buckle started smoking in Gerald's hand as frost formed on its edges. The gray room grew bright. Gerald walked to Cole and flipped the table next to him back on its feet. He set the buckle down on top. Sally turned to Gerald and saw how white the buckle had become. She took his wrist and led him to his sister's chair. She placed his hand in Lizzy's and her fingers squeezed his. When the buckle pulsed with blinding power, a focused beam shot through the breech into the sky above Freedom Square. An m-sphere the size a city block appeared in the path of Red's fighters as they began to retreat. Military drones and patrol pods gave chase out-distancing the SLYcorders flying over the battle. The slowest SLYcorders banked away and returned to show the world what Lizzy's m-sphere had to say.

Gerald watched Abe's island appear and saw the wolf by the black pond with its bloody jowls and glowing otherworldly eyes. He saw the O'Sullivans, Big John, and Lizzy die. When Abe died, the m-sphere erupted into smaller spheres that shot from it like fireworks. Smoldering vignettes of human faces contorted in fear and pain rained down on the people below. It showed Abe as a boy and Dixon as a young man. It showed Brandy being beaten and others Gerald didn't know. In the center sphere, he saw his little sister sitting frightened and afraid as Cole Reaver, the Deputy Director of the FSA, came into her gray room to play for the first time. Gerald watched what the monster did to his sister, knowing everyone in the Freeland with a mole saw him too.

Sally looked away from the spectacle playing above Freedom Square as Gerald scooted his arms under his sister's legs and back. He cradled her in his arms like a baby and squeezed her to his chest. Lizzy didn't weigh much more than a child despite being as tall as any fifteen year old girl. He walked her to the driest corner of the room and sat down with her on his lap. He hunched over her curled body and rocked gently as hot tears dripped off his cheeks into her hair. He whispered to Lizzy without words, humming his feelings as he remembered the locust used to do in the mornings at the Academy. *This is real,* he hummed. *I'm never letting go.*

He hummed for a long time as Sally sat next to him and his sister. She rubbed his back and brushed her fingers through Lizzy's hair, but she didn't say a word. When the sounds of battle died down, Gerald looked up knowing they'd have to go soon if they were to truly escape.

"They're gone," Sally said. "Red's fighters are gone."

"We have to carry her out."

"We have to carry Dixon out too, Gerald."

"Then we'll carry them both," he said, looking at the red-haired man in the chair. "I can't blame him for what he's become."

"Not after what he's been through," Sally said, gazing outside.

"Do you think any of it's getting past the overseers to the sanctioned news channels?"

"Some," she said. "Enough to put him away. Enough maybe, to put Father Rose back in power."

They felt a concussion of air and heard a voice screaming a bunch of words that ended with: *go to the hole, comrades!* It was Pez's voice inside Gerald's mind. Or, more likely Gerald thought, it was Paisley's voice inside Sally's mind. The mental bridge between them had strengthened.

Your escape awaits!

Bloody heroes!

Gerald tried to ignore all the other voices coming to him through his connection to Sally… and then there was a thump in the secret room. The space around the blast hole crackled with dark sparks. "What's going on?" Sally asked.

Gerald smiled. "They didn't leave. They're cloaked."

Sharon materialized in a sparkle of refracted light standing on a cushion of air between a cargo cruiser and the hole in the outside wall. She was on an invisible gang plank with her black cape fluttering at her calves. She stepped down into the room and smiled. "Good work, children."

Behind her, worn out people with guns ran across the space between the cloaked ship and building. In pairs, they jumped down into the room to retrieve the limp forms of Dixon and Cole from their chairs. One hard looking mercenary bent down to take Lizzy from Gerald's arms, and Gerald pulled away. He reached again, and Sally slapped his hands. "Come now, sugars," Sharon said. "We don't have much time."

Gerald shook his head and stood up. "I'm taking her out," he said.

Sharon smiled indulgently and signaled the mercenary to return to the ship. "If you're strong enough."

"I am," he said and followed Sharon and Sally into the cargo ship. He lay Lizzy down on a clean and empty cot between AJ and Mrs. O'Sullivan. Mr. O'Sullivan was squatting between his wife and child holding their hands. He nodded to Gerald who nodded back.

AJ's eyes were open. "Welcome back, Aje," Gerald said.

AJ smiled through split lips and let his head drop to the side so he could get a better look at Lizzy. "So this is your sis, huh?"

Gerald nodded.

"Pleased to meet you in person, sis. Hope you like fish and sharing rooms 'cause Ma's going to take you in. It's what she does with strays needing a home. Right, Da?" he asked, looking up at his dad.

"Right," Mr. O'Sullivan said.

AJ stared a moment longer at his dad and then said, more softly, "It wasn't your fault, you know."

Mr. O'Sullivan looked away and rubbed his eyes. He nodded. "I know."

"And Ma was asleep most of the time. I was there. I saw it work."

Mr. O'Sullivan nodded again. "But you… I didn't know you'd be taken. You had no protection."

"I had protection," AJ said. He looked over at Lizzy lying unconscious next to him. "Lizzy had my back. She had Big John's back too. The wolf hardly ever got to Ma. And Abe…" AJ stared at the giant blond man two cots away. "Abe was too far gone for Lizzy to help him, but he's safe now. We're all safe because Gerald's little sister kept reminding us it wasn't real. When you know that, you're about as protected from the wolf as you can be."

"What protection?" Sally asked.

"I gave Angie an inhibiter," Mr. O'Sullivan said. "A mole that interferes with other moles so she couldn't be forced to vRead. Angie had one. AJ and John didn't."

Sally looked down at AJ and Lina's dad. "So they didn't have to suffer all that time?"

Mr. O'Sullivan pushed himself back to sit on the bench. Mercenaries moved to let Sally and Gerald sit too. "Should have known my son wouldn't let Cole take his Ma away without a fight. He's not good at following orders. He's too stubborn and young to know he can't always win."

"But he did win, Mr. O'Sullivan," Gerald said. "AJ did what he thought was right, and you did what you thought was right. Everyone in this ship picked a side."

Mr. O'Sullivan's didn't look convinced.

"AJ chose to act Mr. O'Sullivan, and it worked. Look at the wolf master now." Gerald pointed across the interior of the ship to Cole strapped to a cot. He was still unconscious and unaware his world had changed, but it had changed. "Now Freelanders will know the truth about him, about the FSA, about overseers and all the rest. There'll be changes made in how we're governed."

"But is change really possible?" Mr. O'Sullivan asked.

"Of course it is," Sally said.

"Got to be," AJ agreed, and then the ship's medical drone ended his side of the conversation with a wave of a blue light that put AJ into a deep, healing sleep.

"Severe dehydration," the drone said, not caring if the patient's family complained. Sharon swept her hands over the hatch to destabilize the energy supporting the gang plank.

Gerald glanced out of the open hatch one last time at the fog coalescing around the freezing buckle he left perched on the table inside the gray room. He could hear the gold plated metal crack and pop as it continued to project Cole's memories over Freedom Square. Icicles had formed on the sides of the table beneath it and thick frost was slowly inching up the buckle's face. With surprising ease, Gerald slipped into y-space and watched a river of radiation shoot from Lizzy on her cot into the gray room where the buckle received her memories. With an understanding he couldn't explain, he knew exactly how long it would take to SLYcast every bad memory Lizzy had stolen over her eight years of captivity. *Not enough time to tell it all,* Gerald thought as the hatch closed and the ship pressurized. The buckle would shatter long before Lizzy could vent everything trapped inside her.

Once the ship pulled away, Gerald saw the radiation change around his sister. The ugly colors powering the buckle leached away from her halo of pinks and blues as new colors began to swell brighter. She was replacing bad memories with good ones wholly her own. There was a yellow flare of something warm and pretty—maybe the budding memory of the day she escaped—followed by a torrent of unpleasant greens and oily browns. Like Dixon, Lizzy remembered centuries of torture and pain, and those memories were packed tight inside her fifteen year old brain. She wasn't going to wake up, not for real, until all her stolen memories were gone. *What have I done?* Gerald wondered, remembering how much he asked of her. *Not just Cole but everybody. Show them the bad, the horrible, the wrong.* There was too much to show.

Lizzy, he thought. S*top,* but it was too late.

There is no justice, Lina had said once.

But there should be, Gerald wished he had said then.

Gerald stared hard at his sister and AJ's mom lying unconscious on their cots. He looked at Sally's cut and bruised face. He watched Sharon give Booker and Pez directions as they flew away from Freedom Square. He listened to the mercenaries talk happily about what they were going to buy with the perks they just earned. Everybody on the ship, for completely different reasons, believed they had picked the right side. Even Cole, Gerald imagined, believed the suffering he caused was done because his side was right. Gerald grew anxious. *What is right for me?*

"Angie?" Mr. O'Sullivan said. "Can you hear me?"

Mrs. O'Sullivan stirred on her cot. "Peter?" she asked.

"Yes," he said, his voice full of relief. "We're here."

"Everyone?"

"Every single one."

"Good," Mrs. O'Sullivan said, drawing the medical drone's attention. "This is good," she repeated, slurring her words as the drone passed its light over her skin. "Good."

Gerald knew then he had never been given a choice between right or wrong. For Gerald, there was only one side. It was spelled out in his DNA and his last name: Goodstone. He'd do everything in his power to do good by his sister, by his mother and father, by the O'Sullivans who had adopted him as one of their own, by Lina and Sally, and by all his friends back in the Glass Lands. He'd remember the genetically enhanced soldiers who cracked the moon and died rather than let powerlords like Cole Reaver take control of their world, Gerald's home, the SLYscape.

ACKNOWLEDGMENTS

This novel took time to write, and there is only so much time in a person's life. So I would like to acknowledge and, more importantly, thank my family for having patience. Without them, I would never have been inspired to finish.

To Gail who told me to just write the thing all ready.

To Garrett who couldn't wait to see what was inside my imagination and once he found out, he helped me with the plot.

To Kerri who reminded me dreams need to be pursued rather than talked about.

To Kristin who has been telling her friends since elementary school that her dad was an author.

I'd also like to thank Judy Ryan for her wonderful editing work and Andrew Schultz for designing a brilliant cover.

Most of all, thank you for reading.

ABOUT THE AUTHOR

John Ryan lives with his wife and three children in southeastern Michigan. He has degrees in writing and literature and spends much of his time authoring technical books and designing software and hardware for the IT industry.